PIECES
OF
EIGHT

BY

Joshua Blair Delaney

To the Bakers —
I hope you enjoy this
old Cape Cod tale!

∞ INFINITY
PUBLISHING

Joshua Blair Delaney

ISBN 0-7414-6479-9
Library of Congress Control Number: 2011922596

Printed in the United States of America

Published June 2011

INFINITY PUBLISHING
1094 New DeHaven Street, Suite 100
West Conshohocken, PA 19428-2713
Toll-free (877) BUY BOOK
Local Phone (610) 941-9999
Fax (610) 941-9959
Info@buybooksontheweb.com
www.buybooksontheweb.com

DEDICATION

To my partner and soulmate Lynne
without whom I would have never embarked upon this voyage.

TABLE OF CONTENTS

LIST OF CHARACTERS

Main
Sam Bellamy – English sailor who washes ashore on Cape Cod.
Maria Hallett – Unmarried maiden with unusual prophetic dreams.
John Julian – Native warrior who resists the English God & ways.

Major
Thomas Baker – Leader of Dutch pirates. Bellamy's rival.
Widow Sally Chase – Aged widow. Midwife. Accused witch.
Lieutenant John Cole – Fisherman. Militia lieutenant.
Mary Cole – Pious wife of John Cole. Dreams of son's ministry.
Justice Joseph Doane – Justice, selectman, militia capt. of Eastham.
Alice Hallett – Recently widowed mother of Maria.
Isaiah Higgins – Owner of Eastham's principal inn and tavern.
Mehitable Higgins – Isaiah Higgins' daughter & tavern serving girl.
Jonathan Hopkins – Covets Maria. Deputy of Justice Doane.
Captain Benjamin Hornigold – Privateer captain. Trains Bellamy.
Elder John Knowles – Church elder. Abutter of the Hallett farm.
Thankful Knowles – The elder's daughter. Former friend of Maria.
Mittawa – John Julian's aunt. The Witch of Billingsgate.
Deacon John Paine – Eastham selectman. Diarist. Finds squid.
Samuel Smith – Owner of the whaling tavern on Great Island.
Captain Edward 'Blackbeard' Teach – Hornigold's star pupil.
Reverend Samuel Treat – Reverend of Eastham.
Palsgrave Williams – Wealthy jeweler. Finances treasure hunt.

Minor
Captain Henry Avery – Famous pirate from Devonshire.
Roger Balfour – Young, starry eyed pirate.
John Bellamy – Farmer in England. Sam Bellamy's father.
Thomas Brown – Pirate loyal to Bellamy.
Johnny Cole – Son of John & Mary Cole. Aspires to ministry.
Mr. Cutler – Cyprian Southack's assistant.
Daku – Dahomey prince & leader of the African faction of pirates.
Thomas Davis – Welsh carpenter who is forced to join the pirates.
Justice Hezekiah Doane – Truro's Justice. Joseph Doane's cousin.
John Dunavan – Irish deckhand aboard the *Mary Anne*.
Doctor Ferguson – Scottish physician who joins the pirates.

i

Thomas Fitzgerald – Irish deckhand aboard the *Mary Anne*.
Francois – French pirate who frequents Boyd's Bog in Helltown.
Samuel Freeman – Coroner of Eastham. In charge of burials.
Samuel Harding – Wreck scavenger & resident of Billingsgate.
Francis Harlow – English shipmate of Bellamy's on the *Josephine*.
Mary Higgins – Isaiah Higgins' wife.
Nehemiah Hobart – Schoolteacher. Covets Maria.
Peter Hoof – Swedish pirate loyal to Bellamy.
Joshua Hopkins – Jonathan's father. Eastham selectman. Tanner.
William Hopkins – Joshua's lame legged son. Town jailer.
Captain Jameson – Bellamy's uncle. Retired naval captain.
Ralph Julian – John Julian's father.
Captain Louis Lebous – French pirate & cohort of Hornigold's.
Alexander Mackconachy – Cook of the *Mary Anne*.
Ebenezer Paine – Palsgrave Williams' kinsman on the *Neptune*.
Captain Prince – Captain of the *Whydah*.
John Lambert – Pilot of the *Whydah*.
William Main – Sailing master of the *Whydah*.
Reverend Cotton Mather – Preaches to pirates in Boston jail.
John Mayo – Old deckhand on the *Neptune*.
Barnabus Merrill – Mary Higgins' uncle. Fixture at Higgins Tavern.
George Newcomb – One of Justice Doane's deputies.
Jacob Nickerson – Deckhand on the *Neptune*.
Captain Pound – Vicious captain of the merchant ship *Josephine*.
Christopher Lowell – Assistant to Governor Shute.
Hendrick Quintor – Dutch pirate who supports Thomas Baker.
Jacques Renneux – French pirate aboard the *Whydah*.
Charlie Sea Eagle – Nauset Christian native. Former warrior.
Jean Shuan – French pirate aboard the *Mary Anne*.
Governor Samuel Shute – Greedy governor of Massachusetts.
Smalley – English squatter on Great Island.
Rebecca Smith – Samuel Smith's wife. Runs the whaling tavern.
Eleazer Snow – Mutinous member of Samuel Smith's whaling crew.
Thomas South – Pirate on the *Mary Anne*. Claims innocence.
Cyprian Southack – Sent to retrieve treasure for the governor.
John Tom – Native Christian Teacher at Indian meeting house.
Simon Van Vorst – Dutch pirate who supports Thomas Baker.
Elijah Wheeler – Eastham farmer whose cows die mysteriously.

Olde Cape Cod
1715~1717

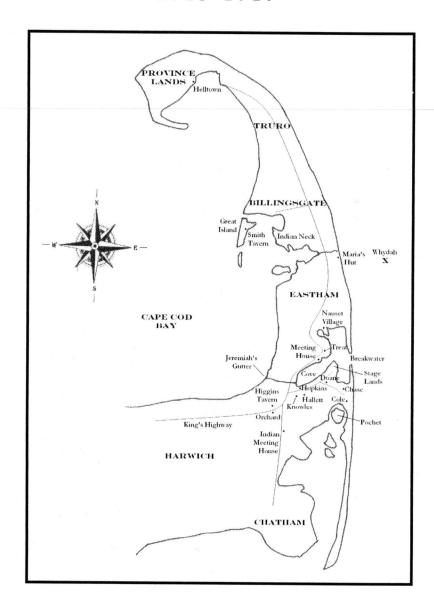

PROLOGUE

The Devil Sea
and the
Plains of the Lord

June 1715

There were times when the sea looked much like a plow field to Sam Bellamy. In the ridges of waves, he could see lines of furrowed ground, such that is fit for planting. The sight of it made him wish he were on a patch of dry land, holding yoke reins, instead of on a ship, hauling the mainsheet and cutting through an immeasurable expanse of water. Sometimes he could not believe that only two months ago he had been standing with soil under foot and chin resting on the nub of his spade, looking out over the hills of Devon at the Atlantic and dreaming to be where he was now.

Farming had become an unbearable toil to him. In the passage of black dirt to crop to harvest and back to seed, he had found nothing but a cycle of monotony that seemed to have no end and no lasting growth either. It was a repetitive rhythm that beat into him until he was sure that he would be in its motion to the day he died. He had thought that nothing in life could produce the same kind of drone until he had been staring at the gray, unmoving line of the horizon for weeks on end.

It had taken Bellamy a fortnight to get used to the pitch and sway of ship life, and it was only then that he could keep the entire day's worth of meals down.

Now that most of the ocean was behind them, Bellamy could almost keep his pace in the smooth, collective effort the crew employed to keep the ship, *Josephine*, moving. It would have appeared an elegant dance but for the flying fists and cudgels of the mates, which kept the men from even thinking of letting the pace waver. There was often an extra blow for Bellamy, the kind that most first time sailors got when they were ten or fifteen years younger, just for being new to the trade. The mates did not often see a thirty-year-old out on his maiden voyage, and they assumed that his late start was due to an easy life that they meant to work out of him. This was his first trip across the wide sea, and Bellamy felt his age coming down on him like the hammer of rain that was starting. He already wondered if it would be his last voyage.

"Ship Ahoy!" came a cry from a man high on the mainsail yard.

Captain Pound stood at the back rail of the ship, leaning out over the water and aiming a spyglass outward. He was a solid-built, grizzled looking man with hair the color of a fading sunset. He grumbled under his breath as he swept the glass to and fro. The pilot came to stand near him, and the two pointed off at some distant shape. Then the pilot hurried back to the tiller, and Pound stowed his glass in his belt.

Pound's eyes flicked towards the mainmast where Bellamy was standing, found Bellamy's own wandering gaze and fastened to it.

"Mind your own work, if you know what's good for you! Hop to it! There will be hell to pay if we are not in Boston on time, and I shall take it from your hide first!"

Bellamy grabbed hold of the mainsheet, stepping next to a man who could have been Bellamy's brother, with his similar black hair and beard.

"What's he see out there? If it is another ship, they're a bit late. I could have used a chat when we were out in the middle of the ocean, traded some mail and tidings. We'll be ashore soon enough now," Francis Harlow said. Harlow was ten years younger than Bellamy, but his legs were already permanently bowed from his work, like an old man who has labored his whole life.

Bellamy looked out to sea and saw nothing but continuous waves and a sheet of black clouds rising out of the east, like a giant, gloomy sail being hauled up the face of the sky.

Then a tiny shape enlarged out of the vast plain of sea and sky. It grew into a dark little sloop, which cut towards them with its one sail cocked at an angle as sharp as a dorsal fin. Harlow groaned. Seeing a shark in the water was bad omen enough, but an approaching ship with the feel of one meant the worst tidings imaginable for a helpless merchant vessel.

"*Pirates*," muttered Harlow. "They'll run us down lest that storm get here first."

Bellamy did not know how Harlow could know that. To him, the ship looked the same as any other. Yet he sensed that there were differences that true sailors could read, akin to the way a farmer knows the best colored earth or choicest cattle.

The cudgel of the second mate came down across Bellamy's back, breaking his thoughts.

"Quit shirking, you sniveling rat!" the man growled. Bellamy risked a glance into the mate's flat, mean eyes, orbs with no more warmth than a fish. He took up the slack of the mainsheet and heaved on it until the mate was satisfied and moved away.

The mates were allowed extra viciousness because of the captain's foul temperament. Pound treated his crew as mindlessly as the other parts of the ship, fit to be bent, beaten and strained, like wood or sail, to expedite the voyage.

"They need more sail," Harlow said, watching the pirate ship buck with the sudden wildness of the sea. He sounded disappointed at the rogues' lack of progress.

"They give a hard chase to find naught but linen in our hold," Bellamy observed. Through the thickening spray Bellamy strained to get a glimpse of the men on the other vessel. He wanted to see what they looked like, these men who had stopped taking life's beatings and decided to deliver their own blows.

Harlow laughed. "If they get nothing but sport, it would be a worthy gain for them! Rough men work these waters. Do you know what they do to those captains who don't reveal where they keep their personal fortune?" Harlow made a hissing sound and drew a finger across his neck.

"I wonder what they will do to old red rooster there," he added, nodding towards the main deck where Pound was busy shouting and turning his face the same color as his beard. The captain marched across the deck, cuffing the men closest to him and howling at them to make sure that they lay every inch of canvas into the wind.

Everyone aboard the *Josephine* was measuring the storm's progress against the coming of the sloop. Some did not yet believe that the other ship was any more dangerous than the one that they were on. But it grew larger and larger until they could see hatches in the hull where the guns would stick out. When they saw its pennant inching ominously up the pole, there was no doubt. Its color was the same as dark smoke or the ashen clouds over head. It sent fear rushing across the deck like a stiff breeze.

"Move, damn you, sneaking puppies!" Pound hollered, lashing out at any man he could reach.

The crew needed no incentive now to try and outrun the pirates. The ship's sails drew up taut, and the hull whisked through the choppy stormwater.

The pirate sloop was easy enough to track through the gaps in the rigging. Soon it was close enough to see the men who sailed it. They were an odd collection in their mismatched outfits of old uniforms, silk sashes and velvet vests. With their strange clothes and their hands piled with liquor bottles and swinging weapons, they looked like a jester troupe at a village fair. It was a surreal image that Bellamy had to remind himself carried a real threat with it. The pirates kept good progress through the waves even though most of them seemed more interested in leering at their prey than attending to the sails.

There was another cry from the lookout, this time for land.

Bellamy spun around and saw a smudge in the distance, which at first looked like a low, gray-hued cloud bank but then solidified into a crest of highlands, which looked not unlike his homeland of Devon from afar.

"Those pirates get as much rum as they can stomach, every day of their lives," Harlow said. They could hear wind-swept words and oaths coming from the pirate ship. It was unintelligible, but it had the sound of drunkenness to it.

"They get the noose if they're captured."

"Are we that much better, beaten like dogs?"

"*Our treatment is an injustice,*" Bellamy muttered. Throughout the journey there had been disagreement between him and Harlow concerning whether escape or revenge was the best response to their plight. Sometimes it seemed to Bellamy that foul conduct was all that made up the world. Misfortune hit one man, and he then lashed out, willy-nilly, at those around him. The next ones in line doled out more misery, which made life into a string of bad deeds that knocked down man after man like bowling pins tumbling. Bellamy aimed to step out of that line whereas Harlow was tallying the blows that he got, so he could repay them later if fate ever put him on the other end of a cudgel.

Captain Pound stood at mid-deck, holding the fluttering edges of a map as he searched for a name for the place that rose up alongside of them: *Cape Cod.*

It had been nearly one hundred years since the Separatists and their little *Mayflower* had first come ashore near this very spot. By the captain's reckoning there was little to show for a century of English life and law in the wilderness. Before him was a stretch of dune and forest with only a few steeples and windmills here and there to show any sign of civilization.

"Four fathoms," called the pilot as he drew up the lead sounding line.

A few yards farther out and the reading had been half the depth. It was a damned tricky body of water, the captain thought. He feared that under every sparkling blue wave was a hump of sea bottom waiting to snag them.

"Hurry up with that sail, Mister Mate!" Pound cried. No matter how much sail they put on, the pirates' faster vessel still gained on them. The men could see the cannon hatches flipping open and the black maws within. They could more clearly hear the sound of the outlaws, an eerie howling not unlike the blowing wind. Even Pound felt a shiver that was not from the chill gale.

There was a dull thud from across the water. Bellamy peeked over the rail and saw a pale cloud pouring from one of the pirates' guns.

A moment later there was a crack like a tree limb breaking, and part of the yard crashed down onto deck, bringing a tangle of rope with it.

Bellamy looked ahead at the land rising up before them.

"What do you know of this place?" Bellamy asked his friend.

"Only that it is but one hundred yards from shore. Why do you ask? I thought that you cannot swim?" Harlow replied.

"I couldn't sail either until a few weeks ago."

"Shut up! Back to work!" the mate's voice cut in. He was trying to oversee them and the repairs of the yard at the same time. He wagged a finger at them as he edged a bit farther away, his eyes coming back to check on them less and less.

The coast of Cape Cod was covered with a sheen of sunlight as if it was immune to the violence of the coming storm. The glow made it seem luminous and newly minted, befitting a new land.

"We could make it," Bellamy said, measuring the distance between himself and the dazzling white beach ahead. It seemed near enough to step onto.

"You could not make it four feet through that surf. And we shall soon be in pirate hands or at Long Wharf, either way dry and with rum in our bellies. *I pray it is with the pirates...*" Harlow added in a whisper.

Bellamy looked along the deck and saw men in a row, hauling on the thick rope that held the sails flapping over head like frightened birds. The men looked like they were tied to the rope rather than pulling it, and the image seemed to Bellamy to be a sign that he would be stuck forever in that bondage of ill fortune that links all poor men together.

His thinking had left him rooted in place again. The captain saw him and drew his pistol, holding it by the barrel end to use as a club.

At the same time Harlow exclaimed too loudly, "I wish that those pirates would take us among them! Then I would have a chance at a good life!"

The words hung in the air between Harlow and Bellamy and, to the captain's ears, seemed to belong to both men equally.

"You would join them! Those be words of mutiny!" Pound cried. Of the two sailors, Bellamy was closer to him, so Pound grasped him by the shirt collar and tried to cast him to the deck. However, Bellamy's natural strength kept him upright for a moment. Had he been on solid ground, he could have held there all day, but his weak sea legs lost purchase in a sluice of water that washed over the rail and sent him tumbling onto his face. When the water cleared, Bellamy felt the sting of Pound's pistol thudding into his back over and over.

Just then there was another shot from the pirates' cannon. In answer, the clouds themselves flashed like a muzzle across the sky. The *Josephine* rocked, pitching Bellamy towards the side. The ocean coursed below, sucking under the hull and looking dark and cold with the shadow of the storm fully upon them.

Pound came at the sailor again, but Bellamy struck first, knocking the captain down.

"You better hope them pirates get you now, lad!" Pound said, struggling to his feet.

If he did not go now, Bellamy knew that he might not have another chance. The clouds fit his mood. He could not face another journey across the Atlantic on this ship, or any other ship, even if it meant never seeing England again. Even if it meant death, he thought as he glanced again at the water.

Closer to shore the sun still glittered brightly upon the sea and seemed almost like words being spoken. Atop the surface were plains of blue and green, which made his head feel comfortably sleepy. He could imagine himself dropping over the side and landing in that welcome bed of light and color.

Before he knew it he was standing on the edge of the rail, which rocked as if the ship itself was trying to shake him off into the water. All he had to do was get to that beautiful swath of shoreline. "It is not far," he kept telling himself over and over until it was an echo in his mind, which rivaled the sound of churning waves or scratch of rain.

He heard the click of the pistol behind him.

Then he stepped off into the air, feeling nothing but a rush of wind under his feet. A moment later Bellamy felt the water surge up around him. His nose and mouth filled with it. The sea rushed over him in a bubbling vault. He looked up into the shimmering dome of water, majestic and peaceful as a cathedral, and thought that he would not care if he did not make it back to the surface. Then the burn in his lungs recalled him to more worldly matters, and he clawed his way upward, trying to think of the water as a substance as substantial as dirt that he could dig his fingers into. When he reached open air, he saw the smoke from the fired gun blowing uselessly away in the wind and the joyous sight of the stern of the ship moving away.

However, his happiness was short lived. His arms and legs began to flail. There was no solidity, nowhere to stand. The under-current snatched at him, and he pounded the surface with his fists to try and stay afloat. The waves loomed more ferociously now that he was among them. His swirling panic made the sea feel that much rougher. After a few dunks he knew that he could not keep himself up much longer.

As the next wave pushed him down, he realized that his gamble had failed. The bluffs in the distance seemed to dissolve in a flare of hot light as if he was falling into the sun rather than the ocean. He could not hear his own breathing, just a humming in his ears that sounded like distant, soothing music. The water pulled him down, but the white light pulled him upward, and he finally stopped struggling, threw his hands up and let whichever direction was strongest claim him.

✠ ✠ ✠ ✠

Seen from above, Eastham was a sprawling, misshapen land, like a jigsaw puzzle with many gaping spots in the design where its many ponds, inlets, bays and harbors cut into its borders. Its firm ground was mostly farm tracts leveled out of ancient, towering hardwood forest by the first generation of Pilgrim settlers and bits of remaining, lesser woods, whose fate would be to fuel the chimneys of the growing homesteads. Life in town was not far removed from that of the pioneers from whom its people descended. For most, time moved with the rise and fall of crops, the run of fish and the reading of scripture on Sundays.

Today was Sabbath day, a cherished time for the man with light brown hair and wide, thoughtful eyes, who sat in his homestead in the southern part of Eastham.

Deacon John Paine paused and laid his quill pen down next to the ink well and open journal before him. He stood up from the writing table and went to the window, cracking it open to let a rush of crisp, cleansed air wash into the room.

There was a strange peacefulness after a storm. He savored the calm stillness in the air, thankful cheerfulness in the songs of the birds and vibrancy to the colors of the world, even the dark ground that glistened with earthy tones. This is what he was trying to capture with his clumsy words - that all of these gifts were ultimately a benison from the munificent Lord.

From his seat at the table, he could look out at the trees standing starkly in groves between him and Great Cove, a huge finger of saltwater that jutted into the center of town. Patches of dark blue hung between the trees' leafing branches.

His wife was still in their bedchamber, preparing and primping herself for the church service. Paine sighed at her womanly vanity but did not judge her harshly. She was a good, pious woman. If one was going to indulge in superficialities like dressing well, then the Lord's gathering was the time to do it, in His honor.

While he waited, Paine flipped through past entries in his journal:

How doth time pass it flies alas, for it hath eagle's wings
It flies away and will not Stay for temporary things
The Sun doth rise mounts up the Skies, but soon doth Set again
Man's born in tears, grows up in fears, his pleasures are but vain
Alas for me how plain I See, my time away doth run
Forty-nine years I've passed here, the fiftieth now begun
O glorious lord wilt thou afford, Me grace this year to Spend...

That year, 1709, had been a good one, as had most before it and the six after it. He was pleased too with the writing that he had done, although he immediately felt guilt for his vain thought and reminded himself that the Lord was the source and inspiration for all of his words. Today it was not his birthday nor had any family or close friend come or gone from this world. Nonetheless, he felt an urge to write. Like the aftermath of the gale, there was something in the air. The Lord felt closer this spring, and Paine felt inclined to praise Him. In the back of his mind, Paine hoped that this praise would suffice to prevent him from writing a more grieving entry later on. *Thank you, Lord,* he prayed silently. *It is indeed yours to give and take away – all of it! But please spare us one more year. I beseech thee!*

As he picked up the pen again, he heard the trilling cries of his beloved children, his brood of Christ's congregation. They were playing outside, under the eyes of the Lord, and Paine smiled happily with the thought that his offspring were, even in their youth, fine vessels for Christ's teaching. That realization spurred him to scratch out the first line of a new verse of praise: *Though they be mine, they remain thine, In humble gratitude your vessels...*

An urgent shout interrupted him, "Father!"

Paine sprang to the doorway and looked outside to see four of his children carrying between them a great length of wood. It looked to Paine to be a section of ship, and he shuddered and mumbled a quick prayer for any poor souls who were lost because of the wood's breaking.

"Bring it here," he commanded, amazed that they could lift such a weight.

As they hauled the thing closer, a darker thought seized him. It did not look like wood from a shipwreck. It was a long curve of timber with smaller cross lengths running the length of it, like a huge, bending comb with bristles sticking out. There was more that had been broken off, but Paine knew what the contraption was supposed to look like even before his young son Nathaniel put his fear into words, "The mill is gone, father!"

It was a section of blade from his tidal mill.

Paine ran towards the shoreline. A sickening feeling grew upon him with each step. Great Cove lay in front of him. Perched upon the marshy edge should be his mill. But he could see no sign of it except a stunted forest of pylons sticking out of the mud. The rest of the machinery had washed away.

"I'm sorry, father," Nathaniel said, slipping a small hand into Paine's own.

If it were not such a bad example for children, Paine might have cried. It would take weeks to rebuild the mill. He would need wood, nails, help.

The grim calculations clicked through his mind, until Nathaniel's grip grew tight, and the boy whispered, *"Father! What is that?"*

Paine turned his wet eyes towards the direction that his son was pointing, and what he saw nearly made him faint.

He did not know how he had missed it before.

There, below the mill on the tideline, wrapped in thick, coil-like strands of seaweed, was a beast.

It was a mammoth, white creature with huge arms, three wagon lengths long, the ends of which were coated in circular suckers, each one larger than a soup bowl. Paine recognized its kind. He had seen smaller versions in the ghostly squid that danced close to the water's surface near the footings of piers when the moon was full. He was aghast that there could be such a monster out there in the ocean.

For a second Paine wondered if this creature had torn apart his mill. Yet he knew that it had not. The beast had been wrecked by the storm in the same way as his livelihood. That it arrived on the Sabbath day, of all days, made it seem ripe with deeper meaning.

Then, all around him, the cries of young voices rose higher and higher, like an appeal to God. It was his children screaming.

Paine was a wise enough man to trust the instinct of children. They were looking at the beast and seeing it for what it was: a creature of unfathomable horror.

He turned and ran back up the hill, his children trailing behind him.

At the top of the ridge, he could see the familiar form of his wife, and she was waving. Suddenly Paine realized that they were late for church.

"Hurry! We must hurry!" he shouted to her as he ran. He was thinking that this was certainly not a day to be lax in communion with the Lord.

✠ ✠ ✠ ✠

Church bells carried on the wind over a simple ten-acre tract of corn, squash and livestock in the pasture. A modest homestead stood in the center of the tract, set off from the road. Stone walls framed one half of the border of the property and a rough line of apple and cherry trees the other. In the front was a fish pond fed by a small stream, and in the back were the stalls and an old barn.

Alice Hallett looked through the window of the house at her eighteen-year-old daughter Maria. The girl stood on the rock wall, looking out over the miles of plowed acreage of adjacent farms towards the small gray sheet of the distant ocean. As usual, her head lay shamelessly bare to the world, her hair twisted into braids, like weaves of loose straw, instead of piously shielded by the bonnet that she twirled in her hands.

The clarion call, at least, snapped Maria from her reverie, and Alice watched her hop from the wall and run off to fetch the wagon before being reminded to do so. Alice sighed, tied her own hat upon her head and stepped out into the crisp spring air.

"Put your bonnet on," she chided as she came out of the house, but her daughter pretended not to hear. Maria pulled the wagon out of the stall and hitched the horse to it, looping them together with a knot that the sailors would do, and then stood back to admire her handiwork for a moment. Alice opened her mouth to make comment on the unnecessary extravagance of the knot work but then changed her mind.

"No, no. Leave the reins…" Alice commanded, pushing Maria to one side of the wagon and reaching for the leather straps that controlled the horse. As the head of the household, Alice felt compelled to drive the wagon even though her daughter had a better hand at it. Lack of skill paled in comparison to the impropriety of arriving to service being driven by her daughter.

They rolled out into a loose procession of other wagons and carts moving along the road towards the sound of communion. Alice talked sparingly as it was, but on the Lord's day her flow of speech nearly ceased unless it was directed at offering prayer to His mighty nature. She expected her daughter to do the same. Although the girl's lips offered no utterance, her eyes plainly showed the course of her wandering mind. They roamed constantly towards the tidy farms that they were passing, with green fields that rolled right to the blue edge of Great Cove. Maria's hands were similarly restless. They were grappling with some mundane preoccupation, twisting around some little trinket, which Alice could not see clearly. Alice attempted to keep her own thoughts fixed on higher matters, but she was too distracted by her daughter's fidgeting.

"What is that in your hands?" Alice demanded.

Obediently, Maria opened her palm to reveal a little button with some string attached. The button had the luster of a pearl, except where it had chipped off in a few places, and Maria rubbed its smooth surface between her fingertips as if it was worth as much as a silver coin.

"I found it in the tide this morning. I thought that there might be something more to explain its story, but nothing else came rolling out of the waves," Maria explained.

"You were at the beach today?" Alice asked, her voice suddenly thick and foreign sounding, even to her own ears.

"Of course," Maria said, glancing over at her mother. "I saw a rainbow in the surf that sparkled when the sun hit it just so. It reminded me somehow of his laughter."

"What beach did you go to?" Alice queried, forcing the words out.

"The one below the Stage Lands that looks out at the breakwater," Maria replied with a reproachful look.

Alice did not answer. She sat stiffly on the wagon's bench. Good posture, she had been informed when she was Maria's age, was the sign of forthright bearing, amenable disposition and propensity for honest labor, which were all pious and admirable attributes for virtuous women. She glanced over at her daughter, who was slumping on her side of the bench, and wondered why the wisdom that she had attempted to pass along had not taken hold.

Maria tucked the button into her apron and pulled her bonnet low over her brow, so her face was covered by the light blue of its brim. Shielded from view was a face that was very similar to Alice's own but without the lines and stiffness that age brings. It was framed by straw colored hair, the same hue as Alice's had been before it had bleached to gray. Alice had been twenty-one when she had brought Maria into the world, only three years older than Maria was now. Along with that act of childbirth, she had to her credit the same as what any other Eastham woman was supposed to achieve with a lifetime: raising children, keeping the homestead running and avoiding sin. Her husband was gone, but the responsibilities remained. She knew that Maria saw things differently. The girl probably thought of her as something akin to the ripped off button, severed from its old carriage and tasks and free to transform into some other purpose, perhaps even turning to silver by some kind of alchemy. Maria had uttered similar nonsense on more than one occasion. Remembering the Sabbath, Alice scolded herself for indulging such blasphemous thoughts, which even her daughter had thankfully avoided mentioning. Part of her felt that she should take the button away from the girl, but it was not a day for insensitivity either.

"This storm is not yet finished. It will be another dark day," the girl said, glancing up at the sky.

Her mother looked at her sharply. "What do you know of it?"

"*Nothing,*" Maria mumbled.

"Do not speak of that to anyone at service. It is a day to ponder the workings of the Lord, not superstition," Alice warned.

"I would not. I did not dream of anything. I know that is what you are wondering."

"*Stop it,*" Alice hissed. "Not on this day!"

Mother and daughter did not talk again until they reached the meeting house where Alice watched some of their neighbors coming towards them and quickly repeated her caution about speculating on the dark clouds as a kind of portent.

The meeting house was virtually the same as that which was built by the first English settlers in 1644. As much a fortification as a place of assembly and worship, it was tightly constructed, and it still had gun holes as if the land was yet swarming with natives. In truth, it was too small to hold the burgeoning population of Eastham, whose borders stretched miles in every direction. Families coming in by wagon from the outskirts of town grumbled about the long distance they had to travel. And there was a stiff fine that the town fathers had imposed on those who missed service. There was much complaint about the fine too. But there was also plenty of talk about the storm.

Just before the service, the sun glided cheerfully through a break in the cover of gray clouds as if anticipating the prayers and benedictions that would soon be offered up to the heavens. For a moment it bathed the dark meeting house with its exuberance, giving a holy coat to the roofline and steeple. Upon the treeless plain the meeting house towered over the backdrop of farms. Its great, gonging bell reached out over the fields and across Great Cove, to the houses on the far shore, to call in the flock.

The structure was set half way between Great Cove and the King's Highway, a muddy cart path that traversed the center of the township. On its front lawn was a collection of graves of the first settlers, set off by a fence. Alongside it was a wooden pillory. The graves were a symbol of the eternal recompense offered by the heavenly father. The pillory demonstrated the seriousness with which His servants on earth made sure that the congregation lived lives that warranted burial in hallowed ground.

There was a native man kneeling within the jaws of the device. He hung like a crumpled scarecrow. His arms and head jutted through the holes in the heavy, interlocking boards, and the lock that fastened the boards together dangled like a necklace beneath his chin. Water dripped off of his clothes and face, from being left there all night in the rain.

A man pinned to a post in front of the meeting house was not an uncommon sight in Eastham. John Julian ended most of his weeks in the pillory's reprimanding grasp, for his refusal to willingly hear the word of the Lord. Julian had such a history of relapsing that he was of little use as a cautionary warning to the townsfolk who hurried past him towards the church door. A man like Julian was practically beyond rehabilitation, a lost cause. They only locked him up within earshot of the meeting house, instead of in the silence of the nearby jail, in hopes that at least his soul might have a chance at redemption.

Inside the meeting house the rows of benches were filled with the eldest members of the families in town. The young and single stood along the walls and in the back of the room.

Alice Hallett pushed her way towards the middle of the congregation, releasing Maria to find a space along the wall, with the unmarried, and advising her that the more loud and earnest her prayers, the better the chance to attract a suitable husband.

Reverend Treat was already standing at the front of the room. He was now nearly seventy and well beyond the years of his youthful vigor when his name rolled off of lips from Eastham to Boston with awed respect for his conversion of the heathen Indians. His height and booming voice still commanded much admiration in the community. However, most of the flock no longer paid attention to his dire words as raptly as they had when Treat first arrived in town some forty years ago because his predictions about the coming apocalypse had proven less reliable than the annual blackfish strandings and nor-easters. For many, the words washed right over them as would a breeze skirting over the fields. Both were a part of life, probably necessary in their respective ways, but hardly worth noting. But as he stood before them at the pulpit, most thought that Treat looked nearer than anyone else they knew to the Biblical prophets of old.

"Around thy head, at the whim and direction of the Almighty Lord, a horde of millions of devils and demons shall persecute the sinners and rip their offensive flesh to shreds in the spirit of His righteous fury! And there will be no water to bathe the wounds, only lakes of fire! And there will be no house to hide in from these beasts, only a wide plain of slaughter! For these wounds are meant to punish and will last an eternity!"

Alice watched approvingly as the old preacher gesticulated towards the ceiling, appealing to heaven for mercy. She kept her eyes fastened to the reverend, except for an occasional sweep in Maria's direction where she caught her daughter yawning unashamed and stifled it with a silent command for obedience.

Treat was famous for invoking the thunderous wrath of the Almighty, striving for such authenticity that his volume rattled the window panes. He shouted, "A pious people is also a vigilant people!

Every blessing of the Lord is countered by a curse from the underworld! Be aware that our duty is not simply to our own affairs and fields, but also to be the eyes of the Lord, righteous and watchful, lest the Devil find inroads into our home!"

As if on cue, the front door of the meeting house sprang open and clattered on its hinges. Deacon Paine stood on the threshold, the gist of his horrific story showing clearly on his strickened face, before he had even begun his tale.

"The storm brought with it a beast from the sea! God be praised, it is dead! But it is an unnatural creature! A horrid thing! Some twenty feet long! Why it has come to us, I know not!" Paine cried.

Heavy window shutters left over from the garrison days of the meeting house made the place feel choked and gloomy. A few lines of dust beamed down through the rafters from the cracks in the upper story windows. Alice pictured them as the unfinished part of Treat's sermon falling like whispers into the chattering congregation. A few women stood and began opening as many windows as they could as if they had not needed light more so than at this moment. As light flooded in, the heavenly beams from above were snuffed out like a candle.

"Well then. The day I long feared has arrived. There is no more need for words, but that of prayer for protection and deliverance, as we make this battle. We need to go see this creature. Even in death it could be a torment for us, and there might well be others of its kind on the way. If nothing else, it is a sign of devilry among us!" Treat said.

Treat led a good many of the men out of the meeting house. He wore an expression of combat, which was not much different from the fiery visage he showed during regular service, except that now there was a trace of vindication in it.

The rest of the parishioners fled away. Some banded in protective groups to wait together until the threat had passed, others struck the reins for home, thankful for any nonsense to release them from the weekly chore.

By chance, Alice and her daughter came up against the shoulder of Mrs. Cole as they worked their way out of the building. Mrs. Cole drew her young children under her arms, like a cautious hen, and gave Maria a steady look as if the girl was as big a threat as the sea creature. Maria did not return the gaze, and for that Alice was proud of her. Alice said nothing either as she shuffled uncomfortably through the throng.

"This was the day of the wreck, was it not?" Mrs. Cole asked, a touch of flint under her words.

"What is done is done. God rest my husband's soul – and the others," Alice replied.

"Yes. Godspeed to them. Odd that this frightful day should occur on the first anniversary of their passing," Mrs. Cole went on, still looking at Maria.

"I see no connection between the two," Alice answered.

"What did thou dream this past night, *Goody* Hallett?" Mrs. Cole asked Maria. She emphasized the general title for an unmarried, of-age girl, with a tone like Maria was something ill who had stained the root meaning of the word.

Alice stiffened but smiled wider as if to create a shield to deflect the accusation. "She dreamt of nothing. And before twas but a childish nightmare."

"I hope as much. Premonition is not listed among Godly works. We are here a year later, and now there is a beast afoot. Perhaps it is mere happenstance."

"What else would it be?" Alice demanded.

Mrs. Cole nodded noncommittally and brushed past them.

"I did not speak to anyone!" Maria said when she caught her mother's glare.

"You did not dream in such a fashion when your father was with us," Alice said with the weight of accusation.

But Alice was not entirely sure about that. All at once, she felt the same devilish chill dance along her spine that she had when she was listening to Deacon Paine describe the beast washed up at his doorstep. A year and a day ago, her daughter had not gotten up to start breakfast, which was her daily chore. She had not replied from the sleeping loft when Alice had admonished her for the neglect. When she finally came down, the girl looked feverish. The illness, it turned out, seemed to be in her mind. She chanted strange, horrid thoughts in a distant, vacuous tone. It was an awful tale, and Alice shouted for her daughter to cease. But the girl did not stop until she had told Alice everything about the storm and the ship that she had seen in her sleeping mind as it slipped headlong into a funnel of waves, like a morsel being sucked into the belly of the sea. The next day dark clouds lay across the heavens like funeral clothes, and Alice learned that her husband was gone forever.

✠ ✠ ✠ ✠

After they released him from the pillory, John Julian walked the mile from the meeting house to his people's village, which sat in a wide hollow with a saltwater pond in the middle of it.

The peel of church bells was the only discordant sound amidst the ageless conversation of wind, water and bird calls around him. The clamor from the steeple signaled the end of service. The white settlers usually considered it a sound of celebration although this time the bell had called something truly terrible to them. Through the open window Julian had heard their worried talk about the monster and was not sure it was a fell thing. Perhaps this beast would drive them from the land, he mused. Perhaps it was the white god himself come to rid himself of his people since, with all of his promises of eternal fire and bloodshed, he seemed to hate them so much. The words of their god and holy man offered as much comfort as Julian's aching wrists. Julian rubbed the marks as he passed members of his tribe who were heading back in the other direction for the long trek to the Indian meeting house in the southern part of town. None of his people met his eyes even when he flashed his bruises at them. As soon as his absence was known at the native service, Justice Doane would come looking for him, and by morning Julian's welts would be a deeper shade of purple. Yet he did not care. If the Nausets were supposed to have their own service, separate from the English, why couldn't they still have their own gods too?

Hawks and crows still circled over the meadow next to the village. Clams still hid under the sand, and minnows and crabs splashed in the shallows where they were chased by laughing children as they had been since the world began.

Wetus, the shelters that his people lived in, still wreathed the pond. They were fashioned as they always had been, with long strips of oak or birch bark tied onto an assemblage of sticks like skin over bone. They were meant to be put up and taken down with the seasons, but it had been many summers now since they had moved from their spots. Fourteen years ago the English said that the natives could no longer roam freely over their ancestral lands or put up their shelters in accordance with the movement of the best hunting grounds – in forest groves during winter, in the growing fields during spring and summer and near the ponds in autumn. Now they had only one spot, and the village stayed there.

Above the village, on the slope of the hill where the white men's first fort had been, Reverend Treat's house stood close enough to almost cast a shadow over the Nausets as if he was ever watchful for any return to heathen ways.

Reverend Treat was celebrated by the English and Nausets alike for introducing the white god to the native people. Now some braves carried Bibles instead of bows. They pushed plows for English farmers and wore the same clothes as the settlers. Some were hardly distinguishable from their English neighbors, except for their tawny color and lack of land, terrain that was once shared by all who are a part of the Great Spirit.

Julian went to the edge of the village and sat on a massive rock on the shoreline of a river that connected the saltwater pond to the great harbor beyond.

He fished a clay pipe and wad of tobacco out of his pants' pockets. The pipe and pants were among a handful of English items of which he approved. The tobacco, of course, was something the English never could have invented in all the time on earth. It was the sacred plant of the Great Spirit. Inhaling its mighty fumes made him feel powerful in the way that he believed that the braves of old had.

While he smoked, he thought about what kind of world the children that he saw bathing in the soft current would encounter. He was only thirty or so summers old, but he sometimes felt as though centuries had passed since his birth. His grandparents had spoken nothing of the English language. Now many of the young had to be constantly reminded of the true names of things because their heads were filled with so much of the foreign tongue. Their notions of the world came out of the white god's book, so they were forgetting basic truths of the world such as the fact that trickster spirits come out with a moonlit fog, animal spirits all have their own demands as payment for killing them and certain seeds and leaves can heal and bring magic to those who know their uses.

No one ventured over to sit and smoke with Julian. Had this been the land of his forefathers, they would not have passed by without doing so. Often he felt as cut off from his people as he literally was now, sitting on one side of the river with the village on the other. Yet if the analogy was to be complete, there would be another – wider – river that cleanly divided him from the English town on the other side of the village, leaving him alone in the middle, his rock a tiny island.

He was sitting on the old sharpening rock. It was a large boulder on the edge of the marsh. All across its surface were grooves, as deep as the tip of a man's finger, from the making of stone axe blades, arrowheads and other tools and weapons. Every generation of his ancestors, beyond counting, had likely laid a hand to the carving of these grooves in solid rock. It told of the Nausets' history the same way that the Bible told the English of theirs. Julian thought that it was no accident that the face of the stone was streaked with lines like the mark of war paint. The land itself was calling for a fight, and Julian wanted to remind his people about its power.

He saw a flash of silver in the water at his feet. There was a gurgling splash on the surface and then another gleam of color as the fish shot away with a flick of its tail. In front of him Nauset Harbor fanned out in miles of marshy inlets, channels and bog until it reached a thin strip of beach in the far distance, which held back the might of the great ocean itself.

The glow of his pipe slowly faded and, with it, his thoughtful mood ebbed away. There would be another hard rain falling. The ground smelled of it. The seagulls told of it as they circled round and round, high in the clouds. It was the kind of weather that made the tide rush fast and high, and the fish would be following it.

He tapped out the blackened, spent coals of his pipe and walked to the shoreline where canoes had been pulled into the tall, green beach grass. A drizzle of rain started, drumming out its rhythm on the bottoms of the craft, which were overturned to keep the water out. These, at least, were kept out in the open for anyone to take who had a need for one, in the manner of his ancestors. He found the one that he himself had carved out of an old oak tree and leapt into its hollow as he pushed out into the water.

He paddled with deft strokes, pulling himself into a flow of current and then letting it carry him for a while. When the water veered away from his course, he poled himself into a more suitable flow. All the water was ultimately heading out through the marshes to the ocean beyond, but each channel had its own course to get there.

The paddle made little eddies, which spun off behind him. Here and there clumps of brown seaweed or crab shells floated by in the current, but there was no sign of fish. At one point Julian saw a long piece of broken wood hung up in the tips of the marsh grass. By its rounded shape and lengths of rope tied to it, he knew it was man-made, but he did not tarry to inspect it. The fish would not be distracted by similar curiosity, and he did not want to miss them.

Finally he could see his weir in the distance where it stood in the shallows on the near side of the white beach that was the barrier to the sea beyond it. There was a break in the beach where the ocean came in and met the more placid harbor in a froth of whitecaps, which Julian did not ever cross through. He had no need to go that far out because the big fish liked to drift along the inner lip of the beach where the current was strong and his weir was waiting to catch them.

In the ebb tide only half of the structure was visible. The sides were tree branches, stuck like poles in the mud, with woven netting - another concession to the white settlers - strung in between to make walls. The opening was a long funnel that led to a big belly of a chamber. The tide drove the fish in. Some escaped, but others became confused and were trapped within the weir. When Julian got there, all he had to do was wade in and scoop them out.

The storm kept the water level higher than usual. When Julian tied off to the weir and jumped in, he was soaked up to his chest whereas normally he could have sloshed through the trap, getting only his knees wet. As soon as he was in the water, he saw shimmering motion in it. Reaching into his canoe, he produced a large hand net of twine stretched across the pronged end of a tree branch. He spun the net through the water and drew up two flapping bluefish, which were the length of his arm.

Their eyes gave him a panicked look as he drew them near, but he spoke soothingly to them, praising their beautiful color and thanking them for the gift of their flesh. Then he laid an ear close to their mouths. Why he still did this, he often wondered, but he did not want to take a chance that the old story was wrong. There were fish that were said to speak and could tell a man's future if he listened closely. But all that Julian heard from this pair was the clack of their jaws as they gasped in the open air. He patted their shiny bellies and loaded them into a sack that he carried.

More fish moved all around him, bumping against his legs, and Julian smiled at the bounty.

Again he aimed the hand net and drove it into the water.

Just then something bumped hard into the small of his back and rolled away with the current. At first he thought that his canoe had broken from its mooring, and he was thankful that it had been caught up in the netting rather than being drawn away into the marsh, leaving him stranded. But he could see the boat out of the corner of his eye, and it was still tied securely.

Julian turned and scanned the interior of the weir and was amazed to see a great white shape bobbing in one corner.

He gasped and sloshed backwards a few steps.

It looked like the underside of a huge fish. His hands started shaking involuntarily as he wondered why it had not eaten him when it had the chance. Perhaps it still meant to, he thought. The canoe was about ten feet away. The fish was an equal distance in the other direction.

Then he heard a strange, choked gurgle as if the giant fish was struggling for words.

Julian's eyes went wide. He trudged a few steps towards it, straining to hear its message. He noticed that its skin looked odd. What was it, he wondered?

As he reached out his hand, the nature of the creature's hide became clear to him a moment before his fingers touched it: canvas. This was no fish at all but rather a clump of sail from a white man's ship.

Relief commingled with embarrassment. A trick of the ocean, he mused. His fingers dug into the material, and he pulled it up out of the water.

Underneath, Julian was startled to see the face of a man looking up at him. A dark beard and hair floated around it like seaweed, and Julian was struck with the uneasy feeling that this was not a good omen.

Then he noticed the gentle rise and fall of the man's shirt, apart from the waves, which showed that the man was alive although he seemed deep in sleep or some fever.

Julian's wrists began to ache again as if in reminder of some unnamed transgression that would land him in the meeting house pillory once more. The mere handling of this white man might be enough cause to bring him grief, he thought, but by the same line of thinking, it was likely too late already. He could look back and see the small point of Treat's roof on the hill across the marsh. He imagined that the reverend could somehow see the goings on in the weir and would hold Julian accountable for the white man's fate. Part of him felt like kicking the defenseless man as if he had washed up into the netting out of spite.

Instead, he dumped him into the canoe. It was foolish to expect that by returning one of the English he would receive some favor from them. Yet his own honor demanded it. He was one brave alone in this new world where bows and arrows no longer worked. His only hope was to keep making offerings to the old and new gods alike. If the beast won, then Julian would be delivering another victim to it. If the whites defeated the scourge upon them, then they would be happy to have one of their own returned to them.

As he paddled towards shore, he continued to ponder the strangeness of this day and the unusual things brought up on the tide – the beast and now this man. It could not be coincidence.

BOOK ONE

The Tale of Goody Hallett

Chapter One
"The Necessity of Proper Education"

June 1715

Alice Hallett stood in the gloaming light of dawn and peered down the long, dark length of Tonset Road. From where she stood at the rock wall of her farm to the black point in the distance, where the road was absorbed into shadow, was empty. Beyond that lay the Stage Lands, a flat plateau of common land that jutted out into the southern part of Nauset Harbor, under which bluff the beast had been found.

Yesterday the road had been filled with men, horses and carts. There was more motion than Alice had ever seen upon the rutted dirt track that cut through southern Eastham. The men of the community had told their wives and children to stay home. They loaded up their carts and horses with nets, fishing knives, axes and pitchforks, with little notion of what weapon might best contend with an unholy sea monster. Those that owned one brought a Bible. Those that did not brought an extra mug of ale. Even the most pious saw fit to keep a flask handy should the knives and books fail to inspire enough courage. Even though she was the head of a household, Alice had not joined the expedition. She stood dutifully by the stone wall at the edge of her property, like a dozen other women stationed at intervals along the road, peering anxiously towards the vacant distance.

It had been one of the worst days of her life, wondering whether men or some beast would come back down the road. Eventually the tale of what the men had found made its way back, household to household, and every woman and child heard that the creature was as enormous and terrible as Paine had said. No one seemed to be able to make sense of the exact meaning of the creature, other than it was a sure sign of devilry afoot. Reverend Treat stood at the great head of the beast and pronounced the Lord's Prayer upon it, after which black blood spewed from the beast's belly, a clear sign of its intentions, according to the reverend. It was a foul, despicable messenger of coming doom.

That night Alice's daughter had slept soundly for once, but Alice had tossed and turned, twisting in the sheets as if the beast had wrapped her in its long, horrid arms. She woke early, feeling groggy and sore. She could not recall what dreams she had spent the night wrestling with, but she felt the ache of them in her back and forehead. She was glad that they had left no further impression, other than a pressing urge to once more check the road to ensure that no further menace was upon the sleeping township.

That is how she found herself again at the wall, bundled in her shawl, in the cold, dim morning. When she finished musing on the terrifying events of the previous day, she leaned back into the cold rock and was comforted for a moment by its solid presence. Long ago her mother had told her to look on such walls as inspiration for the way a woman of Eastham should set the foundation of her life. As a strong line of stone keeps the livestock in and the wolves out, so does a strong, set demeanor protect the private secrets of the heart and keep judgments away. At the moment, the rock itself seemed scant protection against the indiscernible threat that could be carried stealthily by the raw wind or roiling clouds above. What protection was there against devilry, she wondered?

The road was empty. So Alice walked back across the fields towards her house in the distance. As she came inside into the main room, she could hear the gentle respiration of her daughter coming from the loft above. Alice scowled and opened her mouth to shout her daughter awake but then decided against rousing her. For the first time in a long while, she wished to relish the morning quiet.

The coals from last night's hearth fire were nearly black but for a tinge of orange, like the last hue of sunset. She took a ladle full of water from the bucket next to the fireplace and poured the liquid around the hem of her dress to keep any embers from catching fire to it. She had seen enough women with skin like rippling maple bark on their hands or faces to know what could happen should the flames take to her garments. Plenty of graves in the cemetery were of others who took a lick of fire that turned into a sore that would not heal.

When Alice stepped into the fireplace, she felt a slight radiance of heat from the bricks around her. A short-handled shovel stood against the outer face of the bricks. She scraped the remains of the fire into a pile under the iron hook for the cook pot. Then she jabbed the sooty mound with an iron poker, enflaming the coals' color and eventually drawing fresh flame from them. She added a stack of kindling to the fire and brought the conflagration to the proper height to start porridge in the pot.

Water, flax, oats and rye soon bubbled in the pot for breakfast. A second hook held another kettle, which was always full. Any table scraps of beef, fish, bread crust, carrot or turnip were cast into it and mushed together into stew, which was drawn from all week long. It was like a bottomless cup in the way that there was always food within. She did not like to mix the contents, stirring the fresh scraps in with the ones that had been sitting there for days on end. So the bottom layers built up into a noxious crud, which occasionally had to be thrown into the pigs' slop. It was a waste that other women in town would have scorned had they known. But Alice would not suffer eating week old meals as if she was still living on the frontier like her Pilgrim ancestors. However, with the state of the farm as it was, she feared that soon she would be serving such unsavory fare onto her plate.

She reached into the stew pot and withdrew a few chunks of ham, skewered them on the point of a knife and held them over the flame until they were warm.

With her foot she spun the metal grate that held slices of bread. She watched the fire turn the slices brown, then yanked them out with her fingertips and tossed them onto the table.

By the time her daughter had risen and washed her face and neck in the basin on the room's side table, Alice had breakfast on the board and sat down with a sigh. Her first task of the day was finished, and now she had nothing to look ahead to but an endless amount of more toil.

Breakfast was taken in near silence. There was just the sound of chewing, swallowing and breathing, with only the clack of spoons on the pewter plates to differentiate their eating from that of the livestock out in the pens.

Alice let her eyes wander around the room, noting the wide boards that ran straight up the length of the wall and along the floor. It was good, thick oak. The seams were tight and gave her comfort because they had been fashioned by her late husband's hands. Some of the boards were more than two feet in width, making them "King's Wood," lumber that should have gone to England to fit the masts and decks of the royal fleet. Her husband had never seen the logic in the monarch being able to claim trees from a place that he had not once set foot upon, and no tax collector had summoned the courage to press the issue. Seth Hallett had been built as big and strong as his house, and Alice was glad at least that he had left such a solid structure behind because everything else seemed reduced by his absence. Even a little thing, like the taxman on the threshold, made her feel vulnerable and ill prepared. Worse still was the troubling feeling that her daughter often evoked. As for his daughter, Seth Hallett did nothing but dote. It fell to Alice to take the sterner line, where appropriate. Often she wished that her daughter was more like the straightness of the boards in the walls than the wandering spirit that was emerging. Boards could be straightened. With a firm hand they could be bent into truer form, held in place and nailed fast. But it was tiring work.

"Come. Finish quick. There is work to be done," Alice chided even though they were equally close to finishing their meal.

"We shall return to the fields today?" Maria asked.

"Why would we not?"

"Yesterday we spent the day at the wall."

"You know well why too."

Maria nodded. "Could the beast be simply a passenger in the storm, without any aim of mischief? How do we know that it is devilish?"

Alice might have gasped had her mouth not been full at that moment. But she did not get a chance to reply. A sudden loud rap on the door made both women jump.

"Take the fire poker," Maria advised.

Alice felt no need for protection, other than the prayer that she muttered under her breath. For if it was devilry at her door, she could think of nothing but God's will that could save her.

God answered her plea in the deep voice of Elder Knowles, her neighbor, calling her name through the paneling.

She opened the door and saw the severe face of a man about her own age. He was just forty, lean and dark bearded, but already considered one of the town fathers, a senior member of the church, an office holder and a man whose opinion was said to count for much.

"Good. I am glad to see you risen and ushering in the morn without heed to the shadow over us," Knowles intoned.

"Life continues and there are chores to do, are there not?"

"Aye. Plenty of chores."

"Will you come in?"

Knowles shook his head. "Treat has sent a letter to Reverend Mather in Boston, asking for his advice. It was my suggestion, in fact, for I remember Reverend Mather's involvement in more than one defense against Satan. We shall not tarry in our response to this threat," he said.

"Do you believe that there will be another attack upon our shores? Even in the light of day?" Alice asked.

Knowles frowned and glanced up into the sky's dreary contradiction of Alice's words. "All of the town elders agree that it is a warning. If we continue to stray, I fear that this is but the first horror we shall see. The next will likely be worse. But if we comply with the will of the Lord, we may be spared for the final judgment and salvation."

When he had finished his warnings, Knowles peered at the fields alongside the house. "My boys are old enough to help with your harvest, after we complete our own. They can handle the blade and plow. Seth's acreage is manageable for the four of us. There is no reason for you to feel troubled by putting food on the table, Alice."

"Thank you, Elder. You are most kind to think of us so."

"I would have you consider it more than a mere token of neighborliness."

Alice blushed. It had been a year and a day since the death of her husband. By tradition, the first anniversary of her loss released a widow to courtship again, yet Alice still wore her black shawl of mourning.

There was more talk of plans for the farm and insinuations about the future, all of which deepened the scarlet hue on Alice's face.

Knowles then drew himself up to his full height and turned grave eyes towards Alice. "I would add that it is the responsibility of us all to guide our friends, neighbors and family lest any one of us stray. You and I both have children under our roof. And the young have a tendency to misstep on occasion."

When Knowles left, Alice lingered on the stoop and watched him stride across the fields towards his own farm. She had not quite come back to her proper color when she turned and saw her daughter's narrowed eyes peering at her. Alice stared back at her for a few moments, her thoughts rolling inside of her.

"I have not had any dreams recently. That is what you are wondering, isn't it?" Maria remarked.

Alice sat down at the table and bit into her slice of bread to hide her suddenly trembling lip. She had to admit that the girl scared her sometimes. She sometimes wondered if Maria could read minds too. It was a crazy notion, Alice told herself. After all, Maria was her daughter. She reminded herself that it had been but one dream, as dire and frightening as it was. If not for the troubling events of the first anniversary, it would all be forgotten by now. She had told Maria that it was simply a nightmare, a trick of the mind. She told the girl not to think or talk of it, but Maria could not hold her tongue at service that morning after it had happened. *Many of these other girls have fathers on that ship too* was Maria's retort. Alice extolled her to stop, but it was too late. The dream spread along the rapid currents of gossip throughout the meeting house. Later that day the sea pushed out a dozen sons and fathers of Eastham at the very spot where her daughter had seen their doom.

"You are still staring in that way you do when you are troubled by some thought or other," Maria went on.

"It is nothing… For dinner I shall make fish stew. Abraham Knowles caught extra bass in Great Cove yesterday afternoon. He was out there in the water even after all that has happened, brave lad," Alice said with a shudder. Then she stood up from the table abruptly, causing the plates to rattle. "Finish quick so we can get out to the fields before the day is lost."

"Everyone thinks that I am queer," Maria said, still seated and pushing at her oats with a spoon.

"You are simply a girl who grieves her father mightily. That is the nature of the world. That you lost him before his time is the only ill."

"Mrs. Cole considers my dreams more than that."

"She gives in too easily to judgment."

"There are others too."

"I have heard no such talk," Alice remarked. She piled the plates under her arm, brought them to the scrap bucket and roughly scraped them off.

"I sense it. Many people do not think of me in the same manner as before."

"Who? How do you know? Do you dream of this too?"

Mother and daughter locked eyes for a moment.

"I wish that I had not told anyone about the dream," the girl uttered, after a pause.

"That would have been the prudent thing. In time people will forget again. There is much else to worry about these days. We all should be thinking about our salvation, not your prophecies."

"So you believe me to know the future at times?"

"I merely use the word! I do not know what it is. Speak no more of it to me! All I know is that they are not Godly visions, and you should pray that they cease! Your future is nearly upon you, and it will bring you a husband. I wish you would spend more time dreaming of that."

"'Tis another sort of nightmare," Maria said with a scowl.

"It is a necessity! Consider yourself lucky that God favored you with a pleasing face. You will have a better pick of husbands than most," Alice added.

After they had eaten, Alice took her clay pipe from the box that hung by the fireplace. She filled it with tobacco and clasped her teeth around it, making her mouth looked fixed in permanent grimace. Maria took her own pipe, lit it and followed her mother outside.

Alice had a sudden inspiration. "We shall go see Reverend Treat about this matter. He is discreet. He shall not tell another."

"*He sees devilry in everything,*" Maria muttered.

Alice did not look up. "We must look to those who are wiser than us if we are to get any answers."

"And I must go to school for my lessons. I just remembered... I cannot work the fields today."

Alice sighed but nodded in agreement. "Fine. You are indeed in need of lessons." Truth be told, Alice did not mind Maria's absence if it meant an end to their bickering. But as she watched her daughter walk off towards the road, the solitude suddenly did not feel so soothing. In fact, the brighter the sun became, the more the emptiness around her seemed harshly revealed.

✠ ✠ ✠ ✠

Justice Doane liked to say that the body of law, which was his duty to uphold, was akin to a solid oak tree. Its roots held the community firmly in place on the land of their ancestors. Its trunk was the firm structure of moral principles from which laws grew in the directions that best allowed the town to reach new heights. The metaphor was a rare piece of poetry from a man whose usual train of thought was as straight and serious as the line of his mouth or creases on his forehead. His long, chiseled looking face, under his close-cropped brown hair, and his tall, rigid stance made the justice himself seem tree-like. It was for unwavering consistency, rather than inspiration, that most in town turned to him.

Doane lived on Pochet Road, south of Great Cove, near the beginning of that route. The house in which he, his wife and several children dwelled was a modest structure, at least compared to the proud edifice of the man who now stood at Doane's door.

There was a day when Reverend Treat would have noticed the old wood panels of the door, the outdated, diamond paned windows - instead of square, clear glass - and other features that marked Doane's home as a lesser quality construction than his own. Treat was well-admired in town for his success in worldly matters, like trade and investment, which matched his understanding of God's work. He had long pointed to his material abundance as a sign of favor from the Almighty, a reward for his faith and a reminder that a strong work ethic in the fields and on the money counting boards was proof that he was one of the elect, who would receive God's grace. Now his sprawling lands held little interest for him. He did not see how they could much benefit him if they were being overrun by agents of destruction.

When Doane opened the door, Treat saw that the justice was in his dress pants and vest, for he always wore impressive attire, in case he was suddenly called to duty. In contrast, Treat was finding it increasingly difficult to summon the will or concern for his own garb. He often went about his errands bare legged, having forgotten to pull on his stockings before rushing out to visit his flock. He was like this now. The sight of his informality disturbed Doane less than the gaunt look of the man himself. Treat's chest rose and fell, like bellows expelling great gasps of air. Doane saw that Treat had driven himself on the wagon, but he could not believe that the ride across town or walk from the hitching post in the yard to his front door could have caused such agitation. But Treat looked like a man who was taking as many last breaths as he could.

"Joseph. May I come in for a moment?" the reverend asked. His old eyes shone like blue skies trying to break through soupy, white clouds. Doane stepped aside and let Treat pass.

Had this been only months before, Treat might have remarked about the waft of corn scent coming from the Dutch oven where Mrs. Doane was making cakes for supper. The aroma of baking bread also hung in the air, it being Saturday, the day when all Eastham matrons set their loaves and muffins in the cookeries in the faces of their hearths. Treat might have made some mention of that or, on the sly, pinched a bit too much salt into the batter if he could get away with it, or pretended that some fly had dropped onto the skillet and was cooking into the meal. When he was not brandishing the promise of eternal damnation at his congregation, Treat was well-known as a tremendous practical joker. It was one part of his unusual balance, in much the same way that his thirst for material wealth offset his heady pursuit of the teachings of spirit. Today, however, he thumped past Mrs. Doane, with only a slight head tilt in acknowledgement. Then he lowered his ample frame onto the bench closest to the hearth fire, warming his hands over the flame as if testing the force that he was up against.

"I am off to see John Cole's son. His mother tells me that he desires to join the ministry when he is of age. That would be a boon to Eastham in the future. I shall test what kind of mettle and understanding the boy has and then decide if I shall lend my support to his education. Times like these make one think hard about the future soldiers of the Lord," Treat explained.

Doane met his glance. "Indeed."

"The tide has not washed the beast away. Even the birds will not touch it."

"When they are hungry enough, they will peck at it."

"They don't touch the meat because it is rank beyond rot! It is evil flesh, which only the Devil would find palatable!" Treat snapped.

The justice nodded somberly. Treat's outbursts were becoming more and more commonplace and at times incomprehensible. He had heard them sometimes border on blasphemy, if lewdness was considered such. Treat could swear like a sailor when he was of mind, and Doane often wondered how much of the time Treat was still in control of his thoughts.

Doane pulled another bench to the fire and took a bowl of broth from his wife. He motioned for her to fill one for their guest, but Treat shook off the offer.

For a while Treat sat in front of the fire, stretching his legs towards it and contemplating the gray cast of his bare shins. Once or twice he coughed, and Doane expected some discourse to follow. It turned out to be nothing more than a clearing of the throat, the kind of utterance that was more and more frequent from the reverend in recent times.

"Things escape me these days. My poor wife Abigail thinks I have lost my wits. There are times when I cannot find my quill, though it is directly under the parchment I write upon. There are days when the desk itself seems unfamiliar to me. I expect to see the old desk I had as a young man at Harvard, and the one I have had these past forty years seems the stranger. Then I awake in the middle of the night and hear words of a sermon being spoken in my head, in voices not my own, as if I am coming into the middle of an ongoing conversation between angels. They speak of preparation. In my heart I know exactly what they mean. The great final battle is coming to us, and they urge us to be ready. That I should live to see such times…" Treat said.

The justice was well used to the constant preaching of the reverend whether Treat was at the pulpit or not. The rambling nature of it was something new, however, as was the familiarity he showed Doane. In the decades of their acquaintance, they had been close, professional allies, not friends. For all the time that they mulled over the goings on of town, they should have been closer. Yet, in Doane's eyes, Treat was at heart a privileged son of Harvard, while Doane considered himself a product of yeomen stock who had raised themselves to prominence. It was a small, but deep, fissure that had separated them all these years. So the tenor of Treat's personal talk had Doane chewing his lip and searching for the right tone of phrase with which to respond.

Before he could, Treat coughed again and resumed his chatter, "When I first moved to Eastham, the folk of this place offered me fifty pounds per annum, grazing meadows and twenty acres upland. It was a princely sum for a man fresh from university. Your father was among those who welcomed me."

"So I have been told."

"There was a time when Elizabeth, my first wife, wanted to sell the old house on the hill and move here to the south shore, right down the road from you. I remember walking out to the Stage Lands, looking back across the Cove at the land that I now own and seeing how close the meeting house was to my front door. I did not like the fact that there was a body of water between me and the meeting house at that moment. Something about that troubled me, and I could not imagine living with such a barrier between myself and the pulpit. Now look what we find washed ashore at that very spot…"

Doane did not know what to say. So he turned to a subject that he knew well: the militia. He did not have much military experience. But it was enough to earn him the captaincy of the town's defenses, which were comprised of about forty men, a mix of white land owners and local natives. He described the merits, training and weapons of the band, assuring Treat that all of his men lived within a half-day's ride from the heart of Eastham. When he finished, he expected to hear some word of relief from Treat, but the old man kept staring at his feet, wiggling them as if he wished to take off his shoes and spread his toes to the heat. The image stuck for a moment in the justice's head. He wondered if the reverend was out of mind enough to stoop to such indiscretion.

Treat then told Doane of sinful towns wiped clean off of the map by avengers sent by God and others that had met their dooms when they had let Maleficia, the evil doings of witches and devils, spread unchecked. Either scenario did not reflect well on the sanctity of the inhabitants, something that troubled Treat greatly. He wondered if Eastham's collective piety was weakening. They had lapses in church attendance to prove it, despite the new ten shilling fine for such an offence.

Doane reminded Treat that harvest time was approaching and that field work would keep otherwise Christian souls from the Sabbath.

"That is no different than offering an excuse for the ancient, sinful city of Gomorrah," Treat scolded.

"I did not say that I would not punish the offenders," Doane pointed out. But Treat did not seem to be listening.

"Odd, isn't it, that I can not always locate my quill, and yet I can hear the talk of angels so clearly? It is written that angel Gabriel comes with his trumpet at a man's death, to take him if he is destined for the Lord's house. The church bells sound to me like a trumpet at times. I wonder who they call for. I sit and ponder this sometimes when I cannot find my quill to write with," Treat said.

Doane smiled wanly. The reverend's once fine mind was no better than a dog chasing its tail. Doane rose from his chair, hoping the reverend would be inspired to do the same. He did not like to watch such sad disintegration before his eyes.

"I am fully confident in the militia and my deputies. Most men I know in this town are law-abiding and pious. We will provide strength and protection for each other. I do not fear and neither should you. Should another beast, or something of that sort, come upon us, we can beat it back. Even the Great Islanders in Billingsgate would pull their weight if they knew that the threat affected us all. Speaking of that, there will soon be another vote to settle the land division. There is a huge problem of men residing without leave on the island and contesting public ownership..." Doane would have said more about his worry about the squabbles over the deeds to the island off of the northern parish, a threat with potential to unravel them as much as the fear of a strange sea animal, but Treat cut him off.

"This war will not be won with arms and military companies. The appearance of this foul creature is a sign of deeper ill among us. Reverend Cotton Mather encountered witchery in Boston some years ago. In our correspondence about it, he reminded me of the insidiousness of its course. It comes through the innocent, warping them and making them its instruments. The Lord made the simple squid. The Devil warped it with unnatural and unholy size. Its message is that nothing is beyond the power of the Devil's ability to corrupt. Surely a sign as large as this squid indicates that witchery and devilry are taking seed. How else would you read it?" Treat demanded.

Doane inhaled. He did not bother to mention that he was of mind that the squid was nothing more than an overgrown version of the harmless kind that any fisherman had seen a hundred times in the water. "There has been no sign of the Witch of Billingsgate for a decade since my father ran her out into the woods. We have no proof of any evil from the beast or…"

"Proof!" Treat roared. "The proof is here!" He thumped Doane on the chest as he rose from the bench, showing little sign of age now as he puffed up with outrage. "The witch you speak of was of a different kind. She was born under an evil brand. Anyone can be brought under a dark spell and then hide right out in the open, posing as one of our own."

"I know only what I see."

The reverend snorted. "I am late for my visit at the Coles. John Cole is one of your militia, is he not?"

"Yes."

"*Lieutenant* Cole is a man who knows this threat for what it is. Whoever is in charge of the militia or the law should be ever vigilant for any sign of something ill among us. Even if its face seems a flower, look for the darkness underneath! This is the battle for salvation!"

Doane was not so sure. However, he was the only one with the title of military Captain or Justice in Eastham, and he did not intend to relinquish either of them.

✠ ✠ ✠ ✠

The necessity for education was not strong for boys and girls in Eastham. Knowledge of the spade, loom and fishing line was considered far more useful than any skill at penmanship, reading or history. Yet the residents of town did appreciate imparting a base understanding of books, numbers and words, for they believed that comprehension of such facts was part of what set humanity above the beasts of the world. That mathematics and reading were near useless did not undercut this divine duty to raise themselves out of ignorance. If a child came away able to count the sheep in the pen or cite a passage or two from the Bible, it was enough.

For girls, the need for learning was less, yet it was they who tittered excitedly on the floor, awaiting the beginning of the lesson.

They were in the home of John Cole, on the ocean side of the southern half of town. It was a typical two room farmhouse.

Through the back windows there was a view of the sand-strewn Pochet Island and other lesser landforms that only arose at low tide.

Cole was the lieutenant of the militia, Justice Doane's second-in-command. Given that the military band was volunteer, except for the natives, and without a fight for years, it was largely an honorary post. There was little martial in the bearing of the quiet fisherman. His world was among the saltwater inlets at his door. With school upon his house, he was already far away out in the waves, leaving his wife to tend to the two dozen children in the front room.

Mary Cole was of sturdy, humorless Eastham stock. Life for her was comprised of the kind of drudgery that enabled basic survival such as soothing, healing, feeding and teaching her family so they endured the rigors of their material existence and earned their entry to the promised, eternal life beyond. If her own life seemed to be an endless press of repetitive labors, her son's naturally pious disposition promised glory, which would raise him out of earthly chores to the height of the preacher's pulpit. Every day she imagined seeing him standing handsomely at the head of the meeting house and herself sitting in the first row, basking in his virtue and devotion.

Although he was only ten years old, Johnny Cole was already more serious than most of his elders. On Sabbath Day he listened to Treat's stories of the struggle between good and evil harder than most men who were old enough to soon be discovering their eternal fate firsthand. At home he studied the pages of the Bible, pouring through the text for fresh horrors that Treat had yet to mention.

Some of the students were as young as six. Others were as old as eighteen and attending the last of such tutoring. The schoolteacher, Nehemiah Hobart, spent a few months in each hamlet of Eastham, boarding at a local homestead and teaching the children of the area. Then he moved on to the next part of town, making his rounds throughout the year, except for planting and harvest time. For his efforts he received ten pounds per year. The host families received a small payment for their trouble, but for Mrs. Cole the schoolteacher's presence was payment enough. Hobart was a friend of Reverend Treat's and a fellow graduate of Harvard. He had the trust of the reverend and the ear of the town fathers. His word would go a long way towards getting an aspiring young man into his alma mater and then to the post of pastor of Eastham.

At the moment, everyone was waiting for the schoolteacher, whose quarters were out in the lean-to behind the house. Tardiness was one of the man's few flaws, in Mrs. Cole's opinion. Hobart liked to make an entrance, and Mrs. Cole knew that he was making the students wait on purpose, for he was but scant yards away from the noisy racket of the kids and no doubt could hear that his class was assembled. In her son's eyes she saw impatience with Hobart's behavior, and it reinforced her notion of her son's ministerial character. "The Lord does not make us wait on Sabbath day, why should Hobart make us wait the rest of the week," she had told Johnny once, after a fit of fury at the schoolteacher's dalliance. The child had been repeating it ever since.

A group of teenage girls held sway near the hearth where they sat with feet splayed out and mouths slack with gossip, exhibiting the most sinful kind of indolence. Their forbearers had designed seats without arms for women, with the wisdom that a pious woman should always be industrious, never at rest. They would be aghast to see the kind of repose into which their descendants had fallen.

"Goody Knowles… Goody Higgins… Mr. Hobart will be along at any moment. Your minds should be upon weightier matters," Mrs. Cole chided them. But inside she was annoyed at Hobart for fostering such opportunity for mischief.

The girls' tone dropped to near silence then rose up again, building on itself as fresh slander came from their lips and was added to, girl by girl, until all of them were atwitter.

Thankful Knowles, Mehitable Higgins and the other older girls recapped what the men in town were saying about the squid and then quickly moved on to what they thought of the men themselves.

"I want a man with lots of land in the new settlements of Harwich or Billingsgate," Thankful Knowles said. "Father says that soon those areas will be as full as Eastham proper. All that good land will make somebody a fortune. I'd rather it be my husband." She was seventeen and dark-haired like her father, the elder, and brothers.

"And who will that be?" Mehitable asked.

"If only Johnny Cole was a little older," Thankful teased, making the young boy purse his lips.

"I have a sailor lined up for myself. He is staying at my father's tavern," Mehitable announced.

43

"Sailor?" Thankful asked.

"Sam Bellamy. He's the washashore from last week's gale. Have you not seen him? He is only the most handsome man in town!" Mehitable continued.

"That is not a good life. I'd not let my husband treat me with such neglect. He will be gone half the time, and you will always be wondering if the sea will take him," Thankful said, giving a scornful look at the girl who sat in the corner. But Maria Hallett kept her head buried in her Bible although, in truth, the words on the page were a blur to her.

Ordinarily, Mrs. Cole would not have continued to tolerate the noise, but today she did not discourage them. There was something about the Hallett girl that raised her hackles. It was more than the fact that Maria's mother had been a spoiled brat ever since back when she and Mrs. Cole had been in a similar scrum of eager school children some two decades ago. Goody Hallett had an oddness that was disquieting. If she had her way, Mrs. Cole would insist that Reverend Treat make a full study of the girl. If anyone among them was likely to aid the coming of the Devil to their town, surely the Hallett girl was the most inclined. But she had yet to impress Treat with this view.

"Perhaps you should stay concentrated on the scripture, not gossip!" Mrs. Cole scolded the girls as soon as she heard Hobart coming.

Hobart entered a moment later, a smile dancing on his lips. "We shall stand shoulder to shoulder against everything that is thrown at us, be it from the clouds or from hell itself!" he shouted with excessive drama, thought Mrs. Cole.

"Mr. Hobart! Do you mean to frighten these children?" she demanded.

Hobart was just thirty and still a bachelor, a life that suited the kind of peripatetic instruction that he offered. It was rumored that his father's Boston family had money, which would indefinitely sustain him and any wife lucky enough to share his name. In truth, many of the older girls were continuing their lessons only to stay in the mind of the schoolteacher.

There was an angularity to Hobart's face, which gave him the look of a spade or some such sharp tool. He had a long, thin neck with an Adam's apple so large that it appeared as though there was an actual fruit stuck in there. His eyes were haughty and dark and swung immediately in Maria's direction, as they did every class, drawing hard snorts of breath from all of the other older girls around her.

"Good morning, everyone. The Lord smiles upon us once more. There is much to discuss today," Hobart said, looking like all of it was talk that he wished to have with Maria alone.

"Reverend Treat says that the Devil will try to turn us from the path of God. How will he do this?" Johnny asked.

"His influence is sin. Stay pure and true to the command-ments and God's other instructions, and you shall have nothing to fear," Hobart replied.

"But the Devil is strong enough to master even a pious per-son, is he not?" Johnny persisted.

"Well, yes... But only if they relax their virtue. If you have no laxity in faith, then you give him no opportunity to strike," Hobart went on.

"Like *Widow Chase!*" Mehitable hissed. "Look what the Devil did to her! Made her a murderer, he did!"

"A witch," Mrs. Cole amended.

"She was not found guilty of witchcraft, but true, she did stray," Hobart conceded.

"For that, she got the brand on her cheek. Surely, in these times, devilry would receive much worse punishment?" Mehitable asked.

"Any concert with the Devil at this time would be tanta-mount to treason, considering that a heavenly battle might be upon us."

"Unholy premonitions would be among such transgressions, would they not?" Mehitable asked, casting a glance in Maria's direction.

"Perhaps... That would be for the selectmen and Justice Doane to decide," Hobart said. Then, noticing movement out of the corner of his eye, he turned towards the front door and saw a figure moving towards it. "Goody Hallett! You are leaving? Won't you stay among us for a time? Surely, you have some questions about what is going on around us?" Hobart asked.

"I cannot. The farm..." she said, avoiding the smug faces of the other girls.

"Let her go. Perhaps her ears cannot bear to hear the word of the Lord," Mrs. Cole suggested.

"Surely you don't mean that," Hobart said, over his shoulder, to his hostess.

"*Witch...*" Mrs. Cole hissed.

Hobart turned, admonishing words forming on his lips, and saw that Mrs. Cole was not referring to Maria but rather to a figure she glared at through the window.

A tumult of squawking and cursing came from the front yard. The children ran and pressed their faces to the window panes while Mrs. Cole burst out through the door to confront an old woman who was stomping, with equal ferocity, towards the house.

Widow Chase carried much of her youthful vigor in a pair of eyes that emitted a force like smoke and fire. Long gray hair hung forward in such a way as to cover most of her face. Her gait was not normally feeble, but it was made unsteady by the unruly bundle in her arms, a basket full of chickens with a blanket over top, which rose here and there with the poke of hidden beaks.

"Your damned birds got loose again!" the old woman ranted, shoving down at the attempts of the birds to wriggle from their covering.

"You'll smother the life from them!" Mrs. Cole cried, trying to yank off the blanket.

Widow Chase danced away with surprising agility. "I ought to, is what I should do! They have near eaten every last shoot from my garden! I ought to have kept them so as to have something to eat this summer!"

Mrs. Cole glared, unafraid, at the old woman. "I hear that your garden is not as much for the dinner board as for your *broths and concoctions...*"

Widow Chase glowered back. "Bah! Your ears delight in gossip! To you, it is a song more pleasing than any hymn!"

"Oh! Blasphemy!" Mrs. Cole gasped.

"You'll get your chickens back when you give me an apology! Just this once!"

"Blasphemy!" Mrs. Cole shouted, louder, bringing Hobart to the window as she had hoped.

"For God's sake, you fool!" Widow Chase growled and pushed the basket into Mrs. Cole's arms. "The next time I won't be so neighborly. Doing a favor only to be insulted for it!"

The girls watched the two women squaring off in the yard, mirrored by two roosters, drawn by the commotion, which pranced around each other, jutting their beaks in much the same manner as the woman pointed their chins at one another.

"*Speak of the Devil!*" Thankful hissed, drawing Widow Chase's eye.

At that same moment, a gust of wind lifted the widow's hair, like a window curtain parting, but she combed it back in place again before the girls could observe the mark of which they had spoken. Yet the old woman's eagerness to hide her shame drew excited gasps from the girls.

"Perhaps they will hang her," Mehitable suggested.

"You are wicked!" Thankful laughed.

"I would at least throw her, and anyone else who might aid this beast in his work, into jail, before they get a chance to perform their foul deeds. That's what I would do if I were a town father," said Mehitable.

"*You?* A town father?" Thankful chuckled. A moment later all of the girls were laughing, even Mehitable herself.

A wagon was approaching the house from the road, and Mrs. Cole turned eagerly towards it and yelled, "Reverend! You have missed everything!"

Reverend Treat reined up before her and scrutinized the chickens in her hands. She, in turn, was staring at the bare legs of the churchman - as were all the students, through the window.

"What have I missed? Has something happened here? Are the children safe?" he demanded.

"They are safe. Widow Chase came with her ranting and foulness…" Mrs. Cole tried to explain.

Treat was not paying attention. He had turned to face the road behind him and the figure of a girl running down it. "Who was that I passed?"

"Goody Hallett," Mrs. Cole snorted. "Ran out at the beginning of the lesson rather than talk about the punishments of the Lord upon sinners."

"Indeed?" Treat asked. "She had nothing to say on that subject?"

"Same as always: nothing. But I tell you that it is not *nothing!*"

Treat tried to dismount from the wagon but fell back onto the bench and bent over with a cough that made his entire body shake.

On instinct, Mrs. Cole stepped forward and laid a hand to the reverend's forehead. *"You're not even dressed properly,"* she murmured. Then Treat's startled look reminded her of her impropriety, and she hastily drew away.

"Your pardon, Reverend. What will people say of me mothering you like you were one of my boys?"

"They would think my own wife in neglect."

Mrs. Cole's hand shot up to cover her mouth. "Now, I assure you that I didn't mean to suggest that!"

"You didn't, Mary. Be at peace. You have a cool touch, and I am not too proud to have the attention. How did I feel to your hand?"

The truth was that the old man felt as flush and hot as Mrs. Cole's own face felt at the moment, from her embarrassment. These were not the words that she told him, however. "Fine, Reverend. You are a marvel."

Treat climbed off of his wagon and absent-mindedly handed the reins to Mrs. Cole. *"What is that..."* he muttered.

Mrs. Cole bit her tongue. As much as she admired the man, he did not have the same faculties as when he had been a zealous, young minister. A new reverend could not come too soon, she thought.

She dropped the reins and followed Treat. She was surprised to see that he was standing perfectly still in the middle of the yard, leaning towards the sound of a bell ringing near the well.

"Reverend Treat? Are you alright?"

To her amazement, the old man smiled. "Yes. But there is still much to do... Much, much to do."

"I agree!" Mrs. Cole said. When the reverend went inside, she followed the sound of the bell and found one of the hens pecking at the pewter well bucket, making it ring like the call of the meeting house. She shooed the bird away and watched with satisfaction as it hopped and winged off towards the little house on the bluff below her where Widow Chase lived.

✠ ✠ ✠ ✠

After class Thankful Knowles walked home, down Tonset Road. In places along the road, Great Cove was visible in the distance. At one of those spots, she found Maria Hallett staring out at the waves. Were she not so pious, Thankful might have uttered an oath. It was too late to take a different route and impossible to find a shrub behind which to hide on this treeless stretch of road. Not long ago she would have been delighted to still refer to Maria Hallett as her friend. But although raised side by side, they had grown up and branched in two very different directions.

"You do not talk much with the others at school," Thankful observed, unhappy to see Maria stand and get in stride with her. Had Mehitable been present, Thankful would have given Maria the taunting she deserved. Instead, she tolerated the girl but kept a good dozen feet between them, to clearly show that they were not close in any regard, should anyone spy them upon the road together.

"I haven't felt that I have much to say since father died," Maria replied, kicking at rocks on the road. Thankful observed the scuffs of dirt on her companion's boots, with the same critical air that Maria's mother would have had, were she there.

"You did not even remark about the sailor. I would have thought that you would be interested in him. You are always telling me that your father promised to sail you away from here, off to the great worlds beyond the sea." She met Maria's stormy look with what she hoped was an innocent looking smile.

"He did promise that," Maria said.

"The sailor in the tavern hails from England, I hear."

Maria shrugged. "I have not sailed for a year. Father and I used to raise sail whenever we could, even in weather like this. But now I cannot bear it."

Thankful did not respond. She longed to tell Maria that she did not welcome her company, but she could see her homestead in the distance and knew that her discomfort would soon be at an end.

Maria looked again out at Great Cove and sighed. "What manner of man is the sailor at the tavern? Does he tell many stories of the places he's been?"

"Dunno," Thankful replied. "Why does such plight – this devilry - have to befall us when we are in our prime, not yet courted or married? I hope that the elders resolve it soon so it does not bar us from marriage and motherhood. You don't think me sinful for saying such things, do you?" Thankful added, knowing that Maria did not show any strong religious sentiment.

"I think you are a fool is all. Why do you and the other girls talk of nothing else but marriage? It does not seem that wonderful to me. Not like sailing from this place."

"When your father was here, you never talked of leaving *forever.*"

"Well, now I wish to. Few would care anyway, would they?" Maria snapped, scrutinizing Thankful's face for reaction.

"The men would miss you," Thankful said, a tinge of envy sticking in her throat.

Maria kicked another rock.

"That is why the other girls do not talk with you. They are jealous, and they worry you will take their men away," Thankful told her.

"I thought it was because of the dream," Maria said.

"Well, some do wonder," Thankful admitted, pausing to give her companion a chance to make further comment on the issue. Maria frowned when she caught Thankful's hopeful glance.

"I told you what happened! I saw the wreck exactly as it later occurred, even in the same spot."

Thankful's eyes widened. "Exactly? I had not heard that."

"*Exactly.*"

"Have you had other visions?"

Maria nodded. "A few. Nothing important. Things like Mrs. Higgins wearing her blue bonnet rather than the gray one or that a boat would break its mooring."

"Those are still premonitions," Thankful observed.

"Yes, but they are of a different order. It is not as if I dreamed that the cattle in the Hopkins' herd would die and then awoke to them falling over all across the fields," Maria cried, gesturing at the adjacent farm where a group of cows lumbered up to the stone wall to investigate them.

Thankful stared, open-mouthed, at her companion until Maria scowled. "I didn't really see that! It was merely to make the point! I don't *make* things happen!" Then, in frustration, Maria pointed a finger out into the pasture, square between the eyes of one of the herd, and shouted, "You all shall perish! *There!* It is done!"

"*It is done...*" Thankful gasped. "As if you really could ..."

"I don't know how or why the dreams come to me. I do nothing to encourage them. I don't *want* them. Would you tell the other girls that so they don't think ill of me? I do not seek to do anyone harm."

"But perhaps you cannot help it, Goody Hallett," Thankful replied, before running off towards her homestead, leaving the other girl scowling after her.

Chapter Two
"The Unyielding Ground"

The Great Meadow of Eastham lay in the nook of the elbow of Cape Cod itself. Its wide plains were filled with flaxen colored grass, called salt hay, which was thick and dry and good for livestock feed, floor matting, candle wicks and stuffing for the bedding. A network of muddy channels coiled through the marsh, the twisting veins filled with frigid water. Most were narrow enough to be forded by a running jump. The widest of the channels, called Jeremiah's Gutter, could carry a small boat all the way through the miles of marshy plains, during high tide. It connected Great Cove with the massive bay on the other side, thereby severing the top half of town from the bottom. Only a short span of wooden bridge fastened the two halves together.

One could fill an entire wagon with salt hay without reaping any deeper than the very edge of the sprawling meadow. That is where most of the villagers worked, clustered together like cattle fearing the appearance of a wolf. Normally, folks might spread wider and deeper into the hay fields, even splashing through the channels in pursuit of a wandering crab if it seemed of size to fill the cook pot, or in search of a well-laden bed of clams. These days no one wished to venture too far from each other. Many a wary eye was cast on the deeper streams, searching for any large white shapes under the surface.

Reverend Treat wandered among the foragers and scanned the expansive hay fields for any sign of malevolence. A few carts were isolated from the others, their owners' maverick dispositions more powerful than any dread of the harm that such folly could cause them. Treat snorted and stumbled towards them, over a terrain pockmarked with muddy sink holes. This was no time for any one of them to be cut off from the flock.

He reached a cart that was hauled up to the lip of one of the marsh channels, its wheels snapping through a sheet of brown husks, revealing bent green grass beneath. One side of the cart sank into a patch of spongy ground and set the back bed at a canted angle. From a shallow ravine of the channel, a grim-faced, middle-aged woman pitched hay with a long handled pitchfork.

"Mrs. Mayo! What are you doing?" Treat demanded.

The woman did not look at the reverend or break the pace of her shoveling. "What does it look like? I need hay for the cows and covering for the fields. The storm brought cold weather with it, so the foundation might need some more padding to keep that *damned* freezing wind from coming through the floor boards... Begging your pardon, Reverend."

"Foul language is the least of your worries, my dear woman! Is *this* worth your divine soul?" Treat demanded, picking up a fistful of hay and scattering it into the wind.

"You could have put that into the cart!" Mrs. Mayo protested.

"Is your place in heaven worth collecting a wagon load of straw?"

"For God's sake, Reverend, I'm only cutting hay."

"*Because that is what is at stake!*" Treat bellowed. "Go! Continue your harvest nearer the others!"

Then he wobbled towards the other isolated hay gatherers, shooing them into motion like a flock of birds taking flight.

"Stay together! It is too dangerous to work alone!" he told them.

Amidst the tight, protective scrum of villagers, Alice Hallett scooped bits of loose straw into her apron and dumped them into the wagon. Her daughter Maria wielded the pitchfork, throwing as much hay wide of the cart as into it, because of the strong, cold wind. Above, the coal-streaked sky seemed ready to make good on Reverend Treat's promise of more hellfire to come.

There was none of the usual chatter that attended such labor, only the whisk of hay moving from turf to cart, until a young maiden's voice exclaimed, "There he is! He just stepped out from Higgins Tavern!"

Goody Bassett was about the same age as Maria, as were several other girls who stopped work and joined Bassett in looking towards the town center, to the southwest of the meadow. Maria and her mother peered at the small cluster of buildings and farms in the distance but did not see anyone.

"Whom do they see?" Alice asked.

"I don't know. I would guess it is the shipwrecked sailor who stays at Higgins Tavern."

"Oh yes... That is an awful fate," Alice lamented.

"It could have been worse," Maria pointed out.

"Do not try my patience!" Alice huffed. "Back to work! This fellow is only of interest because he is a stranger who came ashore with such drama. None of these young ladies would cast him a second glance if they spied him on the dockside."

"How do you know that?"

"Because that is usually the way of these things."

The Bassetts had moved closer to where the Halletts stood. The matron of the Bassett family, a rail thin woman with almond-shaped, squirrel-like eyes, squinted at the tavern. Her mouth drooped with permanent distaste and the caved-in resemblance of a pumpkin gone to rot. "Men like that take to sea because they are too soft for real work," she declared.

She nudged her daughter back towards the family's half-loaded cart, to remind her of what real work was.

"He's destitute!" Goody Bassett said.

"He's drunk!" Mrs. Bassett spat. "I heard it from some of those who have been with him at the tavern! Them sailors spend every penny they got on ale and fornicating! I don't know why Justice Doane has not seen fit to send him on his way!"

"Here he comes again!" another girl, Goody Brown, sang out.

Mrs. Bassett gave a harsh bark of laughter, for it was suddenly clear where the sailor had been. "He's come from the outhouse, he has! I bet I'd be a rich woman if I had a penny for every time he has made his way out there to piss away the ale! I'd not be hauling hay, I tell you!"

They all saw the tiny figure of a bearded, dark-haired man in the distance, walking the final few paces to the entrance of the tavern. It was impossible to tell if he was worthy of anything that was being said about him.

At that very moment another man was striding towards them from the other direction. Nehemiah Hobart, the schoolteacher, raised his hand in greeting and called out, "Mrs. Hallett! And Goody Hallett! Well met indeed!" His face and gait were filled with happy ease as if he was on a simple stroll through the village.

"May I help you with your labors?" he offered, taking the pitchfork from Maria.

"It would be most welcome," Alice replied, nudging her daughter to offer similar sentiment, but Maria said nothing.

On Hobart's heels came several other young men of town, who were eager not to be outmaneuvered by the schoolteacher. Each offered assistance and then jostled one another to stand closest to Maria.

"More hands will make quick work of the chore," Alice agreed, stepping aside to let the men finish filling the cart. Maria tried to step aside with her, but Alice nudged her back towards her suitors.

"Come! Seems we are in the way," Mrs. Bassett said sarcastically as she drew her daughter away.

A moment later there was a tremendous splash and both Bassett women, along with a score of others, started screaming.

"What the Devil!" Hobart cried, spinning around towards Jeremiah's Gutter. On the north side of the bank, opposite the villagers, stood a native man. At his feet the water rippled from the spot where he had dropped a large stone. Another was already in his hand, and he aimed it towards the first, intent on damming up a small dead end channel in which several meaty fish were cut off.

The native's intentions were unclear to the several Eastham men who charged towards him, shaking their pitchforks. If not an outright provocation, they took the wild splashing to be a prank in poor taste, and they hurried over to confront the native.

"I have seen that man before, but I cannot recall where," Alice said.

"You have seen him in the pillory where, I daresay, he belongs. He is named John Julian. He is a fool, that one. A black mark on the reverend's noble work of taming the savages," Hobart clucked.

They watched Julian let fall two more stones then drop to his knees and attempt to scoop out the fish, but his barrier was incomplete, and the fish slipped over the rocks and back into the current of Jeremiah's Gutter.

By now the Eastham men were crossing the bridge. Julian stared at the flow of choice fish rushing past him through the channel and then at the approaching men. He scowled at both and fled to a canoe on the shoreline, in which he pushed himself off into Great Cove.

The Eastham men gathered in the shallows and shook their fists at the canoe, shouting at Julian to go to the Devil.

Hobart shook his head. "I shudder to think what kind of rotten filth they shall throw at Julian when they next have him in the pillory. I shan't be surprised if someone takes matters into his own hands."

"But he did nothing but try to catch some fish," Maria said.

Hobart turned and smiled condescendingly at her. "He gives us a fright not just because he is so callous and foolish to be splashing through the marsh during these times when we all dread what is in the water. Worse than that, he is a heathen."

The schoolteacher pointed at Reverend Treat, who was hurrying across the bridge to retrieve the vigilantes by the shoreline. "All of his good work threatens to be undone. Julian, for instance, clings to darkness while the rest of the Indians have seen the light. Yet what if his defiance poisons the others and they revert to their ungodly ways? Treat understands how one source of darkness can grow until there is no light for any of us."

Hobart turned pitying eyes on the reverend. "That lightness of his heart, that which we all love, is lamentably strained by these troubled days. Who can retain good humor with what has befallen us?"

He turned back towards Maria, expecting to see grateful comprehension on the girl's face, only to find that she had gone.

✠ ✠ ✠ ✠

Maria Hallett had wandered off towards the edge of Jeremiah's Gutter where the storm-driven water was whisking past into Great Cove and jostling the boats moored there. She had come to try and get a better glimpse of the sailor, but he had returned to the tavern. Instead, she gazed longingly at the anchored boats. She did not notice the presence of the large man behind her until he announced himself with a phlegmy cough.

"You do not fear the water?" Reverend Treat queried, peering at her.

"No."

"That is strange… Did you dream of this storm? Of the beast even?"

She was shifting back and forth on her feet, he noted. Her eyes could not meet his own. He studied her as she fidgeted before him, trying to gauge the source of her awkwardness.

"I did not dream of this storm."

"Only the other one. The one that wrecked your father's ship," he prompted her. If she were indeed guilty, she would flee, he surmised. Yet such a theory was not foolproof. Sometimes the Devil lay deep within, even buried inside dreams, like a snake wintering in its den. Some found it all the more lamentable that the Devil should make his lair in the young, innocent and beautiful. That was his way. The pretty face was the best disguise. The innocent were the choicest prey. After all, it was the very purpose of the Devil to corrupt.

"I did not do anything on purpose... If you don't believe me, what will be done? Shall I be given the brand?"

As Treat stared solemnly at her, a shiver began that Maria could not stop. He squinted more closely at her, trying to discern if there was some unnatural convulsion upon her. But he could not tell for sure.

"The pillory then?" she asked.

"Hell itself awaits those who consort with the Devil. You have heard my description of the lakes of fire in that punishing landscape. The burn of the brand is but a single swift act to forewarn the sinner of the eternal flames that await on Judgment Day!"

He waited for a moment to give her time to reply, but Maria simply bowed her head demurely.

Treat gave an irritated grunt and then reached into a bag at his feet and pulled out two books, one of which was a Bible and the other a thick tome with a black cover and no discernable title. He shoved his hand back into the bag and this time withdrew a small wooden cross and a phial of clear liquid.

"These items verge on Papistry, I admit. But they have their uses. Now hold this," he commanded, handing her the cross. "What does that feel like?"

"Wood."

"No heat? No pain?" he asked, peering at her.

"No."

"Hmmm." He grabbed her palm and poured the contents of the phial onto it.

"Anything?"

"No. What is it?"

"Blessed water. Not holy water. That is Papist. This is water that has been prayed over by a proper minister. Can you read?" he asked.

She nodded, and he handed her a Bible. "Open it and recite the page to which you turn."

Treat listened hard for any telltale wavering of her speech, any quiver in her words that would divulge the presence of an ill spirit within her. However, he heard nothing but her soft, clear voice telling the story of God's challenge to Abraham to sacrifice his son. Treat mused on the text and wondered if that itself was some kind of sign. Only when she had stopped reading did he realize that a small crowd of native children was around him. Their eager faces brought a smile to his lips.

"What are you doing here, little ones?"

"Fishing," one said, pointing back towards the bay where Treat knew many native fish weirs were planted.

"Are you much familiar with our Indian brethren in Christ?" Treat asked Maria.

She shook her head, looking uncomfortable.

As if he had offered them an invitation, the children crammed around him, patting at his pockets.

"Have only two… and I am busy!" he said, withdrawing a sugared plum from his jacket, a delicacy that he imported from Europe whenever he could find a ship to bring some.

"*Make it disappear!*" the children cried.

"Oh, alright…" he huffed, closing the fruit in one fist then raising his hand, palm held towards himself, and dropping the fruit down his sleeve.

"Which one?" he asked. Little fingers pointed eagerly. Most fixed on his right hand.

"Empty."

"*Left! Left!*"

Treat smiled. He had shown them this trick hundreds of times, and yet the children never tired of it. "Empty!" he declared, opening another vacant palm. Surreptitiously, he dropped the fruit back into the hand behind his back.

"And here it is!" he said as he pulled the plum seemingly from thin air. The children squealed and grabbed as he divided up the fruit. Then they asked him to perform it again.

"No, I am busy!" he grumbled, tossing the remaining plum into the crowd of them. One of the oldest ran off with it while the rest of the children looked at Treat with disappointment. He shooed them away and then turned his attention to Maria. She was wearing an odd expression that he could not fathom. It seemed that she had either seen the secret to the trick or wanted some of the fruit herself.

"Where were we?" he snapped.

"I had finished the reading. Shall I read that other book now?" she asked, pointing to the book with the black jacket.

"Heavens no! That is a treatise on Maleficia. Merely a guidebook for me. Well, I cannot detect anything untoward. But what you must know is this: the Devil only gains entry to us through our weakness. When we open our hearts or minds or dreams to him, then he finds an opening to strike. If our heart is filled with prohibited desire, then we give him an invitation. Do you understand?"

The girl nodded.

"I have read that the lack of sleep can thrust away any infiltration of devilry. Do not give into slumber and you will not dream. The Devil tires quickly of closed doors, so he shall soon depart. Then seal the door of your heart to him! Never let your thoughts stray to him!"

"I wouldn't!" Maria protested.

Treat's eyes narrowed in disbelief. "It is well that we are so strong here in Eastham or else one slip could be the doom of us all. Shield your heart to sin!" he repeated, and then, like a squall suddenly waning, he smiled and patted her on the head.

"Dream of a husband, not a sea beast," he advised.

"So I am fine then?" Maria pressed him, noticing that a small group of her neighbors had been drawn by the strange proceedings and now gathered around them. Mrs. Cole was chief among them.

"It seems so, child. Give thanks for that!" Treat said. Then he too noticed their audience, raised his arms and cried, "We should all give thanks and praise! Join me! Our father…"

"*Who art in heaven, hallowed be thy name…*" One voice became a dozen.

"You are still scowling at my daughter. Do you dispute Treat's verdict? Do you deny the result of his testing?" Alice Hallett said over Mrs. Cole's shoulder.

Mrs. Cole glared at her. "Whatever the reverend decides is good enough for me," she grumbled.

"Good," Alice replied. She motioned for her daughter. "Come along, Maria. The wagon is full, and there is much work ahead of us."

Unlike Mrs. Cole, Maria looked ebullient at the results of Treat's examination. For once, she seemed eager for her daily labors. The transformation was so startling that Alice drew breath.

"Off with you now! Your mother is in great need of you these days! Do not fail in that commitment! It is only slightly less sacred than that with God!" Treat called after them.

"I will not fail!" Maria cried back. Passing Alice, she tugged on her mother's sleeve. "Have you noticed? The sun is coming through the clouds. The storm is broken."

Alice looked across the flat sheet of marsh into the wide bay beyond and saw the smoky, gray billow of clouds lined in radiant gold. Thick shafts of light dropped through tears in the overcast sky and settled onto the water's surface like heavenly columns. The sight filled Alice's chest with such hopeful joy that she nearly cried out.

✠ ✠ ✠ ✠

Elder Knowles stood under the shade of cherry trees that formed part of the boundary between his own holdings and the neighboring Hallett farm. To the eye, their line looked straight and true, but he wanted to make sure that their course matched what was written on the deed, which he held and drummed upon with his fingers as he watched the surveyors at work.

Deacon John Paine was on the boundary committee and, in Knowles' mind, was one of the fairest and most competent men of that group. Knowles watched Paine pace off a plum line from a point that he had fixed near Tonset Road, in front of the property, and knew that he would be satisfied with whatever was Paine's assessment.

At Knowles' elbow stood his daughter Thankful. She watched the proceedings with the barest of interest. Knowles knew that she would have much preferred to be in the gardens, checking the growth of the vegetables, or out working the wash in the creek that ran through the woods at the back end of the property. But at his insistence, she stayed at his side, dutiful as she was. Knowles' farm was the same layout as his neighbors' holdings. The fields were plowed in near mirror image to those around him. His four sons walked among the rising green stalks, picking out weeds, as did young men on every field that he could see from where he stood. When Knowles looked at his sons, he caught their pouting glances and felt some guilt at not having them alongside of him as well. He had considered the benefit of having them observe the act of measuring the bounds but ultimately decided that managing the fields was a better education for them. Once the property was measured, that should be an end to it. Knowles fully expected the surveyors to confirm the original layout, and then he would have a substantially bigger farm.

None of that was the reason that he had his daughter standing next to him.

"Trees do not hold the line as well as rocks. They throw their seeds as far as they can. They twist off course. At the time that your grandfather planted this row, it must have looked as steady as a rock wall. But at the end it tapers off, far to the east. The trees there are smaller, thus more recent. They are off the line too. Many of the original trees fell down in my youth. I recall that. The little ones were left to grow as they would, and they grew in the Halletts' favor..." Knowles realized that he was rambling and imparting exactly the kind of information that would have benefited his sons, not a daughter. He stopped and smiled down at her, waiting until his silence caught her attention and she snapped her eyes back from where they had been gazing blankly out at Great Cove in the distance.

"Sorry, father. I was listening..."

"Ah! Do not load lying onto not honoring your father! Your mind wandered because I gave it nothing of the sort that it is used to. I don't judge you for that," he said. He looked at her severely, but in truth, he was not angry at her sin for it was a slight one, without harm.

"Why are you bothering with all of this?"

"Accuracy. That is why. It is always good to know the exact state of things. We could continue acting as we do and our neighbors could do the same. There is no strife between us now, but what of the future when your brothers inherit this land? What laxity we have now might be irreparable later. My indolence could cost them their true rights of ownership."

"Yes, but isn't this wasted effort in light of you and Widow Hallett..." Thankful stopped herself and bowed her head as if in penitence for her brazenness.

Knowles patted his daughter's dark brown hair, then raised her face by her chin. He looked into her eyes for a moment, studying them and amazed anew at the prescience of women.

"Your mother would have guessed the state of things as well," he mused. The thought of his late wife made him clear his throat. It seemed an unsavory thought in light of what he was about to discuss with his daughter.

"You were about to say that when I marry Widow Hallett, these two farms will be joined as one, so it will not matter where the line of trees stands?" he went on.

Thankful nodded eagerly.

He smiled. "There would still be the matter of division later. There are few open spaces for new farms these days. My holdings will likely be split between your brothers. I would not have them fighting over boundaries, after my death."

Knowles then turned and patted his daughter on the shoulder. "You shall not have to worry over such issues as land. It won't be long before you are living on your own farm, though I hate to think on it. Perhaps there," Knowles said, gesturing towards the Hopkins' farm across the road.

"I would be close enough to visit every day," Thankful replied.

"You will not have time, I should think, because you will have a husband to dote on," Knowles stated. "It would be a good match, at any rate. Jonathan Hopkins is a fine man."

"Yes," Thankful agreed shyly.

They stood for a moment and watched Paine and his assistant William Bangs at work. Bangs counted out four-foot lengths, by laying a rod on the ground, while Paine walked beside him, noting his progress in a ledger. Paine sensed the eyes upon him, looked over at the pair and pointed down the row of trees.

"It veers, already, by several feet. By the time we reach the end, I expect that your contention will be correct. We shall see," Paine called out.

Knowles smiled and turned back to his daughter. "There is never any harm in looking closely at a thing that we think we know well enough."

His daughter beamed at him as she did whenever he offered something that bordered on sermon. As a church elder, it was Knowles' duty to oversee the direction and discipline of the church as well as take the pulpit if the reverend was unable. Treat's hardy constitution had given Knowles few opportunities to do so over the years, but the elder still acted as if he was in constant practice. In his heart Knowles was sure that his moment was not very far away.

"Are you fond of Widow Hallett?" he asked his daughter.

"I suppose. She is kind and takes an interest in my education," Thankful said, surprised at the intimacy of the question.

"I would have you and your brothers be happy with my selection."

"It is your happiness that matters."

"Thank you. You are kind, daughter. It is a great virtue of yours. We should all be happy if God wills it. There is no way for a father to raise a brood of six without a mother's influence. You will have another mother, and Widow Hallett is my choice."

"I know. It pleases me," Thankful said although she did not look at all excited by the prospect.

"Then, what ails you?"

"Nothing."

"Speak it."

"I am fond of Widow Hallett, as I said. I wish I felt the same about Maria."

"Maria? Have you not played together since childhood? What strife could lie between you? You were raised as close as kin."

"All true back then. She has changed steadily as she has grown."

The thought of the girl's stunning growth momentarily distracted Knowles. He pictured Maria's appealing form and wondered again whether he was wooing the wrong Hallett woman. He was not too old to take a maiden as a second wife. He knew that it had been done before, plenty of times, by others. The mother was made more attractive by her dowry. The daughter would come with nothing but the clothes on her back, a poorer prize no matter how good she looked in them. In this case, her age might matter. His own children were of similar age, and he did not know if the bond of marriage would give her the power that a mother should have over them.

"She became odd…" Thankful went on.

"How so?"

"Surely you know of the premonitions that she has?" Thankful said. When her father shook his head, she drew up, pleased with a chance to impress him. "Maria saw her father's ship go down the day before it wrecked. And she has had other premonitions since then."

Knowles stroked his beard. He had forgotten that story. Now that he heard it again and thought of it in the context of the pallor of fear and omen in town, it seemed a strong indictment indeed of the girl. There was also the more pressing point of how it would reflect on his own courtship. He did not want to be tied to such tales, true or not. Was it worth the additional acres, he wondered?

"Let us go for a ride," he told his daughter. Thankful's eyes lit up. She could not believe the unfolding of this day. She wondered if her father's unusual, relaxed mood would fade after the marriage, for she felt certain that it was a product of his wooing. Best to enjoy it now, she told herself and hurried into the house to get her favorite bonnet.

A moment later father and daughter were rumbling off down Tonset Road towards the bend in the road that led to the north bank of Great Cove. She knew, without being told, where they were going. That took no magic. Her father's father had been promised the land that Reverend Treat now lived upon, before the preacher's arrival. When Treat came, the land fell out of grandfather Knowles' grasp, and now his son could not get that fine sprawling acreage out of his mind.

Elder Knowles said only one other thing about the Halletts as they rode, "Whatever your feelings towards Maria, they must be put aside if you are to become sisters. Family must bond together like iron even if it is two broken pieces coming together."

She nodded in agreement but noted that he seemed less excited by the prospect as he had earlier.

✠ ✠ ✠ ✠

At the far end of the Knowles' property stood Deacon John Paine and William Bangs. They were debating whether the old white oak in front of them or one deeper on the Hallett property was the landmark mentioned in the deed. When Eastham had fewer souls, farms were marked off using features of the land. The description of Knowles' property was given as "running forty rods in a due south line from Tonset Road to a white oak, then past a large rock, between two beech trees and onward until reaching the Kescayogansett creek." Paine read the line twice and then tried to find the description amidst the tangle of scrub and forest in front of him, thinking that, more than ever, there was a need in town for precision.

Eventually they agreed that only the farther white oak lined up in any discernable way with the bound at the road or could be connected with any rocks or beech trees within the woods behind.

"That's it then," Paine declared. He stepped sideways to align himself with the new angle of the boundary and immediately saw what the shift would mean. He was now looking directly at the Halletts' barn. The vast bulk of it stood off to his right, firmly in Knowles bounds.

"That cannot be! My father built that barn!" exclaimed a shrill voice behind him.

Startled, Paine spun around and looked into the wide, fiery eyes of Maria Hallett. "Good Lord, girl! I nearly had my death of fright!"

"You are in error! We have used that barn since I was a child. All of my father's things are within it!" Maria went on.

"Peace, Goody Hallett! There is no need for this display."

"You will take the barn from us? How will we build another? The animals spend the cold winter months there!"

"Stop this raving! Knowles' deed claims this barn! Your father built on Knowles' land. That is what the surveying says and so goes the law." Paine glanced at the barn. Its shingles hung gray and loose on its flank, and its roofline bowed slightly as though weak with age. The structure appeared to be wilting like a flower suffering from misplanting. Its sad, crumbling condition mocked any debate of its future. Besides, if a mill could be easily rebuilt, then so could a barn.

"That cannot be..." Maria said, her protest trailing away.

"Your father was a truthful man. He would not have done this on purpose," Paine said. The girl's tongue worked with an edge that he had not felt from her before. It made Paine wonder from what source sprang her outburst. He too had heard the rumors of the Hallett girl, and he did not know the truth or falseness of them. He knew that such divination was a dangerous practice, not springing from Godliness, yet he also knew how people's minds made connections that were not always there. He spoke what he believed about Seth Hallett, that he had been a good man. For that reason, he could not look at Seth's daughter as anything other than a poor girl in need of comfort when so much had been taken from her. The fear of such loss alone made him shiver. He could not fathom the real taste of it.

"How are your Bible lessons going?" he asked her gently. He tried to give her a reassuring look.

"Fine," she said, still staring at the building.

Paine wanted to say something more but knew not what. If only he had his pen and paper to aid him, he thought. It seemed that his speech waned in articulation to what he could do with a quill and ink. "All this will pass. You shall see. Then the sun will be out again and the darkness but a memory," he said, thinking that it was a fair bit of sentiment, capturing what he had in his head nicely.

Maria gave him an unreadable look and moved off without a word.

"I will pray for you!" he called after her.

✠ ✠ ✠ ✠

Later Deacon Paine stood in an incoming tide, which lapped at his knees like a dog begging for attention. He reached down into it and pulled on the new wooden footing and was pleased that it had little give. Thanks to the generosity of his neighbors, the destruction to his mill had nearly been righted. That it had been done so quickly and willingly produced a tightness in his chest. It reaffirmed for him the admirable qualities of these people with whom he shared this

God given existence. Such feelings filled him with inspiration, and he sloshed out of the water, eager to set his quill to the task of recording the mighty, heartfelt gestures that he had lately witnessed.

Soon he was sitting at his table. The familiar sight of Great Cove through the window steadied his thoughts in the same manner as ship's ballast. He dipped the tip of his quill into the ink well and then entered a brief summary of the past days events into his journal.

He had just written, *Treat decreed that the remains of the beast be burned, in accordance with the recommendations of the treatise on Maleficia...* when the black line of his script faded away.

Paine tipped the ink well upside-down, and the last three drops of liquid dripped onto the table.

He rose from his chair and went out to his woodshed and squeezed in between a narrow corridor of stacked cords. Behind the kindling was a small space that had been created without purpose by the way that the wood lay. It was just a nook, but now it had other merit, like a space beneath a loose floor board. There was room enough for two buckets covered with canvas. Paine lifted the covering off of the closest bucket and dipped a small glass bottle, which he took from his pocket, into the liquid within. He lifted the jar to the light and examined its contents.

The liquid within it was as gray as charcoal. The sun did not penetrate deep into its depths, but it lightened the outer layers enough to show that the substance had a milky quality. It was an odd substance but one with great usefulness.

Paine stoppered the bottle and put it back into his pocket. He then stepped out of the shed, feeling sheepish and almost sinful.

The black liquid had come from the beast. As soon as he saw it, he knew its merit as ink for writing. The source of his ink supply still troubled him, but he comforted himself with the knowledge that he would be converting its dark origin into words that sang with joyful praise for the light of the Lord's creation. That, he felt, was something of a parable about the way anything black in this world could be turned to light.

Chapter Three
"A Bitter Harvest"

Jonathan Hopkins was a young farmer. His family held acreage across from the Halletts, between Great Cove and Tonset Road. There was enough land, and good corn rising from the black dirt, that he had little reason to supplement the harvest with trips out to sea. He stayed on dry land, and he had a reputation of being good at tending to it. He was due to inherit his father's farmstead, which Alice Hallett could see as she looked out her window, close enough that a strong holler might bring someone out of its door to answer.

In her mind Alice happily listed the young man's qualities as she peeked out at him as he stood with her daughter within the copse of cherry trees in the front yard. The couple stood as stiff and straight as a pair of saplings, reminding Alice of her own awkward courtships in her youth. She remembered the boys who made her wish that time would go on forever and those whose clumsy advances made her long for a quick end to their meeting. All of it was done in full public display, just like her daughter's wooing. It was an uncomfortable, but necessary, passage of life akin to gangly, uncoordinated fledgling birds attempting first flight. With the correct match a young woman could find herself in a comfortable nest as safe and cushioned from the world as one could expect. Deciding on the pairing would be as much Alice's doing as her daughter's because the custom of arranged marriages withstood from the days of the first settlers. To Alice's way of thinking, the Hopkins boy need only ask and she would be content to consider the matter concluded.

Lately the days had begun to grow warmer. Maria was wearing her light blue dress. It was a knit that Alice had created some time ago, with much hope and promise, when the first talk of marriage had begun around the dinner board. It was fine-spun wool, colored with a rare indigo dye but soiled by several long streaks of dirt where her daughter had wiped her hands on the garment. Alice clucked disapprovingly at the stains and the prospect of more soiling to come as she watched Maria sit languidly on the stone wall, her indecency in view of all the neighbors, who were undoubtedly watching through their windows.

Alice had to strain to hear snatches of the courtship carried by the wind. Hopkins was a soft spoken man, and Maria was not speaking much at all, so for a while there was nothing to hear but the chitter of bugs in the field.

She watched her daughter sit on the wall and occasionally kick her legs in apparent boredom. Next to her stood Hopkins, his nervousness playing out in his hands, which twitched and fingered endlessly at the hem of his dress jacket, one that was kept cleaned and pressed for just such an occasion. He did not look comfortable in it, and Alice had an urge to tell him to take it off because she was tired of observing his fidgeting.

The young man's face was thin with a scant scruff of a beard, like the first growth of spring crops. The rest of his body followed this leanness of form. His arms and legs poked past the edge of his shirt and pant cuffs as if he was in the process of growing at the very moment. He modeled himself as a man who would one day be as powerful as Elder Knowles or Justice Doane, and Alice had little doubt that he would grow into his ambitions. She hoped that he was detailing such plans to her daughter and that Maria was seeing the promise in them. But the look on Maria's face disappointed her. She knew well the forced smile that her daughter employed when trying to appear pleasant. She hoped that the boy did not recognize it for what it was. If the courtship held, then he would have plenty of time to become acquainted with it.

Hopkins made some comment and whatever her daughter said in reply made the boy wring his jacket tighter than ever.

Finally she heard Hopkins say, "I have been as far as Boston. My father took me along three times on business. My father considers buying property in that town. We could travel there if you liked, from time to time, and see the great buildings and Long Wharf, which is said to be nearly a half-mile jutting into the sea."

"I would like that. But I would prefer a long sailing voyage to London or Spain," Maria replied.

"Those are hard passages for little use but scenery. A good livelihood can be gained right here in Eastham with less trouble or risk," he replied wisely, in Alice's opinion.

There was a long pause before Hopkins spoke again, "I used to see you sailing in Great Cove."

"Yes, my father bought me a boat. He taught me to sail too. Although we never got past the breakwater. But one day I shall," Maria replied.

At that moment Alice felt like shouting some complaint at her daughter's foolishness. But again Hopkins' good sense showed through.

"I'd be happy to oblige you any adventure we can dream of within the space of the farm. I've got sixty acres. Well, my father does. But at least half is to be mine," he said.

Maria smiled wanly. "My father left us only ten. He never wanted more than that."

Hopkins hesitated and then said, "Your father was a good man." After a time he began talking again, this time not stopping as if he meant to bridge the distance between them with a sheer weight of words. He spoke of the crop rotations, the number and use of the livestock in the Hopkins' holdings, his plans for expansion and purchasing more land.

Suddenly Maria yawned. It came rising up like a bubble coming to the surface of broth. Hopkins looked shocked although his face softened somewhat when Maria said that the rudeness was merely the result of lack of sleep. "Reverend Treat says that I should not sleep in these troubled times," she explained.

Alice bit her lip and watched to see if Hopkins' had discerned the deeper meaning of her daughter's words. But he seemed relieved, then bashful, once Maria flashed him her beautiful smile.

"*Fools… Both of them…*" Alice mumbled although she herself had used such ploys as a wooing maiden. It could have ended pleasantly there, and it should have, in Alice's opinion. Yet Maria would not let things lie.

"I do not sleep because of the dreams…" Maria said, smiling tentatively.

"*Silly, silly girl!*" Alice muttered under her breath. She had hoped that there would be no more mention of dreams after Treat had gotten through with her. She watched Maria peering at her suitor, looking for reaction. Nearly everyone knew the story, and there was no purpose dredging up such dark tidings, other than to undermine this fragile, ill-formed union. Again Hopkins' patience and understanding astonished her.

"I spoke of this with Reverend Treat, before I came to propose. He told me that there is not necessarily evil in it, just a youthful sensitivity that will diminish with proper guidance."

"I do not do it on purpose! It happens only once in a while of its own accord!"

"Be that as it may, it can be cured is what the reverend says. We would not want that kind of ailment to affect the household or be inherited by children."

"Why would you marry me if you think I am sick?" she asked.

The young man went rigid. "You have a quiet disposition that I favor. You are the prettiest girl in Eastham as well. And you are pious enough," he said. Then he reached for the hem of his shirt like he meant to tear at it.

"Is that your proposal?"

"No! Of course not! If you would marry me, you would not want for anything. We have servants who would make your life an easy one."

Then he kissed her, and they looked like two planks being pressed together. But it seemed to give him meager satisfaction, and he stepped back and stood panting a moment, with a look of vindication on his face.

Alice did not hear what was said after that. She assumed the meeting was over. Expecting her daughter to come into the house, she stepped away from the window and busied herself preparing a fat striped bass that the Knowles boys had brought her for dinner. At least the coming day was the day of the Lord. She could not help thinking that the young couple who were groping towards one another in the front field would need all of the help and prayers they could muster.

When Alice next looked up, she was surprised to observe the couple striding off towards town, and she had to stifle the urge to call out through the window. It was a small transgression for an unmarried man and woman to be out in public in each other's company as long as it did not lead to greater sin. The fact that they were courting at all was a sign of providence to come.

✠ ✠ ✠ ✠

Jonathan Hopkins was the son of Joshua Hopkins. Normally the sight of Joshua Hopkins' vast acreage, sloping from Tonset Road down to Great Cove, with its grand homestead and many outbuildings, made Alice Hallett feel small and humbled. However, this day she strode across the road with eagerness in her heart. For once, the property's expanse did not intimidate, but instead inspired her. Indirectly, it was to be her future.

The Hopkins family held enough land to easily feed themselves from it, with ample space left over for pasture to graze livestock, which was shipped out of Barnstable harbor, and a tannery in which hides were converted into leather. Both endeavors added precious coin to the Hopkins' coffers, which in turn was invested in additional lands in the fledgling settlements in Billingsgate and Harwich.

The tannery itself was nothing to speak of, just a rickety, old barn that listed to one side and emitted a foul odor from the urine used to cure the leather.

Inside was dark except for a small fire in the back hearth. What little exterior light trickled in through the open barn doors sufficed for Hopkins, since he only needed to run his fingers across the skins to tell if they were becoming smooth. The dim atmosphere seemed to suit him, and it greatly enhanced his reputation as a shrewd bargainer. He had learned that there was power in hiding one's face, especially if one had a loud voice that came booming like a gale from the shadows.

Alice heard his voice thundering within the structure and then another, lower voice responding, but she was too far away to hear the words. When she drew closer, the discourse was abruptly cut off by a dull thud and a sharp yell.

A moment later Jonathan Hopkins bounded out of his father's tannery, clutching his thigh. He wore a dark brown leather smock, which was stained with tanning oils and shiny in the worn places. It had buffered him from the mallet with which his father had struck him. It was his pride that was most bruised, and that discomfort swelled when he saw Alice standing outside.

"I didn't hear anything..." Alice stammered, astonished at the anger in the boy's eyes as much as his sudden expulsion from the building. He stared at her for a second, his eyes growing round in shock. Then, without a word, he dashed off towards town, in the same direction that she knew that she had seen him traveling with her daughter not half an hour ago. If he was here, then where was Maria, she wondered?

The thought was cut off by a bellow from within the tannery.

"Who is that?" the elder Hopkins growled as Alice was in mid-stride heading back towards her house. She hovered there for a moment, feeling like a fool, for clearly she was infringing upon a family squabble.

"I see you there. I see the hem of your skirt!"

"Mr. Hopkins… It is Alice Hallett. Your neighbor. I don't mean to intrude."

There was a pause before Hopkins shouted, "You'll not find my wife in here, Mrs. Hallett. If you are here to beg for salt or spices, I've got none to lend you out of this stink box. If you are here to set my wife's tongue a-wagging with gossip, I'll ask you to kindly refrain from it so she can get her chores done in a timely manner for once."

Alice struggled to maintain her good cheer in the face of Hopkins' tone. "No, I am not here to ask for salt or spice or call on your wife. I wish to talk to you about your son and my daughter."

She took a tentative step into the tannery. "But if this is not a good time…"

As her eyes adjusted, Alice saw that Hopkins sat on a stool in front of a large, tawny square of skin that was spread out on a wooden table. For a few moments he ignored her. He struck a mallet against the skin, felt out the bumps and ridges in the hide with his fingers and then pounded them flat. Although in his sixties, he was still stronger and broader than his son, despite being slightly shorter.

"We can speak another time," Alice suggested, turning to leave.

"No, stay a moment. Now is no better than any other time," he grunted, thwacking away at his work.

"Your son came to court Maria today. Did you not know?" Alice asked.

"My boy could have his pick, you know," Hopkins said.

Assailed by the murky atmosphere, the stench and Hopkins' churlish manners, Alice felt herself deflate. "I am sure that is true."

"It is indeed! He and I will discuss the matter in due time."

"I believe the matter is already occurring," Alice said, pleased with her fortitude.

The hammering stopped. For a moment she felt that she should apologize for her presumption.

"Your daughter is pretty," Hopkins grumbled as if reluctant to utter the compliment.

"She is that. And she is dutiful, more often than not. She has been troubled since her father departed us."

"Hah! *Troubled* is what you call it?"

"Please do not mock me, Mr. Hopkins. Reverend Treat himself examined her and declared there to be no devilish influence upon her!"

Hopkins smirked and turned his back on his visitor. He dipped a horse hair brush into a bucket of urine and then flung the foul contents across a hide hanging on the wall, taking no notice of the effluent that splashed upon Alice.

"Your daughter may be pleasing to the eye, but beauty fades," Hopkins grunted, glancing over at Alice. He wiped a dirty hand through his thin, graying hair and left a greasy smear there. "My son brings solid worth to any union: land, livestock, a good name. Your girl, well, I ain't entirely certain what she brings besides her good looks. That's the problem. I told him to take a Nickerson girl. What they lack in comeliness, they more than make up for in tracts of good soil in Chatham. Some aren't half bad to gaze upon either."

Alice crinkled her nose at the sharp smell of urine on her apron. Hopkins' words similarly made her cringe. "My daughter would do her share of labor. She and Jonathan have known each other since they were babes. I believe there is some fondness between them," Alice said weakly.

Hopkins arched a brow. "Their romantic feelings are quite beside the point."

"True…" Alice admitted.

"I fear that your girl will give me grandchildren that are soft in the head or perhaps worse than that."

Alice searched her memory for Jonathan's words to her daughter, which she felt summarized the situation admirably: "Reverend Treat says that her dreams will fade in time. It is youthful proclivity that may be outgrown with the proper guidance…"

Hopkins cut her off, "The reverend said the same thing to me and my boy. And I think Jonathan is fool enough for your daughter to believe it." He shook his head in amazement.

As frustrated as she was by the attitude of the tanner, Alice took solace from the strong feelings of his son. It gave her confidence that the union would have stronger bonds than she dared hope. Young Hopkins was exactly what her daughter needed. He was smitten enough to tolerate Maria's oddness and endowed with enough family resources to shield her from the judgment of others.

Hopkins gestured towards the open barn door, and Alice thought that he meant to shoo her out though it. Instead, he gave Alice a suspicious scowl. "You spend most of your life in view of my herd."

"Tis a fine group of cattle," Alice said uncertainly.

"Aye. Everyone in town thinks so. You are not the first to come peddling your daughter with hopes to gain part of it."

"Now, Mr. Hopkins…"

Hopkins spat into the dirt at his feet, then tamped it down with a muck covered boot toe. "I'll speak no more of my son's courting. He and I must tend to other more pressing matters. I suggest that you look to your own homestead in the same fashion." He pointed across the road towards Alice's holdings. "It ain't my cattle that should be concerning you. I hope them bags of bones grazing on your fields ain't the girl's dowry."

"I feel I have been insulted quite enough by you, Mr. Hopkins! Should your son come to ask for my daughter's hand in marriage, I assure you that I will offer him much kinder treatment," Alice said into his smirking face.

"He won't be coming."

"He had better come soon. There are plenty of other suitors for Maria. Mr. Hobart, for one."

"A man who don't even own his own house! But perhaps one day he'll finally bring out all that money he's supposedly got in Boston," Hopkins snickered, his leer growing to more irritating proportions.

"There are others," Alice said.

"Good for you. Now you had better go tend to those cattle of yours before one of them breaks the fence and gets on my land. I don't want any of mine getting what yours got. Then I will be visiting you, and I shan't be so pleasant!"

✠ ✠ ✠ ✠

Alice stood in between the road and the pasture land of her farm, looking askance at both and pleased with neither. Finally she saw the familiar shape of her daughter coming along the dirt track, and she walked to the wall to greet her with a frown.

"Where have you been? I saw you leave with Master Hopkins, yet not long after, he was with his father in his shop. All the while you have been amusing yourself on some adventure."

"Why were you in the Hopkins' tannery?" Maria asked suspiciously.

"Never mind! I expect an answer to my question!"

"I was taking some time to myself. It is Saturday, is it not? I normally receive a few moments of leisure on this day."

"*Resting*, not indolence. Where were you?"

The girl chewed her lip for a moment before declaring, "Higgins Tavern."

"What!"

"Father sometimes took me there after sailing!"

"At which time you were protected by his company."

"I knew everyone present. All but one, that is."

"Nonetheless, it is not very lady-like for a young woman to go alone to the tavern," Alice scolded.

"Are women forbidden from setting foot there?"

"Decency forbids it," Alice said. She glared at her daughter but could not hold Maria's eyes long enough to impart the hard meaning of the look.

"I don't understand. You had just come from courting with Master Hopkins. Why did you leave his company for a filthy tavern? Have you no sense?" Alice went on.

"Half the town has no sense, then."

"If that is how you shall spend your leisure time, then I shall keep you here, for there is much work to be done."

"Perhaps you should ask Elder Knowles."

Alice sighed. "Elder Knowles is a friend to us. And we need help to run this farmstead."

"Today I claimed one dozen eggs from the hens! Yesterday there were fourteen!" Maria countered. "Now I shall go tend to the cows, just as I have for the past year that father has been gone!"

"I shall go with you!" Alice announced. "Perhaps I can open your eyes to the true state of this farm!"

In the distance they saw a cow lying in the dirt. At first it appeared to be sleeping, for it was settled on its haunches in the same position that the beasts assumed before bad weather. Yet the angle of it was too lopsided. When they got closer, they saw the flies, seething like a black scab in the cow's nostrils, and knew that they had lost another of the herd.

Throughout the fields the last dozen of Seth Hallett's animals squatted here and there in weary lumps of skin and bone. For every pound of flesh that withered off of the sickly creatures, and for every one of them that keeled over for good, the Hallett women lost more and more of the coin that Seth had planned to milk out of them.

Three quarters of the fields were left for grazing. It was a dangerous gamble, according to the neighbors who stuck to the traditional equation of half crop, a quarter livestock and a quarter fallow.

If it had worked, Seth would have become one of the richest men in Eastham. After a few seasons of selling milk to the local towns and beef to Boston, he might have been able to buy land in the northern parish. Alice recalled the gleam in her late husband's eye when he would muse upon the potential profit of their investment. It was to be the future of their son who was never born. Now it was the Hallett women's inheritance. In truth, Seth had never liked the feel of land under foot as much as the roll of the deck.

The dead cow lay at the edge of the small pond in the middle of the grazing land. The rest of the herd stayed well away from it except for one. A little calf was standing over the fallen one, hoofing at it in a way that looked, to Alice, as if it was either mournful or hungry.

A week ago the calf was nuzzled under its mother, taking its first suckling tastes of life. Now it appeared weak and pathetic as it sniffed around her carcass. Maria stormed over towards it, clapping her hands and shouting until it danced away.

"The little one should not have to see such a sight. Nor should the neighbors. They already believe that a woman's hand cannot guide field work," Maria said to her mother.

Standing in the sunlight, Alice was reminded of what a pretty girl her daughter was. Although she did not frequent the tavern, Alice knew what they said there, that Maria was the fairest in the entire village. She was not sure if that was a blessing or a mere detail. Years ago the villagers of Eastham had raved similarly about herself, yet it had only resulted in her marriage to an impoverished dreamer from Yarmouth. Eventually he scraped up some pennies, and when they finally had enough to take some comfort from them, he had thrown most of them into cattle and drank the rest away at the tavern. A look at the cows made her wince with annoyance. The cows were dying, and her husband was dead. Now, somehow, it was up to her to provide for the future.

"The dead cow's stench could ruin the drinking water," Alice mused. In that way, the one lost life could spread like poison that tainted all of the others. Every little thing around her seemed so fragile. She wondered how anything made it through a single day with all of the dangers that lurked under every rock and in every ripple on the water.

"I know," Maria replied.

"Then it is best that we move it. I'll go fetch Elder…"

"No, I can do it," Maria grumbled.

Alice shook her head stiffly. "You realize that this dead cow will be followed by the rest, until the field is empty."

"I don't believe that. Why should it be that way?"

"Because that is the nature of the world. When the weak are left on their own, they falter."

✠ ✠ ✠ ✠

The chores passed in time with the long drift of the sun from one side of the property to the other. As evening fell, Alice Hallett closed the windows of the house to block out the dangers of the night air. It was well-known that foul humors that cause illness emerged after dark. After a day's work the clouds of smoke from the cooking lard, tobacco pipes and hearth fire commingled in a vast fog that made her eyes water and every breath feel thick and scratchy. There was a cough that women of the household got, which was almost as a rite of passage. Sometimes it turned into a fever and death, which was then attributed to the night air.

Her daughter was still out in the fields as Alice climbed into the loft to search for a missing weaving cradle, which she thought she might have left there. She found nothing but the straw tick that her daughter slept on and an old sea chest in the corner. She moved, on hands and knees, over to the chest, lifted its cover and saw the wooden toys and straw dolls of her daughter's childhood crammed into it. Except for Maria none of Alice's other children survived, so the box stayed by Maria's bedside long after Maria had grown too old for it, becoming a shrine of longing that Alice could not part with. It just sat there, a sad, closed thing from which no one withdrew its simple pleasures. She took out one of the dolls and examined it, noting the crude little clothes that she had created from scraps of wool. She recalled that Maria had always wished for a button for the outfit. The girl was past the point of such childish fancies now. It was time for both of them to close the lid on the past for good.

That night Alice could find no slumber. Long after the last fireplace embers had gone black and cold, the first rain knocked on the roof and window. She lay wrapped in the coverings and focused on the sound of the rain as it became a hammering and then a loud hiss on the roof and surrounding fields.

Alice rose from bed and stood looking out of her window. She found that she was as nervous as a young bride as she thought about her upcoming wedding. All of Maria's crazy notions of romance were to blame. She recalled her young days with Seth, and she had to admit that she was truly happy back then. There was more to it than contract. Could the same be said of her coming union with Knowles, she wondered? She touched her hair self-consciously. She did not consider herself to be a handsome woman. When she was young, people had called her pretty, but even then she saw too much of her father's square jaw and heavy eye bones to believe it. Now her face looked heavier, the bones starker. Any suggestion of comeliness had faded like spring flowers falling and leaving nothing but heavy, empty branches.

She thought of how similar she was to the wasted cattle and barren ground outside. Across the fields she could see Knowles' light on and wondered if he knew or cared that she could bring no more children into the world. He had plenty of children, but she wondered if he wanted more and would be disappointed if she did not produce them. She could not imagine why else he would be interested in her. It was likely nothing but comfort that they sought from each other, base warmth, shared labor and little more. In fact, she hoped that there would be little other than sleeping in her new bed. She felt her days of love were gone, and the notion made her look to the wedding day with scant joy.

The world could be hard on its women, she mused. That is what she was trying to tell her daughter.

✠ ✠ ✠ ✠

Earlier that afternoon, Justice Doane and Elder Knowles stood by the pillory in front of the meeting house. The pillory had a loose hinge, and when the device was opened, it squealed in a manner that raked the ears. Knowles held the boards flush at the ends while Doane hammered on a new hinge.

They worked in silence, for each was listening to the cacophony of yelling that emanated from within the building where Treat was composing his next sermon. Through an open window they could hear his great rumbling baritone reciting to himself:

"Into the abyss goeth he who turns his back on the word of the Lord, and the Lord will not turn Himself about again to offer the face of salvation to those in that cold loneliness of purgatory awaiting Judgment…"

Doane grunted as he hammered. "There, that should fit snugly. I think it's mended." He gingerly snapped the wooden arms of the device together, and they held tight and strong.

"Fine work. You know your craft well," Knowles said, gazing past the meeting house, up the road in the direction of Treat's Hill where the reverend lived.

Doane packed his kit upon his horse. Then he walked over and stood next to Knowles. The two old friends stood in silence for several moments, listening to Treat's quill scratching madly, inside the house, and watching the swallows dart over the wide hill off in the distance. Knowles ran the fingers of one hand through his dark beard, giving it a slow, contemplative scratch.

"That hill is good land," Knowles finally remarked.

"What of it, my friend?" Doane probed gently.

Knowles was tense. He could not look Doane in the eye as he spoke, "More than one man has owned it, and several who did not own it have *claimed* to own it. Yet my father once held a deed to it, but that deed has somehow gone missing from the record. And now it is *his*," he said bitterly, waving towards the meeting house in which Treat was now yelling again at some complication in his text.

Doane could not believe what he was hearing. It had been years since the town had given Treat a house and the hilly land upon which it sat. It was a small price to pay to attract the first well-respected minister to stand at Eastham's pulpit. He wondered how long Knowles had harbored these feelings.

"It is close to the meeting house for him. Treat did no wrong in acquiring it. The town gave it to him," Doane remarked.

"Yes, but it was *ours* to give. There are other holdings that would have suited him," Knowles said.

"I hear that you might acquire ten additional acres," Doane said, trying to change the subject.

"True, but if I had that hill, I would have far more. That means more cattle, more wealth."

"*Elder Knowles? Are you still about? My ink well is dry, and my mouth is worse for lack of water! Is anybody about to assist me?*" Treat railed from inside the meeting house, not bothering to come to the window.

"I am a church *elder*, not some lowly servant!" Knowles complained.

"Peace," Doane cautioned.

"One day, perhaps soon, he will be gone to the Lord," Knowles said matter-of-factly.

Doane did not know if Knowles meant some vague threat by his statement, but he let it pass. "And we will find another. Your name was once on everyone's lips as his successor." He felt badly as he said it, knowing of Treat's recent visit to see young Johnny Cole.

"*Knowles?*"

Knowles scowled. "I never could stand the idea of leaving this place to go to some seminary in Boston. This is my home. But now we have Nehemiah Hobart of Boston, and Treat has asked him to be ready to take the pulpit should Treat be unable. All because of Hobart's Harvard education!"

"I have heard Hobart remark that he has no interest in the ministry, just teaching."

Knowles gave his friend a skeptical look. "Before Treat, it was good enough to be merely an elder, not a minister, to give sermon. Perhaps we shall embrace such wisdom again."

Doane shrugged. "We are changing."

"Growing too quickly, I fear," Knowles replied.

Doane said nothing. He was thinking of Great Island and the problems that land ownership was raising. It was true that Eastham was indeed growing and overwhelming the limited acres and bounty that God had granted to them. Much of that expansion was from within, generation after generation bringing more and more parishioners into life. That was a good kind of growth, like crops taking root and filling the fields with strong stalks. But there were also men, like some of the Great Islanders and Nehemiah Hobart, who came from elsewhere, adding more seed to the land. Who was to sort out which of the new comers should be granted a place among them, he mused? It worked both ways too. Some of the youth of Eastham had left for the greener pastures of Connecticut and New Jersey where they were interlopers on the claims of the first settlers of those lands.

"Things change, but the law must not alter," Doane told his companion. He was about to say more but another loud holler cut him off. This time it was not the voice of the reverend but an equally strong bellow from the town jail across the road.

Doane stiffened. "Your pardon, John, but the law demands my attention."

"Of course," Knowles replied and watched his friend cross the road towards the increasingly raucous sounds emanating from the building.

"*I see you coming, Doane! The nerve of you, penning up an old woman in this rotten old place! No better than a chicken coop! No cleaner either!*"

"Peace, Widow Chase! I put you in there to give you time to think."

"*Of what? Of where you aim to keep me?*"

"That depends upon you. You have been accused of stealing chickens."

"*But you have no proof other than Mrs. Cole's lying tongue!*"

"You still will not confess?"

"No! Why should I? Ask those school children and they'll tell you that I was *returning* the chickens, not stealing them! Unless they're a bunch of liars too!"

After a pause Doane nodded solemnly and reached for the key on his belt. "Very well. You are right that there is no real evidence at hand... But if I find otherwise, you'll be back in this confinement indefinitely!"

Were it up to Knowles, the old woman would be already on her way to the more secure jail in Barnstable. All one had to do was weigh Mrs. Cole's history of honest piety against the widow's scandalous past full of misdeeds to know that it was the widow who was the liar and thief. At times Doane's adherence to the letter of the law produced in him a blindness, thought Knowles.

"*Knowles! Are you still about?*" Treat's voice roared through the window of the meeting house.

Knowles cursed silently. Then, as quietly as he could, he set off down the King's Highway towards the heart of Eastham.

His way home took him past Higgins Tavern where men of lesser aspirations could spend the hours allowing their ambition to be quenched with Higgins' fare. He gave a disparaging grunt at the thought.

Across from the tavern was a ravine that was planted with apple trees. Their blooms gave a pink and white froth to the hollow, which looked like a colorful tide rolling up to the roadside. The covering was thick, and Knowles might not have noted anything unusual behind its veil if not for a girlish laugh that caught his ear.

He stopped and crept closer to the grove.

There was a flash of light blue and gold, and he was startled to see the upper body of Goody Hallett framed through the branches.

She was not alone.

Knowles stepped closer still. After all, the girl would soon be in his charge, and her actions and disposition reflected on his own character. If this was the measure of her morals, then the reflection would not look good.

The elder began his descent to confront the girl and drag her and whatever ne'er-do-well son of Eastham who accompanied her out of the sinful bosom of the trees. He prayed that it was not a churchman's or selectman's son.

Then Knowles stopped in mid-stride so abruptly that he nearly went skidding down the embankment. The man with Goody Hallett was not from Eastham at all. It was the sailor Sam Bellamy. The storm had washed him ashore in no better shape than a busted ship's spar. Some considered him a victim of misfortune, others questioned the nature of a man who came ashore with no sign of the wreck that bore him. Still others noted the timing of his arrival with that of the devilish sea creature and shivered at the implication. Knowles had as many doubts as any other man. The only thing that Knowles was certain of was that the sailor had a hard edge about him that did not make the elder want to confront him alone.

Chapter Four
"Courtship and Commandment"

In the back of the meeting house, unmarried women were supposed to stand to one side and unmarried men to the other. But the population of town had outgrown the building to the point where, once the main doors were shut, the two groups were pushed tight together in a more general scrum, which always had girls like Mehitable Higgins and Thankful Knowles eagerly elbowing their way towards the edge nearest the bachelors.

Jonathan Hopkins' eyes swept past those eager girls and found Maria Hallett nestled deep in the middle of the pack of young women.

The front door kept opening and closing as the stragglers to service arrived, passing under Justice Doane's stern gaze as he stood sentinel by the door. As soon as Reverend Treat reached the pulpit, Doane would start doling out fines. Deacon Paine stood alongside of him, chatting amicably with the young folk nearest to him but with his ledger open to record the names of those who would receive punishment. Every time the door swung wide, it gave view of wagons rolling along the King's Highway. Some were still too far away to make it to service on time.

The door flew open again, and a loud, age-tinged voice cried out, "Don't even think of it, Joseph Doane!"

"You are not yet tardy," Doane replied.

Widow Chase glared at Doane as if trying to determine if his words were some kind of insult. Hard, shrewd eyes peered out from under hair that was brushed forward to obscure the mark of sin that everyone knew lay beneath.

A native woman was at Widow Chase's elbow. Her face was rough and dark like pine bark, which made it hard to determine her age. She wore a dress like any other Eastham woman, yet she exuded an earthy strength and grace that seemed to outshine the stiff, home-spun wool. Widow Chase clung to her arm as the native woman led her towards one of the front benches.

"Martha is staying this time for service! I am sick of having to wait for her to push through the crowds to get to me. I like to be the first out to my wagon, and I cannot do it on my own!" Widow Chase called out to Doane as she passed.

Doane nodded patiently. It was a routine that was enacted at every service. Servants were allowed to attend the regular service by standing outside to listen through the open windows. The natives had their own service later in the day. But Martha was an exception. Normally she took her place with the other helpers out in the yard, but lately the widow had been leaning more heavily on her, and even Justice Doane would not stand in her way.

"She is not a servant, but a friend!" Widow Chase reminded the justice as she always did.

"And since the lot of us paid one hundred and eighty pounds last time we rebuilt this meeting house, I think any of us should be able to bring whomever we please to this place!" she added.

Many parishioners watched in fascination as the odd pair passed by. As they did, the crowd bulged, and Jonathan noticed that Maria was being pushed towards the seam near where the men stood. Purposely, he tried to squeeze closer in her direction.

The church interior was sparsely decorated, in a conscious effort to reflect the simplicity of the religion itself and the basic interpretation of the scripture without all the trappings of Papist ceremony. Reverend Treat hobbled up to the pulpit, which was the only feature in the holy house that was given an ornate touch. Along its top and base, a thin line of wood was carved in the image of woven tree branches, which was meant to convey the connectedness of church and community, town and kingdom, individual and family, and ultimately God and His children. The truer symbolism of the pulpit was in its raised position looking down on the upturned faces of the congregation.

Despite the intentions of the Protestant church founders, Treat still believed that every flock needed a shepherd. Of course, God was steward over them all, but each small tribe needed a leader who stood a little higher up on the ladder. He was simply an interpreter who spoke slightly more eloquently and purely the language of the divine and so was closer to Him.

Although Treat's voice was scratchy and at times hoarse, it still carried like a drum. It reverberated in the congregation's bones, making them feel like the seats themselves were shaking whenever he enunciated his frequent refrain, "Thanks be to Most Holy God!"

"There is uncertainty and scourge among us. We know that we are the cause of this lamentation and testing! Therefore, I declare the coming day as one of Fasting and Humiliation! In times of joy we offer Thanksgiving to the Lord in recognition of His blessings and munificence. In times of darkness we must humble ourselves and ask for His pardon. We must deprive ourselves and pray for clarity so that we may again see His Holy Light clearly!"

"As the Lord's trusted messenger and the purveyor of His unbreakable word, I urge you to remember and hold in your hearts His essential commandments. Remember the contract that His son Moses brought down from Mount Sinai. Recall it with me so we all may refresh our minds about what we have agreed to, coming into this life in God's kingdom."

Jonathan Hopkins stepped close enough to Maria Hallett to nudge her arm. When she turned, he kept staring piously ahead while surreptitiously rubbing elbows with her. *"Forgive my impropriety, dear Maria, but before the good reverend condemns flirtation, may I be so bold as to ask for your company?"* he whispered.

"Thou shall not covet thy neighbor's wife!" Treat boomed.

"Amen," Jonathan said aloud with the rest of the congregation.

"Respect the property of one's neighbor, be it his plow, his land or his goodly spouse."

"Amen."

"This coming Wednesday evening, I will visit you at your mother's house," Jonathan whispered.

"Honor thy father and mother!" Treat railed. "Should not this directive be infused into us at birth? Should not the first glance into our loving parents' faces seal forever our loyalty and obedience to them, with the knowledge that they have always cared for us and looked out for us, from the time when we were babes and could not take care of ourselves or even know our own names? They have cared and protected and guided us in the same way that God Himself cares for all of His children. So would not our undying affection be planted in our hearts with the first awakening? It should, but it might amaze you that this is not always the case. It would be as if one had turned one's back on the Heavenly Father Himself!" Treat roared.

"Maria. What is your answer?" Jonathan tried again, noting that Maria was shifting uncomfortably. It also seemed that Treat himself had fixed Maria with a righteous glare.

"And once one commandment is broken, it is a simple matter to transgress them all, going deeper and deeper into the pit of darkness, until all sight of the saving light is extinguished and that black place is the only destiny possible! Lust, murder, envy, theft, devilry…"

The front door opened again, and the congregation heard the hard tone in Doane's voice as he berated a late comer to service.

Jonathan Hopkins looked and saw Sam Bellamy at the threshold. The justice pushed the sailor back towards the front lawn and directed him around the corner, to peer through one of the windows with the servants.

"That one is trouble. You should hear what he has to say at the tavern. Among his boasts is that he is wooing a local girl, but he will not say who…" Jonathan muttered, ceasing when a violent spat of coughing, at the pulpit, cut him off.

Treat gripped his throat as if his words had become too much to utter. His wife hurried to his side and ushered him out of a side door. Then Elder Knowles rushed to the head of the congregation, struggling to conceal the inappropriate happiness that lit his face.

Outside, Treat's discomfort rang out across the meeting house yard. Within the building, a chattering started and soon drowned out the reverend's coughing and Knowles' racing thoughts as he tried to make sense of the incoherent scrawl of notes that Treat had left on the pulpit.

"Shadows… Darkness that can take any form…"

Just as Knowles opened his mouth to utter the words, the bell in the steeple gave a great tolling clang.

A few people screamed. A few others leapt from their seats as if to run. Scores of frightened, ashen faces stared at Knowles, who now found his throat constricted with fear and dismay.

The bell was out of sight of the congregation. All that was visible was a black maw that lead up into the steeple and the dangling rope that rang the bell, which swayed just so with the reverberation of the chime. But no one was near enough to have pulled it.

While Knowles stood, mouth agape, in the front of the room, Justice Doane ran out of the meeting house and pointed at the native who languished in the pillory on the lawn.

"You! Did you see what rang the bell?" Doane demanded.

John Julian's position afforded him only a painful sideways glance at the justice. With his neck crooked in such a manner, his grin looked like a crazed, lopsided grimace, which reinforced the justice's low opinion of the man.

"Well?"

Julian nodded towards the sky above the meeting house steeple where a half-dozen seagulls were in flight. An equal number danced skittishly along the roof line.

"The birds? Do you mean that the birds knocked into the bell?" Doane cried.

In response Julian merely shrugged and dropped his head towards the ground.

Doane took an angry step towards the exasperating figure in the pillory, but then he saw Treat come limping around the corner of the building.

"Did you see anything, Reverend?" Doane called out.

Treat pointed frantically at the steeple. "Did you hear it, Joseph?"

"We all did. But none saw anything," Doane replied.

"Of course not! Human eyes cannot see such beings."

"Shadows of darkness?" Doane had heard, through the windows of the meeting house, Treat practicing his sermon in the days prior to service. But Doane's voice was tinged with skepticism.

Treat returned an almost childish smile, which made Doane wonder if some shadow's hand was indeed upon the man's mind.

"No... Angels, good Justice. Angels! It is a good sign, is it not?"

Behind Doane, the native gave a grating laugh, which sounded to Doane very much like the bark of a seagull. And gulls, Doane knew, were clamorous, unhelpful birds.

✠ ✠ ✠ ✠

When Alice Hallett pushed her way out of the meeting house, the sun was already waning. A typical worship lasted four or five hours, without food or drink or respite from prayer. This one had gone on so long that her hungry stomach began speaking louder than her prayers.

Upon arriving back at the homestead, Alice immediately sent Maria to fetch some eggs for dinner. At that very moment Thankful Knowles was chasing the Knowles' flock of chickens, which had burst from their coop and dashed, shrieking in protest, to the rock wall between the two farms. There the two girls came face to face and stood looking at each other for a moment across the ridge of stones.

"Why was Jonathan Hopkins talking with you?" Thankful Knowles asked, her voice trembling.

"It means nothing," Maria replied.

"You do not even fancy him? Yet all he speaks of is you! He longs for you, and there is no room in his heart for another! You have stolen any chance that someone else might give him happiness!" Thankful cried.

"There is nothing between us," Maria snapped.

"The sailor! I saw him staring at you through the window! You are trysting with him! You mean to ruin things for Mehitable as well!"

"She is no friend of mine."

"You are shameless!" Thankful huffed.

"How many men have you dreamed of marrying during these past months?" Maria asked rhetorically.

"That was merely an amusing game to play. All along, Master Hopkins was the one I fancied!"

Around them chickens squawked and were echoed by a rattling cough coming through the window of the Knowles' homestead. The youngest Knowles child, but two years old, was laid up in bed.

Thankful turned towards the sound and said, "'Tis nothing but some food gone down the wrong way."

"I am afraid it is something more," Maria said, shaking her head sadly.

"You lie," Thankful said angrily.

"Did I not dream of the ship wrecking? I was right about that."

"You dreamed of my little sister?" Thankful said, her lip trembling like a fish on a hook.

"The only opportunity I seek is to better myself. I came he[re] [fo]r honest chances, not thieving and conniving."

"*Honest chances?* You jest! You know, there are many in town [w]ho think that you have worn out your welcome. After all, what do [yo]u do for us but slink around stealing our food, our coin, our [w]omen."

Bellamy shook his head. "You know that none of that is [tru]e. You are drunk and upset."

Hopkins scoffed. "We have no kindness for vagabonds and [mig]rants such as you! I am sure that Justice Doane will agree with [me]!"

"Hmmm… So far, the colonies have not much lived up to [the]ir boasting promise. In fact, Maria is one of the few who gave me [wel]come in this town," Bellamy replied.

"Do not speak of her! You seek to soil her!" Hopkins said, [rus]hing at the sailor.

Bellamy grabbed Hopkins and spun him. At first it felt to [Hop]kins like a dance. The motion filled his head, and when he [glid]ed to a stop, he had to turn full circle to aim the blow at [Bell]amy's head.

His knuckles plowed through the air and carried him in an[othe]r circle.

Then Bellamy grabbed his shirt front, steadied him and said, [Eve]rything I have gained is fairly won. Do not sully my courtship [with] your accusations."

The dark bearded face was so close. In his mind's eye Hop[kins] saw his punch moving deft and sure, but the ales slowed his [cele]rity, and the blow glanced off of the sailor's shoulder.

Bellamy's strike, however, landed just where it was aimed. [And] Hopkins fell to the ground, trying to stem the gush of blood [from] his nose.

❇ ❇ ❇

Late August 1715

The summer had been a blur, which now mellowed as the [har]vest was packed away into barns and root cellars. The season was [aging] but not Alice Hallett's resolve, despite the bliss on her

"I did. But I should not tell you."

"You must! You've already said something!"

"No, I know how you feel about my gift, that it is something unnatural."

"Tell me, Maria!"

"The cough will get worse. It is sad… She will not live through the summer."

"You lie! She has had it but one day!"

Maria shrugged. "Perhaps my dreams are wrong for once."

With her face a contorted display of anger, misery and fear, Thankful stared at the other girl for a long while. She did not want to believe that Maria Hallett had supernatural power. On the one hand there was the evil of such propensity. On the other hand there was the unfairness of it. By day Maria's looks gave her power enough, particularly over the men in town. As inappropriate as it was to envy another's sins, Thankful felt a surge of jealousy that Maria might command another potent power while she was asleep.

Another choking spasm came out of the window, and Thankful turned and ran back to the house. She did not tell anyone about Maria's words. Her father had urged her to be sisterly towards Maria, no matter how hard a task it was or how helpless it made her feel, under the doom of Maria's prediction.

❇ ❇ ❇

The young calf gave a pitiful yelp as its twig-like legs slid into the black, sucking mud. Jonathan Hopkins stood at the edge of his family's holdings where a thin rim of brackish marsh connected the land to Great Cove. The little calf, like all of its kind, had been born timid and skittish.

Hopkins felt a tremor of nervousness himself as he contemplated retrieving the struggling animal. It is only ankle deep water, he told himself. It was sunlit water, with light pleasantly dancing on its surface, but he could not push the memory of that awful sea creature from his mind. The beast was dead. He knew that. Yet the image persisted. Shadows from passing clouds seemed like the dark outlines of long, tentacled behemoths gliding just off shore.

The calf squealed as its haunches sank into the mire. Hopkins knew that he had to act quickly. Still he hesitated.

Nearby, a stand of tall reeds shivered, and Hopkins gave it only a passing glance, until it struck him that there was no wind to cause the movement.

Everything seemed to birth a fresh fear.

It is a family of ducks nesting in the reeds, he assuaged himself.

Then he heard voices among the reeds.

"We have a boat. Why don't we sail from here?" a woman's voice cried.

A man answered her, *"Why? I have no desire to go back into those waters. They nearly were the death of me!"*

Hopkins inched closer, along the firm ridge of pasture land at the beach's edge, to try and identify the speakers.

The woman was upset now. He could hear the discomfort in her voice although her words were inaudible except for the plea, *"Take me away from here."*

"We shall go in due time. I have made my promises to you, and I shall deliver. Gold, land… You won't have to worry over anything anymore. Just give me time," the man said.

It was a grand promise to be uttered by a man crouching within a clump of grass, so Hopkins let his curiosity get the better of him. A few more steps and he could almost discern the shapes within the stalks. Behind him the calf belly-flopped into the shallow water and gave an awful snort of fear.

He was about to go back to the calf when he heard the man say, *"Tell me what you want, Maria?"*

At that moment Hopkins longed to cast himself into the mud, hoping it would swallow him whole. But he knew it was too shallow to oblige him. Instead, he sped off towards Higgins Tavern, leaving his father to find the calf and Maria to her treasonous overtures in the reeds.

✠ ✠ ✠

Several ales later, Hopkins had determined that Maria's suitor in the reeds was the sailor Sam Bellamy. He had also convinced himself that Maria suffered merely from youthful inexperience. She was still immature and, he had to admit, unrealistic about the true demands of life. It had made her susceptible to the charms of a man

with no scruples, morals or connections to the communit spell of false claims and pledges.

He thought of Maria's impassioned plea that the her away. He contrasted that with his own awkward cour he had last been with the girl, last Wednesday evening w sat with her on the rock wall of her farm, their usual me He had wanted to kiss her again, but she slid away alc each time he scooted closer. Unwanted images of all of that the sailor might have been taking with her, within t the reeds, filled his mind, and Hopkins hammered on t then stormed out of the tavern.

With his belly full and head a-swirl, Hopkins ened enough for confrontation. He knew that Bellamy be at the tavern, for it was his nightly habit.

As he stood in the road outside the drinking hc was thankful that he had held his tongue earlier. He h any harsh words to her. Those, he knew, would have but products of his pain. He congratulated himself c and composure. That he could see things from a larg marked him as a better man than the one who now a him.

"Sailor!" Hopkins bellowed.

Sam Bellamy's pace slackened, but he kept c "Is that Jonathan Hopkins?"

"It is! I have a bone to pick with you, *sailor..*

"Do you now?" Bellamy responded, stoppi feet from the tavern and waiting until Hopkins came

The walk towards his adversary gave Hop mull over Bellamy's advantage in size, and such thir to sober slightly. Yet there was a larger issue, he tolc fighting for his girl.

"So that sailor's talk was not your usual br seduced the woman that I am to marry," Hopkin voice sounded as though it was breaking with fu emotion that washed through it.

"You have it all wrong, Hopkins. I have sc

Hopkins shook his head. "You surprise n took you for an honest man in need when I first r that you are an opportunist to the core."

daughter's face. She now knew that her daughter had carried on a shameful association with the sailor from the tavern for the whole summer. Word came first from Joshua Hopkins, who had discovered the affair through his son. Soon she was hearing about it from nearly every wag who passed by her on the village roads.

From Maria she had been hearing more and more pleas to allow Sam Bellamy to sup at their board. But Alice would not forsake her better judgment. As scandalous as the relationship was, it would be over soon, Alice told herself. As the good weather faded, so would a sailor's interest in a backwater town. Such tiny villages as Eastham had no shelter to offer a stranger through the winter. It would be best for him to find a berth before the ice kept the ships from running. Alice was quite sure that the sailor would also hold this opinion.

"He has plenty of ambition, mother. Not to grow crops and tend cows but to earn money in shipping or whatever else he would put his mind to. Anything is in reach of those who want it badly enough, he says. You should hear him speak of it. Treat's preaching has no more fervor. We can make our fortune and then travel using our wits and talent to guide us. Why everyone would not want to use their living to see the world, I don't know."

"So he has money?" Alice asked.

"No. Not yet…" Maria admitted.

"If he is interested in shipping, then the place to be is Boston, I should think. There are no deepwater ships here," Alice remarked.

"Mother, you are being contrary," Maria groused. "Perhaps I shall go with him to Boston!"

"And after Boston, then where? He would have you travel the world like gypsies, and they are not well thought of."

"They have their fun dancing and singing. They get a black name because old curmudgeons like Knowles are jealous of their freedom," replied Maria.

"They are dreamers and fortune tellers, whose curse it is to be landless and forced to beg and steal for bread," Alice countered.

"His hands… They are the same square shape as father's. I noticed right away," Maria said softly.

Alice felt like snapping at her daughter once again, but instead, she bit her tongue. There seemed to be no end to her daughter's foolishness these days. It was as deeply wrought into her mind as a fever.

"I thought that I had raised you better than to choose a man by the shape of his hands," Alice snorted.

"That is something I figured out on my own," Maria replied.

Alice stared at the hearth, where the fire's reflection danced on the bottom of the iron cook pot, as she wrestled with the thoughts in her mind.

"Maria, you're at the age when you will soon see what a harsh life it is that we who live on this peninsula face," Alice told her daughter.

Maria folded her hands into her lap.

"You need a family to work the land and a husband to lead the household," Alice declared. "You need roots to be able to hold onto this sandy place."

"I know, mother. But what if I want to leave this place?"

"Hush, child! Jonathan Hopkins has been asking for you. And you should be thankful for that, considering your treatment of him. The schoolteacher Nehemiah Hobart wants to call on you too. I told them both that they are welcome here at any time."

"They are not welcome by me!"

Alice slammed her palms on the table top, yelling, "It is *my* will! That is all that matters under this roof! The Hopkins are a well-respected, hard-working family with deep roots here in Eastham. Hobart is a man who can provide for you. He can give you things that you need, like a home, children and harvest. Don't you want those things?"

"Perhaps. But I should like to live my own life first."

"Your life *is* home, children and harvest. You could have as many suitors as you like if you did not drive them all away! Every unmarried man in town would line up for you! You will end up with nothing if you ally yourself with that impoverished, vagabond sailor!"

"You don't even know him. He's smart and ambitious."

"He wants diversion. He does not care for you, daughter."

"That's not true!"

"I know what he will become. He can't provide. He doesn't even belong here. And he is making us look like fools!"

"So this is about your precious reputation?"

"Maria!" Alice exclaimed. She rose from her seat and pointed in her daughter's face. "Respect thy mother! You *will* honor my efforts for this family and obey my directions. That is the will of God. I will not have this disrespect in my house! I'll put you out into the cold, God help me! Make your own way in the world for a while and see if you don't come crawling back for a hot dinner and warm bed!"

After a silence Alice sat back down. She inhaled deeply and wiped her brow with a napkin. "I don't enjoy that," she told her daughter. "I'd rather that we talked civilly. I am not trying to punish you, Maria. I worry about you. You've been acting a little...wild recently. It's an attitude that can get you into trouble. My dear, he is a sailor."

"Many men here in Eastham make their livelihood from the sea," Maria said tentatively.

"You are young yet, with a child's heart. You don't see all things clearly. No doubt this Bellamy is charming. But these seamen are rovers. They have women in every port."

"Father was a sailor!"

"He was a husband and a father first. Bellamy will leave you as a ruined woman. Mark my words. That will be your disgrace alone if you pursue this. For then no man will have you."

✠ ✠ ✠ ✠

September 1715

There came a day when the Halletts' grazing fields were empty, and Maria burst into the homestead and yelled to her mother that the cattle were gone.

"I know. You would have too had you not been out trysting," Alice said distastefully. "The last living animals were bought by Elder Knowles. Although what he will do with such destitute animals, I know not."

"Sold? For what price?"

Alice narrowed her brows at her daughter. "That is no concern of yours."

"What *price?*" Maria repeated in the irksome tone that she had exhibited since courting the sailor.

"Thirty pounds."

"In coin?"

"Aye. Twas a good bargain for us."

"Where is it then? With that money we can manage on our own for a while."

"Elder Knowles has it in safe keeping for the time being."

"What?"

"If you must know, it is to be a wedding present," Alice said, adjusting her hair self-consciously at the thought.

"At which point, he shall have us and all our money in his coffers," Maria snarled.

"Maria! Hold thy tongue! You have changed, daughter. That sailor has given you a sharp tongue."

"He has helped me find the courage to speak my mind. He has helped me to dream."

"He utters nonsense."

"What does Elder Knowles tell you? If Sam had something to give to me, he would. He would not keep it for himself. The elder gives you false promises!"

"Stop! This is not the day to speak ill of Elder Knowles."

"I speak only of what I see."

"Then you do not see the pain that he is in. Yesterday he lost his youngest child. A fever took her. So be gentle with them. You know well what misery is their loss."

To Alice's surprise, Maria for once looked chastised. Perhaps too chastised. "What is wrong?" Alice asked as Maria edged towards the door.

"The girl died?"

"Yes."

"Of her cough?"

"The cough led to a killing fever."

Maria nodded.

"Where are you going?" Alice asked.

"To think…" Maria replied.

"It is about time!" Alice called after her, but her daughter was already heading down the road towards Higgins Tavern.

✠ ✠ ✠ ✠

First, she looked for him at the old barn that Knowles claimed, where the sailor had lately been sheltering, but her calls fell unanswered into the mounds of hay. Then she went to the field of rushes down by Great Cove, and then she remembered the apple orchard, but Maria Hallett could not find Sam Bellamy.

Finally, after some hesitation, she went to Higgins Tavern. She knew that Sam had worn out his welcome at that place and, therefore, she did not expect to find him there, but just to be sure, she peeked through its smoky windows.

A harsh laugh startled her, and she leapt back from the sill.

Mehitable Higgins tossed the contents of a slop bucket into the pen next to the building and chuckled as she watched the swine trundle over to nose through the discarded rinds.

"I suppose you are here in search of your sweetheart?" she said, turning to leer at Maria.

Maria understood the look. Jealousy. Yet she did not expect the intensity of it. "You and I were never friends. So should I be sorry that Sam chose me over you?"

"No! You should not be sorry for any such thing!" Mehitable's tone bordered on gleeful.

Perplexed, Maria put some distance between herself and the tavern girl. She peered into the tavern itself where men threw dice across the tables, laughed and knocked over their mugs of ale, with all the commotion that she had treasured from her trips there with her father and, later on, the sailor.

"He is not there," Mehitable sang, coming alongside Maria and wrapping around Maria's shoulder a hand speckled with grease from the slop bucket.

Maria squirmed away. "Then I shall be on my way."

"Aye! You shall! And so shall your precious sailor! He sailed this morning, in fact!"

"You lie…"

"Do I? If so, then I suppose you'll find out soon enough when he next comes to your door!" Mehitable cackled.

Maria's heart did not start beating fast until she was home, lying up in her cot, watching the sun's light pooling in the evening shadows under the windows below. She could not remember the last time a day had passed without the sight of Sam Bellamy, some whisper from him in her ear or the warmth of his touch through her sleeve, with all of its exhilarating promise.

A week later her heart had almost drummed itself out, and the panicked shock had been replaced by a dull emptiness. There was no sign of Sam left in Eastham.

She stood on the bluff of the Stage Lands, gazing into the vacant stretch of ocean, which was as unreachable as ever. In her line of sight was the spot where that wretched sea creature had been cast upon them, and farther out, the breakwater where Sam had come ashore and finally the edge of the ravenous ocean that had taken her father. Only days ago, those events had made new, overwhelming connections within her. They had made a line that pointed away from this desolate town, out into the deeper sea and the horizon that had always called to her. Now she shouted into a buffeting wind that smothered her voice. The salt spray stung her eyes. Then the tears came, for she realized that this cliff overlooking the sea was the very edge of her world, the farthest that she would ever go.

Chapter Five
"A Taste of the Coming Fire"

October 1715

The warm days were fading. The descent of brown leaves, trails of orange pine needles and flight of departing birds over head, all pointed towards the coming fall.

The harvest was in, and the annual feasting was finished. Villagers had sat at each other's tables and toasted to each other's good fortune. They formed new bonds of allegiance and friendship as they plunged spoons into bowls of mashed squash and turnip. They pledged aid to each other and for the protection of their town, way of life and God.

At the pulpit Reverend Treat railed as loudly as ever against the Devil's shadow that lay across their doors. "Do not let him in!" the old preacher advised. His voice could still be heard from across Great Cove on Sabbath day by the few who avoided service. But his skin hung loose and gray as if he too was entering a waning season.

As the temperature dropped, metal boxes filled with hot stones from the previous night's fire were laid on the meeting house floor, to use as foot warmers. Dogs scrummed around the legs of others, their heat and fur giving warmth. It was still the middling months when one day could summon the frosty wind and damp chill of winter and the next lay as sticky and humid as midsummer's day.

Outside, the leaves flared brilliantly before they burned out and dropped off of the branches. The languid chirp of crickets and other insects of the meadow was mournful, yet soothing, music that told of how things must necessarily end in order to revive again. The beach grass turned multi-colored, and the greens of the marshy plains became tinged with bands of red and yellow, like a sunset, before bleaching to gray.

The youngest Knowles children worked among a copse of head-high bayberry bushes. Their baskets filled slowly since the berries sat in a way that one could only pinch off a few at a time. It was tedious work that would yield only a few candles. Twelve pounds of berries melted down into a single stick, which was used sparingly.

Alice Hallett watched them through the window of the Knowles' kitchen. Their dark blue shirts and dresses contrasted sharply with the light gray of the branches and berries.

It had been a month since Justice Doane's newest deputy, Jonathan Hopkins, had relayed the welcome news of Bellamy's flight from town.

"Childhood is over for you, Maria. It is time to recall what I have tried to teach you all of these years and live a life of good sense, not folly. Speak no more of rebellion and delusion," Alice told her daughter, on the threshold of their new home.

For the next month Maria hardly said anything at all. She spoke only in response to some question directed towards her, which were few and far between, and then only offered a grunting yes or no. To Alice, such silence was the unfortunate pang of love lost. It was like the painful penitence that throbs after sinful ways, akin to the headaches that her first husband suffered after too long spent at Higgins Tavern. Such afflictions eventually passed as Alice knew her daughter's heartbreak would.

Meanwhile, Thankful Knowles was wary of Maria's withdrawal. She thought of animals that went too quiet all of a sudden, in a prelude to coming violence. At night, thoughts like that mounted and ganged up on her, until she wondered if Maria was more dangerous than ever, and she feared to sleep under the same roof as the girl. She planned to follow her father's example and let bygones fade. But for all of their sakes, she did not intend to let her vigilance waver.

One of the few things that Maria did utter to Thankful was a fumbling apology about the passing away of her sister. Thankful nodded solemnly when Maria tried to explain that, out of anger, she had invented the premonition about her little sister's death and she regretted the fabrication. But Thankful did not believe that Maria's sorrow was sincere.

Alice Hallett and Elder Knowles married in a traditional, simple ceremony in the Knowles' main room, with Reverend Treat presiding. Afterwards there was a brief celebration, during which neighbors shuffled in and out of the house to pay their respects and accept a quick mug of mead. Then Knowles neatly folded his new wife and daughter into his daily routine as if they were no more than a new pair of cattle.

Now they were fixing the Sabbath dinner by the hearth. Knowles and his sons sat by the fire. They all smoked pipes, except for the youngest one who was but ten. Thankful, her younger sister and Maria sliced vegetables into the broth. Alice stood on the other side, speaking of nothing but ingredients and measurements as they prepared the meal.

Knowles chewed loudly on the stem of his pipe, talking through his teeth as he pulled from it. The elder described himself as the primary force that shaped what went on in town. According to Knowles, even Treat often acted upon his good advice.

As part of the meal, the sup bucket was scraped clean because there were extra mouths to feed. Only Alice and the elder had the privilege of sitting at the table. The children sat on the floor around the trencher, a trough-like wooden bowl where the left-overs and lesser scraps of food were cast. Maria had not used the device since she was a child. Alice could see that it filled her daughter with reproach, but it infused Alice with hope that this new, expanded family would demonstrate to her daughter the need to scramble and reach out for anything one could get in this world. Sadly, she noted that her daughter made little effort to compete with the Knowles children and, subsequently, was left with the dregs after the others had their fill.

"You are not eating. What ails you?" Knowles asked Maria.

"I am not hungry."

"You will get nothing else to eat, then. There is no getting up in the middle of the night to fish around in the sup bucket. We sleep in respectful peace, under the eyes of the Lord. We do not skulk around like animals."

"I will not get up later."

Knowles stared at her for a moment. "Good..." he said finally.

In reply Maria let out a loud yelp.

Knowles pushed back his chair and took a step towards the door as if readying himself to flee through it. "*What?* What is it?"

"Tell us what is wrong!" Thankful asked Maria sharply when Maria did not answer her father.

"I'm fine."

"You appear as though you've eaten some spoilt fish." Thankful touched a hand to Maria's forehead and then stepped back quickly. "You're burning." Her eyes scanned Maria, looking for visible stains of illness. "The fever," she said quietly.

"I fear it."

"You'll infect us all!" Thankful exclaimed.

Alice's firm hand clamped over her daughter's forehead. "Good Lord, child! You burn! Why did you not say that you were ill?" Alice cried.

"Get away from her, children," Knowles commanded, pulling his brood up one by one by their arms.

"It might not be fever," Alice went on, trying to conceal the tremor in her voice.

Maria clamped a hand over her mother's. "I am fine. I got over exerted in the fields. That is all."

"Put her in the back room. The other children will sleep out here by the fire. Its heat shall burn away any ill humors that might affect them," Knowles said. There was enough sunlight to go back to the fields where the harvested stalks needed scything. Knowles led his sons away to do that chore and sent his daughters out to put the livestock away.

Alice took her daughter into the back room and made her stand by the bed while she tightened the ropes with a turn key.

"If it is fever, it could run its course in a day or two. Many of the Indians have gotten it and most survived. None of our people have been afflicted. So there is no need to worry. No need to worry at all..." Alice was jabbering.

"Mother! Peace! I shall not recover if you fret over me so."

Again Alice touched her daughter's forehead. "Oh God, you are on fire, child!"

"Stop. I need rest is all," Maria said sleepily.

"Do not sleep too long! I shall wake you for broth in an hour. You must eat something," Alice pleaded as if her daughter had just declared that she intended not to nap but to pass on to the next world.

"Okay. You bring it, though. I do not wish to see any Knowles this evening, please," Maria said softly.

"Child, they care for you."

"We could have run the farm on our own," Maria said deliriously.

"We are ruined, child! Ruined! If not for the generosity of Elder Knowles, we would not survive. If anything should happen to Elder Knowles' good feeling towards us…"

"They are not his fields. They are our fields."

"It is all one now. Go to bed, child," Alice said.

Before her daughter could protest, Alice shut the door of the room. Later when she opened it to leave the broth, Maria was fast asleep.

Alice did not open the door again until the next morning, at which time she had Elder Knowles and most of his children at her side.

"Get up!" Knowles said to his new daughter. Beside him Thankful smirked, her arms folded in triumph.

Knowles led the group to the front door where he leaned down and examined the yellow powder that was spread across the threshold, leaving an off-color look of frost on the floor boards, except where several footprints stood out. The powder, which was fine ground corn, had been sprinkled by Knowles the night before, as a precaution.

"Only Maria's boots match the size of these!" Thankful exclaimed.

"My window was broken," Maria said.

"She admits it!"

"Child, the night air…" Alice began.

But Knowles cut her off, "What business did you have out there in the night?"

"The window in my room was stuck. I was hot and needed air. I was only outside for a moment," she said, giving her mother a pleading look.

Knowles stepped between the two Hallett women. "Perhaps you are not sick at all but merely saving energy for your night's work. Are you already trysting again? Your lust escapes you, it seems!"

"Sam Bellamy was no mere tryst!" Maria cried.

"Maria!" Alice said.

"Where then did you go? Whom did you cavort with if it was not a mortal man?"

"I needed air!" Maria protested. "There was no one! Had you spread the rest of the year's corn meal out doors a ways, you'd see my tracks went no farther than the stoop!"

"Twas meal well spent if it sheds light on your nocturnal wanderings. You shall stay under lock and key from now on. Never did I think that I would pray that a girl under my roof would be fornicating rather than a worse alternative," Knowles said.

"I was not!"

"You have scant reputation to earn you such trust!"

"My belly," she groaned, doubling over. "I feel ill again."

"Pull up your dress," Knowles commanded. Maria instinctively placed her hands over her stomach to protect herself.

"Let your mother see you. The spots of the pox start in the pits, neck and belly," he went on, turning away to give the Hallett women privacy.

Slowly, Maria drew up her shirt and raised her arms, exposing her belly to her mother.

"There are no spots. But there is the mark that Reverend Treat warned us about!" Thankful exclaimed, over Alice's shoulder.

Alice looked and saw a dark blemish above her daughter's navel.

"Father! Look! The Devil's mark!" Thankful cried.

Knowles turned around, his eyes sharp as talons.

Maria brushed at the blemish, and it fell off. "It is a flake of hearth soot or something. How it got there, I do not know…"

"See? It is nothing! You all judge her in error!" Alice said. She turned appealing eyes to her new family and saw nothing but fear in their eyes.

After the children left for their chores in the fields, Knowles wrapped an arm around his wife's midriff, a gesture that nearly took the wind out of her because she mistook it at first for tenderness.

"Reverend Treat is ill. Who knows how long he might last."

"I know. It is plain to see."

"Should he prove unable to man the pulpit, as church elder, it might fall to me to take over temporarily or perhaps for longer," he went on, trying to make it sound like a complaint. "My duties would expand greatly. I would look to you to keep a firm hand here at home, setting a good example for our children."

"Of course," she replied. He was peering at her strangely.

"Our marriage can be undone as easily as it was made. Under such arrangement, I would keep the land of your late husband, and you and your daughter would have nothing to sustain you but whatever charity you could muster. And there is not much charity left in this town for your daughter."

Alice inhaled slowly. "She is misunderstood. She merely laments her father's passing."

Knowles smirked. "'Twas some time ago! I can understand a mother's blindness to her child's failings, but you shield her in error. Too much is at stake for such pampering. With your recent outbursts, I begin to wonder if I was blind to your true nature. I thought you were a pious, faithful woman. Yet you are proving as wild as your girl."

"You suggest that I am unfaithful? Impious?"

"After God, I am to receive your utmost allegiance. Your life is bound to me. As for your daughter, she is old enough that if she cannot find a husband this next year, she shall be put out nonetheless to find her way on her own. Do you disagree?"

"No…"

"Good." Knowles stroked her cheek and added, "Do not despair. It will take time for our families to re-forge as one. These are necessary sparks as we fuse together."

✠ ✠ ✠ ✠

Widow Chase lived in an ancient house that overlooked the ocean that had taken her husband. Inside were all manner of sea chests, lanterns and hanging ropes, which made the interior feel much more like the hold of a ship than the farmhouses of her neighbors. Captain Chase had been a mariner his whole life, leaving for the sea as a cabin boy, returning briefly to woo and marry but spending the bulk of the rest of his sixty years out on the waves. Back on dry land his wife had felt like a widow by her first wedding anniversary. The half-dozen children that she raised had not eased that feeling.

One day her husband left for good, but by then she was used to the absence. It felt no worse than some of his voyages to the West Indies or Europe that kept him away for five months or more. She remembered wondering, when she was a young wife, if the feeling would change when her husband's trips became years instead of months. But the longer that he was away, the less that she missed him as if time was playing a trick on her, wiping him from her memory instead of fusing him into it. These days she could barely recall what he looked like, never mind the more subtle things like how his arms felt around her or his voice sounded when whispered into her ear, something that she had only experienced a few times to begin with.

She had made her way on her own. The harvest brought in just enough to sustain her through the seasons and not an ear of corn more. She made coin as a midwife and by selling the goods that her husband brought back from his travels - strange carvings from the West Indies and barrels of molasses and rum, which were always well in demand.

Maria Hallett sat in Widow Chase's front room, looking out the window that faced the ocean while Widow Chase appraised her with a critical eye and chided herself for not doling out the kind of cantankerous reception for which she was well-known. Instead of showing her the sitting room, Widow Chase now wished that she had offered the girl a view of the wood grain of her front door slamming. But it was too late now, and Widow Chase could only puzzle about her sudden softness, which put her momentarily at a rare loss for words.

They sat in silence for a while, dipping spoons into the broth that Widow Chase had grudgingly prepared. They listened to the sound of the surf coming through the window as if it was washing away the silent minutes between them.

The girl's eyes drifted to the faint ridge of skin under Widow Chase's right eye that formed a distinct "M."

"Lord! It means *midwife*, if you don't know! I've been accused of causing the death of some of the little ones," the old woman growled.

"I...I..." Maria stammered.

"It don't mean *murderer!*" I was never convicted of anything! But that don't stop old Treat, does it! Now stop staring!"

"I didn't think it means murderer. Not exactly..."

"Ah! You think it means some foolishness like *Mistress of Satan!* For they call me a witch!"

"Is it true then? You know spells?" Maria asked.

Widow Chase eyed her young visitor carefully. "What if it were?"

"I'd ask you to teach me… although I am afraid that I have nothing to offer in return."

"*Foolishness!* I am no witch!"

The girl looked disappointed. It had been that way since she had arrived on the stoop, fright and disenchantment parading across her face one after the other.

"Is that why you are here? To apprentice with a witch? For this does not seem like a social call," Widow Chase huffed.

The sudden ferocity in the girl's demeanor startled the widow. "You don't have to pretend with me! I am not afraid. I *want* to know how to make potions."

"*Potions?*"

"I am labeled a witch, and I cannot even make a single spell in revenge."

"I understand your plight, but I cannot help you!" Widow Chase said, standing up in a way that she hoped Maria would see was a signal to leave. "Are you done with your soup yet? I need to be getting on with my chores."

Now the girl wore the sorrowful face again. "Truly? You are not a witch?"

"There are no witches," Widow Chase declared. "Now, hurry along. I have washing still and supper won't prepare itself!"

When the girl still did not get up, Widow Chase took the bowl from her hands. She could see the girl's mind working up fresh questions, and she braced herself for them.

"You must have known my father," Maria said. "Did not your husband speak of him? My father was out to sea for twenty years, starting long before I was born. He sailed with your husband on at least three voyages."

Widow Chase waved away the question. "I don't remember any of them! All I know is that they showed up here, at that door, with big silly grins on their faces, like they were off on some grand adventure! That was the young ones! The ones with more age, not necessarily more *sense*, weren't smiling so much. They knew, after a trip or two, what was waiting for them out there! I can vouch for that."

The girl hung on every word. "So you have been out there with your husband? On one of his ships?" she asked.

"What? Do you think that I am daft? Why would I want to do that?"

"To see the world," Maria replied.

Widow Chase sighed. She did not have the heart to throw her out. After all, she knew what it was like to lose a man to the sea. That much she could relate to. She sat down again, looked at her young companion and felt sorry for her. "I have no trinket to remind you of your father, if that is what you're hoping for."

The girl nodded solemnly.

"Do you know what is out there? Those ships are full of rats and lice and disease. The men have the manners of an old bull. The food is full of worms and the water slick with slime. The waves that you see out that window are but bumps compared to the mountains of water that you find when you are out there in the yonder. It is a life of hardship and death. Is it not? Doesn't what happened to your father teach you these things?"

"How do you know such things?" Maria persisted. "Your husband talked that way about his livelihood?"

"My husband loved his life out there so much that he wanted me to get the full measure of it! I know of what I speak. I did go sailing with him, if you must know. But only once! That was enough to give me my fill. It would not match your curiosity, I'll tell you that. There is nothing out there that is not better found here on land," Widow Chase said.

"Don't your sons or daughters help you?"

"They do not live here!" Widow Chase snapped.

Maria's eyes widened. "You live here alone?"

"Yes, yes! I always have! My friend Martha helps get me to the meeting house, but otherwise, I do everything myself! As for you: one day you'll marry and have a new man in your life. There's plenty coming along the road for you," the old woman added.

"I fear that things will never be as fine as they were this summer."

"You are too young to say such things. I loved my husband when I first met him, but then again, I had only about as much sense as you do now."

"I would have a husband if he agrees to share things half and half. Sam would do so."

"Such nonsense! Wait until he returns home before you count up your share!"

"He will return…" Maria protested weakly. "How come the men in town did not make you remarry?"

The old woman laughed. "After I lost the first husband, I decided that I did not want another. But I was older. My parents were gone, and my children were near grown. I've lived in this house, under my son's name, damn near forty years. Not one inch of it has ever been his! I run this farm. I plant the crops, milk the cow, make the butter and spread the *shit* on the fields – all of it! Damn those who'd try to say this is not *my* farm!"

"I am trying to tell you that you don't need a husband, but you have to think about what that means. You can't run willy-nilly all over town, picking flowers and dreaming of sailors. You have to take care of yourself," Widow Chase summarized when Maria did not respond.

"What will you do when you are older and cannot move around as you do now?"

"I care not! They can roll me over this dune into the surf, for all I care. If I can't move about, I'll be half-dead anyway!"

"It seems sad to be so alone, though. There are good men like my father. He would be here today had I not had that dream…"

A bony hand clamped around Maria's forearm. "I would not talk too much about your dreams, child. It might scare people. You are a good girl. Just get your head out of the clouds."

"Oh, for God's sake!" Widow Chase growled when the girl started wiping away tears on her sleeve.

"I don't want the dreams. I know that I am not supposed to have them. Aren't they evil?"

"Who told you that nonsense?" Widow Chase said.

Maria faltered.

"I lived a long time alone, doing as I pleased. Do you know how? I kept my mouth shut, and when I had to speak, I told the men who think that they run this town exactly what they expected to hear," Widow Chase said.

"But you say whatever you please."

"Of course I do now! But I did not when I was your age. Look at me! I shall be with my fool of a dead husband soon! Who will stop an old woman from saying her peace?" Widow Chase said.

"Come," she added, leading Maria around the back side of the hearth. It was a two sided fireplace. The front of the hearth was hung with the kind of pots and pans that could be seen in any household in the colony. On the other side was a room filled with mortars, tinctures and little glass bottles filled with brackish looking liquid. All manner of strange dried plants, strips of animal hide, feathers and bone hung from the rafters. The Devil's workshop could not have looked more foul and sinister.

Widow Chase saw Maria's look and frowned at it. "I know what thoughts are in your head! If you think to judge me, then I'll send you on your way right now!"

"You do know spells…"

"Are you now suggesting that I am a liar?"

"No."

"Good! You know too little about the world to be judging my place in it!" Widow Chase declared.

Maria swallowed and stood rooted to the floor as Widow Chase came close to her. There was a smell of rankness from Widow Chase's breath, rum mixed with the tooth rot of aging. Maria stepped back farther.

"I don't bite, for God's Sake! Here, let me examine you."

A cold, wrinkled hand pressed against Maria's forehead and then clamped the back of her neck. Fingers dug under the line of her jaw and into her belly.

"Have you been ill in the morning?"

"Yes. I was for some time," Maria said, fear creeping over her. "But I have felt fine this past week. I am no longer ill."

Widow Chase laughed. "Ill? No, I reckon not!"

The widow stepped to the hearth and stoked flame from the coals. She brought water to a boil. Then she moved to a table and began chopping various sprigs of plants.

She measured out herbs and crushed fragments of stone and stirred them into the water, the whole process looking like the making of a witch's brew.

"Without a husband to distract me, I had plenty of time and freedom to see much more of this land than many others. I went to Helltown when I was younger. And it is not the pit of hell that old Treat likes to crow about. There are rough folks there, to be certain. But try talking to a fisherman from Eastham who's just come in from three days at sea, without a fish in the hold, and you'll see just as rough. I pity the women married to that lot," Widow Chase said to the wide-eyed girl.

"I met some interesting people too," Widow Chase went on. "There was a woman, who I knew, who taught me how to do all of this that you see me doing now. She was a native woman. Most called her a witch, the Witch of Billingsgate, but I called her a friend. She weren't no witch. She was just another woman who was too smart to abide by the foolishness that men feed us."

Upon the fire the cauldron bubbled ominously, playing out a ghoulish tune.

"Mittawa was her name. But you won't find many who know that anymore. Even her own people scorned her. *Our* people, yours and mine, ran her out of town. Then, after a few cows and sheep died some years later, we weren't satisfied, so we went after her again, and this time we made sure that she would not be heard from again. I saw what they did to her. Twas nasty business. *Damn fool men...*" Widow Chase said.

Widow Chase stirred the liquid and pulled a spoonful up to her nose for a sniff. She then touched her tongue to it and grunted in satisfaction. "I buried her in the way that her people would have, with a pile of rocks as her headstone."

"What killed the cows?" Maria asked.

"Wolves. Everyone thought they had been gone for ages. But we thought wrong."

Just then there was a claw-like clicking on the floor boards that made Maria yelp, and a dog, as old in its measurement of life as the widow was in human years, came limping out of the shadows. It laid its dark face on Maria's knee and licked her hands as if tasting her in the same manner as its master sampled broth.

"Just kick him away if he bothers you! He ain't worth nothing now. See how well he kept you away from my door!" Widow Chase said. Then she resumed her tale while she dumped more powder into the cook pot, "Them natives ain't fools. Not by a mile. They know how to live off of the land, using every inch of it like it was all just stuff laid up in their pantry. They know the inner soul of all things... Yes, you heard me. You tell your dreams to one of them, and they would know *exactly* what you mean. Does that make them a pack of devils?"

"They are Christian now," Maria said.

Widow Chase cracked a gapped tooth smile and raised a finger like a schoolmarm signaling that a crucial point had been made.

"They keep their mouths shut. We treat them no better than animals, like old Jack here," she said, motioning to the dog. "Yet I wonder if we are the ones who live like we are beasts."

"Taste that," Widow Chase commanded, handing Maria one of the little bottles. She laughed as the girl tipped it to her lips and her tongue curled with the sharp bite of the substance. "It ain't poison! Although, I guess at this point it would not matter anyway!" Widow Chase said, watching Maria force some of the substance down.

The girl pressed her hands to her temples where it felt like an unholy fire had ignited. For a second, in the dim lamp light, Widow Chase's old wizened face seemed broader and darker, her hair shadowy black instead of gray, the ancient lines on her cheeks morphing into a native woman.

Just then the dog at her feet howled at the door, and Maria was so startled that she almost dropped the bottle.

Widow Chase kicked at the beast and then chuckled. "Don't bother about him. Tis just the wolf in him that makes him crazy some of the time. He's a half-breed."

"It is...awful," Maria said of the potion.

"Would you believe that there is poison ivy in that bottle?" Widow Chase said, laughing merrily when Maria tried to spit out the taste. "Don't worry! It is just a touch of its sap, boiled away into the broth. The natives are far wiser than you or I. We see only the scratch that comes from this wretched vine. They see health concealed inside of the stalk. Like the thorn guards the rose, so does the poison shield the medicine. So Mittawa taught me. Mark my words. After drinking that, you shall not suffer again from rash or hives!"

Widow Chase took back the bottle and put it on a shelf. Then she rummaged through the others amassed there until she found one that she wanted.

"This is what will take care of that fever in your belly."

"I am no longer sick. The fever broke," Maria repeated.

The old woman gave her a reproachful look. "Love sick perhaps? Did you lay with that sailor everyone was going on about?"

Maria's blush answered for her.

Widow Chase chuckled again. She held up the bottle and swished its contents. "We call it pennyroyal. This jar is filled with that and some other things. Another one of Mittawa's little secret recipes. Drink it all tonight, and you will wake up free from care in the morning."

The widow suddenly lifted up Maria's apron and pressed a hand to Maria's belly. Then she nodded knowingly.

"What?" Maria asked, her voice filled with panic.

Widow Chase clucked sadly, "There is no chance of freedom now, child, unless you drink the pennyroyal."

"Am I dying?"

"You are pregnant," Widow Chase pronounced as if it were indeed a death sentence. She slid the bottle under Maria's elbow and patted her on the back.

"There will be a lot of blood come morning but no baby some months later. Let the pennyroyal do what it was made for. All of this in God's creation has some use though we, in our arrogance, turn a blind eye to most of it. If you are to live on your own, you must come to know the true meaning of all things, for there will be no man around to whisper his lies in your ear!" Widow Chase said.

When she saw the reaction her words were having on the girl, she added, "You are too young for tears. Had I known your father, I am sure that I would have thought him a fine man, judging by his daughter. Now leave me to my chores. And…you're welcome by the way," she said.

Maria mustered a smile and mumbled thanks as she stepped out of the door. The wind came whipping off of the sea and stung the eyes. Because of it, Widow Chase could not watch the girl from the porch, but she observed her through the window. For a long while she watched the girl stare out into the ocean. Then she saw Maria cast the bottle of pennyroyal over the edge of the dune into a single sweep of white water.

"*Damn fool girl…*" Widow Chase muttered.

Chapter Six
"Defenders of the Lord"

May 1716

Reverend Treat fumbled with the iron key as he guided it into the lock hole in the meeting house door. He cursed the creeping weakness of his aged hands. The step to the front door of the building was a large millstone, laid on the ground, which rocked as Treat stepped off of it, making him feel unsteady and frail. The moon too was like a great millstone, sitting cold and unyielding as black clouds swished by, trying in vain to turn it.

There had been an unusual amount of cold nights this spring. The reverend turned up his collar to shield his shivering bones from the dark wind. His skin felt thin as he shuffled off down the dim line of road towards the dark clump of woods in which his house was nestled. At least the chilly weather had hardened the muddy cart and hoof tracks of the path, making it more passable and reminding Treat that in every grim experience, the Lord leaves faint clues of hope for those chosen for redemption.

Alongside of him, across a length of field and beneath a small slope of hill, the water of Great Cove raced black and choppy. Its noise and color increased the chill in Treat's bones. He hurried his pace as much as two old legs could muster. On the other side of the water, the land was still hilly but cleared into pasture. Under the night sky, it appeared as a long, smooth sheet of darkness, belying its contours. If Treat had been fool enough to have agreed to the town fathers' original scheme to establish him in a homestead on that far bank, he would not be just a brisk walk away from his pulpit. Once again he was thankful to have insisted on having the land on Fort Hill or else his journey home tonight would have been a long trek around the head of the cove in the dark and cold.

No doubt his wife Abigail was positioned at the front window of their home, waiting for him and scouring the shadows for nocturnal terrors. The thought of her sweet, full face made him smile. It consoled him and momentarily beat back his own trepidation. The world held fears aplenty, more so now than ever. At the same time he knew that he should be thankful. After all, this was not the wild interior of his boyhood in Connecticut where a man had a right to be wary of the feral jaws of predators as well as the silent, whistling death of Indian arrows. In Eastham the wolves were dead, and the Indians, thanks to him, knew the Bible.

Yet the branches of the oaks seemed like gnarly living arms reaching into the eerie moonlight. The trees creaked as they rubbed their wooden boughs. Wolves and Indians were one thing, but there was still much to be feared from the spirit world. This night was the perfect landscape for their devilry. That, Treat told himself, was not merely the ravings of the overactive mind of a cold and tired old man.

"Reverend..." a voice said, startlingly close to his ear.

"Aggh! Be gone!" Treat shouted and instinctively threw his cloak out in front of him to ward off any devilish assailant. A dark shape loomed towards him from the roadside, seeming to materialize from the very air. Though in his mind he distinctly heard his own strong voice shout a defiant *No! I cast you away*, only a strangled gargle escaped his clenched throat as he bat at the apparition with weak, old limbs.

"Reverend! It is me!" the figure said as it gradually took on a familiar shape. *Careful*, Treat's mind warned, hovering between tired malaise and crazed, racing mania. *The Devil comes in familiar guises...*

"It is William Hopkins!"

Even in the moonlight, Treat recognized the square bulk of the poor crippled son of Joshua Hopkins. But the murky glow of the moon put a shadowy distortion on the young man. As well as having a useless, bent leg, young Hopkins was half mad too. Perhaps that weakness of mind had allowed the Devil to possess him, Treat thought, feeling vulnerable to be all alone on a dark road with a man who, even in the bright morning light of the Sabbath, seemed something of a stranger.

"Out late chasing some of your father's escaped herd?" Treat asked hopefully. "The shepherd who tends his flock is himself an agent of the Lord, for sometimes the lost are never found unless a single man makes it his business to find them," Treat quoted, like a protective spell.

"I like your sermons, Reverend," William said honestly. "Do you have one for wolves?"

Treat peered into the dark spot of the night where William's head was. "Wolves? Are you out in this night commingling with wolves, young man?"

"No sir!" William said loudly, again startlingly Treat. "I guard the jail, remember? Justice Doane said I cannot be his deputy on account of my leg. I cannot ride a horse well."

"Yes, yes. I recall now."

The wind wrapped around Treat's legs, like a cat, leaving him frosted with its touch. William was suddenly standing much closer to him. His breath filled the air with the reek of fish and ale.

"There is a wolf howling in the night. I've heard it several times! Can you not do something?" William implored.

"*Wolf?* That is not possible…" Treat's voice was undercut by an anguished howl that carried across Great Cove, making both men jump.

"Hear it!" William cried.

"*Shhh!*"

"Aye!"

"*Shhh!*" Treat repeated, spinning towards the sound. It was coming from the edge of the Stage Lands, quite near to where the sea creature had washed ashore. "Justice Doane and the selectmen must be informed at once!" Treat said.

"Aye! They are at my father's tannery right now."

That news gave Treat a shock as fierce as any of the other jolts he had already received this night. "You know this for certain?"

"That's right! Justice Doane was speaking of it, at the jail, earlier today."

"I see…" Treat breathed.

✠ ✠ ✠ ✠

Joshua Hopkins was the only one in the tannery who was standing. He moved along a row of brown cattle skins, which hung from the rafters, rubbing tallow into the hides to soften them and occasionally wiping his fingers onto his grubby smock.

The other town elders sat on overturned crates, which were arranged around a flickering candle. The atmosphere of the room was a stark reminder to them all of their position as a small square of illumination awash in darkness. John Cole drew circles in the dirt floor with the tip of his boot while Elder Knowles, John Paine and Justice Doane perched as straight and motionless as if they were on church benches. In front of each man, a mug of ale stood, lessening with each grievance that was shared.

"A blight is upon us. The fields are black with rot, and more cattle fall nose into the ground every week! Elijah Wheeler has lost cattle. I have lost cattle. Even you have, Joshua, have you not?" Knowles said.

"Aye. There is only one being that could be causing this string of bad fortune, and we all known who he is. Treat spoke of him just this past Sunday," said Joshua Hopkins.

"If it is the Devil, then why does God not aid me? Aren't I a good Christian? Don't I pray as much and earnestly as the next man? I read the Bible every night to my wife and children! And still God would forsake me and let the Devil hex my house?" Knowles replied.

"Only God knows. But the hex was not laid at your door. It was laid on Hallett's land. You have inherited his woe," Hopkins said.

"Yes. That land is cursed," Knowles mused. "The cattle were half dead by the time they came to be mine."

"I have many, many cattle and much land. Yet that will only give a blight more to feed off of. The Devil's hand touches like the spread of pox from one door to the next. We may all look towards Hallett's misfortune for a glimpse of our own if we should not act," Hopkins said. "Ah! Here is the reason why I fret so about the future of my holdings. There will be nothing left for him should I lose them!"

Hopkins waved towards the doorway of the tannery where his son Jonathan had suddenly appeared.

"Good evening, gentlemen," the younger Hopkins said, stepping inside.

"My boy is one of Doane's deputies now. Did you hear yet, Elder?" Hopkins asked, knowing that all in town were well aware of the news.

Knowles fought off a surge of envy at Hopkins' son rising up in society, all that land in the family, all that power. "I had heard."

"He will do admirably, I'm sure," Doane added, making Jonathan shuffle bashfully.

"Father, if I may add something to your discussion?"

"Aye. What's on your mind?" Hopkins asked, moving along the line of skins once more, this time using shears to clip off any rot or tears in the leather.

"With your pardon, Elder… What of Goody Hallett?" Jonathan said.

"It is a good question. The girl is running wild, and even the influence of an elder cannot rein her," Joshua Hopkins mused.

"What are you saying? The both of you!" Knowles cried. While he shared the others' suspicion, he would not have them revel in it. Jonathan Hopkins took a step back towards the entrance of the building, but his father stood his ground and frowned.

"Peace, John," Paine interjected.

"I want an apology from you, Hopkins!" Knowles said, pointing at the tanner.

Instead, his son muttered in answer, "*I meant nothing by it.*"

"She is a young fool, but nothing more," Knowles snapped, glaring around as if daring any of the others to mention the nasty rumors about the girl.

"My boy is right to wonder about her, and you know it!" Hopkins said, pointing his shears at Knowles.

"What evidence is there?" Doane asked.

"The squid, the cattle, the crop…It is not just my land or Knowles' that has been affected. Many around us have black crop and dying livestock. We need to act before it gets worse," Hopkins declared.

"*Whoever* is to blame," Knowles added.

Doane was about to reply, but a loud creak of the door stopped him.

First they saw an old wizened hand. Then the door swung inwards, and they saw a familiar large white-haired head.

Reverend Treat stared piercingly at them. "It feels like a nest of hens planning to cast out the rooster," he grumbled.

"No sir," Paine said quickly. "You were not invited because we thought that you were ill, and we did not want to burden you. We're discussing a range of topics as we are wont to do every so often."

"Including replacing me!" Treat shouted. There was a hoarseness in his voice, which they all noticed, but the sound still carried loudly. "Meeting in a tannery! That is where plotting is hatched! And you have ales before you as well! Treachery is ale's inspiration!"

"We were not trying to be clandestine. This is a meeting of the selectmen *only*," Doane said in his usual steady, take-charge voice.

"I see! And is part of your discourse about the wolf that is now running in the night?"

Treat gazed triumphantly as the selectmen gave each other puzzled looks.

"Well! I am glad I barged in upon this gathering, for it seems that you are lacking crucial news!"

"We must kill it!" Joshua Hopkins exclaimed.

"Of course! But what if it be more than a mere wolf? What if it is bewitched?" Treat countered.

"What matter? It will still die, will it not?" Hopkins said.

Treat puffed out his chest. "Prior to the coming of the beast, there were no wolves. The return of that scourge is grave news indeed. It is not coincidental news either. The Devil does not enlist beasts without also enlisting men and women. We know this as clearly as we know the long history of our battle with Satan. The Devil's ways are blunt and predictable! I call for a vote to authorize witch trials!"

"It is proper to hold such votes in town meeting, in the presence of a quorum of citizens," said Doane.

Treat glowered at the justice, and when his voice roared out, it was accompanied by a series of loud coughs, "Well then? Does a majority agree?"

"This is not the way of law!" Doane declared.

"Do as you are told, Joseph Doane, or else I will put the stripping of your title on the next town meeting warrant! Find us any witches among us and rid us of them!"

✠ ✠ ✠ ✠

All that night and into the next morning, Deacon Paine could not chase thoughts of the wolf from his mind.

He glanced at his black fingers, which were stained with the dark color of the squid ink that he was still using in secret. He imagined it to be a kind of devilish rot that was spreading throughout him. Could the touch of the beast corrupt the Godly hand that brushed against it, he wondered? Part of him wished to run to the shoreline and scrub the offensive blemish from his skin. Then he would dump out the rest of the ink and let the water dispel it into the harmless flow of the current. Finding the ink had been a boon. He wanted nothing more than to think of it as bounty, like anything else given from nature. However, he knew it was not God given. Since the arrival of the squid, things had gotten worse for Eastham.

He blew on his last journal entry to dry it:

In the faces of my children, I see hope turning towards God, like stalks turning towards the sun. My little ones see the worry in their elders' faces, and it troubles them. Yet when I tell them that we fear that God's enemies are about us, they have nothing but innocent faith in the Lord. 'Won't God set it right?' they ask. Within that question is the seed of Faith. Sometimes we need to look to the young to find the wisdom that we forget in old age. Of course, He will redeem us. What man would cut down the crop before harvest? He will protect us and let us grow towards Salvation. All knowing God knows no fear. We who trust Him, through Faith, need not fear either. Once again I am humbled by the Godliness of my children...

His only regret was that the fair thoughts had been pre-served with the blood of the beast.

"*I must wash this,*" Paine muttered to himself, wringing his hands on his jacket and succeeding only in making the stains look more permanent.

A moment later he was kneeling before Great Cove, scoop-ing sand from the bottom, grinding it against his fingers and then running his hands through the cleansing water.

Upon the water's surface a shadow loomed. It was man-shaped, and the rippling waves made the head seem framed with horns. The thing that cast this dark reflection was creeping up behind him.

With a gasp Paine pivoted around.

"Goody Hallett!" he exclaimed. "What a fright you gave me, sneaking up like that!"

The girl watched him for a moment, and he did not take his eyes off of her. He wished he had a closer look at the shadow, to judge if the vision that he saw was anything more than a trick of the sun and water.

"May I talk to you in confidence, Deacon Paine?" she asked.

Paine noted how the girl looked over her shoulder. It was a troubled, hunted look. It was a terrible thing to behold in the face of a youth who should have her whole future life to smile upon. He thought of the rumors about the girl and, without thinking, moved a couple paces away from her. He was sure that she was about to confess.

"Perhaps I am not the right person to hear what you have to say, Goody Hallett. As we speak, the reverend is visiting the Indian meeting house. It is right down the road, as you know."

The girl gave him a puzzled look. "I want to talk to someone who builds and alters boats."

Paine returned a glance full of confusion. "Boats? Well, I do build boats here and there, on the side."

"I know. You built one for my father many years ago."

"Yes… I remember," Paine replied. For a moment he could feel her grief as if it was some kind of wind that encircled her, and he longed to end this meeting.

"I need my little boat made more seaworthy. For a long journey."

Paine's eyes narrowed. "What kind of journey?"

When she saw his reaction, she took a quick step backwards. He could see the fear again. "Perhaps you are right… I shan't bother you."

"Wait! Tell me what is troubling you. What do you intend to do?" Paine called out, but she did not reply. She turned and ran across the fields back towards her family's homestead.

Paine stood and looked at the black stains still on his fingers. He went to wipe them on his shirt, only to discover the fading smear of earlier stains striped across his garment. The evidence of the foul creature was all over him. With a shock it occurred to him that Goody Hallett had likely observed his obvious guilt. Whom had she run off to tell, he wondered?

Chapter Seven
"A Misbegotten Fate"

Early June 1716

Throughout the cold months Alice Hallett's daughter had worn, without protest, the layers of shift, under shirt and apron that she usually decried as oppressive. When spring came, to Alice's surprise, Maria did not shed a single garment. Alice feared the presence of some fever. Smallpox, for instance, could emerge with shivers worse than what was felt in a drafty house in the frozen days of dark February. But Maria rebuffed any attempt to feel out the illness.

It occurred to Alice that the clothes might be a kind of warped protest, an over-indulgence in proper attire meant as a mockery.

"Let the past go, child. We must move forward if we are to survive," Alice frequently told her daughter.

Sam Bellamy had not appeared when the first green promise of spring emerged from the tree buds or the apple blossoms hung thick and fragrant on the branch. It was now June. It had been over eight months since Bellamy had gone. Alice knew that her child was thinking of the rogue. On more than one occasion, she had rounded Great Cove, in the wagon, and seen Maria standing in the shallows of the mooring field, her hands fumbling with the anchor line of her boat, her anger making her clumsy. But Alice had yet to see the girl get into the craft, let alone sail it. She hoped that was a good indication that Maria was on the verge of releasing hold of her childhood fancies.

It was after one of those ill-fated trips past the mooring field that Alice saw a finger of smoke protruding from the distant trees as she rode home in the wagon. It could have been coming from any of the farms within a mile radius around her home, but the thick black haze seemed to point down towards her farmhouse like an accusation. She had known that this day would come, but it was a shock nonetheless. She did not go towards the smoke. Instead, she turned for the Knowles' farm, a twist of the road that she realized had become more permanent than she ever would have imagined.

✠ ✠ ✠ ✠

Elder Knowles stood at the edge of the smoldering ruin, kicking his boot through the thick pile of papery, black ash and harder chunks of charred wood. "Ah!" he exclaimed as he bent down and scooped up something with the sleeve of his shirt.

He held up a square-ended, iron nail and showed it to his sons, who stood nearby. "We shall find hundreds of them in the debris, after everything cools down. Tomorrow I want you to fetch as many as you can. They should not be wasted, for they are worth more than this house ever was."

The house that had been built by Seth Hallett was reduced to a stinging smoke that was sucked away into the white clouds above. Grief, as much as smoke, hurt Knowles' eyes. It had started when he stumbled over a small sea chest that had miraculously survived the fire. Within was a collection of old straw dolls, which reminded him of his little girl who had choked on her last breath before becoming old enough for such fancies. Knowles fed all of the unwelcome reminders from the chest into the last of the spotty flames. Then he set the chest on fire too. Remembering the vigil at his little daughter's sickbed gave him a strong urge for cleansing. Knowles felt his sorrow burning like a fever inside of him. In the conflagration of his wife's house, his pain had found some release. Yet there was enough grief left that Knowles continued to kick at the ash.

"What has happened?" Maria Hallett cried from the roadside as she came charging towards him.

Knowles turned to face her with hard eyes. "I made a decision as head of the household. It is not your place to question."

"You did this on purpose? You set this fire?" She said. Tears sprang from her eyes and left hot trails down her cheeks as she came close to the shimmering wall of heat left from the blaze.

"One homestead is plenty. There is no need to be taxed on a home that is not being used. Mine is the larger one. Now the extra room can be used as field for the cows if any of the herd survive," he said distastefully. "Those are my reasons. Be satisfied with them, for I am not required to give you any explanation for my actions!"

"Mother! *Mother!*" Maria cried.

"Hush, girl! She is away on an errand!" Knowles cried. He pointed towards his own house and shouted, "Get thee to the hearth and prepare dinner, Goody Hallett! Obey me, child! It is your Godly duty!"

The girl did nothing but stare at the ruins as if she did not believe it.

"Your tongue is not so sharp now that your sailor is gone," Knowles observed. He could see the truth of the words in the way that she blanched and could not deny them.

"Mother let you do this?" Maria asked.

"I needed no permission! Now get to the hearth!" Knowles cried, shaking her by the arm.

"Release me! Damn you! You burned our house!"

"What did you say? You damn me? Like you damned my youngest daughter with your dreams! Yes! I know what you did!" Knowles said.

"I made that up only to frighten Thankful..." she protested, her voice faltering for a moment.

"You lie!"

"As do you! Lying about the barn! Whispering lies to my mother to get our land! Curse you!"

Knowles' grip tightened, and his voice dropped to a whisper, "*Insolence...You curse me and accuse me, Goody Hallett? I, your new father?*"

"Oh no...no no...you are not my father!" Maria stammered. "Never! *Damn you!*"

Knowles flinched at the oath. His grip tightened still. "Despite your feelings about it, I am your father. I would rather have respect from you, but the law states that I need only have your obedience."

"You will *never* be a father to me! I will not obey you! I have only one father!"

"We all have more than one father. God is father to us all, above all earthly fathers! Do you call Him your father or is there someone else to whom you pray?"

A burst of crazy laughter came out of her. "You *know* who my father is!" she said.

He dropped her arm like it had burned him. "What are you saying? You rave!"

"My father is Satan…is that what you are asking?" she said, forming claws with her hands and scratching the air in front of him. He jumped backwards, and she laughed again. Behind him, his boys were running hard for the homestead, but he did not think them cowardly. Knowles himself felt a tremor of panic as he faced this awful girl.

"You! That there is this unholy scourge in *my* household! Away from me, demon!" he cried.

"You fool! You are the one under a spell of your own devising! I am the daughter of *Seth Hallett*! A better man than you will ever be!" she hollered.

Knowles was already backing away from her, not daring to turn his back for an instant. "You are unmasked! The truth has slipped out of you! Whatever birth you had, you were re-sired by darkness!"

"You *burned my house!*" Maria yelled, tears of frustration falling.

"Stay away, Goody Hallett!"

"*Damn You!*"

✠ ✠ ✠ ✠

Thankful Knowles saw the familiar form of Maria Hallett kneeling among the blueberry bushes along Tonset Road. She watched Maria grimace and clutch her stomach.

From inside the house Thankful heard the sound of Alice Hallett's voice pushing out a tuneless hum, through teeth that were no doubt clenched on the pipe stem she always smoked when she worked in the kitchen. Thankful did not know if her new stepsister sought a chance to make amends or an opportunity for revenge. Either way, she wished that her father and brothers were not so far away in the fields.

After one more glance along the road, Maria lifted herself out of her burrow and hurried across the field towards the house.

The front door swung inward, and Maria's greeting echoed softly through the room. The cook fires smoked cheerfully under the suspended pots. Enticing smells seeped out of the maws of the pots, in tribute to Alice's deft touch for coaxing succulent flavor from them. The savory odor made Thankful's stomach rumble as she crept along the road, coming in behind Maria.

The back door was still swinging from the motion of Alice going out to the root cellar. Maria hiked up her skirts and hurried in that direction, again calling gently for her mother.

After a few steps she doubled over and fell to the floor. She stood shakily, shuffled to the hearth, filled a basin of water and then went into the master bedroom.

Thankful watched all of this through the open front door of the house. She sprang back out of sight when Maria looked around once more. Then, to Thankful's surprise, Maria began casting off her garments. She lifted off her apron and then her shift, leaving herself naked to the world. Thankful saw the little bulge protruding from Maria's gut, and her eyes widened at the implication.

"Your belly…" she said from the doorway.

Maria screamed and reached for her clothes.

Thankful met her stepsister's eyes and fought off the feeling of pity that she knew was unwarranted. Maria was selfish and criminal and perhaps worse than that. There had always been a feeling that the girl would one day have her dark essence exposed. Thankful could not have predicted the exact form that revelation would take, but now that it was here, she would not yield to sympathy.

"You are with bastard."

Maria was too stunned to respond. Just then, through the window, they saw Alice coming towards the house.

"Let me tell her. That will be punishment enough," Maria pleaded.

"I don't think so. There will be other payments due. Goody Myrick spent two days in the pillory, after it was discovered that she was with bastard."

Maria glared at her. "I will say that I am carrying winter fat. That and the fact that I have grown heavy out of sadness, and you know why."

Thankful smirked. "Oh, I know why. You've no fever but for a dark-haired sailor. We'll see proof of it soon enough when that thing in your belly comes out!"

A moment later Alice came into the kitchen with her arms loaded with squash. She was alone and wearing her usual look of pained resignation.

"Help me, daughter! You're the young, strong one," Alice called out to Thankful.

"Yes, mother," Thankful said, moving to scoop the vegetables from Alice's arms. As she did, she flicked her head back towards the bedroom.

"What?" Alice asked.

Thankful took the squash and stepped outside to peel it, staying within earshot of the open door only to ensure that no ill befell her stepmother by Maria's hand.

Alice turned towards her bedroom and saw Maria, whom she stared at for several long seconds.

"You are beyond shame..." she said finally, watching Maria's movements as the girl threw on her clothes.

"Is that all you have to say?" Maria snapped.

"When were you going to tell me about what you carry under those garments?"

"When I thought that you would receive it with a kind ear!"

"Elder Knowles will never let you back in this house again," Alice said, turning and hanging a large bucket on an iron hook in the hearth.

"Is that all you have to say?" Maria repeated.

"There is nothing to say that would make any difference. You reap the bitter harvest that you sowed."

"*Perhaps that shall be the last thing that you get to say to me. Think on that*," Maria whispered, backing out of the room and then the house itself.

What Alice said in reply was too low for Thankful to hear, but she knew what the words should have been: ungrateful, sinful, harlot...

✠ ✠ ✠ ✠

Widow Chase knew it when she saw the face of trouble. She was looking at it now, in the tear stained cheeks and trembling lip of Maria Hallett, who stood at her door. Every fiber of her old bones told her to keep the door closed and act as though she was not at home. But the girl was so young and foolish. She was too young to be feeling such grief even though it was her own folly that brought it upon her.

The widow meant only to crack open the door, but Maria pushed through anyway, and Widow Chase cursed and closed it tight after her.

"You should not be here!" Widow Chase said, peering through the window. Pochet Road was empty now, but she could already imagine the men coming up it. Husbands she had no fear of, but an angry father, blood kin or not, she did not fancy tangling with.

"I cannot! I have nowhere to go! The baby!"

"You should be at home with those that care for you, as hard as it may seem. I ain't no midwife anymore."

"No. I cannot. They do not care for me as they should. I am friendless. My dreams, the cattle, this baby…"

"Hush! None of that means a hill of beans! Tis all talk. Just talk folks say when they really mean to say something else. They want to bring you in line, is all. Remember all we spoke about. Now get home. This all shall pass and make you stronger though you know it not now."

"Help me! Please!"

"Tis too late. You would have been seen coming down the road. Tis a matter of time till they are at the door."

"My baby!" Maria groaned, doubling over.

Widow Chase bit her lip. It was clear that the girl's pains were real. In a matter of hours, minutes even, the child would be in the world, one way or another. With a scowl she guided Maria into the back bedroom.

"I'll help until the babe is out, then no more! I am too old for any kind of trouble! They told me not to do midwifing no more! This brand shows how serious they are about it! Next time they'll give me something worse, I am certain!"

"Oh God!" Maria moaned. "It's sharp pain."

"Breathe," Widow Chase said. She felt Maria's head and rubbed her back to soothe her. "I've got to get water and swaddling cloth ready. You lie here and keep your mind thinking of nothing but sunshine, hear me? Don't push until I get back here. I'll tell you when to push!"

"GOD DAMN!" Maria cried, her body twisting and her fingernails clawing into the wooden sides of the bed.

Soon there was a scent of steam from water boiling. Then Widow Chase kneeled next to her and dabbed her forehead with water. The widow spread a sticky, sweet smelling balm over Maria's stomach.

"This will protect the baby. Now push!" Widow Chase commanded.

"Ahhh! I feel as though I will burst!"

"It is a strong and stubborn babe. It must be a boy."

"I don't care! It feels like it is killing me!" Maria declared.

"Amazing how the same area can produce so much pleasure and then so much pain," Widow Chase scolded.

The widow lit a bundle of dried herbs and waved the smoke around the room. "This will scare away any evil spirits that try to steal your baby. The baby will be weak when it first comes out. Its spirit may not be settled. Mittawa taught me such things. I had no such knowledge back when I was a midwife. Perhaps it might have helped. But perhaps not..." Widow Chase said with a shrug.

The smoke swirled thickly and set Maria to coughing. "Put that out!" she yelled through her panting.

Widow Chase betrayed no emotion as she unceremoniously extinguished the burning herbs in a bucket of water. "I know it hurts, child. Keep breathing. Steady breath kills the pain for both you and the child. Look out the window at the sea. Keep your eyes on them waves. That should settle you."

In the glass panes the sea rose and fell like gentle respiration.

Maria shook her head. "No... No... I don't want to think about the sea."

She fought the pain for what seemed like an eternity. Her mouth was black with curses and imprecations against Sam Bellamy, her parents, God, even the widow herself. "This babe is a curse! It is sent by some demon to torment me!" Maria shouted.

"Never mind all that. Just get it out, and then we'll see what sort of creature it is," Widow Chase commanded. Her hands shook. But not so much to prevent her from getting a firm grip on the newborn as it finally emerged head first into her arms.

As Widow Chase expected, the babe looked pure and innocent. She cut the cord with a knife and hung it on a rafter, like

Mittawa had shown her, without explaining to the girl why she had done so. Likely, it did not matter now anyway, she figured.

New mother and child gazed at each other in that timeless first recognition that Widow Chase considered the finest part of the relationship of parent and child. After that, life for the two of them would probably all go down hill. She could not help but think that a much farther descent lay in store for this pair than any other she had encountered.

"He looks like his father," Maria said.

"He looks like a baby bird, like they all do," Widow Chase grumbled, wiping a rag across the nose of the babe as he stared around, with his wobbling head and clouded eyes.

"You rest while I get you some tea. You need to keep your bones warm and your strength up. Now that the little bugger is out, he'll want to be eating soon. Eating and eating and eating..." Widow Chase said.

It was not until she was in the other room that the widow blew a whistle of relief through her lips. She had not been sure that she had another birthing in her. Now that it was over, she knew that she would never do another one again. Her hand slid along the over head shelf on the wall until it bumped into a rum bottle that she brought down and drank from deeply.

When the tea was ready, she poured it into a mug and then glanced again at the rum bottle. After a moment's hesitation she tucked it under her arm and brought it out to the girl, scolding herself for how soft she was getting.

"Alright, you can stay here for the night, but you better be on your way come morning. Now it's time to eat..." Widow Chase was saying when she came back into the bedroom.

The only one who heard her was her old dog Jack, who wagged his tail expectantly at the mention of supper.

The girl and the child were gone.

"*Damn it...*" Widow Chase muttered. She sat on the bed and uncorked the rum bottle.

✠ ✠ ✠ ✠

Maria Hallett limped along Tonset Road with her son Samuel squirming in the shawl that she had taken from Widow Chase's.

In one sense, the little creature in her arms did not feel real. Covered in the cloth, it could have been a newborn pup or a squawking chicken. It was not such an odd thought. Maria knew plenty of women who had so many children that they came to describe a new birthing with the same enthusiasm as the coming of a new litter of animals in the fields, a common, unremarkable event.

Maria was more accustomed to watching her poor little brothers and sisters, who entered into the world dead or dying. Until now, a proper birthing was unknown to her. Despite the pain and fear of the process, the moment of new life seemed more magical than anything she had encountered, with the possible exception of meeting the man who had given her the son she cradled in her arms. Sam Bellamy had left her with such emptiness, but some of her love for him rekindled now that part of him had been returned to her in this little form that she held. She felt certain that the man himself would come back too one day. In the meantime all she had to do was feel her son's little body wriggling against her, and she welled with a surge of inner joy and astonishment that had the force of an ocean wave.

She wished that she could have stayed in the widow's house, nestled in the birthing bed with her new babe, getting used to the enormous new pull of emotion that encircled her. But she knew she could not. As fatigued as she was, she worried that little Sam's crying would bring Justice Doane, and with him misery, to the widow's door. She did not want to be a burden to the widow, especially since she sensed that the old woman's help was reluctantly offered to begin with.

Now that Maria was outside, with darkness falling fast and heavy upon the fields, panic fluttered around her, like the crows that jeered in the tree tops along the roadside. She prayed that the noisy birds would at least drown out the hungry wailing of her son.

Three times she stopped and burrowed into the thickets by the road and let the boy feed. It seemed like she could only progress another bend or two along the dirt track before he was famished and howling again.

By the time she neared the Knowles' homestead, she was starving herself. She was exhausted too. Her noble sentiment to spare the widow any risk now seemed a foolish choice. All around her the windows of the houses were warm, glowing yellow squares, yet every door she saw was closed to her. Her own mother was but one hundred yards from where she stood, but that option, more than any other, was impossible. It seemed that her first night with little Sam, as mother and child, would be spent in the unsheltered darkness.

Then the perfect hiding place occurred to her. It was a good, safe spot where Sam's crying would be muffled and his precious little form protected for the short time that she needed to forage the flats of Great Cove, before the day was completely extinguished. She could smell the pungent scent of low tide in the air. Over and over, she calculated the time that she would need to fill her apron with dinner. She estimated that it would take no more than a half-hour. It would be a short parting from her little Sam, yet she almost could not bear it. On the other hand, they both would need their strength if they were to make it through the night. Then they would at least have full bellies when they faced the hard decisions of the morning.

She kissed the baby on the head, marveling at the heat of his skin and the tiny drumming pulse of life she could feel there. It was lunacy to think it, but for a moment she felt that now that they had found each other, there was nothing to fear from the world.

"I shall be back in a moment," she promised her son.

✠ ✠ ✠ ✠

Elder Knowles paused under the massive oak tree by the barn. Leaning his back into the firm trunk, he laid down his lantern and let the water bucket slip out of his hand. He just stood there, gazing into the night sky, with his arms crossed.

The night was still and without sound, except for the far away thud of waves breaking on shore. He inhaled the cool night air, and it filled him like a soothing tonic. There were shadows where the nearly full moon cast gray outlines of shrubs and tree branches among the dark patches of land.

Land… Under the cover of night, one piece looked much the same as any other. But he knew it was a trick of the darkness.

Before him was the great silhouetted bulk of the barn. He peered at it for a moment, imagining the black shape ignited by a blaze similar to the one that had consumed the Halletts' homestead. The decrepit form of the place, alone, warranted its destruction.

Perhaps there was merit in keeping the wood, in case it was needed for some other purpose, he mused. After all, he now had more land to fence in, and there was less and less lumber available in town. There was no need to resolve the debate at this hour. He was here to fetch water from the well near the barn. It was a woman's chore that he took on for the opportunity of a peaceful, solitary moment under the bright canopy of heaven.

When he reached to retrieve the bucket, he heard a clatter in the barn. He left the bucket and crept toward the structure, wondering what could account for the noise. The livestock were all in their pens. He prayed it was a curious raccoon or skunk, not something more sinister. The stars would offer him little protection if it was. Even a raccoon could be dangerous if cornered.

Luckily, he found his pitchfork leaning against the side of the barn. He gripped the handle in his right hand and used it to gently push open the barn door.

At first he saw nothing. His stargazing eyes were useless in this black void. The dark wrapped around him as he walked deeper into the barn. He heard nothing. But he felt a chill, and he spun around a few times, convinced that something was moving stealthily towards him in the dark.

He lifted the lantern, and it brought the barn to life with a startling glare.

Knowles saw the unmistakable glow of rodent eyes, before they disappeared into a pile of hay. He scanned the rest of the barn and saw nothing. He walked towards the back of the building and cautiously peered into the different stalls, with his pitchfork quivering in his shaky hand.

Empty.

Relief flooded into him, and he lowered the pitchfork, feeling shameful to have been so afraid.

Then a bright shape caught Knowles' eye. He turned toward the object and held the lantern out towards it. It was some kind of colorful fabric, partially covered by the straw. Panic rose again. Somebody was here, he thought. He glanced around quickly. Maybe they were waiting outside, hiding and watching. He wondered if that sailor had slipped back into town. The knowledge of the kind of justice that Bellamy would be due did little to assuage Knowles' consternation about meeting the man alone in the barn.

He stepped closer to the fabric. It had bulk. It was a bundle of something.

He poked it gently with the butt of the pitchfork and felt something fleshy beneath. Knowles stooped and gingerly held a corner of the shawl. He took a few breaths to summon his courage. Then he jerked the fabric open and jumped back in shock.

✠ ✠ ✠ ✠

Alice Hallett and her new daughter were knitting by the hearth. The flames cast their knitting needles into giant, blade-like shadows on the back wall, darting to and fro like swords parrying. But there was nothing but laughter and contentment in the room. They enjoyed each other's company. Alice's mild ways and Thankful's cheerful obedience made for little friction in the new household.

"Where is father?" Thankful asked as the evening drew long. At her elbow the flame of the candle towered and brightened before sputtering on the nearly spent wick.

"He went to the well," her stepmother replied. Alice got up to place another log on the fire in the hearth. There was a loud crack as the damp piece of wood popped. Then there was another squeak as Alice settled back into her wooden rocking chair by the fire.

"Shall we start our prayers?"

"Perhaps we should wait for father."

"Yes, I suppose you are right," Alice replied.

Just then the door opened with a crash, and Elder Knowles stumbled inside.

"John, what is the matter?" Alice exclaimed.

Elder Knowles turned towards his daughter and stared at her.

"Father, has something terrible happened?" Thankful exclaimed.

"You must be honest with me, child," he said. He stared at her searchingly.

"*What? What is it, father?*" she whispered.

"Have you been in the company of Master Hopkins?"

"No. He will not speak to me. He still waits and longs for one who has spurned him," Thankful replied, casting a guilty look at Alice.

Suddenly Elder Knowles grabbed Thankful's arms and shook her roughly. "Child! This is no game. Your reputation is at stake! Our name! Your very soul!"

"I don't know what you are talking about!" Thankful cried.

He pulled her out of her chair and dragged her into the front room. Her stepmother stood and covered her mouth with her hands.

"Do you hear me? We will be judged!"

He bent down by the front door and then stood back up with a bundle of cloth bunched in his arms. With the way he stared at them, Thankful wondered if her father had gone mad. Maybe some demon had got ahold of him. Or some witch...

"*Is this yours?*" he whispered, laying the bundle on the table and unwrapping it. Her stepmother screamed, and Thankful stared at it in horror.

The baby lay like it was asleep in the strange blanket. The child was clearly dead. Tiny bits of straw stuck out of its tiny mouth. The lips were stained blue. Its eyes were closed, and its hair stood up in patches of jet black. It was a grisly sight, but Thankful felt relief.

"Sam Bellamy has been gone just nine months," she told her father.

Elder Knowles' eyes alit as he did the calculations. He had thought that it had been far longer since the sailor had been away - too long. But winter could feel that way. Now it all made sense. It was not the sailor coming to town, but his progeny. Knowles slammed a hand on the table and spun towards his wife, ignoring the brimming wetness in her eyes.

"Where is she?"

"I have not seen her..."

"Where? No more lies, woman!"

"I know not...*I know not*..." Alice replied, burying her face in her hands.

✠ ✠ ✠ ✠

The barn was dark and musty with the damp odor of wet hay, a smoky smell like a cook fire. Elder Knowles felt increasingly silly the longer he crouched behind the sheep pen. He watched Maria Hallett push aside the straw to expose the little gully where he had returned the babe, wrapped in its shawl. She lifted the babe gently while cooing quietly in his ear.

Knowles deliberated upon whether to confront her yet or not and decided to wait a moment more. After all, this should be a moment between the girl and her conscience and, of course, God.

It was an awful moment. He heard the quiver in the girl's voice when she asked her child, "Why so quiet, little angel?" She touched a finger to his cheek, and Knowles knew that she would be surprised to find that it was ice cold.

"Sam?" She held a lantern up and looked into a face that Knowles had been unable to shake from his own mind. It was a shriveled, gray face like a little old man.

She screamed.

Then higher and more accelerated became her cries, and Knowles shrank further into the planking behind him. For a fleeting moment he wished that he was not there at all. Was he being a fool, he wondered? *She is a witch...*

"No! Don't take both of them! Don't take them from me! What did I do?" Maria cried. Then she pressed the child to her heaving breast and crumpled to the ground. Knowles waited until her anguish had flattened into a low moaning before he emerged carefully from the shadows.

He was shaking as he approached. His eyes darted around the barn for a weapon, should he need it. Maria squinted at him, her eyes adjusting to the dark and then going wide with vitriol.

"My baby!" Maria cried. "You killed him!"

Hands flew at Knowles. Nails scratched and tore at him. He threw her down on the straw pile and stood over her panting. "Your child is dead! You left him in the hay, and part of the pile fell upon him and smothered him! *You* killed him with your abandonment!"

She lurched at him again. This time he charged into her, his righteousness swelling in proportion to her devilish madness. The wide crossbeam of the back wall caught her square in the back as he pinned her against it. His hands twisted her collar until she could barely breathe.

"You ungrateful little wench! How dare you mock me in front of the whole town! How dare you do this to me, with this farm coming down around my ears! Do you mean to make a laughing-stock of me! Answer me! Answer me! And no lies! Answer me, you worthless cur!"

No word could have made it to Maria's lips through her sobbing terror and Knowles' fingers, which were clamped around her throat.

"You will hang for this! Witchery is repaid with death!"

He shook her as if to make the truth tumble out of her. Then he threw her to the ground. She wailed and pleaded, but the sound of her crying drove Knowles into a greater frenzy.

"NO! You do not get to beg for forgiveness! Even God would not listen!"

Maria cowered on the ground. He hauled her up and held her tightly by the forearm, his other hand coming hard across her face.

"Damn it, the entire town knows! I took you in and showed you kindness, and this is how you repay me! Our farm is in ruins, and you give me nothing but betrayal! Devils and vagrants and bastards!"

His hand struck her again, stinging the tears right out of her.

"Worthless! Worthless!" Knowles was raving. She was on the ground again, and he was on top of her. Then the pitchfork was in his hands. Before he knew what he was doing, he laid the handle hard across her neck. She grabbed hold of it, just in time to hold back some of her stepfather's crushing force.

"Yes, I use the Devil's own tool against you, Goody Hallett!" he seethed. Then he raised his head to the rafters and cried, "God help me! I am burdened by wanton women! Whores!"

It was only when he heard the wheezy bubbling in her throat and saw her eyes rolling white that Knowles came to his senses.

"I am no killer..." he protested, lifting the handle and step-ping off of her while she doubled over, choking for air.

"God help me! God forgive me!" Knowles cried. "Maria! You have erred, but I will not sacrifice myself to scour your sins from the world. Come... You must reckon with what you have done."

He reached for her shoulder, to haul her up to face justice. But at the last moment, his fingers jerked away and sunk down to his leg where the pitchfork tines had passed through his thigh.

"Ahhh!" Knowles screamed.

When his fingers came up again, they were red.

Maria dropped the pitchfork and ran. Knowles could not even limp after her. He took a single step and then collapsed to the floor, his nose pressed against the dropped lantern. The vision of Maria's flight reflected through the glass, making the girl look enwreathed in burning fire. In that moment he had no doubt that she was indeed a servant of the Devil.

✠ ✠ ✠ ✠

The knock came so loud that Widow Chase nearly jumped. Her first instinct was to ignore it. All she had to do was think of the last time that she had answered such summons, and she had no trouble hardening her resolve.

The pounding kept coming, hard enough to make dust cough out from the joints in the board seams.

Widow Chase took a step deeper into her house. She was thankful that no light shone, which would give away her presence. At the same time the moon was already setting into the distant tree tops. Who would believe that she was not home at this hour, she wondered?

It had to be the girl. It was the first night, for God's sake. Now the young fool regretted that she had scurried off, and in her fright she did not care if she brought the whole town running.

The thought made Widow Chase seethe, and as quick as that, she changed her mind and stormed towards the entrance of her house, determined not to help Maria Hallett again until the girl got a good taste of her indignation.

"Alright! Alright! Quit your shouting! I ain't deaf!"

"Widow Chase! Open this door!" Elder Knowles cried. "Justice Doane will see to it if you do not! He is but right down the road!"

Widow Chase froze. But it was too late. The lock was pulled, and she watched in horror as the door latch seemed to lift itself.

"Where is she?" Knowles demanded, pushing past the old woman. His voice was low and rasping from the pain that radiated from his wound. The crude bandage that Alice had made out of a wool shirt and wrapped around his leg was red stained.

"She ain't here!"

Knowles stormed past, audaciously poking his head into Widow Chase's own bedroom, in his search of the dwelling.

She went after him and found him standing on the threshold of the back door, which looked out over the sea.

"Perhaps she has run off to throw herself into the waves," Knowles growled.

"Or maybe the girl has more sense than you credit her with! I'd run from the likes of you too!"

"Were you younger and more hail, I would bring you up on charges of slander, but I don't think your old body would do well in the pillory!"

Widow Chase gasped and puffed out her chest. "Oh! I bet you would too! Bullying an old woman and a recently birthing girl! You are a coward! Add that to your list of charges!"

Knowles wagged his finger in her face. "You are an accomplice! Perhaps you are not deaf, but you are blind! There is devilry afoot in this town!"

"Ha! Devil my foot! You *men* always look for signs of some beast when it is yourselves who are fouling things up!"

She expected some angry retort. In fact, she hoped for it. There were plenty more things she intended to say, and she was happy to have an audience upon which to let loose years of pent up barbs. She planned to let him have them all now that things had gone this far. The thrill of it made her feel younger than she had in some time. Yet Knowles was no longer listening to her. He had that blank, silent look that a man gets when he knows he is beaten and needs time to cook up some fresh lie with which to wriggle away.

"I see more dried herb than is necessary to spice a year's worth of cooking. And all manner of bones and rocks and heathen artifacts," he said, glancing around the room. Malice stretched his face in ugly fashion. "Tell me, Widow Chase, how do you explain all of this?" he asked.

Suddenly Widow Chase found that she could not find a single word to say.

"No wonder you will not condemn devilry. Seems you are a part of it."

"Now, wait just a moment!"

"It seems you've slipped back into your old ways. Good Lord…." Knowles said.

Widow Chase followed the elder's line of vision, which was once again trained on the back door. Through it she saw a small, forlorn figure walking towards the edge of the bluff.

"*Damn fool girl...*" Widow Chase muttered.

Chapter Eight
"Flight of a Witch"

June 1716

No sermon of Reverend Treat's had ever drawn as many willing participants as those who packed into Eastham's meeting house to witness the trial of Maria Hallett and Widow Chase. Folks came from Billingsgate, Chatham, Harwich and even Truro, eager to see what kind of menace lurked on their boundaries.

The reverend stood on the threshold, clasping the hands of those coming through the door and offering each one a look grave enough for a funeral service. It was not inappropriate sentiment because death seemed to lurk in the corners as the audience chattered nervously before the proceedings. Death would also be the fate of the accused if they were found to be in league with the Devil, agents carrying out his unholy crimes. But that was for another day. This day would determine whether there was sufficient evidence to levy the charge of witchcraft. If so, the women would be put on a wagon and sent to the county seat to be judged by the court in Barnstable. This was every bit as serious an examination as that of the official jury. Perhaps more so, because Eastham was a proud town that did not easily relinquish its autonomy in its own affairs even if the fate of heaven and hell stood in the balance.

"This is an inquiry, not an inquisition," Justice Doane chastised the members of the crowd who were calling for a guilty plea even before the first shred of evidence was presented. Some were poor farmer's wives, who were afraid of their own shadows. Others were men who had faced down mountainous waves that loomed at the edge of their ship's bows as demonically as anything that the women on the stand were accused of. All of them should be ashamed, Doane thought.

Treat stood in the center of the room, like the lead barrister, which essentially he was, representing the side of the Lord.

Arrayed behind a long bench were the five Eastham selectmen, Justice Doane among them. Treat could influence only with his arguments and volume. The fate of the two women was squarely in the vote of five hands raised, aye or nay, after the last of the evidence was presented. The crowd's part was merely to bear witness, offer testimony and fulfill the communal spirit that had sustained their community ever since their forbearers had first planted themselves here.

Maria Hallett and Widow Chase sat side by side on the prisoners' bench, which was nothing more than a normal meeting house seat that had been put up next to the pulpit behind the railings that now stood in for cell bars. If anyone questioned the fact of having two possible witches upon the altar, no one said a word. Ironically, the two women had a perspective that no other of their sex had ever had, looking out at the congregation. However, the widow's eyes burned at some spot on the wood floor. She tried not to look at the girl, for the sight only made her flush with anger. The few times that she did, she saw Maria scanning the room for a friendly face and her anger turned into a pang of pity for the girl that even her own mother had not come to her trial.

"This is weakness, not strength, damn them! They strike down that which they do not understand... Like poor Mittawa," Widow Chase mumbled. She was speaking to herself, but Maria answered her anyway.

"I shall tell them that you had nothing to do with anything. It is the truth anyway," the girl said.

The widow's eyes flashed at her. "It does not matter, girl! The truth will not stand in their way if they want us dead! Tis the fate of all women who stick their heads up from out of the grass!"

"But it is all falsehood! It is a sin to lie! They will damn themselves!" Maria replied.

Widow Chase sucked angrily at her gums. "I was a fool to consort with you. You are too young to understand the difference between living on your own terms and trampling on *theirs*."

"If they will listen only to men, then I wish that my father or your husband or Sam was here to defend us," Maria wailed.

"Fool!" Widow Chase snorted.

Treat cleared his throat and began the proceedings, "We have before us an incident that rocks the foundation of this Christian community. An ill wind indeed has blown the seeds of devilry and corruption into our garden. Who among us will be able to look his neighbor in the eye if the Lord of Deceit is allowed to remain in Eastham? Certainly, we must purge this illness from our community, as diseased flesh is cut from the body or as weeds are excised by the root, before they can seed."

He went on in that manner for some time while Widow Chase shifted uncomfortably in her chair.

Then came the accusers, parading one by one to the center of the room to give testimony. Widow Chase snorted again as she watched Elder Knowles limp from his chair with exaggerated drama. She was hardly surprised by the sorry old stories that they had cooked up about dead cattle, evil premonitions and the like. Before long, several dozen men were bobbing their heads in agreement and clamoring to add fresh lies to the toxic brew they were concocting. If it were not all in aim of striking down the innocent, she would have laughed at how much they resembled a flock of squabbling grackles.

So far, all of it was directed at the girl. Widow Chase glanced over at her, from time to time, to gauge how she was holding up but saw nothing but blank stoicism.

"Atwood, Small, Wheeler, Hopkins… all neighbors of yours. All with lost crop and livestock. Seems that whatever killed these beasts spread outward in a circle from your farm, Goody Hallett," Treat observed.

Then the accusers talked of the girl's dreams, and all the while, Treat's tongue flicked eagerly over his lips.

"Most interesting… Terribly and disastrously interesting…" Treat mused.

"We cannot forget the giant, foul squid that washed up on the anniversary of the wreck that took Goody Hallett's poor father!" Hobart said, standing up from the crowd and pointing at Maria. "She told her mother that she dreamed that into being as well."

Next to stand was Jonathan Hopkins, a man whose glare foretold what kind of stories he would tell. After him were other men who had lost crops and women who had lost babies. All of them could step out of their doors and see the Hallett farmstead. All of them now knew that all of their misery had been born of that place and the witch girl that lived there.

"*We are doomed, child,*" Widow Chase whispered to her companion.

Instead of addressing the widow, Maria shouted to the crowd itself, "So we are to be persecuted for all of your misfortunes? A sacrifice! Like Abraham's son Isaac? Did you not teach us that very story?" she said, wheeling on Hobart and Treat. She would have gone on, but a sharp kick from Widow Chase silenced her.

"Goody Hallett, you are not to speak until asked for some defense and reckoning of yourself," Treat scolded.

"*God, child! Have you lost your mind altogether?*" Widow Chase mumbled, but she was secretly pleased that the girl had such spine. It was a shame that it was about to be cracked in half.

"Are you under some spell right now? Does the Devil make you rant so?" Treat demanded, peering into the girl's face. "Why have you continually brought ruin to this town?"

"I have not. I did not summon a squid or kill people's cattle. I do not talk to the Devil," Maria stammered, her voice cracking.

Yes, cry, child. Cry... Widow Chase thought. Perhaps if the girl crumbled, the town would see her as some pitiful thing. Had she tried the same tactic, Widow Chase knew that her fellow residents would have let her crumble and then happily scooped up her dust and thrown it into the wind.

"You say this, but people have testified to your attempts to destroy us," Treat went on.

"I do not! I love this town! This is my home!"

"Yet I have heard that you talk only of leaving Eastham. Where will you go? Off to the next settlement to continue your master's bidding?"

"It is not like that at all. I merely want to see the lands that men of the world get to see."

"You seek to overthrow the natural order of the sexes! You place yourself over men and claim no need of them!"

"No! I love a man..." Maria said and then uttered no more.

"An outlaw! Do you have anything else to say? Your sudden silence weighs heavily against you!" Treat thundered. "You are too much in the clutches of evil for even God to help you. When we are blinded by sin, we cannot see ourselves for the scourge that we have become. The time for forgiveness has past. God now demands your punishment! I am sorry that it has come to this, child, but by your own silence you supply all the evidence any of us would need. You are too far in the grip of the Devil."

"No, no! I am no witch!"

"Let us vote!" Treat commanded.

The reverend turned towards the assembled selectmen. As he did, Deacon Paine glanced at his colleagues and knew at once what their votes would be. Hopkins and Knowles would declare the girl guilty. Cole, he already knew, held the opinion that the beast was a natural, albeit unusual, resident of the deep sea and that the cattle had died of their own accord. About Doane, Paine was not sure until he heard the justice's deep voice declare, "Not Guilty."

Treat swiveled towards the justice. "This is your word?"

"It is. I see no proof of any malice born of this girl. All of it could be explained by blight, famine, storm and the ways of nature."

"Ridiculous!" Treat cried.

Paine nearly cried out too, so surprised and horrified was he to discover himself the determining vote.

"Deacon Paine, what say you?" the reverend demanded.

Paine could not bring himself to look anywhere but into his lap where he slid his ink stained hands into his pockets, out of sight. "I say that I have seen this young woman grow from birth into what she is now. Nay, she is not perfect. Yet I must confess that neither am I. Nor, I would wager, are any of us always so good as we would wish ourselves to be. Aye, Maria has strayed from the true course. Aye, she has sinned. Aye, she has also come to church every Sabbath of her life and prayed most virtuously. Should any of us show such devotion to the Lord and yet still be subject to the whims of His adversary, despite such virtue, then we are all lost. That I cannot believe. Were it my own dear children upon that stand, alone and friendless, I would pray that someone would speak for their goodness. For I know that they have Christ in their hearts, always, even when they are being mischievous..."

"Deacon Paine. The time for discussion has passed. We need only your vote. As you say, she is guilty of sin. The most terrible of sins. So what say you?" Treat said impatiently.

"Well yes... She has sinned," Paine said, looking at the gallery of rapt, angry faces before him and for a moment feeling that he was on trial.

"I have seen her since she was a young girl..." Paine continued, halting at another annoyed glare from the reverend. He was repeating himself in much the same way that the arguments had spun over and over inside his head, like the tide eddying against the pylons of his mill, little whirlpools of thought that kept him stuck in circles.

He had also seen the girl running wild. Sometimes it seemed like there was a touch of madness in her eyes. Yet she had seen him too. She had seen him with the foul, black stain of the beast on his fingers. What would Treat think if he knew that one of his deacons had thought so little of the threat and dire meaning of the creature as to fill up his ink bottles with its blood, he wondered? The girl, witch or not, could tell them all.

While Paine deliberated, a murmur rolled through the crowd. Against the back wall where the unmarried maidens stood, Thankful Knowles exhaled the breath that she felt she had been holding for the past hour. She too found herself adrift in conflicting emotions. She did not doubt that Paine would find her stepsister guilty. Part of her accepted that justice was about to be done. At the same time Thankful could not help but admire how straight and fearlessly Maria Hallett stood and faced her judgment. In that stance Thankful no longer saw pride, wildness or even defiance. For a moment she saw only a girl who had tried to follow her own course, and for that she was going to be struck down. All of a sudden Thankful felt that she could no longer stand being in this meeting house and among this vengeful throng.

Treat's commanding voice suddenly rang out, "Deacon Paine! We will tolerate no more delay! Your vote, please!"

Silence filled the room, except for the sound of Paine clearing his throat.

"I do not consider Goody Hallett to be a witch…" Paine croaked, telling himself that he voted for her innocence rather than to shield his guilt.

Over the gasp of the crowd, Treat rasped to no one in particular, "In this trial I am afraid that we have failed God most grievously!" He sat heavily on the closest bench and sagged as if he suddenly realized that he had expended a lifetime of righteous bluster to no avail.

"And the *widow?*" Doane prompted.

"You were a midwife, were you not?" Treat asked, rising and finding new strength within himself. He would not let two witches slip from his grasp.

"Aye. What of it?" Widow Chase replied, her eyes narrowing.

"We all know that not every mother or child lives through the act of birthing. It is common for midwifes to be in league with the Lord of Death rather than our Almighty God..."

"I helped babes come into life, not death!"

"...bitter, spiteful women who are without the direction of men often turn to such careers of being the Devil's handmaidens..."

"I ain't bitter nor lost without the direction of men!"

"...or sorrowful widows, longing for solace and love. They are susceptible to the Devil's seduction..."

"I was happy to have no man! That bugger did me more harm than good, coming home when he pleased and filling me with babies and then running off again and leaving me to take care of everything. I wasn't sorry to see him go, if you really want the truth out of me!" Widow Chase roared.

The crowd gasped again, and most looked towards Treat in awe at his skill in coaxing such damning admissions.

"How many mothers under your charge were lost, Widow Chase?" Treat asked gravely.

"None by my hand!"

"How many?"

"The Lord took them, on account that it was their time! I didn't take no lives!"

"Blasphemer!" Treat shouted.

"I know of two deaths at her hand," Knowles piped up. "My wife and my just born child. The babe came out purple from being strangled within the womb. The blood would not stop flowing from my wife's womb. Widow Chase sat back and said *we must wait...* while my wife bled to death!"

"It was past any skill but God's to heal!" Widow Chase said. "These questions prove nothing but that life itself can be cruel!"

"Thank you, Elder Knowles. As hard as your testimony must have been to speak aloud, it will not be in vain. It helps us see what kind of evil woman sits defiantly before us!" Treat said.

"That's a lie!"

"Did you not brew potions for various spells to be used against the people and beasts of this town?" Treat demanded.

"I did not. If I am to be condemned for mixing a batch of what you call *potions*, then every native of this town should be likewise condemned. I use only their lore. They, like myself, are a praying people. Will you send them all to the gallows for keeping their medicine? I bet that you would!" she said.

"The Indians have left their heathen ways behind. They do not brew such concoctions anymore," Treat stated. "Who of them taught you this medicine?"

"I learned from several of them."

Knowles stepped forward and whispered in Treat's ear. The old man's eyes went wide, and he took a menacing step towards Widow Chase. "The Witch of Billingsgate? She taught you such craft?"

Near pandemonium broke out among those in the audience.

"She ain't no more a witch than you, good Reverend!"

"She was proved a witch and banished for it, need I remind you! Are you accusing me of Maleficia?" Treat roared.

"I am accusing you of ignorance and foolishness!" Widow Chase said. After her retort she cursed under her breath and bit her lip. She was like a cook pot boiling over, slipping out frothing words that should not be said and would do nothing but burn her.

Treat's jowls shook slightly as he stared at her, considering. "You also harbored young Maria Hallett?"

"I did not. The girl came to me because she was lonely for her father. We talked is all."

"You gave her illegal, unholy elixirs?"

"I did not..."

"You taught her to manipulate her dreams?"

"No!"

"You lead her into unholy alliance with God's enemy?"

"Rubbish! Rubbish, I say!"

"What do you know of the giant squid? Did you call for it?"

"Your questions are ridiculous!"

"*Ridiculous?*" Treat roared. "Is the preservation of God's kingdom so *ridiculous?* Do you laugh at the prospect of our downfall?"

"You are hearing only what you want to hear!"

Widow Chase's hard face sagged and went white. She huffed for breath.

"How much part did you play in the workings of the Witch of Billingsgate? She too was known to have destroyed livestock and crop, by setting an unholy wolf on the run at night!"

Instead of speaking, Widow Chase sat and shook, a shiver that wracked her whole body, like an egg quivering as something inside prepared to break out.

"Have you no reply?" Treat asked. After a gravid silence he slapped the rail in front of her with his palm. "Your silence proves that you cannot deny these charges! Guilty!" he shouted, and this time the selectmen agreed.

"Damn you all!" Widow Chase screamed, rising from her seat and thundering down the center of the aisle without a glance at anyone. She moved towards the open door, the view of the freedom of the road and fields standing in for human comfort. "If I could lay a curse, then surely I would now, you damnable creatures! All of you! God's trials are not so dressed up in men's fear!"

"We are cursed already," Treat said sadly as Doane's deputies moved quickly to intercept her, wrestling her roughly out of the building as if she were the most dangerous criminal they had encountered, which to most in town she was.

✠ ✠ ✠ ✠

July 1716

The moon had crested and was now low on the horizon, dipping behind the glowing treetops. As the light dispersed into the trees, the King's Highway became submerged in darkness. The small jail next to it was nothing but a box of impenetrable blackness against the general gloom.

The jail itself was empty, not just of light but of occupants, including its prisoner. The jailer William Hopkins stood nervously next to the horse that Justice Doane angrily fitted with a saddle forgiving enough to accommodate a crippled rider. Doane's horse stood impatiently next to its partner, exuding the same irritation as its master.

This was not the first time that the inmate had flown her cage. Tonight Doane was determined that the incompetent jailer follow him on the pursuit, hoping that the jarring on the boy's leg might find its way up to knock some sense into his head.

All Doane could think about was the soft bed that was growing cold on one side at home. He always imagined that he was sinking into a billowy cloud in heaven as he slid in next to his darling wife, an angel. No, William Hopkins would not bask by the fire while he trampled through the dark and prickly underbrush after the prisoner, Doane thought.

He yanked on the harness belt, and the horse whinnied protest.

"I am sorry, sir. It will not happen again..." Hopkins promised.

"It has been a month since the trial! You have given me such assurance four times, and she has escaped four times since!" Doane's voice cut, whip-like, through the night, and this time it was the lad who gave a whimper.

The whole trial had been a damned messy business, Doane thought. They had found the girl guilty of fornication. Every one of them had seen Maria Hallett with Sam Bellamy countless times. There was not a person in town who did not know that they had been a pair. Through the interrogation of Widow Chase, they had learned that the girl had also given birth outside of the sanctity of marriage. It could be no clearer that fornication had occurred, and so the vote was unanimous. As punishment, they had given Goody Hallett nine months in jail, to match the length of her sinful pregnancy. It was a hard penalty, but not outside of the law.

The fate of Widow Chase had been even worse. She was now locked up in the Barnstable jail. Doane imagined her verbally abusing the Barnstable deputies, releasing the last of her fire as she headed for her own blazing end. She was a most disagreeable and stubborn old woman, thought Doane. Yet he was not convinced that she was a witch.

Doane realized that if he was not careful, the whole situation could get much further out of hand. If the wisdom and benevolence of the elders did not stop the madness, the townsfolk themselves might go and set up a gallows. Doane sensed the crowd's longing for blood, like a smell upon the air, and it was loathsome. Since the end of the trial, the townsfolk had held vigils outside of the jail. Rumor was that the Devil had gifted black crows to Maria, and she had let them fly to find Bellamy and bring him back to Eastham to save her. Now every superstitious idiot in Eastham was scanning the coast for Bellamy's sail. The thought made Doane snort in disgust.

William's sudden protest interrupted the justice's thoughts, "She must have put some kind of spell on me. Some witchcraft. I had strange thoughts."

Doane groaned to himself. "Tell me, Master Hopkins, what *kind* of strange thoughts did you experience?"

William stammered incoherently and then began coughing. The coughing lasted several seconds and sounded like the beginnings of a cold, but Doane felt unsympathetic at the moment.

"Well?" Doane demanded. "*Lust?*"

"No!" William cried. Even in the moonlight, his face looked flushed. "I was carving. Birds and things is what I usually carve. But Maria looked so sad...and pretty. Especially in the moonlight through the cell window. So when she asked to go outside for a moment to get some air, I thought that I'd like see her with the moon more upon her. Better light. See, I was whittling a likeness of her."

"And the times before that? Did she escape in similar fashion?"

"*It was different things each time,*" William mumbled.

Maria's jail time had been a farce thanks to this nervous, love-struck idiot, Hopkins, Doane thought. Doane knew that the mockery of the girl's escapes could not continue or else irrational fear would infect more citizens of Eastham. They were saying that she flew out of the chimney itself to go on her nocturnal errands. Now that she was in jail, they thought that she was more a witch than ever. Doane advocated stricter measures, some kind of symbol to demonstrate that punishment was being served. His sense of duty told him that something had to be done. Hard decisions were called for, or else the whole town could deteriorate into lawlessness. He would have to discuss the matter with the selectmen.

"Aiding and abetting jailbreak is a crime, Master Hopkins. Perhaps the second jail cell will soon become your permanent home." Doane glanced into the lad's face, pale and stricken in the moonlight, and he grunted in satisfaction that the message might finally be sinking in.

Then something rustled in the underbrush, and William gave a shout.

Doane too felt a stab of alarm. He reached for his pistol in his belt.

A dark shape bolted from its covering, and the horse reared and snorted.

"Wolf!" William said.

"No, no!" the justice railed. "'Tis but a loose dog!"

"Let us go back!" William urged. "Please…"

"Yes," Doane agreed. "You return to the jail and await me! I can make better time alone."

"Alone?" William cried, looking back down the dark road towards the jail.

In answer, Doane spurred his horse off towards Treat's Hill. He rode past Treat's house and up the sloping hill. The image of the shadowy animal kept slinking through his mind, its body crouched low and dog-like. Or was it a wolf, he asked himself?

Then, finally, he crested the hill and rode down the rolling fields to the lip of Nauset Marsh.

She stood at the far end by the waterline, looking out across the marsh towards the sea. A small lantern, taken from the jail, was swinging in her hand. It was a small green globe against a sheet of blackness.

"Goody Hallett! I know for whom you hold that beacon, and I assure you that he is never coming back!" Doane cried.

The girl turned slowly to face him, her face given a devilish cast by the flame filtered through the green glass of the lantern.

"Perhaps I shall fly away from you across this harbor," she said. She too had heard what the townsfolk said of her. She could have hardly turned a deaf ear to it since someone or other shouted it, like a curse, through the bars of her cell nearly every day.

"Ha! Should you accomplish that feat, then you would be put in a place from which there is no escape, only endless torment!" Doane declared.

She looked at him quizzically. "You are starting to sound like the reverend."

"Come along! I am taking you back to the cell! Eight months still await you there!" Doane snapped.

Maria dutifully followed his trotting horse back towards her incarceration, the lantern light forming a little island of brightness in which they traveled.

✠ ✠ ✠ ✠

154

A few days later William Hopkins was blubbering as he stood over the fire, poking the flames with the end of a long iron brand.

In front of him Maria Hallett sat, her eyes burning with indignation. "If you say that you are sorry one more time, I will be tempted to take that iron from you and apply it to your lips!"

The feat would have been difficult due to the ropes that Justice Doane had used to bind her to the chair that sat in the middle of the main cell. But, for a witch, anything might be possible.

"Please, just do it. Do it quickly!" she said yet again.

"I cannot. The fire is not hot enough. It will not leave the mark clearly, and I will have to do it again." His eyes were tearing from empathy. Her eyes welled too, but only from the smoke of the fire. Otherwise, all of her grief had already been burned out of her.

The audience for this part of her punishment was small - only she, William and Justice Doane. Everyone else would see the results in good time, for her punishment and pain would soon be branded upon her cheek, a harrowing initial "F" that would mark her as a fornicator for all time. The selectmen had enthusiastically agreed to the punishment, and Reverend Treat described it as "a brand upon her flesh to remind her of the searing pain to which she has condemned that babe's little soul!" That they refrained from adding an "M" for murderess was again due to the compassion of Deacon Paine's tie-breaking vote.

"Hurry up, it is well heated," Doane instructed.

"I don't know... I don't know..." William stammered. He then broke into a fit of coughing.

"Give it to me! This is an awful business that we all want to be soon through with," Doane snapped as he snatched the iron from William's shaky hands and turned to Maria. "Have strength. This shall take but a moment. Are you ready?"

It took only a moment for her to nod, another to draw a deep breath of steaming air and a third for the searing press of metal to gouge into her. William heard her skin sizzle, sounding so loud that it nearly drowned out her screaming. As instructed, he swung the bucket and threw a sting of water across her face, at which point she looked like she again wanted to strike him. But the water soothed her. Then, to William's astonishment, she began to laugh.

He exchanged a look with the justice, who looked equally startled by the sound of her raving.

"It is hard pain," William sympathized, reaching to untie her. Next to him, Doane stood implacably and stared at the girl.

She laughed harder. "One act of joy brings all this pain and death! Your punishment does not burn it away! It makes it permanent! You fools just made sure it will linger! Forever linger…" she said, her chuckling converting to a choking whimper as she gingerly touched her cheek and its horrid mark.

"Come for me if she worsens. If she seeks flight, come for me still. Just come faster!" Doane instructed before taking his leave.

Outside, the summer morning was cool but warming quickly. Dew glazed the tall, green stalks of grasses in a nearby meadow. The houses along the road looked sharp in the clear air. The sunlight gave glowing edges to the homesteads and tree trunks. It was a fine morning to take the horse out for a long, cantering walk through the village.

He could hear William pleading with the girl, trying to cajole her away from the cell door. She, in turn, begged to be let out. She did not like to use the chamber pot, preferring to step out into the grove of trees behind the cell where it was a simple thing to flee across the back pastures towards the sea bluffs. Doane was about to go inside and settle the matter himself when a flicker of movement along the King's Highway caught his eye. Far down the road, at the bridge over Jeremiah's Gutter, a mob was crossing. They were heading for the jail.

"Good Lord…" Doane said, staring balefully at the throng as it marched steadily towards the jail. He recognized individual faces, knew all of their names, yet the crowd looked like a single, seething thing. A cloud of wasps. Something dreadful and malign.

"William! Is the prisoner secure?" Doane called.

He heard the lad reply, but the words were muffled.

"William!" Doane cried again.

The mob was armed. He could see their simple weapons of pitchforks, reaping blades, knives and hammers glinting in the sun. Yet it would only take a single thrust of an awkward weapon to rend the law asunder. Already they were pointing at the jail and shouting. Much of it was the same taunts of witchcraft and devilry as had been uttered at the trial, but now there were plenty of cries for blood too.

Doane stepped outside to confront the mob and found William at his elbow.

"They rave. All of them! Lunatics!" William said.

Doane frowned at the jailer. "Is Goody Hallett locked tight?"

William nodded.

It did not take long for the crowd to arrive. Among its number were plenty of men who Doane expected to see as well as others that he was disappointed to find in the throng.

"What is this?" Doane demanded.

Elijah Wheeler, a farmer whose fields had born stunted crops, looked at him and spat, "This is true justice!"

"This is law breaking!" Doane roared.

"You cannot arrest the whole town. We have decided on the verdict that you were too weak to give!"

"No! You will all disperse this instant!" Doane shouted.

"Open that cell, Justice!" Wheeler demanded.

Doane spun towards Joshua Hopkins, who stood in the front ranks, his tanning knife in hand. "You are a selectman, and your son is one of my deputies! Surely, you are not intending to circumvent the law?"

"I do not care if you see me among these good folk. What we aim to do is above the laws of man! It is the will of God!"

While Doane was looking at the elder Hopkins, he did not see Jonathan, the son, creep up to the cell window and hiss through it, "*Goody Hallett! Do not think that you can lie away safely within the comfort of this cell! Your reckoning is at hand for all that you did to curse and shame our town!*"

"Jonathan!" William cried, moving towards his brother and trying to peel him away from the window.

"Move over, brother," Jonathan replied, pushing a hand into William's chest.

"Aacck!" William coughed into his sleeve.

"Your cough grows worse," Jonathan noted.

"It is nothing…" William replied, forcing a smile.

"*If that cough is your doing, you shall have me to reckon with, before you meet your end on the gallows tree!*" Jonathan hissed into the dark cell.

"Come away from there… Please…" William said.

A moment later Jonathan gave a shout and sprang back.

Maria pressed her face against the bars. Raw and red shone the gruesome brand that, although lawfully applied, seemed the very essence of the ugliness that the townsfolk feared.

"The *witch!*" Wheeler cried and pointed at the cell. The townsfolk turned and beheld the sight of Maria's mark, and their fear turned to riot.

Doane was spun around by the rowdy mass of bodies that pushed past him. At the same time William rushed to the jail door, flung it open, then fell over as his crippled leg buckled. He collapsed under the onrushing boots of the villagers. Only one of the mob, Jonathan Hopkins, threw down his weapon and hurried to pull William to safety.

The rest found the witch girl already escaping through the open cell door.

They surged after her, leaving Doane completely cut off in their wake. All he could do was watch her flight. As she ran, dirt kicked up in little puffs of dust around her as stones thrown by the crowd landed all around her like hard rain. Those missiles were accompanied by hard, vengeful words as the citizens of Eastham drove her past the meeting house and around the bend towards the northern parish.

Without his horse, Doane had to follow the mob on foot. By the time that he caught up with it, much of the madness had melted away. He stopped a cluster of panting villagers who were returning back down the King's Highway. At first they simply scowled, but after he threatened them all with the pillory, they told him that the chase had lasted for many miles and finally dispersed when she had reached the Billingsgate border.

So she was gone, Doane thought. He did not try to follow her. He was, in truth, not sorry to have an end to it, if indeed they were rid of her for good. But as he headed home, he could not take his eyes off of the dirt-brown stones on the roadside. Each one was a reminder of his neighbors' sharp, primitive judgment, which was its own kind of witchcraft.

Chapter Nine
"The Devil's Pasture"

Maria Hallett did not take time to admire the new terrain that she was traveling through. Her attention was fixed only on the path below her feet, with only an occasional glance behind her to see if she was still pursued. At last there was no sign of her neighbors or any other people. She had never been so glad to be free from human companionship. She did not think that she could look into another person's face without screaming.

She did not stop until she reached the old wooden bridge at Blackfish Creek. Instead of crossing the bridge and heading farther north to Billingsgate, she turned east and delved into the woods where the man-made tracks disappeared under a spread of sand, pine needles and stunted forest. The trees were wind-twisted. The shrubs were meek and malnourished. All of the vegetation clung close to the ground. It could do nothing else because it was constantly cropped and beaten down by the ceaseless ocean breezes that came rushing over a steep dune crest from the sea below.

This was forgotten land, given over to the elements and the small creatures that rustled in the bracken. It was a place where even the seagulls would veer off, gliding just off of the ridge of high dunes and then away again, after a peek at the bleak offerings of the place.

She sat in the meager shade of a pitch pine and probed the raw patch on her cheek and the nicks and bruises all across her body from the villagers' stones. Touch alone told her that the wounds and blemishes upon her made her a grisly sight. Not long ago people were comparing her to a flower coming into its beauty. Now she saw herself as similar to the pine cones protruding from the skeletal branches of the trees around her. There were no budding petals in her world, only the hard, rigid shakes of the cone, which crumbled when she squeezed them and looked like broken, black teeth in her hand. She crushed a dozen of them and scattered them across the barren land.

Funnels of smoke rose out of the forest in the distance, showing where chimneys were planted, but no other people lived within view. She was effectively cut off from her own kind.

It was a voluntary exile, she realized. She had heard shouts from the mob as it chased her. They told her that there was a place for her in Helltown, at the tip of Cape Cod, among the smugglers, whores and thieves. Others urged her to leave the peninsula itself, reminding her of her so often expressed desire for adventure. Still others wished for her to be gone from this world altogether.

At last she had her freedom and, with it, the revelation that she could not even master the adventure of assembling a proper shelter to block the wind and rain.

Eventually she constructed a crude hut from driftwood branches, hauled painstakingly up the cliff side. She had flint, tobacco and a pipe, which the jailer William Hopkins had given her. She used the flint to keep a small cook fire going in the hollow next to her shelter. But she had nothing with which to bring down any of the speedy rabbits and squirrels that she observed around her. So day after day she crouched over the meager flames, feeding them twigs while giving her clamoring stomach nothing.

Soon the world around her felt blurred from hunger. Only her mind retained its clarity, feeling more real to her at times than the wind or sound of surf crashing beneath her. She fed herself on the only bits of sustenance at hand, which were her thoughts. She chewed on the grief and grudges that her friends, family and fellow townsfolk had given her. But it was a bitter meal, which grew poisonous as it aged.

She reviewed her mother's stubborn refusal to believe that two women could run a farm. It was a weakness that appeared all the more glaring when set against the strong will of Widow Chase. The widow, Maria realized, was likely buried in some grave by now, sacrificed to the blind fear of the fools of Eastham. Thinking of the widow's unjust treatment brought hot tears to Maria's eyes and a burning wish that spells were real.

Experimentally, she pointed a finger at a rabbit, which had just hopped out of a clump of bayberry and sat staring insolently at her while it chewed its cud.

"Your death will give me my dinner..." she declared and tried to propel some hex out of her finger tip.

The rabbit sniffed at her and then hopped off, and Maria's next curse was an oath shouted into the wind, but that too was quickly borne away.

All that Maria was ultimately able to kill was time. Some afternoons she combed the sandy terrain, plucking up stones, counting them and, for each one, thinking of a happy memory. "One hundred and one...one hundred and two..." *Picking blueberries with her mother as a child... Her father handing the tiller over to her for the first time... Sam taking her in with his eyes, then his hands, then more...*

"One hundred and ten..."

Damn it, she thought. As if to spite her, the memories turned sour. Soon all she could see was the great bulwark of the back of a sloop sailing away from shore, her house in flames and the rocks stinging her flesh like bees.

"One hundred and fifty..."

The image of a little boy, who looked like no more than a rag doll, colored gray like corn husks left to rot in the sun. Such toys did not take breath, but she knew that this one should. Yet no matter how hard she shook him, he would not stir...

"One hundred and ninety-four..."

After a while she found herself praying. To whom or what, she did not know. God had spared her from hanging but banished her for love and the bitter fruit it bore. Those that exalted and upheld God were the same ones who stole, lied and bent the law to fill their own purses, she mused, with the unpleasant realization that her thoughts sounded like Bellamy's words.

And others just leave when things become difficult...

She picked up another rock and noted that living out in the wild, scrounging for food and water, had made her hands gray and crinkled like an old woman. She caught a strand of her hair and found it dulled and dirty like mud trampled straw. It seemed to her that she was at last seeing the true image of her desire for adventure, and it was unvarnished and faded like weather-beaten shingles.

Perhaps she should have taken the route of marriage, safety and beauty after all, she mused. But that thought created such a surge of anger and sourness within her that she stood up and roared.

More days went by, and Maria marked their passage by the slow emptying of her pouch full of tobacco leaf. It took great resolve to parcel it out. She knew that once it was gone, she would have nothing left from which to seek comfort.

The smoking also slaked her hunger for a time. She had feared starvation at first, but lately she worried about madness. She knew that her wits were fraying when she smelled a sweet smoke in the air, like some herb from Widow Chase's kitchen, which wafted out of the forest as if in response to the pipe smoke that she blew over her shoulder.

After a while it dissipated, and she put it out of mind.

A day later it returned. She made a cautious inspection of the edge of the forest and discovered a strange bundle of smoldering sticks, which clearly had been planted by some invisible hand.

Her throat quivered. She was not losing her wits. She was being watched.

Some time after that she saw the dark fur of an animal flashing through the undergrowth. She threw stones at it until the voice of a man commanded her to stop.

"No… It cannot be…" Maria said. She knew she was foggy-headed from lack of food.

She blinked once and saw only trees and brush. Then she blinked again, and an apparition appeared out of the undergrowth like a dream. It was a native man. He was dressed in English clothes, which made him look civilized, but in her isolation, fatigue and hunger, she could imagine only ill intent from him.

"*Please… Do not kill me…*" she muttered. But he ignored her.

He came closer, and she saw the bow slung across his shoulders and the knife in his belt. There was a grim look on his face and a hard, unforgiving glint in his eyes. He was talking, but she could not hear him at first because fear beat so loudly in her ears. Nor could she hear her own answers to his questions. She spoke as if slipping into a deep dream.

At one point he pointed at her pipe. "You were smoking the sacred smoke."

"I have only tobacco…" she protested, her voice sounding like the thin scrape of foam across beach stone.

"And you are watched by the wolf," he went on.

"Wolf?" she gasped.

The man nodded. "Two wolves. For I am a wolf too. Your people call me John Julian. But I was born into this world as *Ontoquos*. The wolf. We wolves have come for you because you are the witch girl."

Maria stepped back towards the very edge of the cliff. She did not know what to say or do, so she merely looked at the tobacco pipe in her hand like it had betrayed her.

✠ ✠ ✠ ✠

Spring 1717

Slowly, but inexorably, like waves shearing sand from the coastline, nearly a year slipped away. For the first few months, Maria did not see the wolf tracks again. However, John Julian came and went, like the squirrels and rabbits that would occasionally come skitting out of the underbrush and then away again. If he was a wolf, he bared no fangs. His intentions were as strange to her as the primitive necklace he wore of feather, tooth and bone. He did not seem to want what other men did of her – her beauty, her hand in marriage, her labor, her very life. Instead, he left her with gifts of food, then shelter and then, most importantly, learning. She now knew how to hunt, strengthen her makeshift hut and survive. She knew that without John Julian she might not have endured this isolated wilderness through the autumn and winter. However, as grateful as she was, the admission still felt like a defeat, after all that men had put her through with all of their plans, promises and punishments.

Maria thought of such things as she and the native stood on the bluff and took in the vastness of the ocean below them. Its size and power, as it rumbled into the foot of the dune below, made it seem like a living thing. At first it made Maria feel small. She glanced at the native and felt the rising heat of resentment at her dependency.

"More than one man has promised me that ocean. They were to take me across it. But none has fulfilled his promise. I have come to believe that I would sooner stand upon the very edge of the horizon than see a promise come true," she said.

Julian shrugged. "You want the ocean. I want the land. Neither of them is ours to claim."

There was silence between them for a few moments while they watched seagulls float at eye level, just out of reach from where they stood at the dune's rim.

"Why are you doing this? Why are you helping me?" she asked him.

Julian squinted at her and then kicked a spray of sand off of the lip of the cliff. "Because we stand on the edge of what we have and what we want. It is hard to stand there alone," he said.

"Yes. I feel everyone has been trying to push me off," Maria remarked, glancing down the sheer slope of the dune. "If there really was magic, then I could fly. I could go across this ocean on my own," she mused, turning and seeing a gleam in the native's eye.

"Ha! Most of them believe me capable of flight already!" she snorted.

"Are you?" he asked, looking more eager than she had ever seen him before.

Maria laughed. "Not even in my dreams."

His excitement suddenly waned, and she could think of no cause for it. She was still puzzling over the conversation when Julian nodded a good-bye and walked off into the forest.

It was at that moment that she understood that it would not matter if he ever came back at all. She would lament the loss of company, but she would not suffer from it. She was past the point of waiting for men to stay or return. She would survive. Finally, it seemed, she had found her freedom.

✠ ✠ ✠ ✠

April 26, 1717

Several weeks went by, and Julian had not returned. It was his way to come and go, sometimes with many days in between visits. This time Maria wondered if he was gone for good.

"I should not care about this," she scolded herself.

The late afternoon was prematurely gray. Soot colored clouds gathered over head, and Maria lit a fire in the hollow next to the cliff bluff. She sat next to it, watching the flames race eagerly across the crackling branches, raising flickering spires of orange fire from the blackening pile of kindling. It reminded her of another fire, from another time, and soon she was sliding into a reverie as thick and deep as a dream. Back to her house, two summers ago...

From her perch in the loft, she could see the embers slowly dropping off, in black chunks, from the reed candle. She remembered eavesdropping on the couple below. Elder Knowles whispered his inane promises to her mother about how their two farms would be connected, the stone walls retrained and the contents of each brought together. She also heard about his designs upon the land by Treat's Hill. The extent of his ambition surprised her, but her mother's silence did not. She imagined that her mother was overwhelmed by the new world that she was entering. She did not for an instant believe that her mother was feeling any happiness. The thought gave her a malicious thrill, which did not abate even after Knowles had left and she heard her mother stop part way through clearing supper and choke out a hoarse sob.

Then she recalled the words that Sam Bellamy had said to her earlier that evening:

"If we are to travel together, then we need fastening stronger than these merry meetings."

"I don't understand," she had said even though she knew well his meaning. More and more, he had been attempting to kiss her. More and more liberties were being taken as he wrapped an arm around her, always reaching for more. His advances had petrified her at first. But she had grown used to his touch and started to long for it. She was not naïve of what men and women did with one other although the image was a frenetic, misunderstood one based on her observations of the animals in the field. Then there was the tantalizing stroke of the sailor's fingers, which suggested that the true experience was far more than she had been given to understand.

"Sleeping in the barn alone grows lonesome. It must be the same for you, under your mother's eye. We shall have to amend that…tonight if you are willing," he had said. Spurred on by that comment, she climbed down from the loft as soon as her mother was asleep. She could still remember the cold metal of the front door latch as she stepped out into the open air. She did not worry about the dangers of illness that everyone knew could be carried on the night breezes. She hastened towards the barn that stood out in the darkness as a solid, indistinguishable mass, adorned by a pointed crown. She remembered thinking that she was going to give up a part of herself to become something greater. The skin of childhood would be shed in this joining. There was no thought of Justice Doane and the punishment that he would be obliged to mete out should she be caught. Nor did she think of her mother for fear that she would lose her will to continue towards the tryst.

Her throat was so tight that she could not speak when she stepped inside the barn. At the same time her giddiness made the floor feel like it was pitching under her.

Bellamy came towards her and took her into his arms. His hands enacted all of those things that had flitted about in her imagination and more she had not thought of.

She recalled falling backwards into the hay stack as she had done a thousand times as a child. Never had she dreamed of an encounter of this nature in all of that girlish play. Mostly, she wished that the lantern was up higher so she could see the sailor more clearly, lest this moment be confused with some kind of dream that slips away with morning.

Maria could still feel the way it was when they were done. The lantern had gone out. Bellamy held her awhile and repeated his promises, and she smiled and listened, wanting nothing but to hear his words wash over her, to sustain the connection with him. She remembered thinking that he could have said anything as long as he kept talking there beside her…

Once this was among Maria's most cherished memories, but now she could no longer think of it without next recalling that the barn had become a place of anguish, a tomb for her child.

That she had been a mother at all sometimes astonished and terrified her, but it too felt largely like a dream.

She stood and walked to the edge of the cliff and looked out over a sea that was seething like a cook pot coming to boil. Long combers came in from the horizon, the waves matching her own relentless cycles of love, longing and anger. The anger was growing stronger, like the waves themselves. Towering white caps came out of the darkness and crashed onto shore. Another storm was coming. She was determined that this one would not bring her more misery.

✠ ✠ ✠ ✠

That night Maria leaned into a growing wind that held her up, like a great hand bracing her weight, occasionally shoving her back towards the flat plain behind the bluff. Gusts spun off of the swirling ocean below her and almost lifted her up into the air. She kept pushing back against the wall of wind, laughing madly as she did.

Sand scratched on her bare legs as she stood there in the rocky embrace of the gale. Clouds roiled in the sky, and the galloping sea sank its ravenous overbite into the soft hide of sand on the beach at her feet. The wind played about Maria's ears, and she thought that she heard voices in it, whispering spells and dark primordial secrets more powerful than even Julian's people could imagine. The sea and sky were a raging cauldron, and into them she cast handfuls of dried herbs that she carried in a basket.

The herbs, she knew, were simply a ceremonial gesture. She had come to realize that a spell was nothing other than an extreme focus of passion and emotion. She wanted this wind to shear the sadness from her and all the sharp pangs of hope, mad longing and loneliness.

Her feet were on the edge of an abyss. It would be a simple thing to step off the precipice and let herself be swept into the center of the storm. In that way she would be done with this life and perhaps wake into better dreams in the next world.

"No…" she mumbled, in reply to her dizzying thoughts.

The force of the storm seemed to flood into her mind. She felt as though its power was her own; and she could put the wind and waves under yoke and send them off to do her bidding.

She called to the angry spirits of the sea, the doomed ghosts of shipwrecked sailors and the vindictive lore of any witch or woman who had been spurned by the thoughtless cruelty of men. She didn't much care who or what was listening, as long as it was powerful enough to turn the very seascape into a beast bent on destruction.

She could almost feel the savage waves grow in fury as her hand directed them.

Then the mad grief came frothing out of her. She didn't know what words were correct for a spell, but she kept talking and hoping that she would stumble upon a key that unleashed power.

"Damn them all! Jonathan Hopkins! Reverend Treat! Elder Knowles! May their town be washed away into sand! Wipe Eastham from the map itself!" she screamed.

The waves foamed savagely beneath her, like spittle in the ocean's rabid teeth.

"Find him spirits! Find Sam Bellamy! Make him pay! Deliver him to hell, in your clutches of thunder and lightening!" she cried, half expecting the skies to erupt at her words.

"Make him feel my pain! Make him taste my sorrow! Bring the waves upon him! Let them crush him! Let him pay for what he did to me with the same misery that I felt! *Damn him!!*"

As her voice grew raw and wane, she realized that she had nothing left to say. The words that she hurled sounded more and more like one of Treat's sermons, the only difference being that she called for the hellfire that he warned against.

Her anger choked in her throat, tears replacing salt spray. "I *loved* you, Sam!" she cried.

Then she withdrew the last of the herbs from the bag and tossed them into the vortex of wind. The herbs were immediately sucked away into the gray sheet of sky.

In that instant a thunderclap exploded as if in her ears, and she stumbled forward onto the soft ledge of the dune cliff. It gave way under her weight. With a rush she slid down a chute of sand and then rolled log-like to the bottom onto the beach.

The waves seemed to rear up over her head. But they did not touch her. They fell in a line, mere feet away from the wall of the dune. Maria pressed her back against the sand, like she was on yet another ledge, and listened to their sound of grinding boulders. The noise and the violent motion of the storm were relentless. She rose with feral energy and roared back at the waves, "Damn this place! Damn the sea itself!"

Then suddenly a wave crashed into her, knocking her down. It left her skin feeling wet and clammy, and chilled with the terror that her curse had turned upon her.

She scampered up the face of the dune.

Above her, the sky rippled with an unholy, rumbling dirge, and the clouds were burned by angry, crackling fire.

When she reached her hut, she crawled under her blankets and prayed that the cacophony would cease. All she wanted now was peace.

BOOK TWO

The Tale of John Julian

Chapter One
"The Last Wolf of Great Island"

June 1715

One look at the sea creature told John Julian that it was not here for retribution against the English. The lifeless form was strewn in small pieces, from the work of gulls, crabs, tide and a fire that was set upon the remains. All that was left was an awful stink, a patch of black blood leeching into the sand and a few loose tentacles that Julian kicked in disgust.

That this monster did not seem capable of any destruction did not mean that there was no meaning in it. There was always some kind of pattern beneath what men saw in the ordinary look of things. Most people did not see how the signs fit together, but Julian had been fortunate to be shown how to sort through their meaning, by those that had come before him. In the sea creature and the half-drowned sailor, there was a pattern that he could not yet see although it went fleeting through his mind like a shadow.

While he was examining the creature, Julian felt invisible eyes upon him, but when he glanced around at the bluffs and ocean, he saw nothing unusual.

Julian got into his canoe and paddled back through Great Cove, past the place where he had left the sailor. He glanced at Higgins Tavern, with a vague desire of going there and seeing what had become of his good deed. He felt foolish now that he had not lingered with the man to take credit for saving him, but he had been so sure that the beast had come for destruction that he had unwisely chosen the wrong side, as seemed to be the endless fate of his people.

At the southern tip of Great Cove was a channel that wound through the marshy middle of Eastham to a great cup-like bay on the other side. The passage was called Jeremiah's Gutter, named after a white man whose arrogance was so great that he tried to claim not just the land, but the water too.

Coming into the bay, Julian could see a clump of islands to the north. The largest one had a long, sloping face of dune that glowed orange in the late afternoon sun. The whites named it Great

Island and placed it in Billingsgate, which was what they called the northern parish of Eastham.

The sight of the island made Julian's chest tight with the memory of the childhood village that had once been there. Years ago, his father, a Punonakanit man, had paddled back and forth along this same route to woo his mother, a member of the Nauset tribe. Now, in place of the island village was one of the largest buildings that the whites had ever made. It was a big square place, with rows of windows that faced the sea.

Smith Tavern.

It was to Billingsgate what Higgins Tavern was to Eastham proper. Yet Smith's establishment was more secluded and wild. It was home to whalers, fishermen and others who liked the fact that the island lay off shore of Eastham, a little farther out of reach of the strict laws of the land.

Billingsgate had been purchased with things such as metal pots and knives. They were goods that seemed a rare prize to the sachems of old, who had signed away the rights to the land, years ago. Julian knew that to the whites, it was the same as giving away rocks from the beach as payment. They had so many of such pots and knives that it was no loss to them. In their ignorance the sachems thought that accepting such gifts was no loss to the tribe either. Only when they saw the buildings going up did they understand what the whites meant with their pieces of paper, their deeds. By then it was too late. There were too many of the settlers, and the land was lost.

He tried to push such thoughts away as he paddled.

In front of him the long sandy end of Great Island pointed like a great tooth. He paddled past the tip of the island and then along the island's eastern shore, which was a curving stretch of sand with hilly terrain behind it.

In the distance he saw the huge black object buried in the sand. At first he thought it was a rock. But his gut said otherwise. It would not be unlikely for a particularly rough storm or a high moon tide to unearth a large boulder that added new texture to the flat beach. But there had never been a rock of this size in this spot before.

It had to be a whale.

Here was a creature that would bring great profit to him if he could reach it first.

He picked up speed, glancing to and fro as he paddled, to see if anyone else was in the vicinity. He was still several hundred yards away, and the path to Smith Tavern came down to the beach much closer to the carcass than he was now. Surely, someone on the cliff had seen the beast and was on their way to claim it.

But there was no sign of anyone else when Julian's canoe slid onto the beach. He leapt out and ran towards the great dark shape on the shore.

It lay half buried in the sand. It was a little longer than a man and as black as the deepest part of the night. The white men called it a *blackfish*. To the whites, the little whale was a predictable fool that beached itself throughout the year, particularly after storms, and provided easy food and oil. Julian knew that it was one of the oldest and wisest creatures in the sea. They had once been part of the land, some of the old legends said, and they wanted only to return home. That sentiment was one that he could not help but consider noble.

There was a smile on the creature's face that was man-like. To look at it, grinning happily in death, was to think again of its intelligence and satisfaction that it had reached the ground that it had apparently been seeking. That death had greeted it when it had reached its goal could have been regarded as an omen. Julian laid an ear to the smiling mouth of the creature and listened for a moment to hear if it had anything to say on the matter. However, the creature said nothing, so Julian set about carving his initials, "J. J.," upon its rump.

A man's name written in a blackfish's flesh set a claim on the body, according to the custom of the area. If a blackfish washed up in the tide, the first man to reach it received all of the benefits of the beast. That was the tradition of the English. Julian's own people would have shared the animal with the tribe. Its appearance would have been regarded as a gift for all of the people and cause for a communal celebration. But the tribe no longer lived on the island, and now the English made the rules. So Julian made his mark and thanked the beast with a prayer, in the ancient way, looking forward to the modern coin that it would provide him.

He looked up towards the tavern on the bluff above him. There the whale men watched the great bay for signs of spouts, then raced to the whaleboats that lined the shore below the cliff and went out to herd in the groups of blackfish that came in close to the beach. In the old days men waited for the fish to come to them. The whale men had no such patience. In a strange way Julian could relate to their need. After all, working for Smith paid good coin for the catch. Although the rough whale men did not look it, they were some of the better off of their fellows, far better paid than the farmers or sailors of town. Julian often went with them, his skill with a harpoon outweighing any judgment the white men might have about his heritage.

At the moment, there were no boats out on the bay although Julian could see men stationed along the ridge of the island, at various intervals, standing on the platforms from which they scanned the waves for signs of the blackfish. Some were Smith's men, others were not. Many white men claimed ownership over parts of the island. Each one set up a little lookout shack and cut down the woods behind him, to keep his fires going. They all fought over who should own the land and stubbornly clung to a piece of it, ignoring their neighbors' claims. In that way, they ended up sharing the place like Julian's tribe had, although not in the same manner of friendship.

"Hey! What is it you're doing?" came a shout from the hill behind Julian. He turned and saw a middle-aged Englishman running towards him. The man had come down from one of the shacks in the distance. Julian did not know his name. The man's carving knife and long handled blade, meant for cutting the blubber of the whale, were held in such a way as to discourage friendly introductions.

"That's not your whale, Indian."

Julian pointed to the initials on the hide of the beast, but the man shook his head and stepped towards the beached animal.

"This don't mean anything anymore. See that hut up yonder? All of this is my land, down to the water itself. You are standing on my property right now. It is only by my good graces that I was letting you pass. But I won't let you take this prize with you."

"I found it first," Julian said, pointing again to his mark.

"I saw it first, and because it is my land, I can come down and claim it whenever I choose! What you are doing is stealing! The penalty for theft is a good long spell in the pillory," the man went on. "For an Indian, it could be worse."

"That is not the way. The man who marks it gets it." Julian watched the knife out of the corner of his eye. One hand rested on the nub of his own blade. His muscles tensed to draw it although he knew that once he did, everything would change forever.

"When I was a child, I would stand on that spot where you have your hut and watch the whales. When we found one such as this, everyone in the tribe would come down to pull it out of the water," Julian said through clenched teeth.

"I don't care about your childhood, Indian. What you are doing is a crime. That's what the law of this land says!"

"Whoever marks the whale, it is his. That is *your* way," Julian persisted.

"I own this land," the man said flatly. Although the man's face was lined and worn with much living, Julian saw no wisdom in it. In the man's bloodshot eyes, there was no indication that he comprehended that the land owns men and not the other way around. The land can live on without men upon it, and yet men are lost without ground to hold them up.

Julian bent down and scooped a handful of sand. He flashed it in front of the Englishman's face and then heaved it into the water. "Is that still your land?" he asked.

Then he pointed to the tail of the blackfish that swayed with the motion of the tide. "The tail is in the water. Do you own all of that too? All the way as far as you can see?" Julian demanded, pointing out towards the horizon.

"You fancy yourself a clever one, eh?" the man said. He took a step forward.

It did not surprise Julian that it would not be a fair fight. The man turned and whistled towards the shack, and when three other Englishmen came out of the structure, he waved them over.

"Perhaps we can teach you the meaning of ownership," he smirked.

Just then another cry came from farther up the beach. Julian and his adversary both turned to see a small compact man racing along the sand towards them, leading a large party of whale men. His gray bearded face was lean, cunning, sharp featured and handsome in its way. He was nearly fifty, but he looked much older, from all of the toil that he put himself through. One could not keep the respect of a tavern full of whale men without keeping up with them, which Samuel Smith did admirably.

At one time Smith had claimed the entire island. But he had yet to produce a valid deed for his claim, and so interlopers had steadily moved in, muddling the claims of ownership. Four years ago the town of Eastham had officially carved up the island into lots and granted them to certain influential residents. None of those people had yet established any presence on the island. So the squatters continued to draw lines in the sand. Smith employed the majority of the men on the island. Buoyed by his greater numbers, Smith strode across the flats, with a kingly air, waving aside the other white man as if he was a bothersome gnat.

"Smalley! What are you up to? You had better not be aiming to take that blackfish! It's mine, as you well know!"

"The hell it is, Smith! Look! My hut is directly in line with it!"

Instead of responding, Smith motioned his men over towards the whale. Smalley's men, sorely outnumbered, backed off towards their cabin, leaving their leader standing red faced, in ankle deep water, and shaking his weapon futilely in the air.

"Go to hell! You move the lines whenever it benefits you! I have my deed from the original proprietors who bought the land from the Indians. It is all verified by the Barnstable court, for God's sake! I showed it to the selectmen, two years ago!" Smalley shouted.

"I have a deed from the sachem of the Punonakanits himself, and I have been here the longest on this land!"

"Then where is that deed now?"

"I gave it to the selectmen, many years ago! Ain't my fault they lost it! But plenty know that I had it! At a certain point, there must be agreement about these things! Will deeds be honored or not? If they are not, then we are no better than a pack of barbarians! You all are but vultures! But my bones ain't ready to be picked over yet! There is not going to be any meal for you scavengers in my lifetime!" Smith fumed.

"If you had a deed, then it had to have been witnessed. Who witnessed yours?"

"Obadiah Paine and Ralph Higgins."

"Oh! Convenient that they are both dead, so we cannot test their memories!"

"It's a damned nuisance that they are dead!"

"You have no deed! You have been squatting on this land ever since you got here. I bought mine fair and square from the old proprietors. My deed shows that without question," Smalley said, his eyes flicking angrily towards the activity that was going on next to him.

While Smith and Smalley talked, Smith's men carved out long strips of flesh from the whale. They quickly stripped the beast and then began carrying it away in buckets and wooden trays.

Smith dropped his voice to a whisper, "*These damned selectmen divided this place up among them and their friends, and neither your name nor mine was on their list of who's to get this island. It is only because they are afraid of us that we are still here. Perhaps we ought to stick together...*"

"I don't care what the selectmen say! I made a deal with the proprietors, and I can prove it! I've built a home here, and they ain't taking it! You're just trying to weasel me out of my share is all you're doing!"

Smalley's outburst was met with a shrug as Smith turned and marched away with his men. Smalley followed, snapping at the tavern keeper like a barking dog.

Julian sighed and looked at the bones of his blackfish. It seemed unlikely that he would see any of it now.

When they reached the tavern, they saw a sheet of paper on the door, fluttering in the breeze. Smalley pointed towards it and gave a triumphant cry. "We'll know soon enough what the freemen of town think of who owns what! Town meeting is at the end of August. That will settle the land division of this island once and for all! Everything is written there on the warrant!"

"That paper did not get my permission to be on that door! Justice Doane must have snuck it in!" Smith grumbled. He looked around at his men as if he expected to observe guilt on one of their faces for letting the town meeting warrant get pinned there.

"Nor did that door receive any sanction to be on this land," Smalley chided as he headed back down to the beach, moving as fast as he could without making a scene of it. There was enough pride and annoyance for a brawl, but it would not start until Smalley had found a few more supporters.

While he was listening to the men talk, Julian wandered over to the piece of paper on the door. Long strings of symbols filled its face, and Julian could make no sense of it except here and there where he recognized his own initial mixed in with many more indiscernible ones.

He felt a firm hand on his back. Smith was suddenly behind him. "The bastard is gone. Damn his insolence for thinking he can paper my establishment with his lies! I bet he, not the justice, put it up there," he said and went to rip the notice off of the door.

Julian let out an involuntary gasp.

"What's the matter? You can read this?"

Julian shook his head.

Smith chuckled. "Aye! 'Course you can't! What would be the harm in leaving it? It won't mean much to anyone else here neither. Smalley and his foolishness. Every whaler is going to ask me to tell them what this nonsense says. Don't worry about it, Julian. I got the paper that is more important! You know what a deed is?"

Julian nodded. He knew well what a deed was and had even seen its power too. He had seen the one that had taken away this very land from his people when he was a child. The sachem had carried it in his belt, delighting in taking it out to show other tribe members the beautiful design of the words. When he tired of it, the sachem burned it, under a fire, as kindling. But the English had another copy that, enforced with guns and pikes, demonstrated to the tribe the hidden power of paper. It was the only way to get the land back now.

"You found that blackfish out yonder?" Smith went on.

Julian bobbed his head again.

"I thought we agreed that your whaling is supposed to be done through me. If you want to keep the full share, then you'll have to eat the whole damn thing yourself or find someone else to boil the blubber because I won't let you use my vats for your own work. But if you work as my man, then we have something. You need my coin, and I need your lance."

"You have the whale now. It does not matter," Julian said.

"You were going to bring it to my attention, I assume?"

"Yes," Julian said. Then after a moment he added, "The land is still for sale?"

"Of course."

"What about that paper?" he pointed to the town meeting notice on the door.

"Don't you worry about that. Now get up on the viewing platform and find me some whales. If there is one, there is bound to be more. You're my eyes, John Julian."

Julian did not respond. For a moment he had no wish to claim the name that Smith called him. He had always been John Julian to the whites because his father had given him and his siblings Christian names as a sign of peace with the newcomers. It was the same mistake that his tribe's leaders had made since the arrival of the first whites. It was something that he would have to talk about if he finally met his father's spirit.

Julian called himself the white man's name and had been called it so often over the years that he had come to think of himself that way even though it was a false shadow version of his real name: *Ontoquos*. The wolf. At the time of his birth, there had been many signs of wolf medicine surrounding him. It was his birth animal and his protector. He had long suspected that his aunt had much to do with that.

Few knew his real name anymore, let alone addressed him by it. Most natives kept their real names hidden and spoke of them, even to each other, only in whispers.

Bitterly, Julian realized that his whole life's dealings with white men had been a similar kind of guessing game.

✠ ✠ ✠ ✠

It was too early in the season for any but the stray whale that washed up here or there. Julian stayed at Smith Tavern for several nights, watching the dimpled waters, taking an ale with his supper and adding his own output to the pipe smoke that was festooned along the upper rafters of the building. But he did not sleep in the large common room on the second story where the whale men laid in cots. Each night he slipped off into the darkness and prowled the fringe lands of Billingsgate.

There was still much forest there. The English houses were not as thick as they were in Eastham. He could follow deer paths through the woods and almost feel like it was the old days. When he grew tired, he dropped down where he was and slumbered, like there was nothing out there that could do him harm, in the cradling arms of the old world.

One night he slept on the jut of mainland across from Great Island, called Indian Neck by the whites. There the last handful of Punonakanits lived on land given to them by the English. Julian could see their *wetus* in the distance, but he did not go to them. They were content to stay put on this tiny spit of land as if it was truly a gift from the whites rather than their ancient native soil. He would not go to them again until he had the deed for Great Island in hand. Then he would make them choose whether they wished to live in freedom or in bondage to the white men.

In the orange glow of evening, he studied the silhouette of his homeland from this vantage across the water and tried to ignore the blemish of the pointed tip of the tavern. He let his breathing steady until it came in and out of him like a tide. He felt the pressure in his belly from his supper of clams and fish burned over a fire on the shore. He watched the seagulls dance along the flats, their wings keeping them suspended above the ground as if they were too proud to touch the mud, but for their tippy-toes. The sight gave him a vision of his own stance upon the land, just barely feeling it under foot, like he was floating away from it.

Sleep came upon him, with the sound of tree frogs echoing in the stand of woods nearby. He thought of their meaning as his mind drifted away. The frog's song often brought a cleansing rain, to wash away bad spirits and revive the harvest. Tonight the song was deafening, and he felt a smile upon his lips as he lost consciousness. It had rained and rained and rained these past weeks. The white preacher had hollered that it was a return to the days when the ancestors of the English had to build a giant boat to get themselves and their animals away from their sinking land, but Julian knew it was really the call of the frogs.

In the morning he awoke to another message from the animals.

At first he thought it was simply scratch marks from him scurrying around the fire, making last night's supper. Then he saw a distinct four dimpled print with a sharp claw point on each tip.

Wolf...

The tracks ringed the spent coals as if the wolf had been inspecting the remains of Julian's supper.

180

Julian shivered in the weak light of dawn. The trees that had, last night, clamored so loudly with the song of hope now had a dark cast. For a moment he feared to go into them.

But he followed the prints through the woods and back to the beach, until they disappeared into the rising tide. The flats were being rapidly covered with a quick moving blanket of surf. Julian could mark the trajectory in his mind, and if the animal held its course, it was headed for Great Island.

The notion sent a thrill through him. In part it was because he had not seen a wolf since his childhood but, more importantly, it was because of the deeper meaning.

Was the medicine woman still alive, he wondered?

☩ ☩ ☩ ☩

The next morning Julian again woke up on Indian Neck and found wolf tracks. The tracks went into the woods, veering off through dense bramble that Julian had not penetrated during his last tour of the area. He pushed his way through the tearing briars, growing more and more convinced that this was not a beast of the waking world. What animal, even as strong as a wolf, could break through such a thicket without the aid of tools like the stick and knife that Julian employed?

The tracks continued on until they reached a small clearing. There he saw the rotting footings of an old *wetu*. Only blackened stumps stood out from the ground, like the sight of the old medicine woman's stumped teeth from the last that he remembered of them. The rest of the structure had been destroyed. In the middle of the ruin was a pile of stones, ceremonially stacked in the fashion of a Punonakanit or Nauset grave.

He walked right up to the structure and his foot kicked something and sent it rattling away into the surrounding bushes. When he retrieved it, he saw that it was a necklace fashioned of animal teeth, the full bite of a wolf, strung together with thick twine.

So she is dead then, he thought.

He hung the wolf necklace on his belt, for he felt sure that the beast that he was tracking had led him here so he would find his aunt's old necklace. Then he knelt at her grave and muttered a prayer over it. Who or what had destroyed her home, who had buried her and other such questions begged for answers, but Julian had none. However, he knew that, even from the grave, she still had power and servants.

With that thought, he looked around for any sign of the wolf and found none. So he hurried back to the beach, the necklace nipping at his leg as he ran.

Back at the beach he stared at the stretch of sand flats, and the memories came surging back to him. He could see himself with the children of his youth, his playmates, running on the open sand. His parents were still alive. His friends were still growing as if they meant to inhabit the old ways, not turn towards the white man's world. An already old looking woman with startling green eyes, the kind that no other native but his father had, was watching the children play.

Mittawa was her name. His aunt. The medicine woman.

"Come here little one," the old woman said.

Around him the seagulls flew, and he aimed rocks at them, hoping to bring one down. His arm was stronger than most and his throws as accurate as any other young brave. He had the small pile of dead birds to prove it. He thought of the pride that would be in his mother's face when she saw that her young warrior had brought home dinner.

When Julian looked at his aunt, he assumed that she too was about to praise him. He knew that she had been watching him all morning, and when she grabbed his arm and squeezed it, he tightened his muscle to show her how strong he was.

"It is good that you do not miss very often," she said.

"Sometimes I can hit five or six birds in a row, without a single miss," he told her.

"What about the one miss after that? That could be the most important throw of all," she replied.

He looked at her, not sure of her meaning. "But there would be five birds on the ground. That is plenty to feed our *wetu*," he protested.

She laughed, baring soot colored teeth. She was always laughing at times when he could not find anything funny. He smiled as he always did. Aunt Mittawa was good to him. She gave him strange rocks and bones unlike any that he was able to find on his own. Sometimes she made necklaces out of them that she told him would make him feel stronger. They worked too. Other children, even adults, were afraid of her because of her wild green eyes. But he felt sure that the others secretly envied him. For him, she took away as much fear as she gave because she was a powerful medicine woman, and she was his aunt.

"Now they are birds. Someday they may be something else," she cackled.

"How could they be anything but a bird," he asked.

"Because everything can be something else other than it seems to the eyes!" she replied, flashing her own wild orbs at him. "Take a fish, for example. When you find one in your net, you think of filling your belly. But what if you find one on top of your *wetu*? What do you think then?"

Now he laughed and as so often happened, she did not, leaving him as confused as ever about when she was jesting.

"I would think that someone had thrown it there," he replied.

"No. The rain brought it down," she told him.

He knew not to laugh this time. Nearby, a huge flock of gulls dropped onto the mud flats, stupidly drawn to investigate the death of the others. Julian's friends hid in the marsh grass, taking aim, and he longed to be with them.

"I do not understand," he sighed. This was the bad part of having a medicine woman for kin. None of the other children ever got such questions. He answered them dutifully, rarely giving her the answer she was expecting and then forgot her responses as soon as she had strode away. When he was older, he wished he could remember a fraction of the wisdom that she bestowed upon him. Sometimes he felt that he was spending his whole life searching for the answers that she had given him long ago.

"The fish might have been left there by a spirit as a warning. When a fish is alive, his purpose to the fisherman is for dinner. When a fish is on the fisherman's roof, the fish is no longer a fish, but a sign that the man might die in the next storm if he goes out fishing."

"Do you see a fish for me?" the boy breathed, for he loved fishing, particularly paddling out almost out of sight of the village, to where the calm waters of the harbor met the rougher whitecaps that the big fish loved to play in.

"Not a fish. Something bigger," she said. "Listen to me and understand what few men do: a vision always carries within it the clue to avoid its peril. I see a great big fish in your future. A beast with white flesh. There is a man too who is mistaken for a fish. He is more dangerous than the creature although he looks far less fearsome. One day they might come, and you might find the land that you love sliding out of your grasp, like a slippery fish in the water. If they come, you might be lost to the land forever. Look inside for the clue to avoid this fate and save the land..."

He was too scared to ask any questions when she finished her pronouncement. Nor was he ever able to bring himself to question her again about it. He knew that Mittawa did not repeat her predictions twice.

He did not hunt seagulls anymore that day. He did not take his canoe out to his cherished spot either. He went to look for his mother, hoping she was doing something comforting, like pounding corn, something to take the fish and swimming green eyes out of his mind. But when he got back to the village, he found that her hut was closed, and he could hear her screaming inside. A thick forearm blocked him from tearing through the curtain to reach her. The man, his father's friend, pulled him tight, like he was a son, bent to his ear and said, "Give your mother time, Ontoquos. She has lost a husband."

The arm squeezed tighter, the words softer, "Never forget that your father was a good man. He died nobly, and he loved you!"

He could not break free although he tried.

"*Shhh, shhh...*" He heard in his ear, soft and wind-like, until it took on the gentle tone of his father's own voice. Gradually, his strength slipped away from him, and he slumped into the man's embrace, his own voice surprising him as it came rushing out to join the wail of his mother's.

"He loved you," the man said. *I loved you,* John Julian heard. For some reason he thought of the seagulls, such a stupid thing, and the fact that his father would never see how good he had done. Then he thought of fish, of Mittawa, whose eyes were the same as his father's, and of her words. Through his tears he prayed to the gods, all of them, and asked that his father's spirit might return to him as a fish.

That memory gave him comfort as he grew older although he was careful not to let anyone see how he murmured to each fish that he caught and then held to his ear, pretending that he was weighing it, but really listening for his father's words to tell him that he loved him.

Sometimes he found it surprising that he could still eat fish at all. Sometimes he had an awful fear that he might find his father fish and eat it while his father's spirit was sleeping inside. So he never ate a fish right away, but gave each time enough to say what it would. So far none had uttered a single word that he recognized, but he had not given up hope. Enough visions had come true that he was sure of their awesome power. Therefore, prayers too must come true. He felt certain that any man who was under the shadow of some omen also had a prayer or two that could save him. Who better to rescue him than his father, he asked himself?

Chapter Two
"A Land Without Mercy"

Justice Doane stood in the middle of the town's practice field, feeling that his hold on law and order was slipping through his fingers. At the moment, those fingers were encased in thick leather riding gloves, which he raised in a salute that the ragtag band before him barely approximated.

Ten of the native members of the militia were arranged in front of him, attempting to hold their line for the duration of his inspection. Another ten stared this way and that, seemingly more interested in watching cloud formations than preparing for the day their homes and kin might come under enemy attack.

Doane's voice was hoarse from yelling, a verbal bombardment that was much amplified thanks to the stress that these desperate times were causing him. Now he could do nothing but whisper and listen to his second-in-command, Lieutenant Cole, put the men through the drill.

All in all, the natives were not bad as fighting men. Doane admonished himself not to expect too much from them. It would be like faulting children for their youth. English guns, discipline and strategy were so new to these people, it was no wonder that they treated such things like fascinating toys and then, with the attention of babes, soon let their minds wander. The Nausets could not hold formation as well as the white men because it was not in their nature. His father had known this. The committee that insisted on separate places for the native villagers knew it too. It was also not the natives' nature to care about the land. In fact, they had so little regard for it that their chiefs had given it away for mere copper kettles and knives.

Doane did not consider the natives as upraised as Reverend Treat did. It was true that they had embraced the Lord, but he did not believe that they understood His word any better than they did fighting in regiment formation. We are defended by children, he thought.

Defended from what, he asked himself, for the hundredth time? Logic and rationality left little room for the existence of witches and superstition. But the Devil was another matter. Most devilry so obviously came from the hearts and hands of men. Doane saw that reconfirmed over and over in his line of work when he witnessed how greed, jealousy and general pettiness sometimes exploded into confrontation and crime. Did any of it prove that there was a supreme agent of evil behind such acts, pulling the strings and setting the men who committed such deeds into motion? His mind said no, but his lifetime of church training made it continue to be a tricky question. Stick to the law, he told himself. His job was not to gather in the lost flock or determine the reason that some strayed, but merely to punish those that did.

Across from the practice field was the meeting house and the newly mended pillory, which already had its first occupant.

John Julian was one of the few natives who stubbornly clung to his heathenism. It was fitting that he should be the one to christen the improved device.

"You have not once shown up to practice with the militia even though you are of age to fight. You will only attend in bondage, is that right?" Doane called over to him at one point.

"I have not once come to church either," Julian said with a shrug.

Doane gave the prisoner an impatient wave in response, his sore throat burning too much for further speaking.

Before he turned away Julian called out, "A man cannot vote in your town unless he owns land. Yet those who have no land pledge their lives to save the land of others. For this, they still have no say in Eastham." He nodded towards the men practicing in the field.

"It is everyone's duty to defend Eastham!" Doane snapped.

"My father died fighting in this *militia*," Julian said, spitting out the word.

"You should look up to him, then. He was an honorable man for defending his town."

"But there was no war. He was training, like those men in the field, and a gun went off and it killed him."

"That is sad, but accidents do happen on occasion," Doane replied in a softer tone.

"I do not understand why he was made to practice with guns when this town was a place of peace. There was no one attacking this land."

"He was preventing any future threat. That is the same as defending this town."

There was a pause, and Doane was about to turn away from the native. Then Julian cried out in an angry voice, "Can anyone buy land in this town?"

Doane snorted. "How could one such as you afford land?"

Julian glared. "There is no law against it?"

"There is only one law that prohibits it and that is the law of nature. Your people were not good stewards of the land. That is why things are as they are today," Doane said.

Julian burned to say more in return, but he held his tongue. He would have plenty to say when he had the deed in hand.

✠ ✠ ✠ ✠

Julian was left in the pillory all night, and for the first time he trembled as twilight's long, shadowy fingers reached out of the surrounding woods for him. He feared what else might come creeping out of the darkness. Experimentally, he pushed his hands as far as he could through the holes in the pillory, but his scrabbling fingers still clawed uselessly in the air, and his wrists ached more than ever. Should anything ill come upon him, he had not the range of motion even to clasp his hands together in Christian prayer.

That thought brought a bitter laugh from his lips, but it was the sole bit of levity he felt until the sun rose over the tree tops and one of Doane's deputies came riding down the road, with the keys to the pillory in hand.

An hour later Julian was out on the flats in front of his people's village at the edge of Nauset Marsh in Eastham.

He was walking towards his fish weir.

The recent storm had cut right through the barrier beach, leaving a new mouth through the dunes that was only slowly filling back with sand. The wind - the breath of the sea spirit *Paumpagussit* - had come in fast and howling.

The storm left strange things in the mud, like pieces of metal, shards of wood and bits of line. He picked up a piece of round glass, looked at it and was amazed to see his own face staring back at him so clearly that he could see the wrinkles in his skin, the deep eyes that he liked and the pointy nose, like a white man's, that he didn't.

Beneath the sunlit water were stones, some of which glittered bright blue, green or white. His hand fished for them, pulling up the ones that caught his eye, only to see them as craggy, luster-less things when he had them in his palm. Around him the tide had fallen, leaving an imprint of the rushing waves on the sandy flats. All manner of birds worked the shoreline, in the same way as Julian, looking for things stranded by the tide. For old times' sake, he cast a stone at one of the gulls but missed by a wide margin.

Ahead of him were two children who were no more than ten summers each, by the look of their scrawny limbs. They were playing in the sand, building some kind of hut out of mud and sticks that they had found. It looked like the foundation of a white man's building, Julian thought distastefully.

When they looked up at him, their faces stretched taut with surprise and trepidation. Julian knew that he was an impressive, but scary, figure to the young of his tribe. He tried to imagine what he looked like, his shoulders stiff with purpose and his face hard, like a warrior of old. He remembered seeing such men in his own youth and thinking only to emulate them. These young ones looked as though they would be scared off if he said the wrong word.

"What do you build? A *wetu*? Have the elders told you the story of this water and land?" he asked, spreading his hands to encompass the breadth of the marshland, hills and beaches around them.

They shook their heads and Julian told them, "The Nausets have lived here from the beginning of time, when the world was made by the Great Spirit, *Keihtanit*. These hills around the bay were all empty of white people. There were no dwellings of the English. There were only wild grapes and corn fields and summer villages. In the winter the people went inland. During the summer they fished and swam and danced on these sands. They lived in harmony with everything around them. When the white *French* came here, right there at that ocean..." Julian pointed to the breakwater in the near distance, "...the Nausets saw that the whites were not friends, and they drove them away. They were a mighty people back then. Do you know this story?"

In his youth Julian would have responded if a brave had asked him the same question. His answer, of course, would have been *yes*, because he knew the old stories. The two boys, however, merely cupped their hands over their brows and peered through the sun's glare at him, like they could not identify what manner of creature they were seeing.

"What is this you build?" Julian asked, trying to keep the edge from his voice. Part of their structure was a square length of wood. White paint peeled from its edges. There were words written in black up to the point were a large, round splintered hole cut them off. Something had punched through at that spot, leaving only the following symbols: *J..o..s..e..p..h..i...* Julian did not know what they meant, other than they were white men's words from part of a white man's ship. Immediately he thought of the sailor.

"It is meant to be a meeting house, like the one in Potanumaquitt," one of the little ones responded. "These are the walls..." the child began explaining.

Before he could get any further, Julian grabbed the piece of wood, ripped it from the mud and flung it over the little ones' heads into the water. It splashed, went under the surface, then bobbed back up and drifted away, like it was heading for Julian's weir in the distance.

The children both sprang up and raced off across the flats, towards a canoe that was pulled up on the tip of the flat. Julian did not have a chance to explain to them why their creation had angered him so.

He sloshed through the shallows to his weir. The water came only to his thighs this time.

One fish circled fearfully in the corner, unable to fight through the rushing tide back to open water.

He pulled it carefully from the water and put its clacking lips to his ear but heard nothing.

Then he paddled home, unable to enjoy any of the beauty around him because the scene of the terror of the boys kept appearing over and over in his head. *They fear me,* he thought with dismay.

Julian had taken to wearing his aunt's wolf tooth necklace. None of the whites knew its meaning. The few elders of his tribe that did hurried by him on the village paths as if he had turned into a wolf himself. Some had the audacity to cross themselves as they passed. One old man, Charlie Sea Eagle, stopped him with a restraining hand.

"Wolf is from the dark tribe of night," he said as if Julian was ignorant of that fact.

"The wolf of Mittawa is back."

Charlie acted as if he did not hear the words. "The wolf feeds off of shadows. Wear a wolf's tooth on your chest, and your own heart could fill with darkness."

"I wear it to block the darkness. The wolf is also strength and cunning. That is the other part of its medicine. Have you forgotten?"

Dim, myopic eyes seemed to search for Julian's own. The weakness of the glance made Julian's fists clench. He almost told the old man that the wolf's teeth also spoke to him of battle, but even if Charlie understood, he would do nothing with the information but go and tell Justice Doane. Wolves hunted best in packs, and Julian was a man without a tribe. He could not think of anyone who would answer his call were he to follow the advice that the wolf's teeth growled in his ear. At the same time it was dangerous advice. He was close to getting the land back. When he did, he was sure that men like Charlie would see sense again. If he lashed out and was struck down, then he would have nothing. He rubbed the teeth between two fingers, to make sure that he was not mistaken. If they were in fact raccoon teeth, then he would be under the influence of trickster medicine. But his touch was sure. This was the bite of a wolf. The teeth were big. The bone was hard with strength.

"I was paid three pounds per head to hunt wolves when I was younger," Charlie diverted. Julian could not tell if he was changing the conversation on purpose or not. He wondered if Charlie had killed Mittawa's wolf, the tame animal that served as her pet and messenger. That was impossible, he told himself. He had seen the tracks even though it was common belief that all of the great wolves were gone.

"How much are they worth now? I have seen a wolf in the Punonakanit lands. What do I get if I kill it?" Julian said.

"Let me think! Let me think!" Charlie gushed. But Julian turned and strode away, leaving the old fool staring up into the sky, puzzling out the price of bounty on his fingers.

Julian needed time alone. He was tired of the limited thinking of the English and Nausets alike. The whites' views were like a net thrown over the world and the Nausets' a cage that his people had willingly locked themselves into.

He pushed through the deerskin flap of a small *wetu* at the edge of the village, close to the waterline. This was his place although he rarely slept in it, with all of the time that he spent with the whaling men. Most of the time, he took his rest outdoors anyway. A storm would drive him to this shelter, but he took little comfort in the place. Its construction was the same wood and bark design that he remembered from childhood. But anything with walls these days reminded him of being shackled, and he rubbed his neck where the memory of the pain from the pillory flared to life, in response to his musing.

Fatigue clung to him, and for once he was happy for a place to lie down without interruption. It seemed that his days were spent in motion, from the fish weir to the whale lookout to the old lands and everywhere in between. The thought of the omen kept him moving as if, deep inside, his spirit was urging him to run and stay ahead of its purpose. Yet he could not fight off sleep at the moment.

As he drifted away, he thought of Mittawa's words… *the great white fish… the man who comes as a fish… loss of land…*It seemed to be no accident that these words and the wolf were resurfacing right when he was on the verge of reclaiming the old lands. Perhaps they were a boon to him. The great beast had been burned and reclaimed by the tide, its final presence no more threatening than a tiny skate carcass washed up on the sand. The man was still in town. Julian had heard his voice coming through the window of Higgins Tavern. He had even seen him walking along the roads of town. His purpose too seemed nothing dangerous. Yet Julian could not shake a feeling that their destinies were somehow tied. Suddenly he realized that he kept moving as to not cross paths with the sailor. He did not want to risk meeting that man from the sea again. He was not sure of that destiny. Not yet. He needed more signs.

✠ ✠ ✠ ✠

Several nights later Julian looked out into the bay. A bright swath of silver ran out to the horizon where it met the rising moon. It looked like a great skunk's tail.

Off in the distance he could see the fires lit at Helltown, the settlement at the farthest tip of Cape Cod, and the glowing spars of the ship that had been sitting there all day. Knowing the town as he did, he had no trouble guessing the kind of business the vessel was there for. Because there was little law in the remote village, pirates and smugglers made it their home, along with any number of seedy rum peddlers, prostitutes and gamblers, each with a particular brand of skill that justified the moniker of the place. French pirates particularly liked Helltown. They enjoyed the irony of encamping on a spit of English territory to do business with the colonists, defying English law, which prohibited direct trade between English subjects and other Europeans. The pirates had little care for such declarations and neither did some Cape Codders, like Samuel Smith, who felt that a government that was across the sea had little understanding or sympathy for the hard living that had to be done on this peninsula. Men like Smith resented the marked up prices that were the result of England's monopoly on trade. So the pirates were a welcome sight, particularly when the blackfish were not running. It was the underside of Smith's activities, one that was to his whaling as night is to day.

Julian did not care whether he earned his coin in the light of the sun or the moon. Men like Justice Doane found more virtue in the day but only because such men could not see anything that was not right in front of their faces. Smith was the one who paid Julian his coin. It was also Smith who would sell him his land. Then he would have the deed, and that was all of English law that he cared to know. If Doane caught them, they would all suffer and all could be lost. But within the windy clutches of darkness, he did not worry about Doane.

Other than the risk to his land, Julian felt no qualms as he sat in the bow and listened to the chatter between Smith and the shadowy men in a small sloop alongside of Smith's own two craft. One boat held four of Smith's whale men. The other contained Smith, Julian and enough space for the illegal wares that Smith was purchasing and would soon be selling to his customers from Eastham.

The voices from the sloop were haughty and accented. Frenchmen. Pirates. Julian felt the tension between them and Smith's men. He felt none of it himself as he calmly gazed into the murky horizon, thinking that the clamor of voices was a squawk similar to a pack of blue jays squabbling.

His job was to keep a lookout for the navy warships that occasionally cruised the coast, sniffing for such clandestine trade as this. Everyone had stories of the great men-o-war appearing like silent, dark mountains out of the gloom, but Julian had never seen one and felt no fear from the tales. Shore was only a short one hundred yard swim away. Once on dry land, in the dark and following the ancient footpaths of his people, no navy man had a chance to find him.

"This is robbery, Smith! There are ten barrels of wine, alone! Then there is the iron and the silk!" a voice snarled.

"Robbery? *Robbery?*" Smith mocked. Around him, men laughed - his own crew first and then even some of the Frenchmen, for reasons of their own.

"Even among thieves, there must be some honor!" the Frenchman replied.

"I do not go back on my word!" Smith replied. "Last week the price was five hundred pounds!"

Julian balked at the amount. It was enough to buy the entire acreage of Great Island. But the French pirates were not convinced by Smith's argument.

"Now there is much more cargo that you are receiving! Six hundred!"

The bickering continued, making all of the men observing in the boats grow restive. It was the kind of noise that always accompanied such negotiations.

Then Julian heard a different sound: a cold click of metal, echoing across the water.

"What the Devil are you doing?" Smith roared.

"We do not give these things away for free, old man!"

"Without me, who will you sell to?"

Another metal scrape resounded, which Julian was sure was a blade being drawn by someone on the French sloop. Instinctively, his muscles tightened.

"Pay us! You already promised this!" the Frenchman shouted.

"Damn you! Damn you! Damn you! I'll not be treated this way!" Smith cried.

There was a sudden commotion. Julian saw two dark forms leap into the boat, between him and Smith. One Frenchman scampered around behind Smith and locked Smith's head between his forearm and a dull, glowing sword. The other pointed a gun into the darkness as he peered around, looking for Julian himself.

Before the Frenchmen could speak a word, Julian was among them. He pulled back the arm of the man nearest to him and felt a rush of wind blow by his ear as the gun discharged.

Then he peered into the startled face of the man and pointed his knife between the man's eyes. He already knew that his captive was the leader of the pirate band, their chief negotiator. Most tribes strove to save their chief. Julian hoped that these pirates were the same way.

The pirate before him chortled and shrugged. "So I miss…" he joked.

"Get back to your boat," Julian ordered the other pirate, who held Smith. "Then I will let this one go too."

For a moment the pirate's blade quivered, and Julian feared that his command would be in vain. Then the man with the sword bared his teeth and stepped back over the side of the sloop onto his own boat. As he did, he flicked his blade, and Smith gasped and touched his fingers to his cheek.

"Bastard cut me on purpose!" Smith railed, dabbing a thin slice on his face where the departing pirate had left a bloody signature.

"This does not help the situation. We still have the problem of payment," the French pirate captain said. He was talking to Julian now. Julian could not help but feel a surge of pride in the position of power that his knife had put him.

"Five hundred and fifty," Julian declared.

Both Smith and the pirate exhaled in disgust.

"Half what you want, half what he wants," Julian explained. He pressed the knife harder against the pirate's nose, wondering if he should leave some mark there in revenge for Smith. Before he could decide, the pirate laughed again, heartier this time.

"Ah! Your secret weapon, Smith! Had we known you had a cannibal among your ranks, we would have compromised much earlier! Do not let him eat us, eh?"

Julian's blade flashed, and the pirate's eyes dipped out of focus for a second. But the crazy man kept grinning as the blood trickled down the length of his nose. A cut for a cut, Julian thought grimly.

"We will remember you, cannibal…" the Frenchman promised menacingly. Then he stepped quickly over the side of the boat. "Five-fifty!" he said.

The dispute was settled, and the crates were passed quickly from one ship to the other. Then the pirates glided away into the murky night.

"Five hundred and fifty! I only tolerate it because I have to keep the peace, to do business with them," Smith grumbled, but he did not sound that displeased. Nor did he offer any thanks for Julian's intervention.

The quiet night seemed poised to enfold them again. Then suddenly there was a flash from out in the water. A second later the water erupted in front of Smith's boat, throwing a plume of spray across Smith and Julian's faces.

"Shit! Those damned Papist swine!" Smith hollered.

Out in the dark they heard the sound of accented laughing.

A short while later there was a swish of oars that stopped a dozen yards from the boats. The smugglers eyed each other warily, unsure if the approaching vessel had slowed out of uncertainty or stealth.

"Who's there?" Smith shouted. Julian was sure that he heard a note of stress in the man's voice.

Smith shouted again and was answered by a cry that sounded youthful and timid, despite its attempt to be otherwise.

"*Knowles…*"

"Can't see ya? Is that Elder Knowles?"

A few oar strokes later, a small boat pulled into view, with two small shapes at the oars.

"Ah! The elder's sons!" Smith crowed.

"Abraham and Thomas," the older boy responded.

"What can I do for you two gentlemen? The same order as usual for your father? Snuff, silk and iron?"

The two boys nodded as one, and Smith looked like he could barely restrain himself from laughing.

Later, when they had hauled the boats back on shore in front of the tavern, Smith and Julian ended up side by side for a moment. Smith still did not offer any word of thanks, but Julian did not expect him to. He knew Smith to be an ornery man without much surface warmth. He was like a skunk in that way, emitting harsh defense to give himself space to live life his own way. But after what had happened, Julian felt that this might be a time of more acknowledgement between them.

"They took us by surprise. The next time we will be better armed," Julian said, in case Smith felt foolish at being taken so unprepared.

"What? No need. They are truly devils, but they would not have cut any of us down. They need us desperately if they are to sell any of their stolen wares. Now get the rest of these cases into the root cellar before Doane arrives. Unfortunately, he is not one of my regulars."

"I do not trust those French," Julian went on, determined to make some deeper connection with the man. After all, one day they would be neighbors and equals, and then their relationship could not be as it was now, with overtones of master and servant. On that day Julian would have no more need to make coin. The fish and the earth would sustain him.

"Nickerson! Rogers! Help Julian bring the crates in and be quick about it!"

Smith began to move ahead of Julian, but Julian strode to keep up with him. He felt anger rising, despite all he had just told himself about not minding Smith's prickly ways.

"The land…" he began.

"Not now, Julian. I must get this money safely away, before anyone gets their greedy eyes on it."

Julian nodded. At least there was that. Smith evidently trusted him enough to carry the money out in the open.

"I am almost at fifty pounds," Julian said.

"*Fifty pounds?*" Smith repeated, looking at Julian like he had stolen the money from him.

"Yes. The money I am saving to buy the north of the island," Julian said, impatience swelling again.

"You have fifty? You *kept* it all?"

Julian did not register the man's incredulous tone. "Ten more pounds and I will have sixty. By the end of the summer, I will be ready to pay. Have you found the deed?"

He peered at the man. There was a deed. He was sure of it. He had *seen* it as a child. Smith had it in his possession too. That he had to take more on faith. But he could feel the rightness of it in his bones. There would not be a building here if Smith's claim was not true. In Julian's experience, buildings did not go up without those official papers holding them up.

"The deed? Of course. I will have it when the time comes. *Sixty?* That's not far off the mark."

Julian's skin grew hot. "What is the price of the land? You said sixty last summer."

"I know...I know...but it is just that taxes have gone up, you see. And Doane has been fining me for anything he can think of. That land is my wife and my future. Should anything happen to me, Rebecca will need that money to live off. You would not want to see her turned out into the cold night air to sleep, would you?"

"What is the price?" Julian asked, keeping his voice steady.

"Oh...seventy. That's fair, I reckon. A few more runs such as this and you might have it by harvest time," he replied.

Then he hollered along the beach again, "Nickerson! Where the bloody hell are you? Them crates need moving right now!"

"I must go," he told Julian and then scurried up the path towards the tavern.

When he had gone, Julian kicked the sand. Every year the excuses had come out and the price had gone up. Sooner or later Julian would have enough coin that Smith could not refuse. He had seen the look in the man's eye when he was talking of money too many times to think otherwise. Yet the conversation left a bad smell in the air. *Skunk...* What a wretched, skulking creature it was, Julian thought.

✠ ✠ ✠ ✠

Over the next few days, Samuel Smith spent much of his time gazing out of the tavern's front window at the wide bay. Ever since the exchange with the French pirates, he squinted at every boat on the horizon, trying to discern if it was some launch from

Helltown. His own sloop stayed anchored off the inner shore of the island. The whaleboats were on the sand on the other side of the island, at the foot of the bay, flipped over from lack of need. The whale men wandered the shoreline, trying their hand at casting for bluefish and stripped bass, or sitting on empty barrels down by the try works to play cards, drink and wait. There might not be more whales this season, but there would be plenty of the other nocturnal work. Yet to John Julian's eyes, the old man seemed less sure of himself than ever.

Dusk slid across the beach as if propelled by the darkening waves of the bay. It was pooling in the corners of the tavern.

Rebecca Smith wiped her arm across the deep grooves of her forehead, pushing back a loose sprig of her fading copper colored hair. She stood at the table by the hearth, filleting fish and piling the meat on one side, the heads, tails and bones on the other. Julian watched her and wondered if she would throw away all of the gurry, in her ignorance of the wide range of uses it had to cure illness, fertilize crops and summon spirit energy. However, he did not intend to find out.

He could not spend too much time in the tavern. Like all of the English buildings, the boxy, closed space depressed him if he lingered too long. Why look out a window at a shore that could be much better seen and appreciated by stepping out into it, he thought? So he declined when Smith offered him an ale. The drink was not worth the loss of coin. Then he told them that he was leaving.

"You could sleep here tonight," Rebecca said.

Before Julian could reply, Smith growled, "He don't want that. Julian likes the open air! Ain't that right, Julian?"

"Surely it wouldn't kill you to lie on a bed for a night? The weather has been most foul and yet another rain comes. Don't you get tired of being soaked to your skin?" Rebecca asked Julian.

Julian nodded towards the tavern keeper. "I will go to the tip of…Great Island," he replied, stumbling on the name as he always did. In his childhood the place had no name because it had not needed one. Everyone knew it as the place where the tide wrapped around a spit of sand and the fish were thick and the forests full of deer. That was all that was needed to know.

"Fine. Suit yourself," Rebecca replied.

"I slept under the sky when I was a child. The ground feels as good a bed to me as those cots upstairs," he explained, smiling to show her that he recognized and valued her kindness.

"While you're out there, keep an eye open for any boat that might come creeping in," Smith told Julian.

"You think Justice Doane will come here at night? Has he got that kind of nerve nowadays?" Rebecca said.

"Not Doane. Them French pirates. I don't trust this lot. They're more unpredictable than the others I've dealt with. Mad, they are."

"You fought with them, Sam! No wonder they shot at you!" his wife said.

"I was haggling, woman! That is how it is done. They're the ones that made a fight of it! Ain't that right, Julian?"

Rebecca's hard eyes swung towards Julian, daring him to lend credence to her husband's claim, but Julian knew the truth of what Smith said, and he confirmed it.

"Perhaps Justice Doane should concentrate more on driving away the pirates than breathing down our necks. Seems a larger issue to me," Rebecca said.

"Why would you say such a thing? That would cut into half our profit! We need them pirates, since there's no whales this year!" Smith said, breaking off abruptly when he realized that he was about to start discussing his ledger books in front of Julian. "Well, Doane can do naught there anyhow. Old Helltown don't belong to no law but its own. The colony isn't rushing to clean it up. Besides, those French have been here longer than we have, probably one hundred and fifty years they've been coming to camp and fish on these shores. Great Island too. I wouldn't be surprised if *they* start flashing deeds around, one of these days!"

"I saw no French when I was a boy," Julian said.

"Really? You're probably related to one of them! Those Frenchies love Indian women."

"Leave him be, Sam. The man wants rest. He'll be up all night if you fill his head with more of your crazy notions," Rebecca said.

It was dark as Julian walked through the north woods of the island, but his feet knew the way and did not stumble upon any of the unseen roots or rocks. The night was cool and crisp, and a soft wind lamented the loss of the old ways as if it too was gradually losing the language of the earth.

Sure enough, Smith's words hung in Julian's mind as he watched the stars slowly inch across the night sky. He had known that other white men had come and gone from the land, long before the English settled here, but the thought of them coming year after year was something new. He felt certain that Smith had his story wrong. But he could not quite convince himself. Mittawa's green eyes kept flashing in his head. The eyes of his father, her brother, were the same color. *They love those Indian women...*

The wind made the summer air cool. Julian started a small fire to warm his bones. He did not care if the blaze alerted any skulking French pirates to where he was or if Smith took issue with his little beacon. When the fire was steady, he skewered an offering of fish and set it over the flame. It was a good strong bluefish, whose oily scent was like the scent of the sea itself. He danced around the blaze, chanting the old songs as he banged out a rhythm on two sticks that he had dug out of the brambles. He spun and danced and let his thoughts whirl out of his head as if the motion of his movement was flinging them out of his very skull. Soon he felt nothing but the stretch of his muscles and a pleasant hum in his brain. After a while he noticed a sensation at his back, the firm but unseen touch that told him that the spirits were joining him. Then they all danced together, and Julian let a single question dangle in his mind: *Tell me who I am...*

It was a big question, he knew. But he was sure that the spirits could answer it. When he was too dizzy, he fell to the ground and lay there, with his face pressed into the cool earth. At the same time the fire's heat ran along his leg like warm fur. He sensed the power of the wolf around him.

Mittawa...Aunt... Her presence was close.

His mind filled with her, a scene of color vivid enough to be a waking meeting. She had come from across the divide of the spirit world, and she was lurking in the woods around him, just outside of the fire.

"Mittawa..." he said aloud.

He got up and took a step into the trees, and he could feel her spirit floating away before him. He took another step and felt the woods close around them, the sensation bringing an unusual pang of fear. He wondered if she was luring him away from the fire for some devious purpose. After all, her motives had never been clear in this world, why would they have changed in the next, he mused?

The woods gave way to a meadow that stretched towards the tip of the island, where it met the water. Coming quickly out of the field was a pair of glowing green eyes that froze Julian in his tracks.

The eyes came towards him, and Julian pulled his knife from his belt. The eyes were sharp and sure in the night, and he feared that the creature would have the advantage. Julian sprang back into the forest and searched for a low branch to hoist himself up on. But the creature was quick and leapt upon him, pinning him with heavy furry feet, the claws pinching his skin.

It was a wolf.

Its breath fogged his very brain with the stench of death. He closed his eyes and expected the tear of teeth that would end him. Instead, the breath slowed to a lullaby-like rhythm.

When he opened his eyes, there was no longer a wolf sitting upon him but a woman. A woman who he knew well. Her skin was lighter than his but still dark. Her eyes were green, like leaves unrolling in spring time.

"*The wolf...*" he muttered. *Had his senses betrayed him?* The claws, the animal's breath... it had all seemed so real. Once again Mittawa's magic astounded him.

"*If you want the land back, the answer lies inside,*" Mittawa said, standing up.

"I have been looking for you. I am glad I found you."

"*I came to you to say that you are reading the signs wrong.*" Her green eyes blazed.

"Tell me what I should know!"

"*Every time the tide rushes onto the beach, it eats away some of the sand, and the island gets smaller. But the tide leaves the sand somewhere else, making new land,*" she told him.

"New land? I don't understand..."

"*Bah!*" she yelled and shook the bone she bore at him. "*You forget our ways and can no longer catch the big fish.*" She gestured out towards the empty bay, which the whales had been avoiding.

"The big fish will come," he said in their native language. "I keep more of the old ways than any other in our tribe!"

202

She snorted. *"You need me to read the ancient signs for you because your eyes are now too white to see them! No land stays the same. Remember that when you consider what you want."*

"I want the old land of our people. Does that count for nothing? But one must be like the white man, talk like him and trade like him to get what is ours back from him. I know his way, and so I will get our ancestors' land. You were driven out! You were left with no land but fields so poor that not even the pigs will graze there! You failed! I use his language! His tools!" He took a silver coin from his pocket and shook it at her, like it was some kind of talisman imbued with powerful spells.

"Bah!" she said, showing him her tongue. *"You are deceived! You think that you are gaining something with those coins, but you merely sell yourself for poor payment! I have seen this all."*

"If you see all, then why is it that the beast came and did nothing? The man came and did nothing?" he demanded. "If they do not mean harm, then they must bring good. Their message is that I will get back the land. Afterwards we shall take more of it, the same way, until the balance is restored between the English and our people! That is what you saw, isn't it? Tell me!"

"This is all that is left of me or my visions," she said, shaking the bone that she carried. *"I will not tell you what to do. I live in the spirit world! This land means less to me than it did. But it is still your world. Is that what you want? Open your eyes!"*

Julian wanted to shoo her away. Foolish old witch, he thought. She had told him nothing. He had already seen the signs when the wolf came. A child could read them. He braced himself for a spell but none came.

"Then tell me of the French who lived here!" Julian cried, suddenly recalling his question.

"They were the first to try and take this land. But they did not stay."

"I know this! Did they *take* anything else?"

Mittawa stared at him, her teeth bared as she laughed. *"No. We gave ourselves to them. We were blinded to the trickery of the whites even then."*

Julian put his hands to his face, wondering if he was hearing correctly.

"*You do not need me to tell you such things. My eyes do not come from a Punonakanit father?*" she said. She hissed at him and began to disappear into the fire's smoke.

Before she completely dissolved, her green eyes erupted at him. She pointed at him and then jabbed her finger at the ground. The connection could not have been more clear. He would stay. But the land felt somehow different as if it did not hold him up as surely as it once did.

The sunrise gave him no comfort, for the words that he had heard that night were burned into him. He felt raw. Betrayed. Catching sight of his familiar reflection in a puddle of water, abandoned by the retreating tide, he saw the native man that the world saw. But that was an illusion. Inside he was like a clam with a nasty surprise of mud within its shell where the succulent meat should be.

French... He did not even know how to measure their worth against other white men. The few he had seen had no law or respect at all. It seemed as though he was spawned from the worst of the white races.

Chapter Three
"Deeds and Words"

September 1715

The Potanumaquitt Indian meeting house looked much like the English one. It had the same side boards, glass windows and stone steps leading to the front door. All it lacked was a steeple, such as the Eastham church had, as if it was unable to reach as high towards the Lord as its white counterpart.

It stood on the side of Old Wading Path, to the south of the English settlement, towards the Monomoyick lands.

John Julian opened the door and walked inside where the empty benches faced a wooden pulpit. There a native man was standing, reciting from the Bible to the vacant room.

John Tom was about eighty as near as Julian could reckon. While the whites had a reverend, the natives had a *teacher*. It was a better name as far as Julian was concerned. All Treat did was lecture to his flock. And the congregation never grew more intelligent than sheep, droning back the words that Treat fed them. Sheep got easily lost without guidance, Julian noted.

Julian had always heard that John Tom had been a wise man and one of the strongest Potanumaquitt braves, before he had taken up the white man's god. He hoped that John Tom had some of that wisdom left.

The old man came down to the meeting house floor, with more spring in his step than Treat could muster. That gave Julian hope. John Tom's grip on Julian's shoulder was firm too, and it reminded Julian of the connection his people had with the land.

"I know you. You are Ralph Julian's son," John Tom said.

Julian nodded appreciatively. Few from the other tribes remembered his father. This too gave Julian hope that perhaps the tribes were stronger and more connected than they appeared.

There were signs of this occurring already. The nearly decimated Pamet and Punonakanit tribes had largely joined with the Nausets. Julian himself lived in Nauset village because his mother had brought them there after his father died. She had kin among the Nausets. The tribes had become too thin to squabble over bloodlines. They had all been cousins before. Now it was time for them to start acting like brothers and sisters.

All of the tribes, from Pamet to the southern tip of Monomoyick and out to the Sauquatucket lands in the west, were welcome to gather at this meeting house for service. But many had their own teachers among them, who gave sermons under simpler bark roofs. Others waited for Treat himself to make the rounds through the native villages as he did from time to time. John Tom too had been to Nauset village many times. Not just to preach, but to actually sit and break bread at Treat's table, a privilege few natives had experienced.

"It is an honor to have you here in my church all the way from your homeland," John Tom went on, spreading his hands wide, in the same way that Julian had found him doing up at the pulpit. Despite its intent the greeting made Julian wary. Surely, the old man had long waited for this moment. Julian wondered how often John Tom, Doane and Treat had spoken of him.

Julian looked around at the interior of the building. The beams that held the roof were straight and long. The walls were smooth and painted white. The floor was wood with grooves. It was all so perfect and orderly, unlike the twisting branches that held a *wetu's* top on or the rough bark that were its sides. In his mind's eye, he could see old wisemen like John Tom passing the pipe around the fire circle, within the *wetu*. Seeing a wiseman here in this great box did not seem right at all. It made him feel much worse about what was happening to his people.

"What are you going to tell the people when they come?" Julian asked.

John Tom tapped importantly on the book that he held and smiled warmly. "The whole thing speaks of the works of the God behind the gods. The one God that created everything from the white man's world to ours to ones that we will never see, that lie over the water."

"That book speaks of *our* land?" Julian asked in surprise. He had not thought there was anything as impressive as that in the book's pages.

"Well, no. God had written the book before we were discovered."

Julian frowned. "But this god must have known of us if he had made us and all of our gods. That is what the whites claim!"

"Of course! He did make it all! Then he went away and did great things that were written down here in this book while we slept and waited for Him to return!" John Tom took Julian's hand and placed the book in it, patting his hand like he was a foolish child.

"Have you read it?"

Julian shook his head. The book felt as heavy and dense as stone in his hand, which made sense because the book was meant to be a weapon or a tool for the people that used it. He flipped through its pages, and they fluttered like a bird's wings in motion. He inserted a finger into its flow and looked at the open page. There he saw the same strange symbols that were on the signs of certain places in town or the papers that the white men had given the Punonakanit sachem in exchange for Great Island.

The teacher took back the book and began reading. To Julian's surprise, he spoke in Wampanoag.

"It is in our language?" he interrupted. He did not know that his people's words had been written down.

John Tom nodded solemnly. "See? The Lord has not forgotten us. Nor have the whites. Reverend Treat translated the book for us."

"My father was born without knowing of that book. He came to believe in it, and he died preparing to fight the white man's wars. Others in my family did not believe it. Like my aunt Mittawa. She said it was filled with lies."

The old man snapped the book shut and tucked it under his arm. With his thin, flabby arms and his clean, wrinkled face, he looked suddenly as weak as a little child, clinging to the book as if it could give him some kind of strength.

"Mittawa gave me a vision when I was young," Julian said. "She talked about a man and a beast, whose coming will decide if the land can be saved."

"It is all in here!" John Tom exclaimed, lifting the book into the air.

Julian was shocked. "Did she read it there? She hated the white man's religion."

"She was a fool! The white man's God belongs to all of us and all of us belong to Him. You should come to service, before it is too late for you!" He tapped a bony finger on Julian's chest.

"What does the book say about the man and the beast?" Julian asked. He felt like grabbing the old man by the neck, not letting him walk away, wringing out the answers if he should not offer them.

"The beast, God says, will kill us all. Its coming means that the last days are coming. Those who believe in the man will come back from the dead and be saved."

"We will be spirits and then live again?"

"Come to service, and you will hear more," John Tom replied.

Julian sighed. The old man was back at the pulpit, raising his hands to the sky, in the way of the old sachems. The image looked so out of place in this strange building that Julian had to blink his eyes to believe it. That the book told of Mittawa's words was hard to comprehend. For the first time, he had some respect for the white god. He was evidently more knowledgeable than many of his followers even knew.

"Was this beast white?" Julian asked, pursuing the teacher up to the pulpit.

"It is whatever color it wants to be."

"So the beast that washed up is the same as the one in the book?"

"There could be no other meaning."

"The man. He washed up in my weir!" Julian said. Then an odd, terrible thought seized him. If all of the other details were in the white man's book, then the rest of his fate should be written out there on its pages too. He lifted the book out of John Tom's hands and leafed through it again, somewhat thankful that the symbols were indiscernible to him.

The teacher took the book back and laughed. "The man's name is Jesus Christ! He did not land in your net. He has not come yet. But you would be lucky if he washed up in your net. You must beg him for forgiveness for your sins. Then he might save you from the beast, for the beast will come again! Now go. I must prepare for the service. We will talk more then."

When Julian reached the door, he called out the other question that was nearly as important as the nature of the beast and the man, "Did you know that the French white men shared land with the Punonakanits long ago?"

John Tom tapped upon the book. "The French do not read the book well. They stray from its teachings. Many Punonakanits strayed too. That is why they found comfort with each other."

"You knew about my father and Mittawa? And of the French…" Julian asked, heat gathering around his face and neck.

"Come to service. It is not too late for you to join this new world."

✠ ✠ ✠ ✠

Later Julian made his way back to Great Island, to the very northern edge where the incoming tide wrapped around the spit of land, whittling it down to a tiny sharpened point, which reminded Julian of a spear head. He lay on the sand and looked up into the stars. He saw new shapes in them. The letters from the white book seemed scrawled across the heavens as if they had always been there, hidden under the familiar images of bear, Great River and fish. He still did not know what they said, but he tried to take comfort in them, drawing his own conclusions from the images formed by the sparkling points of light in the sky. If Mittawa's omen was taken from the white book, if they were one and the same, then it was men like John Tom who were leading his people in the right direction and he, Julian, was being left behind in darkness. If that was so, then perhaps it was time to understand this white god, Julian decided, fighting back the doubt that fluttered in his gut.

Around him the wind played a haunting tune in the reeds by the water. When he was with the teacher, the words of the white book made some sense, he had to admit, and the claims of his aunt rang hollow and false. Now, in the dark, John Tom's assertions were no comfort, and every creak in the forest behind him made his eyes pop open and expect to see ghostly shapes in the night. He wondered if Mittawa would come to him this night and how she would explain what was written in the book. Perhaps that is what Mittawa had meant when she told him to open his eyes and when she talked of new land forming. Yet he still did not understand why

Mittawa had never mentioned the white god's book before, other than with venom. He fell asleep as confused as ever.

The next morning the paths through the marshland looked peaceful and safe. It made him wonder if there was anything really to fear from the spirits and their vague omens. The ground felt solid once again. But every few steps, he seemed to mistrust his footing. It was solid ground, but it was new ground, a new world. Nothing was the same, not even the blood that ran within him.

These thoughts made him so distracted that he did not notice the man at his campfire, until they were practically standing face to face.

Sam Bellamy reached into his pocket, pulled out an arrowhead and showed it to Julian. It was a token that the native had left with the sailor when he had dropped him at the edge of Great Cove. Julian gaped and wondered if the gesture was meant as a sign of recognition or threat.

"I still don't know what I am supposed to do with it," Bellamy said with a half-smile.

Julian stepped close to the sailor and plucked the stone from his palm. Originally it had been a token to mark the man and remind him of Julian's willingness to fight. After last night he felt no less fire in his belly, but he no longer knew exactly where to aim it.

"This is made for hunting. Without wood and feather it will not fly," he said and dropped the object to the ground, to emphasis its useless weight.

"I hear I owe you a debt of gratitude," Bellamy said.

Although he did not show it, Julian felt a twinge of caution. What was the name that John Tom had told him...*Jesus*. He wondered if he should make some gesture of homage, just in case the old teacher was right and Mittawa was wrong. He stooped, picked up the arrowhead and returned it to Bellamy.

"*This was a gift*," Julian mumbled.

"You said it was worthless!" Bellamy chuckled, causing Julian to burn with embarrassment.

"Are you a Frenchman?" Julian asked.

Bellamy crinkled his nose. "I am not. I am English through and through. What manner of man are you?"

"Punonakanit and Nauset..." Julian said. He could not bring himself to explain the rest of his heritage.

The words meant nothing to Bellamy. After a pause the sailor pointed towards Smith Tavern and asked, "You know that place?"

"Yes."

"What of it? Can I make a living there, for a time? I hear that the owner hires men to run his boats for fishing."

"Not this year. There are few fish."

"But you work there?"

"Sometimes."

"Will you take me there? Perhaps it is greedy of me to ask more of you, after you have saved my life. But if you give me an introduction to this Samuel Smith, I promise that I will eventually make all your favors up to you."

Julian nodded absently. The sailor was nothing like he expected. No sense of power emanated from him. Spirit or white savior, there should be something more.

"I do not know your name. Is it... Jesus?" Julian asked tentatively. By the way that the sailor threw his head back and laughed, Julian had his answer.

"Forgive me! I did not expect one such as you to have a sense of humor!"

The man smiled, and Julian tried to return it. Now he was sure. This sailor was nothing but a man. So the omen was not what Mittawa had said it to be. A few days ago such news might have made him happy. Today it did nothing but conjure new fears. Was his fate now tied to a book that he could not even read, he wondered?

Just to be sure, Julian lingered for a while after he had brought the sailor to Smith Tavern. He nodded to some of the whale men at tables that he passed, making his way to the far corner, where he would be alone to smoke his pipe and observe the sailor from across the room.

Bellamy told lively tales that eventually drew some grins and even a few drinks from the whale men. But overall, Julian noticed that the whale men did not seem much impressed by the newcomer, least of all Smith himself, who scowled when Bellamy announced that he had not a single penny upon him.

"However, if you'd give me a draught on account, I owe that Indian a mug for the service that he did for me," the sailor announced. Then Bellamy turned and scanned the room, and Julian exhaled a screen of pipe smoke just in time, before the sailor's eyes found him.

"Perhaps he's left..." Bellamy said.

"He don't drink much anyway," Smith growled. "Nor do you, unless you can pay with other than tall tales!"

The sailor stayed inside with the rest of the white men. Julian slipped away, without a word of good-bye to any of the others.

When he reached his camp site, he pulled out the Bible that John Tom had decided to give him. Only a handful of Bibles written in Wampanoag existed in Eastham, making it a prized possession. Julian had reminded the teacher that he could not read, so the gift would be useless to him. John Tom insisted, claiming that even unread the book had power. "Just carry it around with you for a time and see how you feel," the old teacher had said, pushing the book into Julian's hands.

"Hell... A place of endless fire deep in the center of the earth awaits those who don't believe this book!" John Tom had told him.

Mittawa promised him other equally unpleasant tortures should he turn his back on the ancient path of the Old Ones. But the old witch was wrong about the sailor. There was no special power that Julian could see in the man.

The book, it turned out, fit nicely under his head, and Julian was content to simply lie quietly in the solid palm of the land, feeling more relief than he had in some time.

⚜ ⚜ ⚜ ⚜

In the candlelight Rebecca Smith bent over a piece of parchment. Her arm cast long disproportionate shadows as it moved back and forth. From behind, it might have looked like she was weaving the shadows themselves into some kind of tapestry.

Her husband appeared behind her and peered over her shoulder, grinning to himself as he did.

"*What a fine hand you have, dear one,*" he murmured.

She glanced up at him and shook her head reproachfully. Samuel Smith knew that she did not have the heart for this kind of creation. She did it only because he had convinced her of the need.

Looking at the words taking shape on the paper and the little diagrams of bows and arrows and fish that were the old Punonakanit sachem's mark, he lamented the waste of her talent. Had they thought of this before, they could have drawn to themselves a fortune.

"Very good...very good. That looks as real as if the old bugger had put pen to paper himself," Smith remarked. Before he could stop himself he added, "I always thought that children could draw better than them Indians. Yet I suppose it is better than merely leaving an *x* for one's mark." He meant the words to be conversational, but they brought another admonishing look from his wife.

"Perhaps you ought to go find a child to complete this task, then."

"Ah, Rebecca! I do not jest! You do beautiful work. Beautiful!"

She did not reply. The quill tip dipped into the ink well and then scratched out another crude arrow.

"You've no quarrel with smuggling. I see no difference..." he began but another look from her stopped him. He knew her views well enough to understand that she accepted smuggling as a necessary reaction to an unjust plight caused by callous government policy whereas forgery was, to her, less justifiable.

He heard footsteps upstairs. One of the whale men moving about.

"Doing a bit of writing in your journal, dear?" he said loud enough that if anyone was listening, they would not begin to wonder. Neither Rebecca nor himself were much known for an interest in writing, particularly by the light of midnight oil.

His wife answered him in a whisper, "*Samuel Smith. You don't have to act all innocent! None of these men know anything of deeds...*"

"Deeds! What a cursed word it has become! There was no need of them when we first came here. Doane and his cronies never cared one whit about this place back then."

"Let us hope that this is the end to it," Rebecca replied. Then she stood up, put her hands on her hips and glared down at her work. "It is done."

Smith could not help himself from smiling. He grappled his wife and kissed her on the cheek. "A man could search all the world and not find a finer woman than my Rebecca!"

"Get off of me! Time for bed. And know that I have had enough buffoonery for one night!" she warned.

He laughed and kissed her again. "All of this will be yours! Didn't I always tell you it would be so?"

She might have scowled again at the comment, but this time she merely gave a half-smile and patted him on the cheek. "To you, all of the world is ours already, whether it is rightly so or not."

"That's right! That's right!" he exclaimed.

Rebecca slipped off towards the bedroom, and he was eager to follow her but not before one more glance at her handiwork. It was a deed that looked as real as any of them had been, he thought.

From the table, he took out the scrap of paper that he had for so long carried. On it were scratched out the signatures of the dead native leaders. He had reproduced them as best he could from the deeds that he had seen in John Paine's care, and then his wife had brought them to vivid life. He had no doubt that they would trick even the discerning eyes of Paine, Doane and the other town fathers.

Then Smith eased himself into the chair that his wife had been sitting in and listened for the sound of movement coming from the bedroom. It was his ritual, before getting into bed, to sit by himself with a mug of ale and clear his head of the problems of the day. His wife would not come to check on him, which was just as well, for there was one more problem with which to deal.

He pulled the ink and a blank piece of parchment towards him, consulted the native signatures once more and began to write. It would take far less skill to make this creation because it was meant for a less discerning audience.

✠ ✠ ✠ ✠

The next morning John Julian was surprised to see the old man stomping towards him through the beach grass, under the first glow of dawn. He got to his feet, and Smith came and stood next to him. For a moment the two men kept to their own thoughts, each gazing out at the woods, marsh and beach in front of them, like it was a picture too potent for words. Silence did not bother Julian. In truth, he could have spent quite some time entranced with the view. He already had for much of the early morning. Yet Smith was not good at repressing a need when it was in him, and Julian could feel some kind of urgency radiating from the whale man's body.

"How close are you to getting the coin for this land?" Smith asked finally.

Julian did not mind repeating his situation yet again. Better to be asked at all than forgotten, he told himself. "I need ten pounds more."

"And then you will have seventy-five pounds?"

"Seventy is what we agreed."

Smith went silent again for several minutes. Birds made their plays for each other in the bracken, and the surf grew louder with the coming light as if the sun gave it additional volume. Joy welled up in Julian. He wanted to shout and raise his fists into the air. When Smith finally spoke again, Julian could almost hear the words before they left the man's lips.

"Here. The land is yours."

A piece of paper was thrust into Julian's hands. His fingers massaged the surface, feeling the rough surface, itself a texture like a miniature landscape. All of the terrain lying out there in front of him was somehow contained in these obtuse little words. It was all there. John Julian's land.

"The next time we go on a run, you should make enough to cover the difference. But you can have the deed now. I trust you," Smith said.

Then Smith nodded and left. Julian lifted the paper to his nose and inhaled. The scent of ink was strong and acrid, but it was solid and permanent. And it was the first time that any white man had thought so highly of him.

✠ ✠ ✠ ✠

October 1715

For the full life span of a moon, from its growth from a dark patch in the night sky to a ripe, round glowing ball and then back to emptiness, as if the darkness was a tide scraping away its shores, Julian reveled on his land.

He too felt reborn from blackness into shining light. He paddled the length of his beach, hunting crabs and oysters. He stalked the flats, with pockets full of rocks, and brought down a half-dozen gulls for dinner. Most of all, he sat among the whispering reeds in the marsh and gazed around at the empty stretch of sand, beach grass and sparkling water. There he pretended that he was hiding in the thickets of his youth and the wind muttering in the vegetation around him was the hum of the voices of his long gone people, once again filling the island. The lack of any tribe to share in his victory was the only thing that diminished his joy. The rest of it felt as blissful as waking to a world the way it was, without the shadow of Smith Tavern looming behind him.

Julian rarely glanced in that direction. He had no need of the tavern keeper or his rapacious whale men anymore. He had paid Smith his coin. Should a blackfish wash up on this side of the island, *his* side, there would be no dispute over its ownership. Julian relished thinking of the prospect.

Apart from that indulgence, Julian thought about the white men as infrequently as possible. Often he heard them shouting up on the ridge or out in their boats, but it was as if they lived in another land. Even the sailor had almost passed from his mind, until one day when he saw the man coming down the beach.

"You!" Sam Bellamy called out. "I have come to repay that favor I owe you! You can sail can't you?"

The sailor's wide grin made Julian cautious. "Yes…"

"We are preparing for a journey. We need more hands."

"I do not work for Smith anymore," Julian replied.

"Not Smith! Me! Smith won't help, so I am going out on my own," Bellamy said and pointed out towards the horizon.

"Away from the land?" Julian asked. With a stab of alarm, he remembered the omen once again. *When the man appears, you may be lost from the land forever…*

"For a time, yes. Ah! You are thinking about it! Good! You of all people have little to gain by staying here under Smith's thumb! On the sea you will be an equal. And if what I have heard is true, we will all return as rich men. You will have more coin than you could spend in a lifetime!"

Julian held up a hand to stop the sailor. "No. I stay," he said. He had no more need of coin. He had the land. He was equal. He was more than that. He alone belonged here. *All* of Julian's blood cried out to that fact.

For a moment the disappointment in Bellamy's eyes almost convinced him to reconsider. The sailor desperately wanted him to go. So much so, that Julian wondered if Bellamy had some hidden knowledge after all. Then Bellamy disappeared, and Julian told himself that the sailor was simply a flesh and blood man who was sailing away from this land and taking any hint of omen with him.

He turned his attention back to the little spit of sand at the end of Great Island.

✠ ✠ ✠ ✠

November 1715

The trees took on their bare winter skins and looked like massive woven fish weirs instead of forest. The sea too changed color. It became darker, in reflection of the brooding sky, which was more and more often gray with clouds. But today the sun was warm and bright like a memory of summer.

Julian had yet to build a *wetu* on Great Island. The structure seemed far too indulgent without a tribe or family to fill it. For shelter he had constructed a simple lean to, nestled in the marsh grass, with bark laid over the wooden frame to shield him from wind and rain.

He went inside and dug into the sand until his fingers found the corners of a small wooden box, which he had found washed up by the sea. He pulled it from its hiding place and lifted the lid. Within it was the Bible, written in the Wampanoag language, that John Tom had given him.

Julian went back outside, sat on the beach and let the book fall open to a random page. From afar it would have looked like Julian was deep in thought, absorbed in the message of the Godly words. Really, it was the reflection of the sun that he studied, the way that the gleam of light made the writing seem like carving in a stone.

John Tom had taught him a few words, including: *Christ.* The Son of God. He was a fellow fisherman, who had been pushed aside by his people yet had come back to them in the end to save them from a great, terrible beast. He liked this man. The man from the omen.

Then he flipped open the Bible to its very center and withdrew a loose sheet of paper. He could not read the words on this paper, but he had made John Tom say them over and over to him until he knew every one by heart:

I, Samuel Smith, do hereby sell my ten acres of the north quarter of Great Island to John Julian, native of the Nauset Indian village, on this day, September Eight, year of our lord Seventeen Hundred and Fifteen, anno domnus. Said acreage of Great Island is bound on the south by Billingsgate Creek, to the East by Billingsgate Harbor, to the West and North by the Great Bay. I do hereby grant and convey all ownership, rights and privileges of said land to John Julian and his heirs in perpetuity...

The native teacher could not tell him what all of the words meant, but Julian understood the basic implication. The land was his, and he had invited John Tom to come preach there at any time to the Punonakanits and Nausets that he expected to join him there.

"I give this Bible more weight than that deed you got," John Tom had told him. The teacher scowled, like he considered Julian's ownership of the land improper.

"This is the way that the English split up the land among them," Julian replied.

"Once you know *this* then you may be ready for land. What do you expect our people to do out there on that island? Dance and sing by the fire like heathen people!" John Tom spat. "This has *more weight!*"

In one hand the Bible sat heavy and admonishing, and in the other was a sheet of vellum as light as the feet of a dragonfly. Julian rested one in each of his palms and, despite the obvious differences, he still considered the flimsy paper to be the more valuable object.

Chapter Four
"All That is Left is Smoke"

July 1716

The marsh that surrounded Nauset village was green, and its channels were filled with oysters and clams. Most of the tribe was knee deep in the inlet that led to a saltwater pond, gathering armfuls of the shellfish.

They were not his people, but they were his cousins, and John Tom watched the clam diggers' industry with pride as he passed. He hoped that the man behind him observed the way that the people were singing the psalms as they worked and was equally impressed.

That man was Justice Doane, who in fact had other things on his mind. All winter and spring, he had been stewing over the goings on at Great Island. Bellamy had slipped through his fingers and apparently was now off on some voyage orchestrated by Smith. It was clear that Smith had harbored a fugitive, but Doane could not think of any way to force Smith to bow to the law without causing a near riot among his Great Islanders. Perhaps the sailor would return and provide an opportunity for further investigation. In the pit of his stomach, Doane felt that scenario denied. With all the time that had passed, Bellamy could be halfway around the world by now. Doane was quite sure that Bellamy was gone forever.

"Here!" John Tom said, throwing open the deerskin curtain that hung over the entrance to a bark covered *wetu*. "It is empty. He took everything with him."

Doane ducked inside the dwelling. It only took a moment to confirm what John Tom had said. Apart from a few blankets in the corner and a dark patch of charcoal under the smoke hole in the center of the structure, the place was barren.

"Whose hut is this?" Doane asked.

"He used to stay here from time to time. But he has not been seen for many moons. No one will live in his *wetu*, in case he comes back. This is what the Nausets tell me."

"Who?" Doane demanded, exasperated at the way the Indian teacher insisted on squeezing every bit of drama from everything. Apart from his skin hue and rough mismatched garments, John Tom was not so different from Treat, Doane mused.

"John Julian."

The name sounded familiar to Doane, but it took him a while to place it. *Great Island, the pillory, the one who found the sailor...* It was all beginning to make sense.

"You asked me to tell you who had been speaking of Helltown or Great Island," John Tom said eagerly.

"Yes, yes. Very good."

"He spoke of both. He asked for forgiveness. He has bought part of Great Island, and he wanted the blessing of Christ upon it. I told him that he had to renounce all sin attached to his getting of it, and that is when he told me about the French pirates..."

"Wait...he bought *what?*"

"Great Island."

"From who?"

"I do not know," John Tom said.

Doane, however, was quite sure who had sold the land. If so, then finally he might have something to work with. It should make his case go that much smoother at town meeting.

When Doane stepped outside, his boot kicked something from the grass that spun, sparkling, ahead a few feet and then came to a rest on the dirt path that connected the *wetus* to each other.

Doane picked it up and saw that it was a necklace fashioned from sharp animal teeth.

"No!" John Tom cried suddenly. Before Doane could react, the native snatched the necklace from his hand and flung it far into the inlet where it splashed among a flock of frightened seagulls.

"What is this?" Doane cried, spinning on his companion. "Why did you throw away that *evidence?*"

"Bad, bad necklace," John Tom said. "I know this necklace. I know why John Julian carries it. It bears the mark of *her*. She gave it to him."

"Who?"

"His father's sister. She does not pray to God. No, she prays to the spirits still. Very bad."

"What is her name? Where is she?"

"Mittawa. She lives on Great Island too."

Doane was thinking fast. Unwanted images of the great beast and the dead cattle came to mind. They made unbelievable connections that Treat, Knowles and others so vehemently asserted as truth, that there was a devilish conspiracy in town. In *Eastham* of all places. It did not make sense. There was no logic to it, only superstition. But if there was proof, that was another matter.

"Can this woman draw strange beasts from the sea?" he asked the native.

John Tom looked puzzled.

"Can she call to monsters of the sea and make them do her bidding?"

"She talks to the old sea spirits."

"Like the monster that washed up. Did you see it?"

"I saw."

"Like that?"

"Maybe…"

"Does she fly? Has anyone ever seen her flying in the air?"

John Tom shifted uneasily, eager to please but confused. "People see her eyes at night. They glow green. We see her wolf. It has green eyes too. If you see it, you must run. Even still, you may be doomed," he explained uncertainly. Then more forcefully, he cried, "But that is not the way of God. I know that is the old bad way. I do not believe that anymore!"

"Yes, yes. Green eyes…wolves…" said Doane thoughtfully. It all led to one impossible but increasingly undeniable explanation.

"Could she make animals die?" he asked the native.

"Yes! She kills them as sacrifice to the spirits!"

"Really? Could she possess a man and make him do her bidding? Is that what the necklace was for? A spell?"

"She knows spells!" John Tom said eagerly.

"She is a witch then," Doane concluded. And she was in Eastham.

"The Witch of Billingsgate," John Tom replied, remembering the name that the whites had given Mittawa.

"No, no, no! She is dead!"

"Half dead," John Tom said. "Her spirit lives. Very bad spirit!"

"She is completely dead! No one is half dead! Are you not the teacher of the Bible?" Doane said.

John Tom shrugged, "She is alive, then."

"John Tom. If she lives, you must lead me to exactly where she lives. Can you do it?"

The native nodded his head fervently. "Bring many men. She is…what do you say? *Witch*."

As he rode back towards town, Doane thought about the Witch of Billingsgate. It had been so many years since there were eerily similar sights of cattle dying and other strangeness in town. The witch had been driven out by Doane's own father, who had been put in charge of dealing with the matter. Doane had assumed that she was dead, but now he wondered if his father's fight with the Devil was to be his inheritance. Same fears, just new faces, like Widow Chase and Goody Hallett. It all seemed so unreal. Was it even possible, he wondered?

He passed Higgins Tavern and felt briefly pulled towards it by the burning lanterns and rolling sounds of many conversations coming from inside. It had been quite a while since he had sat as a neighbor and friend and raised a glass with his fellow townsfolk. Not since he had taken his post had he spent a day drinking to the harvest and worrying about the simple issues of most men such as planting, reaping and raising children.

The cloudy midday fields of Nauset felt wide and lonely as he rode, but he did not regret his station. Every town, every era needed a few men to be out in the world acting upon it while the rest sat in taverns and talked about what was being done. He had always been a man of action, and so he rode by the tavern.

When he got home, he found another man of action on his doorstep. The man had a long, dour face similar to Doane's, only a bit more wrinkled and gray. It was his cousin Hezekiah, the Justice of Truro, the town nearest to Helltown. Typically, they did not see each other more than a couple times a year. Over twenty years ago Hezekiah had moved to Truro to hunt whales. He had set down roots in that fledgling northern town, raised a family and become a stalwart pillar of the community. He had little reason to return to Eastham.

"What a pleasant surprise, cousin!" Doane said, feeling quite the opposite. There was something unusual and foreboding about his cousin's presence on the stoop.

"Good day to you, Joseph. I have spoken to your dear wife, and I am glad to hear that all is well with your family. Mine is also well though little else around me is," he said, reaching into a sack on the ground and pulling out a mangled rabbit, which he held out for Doane to see.

"What is it?" Doane gasped.

"Wolf did it, by the look of it."

"There are some left?" Doane asked.

"Hardly. The bounty on that animal hasn't been paid, up our way, for five years. I imagine it is the same in Eastham."

His cousin was right, but Doane wondered what Hezekiah thought it meant. "You've heard of our troubles?"

"Of course! That is way I am at your door. Been a wolf in Truro and pirates warring in Helltown. Damned if I care if the lot of them wiped each other off of the face of the earth. Folks say they saw Great Islanders among the fray. That's the work of Sam Smith, then. I thought that bit of news would be of interest to you, cousin."

"Aye, aye, tis…" Doane answered vaguely.

"And there's more," Hezekiah said. "That old Indian witch was spotted in the highlands not more than a week ago. Thought your father had buried her in the ground, but my deputy Silas Eldredge saw her plain. She ran like a rabbit when he did. She just plain disappeared. Searched high and low for her for three days but found nothing but this dead carcass. Strange times afoot, cousin."

"Indeed," Doane sighed. "But you must be hungry. Come in and sup with us, and we will talk further."

"I'll eat, but no more talk. Tis not the tale for the ears of women and children."

"Hmmm," Doane replied. His cousin stepped inside the house, but Doane lingered at the door for a moment, looking into the russet landscape of growing evening shadows and expecting to see demons and devils lurking behind every rock and tree.

✠ ✠ ✠ ✠

John Julian was standing on the edge of his land on Great Island. His head was bowed in prayer as he gave thanks for the ground that he stood upon. He told the land that he had not wanted it to be this way, him laying claim to the sand and water as if he presumed himself some kind of god. He wanted to remember what it had been like when he had awoken in the *wetu* with the chill of coming winter seeping under the walls. As a child, such coldness signaled a time of moving, in search of inland shelter in which to wait out the winter. And he wanted to remember the feeling of coming back to this place, after the snow thawed, when the tribe would return and spend the warm season living next to the water. Now he would stay here all year round. He would not return to Nauset village anymore. This was his place. In a way, he had paid to tie himself to the land in a similar fashion as the whites did with the homes that they dug into the earth. Yet it was not the same. He would build no house here. There would be no trace of him other than footprints, campfires and perhaps, one day, a small *wetu*. He pledged this to the land and sea.

"Hold! Hold there, Indian!" came a cry behind him.

From out of the bay, a boat was heading towards him. So deep was Julian in his reverie that he had not seen it until it was a stone's throw from him. Five men were in the vessel. At first Julian wondered if they were the French pirates coming for revenge.

Then he saw the man in the bow and heard his sharp baritone.

"Stay there, John Julian! In the name of the Governor of the Massachusetts Bay Colony and the king himself, I order you to stand still and await our arrival!" Justice Doane cried.

Julian stood motionless in the water, nothing but his mind moving, and that at great speed. He had attended church faithfully since the day of his conversion. He had fished and hunted peaceably, careful not to tread upon the English common lands where the white men said no native was allowed. He had paid Smith fairly and been given the deed for this land, on good faith. He had not aided the French enemies of his English neighbors. What was left, he wondered? *The smuggling with Smith? His refusal to join the militia?* That he could follow so many of the English rules correctly and still be persecuted for the few that had escaped him made Julian rage.

He splashed back from the water's edge, noting that his canoe and the coming ship were equally far from him at the moment. The boat, however, was on the bayside and the canoe on the shore of the harbor. Doane would lose time circling around the tip of the island, and the deeper draft of his vessel might ground in the shallows around the harbor side of the island. Unfortunately, the tide was just past its height, which meant that Doane might stay afloat after all, but he would still have to be careful. The sail was speedier than his paddle, but all in all, Julian had a good chance to cross the harbor first. Once he made the creek on the other side, there would be no way for Doane to follow.

As soon as Julian had taken a step, Doane's voice grew more shrill, "Accept your summons peaceably, and the court will look favorably upon you!"

Before he ran to the canoe, Julian turned to look at the justice. The braves of old might have judged the unfavorable odds the same as Julian and likewise fled, but they would have at least met the eyes of their adversary, and Julian would do no less. The justice railed at him, drawing his pistol as he did, "You are resisting arrest, Julian! Such flight will add to your punishment!"

Julian's sore wrists testified to the ill intentions of the man. Had he any weapon, other than his knife, he would be tempted to stand and settle the matter once and for all, despite the stronger force gathered against him.

Doane was still shouting as Julian pushed off and paddled as fast as he could across the slick of blue water. The only thing that caught Julian's ear was "...Witch of Billingsgate."

But whatever Doane was saying about Mittawa was soon buried beneath a more desperate fear. The air cracked with the sound of musket and pistol fire. Around Julian the water splashed as if fish were jumping. The bullets sank away into the water, and the current pulled Doane's boat around the island, out of range. Julian looked back as he paddled, waiting to see how quickly the white sails would re-emerge from behind the dune at the tip of the island. It appeared faster than he expected, and now there was nothing to slow it down but the hidden sand flats under the harbor. If the boat passed over those, then Julian would be lost. He had not gotten far enough ahead.

To his surprise, Doane's ship did not come after him. Instead, it tacked to shore, and the men in it threw anchor. A few moments later they were splashing ashore at the very spot where Julian had been standing. Doane was far enough away that his face was unreadable and his words too soft to hear. Julian watched the justice bend to the ground and lift something up from the sand. He saw something fluttering in Doane's hand, and then he recognized the Bible that he had dropped in his haste to reach open water.

Doane drew a single sheet from the middle of the book, and it snapped wildly in the wind, like a bird seeking flight. He watched Doane wrestle with it for a moment, holding it out before him as if he was reading it aloud for the others. Then he ripped the paper in half and in half again, and then the scraps rose into the wind and disappeared into the water as suddenly as a flash of sunlight on the waves.

✠ ✠ ✠ ✠

After leaving Great Island, Justice Doane aimed his ship towards Indian Neck.

John Tom was the first to disembark and splash through the shallows. He led Doane and his men along the faint paths through the pine trees, deep into the heart of the forest.

"Be careful! She might have already seen us approaching. The birds and animals that fly before us might bring word to her. We will not surprise one such as her," John Tom explained.

Doane glanced around him and saw more fear on the faces of his militiamen than he would have expected. Some of the native members seemed downright terrified. Yet he felt only annoyance rising. With every turn through the woods, the place was becoming more familiar to him. The trail was changing from a confusing, wandering maze to a direct path back to his youth. He could recall coming here with his father. He had been a young militiaman, much like the ones that he had in tow at the moment. He had not been present when the witch was subdued, but he had seen the aftermath. The witch's *wetu* had been burned to the ground with such great flame that it left a twenty-foot wide ring of scorched grass around it. She had not received warning of their coming on that day.

The party broke out of the trees into a little clearing, and Doane saw the remains of that old hut and knew at once that no soul had renewed lodging there.

"*Quiet...*" John Tom advised.

"This is a waste of time," Doane declared.

"*Shhh... She could be watching from the woods...*"

"She cannot see anything because of all of the stone piled atop her," Doane replied, turning the native teacher to face the grave in the middle of the meadow. "She is dead. I should never have let you seed doubt in me. I see no evidence of any witches."

"You saw the necklace. You saw John Julian flee. He is guilty."

"True. But his offence is something simpler than witchcraft. He is a smuggler working with Smith's band. For that despicable service he was rewarded with an illegal grant of land."

"But the *necklace!* It is a sign of devilry!"

"To that I say: *people*, not things, become infected by Satan. To imbue an object with mystical powers is to give in to superstition as base as any pagan's creed. It is akin to throwing salt over one's shoulder to keep away bad luck! Besides, if these necklaces are so vile, then why are all of your Indian brethren wearing them?" Doane pointed towards the far edge of the clearing where several of the Punonakanits were stepping out of the woods. They had heard the commotion of the militia and had come to investigate. When they saw John Tom, who was well-known to them, they began bowing. As they did, various strings of bone, teeth and bead bounced against their chests.

"They are Christians, are they not?" Doane asked John Tom.

"Of course!"

"Then it stands to reason that these decorations are harmless or else these men could not embrace the way of Christ," Doane replied. Too many people were too quick to string together all of the strange events occurring around them and assign to them some awful demonic power. Not all of it fit together, Doane knew. It took a rational mind to sift through the facts and break the leash of hysteria, which could lead them all to ruin as surely as actual devilry.

"Yes, but John Julian's necklace is different!" John Tom protested. He turned to the Punonakanits and exclaimed, "Tell him!"

But Doane waved them silent and ordered his men back to the ship. "All of these necklaces look the same to me."

✠ ✠ ✠ ✠

After being run off of his island by Justice Doane, John Julian fled through the village of Billingsgate and came to a stop in the center of the King's Highway.

Looking north, Julian considered the merits of going to Helltown, some twelve miles distant. Helltown was named after the land of the whites' bad spirits, those that burned for the kind of sins in which the inhabitants of the place regularly indulged. Even the fishermen were more interested in using their boats to row out to the anchored pirate ships to try to barter liquor for easy money rather than spend their time on the trail of the beasts of the water. Julian noted the irony of his thoughts, for he too was a fisherman who sought coin. But there had always been greater purpose behind his search for wealth. The men of Helltown simply turned over their money to the first tavern keeper or harlot ashore. Julian had been to this place and seen its wicked culture, so he turned south where the road led back to Nauset village, a place that he guessed would be under the watchful eye of the English lawman, and even his own people for that matter. He was not confident that any of his tribe would look upon him with any more favor than the English.

Yet part of him yearned to return to the southern villages, to John Tom's meeting house, to be exact. He had seen the shameful old native teacher hiding in the back of Doane's boat. Julian could not believe that one so skulking and false could have ever been a tribal warrior. For a moment he entertained the thought of confronting the old man and making him suffer for his treachery. The notion ultimately made Julian somber. John Tom was the same as many other native people who had given up their pride and would just as quickly give up one of their own. Revenge, Julian decided, would be a meaningless gesture for such lost people. It would only achieve more suffering among the tribes. It would be the English who had the ultimate victory. It was the English who should pay. First he had to make sure that Justice Doane did not find him.

So he stepped off of the road into a wall of thick bracken.

The branches parted easily as he pushed through them. After breaking through the first wall of trees, he discovered that the ground was clear of undergrowth. There was even the faint scratch of a trail running through the woods. Around him was only the press of leaves and branches. It was as empty as the first forest in the beginning of the world.

Julian walked towards the southeast, through a place of ponds where his father's people used to come in the autumn and winter months when the wind grew too icy to stay on Great Island.

After a few miles, the forest gave way to scraggly brush and then to a wide plain of sand. In it were lone trees with limbs warped and stunted by the incessant wind, clinging to the endless sandy highlands overlooking the ocean. Other twisted shrubs and briers lay here and there on the plain but little of the environment looked hospitable or even friendly. The land itself was as flat as a table set at the feet of the mighty sea spirit.

The land that Julian was traveling into was known as the Devil's Pasture, an appropriate moniker for the barren, desert-like area before him. Julian did not use that name. To him, this land would always be Punonakanit land.

With the Punonakanits diminished and clinging to their tiny village on Indian Neck, there were few who came to this place anymore. Normally the emptiness around him would have been sorrowful, but today he was glad that nothing existed here, except for the memories that were thick around him.

He dropped to the ground and sat cross-legged in the sand.

Keihtanit... Great Spirit... Open my eyes and heart and show me the proper path... Lead me in the direction that will save my people and restore our lands... Give me strength for the struggle ahead... Julian silently prayed.

When he opened his eyes, he saw nothing. No mighty spirit risen from the sea, no animal messenger, not even his aunt.

With a sigh he closed his eyes again. It was then that he realized that there was a trail of smoke in the air. The scent of flame blew towards him, from the strip of land to the east where the bluff overlooked the sea.

He began cautiously walking towards it. He had no idea whose lands these were anymore or if they were friend or foe or even living or dead.

There was a sweet tang to the smoke, and with a start he noted that it was not from a cook fire but rather a whiff of tobacco, the sacred smoke. He followed, with his hope rising. These days the sacred smoke was not reserved for ceremony alone. Both whites and natives took to the pipe whenever the desire overtook them. Yet Julian smiled because he did not see how such special smoke could be an accident as it wafted out from the sea, in the middle of this desolate land, in answer to his prayer.

Were there other braves living out here, away from the settlements, waiting for the time to strike back at the English, he wondered?

Soon he saw a crude hut, one little better than the Nauset children might make on the shoreline, playing at building their own *wetus*. It was set in a little protected gully of sand, set back from the lip of the dune cliffs. The basic structure was a box of limbs, wind gnarled and weather worn, with piled stones around the base to keep the footings strong. Other tree limbs and shipwrecked boards were lashed, in crude skeletal crisscrosses, onto the sides and roof to make basic walls. Bark and moss were stuffed into the cracks in the walls to block the wind, but the ocean gusts had already knocked much of the insulation out, leaving the rest dangling and bobbing ineffectually in the breeze. There was none of the sense of artistry and form that a true *wetu* exhibited, which told Julian that this was no native dwelling. More white men, he thought bitterly.

Then he saw the girl standing on the bluff next to the hut, gazing at the sea. She had a crude pipe clenched in her teeth, the tobacco streaming out of it in search of him. He knew that the powerful smoke had not led him here in vain. His prayer had been answered.

The spirits had brought him to the *witch girl*, a powerful medicine woman who even the whites themselves feared. But he did not understand why.

Chapter Five
"Of Good Magic and Bad"

The witch girl looked much the same as she had during the trial. At that time, John Julian had been passing by on the road, defiantly glaring at the pillory on the meeting house lawn, when he heard his aunt's name shouted through the meeting house window. He elbowed his way towards the sound, through the crowd of natives who were trying to peer through the windows from outside the building. Most gave Julian hostile glances and indignant whispers as he passed. Despite his conversion to the white man's god, his fellow natives were not convinced, and they treated him with the same indifference or suspicion as ever. However, none had the courage to block him from pushing right up to the glass. Inside he saw the old witch woman shouting at the humorless white town fathers, telling them about his aunt. Julian was surprised to hear much wisdom in the old witch's words. The young witch, however, was even more impressive even though she did not say a word. She just sat there and, to Julian's amazement, the white town fathers could not look her in the eye, so great was their fear of her.

"*There have been no witches from among the Nausets! Only the Puno-nakanits…*" Julian heard Charlie Sea Eagle muttering to his woman, in the crowd behind him.

"Mittawa was a wise woman! You all feared her because you are fools!" Julian scolded them as he shoved his way back through the throng. No one uttered another word. Julian was pleased that the truth still carried some power. Perhaps not enough to knock sense into them but at least enough to silence their foolish words.

By chance, he later saw the old English witch being loaded into a ship bound for Barnstable. He had been at Rock Harbor, the ancient land of the Namskakets, when they dragged her, chained and screaming, onto the vessel. Julian could not help but be impressed at the raw vehemence of the woman's curses, useless as they proved to be.

He had not seen or heard what had become of the young witch until now. He watched her start a bonfire on the lip of the dune crest and then stand overlooking the sea as if offering prayer. Between him and her was the flame of the fire. The smoke of the blaze clung to her and, from a distance, made her look hazy and

231

spirit-like. When Julian crept closer, he noted that she was merely tired and hungry. She looked weak for a witch as if she was entirely unable to talk to the spirits and ask for their help to find food and shelter. Julian pushed away his suspicions, reminding himself that white spirit women might be entirely different than those of his tribe. Yet it seemed that even the scratch of birds, squirrels or rabbits in the under growth around her hut would startle her.

He decided to wait and watch the girl to see if indeed she had the power to call the spirits to attend to her. So he withdrew into the forest, leaving behind a little bundle of herbs, tied with some twine, sticking out of the sand at the edge of her sleeping area. When it burned, it gave off a sweet scent, which was enticing to the helpful spirits and repugnant to those of ill intent.

She found the herbs the next day and gave a little scream, which was so feeble as to be quickly drowned out by the birds in the bayberry bushes in which Julian hid.

A short while later she yelled again, this time filling her lungs with the sound. After she had gone back into the hut for some time, Julian came out to investigate and found a sight that nearly made him shout as well.

Wolf marks.

Mittawa...

The animal was large. It had left its mark all over the area where the witch girl had been sleeping. It had been circling her in the night.

Julian crept away from the girl's hut, his mind spinning with thoughts, like seagulls wheeling through an endless sky.

There was a spirit around this girl, and it was not just any spirit but his aunt, whose mad eyes could penetrate the mist of the Great Spirit and see what was to come. It was Mittawa who led him here. That was as clear as the claw marks in the dirt, a message as readable to him as the words in the Bible were to the white men. Deep in his heart he knew that the girl would have some part to play, but although he burned tobacco in a sacred fire, he could not summon Mittawa to find out what he was to do next.

All that night he stared into the darkness, until his eyes grew soft and his mind hummed from the unanswered questions.

His faith in the white god was wilting like a young plant shoot suffering in drought. The fantastic predictions of the white man's book did not appear close to coming true. In fact, some of the Christian natives had admitted to him that even the whites had been waiting for many, many thousands of seasons for their god to return to them. Julian saw little promise that the world would be remade by the white god in his lifetime.

He wished that he was still in possession of his Bible, in order to tear up its pages in the same manner as Justice Doane had ripped up his deed. Then he would toss the paper onto the fire and see for himself if the white god could be summoned.

The white god did not seem to care what a man did or said as long as he bowed his head and prayed long enough in the meeting house. Even then, the utterances of his own English people seemed to please him more than the small pleas of his native flock. Julian had prayed and prayed. Nonetheless, his land had been snatched away from him by the English.

Now his aunt had returned, and that knowledge made Julian's face burn with guilt because he knew that she had cause to chastise him.

Sure enough, when sleep finally came, it delivered a dream to him in which Mittawa towered menacingly above him, in furs and feathers, shaking fish bones and demanding that he wake up - wake up *inside*. *"Let the girl do the dreaming,"* his dream aunt had said.

The girl is a dreamer...

Upon waking, Julian remembered that the witch girl had been exiled because she could dream things into being.

A new plan began to form in Julian's mind. Perhaps it would take a white witch to deal with the whites themselves. He knew that he would have to be cautious. He also knew that the fatigue and weakness of the girl was only a mask. It did not matter that she seemed so helpless during the day, for she wielded her power when she was asleep.

✠ ✠ ✠ ✠

The next morning Maria Hallett bent to inspect the latest burning offering at the edge of the forest and found herself suddenly covered in shadow. When she looked up, John Julian smiled down at her and kept smiling until she had finished screaming.

"It is protective smoke. Where it blows, no bad spirits can follow," he explained as he nodded down at the burning twigs.

The girl gave him a slightly crazed look, and for a moment he worried that she had been driven out of her home simply because she was unbalanced in the head. Then he recalled that Mittawa herself had seemed out of mind, more often than not. He decided that a tinge of madness might be common to all wise women and witches. Perhaps it is what happened to anyone who tried to live in the living world and spirit world at once, he thought with a shudder.

"The man from the pillory…" she said, standing up and taking a few steps away from him.

"Yes."

"You were being punished for missing service, were you not?" she said, her eyes swimming with worry.

"Yes," Julian said.

"It was not for anything worse?" she asked.

"No… The English stole my land and punished me for praying to my own gods – the spirits," he replied.

"That is all? You took no revenge? You were merely a victim?"

"I did nothing," Julian said sadly, feeling a touch of shame at his lack of response to what he had suffered. "I mean you no harm," he added. He knew that she too had been force fed the bitter taste of injustice.

The girl nodded solemnly, but she also looked relieved.

Julian dropped down to the ground, to run a finger over the wolf prints. They were not warm, but they had held their shape despite the blowing wind. He judged them to be no more than half a day old. "The wolf is close by."

"I thought that they were all dead! Is it not just a large runaway dog?" she gasped.

"No. It is a wolf," Julian replied. Then, noticing her renewed fear, he told her, "The wolf led me to you. Now I will try to lead you as far as I can. You know of the spirits of the plants and animals?"

The girl looked at him blankly.

Julian frowned. "How have you survived if you cannot hunt or find other food?"

"I've had nothing but blueberries since I got here! Do you have food?" she asked eagerly. Then, amazingly, she dropped down in front of him, begging for something to eat. He could not imagine Mittawa having ever suffered such a position.

Startled, he asked her nothing else until he had returned with two full grown rabbits and laid them in front of her. He waited for her to say a prayer of thanks. When she did not, he did not know whether to thank the old gods or the new one for the bounty, so instead, he simply thanked the spirits of the beasts themselves, in his own tongue, and she did not inquire about the words or meaning, only stared avidly at the meat.

They ate in silence, except for the thrum of the incoming waves. After dinner he pulled out his pipe and tobacco. They shared the pipe, and she inhaled it and spewed it out, without any sacred rhythm or prayer to gods of any kind as far as he could tell.

Finally he could wait no longer. "What is your magic?" he asked.

This time, she looked at him and laughed.

✠ ✠ ✠ ✠

For the next weeks Maria Hallett would not tell John Julian her magic. In fact, she denied that she had any at all. Only when he spoke of dreams, did she color red, the way those of her race revealed their secret shames, and he knew that he was not spending his time in vain. Yet he continued to tread carefully, winning her trust and gauging her power. It was he who was the teacher in those early days, showing her everything from how to shore up her hut, how to hunt, and most of all, how to invoke the hidden spirit of the things around her.

"You do not see much of what is offered to you in this place," he said as he blew on the coals to bring a lick of red flame from them. An iron cook pot, which Julian had found, dangled from a branch that he had suspended over the fire. Two more rabbits lay on the stones near the fire, already thanked, skinned and rubbed with cooking herbs.

"Rabbit stew..." he said. "You cannot eat blueberries all winter."

"What is your true purpose for coming to find me?" Maria demanded as she watched Julian cut up the rabbits and drop them into the pot.

"I did not come to find you," he said with a shrug. He dipped a finger into the cook pot and then touched it to his tongue. He frowned, got up and walked over to a swath of shrubs. Then he plucked off a green leaf with a ruffled texture and held it up. "Mint," he explained. "I give you the English words. Go on. Eat. It is not poison."

Tentatively, Maria placed it in her mouth and bit down. A cool, sharp taste burst on her tongue.

Julian smiled.

"It's wonderful," she gushed.

"It brings life to the mouth when food is scarce or meat is old. It does much more too. A medicine woman can crush it, breathe in its scent and use its medicine to talk to the dead," Julian explained, giving her a moment in case she was ready to share any of her secrets with him.

Maria did not reply, but to Julian, she looked thoughtful as she stared at the mint leaf.

Encouraged, Julian foraged among the grasses and weeds, looking for more herbs. "We must hope that the spirits have placed what we need in reach."

"I know inkberry," Maria said, pointing at the long stalks with gravid purple berries clustered on the end.

"Boil it and it will get rid of a fever. Also it will protect you from evil spirits," he replied.

He showed her sassafras, Solomon's seal and bearberry, to be used respectively for general healing, inducing romantic love and curing infections.

"And of course, tobacco… This is the Great Spirit's favorite plant. It is my favorite too," Julian said. He pressed a handful of tobacco leaves into her palm and nodded for her to accept the gift. Maria took them happily and immediately put them to use, walking beside him with her pipe dangling from her lower lip in a most disrespectful manner. But Julian said nothing. Her ways were not his.

"Can you kill the wolf for me?" she asked him.

Julian scowled at her. "I would never do that."

"But…"

"The wolf is a good spirit."

The girl came to a stop and demanded, "Why are you helping me?"

"We trade. I help you hunt and learn about spirits. One day you can help me."

"But I have nothing to offer!" she insisted.

Julian turned his back on her. "Come. I will show you where the rabbits live." Then, realizing that she was not following him, he turned and asked, "Do you fear me?"

Obscured in pipe smoke as it was, Maria's face was hard to read. *"No one else has taken interest in my welfare..."* she muttered.

"Then come."

They strolled through the rough pasture of the Devil's land as if they were simply two Eastham villagers walking through a commons.

"Why do you not live with your people?" she inquired.

Julian told her of his people's disintegration, his purchase of Great Island and then his outlawry that had made it too dangerous to return to his reacquired land.

"I do not know much of your people, I admit. I have never even been to Nauset village, if you can believe it, even though it is but a few miles from where I was born. Although, I have sailed by it. So it seems as though the men of Eastham have been spreading out misery to more people than I ever knew."

"Yes," Julian agreed, his excitement growing. "What will you do?"

"Me? Wait here until Sam comes back, I guess. If he does not, then I will simply hunt for plants, with you, until the wind one day sweeps me off this bluff. What will you do? We are both outlaws, it seems. Will they come looking for us one day?"

"No. They do not care for this land. There is nowhere to grow good crops or graze animals," he said despondently.

She peered at him, misreading his disappointment in her for a more general sadness. "Ah! You are lonely too! It is a sorrowful state. I can attest to that. Yet now we know that we are not alone. We are alike in our exile and misery."

"Yes, we are much alike," Julian sighed. She would tell him when she was ready, he assured himself. "Except that you do not know how to catch a rabbit."

"Can you teach me to catch one, then?" she asked.

Julian looked at her. "Rabbit is the animal of fear. Once you have no fear, then rabbit comes to eat out of your hand."

By the end of the afternoon, Julian had taught her how to make a bow and arrow and how to take down the rabbits when they wandered into the open meadows. By nightfall they had several animals skinned and ready for the fire. As Julian cooked supper on a spit, he continued the conversation that they had been having all day, one that examined the injuries against each of them over and over, until they were both convinced that they were the two most wronged people in Eastham.

After the meal he got up abruptly and began to walk towards the darkness.

"Where are you going?"

"I sleep in the place of my people," he told her. "You sleep in your hut. It is a good one now." He glanced at the dwelling as he spoke and nodded approvingly at the way they had refashioned it into something much closer to a *wetu*.

"You are *leaving*? I thought that, each night, you slept by the fire!" she said in alarm. "If you prefer, you could share the hut. I don't like being here alone. Sometimes I have... *bad dreams*."

At the mention of her dreams, Julian's heart skipped. But, as eager as he was to hear more, he raised his hands to cut her off. It was too late now to speak of it. He wanted such council shared under the clear light of the sun, not the shifty gaze of the moon. Then, once they had a plan, she could enact it under any conditions that she wished, he thought, glancing up at the smoky clouds drifting across the face of the bright orb above them. "I will not be far away. If you shout, I will hear you. Sleep now and do not fear the dreams. You can catch rabbits now. You have nothing anymore to fear."

The girl looked skeptical at his words, but Julian felt ebullient at her admission. *Yes, she is a witch after all...* And her enemies were the same as his: Justice Doane, Samuel Smith and Reverend Treat.

✠ ✠ ✠ ✠

Sometimes Julian would leave for days or weeks at a time, telling Maria nothing of his journeys, other than that they were meant to reveal the nature of his purpose to him. In truth, he still did not know what this land wanted from him. More and more, he believed that the girl had some part to play or message to deliver, but he did not want to act rashly. He would tend to her growth, like the plants that he was teaching her about, and wait to see what would flower.

One day Julian took Maria to the edge of the white cedar swamp that lay to the northwest of Maria's hut. The trees were set in a long sloping gully. They stood close together, emitting a murky gloom, which suggested that a state of permanent twilight existed within. Maria appraised the gnarled woven branches, the bark that looked like an old man's skin, bearded moss that hung from great, face-like growths on the trunks and all of it made her shiver. When Julian informed her that the place held great knowledge and hidden magic from the beginning of the world, Maria said that she was not surprised to hear it, but she admitted that the look of the place made her loathe to learn its secrets.

Julian hovered at the edge of the swamp for a moment, inhaling its earthy smell. To him, the swamp was as hallowed as the white man's meeting house. But it only passed along its wisdom to those who were ready.

"Let us go," Maria said. And Julian reluctantly nodded and led her away.

They gathered herbs from the edge of the forest, from which he promised to show her how to make more remedies to heal cuts faster, help with sleep and keep away unwanted spirits. She told him that Widow Chase had given her a glimpse of this kind of medicine, but he strove to enhance that knowledge, turning the world that had previously seemed to be nothing but a boring wall of interwoven, nameless plants into a living apothecary, as the girl referred to his teachings.

"I remember that Widow Chase gave me a drink made out of pennyroyal. She knew much of what you are showing me," Maria mused as she and Julian sat, peeling the leaves from stems of plants.

He could hear the guilt and worry in her voice and nodded solemnly. "You do not need to worry. Men spoke of this in Smith Tavern... Widow Chase lives. They did not believe her to be a witch," he said of the verdict of the Barnstable court. He shook his head, surprised that such men were capable of such wisdom.

"That is *very good*," Maria breathed. "I did not believe that she could do magic."

The native frowned. "This... *this*... *this*... all is magic," he replied, pointing in turn to the twisted pine trees, a line of ants crawling along the path and the massive ocean.

"That is not how Reverend Treat explains it."

Julian scowled at the remark. "Treat does not believe in spirit medicine. You must believe for it to work." He pointed towards a cedar tree in the distance. "Burn the twigs and make smoke, and then you can *see* spirits."

"Ghosts?" Maria asked.

"Yes, yes, they are there even if you cannot see them," Julian said impatiently. "To see them or talk to them, your mind must be calm, like a pond, and your heart like an open field. If you are too angry for magic, you will call the thing that you fear. You know much of this even if you do not know what it is. At the trial they spoke of your dreams and visions. I heard this from those that were there," he told her.

Maria backed away from him. "Oh no, no... You are in error. I do not prophesize. I am no witch."

"*Witch* is Treat's word! He gives it to those that he does not understand! Mittawa is *dead*. But she still sees! The gift of sight cannot die! It is a thing of beauty, not fear! Magic is part of everything. I call it *spirit*. Your people do not know what spirit really is! You cannot help but have it inside of you! You cannot help but be who you are! Have I taught you nothing?"

"To you it is magic, to me it is misery!" she cried and ran off into the scrublands. Julian did not follow. All he could do was keep shining the light of knowledge upon her, like sun falling on the petals, and hope that she would reveal her inner self to him. Witch... Medicine woman... He knew that it was not the words, but the wisdom, that made magic real.

✠ ✠ ✠ ✠

It was several nights before Julian came back to Maria's hut. He found her tending the fire. Unseen, he watched her walk around the blaze, constantly touching her belly, patting it as though there was an emptiness there. He remembered that she had talked about a baby. He crept closer to the fire, sensing that something was at last unfolding inside of her.

The fire was huge and mesmerizing even in the hollow. It called out to those at sea and even those passing by on shore although none dared cross the Devil's Pasture by day, let alone after dark.

Then something extraordinary happened. Julian heard the girl calling for the spirits. It was a clumsy first attempt, but the desire was clear, and he felt his heart thrum with the possibilities of her summons.

Sure enough, he watched her toss sticks onto the blaze, and then he caught the scent of cedar burning, beckoning the spirit world.

She also had a handful of mint leaves. Several times, she raised the leaves towards her nostrils and then dissolved in giggles, unable to go any further.

"This is ridiculous!" she cried.

"No... Feel spirit..." Julian whispered in encouragement, looking around himself and straining to feel some sense of spirit gathering.

Finally she pressed the mint up to her nose and inhaled deeply. Julian knew that she was feeling the mint scent shooting, like a finger of ice, into the space between her eyes. He could tell that her head was throbbing from the intensity of its essence. He knew too that it takes a strong jolt from a powerful plant to connect with the other world.

As if the power of the leaves was too much to bear, she lay down on the cool, sandy earth and closed her eyes for a time. Her breath became slow and gentle.

Then she abruptly stood up and went closer to the fire. She stood over the flames and began chanting, slowly and rhythmically, her body swaying. The words were nothing that Julian recognized. But the *sound* of them was kindred to an old prayer that he recalled from his childhood:

Let the wind carry my thoughts, let the ground lead my feet...

More and more, the shadows seemed to converge around the girl, making her seem a part of the night.

Let the sun be my eyes and the moon be my memory...

As she danced, Maria raised her arms and let herbs sprinkle out of her hands and drift down into the fire. The flames devoured them, and the fire expanded, crackling and furious. The sweet odor of lavender and beech leaf spread into the darkness, reaching Julian's nostrils and making him giddy.

Up in the sky a silvery full moon shone in the darkness. Thin, dark clouds streamed across the face of the moon. Each time the shining orb broke through the black clouds, it felt to Julian like laughter.

Julian looked back at the girl and listened to her sing more. There was only one way that she could know that ancient melody. It was being sung into her ear by spirit. By one particular spirit.

Maria suddenly stopped singing. She opened her eyes, as if in shock, and exclaimed, "You are dead!"

From deep in the dark bracken behind him, a wolf gave a plaintive cry.

Mittawa.

Right alongside of the girl was a flash of the waving brown arms of another dancer, clothed in a dress of furs, spinning around beside her. The image came and went, like the flicker of the flame.

Over time, the spirit grew stronger. His aunt was speaking to Maria, but Julian could hear the words plainly.

"*Can you see him?*" Mittawa asked.

"Who? Who is it?" Maria said aloud.

"*Next to you…There is someone else here…*"

Maria glanced nervously around but could discern nothing but the spiky outlines of brush and pine in the darkness. "*Where?*" she whispered.

"*Next to you…*"

"What?" Maria exclaimed, nearly tripping over. Again she saw nothing around her but sand and clumps of undergrowth.

"*A little boy… With dark hair… A little boy…Your boy…*"

"Stop it! What you say is impossible. You can't see my son!" she shouted.

"*Forgive… That is what he says. He wants you to forgive…*"

"Where are you, little Sam? Where are you?" she cried into the night.

The dark void around her gave no reply, and the moon twinkled impishly as if it knew, but would not part with, the answers to her questions. Julian watched in awe.

"*Forgive…*"

Tears rolled down Maria's face, burning like fire. She circled faster and faster. A mournful moan seeped from her wide open lungs.

The mixture of scent, fire, motion and swirling stars made Julian want to dance too. But this was her trial, her cleansing. He could tell that she was shedding the weight of her ordeals, flinging off more worries and fears each time that she spun around. She was not afraid of magic anymore.

Maria hiked up her skirt because it was tripping her as she danced. She threw her hands up in the air and released the last of the herbs that she carried. They rained down into the fire, and Maria yelled with delight.

As the flames roared to life, she suddenly crumpled to the ground.

"My baby!" she yelled, clutching her belly and rolling onto her hands and knees. "It feels like I am giving birth again… Ahhh!"

"Joy and pain are inseparable. Two sides of life." Mittawa pressed her palms together to emphasize the point. Then the spirit receded.

Tears streamed. Maria's voice shook and howled like a tempest. She lay on the ground, curled into a ball and stayed that way for some time.

Then, seized by sudden inspiration, she began crawling around, looking for stones.

Cautiously, Julian came out of the shadows and stood in the fire light, gazing at the witch girl with an intensity equal to that of the fire.

"I danced with her…the *Witch of Billingsgate*," she said when she noticed him. Then she quickly turned her attention back to the ground. "More flat stones… I need more flat stones…"

"My aunt. Mittawa," he said, coming towards her.

"You were right! She is somehow alive! I *saw* her!" She dug into the sand, exhuming fist-sized rocks and piling them up in the way that the lingering energy of the dance guided her. Some of the rocks looked as large as the little boy for whom the shrine was in honor.

Julian nodded at the monument. "Any spirit would sleep well under such care."

"Why did the cows die? Or the squid arrive?" Maria asked urgently. "Do you know? Perhaps you could reverse the magic and return my father's fields as they were? Could you bring Sam back? Or my baby?"

Julian gave her a pitying glance. "Why your sailor or your baby or the cattle were taken, I do not know. But there is a reason."

"You must know! They say witchcraft did it! You know about these things. Tell me! Tell me what is to become of me! Do I die here, alone and miserable?"

Julian lifted up one of the herb leaves that lay scorched on the ground. "No plant can let you know the future. Only spirit knows the future. But not all spirits. You must make sure you are talking to a spirit that actually knows something."

"But the spells."

"Spells, spirits… They are as real as this fire or the night sky above us. They are real as dreams. You can *see!*"

Maria was silent. She laid the last stone on the pile and stood up next to it. The mound of rocks was no more than a couple of feet high and probably barely visible to any ship that might be passing off shore. There was no name carved into the monument. A swift kick could send it tumbling out of form. But it was something. She patted the top stone like it was her babe's little head. After sitting next to the fire, the rock was as warm as if it had life in it.

Later she went off and stood on the bluff and looked out over the ocean. Julian could not tell what her expression was. A day ago he might have thought that she was still pining for her sailor, her lost baby or her life before exile. But he knew that could not be the case now. She had transformed. It was not a fearsome change. It was more akin to a butterfly hatching from a cocoon. But she could not go back.

Chapter Six
"The Omen of the Wolf"

Autumn 1716 - Winter 1717

Autumn came but had little visible effect on the harsh land-scape of the Devil's Pasture. Some bushes browned and some pines went to rust and dropped their needles. Birds flew over head, in great arrows pointing south. The wind off of the sea carried more ice than water in its touch.

The witch girl changed but not in the way that John Julian had expected. She did not embrace her connection to spirit or send havoc to the English, with her powerful dreams. Instead, the fire dance seemed to have burned much of the anger from her.

The two of them spent most of their time sitting with their feet dangling over the edge of the cliff, tobacco pipes clenched in their teeth. Now and then, he might nudge her and point wordlessly to some bird scurrying across the sand or a stretch of clouds in the sky that looked like fish scales. They would nod at each other and then lapse back into quiet, letting the soft scrape of tide on the beach below and endless whisper of wind speak instead.

Julian continued to teach her the lore and lifestyle that he knew. The irony of passing on such wisdom to an English witch was bittersweet. His lore was not the way of the rest of his people. It was an older, vanishing philosophy of living. When he was gone, he did not know to whom she would hand the stories next, but he doubted that it would be a Nauset or Punonakanit.

Maria often declared that she was coming to prefer the style and wisdom of the natives better than the culture that she had grown up in. She said that it seemed more sensible to her, with its notion of fitting in with the world around them rather than plowing it under foot.

They were outlaws together, both rejected by their people. At times it felt as though they were taking what pieces they found useful from the lives they were leaving and forging a new kind of culture between them, in which they both fit perfectly and were completely understood. Perhaps it would have sustained them indefinitely, but Julian could not help but mention the grievances against them whenever those wrongs seemed in danger of fading away.

"I cannot forget what the townsfolk did to me. Knowles, Treat, my mother..." she would admit. From her tone Julian knew that she would not forget, but sometimes he worried that she had already forgiven her foes. Perhaps she even dreamed well of them.

Julian could never get the girl to tell him what she saw in her sleeping mind. Yet he continued to ask her about it, more out of habit than any hope that he would be answered. If she responded at all, her reaction was worse than ever. Whereas before she seemed too terrified to reply, now she scowled as if the question was a betrayal.

In truth, he did not care as much as he used to. By winter the wolf tracks faded away. The absence of the wolf confused and depressed him. He found no trace of it around the hut, swamp or forest. At times he felt as though he could barely even detect the voice of spirit in the wind or ground beneath him. It was like the waning beat of a dying heart.

The cold settled in for weeks, making his muscles feel like lead and his thoughts and willpower stiff with ice. He spent much of his time resting and sleeping in the rickety lean-to that he had constructed in the wedge between two crooked, gnarled white cedars, with no extra hope in his heart, just a flicker of restlessness that there was *something* that he should do. What it was, he did not know. For all he knew, some white man had, by now, built a house on his land on Great Island. Sometimes he imagined fulfilling the omen and leaving the land altogether, but the more he pondered the idea, the harder it was to find the energy to move at all. At times he wondered if there was some kind of curse upon the land that prevented him from leaving.

One morning Julian woke with a start. Snow dribbled through the weave of branches over his head. The snow's wet touch on his forehead was cold and quickly drove off the dream that had woken him. All he remembered was that he had been talking to his aunt. That in itself was an occurrence. It was a pity that he could not recall anything that she had told him.

Then he saw the mark, the padded depression and claw pricks, like the image of a spiky flower petal, in the snow.

Some instinct told Julian to go see the witch girl. He dashed across the field of white powder towards her snow-mounded hut.

"Wake up!" he called into the dark interior, thrusting the deerskin curtain door open. "I saw wolf tracks!" he cried joyfully.

The girl was curled up in bed next to the cold, black coals of a spent fire. Ice skimmed the surface of the cook pot, which sat on the coals, and the freezing wind whistled through gaps in the walls.

Maria lifted her head to look at Julian, and he was amazed to see fear and incomprehension in her eyes as if she did not recognize him. She pulled her covering of furs tight around her and scooted away from him, deeper into the corner of the hut.

"What is the matter?" he asked.

"Why are you here?" she asked back, staring intently at him.

"The wolf is back. It is a sign." He thought that her face, for some reason, looked somewhat paler when he mentioned the wolf.

"Why are you here *today? This morning?*" she implored.

Julian was confused. He wondered if the girl's mind had been swept away by the cold winter winds. "Do you want me to leave?"

"She said that you would come today. She said *the wolf will come too.* I cannot believe it... I *won't* believe it!" Maria went on.

Julian glanced around the hut and, of course, saw no one. Nor were there any footprints in the snow outside except for his own. Besides the two of them, none came to this spot. None that were of the living world that is. All of a sudden, Julian thought that he knew of whom the witch girl was speaking.

"Who told you about me? Were you speaking to Mittawa?" he asked eagerly. When her eyes went wide, he knew that he was right. "You saw her again? Like you did when you danced around the fire?"

Slowly, the girl nodded. Julian could see the hesitation in her face. But then she said, "I dreamed of her."

Julian's jaw dropped. The long awaited moment had arrived. He felt his skin tighten, and the sensation was not from the chill air around him. It was the same kind of feeling that he had experienced long ago, on the sand flats as a child, when Mittawa had told him about the beast and the man who would come from the sea. "*What else did she say?*" he breathed.

"She told me that she had come to take away the winter and that, over the next few days, planting time will come and, with it, turmoil."

"Something bad is coming for the English?" he asked.

The girl shrugged. "It sounds like it will be unpleasant for somebody. I don't know… She also told me that you would be coming here this morning. And here you are. I don't like these dreams."

Julian was too excited to notice how tense and rigid the girl was. If he had, he would have assumed that it was due to the power of the vision. "What are we to do when planting season comes?"

"I don't know!" Maria wailed.

"Try to remember!" he urged.

"No. Let me sleep," she protested. "Let me sleep and dream of nothing."

"A vision will give you no rest," Julian told her. "Come outside with me, and we will build a fire and dance and ask for Mittawa to come and remind you about what she said in the dream."

She turned her back to him. "What is the use? It is the middle of February. Spring won't arrive for weeks!"

Julian gave an exasperated sigh. "That does not matter! The spirit world spoke to you! We must listen!"

"Let me sleep!" she cried, pulling the furs over her head.

"Do you not want to avenge yourself on those who hurt you? Maybe this dream will tell you how to do that!" he shouted.

She said nothing for a long moment. Finally, from under the blanket she mumbled, "*I want to sleep…*"

Julian nodded glumly and stepped outside. He could tell that she would not be persuaded. The wind was driving hard off of the ocean. By the time that he had wandered back to the swamp, the wolf prints had been swept away as smoothly as the tide rolling over a beach. But he did not despair. He gathered fallen branches from the swamp, lit a fire and did a ritual dance around it, asking the spirits to help make Mittawa's vision come true. He felt sure that whatever his aunt had in mind would bring sorrow to the English.

The next day the air was warm on his skin. The day after that it was warm again, and the snow sheets started turning to water. By the third day, he left footprints in the muddy ground, which had thawed all around him. Soon after that the soil was soft and fit for planting, in a time when the ground usually sleeps under ice and cold. Julian rejoiced at the favor the spirits had shown them. The dream spell had worked.

When he next saw Maria, she was staring, bewildered, at the dirt outside of her hut.

She looked at him with astonishment but also a trace of horror.

"It is impossible..." she gasped, pointing down at the ground where the heads of small green shoots were poking through.

Julian smiled with happiness. "I have been thinking about the vision. Maybe it is a trick to make the English plant all of their crops early. Then the snows will come again and destroy them and leave them with nothing."

"Yes, winter will come back. Everyone knows that. That is why no one would be fool enough to plant now," she responded in a dream-like voice.

Julian shook his head in frustration, but he had to admit that the girl was probably correct. "Then perhaps it is simply a message from the spirit world. They are trying to give us hope! A *dream* did this! *You* helped do this!"

Both her eyes and voice sharpened with anger. "If that is true, then perhaps *I* am the one who is cursed. Perhaps Mittawa has been cursing me all along, by giving me these wretched dreams!"

"What about the dance around the fire? You were healed," Julian protested.

"All I know is that my dreams bring unhappiness. Your aunt said that this thawing would lead to *turmoil.* To me, turmoil is usually grief!"

"Mittawa would not want you to have grief. The spirits show us visions to give us warning, hope and teaching. I think that she came to you because you have great dream power. She is showing you that you can dream bigger and better!"

"I keep telling you that I don't want this! I dreamed of my father dying and then he did!"

Julian softened for a moment. "We are not wise enough to know why that happened. But not all dreams are bad. You should not be afraid of your power," he said soothingly.

Maria shot him an angry glance. In a voice like a curse, she declared, "These plants will die in a few days! It is still winter!"

Then she stormed back into her hut.

The girl, it turned out, was right.

The unnatural warmth lasted for two weeks, bringing tree buds and fledgling crops but no lasting switch of seasons. Abruptly, it ended, under dark clouds of snow, which piled up higher than a man's head. It was more snow than they had received all winter.

The snow stayed longer than it should have, well into the time when the trees should have bloomed on their own, and Julian could not help but feel responsible because of his part in it, his ritual dance. It looked like yet another one of his appeals to the spirits had gone astray. In the end it seemed that all he had done was create a little space within winter, which had since been covered over by snow tenfold, like the interest that the whites demanded for the borrowing of their money. Cold, warm, cold. The strange weather was mirroring his emotions these days.

It would have been so much better had he stayed on Great Island, he thought. He would have been safe and warm in the *wetu* that he had hoped to build there. As soon as it was okay to return to his land, then perhaps he would take a wife. Maria showed much promise as a partner, but it was a shame that she was English. He had not enough white blood to seriously consider the notion. Besides, he was bitter at the girl. She had a gift worthy of a great medicine woman, yet she was throwing it away.

His plan, it seemed, had failed. The witch girl was no use to him. The fight for his land was his alone. But, at the moment, he had no strength for it.

✠ ✠ ✠ ✠

March 28, 1717

Earlier in the night, John Tom had been in his glory. His cousins of the Nauset tribe had welcomed him like an honored guest. Inside the *wetu* he sat next to Reverend Treat himself, and the reverend bestowed upon him the additional honor of asking him to explain the intricacies of the prayer for the coming harvest. He told the reverend that it was based on the old tradition of asking the spirits for bounty in the coming year, yet it was now appropriately offered as a prayer to the Holy God rather than some ignorant spell.

Normally Treat was fascinated by the culture of the tribes. John Tom expected the reverend to ask him endless questions, in Wampanoag, about everything from the spices in the fish stew that was being served to the prayers that the Nauset elders were offering to their ancestors. He would not have been surprised if the white man had jumped up and joined the native children as they danced around the cook fire in the middle of the *wetu* or played blind man's bluff with the youngest ones, as Treat had done when he was younger and first getting to know the tribes. But this night the old man's eyes wandered, and eventually John Tom's own enthusiasm began to slip away.

The snow fell by the foot, and John Tom realized that he would not be walking or canoeing back to his own village. For once, he felt annoyed at the old reverend. Treat was acting like a child by insisting that he walk home in the face of the wind and snow. Even though Treat's homestead was a short walk through the woods and up the hill, it was the kind of storm that could swallow a man after only a few paces. He watched the old man go, his great bulk quickly reduced to nothing, in the sheet of white.

By morning the fields were covered in a white veil as quiet and still as death, and John Tom felt nothing but love and grief.

He had not been the first to hear the keening, but after the young woman who first noticed came to fetch him, he knew what the cry meant.

It was coming from Treat's house on the hill.

He did not want any companions, for he relished the privilege of being the emissary to the white preacher whether to receive good news or bad. But he could not stop the natives who filed in behind him. They all loved Treat.

Mrs. Treat was howling like a wounded beast. They could hear her through the windows, then see her face pressed against the glass. Her features were a mask of pain and fear, staring out at them, distorted by the rough cut of the window pane to look like a yowling demon. The snowdrift at the front door had trapped her inside. It stood larger than a man, and John Tom set several men digging to open passage.

But the natives did not have to be told. More hands than were needed tore at the snow, carving a trench to the door through which John Tom prayed he would be first to enter.

The diggers worked in a frenzy, and as soon as the hinges were cleared, the door sprung open and Mrs. Treat fell, sobbing, into the arms of a young brave.

"He is dead! My Samuel!"

The inside of the house was as dark as a tomb.

John Tom stepped across the threshold and saw the great man laid out on the floor. His body was stiff as if frozen.

He was gone. It was like God Himself had left them, John Tom thought bitterly. What would happen now, he wondered?

✠ ✠ ✠ ✠

One day in mid-April John Julian came out of the white cedar swamp and knew that the ground's thaw would stay until next winter. Everything from the warm, scented air to the green push of new growth on the trees spoke of it.

He was breathing in the full brew of the morning breeze, so he did not notice the tracks on the ground, until he had walked over half of them.

Wolf...

Relief flooded through him. It was a new sign from spirit, a new direction, and he told himself that he would follow it wherever it led, and he would be content. The tracks, it turned out, headed away from the swamp towards the west.

He touched fingers to the prints and found there was still warmth in them. The creature was not far ahead of him. He scrambled after the animal, through the bracken, leaving the witch girl behind him, on her lonely perch over the ocean.

All that day he followed the trail. To his surprise, the animal led him to the water's edge across from Great Island.

He stood and marveled at the way the island seemed to literally float on the surface of the ocean. He felt as if he were beholding it for the first time.

The wolf did not stop there. It went south on colder tracks. He was falling behind. Yet that knowledge did not trouble him.

He found signs of it again, the next day, just over the bridge that spanned Blackfish Creek. On the other side was the southern parish of Eastham. Only then did he hesitate. Yet the sign was clear. The wolf was leading him onward.

By the afternoon of the second day of his pursuit, John Julian was standing on one of the two hills that overlooked the north side of the saltwater pond next to Nauset village. Below him, his people were planting corn and squash in the time honored way of setting the seeds so the climbing vines would twine around the corn stalks as they grew out of little mounds, each planted with a single herring fish to act as fertilizer. It had been so long since he had taken in this view that it came to him with fresh eyes and a light heart, born from the promise of his animal guide.

Not long after he passed the saltwater pond, the trail disappeared. By Julian's reckoning he was only a half-day behind the wolf. Somewhere close by, the creature still lurked. If he could find some mark of it, he could continue the journey. If not, he did not want to think about it. Too many omens and signs had gone off track for him lately.

The Eastham meeting house stood, stark and dreary, next to the King's Highway. As Julian trotted towards it, the sight of it made his wrists ache, with the memory of too many days spent writhing in the pillory under its shadow. Today there was a different man trapped in the device. A white man. Julian gave a little chuckle. If nothing else, the wolf had shown him this pleasant irony.

Old Barnabus Merrill had not slept well, having been pinned up in the pillory all night, for public drunkenness. His throat was parched and felt like hell. When he saw the native man coming towards him, he did not care what kind of abuse the fellow had for him as long as he also offered a bit of something to wet his tongue.

"Be a good sport now and give us a bit of ale, before you have your fun!" Barnabus cried. Around him were the rinds of well-rotted fruit. Lack of crop made meager pickings for vegetables to hurl at those in the pillory. The limited choice did not make what was thrown any more inviting. The local children had raided the compost piles and shell heaps for their missiles. So the stuff that stuck to the old man's face and clothes was rank meat and fish guts so putrid that even buzzards would not have touched it.

Julian lifted his hands to show that they were empty of either help or projectiles. Outside of the meeting house was the town well. Julian headed that way to fetch a drink of water but stopped when Barnabus complained, "Oh no! Can't you get me anything stronger?"

The native turned around and came back towards the imprisoned man. As he did, two things came into sharp focus. One was a murmuring sound coming from the building behind him. The second was a salty tang in the air that smelled of blood. He sniffed close to Barnabus, and the old man hissed at him.

"Get away from me! What are you going to do, lick the dung off of me?"

"Blood?" Julian asked.

"Those little hellions, the Mayo boys. Threw a damned pig's leg at me! Freshly cut too! I don't mind the blood. Tis the bone that hurt me! Another inch and it would have damn well taken my eye!"

Julian cocked an ear to the sound coming from the meeting house.

"Town meeting," Barnabus explained. "Can't hear much of what they are saying, except for when they get riled up about something."

There was a fluttering in Julian's stomach that he assumed was nerves. Justice Doane was likely right behind that door. It could open in an instant, and then Julian would have to run for his life. Then he realized that his shudder went deeper. *Town meeting...* He recalled the notice fluttering on Samuel Smith's door.

"*The land division...*" he muttered.

"Oh yes, they're going on and on about that again. Every year, it seems, that comes up."

"Every year?"

Barnabus laughed. "Almost! You wouldn't know, would you? Indians don't get invited to such meetings. Well, four years ago they divided it up. And two years ago they did it again. Since then, some folks keep protesting the new ownership. Foolishness! That is why I sometimes wish I'd stayed at sea!"

There was another sharp whiff of blood in the air, but it was not coming from the direction of Barnabus. What was it, Julian wondered?

It was coming from the meeting house. Something fluttered above the door, drawing Julian's eye.

A pack of crows. Their black feathers merged easily with the dark stain of the meeting house walls. What he could see most clearly was the red flecks on their beaks.

The foremost one hopped over a strange furry clump that was pinned up over the door. It thrust its beak into the mass and drew out another bloody red gulp.

A wolf's head.

From its perch, the wolf aimed hollow sockets down at Julian. A crimson line at the neck was all that was left of the rest of its once proud body. The crows would make quick work of the rest. Its jaws were slack, giving the creature a jaunty smile as a death mask.

Everything about it, from its blackness to its foul blood to its grisly end, churned awfully inside Julian. The sight hit him with such impact that he nearly fell over.

No...

Merrill's voice cut in, answering his earlier question, "Ah yeah! The bloody land division! That caused a damned uproar, let me tell you! I heard the whole thing through that danged window. All the dithering they did was punishment enough on top of where they already got me! They spent an hour dithering. I heard a whole lot of whining from that Sam Smith. He tore out of here, cursing so much that I was shouting for the justice to put him in the pillory. Coarse language in public! That's a fine too, you know!"

"He owns Great Island," Julian said. He could feel the scent of the dead wolf seeping down into his stomach and twisting sickly there.

"Ha! That's what he thought too! But it's all divvied up now among the proprietors...John Knowles, Justice Doane...all the usual lot! I don't care, though. The ale Smith serves ain't worth the time it takes to get there!"

"I have a deed."

"What you say, lad?"

"I have a deed. I paid Smith seventy pounds for it." Julian looked Barnabus straight in the eye. For a moment their eyes locked and there could have been some understanding between them. They were two men who had never owned any property. But Barnabus had drunk enough that there was still some fume of it left on him.

He started laughing. "Seventy pounds! That land ain't worth half that much! In fact, it ain't worth spit! Smith never owned it to begin with! All you got is a piece of paper, Indian!"

Inside of him something took hold of Julian, like some inner spirit was controlling him. Before he knew it, he had struck the old man.

"Hey! What was that for, you bastard?"

Julian hit the old man again, and Barnabus' eyes went wide with the kind of fright that his ancestors had in the years when they looked out through the garrison windows at the hostile land, with primordial fear. "You bloody savage..." Barnabus breathed, in horror.

Julian hit him again and again.

He did not stop until he heard no more oaths or cries, just a soft wheeze of unconsciousness.

This should be Smith or Doane, he thought as he at last came to his senses. His own dread came to life as he realized that now he had given the whites an actual crime to pin upon him. For once, there was reason, he thought as he tried to wipe the old man's blood off his knuckles using Barnabus' shirt front.

At any moment he expected to see Doane and his posse come triumphantly out of the meeting house. He needed to get to Great Island...or somewhere. He did not know where to go anymore. But he could do nothing but stand there and seethe.

Damn it, this was his land. And damn Sam Smith and Justice Doane and the endless lies of the white men. Even their laws and deeds were false promises!

The old man's bleeding face gave Julian a surge of remorse. He hurried to the public well and brought back some water, in the cup of his hands, which he dribbled over Barnabus' lips. Then he put some crushed sassafras on Barnabus' tongue, for healing.

"*I am sorry*," Julian muttered.

Still, the thoughts in Julian's mind stung like a swarm of bees. He longed for revenge on those who had wronged him. He wished for one more chance to talk with his aunt. But he had a strong feeling that he had seen the last of her. He knew that if she indeed had left him, it was because he had failed her.

The wolf's tongue lolled in its dead jaws, mockingly spilling the final truth of Mittawa's omen. So it had come to this. He had read the signs all wrong after all. He was to be driven from the land. It was over, and John Julian had lost.

Chapter Seven
"Return of the Warriors"

Mid-April 1717

The dwelling was not much more than boards leaned together, nailed here and there for more support but largely left to angle and gravity to keep it upright. Rain poured off the roof, and some through it, but the weather did nothing to quell the raucous sounds within. In its way, it fit in perfectly with the other establishments and dwellings of Helltown.

One did not knock to enter such a place. John Julian pushed aside the wooden planks that hung like loose teeth in the hinges of the door and walked into a room that looked like a miniature Higgins Tavern. Instead of tables, there were great wooden stools that men and women stood around, balancing tin cups and mugs while they smoked, laughed and poked at each other. At first glance it was impossible to tell who owned the establishment or served the liquor because the owner and the serving girls were mixed in with the rowdy patrons and drinking the same share as the others.

It was the kind of place where everyone sized up the next drinkers who came through the door. Some might offer a place at the stool. A woman might hike up her dress and offer a peek at her leg if the newcomer looked handsome or rich. If company was declined, then there was no further trouble. A man could stand and drink at his leisure, help himself to refills of ale if he was being neglected, and mind his own company, until a fight broke out, then everyone was served equal measures of the brawl. That was simply the tradition at Boyd's Bog. The best way to start a fight was to forego dropping a coin into the glass beaker that stood atop the ale barrel. Boyd Christie preferred drinking with his customers than serving them, but no matter how deep into a drink or tale he was, some part of him was always fixed on that coin glass. No one yet had gotten a free ale.

Ships were in the harbor tonight. Julian had seen their towering silhouettes in the darkness as he walked up the King's Highway and then across the flats where the king's men had stopped the road, feeling that no more civilization could be reached by it. Past that point lay Helltown. One had to cross the open flats to reach the settlement, tucked in as it was around East Harbor, under the curling knuckles of Cape Cod. There were other places to drink in Helltown, most notably the wide stretch of sand next to the harbor, but Boyd's Bog was the most popular and, considering all of the ships at bay, Julian was not surprised to find the place packed.

Julian nodded, but said nothing, to those who greeted him. He wondered again why he had come to such a place. There was little pleasing about the company. If he listened closely, there was information to be gained, which men in Eastham might pay for, such as rumors of rebellions, land speculations, talk of pirates, where-abouts of outlaws from Eastham and the like. Julian was not above adding to his pile of coin to set white men upon each other. To him, it seemed a beautiful kind of justice, since the whites had so long made it their practice to set themselves on his people. He had little need for coin now, except for a handful of pennies to deposit in Christie's glass jar. The coin was good for nothing but the ale that the white men were so fond of and the hazy oblivion that it promised.

Since there was no empty seat, Julian joined the table with the most open spaces.

"Another Indian," the man next to him told his table com-panions. Julian noted the lilting accent as well as the knowing look shared between the men. Both made him wary. Foreign white men had no ties to the area and so could be the worst of their kind.

There were natives here too. Some even with Punonakanit blood, who might have been worth talking to if only to soothe his feeling of homesickness. But they only stared and pointed at his face and would come no closer. Their fear reminded him of the Nauset boys on the flats, who had run from him.

Julian sat and drank and listened to the unusual accents around him. The more he listened, the more his suspicions grew that these were the kind of white men to whom he could be distantly related. His table companions spoke in the manner of the French pirates who he had met with Smith. They were a scruffy and tar-caked ship's crew.

They were talking of war, like men of all colors did so often at Boyd's Bog. Many of the patrons were veterans, lapsed militiamen, privateers or scouts. They were all weighing where the profit lay in the next conflict and how dangerous it would be to get a piece of it.

The French sailors did not address Julian again for some time. Only when they tired of their own talk did one catch Julian's eye and languidly say, "What is this on your face? Don't tell me...I have heard of such decorations before. Ah! The colors for battle, eh? Very nice, very nice!" The Frenchman's friends erupted with laughter.

Julian touched his fingers to his cheeks and felt smudges of blood from the wolf's head that he had ripped down from the Eastham meeting house.

"I am joking, my friend! Drink! Drink and be happy! There is ale, there are women and there may be fighting if we are lucky. Why are you looking so sad?"

"You talk of your wars. I have none," Julian shrugged.

"No, no! There are many Indians who fight in Quebec for our king! These English pigs have some too. But you would die sooner from their food than from an enemy musket! So you see? You did not get dressed up for nothing. There is always plenty of war, my friend!"

Julian shook his head. Half-formed questions spun through his mind. He did not know exactly what he would ask such men or what they could tell him that would help him know anything important about his ancestry, yet he wanted to hear them speak more, gauge them and understand them. He hoped they held some clue that he would not have otherwise found. It could not be coincidence that he had sat next to this group, of all the others in this place.

"Don't such er... designs... help you drink better, my friend? Make war on that ale! You have not once gotten up for another? You are not thirsty this night?" the Frenchman asked.

"I am not thirsty."

"You are out of coin," the man continued with a sly look.

"If he has no coin, then why waste your breath, Francois?" another said with a laugh. "If you want to talk to an Indian, how about her? She is cleaner and far more beautiful." He pointed towards a pretty native woman sitting on the lap of a fisherman towards the back of the tavern. Julian did not know her. She could have come from any tribe, anywhere, with the way that people came and went from this place. He did not care, for that matter. The Frenchman's talk sent a strange image through his head of his

French grandfather chasing his native grandmother through the marshy reeds of Indian Neck. He studied the image in his mind, trying to decide if it felt like love or more like the lust he heard in the Frenchman's words.

"I am too tired from the English whores to go for another, at the moment," Francois said. "You go have your fun, but I will not fight that one she sits on just so you can get your prick wet," he added.

His companions got up from the table, sniggered at each other and clumsily pushed their way through the crowd, nearly starting a brawl before they were halfway across the room.

"You! Why do you not go try to woo this woman? You might even be the cleverest among us, eh? That is, if you ever said anything."

"I did not come here for any woman."

"No? You come for the conversation?" he chuckled.

"Why are you here?" Julian asked.

The Frenchman raised his eyebrows. "I serve on one of the ships in the harbor. We stop here frequently when we are in this place, between sailing here and there. You know how it is."

Julian nodded. He could guess more than the man was likely to tell him. Common seamen were not as well-armed with knives and pistols as this one was. He was likely a smuggler or worse. Julian looked hard at the man, and his features seemed identical to that of the French pirate leader who he had met out on Cape Cod Bay. Yes, there was the thin cut down the line of his nose that Julian had given him that night. It was clear that the Frenchman did not recognize him in turn. He could not tell one native from another, even one who had put a knife to his face, Julian surmised. The fight had been at night under the tricky light of moon glow, Julian told himself, but nonetheless, he was disappointed to be so indistinguishable.

For a mad instant Julian wondered if he should tell the man about the other Frenchmen who used to spend the summers on the Punonakanits' lands. Perhaps this man's own grandfather was one. Perhaps they shared the same grandfather, he wondered, peering into the grimy face to see if he could recognize anything of himself there. Soot blackened the Frenchman's face to a color near Julian's own, but still the features were too sharp and small to show obvious kinship.

"Why are you staring like that?" Francois demanded. "Is there something on my face?" He gave a drunken laugh. "Come now! What kind of stories do you know? Tell me something to pass the time. I shall have to wait here for a while, till my friends do their business."

Julian considered what he might say. The pain of hearing the news of Great Island still pierced him. He wanted to tell this stranger about Smith and the greed and the foolish pieces of paper that had stolen the land from under him. He wanted to make him see that it was outrageous enough to demand vengeance. He wished that everyone in this makeshift tavern would feel the injustice of it, and that they would help him get the land back. He felt that little French part within him stir as if it wanted to say to his companion, *"This was your people's place too! Are you not ashamed and enraged?"*

Then the ridiculousness of the thought occurred to him. It was not the Frenchman's place nor, likely, did he care. And Julian knew that his own French blood was there by accident. It should not be in him anymore than Smith Tavern should be on Great Island.

Instead, Julian told the man about the Great Spirit, *Keihtanit*, who took sand from the sea bottom and created the Punonakanit land and then populated it with the first animals and people. He told him of the great sea spirit, *Paumpagussit*, who provided fish to feed the first people and the spirits that kept the ground producing corn. As he related these things, he felt his eyes moisten and thought at first it might be the sting of the pipe smoke all around him. But he knew it was not. He was crying for the loss of his land and for the exile that he felt coming over him as it had for Mittawa. He had thought that the horror of her omen would be his death, but now he found it was far worse than that. He was being cut off from the land. Even the words of the story, as they fell from his lips, seemed to slip away in the air. He knew that he would never tell anyone such stories again.

It seemed fitting, then, that this Frenchman, who he did not know, should hear the final tales about the old ways that Julian would utter. Just as another Frenchman, who he never knew, had likely set the whole prophecy of Julian's life in motion all those years ago. He was now certain that something in his blood had contributed to his downfall. He realized that he did not feel like anything anymore, not a Punonakanit, a Nauset or a part-French native. He felt like a man whose spirit has already left him though his body yet lives. He felt like the land he had fought to save had betrayed him in the end. The words that his aunt had laid upon his young head had been a curse after all, from a half-breed like himself. They were both creatures who were unnaturally made, whose very being rent the way of the old world. Normally he would have felt foolish for taking his thoughts to such crazy extremes but his head swam with drink. The dried blood on his face made his whole skin itch for action.

He fell silent and sat there until Francois had returned with two mugs of ale and set one down before him.

"That tale deserves a reward. I have heard many stories in my travels but none like that," he told Julian.

"My father told me many such stories," Julian said. Then, before he had barely thought the words, they came out of his mouth, "He was half-French. But he never told me anything about that."

Francois snorted out part of his ale. "You? Part French? You tell jokes as well as tales!"

A look at Julian's expression told him otherwise, and he reached out as if he wanted to touch Julian's face, probe it for authenticity, but then he drew back and concentrated on his ale instead.

"I never would have known," he said. "Wait! We could make the others guess and charge them a coin if they are wrong. We would split it, you and me! Can you prove it?"

Julian shook his head, and Francois clicked his tongue. "Pity," he said. "Have you ever been to France?"

"No," Julian said. Suddenly he knew why he had talked about his heritage and what he wanted to hear. If the world of the Punonakanits was lost to him, then maybe another one would open to him. He wanted to know what France was like.

"This area is all English! I don't know how you stand it. We like to plant trees and flowers and lots and lots of grapes," he said, raising a mug to clink with Julian's. "Wine is better than this rotgut! You would love it! It is in your blood, no?"

"I am from the south near the sea," Francois went on. "There, the fields roll out as far as you can see. There are stones from the old castles, which we make walls with. There are grapes and wheat and poplar trees in groves. We have cities, not as big or grand as Paris, but older! Much older! Roman cities! Not some somber city of the Franks!"

Julian nodded, trying to picture cities and Romans and fields of grapes that stretched into the horizon. None of it felt at all familiar or comforting, but he liked Francois' enthusiasm and heard in it the sound of a man who knows and loves his land and his gods. If all French were like that, then maybe they were not that different than Punonakanits after all.

"We own islands too. Down south in the West Indies. That is where we go next. That is something that you should see! The water is so clear that it looks like it came from a spring, not like this muddy water out in the bay! The fish are bright colored, blue and orange and red! You cannot imagine! There are Indians there, same as you! In fact, many a Frenchman I know has taken an Indian wife, so there are many like you, half-Indian, half-French!" Francois said, growing more and more excited.

Julian was growing excited too. Fish. Half-breeds like himself. It sounded like the perfect place for exile. He wished that it were light and that he could go outside and look around at the familiar view of the bay, dunes and all the things that he knew he would long for later. Francois told him that they would be sailing before dawn. Julian told the Frenchman that he knew the waters of Cape Cod as well as Francois knew the corners of his own ship. He told him that he could lead them around the dangerous shoals, past the breakwaters and back to the sea. With another clink of their mugs, Julian was going to the West Indies to start his exile.

When the morning sun came sliding through the cracks in the roof and walls of Boyd's Bog, a finger of it found Julian's eyelid and pressed hotly upon it until he awoke. Around him, he heard the groans of those who had likewise been drawn from sleep and the snoring of the lucky ones who hadn't. He found himself slumped over on the table top, the mug spilled over on one end, and the sharp smell of old ale in his nostrils. Another half-dozen ales had gone into the celebration, twice as many as Julian could remember ever drinking. His head beat like someone was cracking clam shells against it, and when he stood up, he had to cling to the table for a moment before he could walk around.

It took only a few minutes to explore the length of the tavern and discover that none of the Frenchmen were still there. He stepped outside into the bright dawn, with a sense of panic rising out of proportion to the speckled rays of light trimming the surface of the bay. He saw the little fishing boats first, their bows nudged into the sand where they had been run aground for the night. Then he looked past them and saw nothing but blue water. The great ships had all sailed without him.

I have no tribe, he thought. He was not even angry with the Frenchmen. Daylight returned enough sense to him to know that they were likely not the kind to sail with anyway. If they had not left him here, who knows where they might have dropped him out there in the ocean when they had tired of him.

In front of him the bay was as radiant as ever. His eyes naturally followed the birds skimming over it, knowing that they were already on the trail of fish. Far in the distance, Great Island was emerging out of the morning mist. He could not quite see it, but he could picture the crown of Smith Tavern taking dark, distinct shape out of the milky hue. Julian sighed and stroked his head, trying to wipe the ache from it. Then he began walking south, wondering what it would be like to grow old as a whale man in a white man's tavern.

✠ ✠ ✠ ✠

Julian left the blood on his face. He stood for a long while and stared out at Great Island, from the shore at the edge of the village of Billingsgate. He counted the whale men over and over and each time arrived at a number that seemed to outweigh any effort he could imagine mustering against them. Twenty to one. Even the greatest braves he had ever heard of had not claimed to have beaten such odds.

Once, he saw the old smuggler Smith come out of the tavern and stride around the bluff, snapping orders. The sight made Julian's hand tighten on the hilt of the knife in his belt. He considered again: *twenty to one...*

Then he turned his back on Great Island, with the knowledge that he might never see it again.

By afternoon he was sitting on the sharpening rock outside of Nauset village. His clothes, the heavy, itchy material of the English, lay about him in piles, like great colored heaps of seaweed suspended on the tips of the marsh grass.

At his feet were three wooden bowls. One was filled with black mud, another with a pigment of orange clay and red berries, a third with white chalk. He dipped his hands into the bowls and then drew circles upon his cheeks.

Then he thumped his fists on his chest and raised them up to the sky. *"Give me strength, Great Spirit..."* he muttered in his people's language.

Children from the village stood at a distance, shuffling nervously as they peered at him. Their mothers came swooping in behind them and hauled them away.

He spread black mud on his forehead and chin. A thump and a raise of the arms. *"I draw on the power of the sky to lift my fears..."*

Long white chalk streaks down his arms and legs. Thump and praise to the ground. *"I draw upon the might of Mother Earth to hold me up..."*

"Julian!" came a cry. John Tom's voice sounded frail and weak to Julian now. It was nothing compared to the deep resonating hum in Julian's throat. As the teacher approached, Julian did not look at him. His chant grew louder and louder. The old man knew exactly what it meant. He had heard it long ago when he had been young and strong enough to respond to the war cry.

"Stop it! Stop it! You will get us all killed!" John Tom hollered. "Peace, not war, is the way!"

Julian smeared red-orange color upon his chest, sketching the rough shape of a wolf. Then he took up the instrument that he had created, a wedge of rock with a sharp tapered edge, which was tied with cord into the nook of a short, strong tree branch. The kind of axe that his forefathers had used. The kind of weapon that had been woefully clean of English blood for far too long.

He braced the stone blade against one of the grooves in the sharpening stone and flexed it back and forth, the din of scraping adding a discordant counterpoint to his droning intonation of war.

At his hip was a bow strung with horse hair and a quiver full of arrows, fashioned from pointed rocks that were fastened to lengths of dogwood. He ran his hand through a pile of stone tips that he had yet to turn into arrows, his fingers making a vague calculation. No more than fifty.

Then he stood up on the tall rock and lifted the bow over his head. "Great Spirit, let my aim be true!" he shouted.

John Tom's hand clamped onto his ankle, and the old man rasped, "Think! Think of what you will call down upon your people if you do something stupid! We shall all suffer for your vengeful pride! The English will see us as one in the same!"

In a flash, an arrow notched onto the string, and the bow pulled open and spun towards John Tom's face. Julian's eyes sighted down the length of the arrow shaft. His speed and reflexes felt good. *Thank you, Great Spirit…*

"*People?*" Julian snarled. "Who are my people? I see none who stand with me now!"

"Julian…please…think!" John Tom said, shielding himself with wrinkled, shaking arms.

Julian's fingers lightened on the bow string until only the tips of them held back the old man's death. He let his grip slide to its farthest point and left it suspended there for a long moment as he watched the teacher shake, in his pathetic attempt at bravery.

"The white man's book is a poison. I should shoot you in the way a sick beast is put out of its misery. But I will not. Your teaching was meant to spread misery, like an illness, to our people. Your curse shall be to live on and see how your work will cause everything to die away."

"You are wrong, Julian. This is the only way."

The arrow whistled past the old man's cheek, causing him to yelp and jump back. "Go!" Julian shouted at him, notching another arrow, which he meant to aim true if he was not obeyed.

He watched John Tom's retreat with sadness, not a feeling of victory. This was not where the battle should be, he told himself.

Then he gathered his weapons and sprang off of the rock.

Behind him was a hill. He sprinted up and over the crest and into the meadow that lay between the village and the late Reverend Treat's house. Treat's fields were a rolling plain, and it was not until Julian had reached the second crest of the terrain that he could look out and see the surrounding holdings of the next closest white men.

He wished that Treat had lived to see this act of defiance, the old ways finally being thrown back into his face. But there were only a few farm boys in the distance on the neighboring farm. When they first looked up, they shielded their eyes as if squinting to see him. But Julian could tell that they were too far away to get a clear view of him.

See me and know fear, he thought to himself.

"*Hi-hi-hi-hi-hi-hi!*" he cried and charged halfway towards them, his axe swinging around his head. Plows dropped, hats flew off and, as easy as that, the boys turned and fled. In mid-stride, Julian fired off a few arrows at the figures, but the distance was too great, and the shafts sunk harmlessly into furrowed field. He spit in the direction of his quarry, to show what he thought of their cowardice. Then he looked to and fro and saw no other English to take mark on.

A few minutes later the meeting house bell began gonging. The farmers must have fled straight to the old garrison, Julian realized. Soon the militia would be sent after him. The war had begun.

"There he is!" John Tom shouted. Across the meadow a dozen native men burst from the treeline that hid the village and came hooting after him. The sight of them in full fervor nearly brought tears to Julian's eyes. *If only they had found this strength sooner and directed it where it was really needed...*

A whizzing arrow punctured his thoughts. Its feathers fluttered as they passed.

He ran down to the waterline where his canoe was waiting.

Then he was out in the water, pulling for the deeper channels. The men splashed some ways into the shallows and fired off another round, but he was out of reach, and they did not follow.

Julian felt proud about his action although it was a small, ineffective gesture. Now they knew who he was and where he stood. There would be no more hiding. However short his war was, he would die with honor and, in that final act, achieve something that the whites could not take from him.

In the meantime his battle would have lasted mere heartbeats longer had he stayed to face the combined might of the English and his traitorous kinsmen. He needed men who would fight for the old ways. He was not even sure that any such braves still existed. But he intended to find out. Then he would come back with all who responded to his war cry and the matter would be settled once and for all.

The paddle felt strong in his hand. Whenever he was out on the water, he felt seamlessly connected to it. But as he passed the land, which presently lay under the yoke of the English, he saw it as the prisoner that it had become. The English houses, like fence posts, pinned it down. Lines of stone walls sat heavily on its surface, dividing it up into broken pieces. There was nothing whole about it anymore. There was nothing of the old place left that he could recognize. The sight made him wonder why he wanted to stay here any longer.

His people too had been divided and broken. Those that had not been poisoned in mind or stricken in body by the diseases and crimes of the whites had been herded away, like sheep, into villages that were no better than the pens where the whites kept their animals.

Julian did not know what was left for him in this world. He paddled along the ocean side, breathing in the hard, tangier air that came from the sea. Eventually he came upon sandy terrain that extended for long stretches, free from the scourge that had ruined the rest of the ancient lands.

He kept going farther south where the sand stretched like a long fin into the ocean. Monomoyick land. It was once the homeland of a proud people, who had driven the French away from their shores, long before the English had arrived to stay. Like all of the old people, the Monomoyicks had not fought fiercely enough. When the English came, they offered kindness when they should have given only arrows and spears. Their foolishness had led to the Monomoyick lands becoming Chatham, another stronghold of white villagers.

Julian did not like criticizing the old ones. After all, it was to them that he continually appealed, asking for their help to get back the land. Only with time did he realize that they too were as ignorant and stupid as the Nausets who prayed to the white god. No wonder their spirits had not been able to aid him when he had most needed their help, he mused. Their promises held no power, just like their defense against the whites had been feeble or nonexistent. That is why he was out here on the edge of the sea, scouting the land for some village that remained untouched and unspoiled. He had heard the whale men say that the white settlements went on and on, for hundreds of miles, well past the farthest land in sight. But whale men were often drunk, and if their stories of the size of the fish that they caught were similar to their tales of the extent of white land, then he knew that they were not telling the whole truth. He did not believe that all of the land was overrun by whites. How many of them could there be, he wondered? Sooner or later he would find a village that had not succumbed and he would join them.

The surface of the water began roiling in great swells that made it feel like his canoe was sliding down the face of dunes. A fog gathered in front of him, and soon all he could hear was the hiss of surf crashing somewhere to his right and the gurgle of the large waves as they rose up under his paddle. In breaks through the mist, Julian saw sections of the beach. The land was flat, lifeless sand, except for where colonies of gulls and black-feathered birds stood with their backs to the wind. They looked ghostly in the fog and made Julian wonder what spirits were amassing in that veiled bank of mist.

He kept paddling. The sand continued on and on until, finally, it abruptly ended in a massive, churning field of water, beyond which was no sight of solid ground as far as he could see.

Julian pressed towards the beach, but a strong current dragged him out of reach of the mainland. The fog quickly closed in around him, and he realized that even if he could break the pull of the water, he did not know in which direction lay land.

Mist wreathed him, muffling the noise of the sea and quieting his thoughts, until it seemed to him that he was passing into sleep. The venom began to drain out of him. The haze seeped into his mind, talking to him in a soft, ancient voice. It told him that it was the source of the beginning and end of all things. He knew all meaning and wisdom, but his brain could hold onto none of it, except a feeling of contentment that belied the cold touch of the mist.

His paddle began to feel weak in his hand, and after a while he brought it into the boat and laid it over his knee, in a kind of ceremonial position. Then he lay down in the bottom of the canoe and looked up into the vapor that poured like smoke over his head. He imagined himself in a pyre, returning to ash and smoke and disappearing into the great mass of fog above him, his soul absorbed into all that constituted it. Then he thought of himself as the tobacco in a peace pipe, funneling out in completion of a gesture of contract. The thought made him feel better about his place in this world than he had in a very long time.

Julian did not want this to be the end of his journey in the waking world. Yet he no longer cared where he was bound. He would leave it up to the white fog and dark blue water to take him to a place that only they knew.

A splash at the edge of his canoe caught his attention. He did not turn his head to look, for he knew in his heart what it was and the notion drew a hearty, cleansing laugh from him. The father fish was here...

For once, he appreciated the irony in the way that spirits wait until they are ready. They do not respond to the impatience of living men.

He cocked his ear to the sound and let the words he had so long waited for rise up from the water, "*A true warrior does not give up... The seasons change but, underneath, the Great Spirit remains... Do not fight for time but flow through it...*"

Julian dropped his hand over the side of the canoe and trailed his fingers through the water. The gesture gave him a sense of his father's meaning. The cool touch of the water trilled through his fingers, and Julian smiled. He was not abandoned by spirit after all.

"*Thank you,*" he whispered over the side of the canoe.

He did not hear the father fish's reply because it was drowned out by another louder noise. A great roar snapped Julian out of his reverie.

The growl of water grew louder, and he wondered if he had been turned around and was approaching the surf on shore. Had his father pushed him back towards the beach, he wondered?

He heard the sound of voices, and he grew more confused. They were not speaking the Wampanoag tongue. They were white men.

A shape loomed out in front of him, looking like a massive, dark boulder. Around him the sea churned so much that he thought that he would be thrown over. He heard the rush of water along the keel and then the flap of sail high above him and men cursing the weather.

Then he saw lights. Lanterns bobbed off of the stern of a great ship.

The giant vessel raced past him. He could see the wood grain on its flank as it roared by. Behind it came a curtain of rain, which the craft seemed to fly like a dark flag. Julian clung to the canoe as he watched the ship veer off and mumbled for his father to save him.

"*Look there! A fisherman!*" came a cry from the stern of the ship.

No...no...no... came the chant in Julian's head. *Protect me, Father... Protect me, Great Spirit...* All of a sudden he did not feel like any more fights, any more challenges. He wanted the peace that he had felt in the fog. It was an ageless promise more beautiful than even the old splendor of the living land.

The boat disappeared into the mist. But a short while later, he heard the splash of oars, and then a craft the size of a whaleboat came out of the veiled bank. Rain punched the surface of the water and filled Julian's canoe.

"Looks like we have found ourselves a guide for these waters," came an accented voice.

Julian let the men pull him into their craft and watched them kick his canoe away so it drifted unmanned into the fog bank.

The men were bearded and foul. Their skin stank like a carcass and was black with grime, except in a few patches where their whiteness showed through. They were armed with all manner of weaponry, which they patted ominously as they cackled at each other.

"Aye. Welcome aboard, pilot! You are now a pirate," one said, his accent marking him as a Frenchman.

Julian gaped at him but did not recognize him as one of the men from Boyd's Bog. But it had to be the same ship. He could not believe it. He wondered if the next land that he saw would be the tropical island paradise that Francois had spoken of. Then, with a shock at all of the water racing under him, he realized that he could be taken anywhere. When he looked back into the fog, he could see no land at all. In fact, he could see absolutely nothing at all.

"Where are we going?" Julian asked.

"We were hoping that you would tell us that," the French pirate responded cheerfully. He pointed back towards Cape Cod. "We need you to take us to Great Island."

Julian was too stunned to speak.

"You don't agree?" the pirate asked, raising a pistol and pushing its tip against Julian's forehead.

Reluctantly, Julian nodded.

"Good. Now go up front and report to the captain!"

Julian walked to the rail, fingering the round indentation where the gun barrel had been. He glanced over the side of the ship and wondered if he had been led astray once again. He turned towards his captive and asked, "What is the name of this ship?"

The pirate cocked a brow. "Name? That's no concern of yours!"

"What is the name?" Julian demanded. Some inner voice insisted that he know.

The pirate's mouth fell open. "A brave man, eh? Well... this ship does have a name but few of us but the captain use it. The rest of us have a nickname for her. We call her the *Wolf of the Sea*... Now get moving!"

Julian nodded and let his captor lead him away. But he could not stop from smiling because deep inside he felt his stubborn hope revive once again.

BOOK THREE

The Tale of Sam Bellamy

Chapter One
"From the Belly of the Beast"

June 1715

Broken images floated through Sam Bellamy's mind: pirates cutting through sheets of rain, water closing like a fist around him, his fingers reaching for a fragment of ship's spar, a fishing net, a savage face glaring into his own...

Then he started to awaken, his awareness rising up through the swirl of dreams, like he was reaching his face towards the surface of water.

When Bellamy opened his eyes, he was surrounded by darkness. He felt rope cutting into his back, touching the tender spots from the mate's whippings and the beatings of the sea. The rope was from bedding, not hammock twine. It was a bed with no sway to it. The room that he was in was very much like a ship's hold. He could sense the closeness of the walls, even in the dark, and hear dripping somewhere close by. Yet the atmosphere lacked the hacking coughs and putrid smell of an under-deck. The drips were hitting glass, of which there was little aboard a ship. There was no doubt that he was on dry land, in a bed and with no memory to account for how he came to be where he was.

There was a scent of fish broth in the air. Bellamy inhaled hungrily. There was a bowl on a table, within arm's reach, but it was empty, and the notion that he had likely eaten from it sometime during the night was no comfort to him.

The rectangular outline of a window took shape in one corner. Its panes were smoky glass, which gradually filled with color, a gray smudge at the bottom and several shades of blue that Bellamy judged to be the sea and sky.

Bellamy swung his legs out over the edge of the bed. He gingerly trudged to the window, opened it and looked out at a landscape that fit the fragmented pictures in his head. All around him was nearly treeless farm field, lined with dirt tracks that seemed destined to lead to more of the same kind of terrain. The houses were few and gray-shingled. Only a handful of other structures stood among them, a steeple and a couple of windmills with arms paddling languidly through the sky. A long, finger-like cove reached to within a quarter mile of where he leaned out of the second story window. Boats were anchored at its tip. Off in the distance was a marshy harbor and, beyond that, the ocean. Bellamy guessed that this was the route by which he had traveled to shore. The length of it stretched his eye and his comprehension. He could not believe that he had made it through all of that water.

Beneath him was an arm of wood that dangled a carved, wooden sign out over the road.

Higgins Tavern, it read.

Not long ago Bellamy had been sitting in a similar kind of place, far across the ocean, draining the dregs of one ale too many as he listened to the ravings of a recruiting man for the *Josephine.*

"As far as you can look to the horizon is naught but a drop of what is out there. If it fit in your ale mug, you'd have another fifty mugs waiting for you, afterwards, before you had drunk up the whole ocean," the man had said. Bellamy recollected their shared laughter at the image and the knock of their mugs together.

"The money you'd make at sea would take you a lifetime of plow work to yield the same. And the riches of the fair, balmy isles that you'll be seeing are such paradise that they'd make a preacher at a loss for words..." The recruiting man reached his mug out a second time, and when Bellamy touched his own to it, he did not know that he had just signed himself away from his homeland forever.

By the time he staggered out of that dockside inn, he would have sailed to hell itself had the recruiting man recommended, so agile and poetic was the man's talk. Instead, he was brought to the ship he came to know well. The recruiting man did not board with him and in fact did not seem to know the captain much at all. Bellamy wondered why the two dickered in the stern, until he saw the captain press some coins into the other's palm. By the time Bellamy realized that he had been bartered aboard, like a piece of cattle, his drinking companion was headed back to the tavern, no doubt to sweet talk another farm boy. Bellamy was left watching the docks slip out of reach and about to receive his first taste of life at sea, bludgeon end first.

Bellamy's thoughts came back to the tavern room in which he was standing. He caught another whiff of broth and wished that it were grog instead. He shook his head at the thought. What better place for a man, with the rest of his life before him, to have washed ashore than a drinking house? It took over a dozen mugs to get him aboard the *Josephine*. How many would it take to start him off on his next foolish errand, he wondered?

✠ ✠ ✠ ✠

There was a knock on the door. Bellamy turned from the window, but before he could reply, the door swung open and a white-haired man burst in, nodded curtly and sat down on the edge of the bed, wheezing from his climb up the stairs.

There was something in the man's large frame that reminded Bellamy of some of the dockside workers he had known, but none of them had carried a Bible.

Behind the first man came a tall man with a drawn, grim face and an uncompromising air, like that of a tax collector.

He was followed by a stout, rumpled fellow who exclaimed, "He is out of bed! About time too! He has drunk more soup and rum in his feverish state than most men can drink whilst awake!" Then, casting a look at his companions, he unconsciously patted down the folds in his apron and added, "God left this poor sailor upon my doorstep, so who am I to give a cold shoulder to His request? Anyone would have done the same."

The tall man looked at Bellamy. "If this is the first time that you have come fully awake, then no doubt you have not properly met your host Isaiah Higgins." He gestured to the portly tavern keeper and then pointed to the man on the bed and continued, "This is our esteemed Reverend Treat. I am Justice Doane. We are here to discover who you are."

Any last vestiges of slumber evaporated from Bellamy's mind. The presence of this kind of men did not bode well. The possibilities came in a flash: the *Josephine* in port nearby, Captain Pound bringing wild charges against him, imprisonment, return to England in chains. He would not let it happen.

"I was washed ashore in the storm."

"We are well used to men wrecking on our beaches but not men who wash up without the ship that carried them," Doane said.

"Aye! There is no wreck. I have been out to the bar and found nothing," Higgins added.

"Really?" Doane's eyebrows arched.

"It's true!" Higgins replied.

From the bed there was a hacking sound, and the other men turned towards the reverend, who spat into a handkerchief and then motioned for Bellamy to come nearer.

The old man flipped open the Bible and read, "I saw a beast rising out of the sea, with ten horns and seven heads, with ten diadems upon its horns and a blasphemous name upon its heads..."

He went on to describe floods, tidal waves and other such devastation, leaving Bellamy stunned and thinking it was the oddest start to any conversation he had ever had.

"You have come on a large stormy tide, haven't you, Bellamy?" Treat asked.

Bellamy was not surprised that they knew his name. He had vague recollections of murmuring answers to questions asked by those who had taken care of him in the night. He was not able to recall what was inquired or what he had told them. He could not help wonder what else they knew. If he could find out fast, he might better figure out where he stood. "Is there word of my ship? And the pirates that attacked us?"

The justice gave him a steely eye, but Treat flipped through some more pages of the Bible as if he knew of a chapter that would answer just such a question.

"Do you know any of this book?" Treat asked Bellamy as he continued searching through the Bible.

"Yes," Bellamy said and recited the only passage that he could recall from his childhood lessons, "Do not neglect to show hospitality to strangers, for thereby some have entertained angels unawares."

"Do you believe that the opposite can be true? That a man might entertain devils and be unaware of it?" Treat snapped.

"Yes," Bellamy said, watching with satisfaction as Treat nodded gravely. It confirmed Bellamy's belief that captains, preachers and lawmen were all cut from the same cloth. The answers they liked best were the ones that agreed with them.

The story that Treat then told him was not one that he would have expected from a man of God. It was sailors who usually ranted about sea monsters and murderous storms, and those tales most often needed a few rounds to get them started. While he talked,

Treat stood and walked to the window, glancing furtively outside as if he expected to see new horrors out there.

"What do you say to all of that?" he asked Bellamy.

"I saw no such creature during the wreck nor have I ever seen such a beast."

"Why was your ship destroyed so utterly? What was your trade that God would seek to blight it from existence?"

Bellamy gaped at the preacher, wondering if the man had all of his wits. He had heard of small farming towns that fell under the sway of demented old frauds, who poisoned the congregation, swindled them, even led them in the exact kind of debauchery that they were sworn to defend against.

"We carried linen," Bellamy responded. He looked from face to face, waiting for more explanation of the fate of the *Josephine*. Higgins did not meet his eye. The justice merely peered at Bellamy as though he could glean all he needed to know of the sailor with his eyes alone.

"Are you of the true church, then?" Treat asked.

"I was christened long ago in the Church of England," Bellamy replied.

The etched wrinkles of Treat's face were deep and made his face sag as if he was permanently disappointed.

"You make your church attendance sound past tense. Are you not of practicing faith?"

Bellamy smiled. "I make my own peace with God."

"Your *own* peace? What blasphemy is this? It is bad enough to cling to the Church of England over more enlightened paths such as our own. But to choose nothing!"

"It comes from what I have experienced in the world. There is no answer, in that book you are holding, for what I've seen."

Treat's face flushed red, and his jaw quivered as he struggled to rise. "It would behoove you to attend my service this Sabbath. That might mollify the Lord…somewhat. Let us go, Justice Doane. I have nothing else to ask this man."

Before he left, Doane turned to the sailor and warned, "We take seriously our heavenly charge to offer assistance to those who come to us in need. In return we ask only appreciation and respect of our ways. Do not mock our courtesy."

"I wish only to mend and then be on my way in search of some of the promise that I have always heard spoken about these colonies," Bellamy said.

Doane nodded in approval. "Godspeed to you, then. But muse on this while you mend: the law is much prized and enforced here in the colonies. Perhaps more so than in your own country, for we are new towns. Our grandfathers carved Eastham out of the savage wilderness. The law tamed that wilderness. It tames all of those who would take us back to savage times."

"I am here for opportunity, not strife," Bellamy replied.

"That is well."

When they got outside the room, Higgins laid a hand on Doane's arm. He nodded towards the stranger's door. "What of him? He is not the typical boarder in these parts. Most of mine come from the packet boat, not like Jonah from the whale. Not a half-penny on him. I know the truth of it. He had naught but his clothes, and they were as slick as otter's skin."

Doane nodded. "In a day or two, someone will make a run to Barnstable or beyond and might ferry him along so that he can make his own way from us. Do not fret over it."

Higgins cleared his throat and said as delicately as possible, "He might stay here for days, before he is well enough to travel. Of course, I will provide room and board…"

"Perhaps there are poor house funds that can be directed to you, for your good will. The selectmen will discuss the matter at our next meeting. I shall try to put it on the town meeting warrant." Then Doane walked out into the night, sniffing the air and noting a smell like a turned field that meant more rain was coming.

The sky foretold nothing of its future intentions, but Higgins too understood what the tang in the air meant. He rubbed his hands together, imagining the coin that would soon be pressed between his fingers. He knew that rain and rum tended to run together in equal proportion.

✠ ✠ ✠ ✠

Bellamy lingered in his room, nursing his pains. It seemed they had not yet discovered the whip marks, and he made no mention of them. He had decided that there would be no benefit from such disclosure, for he did not know if these people sympathized more with crews or captains. It seemed like their chief concern was the enforcement of church service and their precious laws.

Rain began coursing down the window panes as the weather went foul once again. Bellamy stared at the view outside as he stewed over his meeting with Justice Doane and Reverend Treat. Through the window, he saw figures in nearby fields, and their rain-blurry forms coaxed old memories from him.

Some of those memories he would have just as soon forgotten forever, such as frozen winter nights spent listening to the raw rain drip through the thatch and lift the smell of sheep dander and hog sweat into the air as his family and he, and all of their animals, huddled together in their small shack. He could see his mother as she went into the house to deliver his baby brother and never came out again. He saw himself not believing it and straining for a glimpse of her, but the dark cloth thrown up over the doors and windows barred him from any sort of farewell. That day he heard his father cry. At eight years old, he had been startled to hear such sound come from a man.

He heard it once more when he was a few years older. He and his father stood at the edge of the field that they worked. His father eyed the steep pitch of the contours of the land and voiced his usual hope that this year it would be easier to plow. They looked at the rocks, some as big as a cart bed, strewn throughout, and his father declared that they would soon have them all cleared. Bellamy felt his hair tousled and looked into his father's eyes, which were like old gray stone, flecked with just a touch of sunlight.

"Look out yonder," his father said, pointing his rake out towards the shiny surface of the ocean in the distance. Like Eastham, the water was always in view, always beckoning to some and teasing others who had not the spine to brave it. There it sat, with all its promise of escape, and his father's eye would often wander to it. "The docks are at the foot of the hill. In a few years we could walk down there and find you a fine ship to join. You could come back here and buy this land from Radford. Imagine that, son! You the owner of your own holdings! Think on it! Otherwise, this little plot, fine as it be, will not divide enough to keep you, your brothers and I all fed or feed the families that you will one day have."

Bellamy did think of the sea. His mind went to it like a gull circling. He fed off of its motion and woke to its fresh scent through the window.

"Captain. That's what a lad can be that sticks with the trade. See them fancy houses down by the Plymouth docks? They are all bought with merchant money from running ships throughout the Empire. They are men who made something of themselves. Plenty from this very county have gone on to fame and fortune from that dock: Francis Drake, Walter Raleigh, Richard Grenville, Humphrey Gilbert..." Bellamy's father pointed to the line of stately buildings that ringed the harbor below them. Each one could have fit a half-dozen of the type of hovel that he lived in, within its walls. "Ours is borrowed, rented land that could be withdrawn on a cruel whim. Those houses are as good as castles for their owners."

They did not clear the rocks that year. A hard rain made planting a struggle, which took all his father's fight out of him. Roots rotted in the ground. By midsummer it was plain that the harvest would be a poor one. Folks were hiding their scraps, which in better years would have been fed to the livestock, for fear that any surplus would be enticing to their neighbors.

Lord Radford, the landlord, had holdings across the county, including areas which were not as ruined by the weather. He ran his ledgers as if all of the little boxes on his property map were of uniform mint rather than as different as the Bellamys' rocky slopes and stone-less plains of good earth that lay on either side of it. Lord Radford himself did not deign to come around to directly inspect his land. The closest Bellamy saw of the man was a tiny figure coming out of the large manor house on a hill in the distance, climbing into a carriage with a roof and door, and riding away towards Plymouth.

It was his hirelings that rode up on their horses, the hides of the beasts and the red cheeks of the men's plump faces a similar glossy sheen of health that made Bellamy itch with envious fury.

He remembered the fire crackling, early one morning. His brothers were still in bed and he, the oldest, was proud to be up already, adding kindling under the cook pot.

"I should find a wife to do such things. You are of age to be joining me more often in the fields," his father mused as he inspected the edges of his hoe and spade.

It was the first time that it had occurred to Bellamy that it was possible for him to have another mother. Yet there was little time to dwell on such notions. There was an impatient thud on the door, and when Bellamy's father opened it, one of the lord's men was standing on the threshold.

"Where are your wits? I have children sleeping in the back corner! It is just dawn outside, and you come banging on my door?"

"Lord Radford's business comes when his lordship demands. By his grace, your children have a corner to sleep in at all."

"Speak then! What errand is so important, to wake us with your racket?"

"This season has been a ruin for the lordship's stock."

"For us all…"

The lord's man gave a cold smirk and shook his head as if he could not believe the degree of insolence of which the elder Bellamy was capable. "Hold your tongue, John Bellamy. There are plenty who have not the fortune that you have here! His lordship has added three extra bushels of wheat to the rent. Good day."

"What?" John Bellamy exclaimed. "In this kind of poor season, I cannot raise the old number. If I give you three more bushels, my family will not eat!"

"If you do not want to be driven out, you will provide."

"Send Radford to look for himself. He would see that it is unjust to place this burden upon me!"

His father followed the lord's man outside and gestured madly around him, trying to show the state of the fields. The lord's man did not glance over. He was focused on his orders and did not waver for anything or anyone.

"Many eye your property. New leaseholders must pay five additional bushels! Lord Radford shows you favor!" the lord's man scolded.

"Favor! His favor will be the ruin of me! Send him, and he will see this is folly! The land will not yield the rent! Radford does not know!"

There was a click that sounded to Bellamy like a door latch being lifted. Then he saw his father stagger back a few paces from the horse of the lord's man, and raise his hands up in the air. Meanwhile, the lord's man had nosed the horse around to face John Bellamy, and he pointed a pistol at the farmer's face.

"Any other complaints? If you continue in this manner, we will bring you to Lord Radford directly, and I assure you that his ear will take your grumbling less well than I!"

John Bellamy said nothing. The lord's man sighed audibly and holstered his weapon, giving a tired wave to send his party riding off to the next leaseholder.

At that moment the sun broke through the clouds, but the older Bellamy took no comfort from it. He threw his hat to the ground and stomped on it. There was wetness in his eye that his son swore were tears forming although John Bellamy ascribed it to the brightness of sun, and they never spoke of it again.

A month later Bellamy's father was dead. The dampness seeded him with a cough that sunk deep into his chest, leaving him as wracked and ruined as the land around him. Lord Radford promptly rented out the plot to a neighboring family. Bellamy and his brothers were packed off to a foster home, with no inheritance but his father's crazy belief that the sea could make something of him.

✠ ✠ ✠ ✠

The downstairs of Higgins Tavern was a great open room filled with tables and chairs and a huge fireplace on one wall. Across from the fireplace was the main entrance and a set of stairs to the top floor. The ale vats and a small cooking hearth were in one corner, behind a long bench where the family prepared meals.

Mary Higgins and her daughter Mehitable tended the cooking hearth while Isaiah Higgins poked at the flames in the large fireplace with an iron rod. When he was satisfied that the wood had taken flame, he stood to his full height and wiped his peat-blackened hands on his vest.

Higgins turned towards his wife and nodded upstairs. "I keep wondering how he got here."

"He's here, ain't he? What more do we need to know?" Mary replied.

"I wonder all the same. Did a wave knock him over the rail? Did his captain heave him into the ocean because he was a mutineer? Or does he have something to do with that sea creature..." Higgins mused.

A phlegmy, old voice, from one of the tavern tables, interrupted him, "Bah! Tis nothing but a sea fish! I've seen many a similar one in my travels. Much larger too!"

Higgins turned around to face Barnabus Merrill, the uncle of Higgins' wife. When Higgins looked at Barnabus' spindly white beard and glazed, rheumy eyes, he felt regret for agreeing to house the ancient fool. It was an out-of-character act of charity that he knew was unwise, from the start. He glared and waited, but Barnabus did not elaborate further. Instead, he raised his empty mug to Higgins and said, "Give us a bit of ale to toast the first guest this damned place has had in years!"

Higgins had to admit that the old man was right. Few strangers came to Eastham since there was little in town to draw people from afar and next to nothing of interest beyond its borders to warrant passing through. It was a dead end in the hinterlands. And it was just his luck that his visitor had not a single penny on his person. Higgins had checked twice, just to be sure.

"What are you doing with *that?*" Higgins exclaimed, yanking a bottle of rum from his wife's hand as she passed by him.

Mary turned unrepentant eyes towards her husband. "It's the best way to help a sailor heal that I know of," she said, snatching the rum back out of Higgins' hand.

"Rum is expensive, woman!"

"The sooner he is fit, the sooner he will be on his way," Mary sang out as she stomped up the stairs.

Muttering to himself, Higgins stepped over to the main window and looked up into the clouds, which were once again thick across the sky. The rain crackled on the shingles. Higgins knew that the farmers in the fields would soon be hanging their tools on the wall pegs in their barns and beginning a procession towards his establishment, from all corners of Eastham. That was something to be thankful for, he mused.

By midday Higgins' prediction proved correct. Wafts of pipe smoke and the aroma of ale and fish stew filled the dimly lit tavern. Gusts of wind shook the building, causing the glass panes to rattle. The candlelight jumped and flickered in the tiny spurts of wind that seeped through cracks in the eaves and window sills. But the interior of the place rang mostly with sounds that were pleasing to the ear such as laughter, playing cards being laid upon the table and the clink of coins in Higgins' pocket.

The patrons talked loudly and boisterously as if they meant to drown out the storm with their voices. They were a group of men who did not normally have much to say. They were accustomed to long hours handling lines or plows, and their voices seemed tools that they had little use for. Then the storm came. That itself was no cause for comment because every man there claimed to have seen worse and some actually had. But not every storm brought a washashore. None that anyone could remember had washed up a sea monster besides. The incident had inspired the patrons of the small tavern to unprecedented levels of discourse.

Higgins hopped between the tables, doling out ale, rum and a flattering word, depending upon what was most warranted to make his storm-captive guests eat and drink more.

Finally the sailor himself came gingerly down the stairs. His heavy tread echoed across a suddenly silent room, an atmosphere akin to a sail going slack in sudden irons. Dozens of eyes looked askance at Sam Bellamy as the sailor scanned the room for an empty seat.

"Here! By the fire," Higgins called out, ushering the man towards the main hearth.

"That and some broth will warm you up," Mary declared, coming up behind her husband and laying a bowl of soup in front of the stranger.

Higgins began to protest, but an unmistakable look of contempt from the sailor silenced him. "I did not ask for the reverend and justice to look in on you if that's what you are thinking! Tidings of your presence here have already spread about town. I should expect that every man of standing will want a word with you. Mind you, that is not the typical reception you'd get under my roof. But these are strange times!"

"Because a squid washes up onto the beach? I did not expect such ignorance here in the colonies. My father always claimed that this place drew only those of foresight and free thought. I am glad that he never had the chance to come here and have his illusion shattered," Bellamy replied.

"'Tis a dark time, lad. You can believe it or not. It makes no difference to me. We here believe Reverend Treat when he tells us that there is evil work among us. There are some here that feel that you are a part of it."

Bellamy nearly choked on his broth. "Me? Why would anyone think that? Can they not see that I was flung out of the sea? I have naught but the clothes on my back!"

"What we see is not often the whole truth of things, so says our Reverend Treat," Higgins said with a shrug.

The tavern keeper moved away from the stranger. Gradually the more curious and brave of the patrons made their way to Bellamy's table.

It did not take long to extract the basics of the sailor's story and for increasingly incongruous versions to echo throughout the room:

"He says the beast wrecked the ship."

"I heard him say twas French pirates. My cousin in Truro saw a rogue ship with a fleur de lis on the mast, some weeks ago out by Helltown."

By evening the tale was gaining a life of its own, and most men would not believe that the *Josephine* had survived both scourge and storm. Eventually Bellamy himself wondered if the pirates had been successful in their work and the *Josephine* really was lying there on the bottom where, by rights, his own drowned body should be. If not for the deaths of the innocent crew, it would be a just end for the ship.

Bellamy told them again the rough coordinates of where he was when he had gone over the rail. The local men debated the position of the supposed wreck.

It was blasphemy to say such things, but the sea was a bit like the Lord Himself to the folks of Eastham. With one sweep of waves, it could cruelly take away a ship full of local sons, and with the next, deliver a fully laden hold of wares, like a gift left on the doorstep. For most men of Eastham, understanding the rationale of the ocean was as taxing as trying to fathom the depths of God's mind. Yet they knew that a wreck meant lengths of rope, good timber and casks of God-knows-what washing up with the seaweed. As they watched the dark-haired sailor sitting by the fire, many felt that they had been cheated somehow of their due.

Pipe smoke, coarse bursts of laughter and the pungent fume of chowder and beer swirled around Bellamy. All of that, and the hearth at his back, made him feel groggy, and the events of the day pressed heavily upon him. He tried to focus on Mehitable Higgins as she made her rounds. When she went out of sight into the back of the room where the food was prepared, he raised his mug to his lips and found nothing but air.

"You had better drink fast! As soon as everyone tires of hearing your tale, Higgins will show you to the door, my friend!" said an old man, who dropped into the chair next to the sailor, tapping his own mug against Bellamy's in an absent way, like it was a ritual that demanded doing.

"I'll be happy to be on my way," Bellamy replied, hoping that the old man was about to offer him another ale. But Barnabus Merrill gave him only his name and a handshake.

"The justice, the reverend, all of them are busy bodies! They don't like a man to sit idle. That leads to the Devil's work, they say. They'd sooner see you sitting in jail than sitting around in this tavern, doing nothing but eating and drinking," Barnabus cackled.

The old man seemed harmless, so Bellamy lowered his voice and said, "They are a pimp of a parson and a fetching dog at his heel. I've seen plenty of their like, and every last one of them is the same in temperament."

"I can tell you are a lad who likes to take his whippings," Barnabus chuckled. "I was a sailor too! I'd be out there still, except I'd be coming down the mast every hour to take a piss. Don't get old, lad! The good life is for the young."

"How did you stay out at sea for so long, then? It's no better out there. Replace the reverend and justice with the captain and mate, and you have the same pack of hens but ten paces from you all ocean long," Bellamy said.

Barnabus winked. "I drank my fill, and then some, every day of the week, is number one. Number two: I was the captain, see? Round here, a seaman who ain't captain by twenty-three is a busted up failure, plain and simple!"

Bellamy scowled although he could see the wisdom in the answer. He was now seven years past failure, according to Barnabus' terms. Even though he had stayed on land, it was enough time that he could have completed an entire apprenticeship, had a trade and been his own man in the world. Thinking of his prospects made him gloomy, and he wished that he was awash with more of Higgins' ale, drinking as if to bleed the tavern keeper of every last bit of generosity he had. If they were going to throw him out, he wanted it to be according to Barnabus' first principle.

The next townsfolk to take a seat at Bellamy's table were some of the local young men. They brought a set of dice with them.

Gambling was the first small success that Bellamy achieved in the New World. The farm boys' grim mood, with all the talk of squid and devilry, seemed reflected in their throws of the dice. It was working to Bellamy's benefit for now.

"Another ale?" came a sing-songy voice in his ear. Bellamy turned and looked into the beaming face of Mehitable Higgins.

"Indeed." With the ale swirling, she was looking finer and finer, Bellamy thought. "Will you join us for a throw, after you've brung it?"

She laughed and cast a glance over her shoulder at her father. "I am not so easily won as with dice, Bellamy," she chided him, with a smile that said otherwise.

Bellamy shrugged. One big win is all he needed, and then he would leave the old world, and even Eastham, behind him.

Chapter Two
"The Other Side of an Old Life"

June 1715

Barely one week had passed since he had come ashore, but Sam Bellamy noticed that his ale mug was filled a little less often and the broth in his bowl did not reach the lip as it once had. Isaiah Higgins had hinted that Bellamy's room might soon be needed although the sailor got the sense that not a single other traveler had passed this way in some time.

Any profit Bellamy had achieved with the dice had transferred to Higgins' greedy hands. He could not win enough coin to pay his way to the next township where perhaps his fortunes would improve.

Reluctantly, Bellamy had agreed to help Higgins tend his fields, which lay adjacent to the tavern.

The days were starting to slip past, and it seemed that if he was not careful, he might be working each day, to pay for the previous day's food and lodging. It felt like just the sort of trap that the landlords of England would have employed.

Higgins was happy enough with the arrangement although Bellamy knew that his contentment and generosity would dry up after the harvest was in. The sailor wanted to be in some place of his own before winter. He did not know how the destitute fared in this new land, but he recalled the time of his youth spent in the Poor House, before his foster father had found him, and it was a place with no more comfort than a prison. He had staked his life on the chance for new prospects, not the same old fetters.

This is new land, he kept telling himself although he worried that putting too much faith in land of any kind was folly. Yet that only left him a fickle sea that he had little wish to contend with. It seemed that the only way to leave this place was to risk open water again.

The waning afternoon light crept across the wooden floor boards, until it lapped at Bellamy's feet like a tide. The sun was part way through its arc across the sky, but Bellamy was unable to begin his own journey. Now and again, a cart rolled past the open door, carrying a farmer off on some errand or other. Bellamy watched them go with increasing despair. Their motion made his lethargy feel more and more powerful.

Beside Bellamy sat Barnabus Merrill, an ale mug poised in its usual position on the edge of his lip. He drained it and then turned it upside-down. As the last drop of ale dribbled onto the table, his face drooped with despair.

"This road out front... Where does it lead? There must be a port around here somewhere. One deep enough to hold a ship bound for New York or the like?" Bellamy asked. He had heard the name of that city, in the smoky taverns back home. His plan had been to head to New York after the *Josephine* brought him to Boston. Some men claimed that New York was a place where a man could gather a fortune to himself, in a matter of a few seasons, although none had offered insight on the exact method of such men's success. Still, it seemed a better prospect than what faced him in Eastham and Higgins Tavern.

"A deepwater port? Bah! There's naught here but marsh and sand flats. I'd go sit in the orchard, if I was you, and pretend that my bones was still broken, lest they drag you into more of their foolishness, like building them another windmill."

"Then where is the nearest port?" Bellamy persisted.

"Probably Plymouth."

"Ah yes! The place that the Separatists founded after they departed from Plymouth in Devon, from which I hail. My father spoke of it every time he took me to the harbor. 'From this very spot, men went off to discover new worlds. Why could not you do the same?' That is what he would say to me."

"Aye. Well, you're a bit late. This Plymouth was founded near a hundred years ago. I wouldn't bother with it myself. It is not much different than Eastham – sand, sea, fields, ale..." The old man hoisted his mug, at the conclusion of the list.

Bellamy thought about the two Plymouths, an ocean apart from each other, and he could not help but feel a sense of defeat in their commonality. New York had at least added some sense of novelty to its moniker. This new Plymouth seemed content to aspire to nothing better but the tired old world. He had to keep telling himself that it was merely a stop along the way. As such, it was a good fifty miles northwest towards Boston. By Bellamy's calculation, it was about a three-day walk overland or a half-day's sail.

Bellamy dropped his voice to a whisper, "I'm getting tired of sneaking around for scraps like a starving hound. Is this the way of the colonies?"

Barnabus arched his brows. "It is the way of my niece's miser of a husband."

"I need a boat," Bellamy grumbled.

"You can sail with me if you like! Just remember that, as captain, I give the orders!" Barnabus sang.

"You have a boat?"

"Aye! In the Cove."

Bellamy frowned. He had seen the tiny craft that were moored in the small anchorage of the Cove. "Is it large enough to bear us to New York?"

"Nay. But it would be an easy passage to Plymouth," Barnabus replied.

Such an arrangement would mean signing on, at Plymouth, with another merchant ship, to take him to New York, Bellamy mused. But it was better than nothing, and with luck his next berth would prove an easier time than his ordeal on the *Josephine*. He raised his mug to toast to their journey, but Barnabus yanked his own mug away.

"Oh! What am I doing? Tis bad luck to be sitting with a man thrown from a boat! Next time I sail, tis at my peril for knocking back too many ales with you!"

Bellamy snorted derisively. "That I survived was luck and nothing more. But I will take it all the same."

Barnabus stroked his chin and considered the matter. "Luck or miracle, I wonder which? Now, a shipwrecked man is a boon for certain. That is fate throwing him from death to shore. But a man who falls off the rail..."

"I jumped," Bellamy corrected.

"Well then, that ain't the same as falling from a boat at all!" Barnabus said happily.

Bellamy shook his head at such backwater superstition. "Can we sail tomorrow?" he asked irritably.

"Tomorrow? Only if the day is bright and calm. I won't risk four-foot waves and a sea spitting foam, with nothing but your luck to save us!"

"My luck will hold," Bellamy predicted.

✠ ✠ ✠ ✠

The ale was building up in Bellamy, and it made his bladder clench as bad as his guts sometimes did when he thought of returning to the ocean.

He put his head out of the open door of the tavern and was confronted with a mix of scents: apple blossoms from the orchard on one side and the salty tang of ocean water from the other. It was farm and sea flowing together, catching Bellamy in the cross-current of his lifelong dilemma.

Outside, the sunlight was mellow and pooling in the long, soft shadows of afternoon. A hue of deep cobalt colored the upper sky. On the horizon the clouds were a fluffy white, occasionally emblazoned at the edges with gold. Seagulls spiraled through the sky, their under-wings flaming from the waning sun. All of these gentle sights lifted Bellamy's spirits, until he was convinced that he was finally on the cusp of discovering the true promise of this new land.

In the spirit of that revelation, he decided to head into the apple orchard, instead of facing the grimness of the outhouse.

Bellamy walked across the dirt path towards the orchard, feeling buoyed by the ale and food. The orchard was set within a ravine. Bellamy ran down the slope, something about the joyful call of the birds and the music of the wind through the trees making him feel giddy. Or was it the drink, he wondered?

The trees' perfume masked Bellamy's own stench as he relieved himself. He finished up his business, hoisted his britches and then followed the apple scent deeper into the grove. He walked under the boughs, with petals falling about him like rain.

He thought that he was following the song of a bird, but he soon realized that it was the words of a song, playing out lazily and seductively before him. It was a woman's voice, the kind that men dream of during long voyages, with nothing but the empty water and each other to look at. What's more, she was singing a sailor's song. It was one that they sang while manning the lines and trimming the sails, one he himself had recently learned. This was a sweet dream indeed, he thought, chuckling to himself.

Bellamy circled a tree and then another, each time expecting the singer to come into view. Gnarled apple trees twisted their boughs into each other, in the tangled orchard.

He still couldn't see her, but the voice was loud, clear and quite close:

"A-roving, a-roving I will go..."

Then he spied the hem of a blue dress moving in the row of trees before him. He did not know if he would find her as enticing as her melody when he finally saw her. But there was comfort in the voice, a sweetness that made his blood warm in a way that he hadn't felt in ages.

"Stay! Stay! You saucy sailor boy,
Do not sail afar,
I love you and will marry you,
You silly Jack tar."

Then he saw her cross between two rows of apple trees, and his blood came near to a boil.

She was just a young girl, not yet twenty, he reckoned. But her beauty was ageless, classical and perfect. He would not have doubted it if she had strode over to him and announced that she was an angel. All he saw was her profile, which was delicate and alluring. Her hair shimmered golden, like it had stored up the last of the sunshine. Then she was gone behind another row of trees, her singing voice trailing behind her, *"I'll make you a comb from a codfish bone if you'll stay here, darling, beside me."*

He felt intoxication rising again but also a strange fear that surprised him. In fact, it was crazy. He had grown up near the docks of Plymouth where women had begun tousling his hair when he was a mere pup, and later he tousled back at them, in the taverns and boarding houses along the dockside. Why was he afraid of this young colonial girl, he asked himself?

He reached down and plucked some dandelions and violets and gathered them into a bunch. Ducking under the branches, he trotted after the girl.

A wagon rumbled by, and her singing abruptly stopped. He saw her crouch, apparently hiding from whoever was riding by. Bellamy almost laughed out loud, at the notion of her singing sailor's songs right under this proper town's nose. He liked her already. Instead of a laugh, he let out a loud crack as his foot trod upon a broken limb covered by the thick grass, and in his embarrassment, he called out something foul.

Immediately she sprang up to face him. If he hadn't been leaning against a tree, he would have tumbled over. Her beauty washed over him like a tide. A burning feeling raced from his head through his heart like a cannon shot.

Her blue dress was trimmed with lace. It breathed in and out slowly, with the gentle puffs of wind, as she watched him. Upon seeing the way that she was clad, he wondered if she was more than a mere farmer's or fisherman's daughter.

"Don't stop on my account! I would very much like to hear what became of those two you sing about," Bellamy said, stepping closer to her.

"You are the sailor," she guessed.

"And you know sailor's songs. Where do you learn them?"

He thought she might be blushing. However, the air was fresh and could have marked her cheeks with its vigor.

"I hear such songs sometimes coming out of the windows of Higgins Tavern," she replied. "Do you have any you can teach me?"

He liked her spirit. It was not the kind of flirting that he was accustomed to. Tavern girls tried to make a game of it but the end was a certainty. He realized that he barely knew how to talk to a girl in such well-spun clothes, which looked finer than the garb he had grown accustomed to seeing in these parts.

"Well, have you anything else to say?" she asked, shaming him with his silence.

"A few words come to mind, on a day such as this. What could I say that could compare to the songs in the air, yours included, or the fragrance of these trees?"

"But you have had plenty to drink, I see," she said. "It is okay. I know the smell, from my father's visits to the tavern. Women are allowed in there but not encouraged. Otherwise, we might have met before this," she explained.

"I would have hated to meet you in there. The gloom of that place does not suit you. You are better seen in the sun if you don't mind me saying so," Bellamy said, wondering where all of this poetry was coming from.

"Yes, you have been drinking," she said. "But it affects you better than most men."

"So much so that I have yet to ask your name."

"Maria Hallett," she replied. "What are you doing out here?" A suspicious look came into her face for a moment.

"Merely exercising. I am due to leave tomorrow. My leg is mending, and my welcome has worn thin, I am afraid," he said, wondering if she would care at all about such news.

If she cared, she did not show it. "Oh. Then I shan't keep you."

"And you? Is this the place you come to perfect your songs or have you lately learned another? I was just inside the tavern, and I don't recall anyone singing."

Maria smiled and Bellamy noted, with amazement, how the simple gesture made his whole body feel lighter.

"I am out exercising too, I suppose. There is really no reason I should be away from the farm, with all that needs to be done. My mother worries, with the strange goings on these days. But my mind feels crazy sometimes, with nothing to look at but the plow rows, the house and the roads that lead off to exactly where I know they shall go…" she broke off bashfully. "There is no reason to tell you this. I should tell you that I am glad that you survived your ordeal. It must have been terrifying to have gone through it."

"I live. That is what matters."

"You have some kind of angel attending to you, then."

"Perhaps."

Her gaze drifted, and Bellamy kept talking, eager to keep her there, trying to get any information out of her that he could, "Where is the farm that you speak of?"

When she pointed to it, he tried to imprint the direction on his mind, hoping he would have need of it later.

"I should be going home," she told him.

"Are you sure? The day will hold like this for an hour more at least."

"My mother will need me. I've been away too long as it is," she said. "If you are leaving, then I suppose this is good-bye."

"And if I am not," he said, his throat constricting like he had never felt before.

Maria studied him for a second, looking much older and wiser than he judged that she was.

"Are you are a church-goer?" she asked.

"Yes," Bellamy lied.

"Tomorrow is the Sabbath. If you are still in town, perhaps I shall see you there."

"You shall. Since I have been here, I have missed service only due to my injury. Now that you mention it, I should not want to make a voyage without the benefit of scripture first."

She smiled cryptically, and he could not tell if he had pleased her or not with his fumbling.

Then an inexplicable surge of guilt prompted a quick confession from him, "In truth, I do not much cross any church's threshold. And if I may say, you seem too lively to fall for such a ruse."

The girl looked embarrassed. "I am not usually this lively."

"Perhaps you should be," Bellamy replied.

She said nothing. Instead, she gave him a flicker of a smile, merely a twitch of her lips. Then she hurried off through the trees, and he bent his will upon her back, hoping to get her to turn again, but the branches folded around her and she was gone.

✠ ✠ ✠ ✠

The next day Bellamy awoke to the sound of a bell clanging. From his window he could see the slow procession of wagons, pedestrians and even some boats in Great Cove, all heading for the meeting house on the far bank. The obedient flow of people, many heads already bowed as if the air itself held some extra weight this day, made Bellamy wish to flee in the other direction. It would have been the ideal day to make for Plymouth had he not remembered who was waiting for him. She was the sweetest reason he had ever had for attending service.

"You are still here? I assumed that you would have been gone from us by now," Justice Doane asked the sailor when the two met on the meeting house doorstep. Ordinarily Bellamy would have been amused by the moment. Usually people like Doane were busy trying to get him into service, not hold him from it.

"I am here. For the time being at least," Bellamy replied.

Doane eyed him suspiciously. "Well, you are late for service. Did you not hear the call of the bell? I have never before heard of a man getting lost on his way here from Higgins Tavern," Doane remarked, pointing across Great Cove at the tavern, to emphasize its nearness.

Bellamy sighed. "Are you going to put me in that?" he said, gesturing towards the pillory on the front lawn where a native man was pinned.

"Missing part of service is a fine. But only for residents. If you intend to linger here, then you had best not be late for service again. We shall be keeping watch on you, until you prove yourself to the town..." Doane went on, until he noticed that the sailor was more interested in waving to someone in the crowd than absorbing the good advice that he was giving. He could not see who Bellamy hailed, but he did not let Bellamy join his companion when the sailor attempted to enter the building. "Late comers, servants and Indians do not go in but instead stand outside and look through the window."

From that vantage point Bellamy could not spy Maria Hallett in the throng of worshippers.

After service the crowd cleared quickly, and by the time Bellamy caught sight of the girl, she was already being carried away in a wagon.

Bellamy began walking down the road that Maria had taken, feeling at once buoyant and silly. She would think him a simple puppy dog when she saw him trailing after her. But an overwhelming sense of gladness propelled him on. It made little sense. His boat was lost, his wages with it, he had nowhere to stay nor means for a single cup of fish stew, yet here he was, fighting off a mad urge to skip along the cartway or sing at the top of his lungs. A girl had done all of this to him. A very young girl. There was no end to the odd occurrences in this place. Maybe it was under the sway of devils after all, he mused.

As he passed the orchard, he looked down into it and thought about his meeting with Maria. He felt that his conversation might have improved had he stayed for one more round of ale before coming into the orchard that day. At the same time, everything around him, during that encounter, seemed more vivid and full of feeling than it ever had with any quantity of drink.

At each house he passed, he tried to get a look through the windows, hoping to catch sight of her face. He did not pass a single home in which there wasn't a face looking studiously back through the panes. And each farmer in the fields invariably paused and watched Bellamy pass by. None offered more than a nod although Bellamy recognized several of the men from nights at Higgins Tavern when some of them had been deep in their cups and slapping Bellamy on the back like old shipmates. He could recall few of their names, and he figured there would be no re-introductions with the men's wives within earshot.

There was an old barn set back from the road, surrounded by tall grass and a thicket of trees. It was in a sorrier state than many ships he had seen rotting at anchor. The roof was caved in at one corner, and its side boards hung askew. Its apparent abandonment gave Bellamy an idea, and he noted it in his mind as a place that might provide refuge in a tight spot.

After that he came upon a field where several cattle lay on their haunches, looking worse than the barn.

Bellamy felt certain that whoever owned this place was a man he had seen regularly at the tavern. He expected that it must take a lot of ale to cause the kind of neglect which reduced livestock to such a state.

Off in the distance he saw a middle-age woman in the garden. She had fading sandy colored hair and a hard face that, at a certain angle, left no doubt that Bellamy had found his destination. He did not know Alice Hallett by name, but he knew that she had to be related to the girl. He walked towards her, with no thought of what he would say to her, only that his longing to see Maria had become an ache in his chest.

He was just about to open his mouth when a voice hissed at him, from a copse of cherry trees at the edge of the farm's rock wall, "*Shhh! Do not hail her! If you do, she will shoo you away, like a stray raccoon that has wandered into the fields.*"

Bellamy peered over the stones and grinned at the crouching form of Maria Hallett. "Raccoon?"

"*Quickly! Cross the road and go down to Great Cove where there are tall rushes along the edge! I shall meet you there!*"

Bellamy crossed the road and entered open farmland. As he walked through it, he expected its enraged owner to come charging out of the homestead in the distance. But he reached Great Cove without incident and found the dense pack of reeds to which the girl had sent him.

A moment later he was within the wall of reeds, surrounded by its murmuring sway. Soon after that he heard the crunch of footsteps, snapping the reed stalks. Then the wall parted and bounding in came Maria.

"Do you relish the privacy or are you attempting to keep our meetings hidden away?" he asked, bemused.

She looked nervous and kept some space between them. "Mother... She would not understand."

"Ah..."

"So are you ready to sail? You are leaving today, are you not?"

Bellamy suddenly recalled his last words to the girl. In truth, he had postponed his sailing. At least until the end of this meeting.

"Where are you bound? I could sail you to Plymouth if you like," Maria went on, trying to hide the distress from her face.

"Maybe I shall take your offer, but I have not yet made up my mind how long I shall linger." All he had to do was steal a peak at Maria's lithe figure, as she stood next to him, and he felt committed to remaining in this town more forcefully than before.

"*So you are not leaving soon?*" she whispered.

"Nay, Maria," he said. Her name released from his lips like a piece of music.

"Why did you come looking for me? I did not think that you would really come to church," she stammered.

Bellamy inched closer to her. "There were plenty more things that I wanted to tell you at the orchard but did not," he replied. "I did not get to speak with you at today's service. I will not take that chance again. Besides, some of the things I would talk about are the sort of things that would need forgiveness on the Sabbath Day."

"Like what?" she breathed.

"I was thinking of laying you down in that grassy orchard and spending the day looking into those magnificent eyes of yours, watching the petals fall upon your pretty face and making up a few of our own songs to pass the time."

"You are telling me what you want to do with me, not what you want to say to me," she pointed out.

"How about this: I've been to sea but once. Little did I suspect that I would wash ashore in a little colonial town and discover a girl who puts all the others to shame with her beauty. It would be like pulling out this reed and finding a gold piece in the dirt," he concluded.

"You are not a sailor, then?" she asked.

The disappointment in her voice surprised him. "That's right," he replied. "Do you believe that fate might cast a man into a particular place for a reason?"

"I don't know what *fate* wants or why it does anything."

"Or if it exists at all," Bellamy pointed out.

"Something is moving us around like checkers on a board. That I am sure of."

Bellamy was enjoying himself more than he had since he first woke up and found that he was still alive. Most girls' banter would have grown tiresome by now, but this one had a keen mind to go with her looks. The combination stirred him more than he thought possible.

"Will you and your mother survive this harvest if the cattle fail?" Bellamy asked her.

"I don't know," she said.

"I know the scene all too well. The farm that I grew up on was half this size with three times the rocks and weeds. Pitiful ground. When the good land was full, the poor like us were pushed into such places where a man was lucky to find space fertile enough for a row of peas. Some of our neighbors turned to sheep. They are a bit like cattle. If nothing else than in the fact that when they die, they damn near kill the owner too. I know that feeling of watching everything you have falling down dead in the fields."

"We will be alright. And you? Life at sea pays better than this. I should hurry back to it if I had the chance," she said, thrumming a stalk of reed.

"It may pay well, but I did not stay aboard long enough to collect my wages," he smiled.

"Oh! I forgot!"

"No matter. Payment would have had to be thrice the amount I signed on for, to be fair trade. These days I wonder if I have had my fill of the sea."

Maria scrunched up her brows and Bellamy added, "But the sea did bring me here."

"Perhaps we can go sailing some time," she suggested. "To me, you are a sailor."

Bellamy smiled. "As you wish."

He took another step closer, but Maria danced away, her ear trained to the sound of her name being hollered in the distance.

"My mother calls. I must go," she said, her face turning as pink as the light that shone through the reeds around them.

"Will I see you again?"

"Unless you sail away," she said as she slipped off through the rushes.

He could not help but notice that every farm in the vicinity lay in direct view of the sparkling ocean, a view of thousands of leagues that eventually splashed ashore in Devon. He wondered how many people in Eastham had spent their lives dreaming of trading their lot here for the promise of what lay on the other side of the sea, which was, in fact, nothing but a land of poor farms, like the one he had been born on.

✠ ✠ ✠ ✠

That night Bellamy found the door to Higgins Tavern closed down to a crack, which the tavern keeper's head stuck through.

"The fields are close enough to harvest that we can manage alone. Our debt is settled, and I cannot keep supporting a man without a penny to his name," Higgins said in a rush. Bellamy noticed that Higgins' face shook slightly, and he wondered what would happen were he to force open the door. No doubt it would lead to an appearance by Justice Doane.

"So ends your charity? I did not expect it to stop so abruptly," Bellamy said.

"Alas, I would keep you on if I could, but it would be the end of me."

Bellamy tried to bite his tongue but could not, "Doane has commanded this of you."

"No, no!" Higgins said. "I made the decision! I have the right to serve whom I want! I don't need Doane's blessing on that!"

"So *you* want me out then?" Bellamy said, making Higgins' face go white.

The tavern keeper showed surprising mettle, despite his obvious fear of the sailor. When Bellamy saw Mehitable sniveling in the corner behind Higgins, everything made sense.

"I showed no impropriety towards your daughter. Nor did I give her reason to hope," Bellamy said.

Higgins snorted in disbelief. "You'll not get far with that Hallett girl," he warned.

"That is why I must go?" Bellamy asked.

"Well yes…and also because guests of healthy body are expected to pay. You are obviously completely fit!"

"And you need no more help on the fields," Bellamy recounted, more to himself than Higgins.

"Seems you found another field to plow," Higgins said darkly.

Bellamy walked back out into the dark and tried to determine where best to find shelter. The Hallett house was visible in the distance, its windows glowing warmly. But he knew there was no real welcome there, not from the mother at any rate. Above him the stars blinked coldly in the unusual chill of the air. He crossed the road and headed into the orchard, counting on the memories of his last visit there to keep him warm through the night. Perhaps those visions would help him decide whether to stay or go, he mused.

✠ ✠ ✠ ✠

Late August 1715

Weeks piled on top of each other, yet Bellamy felt no weight from them. During his moments with Maria, all sense of time's passage was lifted, blown away like corn husks rolling off on a breeze. There was only a long single moment, sun-baked and dreamlike. He did not even have a spare second to wonder where it would lead or if it would ever end. It was as if the summer was their private season, which existed simply to please them. He thought it a pity that they had to hide their joy, but he understood the need for some discretion. He saw the suspicion and recrimination in the faces of the townsfolk. It was mostly wordless frowns and flicks of the eye. They called the courtship improper because it was not sanctioned by the church or the girl's mother. In turn, Bellamy and Maria considered the townsfolk's disapproval unjust. However, it all derived from jealousy, Bellamy knew. Those that glared at the couple, as they did something as innocent as dig clams, only added the spice of rebellion to his already overflowing feelings. Whether he would pay later for this freedom of spirit, he did not know. That moment seemed as far away as the end of these long summer days.

In truth, it was almost September, and the summer heat had turned the high stalks of elephant grass brown. But he barely noticed on those days when he and Maria walked the sands, with a bucket filled with quahogs in hand.

Usually Bellamy slept on the beach, tucked within the reeds. If it looked safe to do so, he would sneak into the old barn near the Hallett farm where the straw covered floors were a luxury compared to a bed of muddy peat.

During this particular twilight a faint lantern glow emanated from the structure, a signal that told him that a most pleasurable night with Maria waited inside. They had recently come to know each other in the way that the town elders forbade for unmarried couples.

When he pushed the barn door open, Bellamy sprang through it, his lips curled with sweet words, which fell away when he saw the figure of Elder Knowles standing amidst the hay piles.

Elder Knowles, in turn, looked like he had been struck. It was the kind of feigned indignation that made Bellamy want to knock the man down, had he not been trespassing in his barn.

"You look like a snake coming home to its den," Knowles snarled. "Is my barn your place of refuge? Under my very nose?"

"There are no livestock housed here, so it does not seem that you are in need of it after dark," Bellamy replied. "But I should have asked…"

"Twas the polite thing to do," Knowles replied, inching closer to the wooden pegs where the pitchforks and scythes hung, in case he would soon have use for one.

"Well, I shall leave to find shelter elsewhere."

"Really? Higgins Tavern is closed to you. And I doubt that any other farmer in town would accept a vagrant under his roof."

"What did you call me?" Bellamy asked. He was no longer moving towards the door.

"Anyone without a place to stay or coin in his pocket is a vagrant and is warned out of town. Justice Doane's men will escort you to the town border. If you return, you will find residence at the town jail. I don't imagine that you have any coin. And I hear that no one needs extra hands this harvest."

"No. Even though there is reaping to be done. I have a hand for it, but it is as you say. Strangers are not welcome in this town." He too walked towards the sharp, pointed tools just to see how Knowles would react. As he expected, the elder danced away towards the door.

"You look like you wish to run. You do not trust me?" Bellamy snickered.

"I do not know you or anyone who could vouch for you. Perhaps Goody Hallett bade you stay, but her word carries no weight. If you will not leave willingly, then I will have Justice Doane take up the matter with you."

Bellamy was not good at keeping his true feelings locked inside. Captain Pound of the *Josephine* knew that. The scars on Bellamy's back occasionally burned in reminder of Pound's reaction to his criticism. He did not know what kind of force Knowles had to back up the lashing of his tongue, but such ignorance had never stopped Bellamy before.

He took a step towards the elder and was pleased when Knowles again backed off a pace.

"To me, it sounds like I am the one who has caught the criminal," Bellamy said, coming to stand face to face with the elder. "Your jowls shake, like one who is caught red-handed. I imagine that is because you are in the midst of thieving the land of a poor widow and her only daughter. It is so obvious that I saw your true intent after being here but a few weeks."

"How dare you! Are you not stealing an impressionable young maid's heart? You are not one to cast stones!" Knowles stepped out of the barn and backed away along the rock wall of the property line, with Bellamy following him.

"Nay, we took each other's hearts. You will not fight me man to man?" Bellamy said, leering.

"I do not have to. The law is on my side."

Bellamy gnawed his lip and sighed. "Your law only serves your lies! I have seen this all before. Thieving landlords, corrupt ministers, greedy neighbors. A pack of blackhearted devils is what you are. I shall not be sent away by the likes of you! There is more justice in this world than what your Justice Doane offers, and I am willing to administer it to you if need be!"

They had come up alongside of the Halletts' house, and just then the door swung open and Alice Hallett came outside, worry framing her face. "What is this commotion?"

It was Knowles' turn to smirk. "Go ahead then, Master Bellamy. Tell her…"

"What is going on here, John?" Alice demanded of Elder Knowles.

"Master Bellamy wishes to take lodging in my barn as to be closer at hand to woo your daughter."

"How dare you!" Alice seethed at the sailor.

For the first time Bellamy was face to face with the mother of Maria Hallett. Despite her wrath Bellamy felt his own venom draining out of him. "Ma'am… Elder Knowles makes my courtship sound a tawdry thing. It is nothing of the sort."

"No, it is not even courtship, Master Bellamy. It is the rebellion of a wanton child, which will cease as soon as you are on your way."

There was no chance to offer any protest or explanation. As quickly as she had appeared, Mrs. Hallett withdrew into her house, and the wooden door clicked shut as firmly as the gate of a castle.

"Go on! I would head west and not stop until you have reached Barnstable if I were you!" Knowles said.

✠ ✠ ✠ ✠

The next morning Bellamy and Maria met at Amaziah Harding's mill, which stood on a hillock not far from the Hallett homestead. The building was filled with the whir and clack of wooden machinery and the soft hiss of corn meal coming out from the press of turning stones. A sand-filled hour glass slowly draining would have a similar affect on the mind, thought Bellamy. While waiting for the grind to finish, there was little to do but watch the empty road, beneath the structure, or look in the other direction, down the slope towards Great Cove, eyes drifting mindlessly with the cut of some sloop out on the water.

Bellamy noted the relationship between farmer and miller as one of great mutual benefit. The farmer tends to the planting and the miller to the grinding, neither having to worry about the other part of the equation yet both ending up with a winter store, for the larder, without a penny changing hands.

"That is the way that men can be an advantage, rather than scourge, to each other. The parson is quite the opposite. He takes his tithe and then promises men nothing but eternal hellfire as a reward. If one listens to those lies and believes them, there is nothing to look forward to in life but a short race towards a bitter, black end," he said with a playful arch of his dark brows, but he could not draw a smile from the girl.

"What ails you? It is a glorious day, and we should revel in it," Bellamy said.

"I was within the house when you and Knowles were shouting at each other," she said.

"Then you heard me defending you and your mother as I should have done long before. I am sorry that I did not. But I believe that I have given Knowles something to think about," Bellamy replied. He did not want to talk about the confrontation. His moments with Maria were akin to the precision and entwined grip of the mill gears, their twirling progression resounding like a heartbeat. In contrast, Knowles, poverty and the suspicion around town were to Bellamy as jarring as jamming a pole into the cogs.

"You are not listening! Warning out is serious business!" Maria said.

"I do not care about Knowles," Bellamy said.

"You should care about his threat. What are we to do? They could send you away at any moment! We need a plan at least!"

Bellamy waved away her protest. "I have been without money for weeks now. The clam flats provide my dinner, the reeds my bed and you make the hours in between worth suffering the rest of it. If Justice Doane wanted me warned out, he would have done it long ago. I think my attendance at service has put me in good stead," Bellamy said with a wink.

Maria pouted in response. "Now that you have riled up Elder Knowles, he will prod Justice Doane. Perhaps they merely wait for winter to come and deprive you of your dinner and bed. But it doesn't matter! We need a plan!"

"I will come up with one," Bellamy assured her. He drew Maria around to the back of the mill where anyone on the water with a keen eye would have seen him press her up against the shingles and lay his mouth upon hers.

The kiss was warm and scented like Johnny-cakes, from the fine powder that had accumulated on them from being in the mill. There was a vague taste of ale in Bellamy's mouth too, adding to the feeling that the kiss was a kind of sweet feast. She returned it with a quick, hungry burst and then pulled away, brushing off her apron as if later someone might see signs of their indiscretion shaped there among the corn powder.

"No one on Great Cove can see us. I know that Reverend Treat's eyes are not that strong," Bellamy said, grabbing her by the elbows and reeling her gently back towards him.

"You need some money," she said.

Bellamy threw up his hands. "Where shall I get it? You heard what Knowles said yesterday. None will hire me. They are in league with each other to block me out."

"And you believe that they won't one day warn you out? They wait only to make it less pleasant. They hope that you will leave on your own. But now you have pushed them, and they will surely push back."

"So what is the use of obtaining money?"

"You are no vagrant if you have coin. The law will protect you."

Bellamy shook his head. "You have much to learn, my sweet one."

"Then what is your plan? They will send you away!" she cried and stormed off down the hill.

Bellamy followed her, but not until later, after Harding had finished and handed the sailor the ground corn. He left the sack of meal on the Halletts' stoop and then peeked into the windows to see if Maria was within and if she was alone.

"*They will see you!*" came a hiss from behind him. Maria glared at him and then began walking along the stone wall in front of the farm, towards the heart of town.

He followed after her, whispering, "*I will not run from them!*"

"You want to stay because of me too, don't you? You are not simply being stubborn and defiant," she asked.

"Of course!" Bellamy replied.

"Just walk beside me and hold out your hands," she commanded.

"Maria. You would think me a coward if I ran. Were I to do that, I would not deserve your affection. You ought not grant it to me were I to flee this injustice."

"Hush! I am giving you *this*..." She placed an object the size of a bread loaf into his hands. It was covered with a blanket and caked in dirt. Bellamy took it, shook free the clods and peeled the covering off. Underneath was a small leather box.

He looked inquiringly at the girl.

"Open it. Quick!" she demanded.

When he did, its contents bedazzled in the sun. A pile of gold, silver and copper coins. "What is this?"

"It is the coin that Knowles made selling *my father's* cattle! I saw him bury it in his fields."

Vindication shone in her eyes. Bellamy stared at the coins, like he was receiving a missing clue to the meaning of all his striving.

"Now Doane cannot send you away," she added.

He hugged her. "I will return this coin to you and your mother with tenfold the interest."

"Promise me only that one day you will bring me with you when you leave this place."

"I promise," he said.

✠ ✠ ✠ ✠

That evening Bellamy stood outside of Higgins Tavern. At his hip was the box that Maria had given him. He shook it to hear the contents give a satisfying rattle. Thirty pounds worth of coins lay inside. He had counted them three times, just to be sure. It was more wealth than he had ever made on his own. He ruminated on what the coin could do for him and what they could not. With them he could book passage to New York or beyond. He could purchase a new set of clothes. Even a small tract of land in Eastham might be in reach. What he had in hand would suffice for some time, but it was not the stuff of dreams.

Before he could do anything, he needed more coin in the box. After all, the money was not even his, at least it was not fairly earned. It is a loan, he told himself.

He had turned his plan over and over in his mind and decided that there was nothing but merit in it. The local men had shown no skill at cards or dice. Over the course of an afternoon, his new found prosperity might double or triple in size, depending upon how poorly the others picked their cards.

"Oh, you have some cheek, you know that, Bellamy?" Isaiah Higgins huffed as the sailor came through the door. "Did I not make myself clear? You are not welcome here..." The tavern keeper's voice fell away at the sight of Bellamy's unexpected wealth.

"I will not even stay the night," Bellamy assured him.

"Okay! *Quick! Quick!* Just for a couple hours!" Higgins said, holding the door shut, for an extra moment, while he turned and shooed away his daughter. "I can handle this lot. Go out and tend the fields till the light is lost!" he told her and stood blocking her view of the sailor, until she was safely out of the back door. After that, he brushed off his apron and could not suppress a whistle from seeping through his lips.

On one wall was a box with stems of clay pipes sticking out at various lengths, from stubs no more than a hand width long to others of a foot or more. It was a communal stash from which patrons could draw. Bellamy pulled out one of promising length. To his disappointment, the end was mushed, from the chewing teeth or gums of the last one who smoked it. A pair of metal clippers hung over the box. Bellamy snipped off the end of his pipe, making a clean, round opening. Then he gave a coin to Higgins in return for a roll of tobacco, some of which he thumbed into the pipe's mouth and then tamped down with the metal nub that stuck off of one side of the clippers, for exactly that purpose.

It was the same ritual that he had done hundreds of times at different taverns, but with coin in hand, he went slowly, enjoying every detail of the procedure with fresh enthusiasm.

Bellamy tried his hand at dice with some of the young men of town and was able to win a pile of pennies before dinnertime. It looked like a pitiful stack in the watery light of the evening's lanterns, but even that little mound discouraged the parsimonious men of Eastham, who all took their leave before they slipped further into loss.

Bellamy added what he won to his own pile and did a quick calculation. The winnings accounted nicely for the pipe and drinks, leaving him roughly where he had started when he had first come through the door. Part of him suggested that he stop now, but the ales were going down by the handful per hour, and Bellamy felt that familiar feeling of buoyancy in his mind. Not for the first time, it occurred to him that his journey through life could always be this smooth were the ales to be continuously flowing. That, though, took hard currency, which was attained only by engaging in the general viciousness of living. An endless circle, he mused, drawing out another coin and clinking his mug for a refill as if he were some idle lord who could dismiss the hard facts of existence with such a nonchalant gesture.

There was a clatter of hooves outside. Bellamy went to the window, with the few remaining patrons, to watch a driver climb out of a wagon and help a well-garbed, plump, middle-age man down from the riding bench. The onlookers chattered about the fellow, pronouncing him the finest dressed guest ever received at Higgins' place. One of the men recognized the stranger and said that the stranger's name was Palsgrave Williams. "I hear he is a frequent visitor to *Great Island*," the man added, and the rest of the patrons nodded knowingly.

Williams and his driver came in without any baggage in tow. When he realized that he was receiving them just for dinner, not lodging, a flicker of disappointment creased Higgins' face.

"We are bound for Billingsgate. I am told that I shall arrive before nightfall," Williams explained. He shook off his coat and beamed around him, like he was reflecting the radiance of old friends rather than blank faces.

"After all the rain, some of the King's Highway is likely washed out. A start in the morning would be the safer plan," Higgins suggested.

"Perhaps. But we shall make the attempt nonetheless," Williams said. He looked around for a place to sit, and Bellamy had the feeling that he was assessing the company as much as the table placement. Instead of sitting by the roaring fire, he took a seat at Bellamy's own table.

Williams introduced himself and extended a large, fleshy hand that was wet and warm as it wrapped around Bellamy's own. Williams was garbed in a velvet vest and high-crowned wig, typical of an aristocrat. Yet his face was full and loose and moved liberally in all directions when the man chuckled or smiled, which was frequently. He had entirely too much mirth and twinkle in his eye to fit Bellamy's notion of the upper class, and only that kept Bellamy from rising and heading to bed early without making his acquaintance.

"You look like a man who thinks he knows something that the rest of us don't," Bellamy said.

In response Williams offered his widest smile yet, a truly magnificent stretch of cheek and teeth. "Perhaps...Coming here was the first good idea I have had in some time. If it is a sort of illumination, so be it. However, it is no secret. This place soothes the soul. I smelled the fish running as we came around Great Cove," the man said, breathing deeply as if he could still catch a whiff of the fish scent under the heavy clouds of tobacco and hearth smoke that filled the room. "Tomorrow I might set a pole out and try my hand at reeling in cod or bluefish," he added.

Bellamy's own cheer faded somewhat. Within moments this stranger had made him feel like a fool, one for whom landing a codfish was not sport but instead might determine whether or not there was dinner.

"How is the chowder this evening?" Williams called to Higgins.

The tavern keeper promptly appeared at Williams' elbow, displaying an obsequiousness that made Bellamy cringe. "Freshly made and the best in the county, if I do say so. An ale would go nicely with it."

"Fine! One for me and another for my friend here," Williams replied, including Bellamy in his gesture.

As Williams leaned across the table, Bellamy worried that he would have to pay more in idle chitchat than the free meal warranted. Sure enough, the man asked all about Bellamy's seafaring experience, his time in Devon and anything else he could think of. Bellamy got talking reluctantly, but his audience was so keen and rapt that he found himself revealing more than was prudent.

"The captains of such ships are no better than thieving criminals. I'd not cry to see Pound strung from a line on the Wapping gallows. God knows he deserves it!" Bellamy remarked, slurping from his ale.

"I thought that you lamented how men put misery upon each other as a matter of course?" Williams pointed out.

"Ah, who cares? Tonight I'd not weep if Pound got his due!" Bellamy scowled, annoyed at the way his drinking companion seemed to delight in catching him in contradictions.

"Keeping ships afloat is no easy task whether one stands at the tiller or sits in the counting house."

"You are a shipping merchant?" Bellamy snarled.

"No, my father is. We have many ships in our employ. I handle the currency for the family business, but I am a jeweler by trade. This is Swiss metal. The diamonds are from Africa. The design is my own," Williams said, pulling a golden watch on a chain from his vest pocket.

"It is a sight to behold. Must be worth a fortune."

"The art of it is its true worth to me."

Bellamy nodded mutely, thinking that it was the kind of comment that only a man who had never lived with want could have made.

"You disagree?"

Bellamy told Williams what was on his mind and was surprised to hear another burst of laughter, a loud rumble like water among breakers.

"You speak like a fellow who is in need of money!" Williams hollered.

"To me, it is no jest but rather a matter of life or death. But not so much today. I'll warrant that."

"Do you play dice?"

In response Bellamy grabbed randomly into the box of coin and laid a pile of pennies onto the table. Williams' figured their number with a mere flick of his eyes.

"Ah! Twenty-two pence! The savior's soul was sold for less! It is a good start," Williams said, ignoring the ripple of comment around him at his blasphemy.

"Can I get you any more to drink or eat?" Higgins chimed in over their shoulders.

Williams turned and beamed at him. "Keep these mugs well filled. That is all I require!"

The tavern keeper nodded and moved away. Then Bellamy grabbed the dice from the table where he had last played and they began their rolls.

The sailor won the first few games, and again a warning to quit while he was ahead sounded in his mind. But it was soon washed away by the next round of ale. It would be worth it if he won more coin. What he had so far was not enough, he told himself again.

He rolled the dice. They bounced all the way to the lip of the table and landed right in front of Williams. The jeweler gave a haughty laugh, and Bellamy did not have to look at his roll to know that he had lost.

Bellamy won the next game, and again the jeweler gave the same chortle, win or lose. Bellamy had the distinct impression that the man had little idea of the true stakes of the game.

"Gambling is something of a habit of mine, I suppose. It is a luxury, I admit. Yet I can't seem to shake it," Williams said and chortled again.

The more Williams laughed, the more that Bellamy's throws rolled past the winning number. Losses began to outweigh victories.

"What a rotten streak!" Williams guffawed.

Bellamy would have predicted that a man of Williams' station would not have skill at the game. Poor men in mean hovel taverns were the kind that seemed to excel at such sport, men with everything to loose. Williams kept winning, and Bellamy saw his pile reduced to his final coin, leaving a bitterness that not even the free ale could quench.

"Is that the end of your entire fortune? I hope that I have not tempted you to squander it," Williams said.

Bellamy tried to match Williams' casual tone even though his fingers now rested in a nearly empty box. The feel of all that space so suddenly there in place of the hard coin took his breath away.

"Have you a wager?" Bellamy asked.

Williams put the dice down in the center of the table and wagged a finger at Bellamy with an avuncular air. "From what I gather from your tales, you are stuck here in this tavern, after being washed ashore in a foreign land with only the clothes upon your back. You are even perhaps down to your final bit of wealth. You have nowhere to go, no means, no livelihood that entices you, correct? Yet you will risk all for the sake of a few ales and a promise of coin falling into your lap unearned. There are works of literary men that fail to capture such pure drama... I do not jest. Yet I will not strip you of your last means over a meaningless game."

"What do you wager?" Bellamy repeated, his face darkening.

"Drink up and eat. Let us talk more of places you and I have been. Such conversation is more interesting than sitting here, watching to see which black spots turn up on the dice."

"Your concern is wasted. I have coin enough left. A decent man would allow me the chance to win back what has escaped me."

Williams sighed and shook his head. "As you wish." He drew out the gold watch again. "This is my wager..."

The first thing that Bellamy thought of when he saw the device was its purpose, to wind away great lengths of time, like a reaper cutting down wheat. It made him wonder about the state of the fields that he had left behind in England. He did not even know who currently held the lease, but he knew that if they had any skill at all, the soil should be laden with crops, ready for the harvest table by now. His own life felt stalled somewhere in early autumn with no harvest in sight. Imagining himself with the watch did not make Bellamy feel in possession of even a minute extra of time, yet he imagined that there was something comforting about carrying it, saving it for a dire need in the way that country folk had dishware and doorknobs made of silver, which could be melted down to pay for some emergency.

"It is worth more than all of the coin that has yet passed between us. It exceeds what I carry too. You mock me," Bellamy said, trying to get Williams to give him an idea of its monetary value.

"No, no. I admire the chances you've taken. I merely emulate your brazen play."

"You have plenty of coin to part with first."

"I do not plan to part with any of it," Williams chuckled.

"I call seven," Bellamy said and picked up the dice.

He saw the dice turning across the table, the winning numbers rolling into view and then away again. It was over in an instant.

"So it ends…" Williams said, sounding sober for the first time all evening.

"I am finished then," Bellamy groused.

"Don't say that, friend! You are such a good sport that I shall buy the next round!" Williams said.

Bellamy rose from the table. "No. The money is yours. It was fairly won."

"Nonsense! I want to treat you."

Bellamy shook his head.

The jeweler's face fell. "Then if there is no more amusement to be had, I shall go as well. I doubt that I shall see you again, but were you to tire of this place, I shall be at Great Island and always up for a game if you find anything else to bet with," Williams said, again grasping Bellamy's hand. The jeweler then walked unsteadily around the room, looking for his driver.

"No better than you started. You had better take him up on his offer," Higgins clucked in the sailor's ear. He held the front door open until Bellamy stepped outside, onto a road that was empty except for a wagon rumbling away.

Chapter Three
"Drift Highways"

September 1715

The bright sun of morning, the promise of a box full of coin and the warmth of young love all should have buoyed Sam Bellamy and Maria Hallett as they stood by the mooring field of Great Cove. Yet Bellamy experienced only discomfort. The money was gone, and he didn't know how to tell her.

"Why don't you make a proper sailor out of me," he said.

Her eyes lit up. "Really?"

"Aye."

"Right now," he prompted her. He composed himself and looked out towards the water. "Is that not where your heart lies?" he added, gesturing towards the horizon.

"A man of this colony spends more time traveling by water than land. I cannot imagine a man who does not know what to do in the water." Maria said, a smile breaking on her lips.

She led him to a small vessel, tromping through the water with no concern that her skirts were floating up like a jelly fish. "My mother will find out one way or the other. There is no sense in trying to hide the fact," she said.

"Yes. We are quite out in the open," Bellamy remarked, noting the houses overlooking them from the bluffs on all sides, their windows looking like prying eyes.

Maria did not look around. She kept trudging towards the anchored craft. "It is a well built boat. But it is small. It is probably too small to sail to New York. But we could try if we wish!" she exclaimed. "Make yourself useful and get us to deeper water."

He pushed the boat off through the shallows. Then he waded quickly behind it, hopping madly, like a deer bouncing through the meadow, in his effort to catch up. He scrambled aboard the stern and flopped into the hull, panting and clinging to the gunwale.

"It is not even over your head," Maria laughed.

"I know," he replied with a wan smile.

The boat was simple to manage. It was wide keeled and forgiving. Great Cove was sheltered enough from heavy wind, and the breeze was moderate even when the vessel broke through into the harbor.

Bellamy showed good instinct with the sails, keeping them fat with wind or cut close, depending on what was warranted. But Maria did most of the sailing, giving Bellamy time to look about at the long fields of green marsh grass swaying in the wind and current. A brown line cut neatly across the stalks, about three quarters of the way towards the tip, showing where the last high tide had been. From the line down, the stalks looked like weathered shingles. The mud and peat stank like manured fields. The holes of little crabs dotted the mud bank, and the creatures went about their business in a mad scurry, which seemed a reflection of the atmosphere of the whole of Eastham. Drifting through the firm clasp of marshland wasn't so bad, Bellamy decided. It had none of the distress of being pushed across a sheet of water that took months to traverse. He tipped his head back and watched the blue sky glide over the tip of the mast. Next to him, Maria pulled in the mainsheet, and from where he lay it looked like she was holding the clouds on a string.

After a while Bellamy wished that the sea would bear him away forever. Part of him longed to cast himself overboard, knowing that he would not likely escape fate twice. It was a fitting end, he felt, for what he had done to this girl and the gift she had given him. Much of last night was a blur although he had the hammering in his head to remind him of the gist of it. He was trying to stay cheerful, but he could tell that she sensed something. The dilemma made his hands sweat in a fashion that he had never experienced before. He could imagine the broken look of disappointment on her face when he told her, and he did not feel strong enough to bear it. All morning he searched his mind for a way to replace the coin, including tracking down the jeweler and making him play for it again, but he had nothing to gamble with except his life itself. To get the money, he would have to do something that might put him on the gallows. It was too much to make another man pay for his error. The waves lapped against the side of the boat, and it sounded to Bellamy like they were urging him to be done with it. Throwing himself over would at least grant him a final piece of honor. Yet that too displeased him. He had not survived the ocean only to cast himself back into it. He would confess, then he would make it up to her. He would do right by this girl, he decided. He would get her a fortune twice as big. God knew that she deserved it, he told himself.

Farther out, the marsh grass thinned. A long strip of white sand, without a single footprint upon it, came into view. Birds became the dominant resident. All manner of them hopped about the water's edge and swooped and dived at the surface.

The breakers were coming up fast. They sounded like the noise of water boiling as they churned through the wide inlet that cut through the sand. The tufted water came in row after row, relentlessly. The span of waves seemed too wide to pass through, and Bellamy wondered if he would look like a silly fool if he suggested that they turn back now.

The French had dubbed the spot *Mallebar,* dangerous shoals, when Samuel de Champlain and his crew had run a much larger ship through the breach in 1605. Many ships since had been pulled under by the endless hunger of this shallow, wave-swept stretch of water.

"*I know this place...*" Bellamy muttered. The water's sound was a throaty roar. The chill of the water that splashed over the side onto him made his very blood feel like it would freeze.

"Yes, the harbor mouth leads to the sea. You washed in through this passage, they say," Maria said.

Bellamy drew a small flask from his pocket and showed it to her. "Ale grows wearisome on the tongue after some time. I won this from old Barnabus Merrill last night. It is sure to get our minds off of any troubles."

He uncorked the top and passed the bottle under Maria's nose. Then he took a sniff himself. The sharp slap of rum shot into his nostrils, and then the rest of the way into his head, making his mind ache with the flavor.

"There are plenty of songs about this drink. In fact, men at sea seldom sing of anything else except, of course, women."

"Is this what you drank aboard your ship?"

"Aye. Whenever I could get it. Grog is but a watered down version of this. This, though, is genuine," he said and took a long drink. He handed the bottle to Maria.

"A sailor's drink..." she mused.

"Drinking is the best part of sailing as far as I am concerned," he told her.

She smiled and tipped the bottle back. "It is strong... But good too. I feel it has wiped away everything in my mind."

"That is what it is supposed to do," Bellamy replied with a grin.

"I feel that I am finally going to make it through the breakwater," she announced.

He took a swallow and then handed the bottle back to Maria. By the time that the rough water was upon them, the liquor had risen into their heads like a mist, and they no longer cared about the consequences of misjudging the channel. Maria cried, mimicking the chorus of birds that had begun squawking at their approach.

The boat bucked in the large waves. The sail jostled and shook the lines like loose horse reins. The next row of waves made the bottom of the boat bounce and slap the water.

The wind picked up volume as they neared the open ocean.

"Give me the sail!" she cried. She took it from him and pulled it as tight as she dared. The canvas caught the wind hard and pulled Bellamy's side of the boat precariously towards the frothing water. Bellamy hollered and clutched at the mast, pitching them the other way and almost rocking them all the way over.

"Stay put! Just shift your weight is all!" she cried.

He settled himself in the middle of the boat and stole another drink of rum, looking miserable as they cut deeper into the channel, the sand slipping quickly past them, and the enormity of the sea racing to meet them.

"The rum loosens my grip! I have a feel for the sails like never before! It feels easy!" Maria cried. She beamed at him. "I should tell you that this is not the way to Plymouth!"

Bellamy smiled as best he could, but his expression was as rocky as the wake around them.

The waves became more harrowing, and the boat dipped sideways into the surf, scooping out great volumes of it. Bellamy and Maria scrambled up the other side of the craft. Then the bow pitched dangerously high as they glided up and over the crest of the wave, and again the mast quivered as they hit the other side.

"Damn this ocean!" Bellamy cried. He finished the bottle and chucked it over the side.

"We are so close!" Maria hollered through the wind.

Bellamy's jaw was clenched so tight that he could do nothing but bob his head in reply. Below him the water sloshed wickedly against his boots. In front of the bow, some fifty yards of treacherous waves stood between them and the equally rambunctious open ocean, beyond the last spit of land. There was enough rowdy water around them to make Bellamy wonder why the girl longed for more. There did not seem to be any pleasure in it.

Maria strove to keep the boat on a point where they could catch the wind without toppling from it. But the waves worked in conjunction with the air, the two smashing into each other, leaving no room for the boat to thread through. Soon the listing was so great that she had to let go of both sail and tiller.

A strong arm of current threw them, and they surged towards a flat stretch of sand so well hidden by the motion of water around it that Bellamy did not see it until they were nearly upon it.

The boom swung like a sword at their heads. Bellamy lunged and toppled into the cockpit of the boat, landing with a splash in the accumulated water. He heard the rip of sand as the boat ground over the tip of the bar and then back into deeper water on the other side of it.

Then they were locked in the rough push of wind, going with it but heading back towards land. The breakwater had completely turned them around. Maria looked devastated.

"It was a good try… I have not met your like before, Goody Hallett," Bellamy choked out.

"I cannot believe that we failed," she said so sorrowfully that Bellamy dreaded what her reaction would be to his own ill news. He looked around for anything that might distract them. There was little but tide-swamped marsh grass, houses on the distant hills and the blue swath of sea around them. His eyes roved back to the sandbar that almost snagged them, and he pointed to it.

"We shall find some little island of our own. It will be something like that one but larger. Perhaps ours will be among the islands that my shipmates spoke of seeing in the southern waters. Imagine the sun beating endlessly down from the heavens, not a trace of rain for weeks on end and that which comes falls as bathwater on the fruit trees and naked villagers…" His voice was coming back to him, and his imaginings sparked a warmth in him, which burned away his panic from the attempt on the breakwater.

"There are islands where no person has set foot. When we go on our travels, we shall find one and settle there, and you shall rule as queen of it. *Isle of Maria* is what we shall call our land. We will have our fill of fish, wild pig and anything else that grows there. You can sail your boat through crystal waters to your heart's content. There shall be no church or taxman or landlords or stuffy fools to make wretched our happiness. Can you picture that?" he went on.

"*You are losing your wits altogether,*" she muttered.

"We shall run through that wretched breakwater on the next try. Do not despair of it."

Maria smiled wanly. "You shall need more practice with the sheets and tiller if we are to go searching for this island."

"Ha! You shall do the sailing. I shall lie out on the bow with a bottle in my hand!"

"Just remember that you promised to take me with you the next time you sail away," she said seriously.

"Yes... I shall," he said.

The wind and water now pulled them as if the boat was hitched to a line and being hauled towards Great Cove.

"We can leave right now, can't we?" Maria said. "We could live off of the coin I gave you, for some time."

Bellamy said nothing. The liquor was waning, leaving his head feeling sleepy and slightly pinched from the excitement of the sail.

"But I suppose we should wait. It is too late in the day to start such a journey. I would not want us stuck out here all night. Remember that squid? It was a nightmarish creature. I shiver to think of what else might make a home out here," she mused.

"Is it true that you make predictions through your dreams?" Bellamy asked suddenly.

Maria gave him a worried look. "I knew that you would hear word of that sooner or later... When did you hear it?"

"I have known for some time."

"But you have said nothing."

"Did you dream of your father's death?" Bellamy persisted.

There was a pause and then Maria nodded. "He died right off this shore. Had we sailed a bit farther, we would have gone over his grave."

His hand closed over hers. "My grave would have been there in the sea too had I not been lucky. That is all it is, though. Sheer luck. Any other notion is lunacy. Dreams are spineless, watery things."

Still holding her hand, he went on, "My father died too. I recall the day that I awoke and found him bent over in the fields like an old man. The lord's men came, wrapped him in a sheet and slung him onto the back of their wagon, like he was no more than a sack of ground corn. The grave they gave him was but a rut in the ground, filled with other paupers from town who had laid there for a week already. The lime barely covered their stench. He was but five years older than I am now... Here in the colonies, my work will get just rewards. I would even go back to farming if I could find no other work. Yes, one way or the other, there will be just payment. Then we shall be gone to that island forever." In fact, he did not know what kind of work he could stand anymore. Anything that he could think of seemed to place him far down at the bottom with a long climb to reach prosperity. Despite his pledge, in his heart he was counting on the roll of the dice to save him. He cursed that missed seven that had lost him his first and only fortune.

Maria said nothing for a while after Bellamy had spoken. They drifted through the channels towards Great Cove at high speed, like the marsh itself was hurrying them inward.

"When we get ashore, will you go fetch the coin I gave you? I am in need of some of Higgins' ale," Maria said, glancing forlornly back at the breakwater.

"The money is gone," Bellamy blurted out. In the few seconds that it took him to explain what he had meant to have happen and what actually occurred, her face contorted into the painful look that he had imagined.

"I will repay you with interest. Enough to fill an island," he went on, but her only response was to let the tiller and sheets fall from her hands and slouch back against the rail.

Bellamy steered towards the mooring field, running the boat to a crashing stop against the embankment of the shoreline. He could see Doane and his men in the distance, on the northern shore of Great Cove, by the meeting house. It did not appear as though Doane had spied them yet.

Maria saw nothing. She buried her head in her hands and did not speak. Bellamy looked up the road but could not see Doane or his men because the homesteads in between blocked them from view. Nonetheless, he knew that they were close. He pulled Maria's hands away and gave her a meaningful look. "Come find me in the apple orchard! I will wait for you there!"

When he kissed her, he felt a flicker of response, and he hoped it meant that he would be forgiven. Still she said nothing. He could not linger a moment longer. Already he had waited too long. By the time he reached the road that lead to the tavern, he was out of sight of the girl but completely conspicuous to the justice and his deputies, who bore down upon him.

✠ ✠ ✠ ✠

There was a time when Bellamy could not wait to be away from the town of Eastham. Now that he was outside of its border, blocked from returning by the wall of Doane and his men's horses, he felt as wronged as any other time before in his life.

For good measure, Doane had brought him through the adjacent town of Harwich as well, leaving him on the edge of Yarmouth and that much farther along on his way.

Little was said when the posse led him to that boundary, an indistinguishable line that cut through identical looking farmland. They were on the King's Highway, near one of Cape Cod Bay's many creeks, without even a marker to indicate if they were where Doane said they were or if they had traveled a fair distance beyond the margins of town.

Doane's parting words were a predictable warning that the severity of the punishment would increase twofold were Bellamy to be captured within the confines of Eastham again.

Obediently, the sailor turned and walked down the road into the Yarmouth farmlands until he was out of sight of the deputies, who sat on their mounts, smoking their pipes.

When Bellamy crept back at nightfall, he saw that only Lieutenant Cole was present, sitting contemplatively on his horse and staring not down the length of road but out towards the distant bay as though he was comparing its worth to the ocean side that he lived on.

With darkness to hide him, Bellamy had no trouble cutting through the nearby farms, avoiding the territory where hounds roamed and crouching like a fox lest his moon-shadow give him away. Cole did not so much as look over at him, so entranced he was with his own thoughts. Had he turned a little to the north, Cole might have viewed Bellamy's destination in the distance across the bay: Great Island.

The island was illuminated by a pearl-like luster of moonlight. The lights of its tavern stood like beacons as distant and alluring as stars. Bellamy had heard men speak in whispers of the island, its tavern and what went on there. A place of whispers seemed the perfect spot to wait in the shadows while he figured out what to do next.

He wished he had Maria's boat, for the ride from Jeremiah's Gutter to Great Island was no more than a couple hours with a good wind.

Instead, he walked north through the night. After midnight he was on the road towards Billingsgate, a drift highway burrowing away into the darkness of night, with no outward indication of where he was going, other than towards the water - eventually. Every road in these parts sooner or later led to the water.

They called them *drift highways* because one never knew where the exact lay of the road would be from year to year. The courses ran through sand, which was pushed and piled up by the wind into great, mounded crests that buried the rutted lanes. The next travelers skirted such obstacles, their wagon wheels quickly carving new tracks at new angles that eventually brought them to the same old places. The King's Highway became such a route after it crossed the bridge at Blackfish Creek. Many side roads meandered off to the sparse settlements of the area, sometimes to a single homestead or a woodlot filled with stands of pine and scrub oak grown only to feed the hearth fires. One road turned through the heart of the nascent village of Billingsgate, a community not quite large enough in size to declare its freedom from the motherland of Eastham.

Soon he saw the dark point of a steeple off to the west, and he took the road that seemed to lead to it. The highway passed a scattering of homes and waterfront shacks where fishing and boat building were done. There were wharves along the marshy banks of a great inlet that loomed out of the night, moon-sparkling water showing its vast outline. Soon islands were taking shape in the milky glow of approaching dawn.

Love was guiding his steps and sustaining him through the night. The very thoughts in his head gave him warmth. No hearth could have heated him like the image of Maria's face, which he kept in his mind like a lantern. Was it really love though, he wondered? Their time together could be measured in weeks. It was too short, it seemed, to give birth to such a powerful word. But he knew not how else to describe what he felt about the girl. She had made him linger here and change his plans. No other had ever held him in place like that before. Surely, that told him all he needed to know of what he was feeling.

By the time he reached the span of water that separated the mainland from the northern tip of Great Island, he was still aglow with his amorous feeling and content with his decision even though his legs had softened to jelly. He had not completely turned from his path. He was still determined to make something of himself here in this new land. Something befitting the size of the grand young colonies. Something that transcended the narrow minds of those who were trying to confine the place in the limited thinking of the old world, men like Doane, Treat and Knowles. So far Maria fit beautifully into that vision. He hoped that she still would later when his opportunity arrived, for he could feel the coming of one. He had not risked so much in order to fail now. He hoped that there would not come some fork in the road at which his ambitions ran straight while her way veered off like one of these drifting roads.

The water would have stopped Bellamy cold if it had been any higher than his chest. As it was, he could ford the two hundred yards of its width, without his feet leaving the bottom. A higher tide might have made such passage impossible, but luck was with him. Soon he was shivering on the island's bank, inspecting the rolling scrubland and pockets of forest for a place where he could sleep in shelter until the sun fully rose.

He found a little dell, a short way down the spit, just before the terrain opened into a wide, bowl-like marsh, which connected the spot where Bellamy stood to a larger upland to the south, over which the tavern presided like a castle rising into the sky.

To his surprise, the place seemed recently inhabited. There were signs of a fire, and the grass was tamped down in one spot as if someone had lately laid there. He wondered if some of the islanders kept vigil on certain areas of the island. An instinct told him to be wary. No man's mood was at its best when he was taken unawares in the dark. So Bellamy crept carefully to the black pile of coals, from which all smoke had risen. Over it was a crude support of sticks, which held a cooking spit in place. Chunks of fish still clung to the shaft, and they caused an uncontrollable rumble in Bellamy's gut. Disregarding all prudence, he walked over to the cooking spit and began tearing off the scraps of food, not noticing the strange, clawed prints that spotted the sand all around or the shadow that separated from the larger mass of dim, pre-dawn light.

"*This is my land*," a voice said from the gloom.

Bellamy gave a shout and grabbed for the cooking spit, the nearest thing to a weapon that he could reach.

The shadow took the form of a man. As he came closer, Bellamy recognized the face of the native who had saved him and laughed in relief.

"Perhaps you are my guardian angel! You appear whenever I am in dire straits, it seems!" Bellamy cried.

John Julian gave him a puzzled, almost suspicious, look.

"I don't fear you, Indian. I enquired about you around town. They say you do all manner of chores if there is coin in the bargain. I am sorry that saving me did not bring you much profit!" Bellamy grinned.

This time the native snorted, and Bellamy wondered if the man was in command of all of his wits. Bellamy thanked him for his service, apologized for taking his breakfast, even slandered the name of Justice Doane, having heard that the Great Islanders appreciated such sentiment, but he received nothing but short, grunting answers in return.

But Julian did provide him an escort to Smith Tavern.

They walked along the beach next to the great bay. Wane morning sunlight was rising up the dune face beside them. Long benches for cutting blubber, iron cauldrons for boiling whale fat into oil and the try works that held the pots stood unmanned along the sandy beach. They walked past a neat row of whaleboats, whose hulls were more accustomed to the slick of bird droppings than water these days.

A path ran straight up the length of the cliff at such an angle that, at certain points, they had to dig their hands into the sandy side of it to keep their balance. All the while Bellamy examined his surroundings with a smirk on his face because the island was revealing itself exactly as he had expected. As Bellamy looked around him, he saw an opportunity that he could take hold of. In the distance he could clearly see the curved outline of the coast as it bent into the heart of Eastham. With a chuckle he realized that he had found himself a little island.

The only thing that surprised him was what he encountered when he raised his head over the top of the crest.

"Who the hell are you? Run along and tell Doane that I will not suffer any surveyors on *my land!* Get going and tell him or else I will send you back with a hole in your belly!"

Bellamy saw Samuel Smith pointing a blunderbuss at him, its wide open mouth stretching like it was in mid-shout.

"You have the wrong man!" Bellamy replied, throwing his hands into the air.

"Do I? Are you from over *there,* then?" Smith cocked his head towards Helltown.

"He is the one who I found in my net," Julian said, coming up behind Bellamy.

"Julian? What are you up to, putting a scare into me like this? These ain't the best days to be scampering up the rise in the near dark!"

"He is the one who came ashore in the storm."

The gun lowered slightly. "Ah, I heard something of you. Thought you'd be long gone by now. Can't imagine what would keep you here among us if you have some other life to go to," Smith said to Bellamy.

Then the man grabbed Julian by his shirt sleeve. "Tell me, did you see anything out there last night?"

Julian shook his head.

"Good, good…" Smith replied and turned back towards the tavern as if he had forgotten all about the two men trotting along in his wake.

The tavern stood on a high plateau on the eastern side of the island. Beyond it Bellamy saw the harbor of Billingsgate and the mast of a ship moored just off the island. It was not as large as the *Josephine*, but it easily had enough room for two dozen men and one hundred tons of cargo. He saw men upon it now, scrubbing the decks and coiling the lines.

"Is that your vessel? I am a sailor. I can work the sheets," Bellamy said, coming alongside Smith.

"Don't need any men."

"I've sailed across the Atlantic. I can handle any kind of weather."

"The wind must have blown out your hearing. *I ain't hiring any more hands.*"

"You must need some help," Bellamy persisted. He followed Smith into the main room of the tavern. Inside, its walls were higher and filled with more windows than Higgins' place. The view all around was sky and water, as if in reminder that harvesting the sea was the main business of the place. Its feel was open and inviting, yet it had the opposite effect on Bellamy. His frustration flared when he realized that once again he was without means and this time the surly tavern keeper will not even let him work for it.

"Pipes are free, tobacco isn't. Food and drink and lodging ain't either. You can sit here till light runs out tonight, and then you can crawl back out into the marsh and sleep out there with your Indian friend," Smith told him. He walked over and kissed the cheek of his wife, who was tapping an ale barrel.

"The alarm was false," he explained.

"Who is he?" Rebecca Smith asked her husband.

Bellamy stepped forward and introduced himself. Then he asked for Palsgrave Williams, feeling certain that the jeweler's name would significantly alter the kind of reception he was getting.

"He's out at Helltown..." Rebecca started.

"He's on an errand and never you mind what, Bellamy!" Smith cut in.

"Samuel! There's no secrecy to it!" Rebecca protested.

Smith grunted and addressed Bellamy, "Why? You acquainted with Palsgrave?"

"Aye. He invited me to join him," Bellamy said.

Smith did not seem impressed. "He won't be back for some time," he said curtly. Then he walked back out the front door. "I'll be back for dinner. I must make sure those nitwits don't ruin my boat," he added and then shut the door behind him.

Bellamy sat at a table next to the window and gazed out towards Eastham, without the same excitement at the nearness of the place. It had only been hours since he had left Maria, yet he felt the time apart already pulling at him. The bay itself seemed to capture that feeling for him somehow, the flat water, the throbbing sun upon it and the horizon that seemed to melt away in the growing heat. One month could lead to two, then to God knew how many more. He had not felt the bite of a New England winter, but he had heard enough, from men who had been here, about the chill that it put on a man's bones.

If he could not find a way to support himself, he would not last but a few days more. Well before winter, he would be reduced to begging. Something had to be done before that, and the answer, he felt, lay in the small stretch of sand off in the distance that they called Helltown.

It was a place that the few in Eastham who spoke of it called evil and full of unspeakable sins. He asked Rebecca Smith about it, and she was happy to enumerate what those sins were. In between the strokes of the tap mallet Bellamy discovered, as he suspected, that they were no worse than those of any dockside community: thieving, whoring, fighting and the like. It was really but a village set up in the most temporary fitting of boards, tents and netting by transient fishermen. To them were added the occasional pirates, brave French or Spanish merchant crewmen, displaced natives, outcasts and hermits from the southern towns. It seemed a place ripe for mischief. Bellamy imaged that there were enough new faces cycling through to provide many card games to come. The only disadvantage was the extra leagues it placed between him and Maria.

"Here. Drink it quick. Later I'll give you some broth if you can keep it out of sight," Rebecca said, sliding a mug of ale towards Bellamy.

"I will pay you for it sooner or later," he promised.

She waved a hand at him. "I'll take a story or two to pass the time. Cleaning this place gets to be dull work when I've got nothing to listen to but my own thoughts."

Before he knew it Bellamy found himself speaking of Maria, describing her in a way that a man might craft a poem, likening her beauty to an effect produced by the sun off of the waves, her kindness a touch like a soothing breeze and her laughter a lightness like birds taking flight.

"She sounds like no girl of Eastham, that's for certain. All the young ladies I know in these parts are better at spitting tobacco than sweet talk," Rebecca said when Bellamy had finished.

"I know not how to speak of it."

"How old are you?"

"Thirty years."

"Yes! You seem more seasoned than this puppy love you speak of. If you are this hot under the collar, than why have you never married before?"

"I said to myself that I would not until I had something of my own, like land or earnings. The farm was but borrowed ground. I knew that it would be yanked out from under me sooner or later."

"So you came all the way over here? To find what, I wonder?"

"I heard that this was a place where a man could find payment in accordance with his merit..." Bellamy replied, stopping when Rebecca's laughter cut him off.

"You are young and fine to look at. Were I a man like you, I would let the sea keep taking me onward and onward to see what places I washed up on. Why pine for a farm girl? As you say, farming is hard living. You'll spend your whole life trying to make good on your promises. And she'll have nothing in her hands but these," Rebecca said, showing him the calluses on her palm.

"What this girl and I have would make even farm toil a delight."

"Oh, then I pity you. This one has you in a spell, no mistake. Would that I had ensnared a fool such as you in my youth. I did pretty well as it stands, but dear Samuel never uttered such mad fondness for me, I am certain."

✠ ✠ ✠ ✠

Bellamy got through six days on the crumbs slipped to him by Rebecca Smith. By the seventh day he considered himself no better than vermin haunting the kitchen, and Samuel Smith wondered aloud how long a man could sustain himself on nothing but air. After such speculation he would give Bellamy an eye that said clearly that he did not believe that air was Bellamy's sole means of sustenance.

The whale men were surprisingly tight-lipped, even when the drink was upon them, but Bellamy heard enough to know that Smith's main business was not catching blackfish or brewing beer. Flowing under those activities, like a vein of well water, was a thriving business of moving contraband items. He looked at the closeness of Helltown in the distance and the towns dotting the rim of the bay in either direction and realized how perfectly situated Smith was for easy access to innumerable customers for his cheaply priced goods.

Bellamy imagined that there were another hundred men like Smith spread out along the coast, doing just what he himself would have done had he been put under the thumb of such a declaration as the Navigation Acts. For he knew that such laws were a device created by the rich to squeeze more out of those beneath them. That didn't soften his outrage at Smith. He judged himself as good a worker as any of the drunken oafs in Smith's employ. The whole operation struck him as clannish. He decided that he would wait another day, and if Williams had not returned, then he would head to Helltown.

✠ ✠ ✠ ✠

The next morning Bellamy awoke and saw two ships on the leeside of Great Island. One stood swaying at anchor, and Bellamy did not recognize it. The other was Samuel Smith's sloop, and it was already in motion towards another errand to which Bellamy had not been invited.

Bellamy hurried down the dune towards the shoreline, his anger rising with each step. It was too late to catch Smith's vessel, but it was close enough to at least hurl a few oaths after it.

To Bellamy's surprise, Palsgrave Williams stood at the edge of the tide, without his wig and fine vest, watching both ships with a satisfied expression on his face. Next to him, Smith himself paced back and forth on the beach.

"Good Lord! If it isn't that shipwrecked sailor! My gut told me that you would be along to join us one day!" Williams cried, patting a belly ample enough to hold much in the way of wisdom or anything else for that matter. "Are you inclined to play another game of dice?"

Smith gave a barking laugh. "He has no money! Somehow, he has been sweet talking dear Rebecca into feeding him the table scraps. The dog is suffering for it."

"Once again there is no place for me on that ship that just sailed?" Bellamy shouted at Smith.

"Get away from me, ruffian! I decide who stays and who goes on my errands. I have no work for you," Smith replied. He tried to push past Bellamy, but Bellamy grabbed his arm and held him fast.

"Some here find amusement in shutting me out of anything but the crumbs on the floor!" Bellamy cried.

"I decide who works for me, and it is no more complicated a matter than that! I only hire men who can do this kind of work!" Smith said, yanking his arm out of Bellamy's grip and rolling up his shirt sleeve so Bellamy could see a long scar running up his forearm. "That was from when I was pinned between falling crates, loading them onto a sloop, with a gale coming down on us. If I hadn't, a year's worth of investment would have been lost. Or this!" He probed his thumb into a gouge under his ear. "That was where a pulley sprang loose and nearly had my head off. I was manning my own ship, making my fortune, piece by piece. All before I was twenty-five! Everything I have came from sweat and toil," he said, glaring for a moment at Palsgrave, who huffed and turned away.

Bellamy turned a fist into Smith's shirt. "Give me a chance to work, then."

"Let me go! I have no use for a fool who can do nothing but cry for his meals!"

"*Cry?*" Bellamy hollered. He felt a craziness rising in him. He scanned the beach and spied some crates lying about, cargo awaiting the next of Smith's shipments. He ran over to them and lifted the first box over his head. Whatever was inside was heavier than he expected, but with a groan he hoisted it and stacked it on another box. Then he grabbed a second crate and screamed as he threw it up on the pile. Arms aching, he ran to the fish bench, found a knife there and went madly down the line, lopping the fish heads off with swift precision, then turned and hurled the knife at the stack of boxes. The blade stuck into the wooden side of a crate and stood quivering as wildly as Bellamy's nerves felt at the moment.

"I can do any work you require!" Bellamy declared, breathing hard.

"Foolishness! I'll never give you a place on my ship! But perhaps you are just crazy enough for old Palsgrave's wild errands!" Smith spat and began striding up the hill.

Bellamy made a move to follow him and thought of taking the knife with him. Part of his mind flashed red and urged him to use it. "Now you have two ships, God damn it! You *need* more men!"

A meaty hand restrained him and he turned, panting, to look into the large brown eyes of Williams. "Let that ship sail. Let Samuel Smith walk away as well..."

Bellamy flung Williams' arm off and sat down on a fourth box, which had not made it onto his pile.

"Damn him! There is nothing left but Helltown now, unless you will play for double or nothing," Bellamy said.

Williams wagged a finger at him. "You must ply me with ale before I shall open my purse again! But I shall do you the good turn of having a go at winning your money back."

Bellamy pointed at Smith's departing ship. "I have nothing to bet with, until Smith gives me a chance! Other men have come here and been hired on since my arrival. Seems there is room for anyone who comes through that tavern door, except the one who does not hail from here. When small towns turn to lording over each other in the same way as the men with fancy titles, they make themselves into the same kind of scoundrels! I would do honest labor if I could get it. I would even do a dishonest deed or two if it were not too repugnant and did no harm to the innocent," Bellamy ranted.

Williams brows arched in amusement. "Is that so?"

"Yes, damn it! And where the hell have you been?" Bellamy snapped.

Williams pointed to the sloop that was still at anchor. "As of this morning, it is my ship. I bought it in Helltown. A fair deal too," he said in response to Bellamy's dubious look.

"Where are you bound?"

"In a moment…" Williams said, drawing up another box to sit upon. "When you gave that delightful little speech just now, I was thinking of my own youth. I had my own travails as I rose up in life. Granted, I started quite a bit higher than either you or Samuel Smith, for that matter. What neither of you seem to understand is that there are arenas of mankind that are far more dangerous and tricky than the world that you enjoy. See these?" He held up his hands, and once again Bellamy saw how unspoiled they were, clean and unmarked as the worst idle lord.

"You should wear gloves. The saltwater will crack them in no time," Bellamy growled.

"These are as scarred as Samuel's or your own. You just cannot make out the damage. My work is with metal, pen and paper. When I was an apprentice, learning how to work with silver and gold, I did incur a scar and burn here and there although they were slight and left little trace. You would call me fortunate perhaps. My father was indeed a man of wealth. I had access to clients who left vast amounts in my care. I signed notes for it. I signed notes for the cargo that I began investing in. Some of those notes were called in, and some of those ships sunk into the sea. There was a time when I had my whole fortune upon the waves all at once. I gambled everything in two small ships, carrying bails of silk in from Madagascar. Do you know the kind of place that is and the kind of dangers that lurk there? Can you imagine pacing the docks, wondering if your gamble would make you a pauper or rich beyond your wildest dreams?"

"It appears to me that your ships came in," Bellamy remarked.

"Yes," said Williams blandly. After a pause he continued, "I don't sport much with the men of Billingsgate. Most of them are wary of my station, like you, I suppose. They don't judge me for it, but it is disadvantageous enough to be Samuel's old friend. They don't offer me a chair at the table as often as I would like. But I am accepted to whatever degree. That is all I could ask for. When I want a bit of sport, I go where no one knows me or cares which kind of games I desire to play," he said, pointing at Helltown in the distance.

"Helltown…"

Williams gave an impish chuckle. "With all of your talk of how a man should not be judged by the circumstances of his low birth, his lack of wealth or meager occupation, I'd think that you'd understand that the inverse is true as well. So far we have rolled the dice once, and it seems that I am the better gambler."

"I have invested in ships but never owned one until now. Five hours ago to be exact," Williams added, making a show of pulling the ornate pocket watch from his vest.

The sailor groaned openly. Williams just peered at him. "You don't like fine things? Do they offend you?"

"Their use can offend me if it is done to rub other men's faces in it."

"Is that you what you think I am doing?" Williams replied. He peered at Bellamy for a moment as if deciding how he was going to summarize him in one of his ledger books. "You would do anything to get a gold watch such as this?"

"I would earn that watch on my own accord or hope the dice favor me with it."

"What of the Spanish? They have long been our enemies, so would it matter to take from them?"

"That I can live with."

"Hmm. I think you may be worth gambling on once more, Bellamy," Williams said.

"Meaning what exactly?"

"Samuel Smith and I disagree upon a venture that I plan to embark upon. Samuel may look daring, smuggling goods in under the nose of Justice Doane. But he is a recluse at heart. His risks are manageable and contained. He doesn't like to spread his wings if he cannot see the easy profit in it. The news that I heard in Helltown last week is for a man with far reaching vision."

"Helltown?" Bellamy laughed, amused at how naïve the jeweler was. He could imagine some drunken fool spinning yarns and Williams' nose buried in his parchment, writing every lie down.

"Then I received this yesterday! It confirms the veracity of the story."

Williams held a letter out to Bellamy. He could see the flourish of the government seal upon it and the cracked wax where it had been opened. He slid the paper out and read:

Dear Palsgrave:

What I am about to write to you is done so in the strictest of confidence. Whoever told you of the Spanish wreck is correct. Eleven vessels got caught in a storm most violent. Millions and millions of pesos lie on the sea bottom. Daresay that it is a stroke of luck if we can get our hands on it. The water is shallow, so the cargo is reachable if it has not been recovered already. Spain will be hard after it, as you know, for her debts of war were to be paid from this treasure, and without it her entire coffers may run dry. Best for me not to elaborate more on the details. You will hear more about it soon enough. I hope that satisfies your curiosity. We shall be delighted to have your company when you return to Newport this autumn.

Regards, X

The paper was shaking when Bellamy had finished reading it. "Is this true?" he inquired.

"Of course," Williams snorted.

"*Do you swear it?*" Bellamy asked, his hands wrapping into Williams' shirt front.

"The correspondence is anonymous, but I assure you that it is completely trustworthy. My family is well-connected, you see," Williams said with a chortle.

Bellamy waved the letter at him. "What else do you know?"

"I hear that it was fifteen ships, not eleven. But you know how such things grow, pint by pint, in a tavern. The Spanish were hauling specie from their South American colonies. Poor devils were ravaged within sight of a place called Playa Verda. I figure that it is about four weeks away if the winds are with us."

"Specie... that's coin, right?" Bellamy asked.

Williams laughed. "It is, my friend. All sorts of gold and silver such as pieces of eight, the Spanish coins."

When Williams reached for the letter, Bellamy did not want to let it go, fearing that what was written on it would disappear if he let it out of his grasp. He considered the risks: the weather against them, competitors for the treasure, the vicious Spaniards who would be sure to try and reclaim it. Even if there was just a little left, the scraps could make a man rich.

"When do we sail?" Bellamy asked.

"We?" Williams smiled. "Welcome aboard, then!" He slapped Bellamy on the back, like he had been waiting to do that all along.

✠ ✠ ✠ ✠

A few weeks later Palsgrave Williams and his crew were ferrying cargo out to Williams' ship, loading it in preparation for the voyage south.

Bellamy had gone to the whale men of Great Island individually, in the tavern, pitching the idea to each man, one at a time, tailoring the news to what Bellamy knew of each one's needs and tastes. Bellamy figured that some of them must have their own Maria, a love to whom they had promised the world but had not yet delivered. Most of the men looked uninterested in anything but their meals. There was nothing but pipe smoke in their eyes, no fire left there.

Maria had also been much on his mind. The gold and silver, he realized, would solve everything. It could buy up the whole of Great Island, he reckoned. It was a sweet vision to imagine buying the tavern for Maria and himself and having a view of his very own sloop below. The treasure was simply sitting there in Florida, in some undersea vault, waiting for him to collect it. And the ship to take him there had come to him out of nowhere. Everything seemed aligned and in place for the voyage. It fit so neatly together that he did not believe that even the mighty sea could hew it apart. It was luck so strong that it almost seemed like some larger fate was behind it, had he believed in such notion.

Eventually seven men signed on. To those were added Bellamy, Palsgrave Williams and Williams' distant relation, Ebenezer Paine, a fifty-year old, hard-edged veteran coastal sailor, for a total of ten hands to run the ship. The crew was almost too lean for the job, but it was a good number for splitting the wealth. He would just have to trust his luck a little more than usual, Bellamy reckoned.

"Heave!" Williams cried with delight as they hauled aboard the last crate of supplies. "That concludes the loading. We are ready now to raise sail whenever we wish! There is light enough that we could depart immediately if we want! Why should we linger, eh?"

"Tomorrow... First light tomorrow," Bellamy said.

"What? Why?"

"There is a woman who has spent the past month waiting for me in an apple orchard. I cannot take leave without telling her that I shall return in due time. A promise is owed to her."

"We are preparing to weigh anchor, not add more chains!" Williams chuckled.

"She is no shackle. I have been in irons and so know the difference."

Williams' hand latched onto his arm. "Wait! Do not go!"

It would have been an easy thing for Bellamy to shake loose the jeweler's grasp. In a couple hours, he could be ashore at Jeremiah's Gutter, then on his way to find Maria, explain himself, ask for forgiveness and mend the ugly parting that stood between them.

"*Justice Doane is upon us…*" Williams muttered.

"What?" Bellamy cried, spinning around towards land where a group of horsemen galloped towards their anchorage, a tall figure in a dark cloak in the lead.

"Raise sail! Raise anchor!" Ebenezer Paine shouted to the rest of the crew.

"I shall hide, and we shall wait until he leaves. I doubt that he is looking for me anyway," Bellamy said.

"We cannot wait! He could be coming to harass Smith, or he might have heard that you are still in town. Such is the trouble with small towns. It does not take long for gossip to make its way from one side to the other. Do not forget that Billingsgate is part of Eastham! I assure you that fact has not been lost from Doane's mind," Williams told Bellamy.

With a curse Bellamy mounted the sloop.

Around them the small crew was already in motion, propelled by the orders of Ebenezer Paine. Bellamy's decision was made for him. The boat floated away into the gentle current as the galloping horses came charging up beside it. Soon the terrestrial path ended in a spongy swath of marsh grass. The horses came up short, and the boat drifted past them out into the flat, blue plain of the bay.

Chapter Four
"Treasure in the Tide"

October 1715

The dunes of Billingsgate receded quickly from their ship, and Doane's form shrank as Great Island was left in the wake of the departing sloop.

Sam Bellamy was suddenly reacquainted with the lurch of forward motion, the sting of salt spray in his eyes and the unsteady footing of life at sea. He had to recall all of the maneuvers for handling the ship. His sailor's legs came back slowly, and the lines raced through his awkward hands, bruising them since they had grown softer, over the summer, than a true tar would allow. He found himself constantly in the way, getting shoved and snapped at by Ebenezer Paine for his clumsiness. It was Palsgrave Williams' money, but it was Paine who took control of the vessel, by virtue of kinship with the jeweler and being the most seasoned sailor of the group. Soon Paine began wondering aloud whether Bellamy's limited contribution entitled him to an equal share of the wealth as the others. Bellamy could not look at the man without thinking of the mates of the *Josephine*.

Only Williams was as unhelpful and unproductive as Bellamy. He constantly looked like a boar gotten loose from its cage. If he was not barreling down the gangway, too late to grab one flapping line or another, then he was hanging precariously in the netting, watching other, more surefooted, men scale past him to attend to the sails in a timely fashion. Had he not been owner of the boat, the others would have taunted him mercilessly. Instead, Bellamy bore the brunt of their mockery. The words were easy to bear with no whip to drive them home. If they found what they were looking for, the fools could curse at him all the way down and back, he told himself. He would be the one laughing in the end. And he would get his full share. Of that, he was certain.

Soon Bellamy's anxiety returned. It took a while to get close to the rail without reliving the sensation of going over it. He felt mild panic at the feel of the thrumming deck boards and the thought of how much ocean was rushing under them. The distant horizon was dark blue, and Bellamy knew that it would remain that way for what would begin to feel like eternity. He kept his eyes locked on the vast openness and dreamed of gold and silver coins, far away, gleaming on the sea bottom like a beacon. Sailing was not that bad when there was a good and willing cause for it, he mused.

With a pang he realized how much Maria would have loved this moment. *There had been no way to get word to her...* That refrain played over and over in his mind, accompanied by the image of the girl sitting hopeful and alone in the apple orchard. She was somewhere in the middle of the long stretch of terrain behind them, unaware that the man for whom she waited had left the land itself.

"Damn it!" Bellamy cried, kicking at a pile of loose line at his feet.

"You'll not get it coiled that way!" Paine scolded, coming up behind him.

"Damn you too!" Bellamy told the man.

Sunset looked like a fire across the heavens. It extinguished in an ash of dark clouds, which blew in with the coming dusk. As night fell, the steady wind carried the ship as sure as a cradle.

That night Bellamy listened to the crewmen's boasting and boisterous talk of fortune, women and the easy life. Their voices hung in the darkness, like they were in the hall of some tavern rather than alone in the middle of the ocean.

"I found a worm in the water barrel. I hope it's not a bad omen," said Jacob Nickerson, a gangly, sandy-haired man of about Bellamy's age.

There were gasps of alarm from some of the other men, but Bellamy's laugh cut through them. "You actually believe such nonsense?"

Nickerson shrugged. "Aye! And you've sailed without saying farewell to your girl. Tis a bad omen. You're not likely to see her again."

"*Superstition!*" Bellamy scoffed.

"Oh! And now you say that you know the way of all things!" Paine shot back.

"I know that men, not fate, cause most of the misery in this life," Bellamy said.

"We had red on the horizon tonight. We should have clear weather to make decent headway tomorrow. That ain't no superstition, but plain fact," the dour old sailor John Mayo broke in.

Bellamy only snorted and moved away to the bow of the ship in search of peace and quiet.

Footsteps resounded behind him, and he heard Williams's voice, "If this voyage was a game of dice, what number would you say that we have rolled thus far?"

"The dice would be still bouncing. But this is no game. It is business to me," Bellamy replied.

"If I may give you some advice: do not get too enthralled with the activities of *business*. Life itself can be a most enjoyable business. Keep rolling the dice. It seems you are partial to it already," Williams noted. Seeing Bellamy's reaction, he remarked, "You glare at me now, but you have not seen it from where I was sitting for the last two decades. I know I must seem an interloper here. You would all have me stay at home chained to my desk, handing over the investment money while you come out here and have your fun."

Bellamy shrugged. "You are captain. You can do as you please, as all of them do."

"I am captain in name only. It is, in fact, *you* whom the men hold in respect."

"They think me an outsider," Bellamy said in refute.

"Be that as it may, I know their type. They are too stiff to show their admiration other than by spite. They feel that you add good luck to this voyage by virtue of you having so dramatically survived the sea. Even Ebenezer feels this way."

Bellamy snorted. "Don't tell me that you are superstitious as well? Are there no enlightened men in the colonies?"

Williams chuckled. "I do not claim to know everything about this world. That is the joy of it! That is why I sail into the unknown!"

"I sail to gain the comforts that you are so willing to gamble away," Bellamy replied.

"Ah! But should you achieve such comforts, you may find them a lifeless prize! There is far more to savor in the dreaming and striving for comforts than the gaining of them! Think on that as you muse here in the dark!"

Had it not been dark out, those watching their boat pass by would have seen the word *Neptune* stenciled onto the stern in proud, tall letters. The name was chosen by Williams from some ancient book, which none of the other men would ever read. "We mean to sail these waters as if we are the Gods of the Sea," Williams had declared at the christening. The choice caused Bellamy to wonder anew if the jeweler had any loves of his own, other than books and fine watches, for most men were prone to calling their craft after their sweethearts.

Mostly, Bellamy ran through his calculations again and again. The Cape Codders said that the run south and back would be no more than two months if the weather held. Bellamy did not believe that Maria would begrudge him the time. The treasure would make all forgiven. As far as sea voyages went, it was a short one. Two months and then he would be anchoring in Eastham with wealth beyond counting. Coin and jewels enough to fill the night sky. He smiled at the thought. In the clear sky above, the stars were as easy to follow as a highway.

✠ ✠ ✠ ✠

The next day was the first of several that dawned clear and bright, revealing a changing terrain. They saw row houses in the distant harbor of New York, fishermen's huts along the coast of New Jersey and then the bustling entrance to the Chesapeake. They glided past all of it without more than the occasional hail to a passing ship.

Then the tidewaters and coastal hamlets of Virginia streamed by alongside of them, on the distant shore. All around, white sails cut, to and fro, across the sea. Little coastal sloops tacked by them, their occupants squinting a look at the crew to assay their identity.

Circling the deck, Bellamy came across Paine and Mayo huddling against the rail and passing a glowing pipe between them. Its red ember smoked thickly, but the scent was yanked away by the wind.

"I'll be damned if we get down there and the coin is picked clean because that fool Williams refused to stop along the way to talk to any tars and find out if there is anything still worth chasing. The Spanish could have it all safely picked up by now. We could be wasting our time," Paine told his companion.

Bellamy strode over to them and without preamble said, "And if we tarry here for a night and are but a day late for the treasure, then what will you say?"

"Nothing to you."

"Aye. You would not, old man. Don't forget that without Williams there would be no trip," Bellamy said.

Before Paine could respond, Mayo shouted, "Tis a God damned man-o-war!"

Behind them, out of the sunrise, came a huge warship with a black, bulwarked frame and dozens of guns protruding like fangs from its hide. A large, fluttering flag, with a red cross for St. George and the Union Flag colors in the canton, indicated that it was part of the royal fleet. It would be hard to mistake it for anything else. Its sheer size and the number of formicating crew, on the deck and in the spars, set it apart from any other vessel.

A cold fear scampered across Bellamy's skin. He had seen these monstrous craft up close, hovering off of the shores of Devonshire. Now he could not believe that during Queen Anne's War he had dreamed of climbing the ropes of one of these ships. He had seen the merchant captains' capricious cruelty and had heard that the naval men far exceeded their merchant colleagues in violence and arrogance.

There were dozens of ships within sight, but the man-o-war appeared to barrel through the waves in a straight line towards the *Neptune*.

Williams stood at the rail, watching the coming ship with a mixture of dread and wonder on his face. Above, the men in the ratlines cursed as they yanked and hitched the lines as if they were enraged with the *Neptune* itself.

"Can we outrun it?" Williams gulped. His face blanched as if answering his own question.

Mayo nodded his head in agreement. "Aye! That's how we kept scarce from his majesty's bastards on the Cape! We could head to shore and look for an inlet that's too small for that ship to enter!"

"No," Paine spat. "We are too far from shore, and even if we outran the warship, we do not know these creeks well enough to know which might shelter us. We should have stopped along the way! We would have found out the good hiding spots, and more importantly, known that there is a navy ship about!"

"Who says it's coming for us? Likely, it is on patrol and will pass by without incident," Williams offered.

"Of course it comes for us!" Paine snapped. "We have no flag of Virginia."

"But we have nothing to fear! We are not in the midst of smuggling. Surely they won't harass us when there is no provocation?" Williams said.

Paine gave his kinsman a look of disgust. "We have an empty hold. How will we explain that? What kind of trading vessel sails unladened from New England to the south?"

"You don't think our tale of treasure will be satisfactory explanation? We move against the Spanish. It could be seen as a strike in support of the English crown."

"No. That navy captain will likely delight in breaking a boatful of colonials and dreamers of their notions of treasuring hunting. It will be like confessing to piracy."

The warship was only a few ship lengths from them, tearing through the water at alarming speed. Its bulk seemed to rise like an island out of the water. Its crew scampered through their duties as if they were living extensions of the huge intricacy of the ship.

In contrast, no one was manning much of anything on the *Neptune*. A few men hissed through their teeth, another gave a little whimper. Everyone in the crew stood and stared at the warship with dread.

"We're merchants. We've just sold our cargo of cattle, rope and rum in the Chesapeake, and now we're headed to the Carolinas to trade for tobacco before heading home," Williams said.

"*Drop sail and anchor!*" came a crisp, wind-blown command from a mouthpiece on the deck of the approaching ship. With the sun behind it, the monstrous vessel cast a shadow that slipped over its prey like a dark cloud.

The *Neptune* circled to a stop, and the warship came alongside, fluttering its huge sails like a gigantic bird landing. The voice commanded that the Cape Codders wait for a longboat to come retrieve them.

When the longboat came, it slithered across the waves like a snake. The men who propelled it had faces as sharp and mean as fangs.

"Come on down here, Cap'n, whichever of ye farm boys be him. And bring with ya yer *officers*," one of the men in the boat said, turning to share a laugh with his mates. Short rifles lay across the laps of the two men in the back. When no one from the *Neptune* stepped forward, the face of the man who had spoken colored red. Patience was not a prized trait among the men of the King's Navy.

"Hurry up now, ye bloody miscreants! Are none of ye swine Cap'n? That figures!"

"He is!" Paine turned and pointed at Bellamy like he was condemning him.

"What?" Bellamy exclaimed. He started to protest, but at that moment, Williams stepped forward and said to the sailor, "I am the owner of this vessel. Why have you detained us?"

"We'll be asking the questions, not you! Come on! Both of ya!" the sailor snapped, pointing at Williams and Bellamy. "Get the bloody hell in here! Our Cap'n don't like tarrying for poor bastards such as you!"

There was little choice but to climb down into the longboat where another of the sailors shoved Bellamy and Williams roughly onto a forward plank.

"Better enjoy this seat, mates. Aboard the ol' *Foxhound* ye'll likely be standing on the yardarm for the rest of yer lives."

"These ones will be lucky to be used for anything but shark bait. I've never seen such weaklings!" said the sailor who had first spoken. A few minutes later, when the longboat thunked into the towering side of the warship, the sailors' laughter was still ringing out.

For several minutes Bellamy and Williams were forced to wait on the main deck as if the warship's captain was too busy with other engagements to meet them promptly. Bellamy knew that this, like the sailors' coarse jibes, was calculated to intimate them, so he glared defiantly around the ship.

Standing among the endless web of rigging, tall trunks of masts and layers of sail, the warship was as overwhelming and impressive as it had looked from a distance. The sheen of the painted deck, the size of the sails, piled on top of each other, and the cabins that rose from the deck as large as houses combined to humble Bellamy. He found himself wondering what kind of speed the ship could reach, what were the number of her guns and the like.

Around him were sailors in faded white shirts and tar slicked pants, cut high above the ankle. Most of the men ignored Bellamy and Williams, but a few cast looks of sadness or pity in their direction.

Farther along the deck, crewmen were roughly pushed aside as a contingent of fancier dressed officers strode towards the main deck. It was the captain and his aides. Their arrogance made Bellamy resolve to stand firm and not give them any more satisfaction than they wrangled out of him.

A moment later the captain stood before them, inspecting them like they were a pair of beasts to choose from. His eyes flicked covetously over them, lingering for a while on Bellamy.

The ship rolled with the pendulum-like swing of the waves, the rhythmic slap of water on its hull tolling in warning.

"Which of you is *captain?*" He said in a reedy gentry accent, throwing the title at them like neither of them deserved it. He was not a large man, but the plumage in his hat and the resplendent medals on his sharp, pressed uniform gave him an ostentatious badge of authority.

When neither Williams nor Bellamy spoke right away, he peered into Bellamy's face, scrunching his nose as if the scent of the man reviled him. "Are you a band of rovers? Speak, man! Which of you is captain?" he demanded.

"We both are," Williams replied.

Ignoring Williams, the naval officer sniffed the air in front of Bellamy for the scent of booze. "What is your name and the name of your ship?"

"Sam Bellamy of the *Neptune.*"

The captain leered. "Ah! *Neptune?* So they actually teach history and letters to quaint country men of this colony. Oh! But you're English. Is this an English crew? Where are your sovereign colors?"

"I am from Devonshire. The crew hails from Eastham in the Massachusetts Colony."

"Hmmm, a typical colonial mishmash. Well, no matter. You are all the king's men after all. And I am Captain Mathison of the *HMS Foxhound.* As the king's servant, I demand a true account of your voyage, cargo and intent. Any duplicity on your part will be considered treasonous and grounds for the strictest punishment! Well, what say you, Captain Bellamy?"

When Bellamy told the story they had concocted, Mathison looked at him with spite nearly dripping from his face as if he could taste the boldfaced lie.

"Well, *Captain*," came Mathison's mocking voice, toying with them. "I will take you at your word. But there is one thing... We are a little short of crew these days. We had a spate of coughing illness, which is all too common here in these infested backwaters. No doubt you have no problem with contributing to His Majesty's needs?"

Just then Bellamy heard another longboat pulling for the *Neptune*.

"You cannot force us," Bellamy said slowly.

A dangerous threat flashed across Mathison's mien, but he stifled it and replied, "I did not say anything about force. I merely asked for your willing help *in the name of the king*."

"Our crew is small, sir. Undoubtedly, you understand that were we to lose any of our crew, we should not be able to handle the vessel adequately," Williams interrupted.

Mathison peered closely at Williams for the first time. "Lucky for you that your ship is empty. It should, therefore, be much easier to handle, even a man or two short."

"Well, perhaps. Yet I have hired all of these men out of the company shares. You know how it is. The loss would make our profits suffer grievously."

"So you are the investor on this little voyage? What are you so eager to collect that you felt obliged to accompany your own vessel?" Mathison said icily.

"Cattle. Now we are headed to the Carolinas..."

"To trade for tobacco. Yes, yes, I heard that little story. So if the hold is empty, surely your pockets are not."

"Sir, you put me in a hard place," Williams said honestly. "The need of the king is above all other, of course, but to lose these men would be like coming home with partial cargo. I would likely have to bear the difference out of my own wages. I beseech you not to take any men from us. Our loss of crew might jeopardize the journey."

"Let us see your manifest."

Williams hesitated.

"We have been paid in gold, sir. It is the nature of our business with our clients," Bellamy said. He pointed to Williams' jacket, hoping that there was still some jewelry within.

Williams sighed and withdrew the fancy watch that he had wagered at Higgins Tavern and a handful of glimmering necklaces.

Mathison's eyes narrowed. "As you say, His Majesty's mission is of far greater import than your puny profit. In fact, I personally care not for your voyage or even your lives. I could place you all in my ranks this minute, with full condoning from His Majesty. *That* need suffices! In the name of His Majesty, I'll take what men I deem fit! Then maybe your mind will better comprehend His Majesty's generosity, as well as mine, and you can part from us, knowing in your heart that you have done service for your country as well as kept your liberty. These are not quite the kind of tokens of trade that I recognize from these parts," Mathison said and snatched the gold watch and necklaces from Williams' hand.

"A gift to the king!" the officer declared.

"*Indeed...*" Williams muttered.

Bellamy looked down at his hands as if to gauge if he could trust them to fight his way out of the predicament. But he knew it was useless. Dozens of men, all armed, stood on deck. Even if they made it off the ship, the bristling promise of death from the rows of cannon showed how foolhardy any attempt at confrontation was.

Alongside of them the second longboat was returning with Mayo and three other Cape Codders in the bow.

"Four men? That's too much!" Bellamy shouted.

Around him bayonets came level with his eyes.

"I consider the rank of captain, no matter how liberally it is spread, to be a sanctified post. Captains do not rise to their positions without full mastery of their craft. This vessel surely can be handled by *two* such experts! I am not an ungenerous man. I have even left three crew members to assist you," Mathison said, pointing across the water to where Nickerson and two others stood forlornly on the *Neptune's* bow.

"You bastard!" Bellamy wailed. He only got a few paces before a rifle butt brought him down.

"Don't try my patience!" Mathison roared. "I know that, by rights, I could have you all in front of the Admiralty! No one trades for gold watches and chains but a smuggler! Yet this time it will suffice to save the rest of you!" he said, shaking Williams' jewelry in his fist.

Bellamy and Williams were ushered away in the other direction towards another longboat that was waiting to return them to the *Neptune.*

"What the hell happened?" Nickerson asked as he helped hoist them onto the deck of the *Neptune* a few moments later.

"We have been fleeced by the king's men, and our shipmates are as good as dead," Bellamy said flatly. When he saw Paine standing behind Nickerson he added, "Did you hear what I said? We lost four good men!"

"And I suppose you consider that to be my fault?" Paine demanded.

"It matters not anymore. We're damned lucky they let the rest of us go. Although I am surprised that they did not choose you. You are the most skillful sailor of us all," Bellamy said.

For once, Paine had nothing to say. Instead, Nickerson answered for him, "He hid below while the rest of them were rounded up." Nickerson then turned away in disgust.

"And you told them that I was captain because you thought that they would take me? I was to be a sacrifice?" Bellamy asked. He was surprised that he did not feel more fury at the man. Instead, he could see plainly that Paine's shame would be punishment enough although Paine still bristled outwardly.

"I had no idea that they would take any of us! But in case they did, I knew that you are the worst seaman of us. We could afford to lose you. I needed to make sure that we had experienced men left to complete this voyage."

"And in the process you made me captain. So I order you to let out the sails so we may put some distance between us and the *Foxhound.*"

"*Captain?* You're not captain!" Paine exclaimed. "I just said that to be rid of you!"

"But the title has stuck," Bellamy replied.

"The hell it has!"

"I say he *is* captain," Nickerson interjected.

"What?" Paine cried. Around him Nickerson, Williams and the last crewmen nodded in agreement. "You are all fools! We will never get there under his command! What say you, Palsgrave? You and I have known each other for a long time. We are kin, for God's sake! Will you let us be led by this bragging nitwit?" Paine asked Williams.

Williams shrugged, "I say we roll the dice on Captain Bellamy."

Paine glared at Bellamy for a moment but then turned dutifully away. "*Damn you, Bellamy,*" he muttered under his breath as he went.

The *Neptune* sailed on, for the rest of the day, in near silence. The coming night felt as wide and cold as a chasm. Here and there bobbed a warm globe of light, revealing a vessel closer to shore. Such lights were usually quickly extinguished as the *Neptune* came within sight. Along the coast glowed dim squares of light from individual houses and the occasional cluster of illumination from villages. They revealed little but the faintest detail of life and nothing of welcome. The sliver moon was likewise obscure and indifferent to the *Neptune* as she slid uncertainly over the rippled water.

That night Bellamy pondered the respective fates of Nickerson and Mayo. Nickerson had found a worm in the water barrel and considered himself marked by bad luck because of it. On the other hand, Mayo had looked to the red sky above them as a promise of clear sailing to come. And yet Mayo was now essentially a slave on an English warship while Nickerson sailed on towards fortune. *It is nothing but dumb luck*, Bellamy thought, feeling thankful that his own luck still held. He had been shielded from conscription by the title of captain. For the first time, he appreciated the power of the position and saw some merit in it. Added to the feeling was the vague responsibility that he felt as he remembered the scene of Mayo and the others, men he barely knew, being led off to a despicable fate. But he was not really a captain, he knew. That position belonged to Williams, for it was Williams' ship. As far as Bellamy was concerned, the jeweler could have both the ship and the title. Captain was ultimately for men who sought power, Bellamy thought. All he wanted was a bit of treasure and then to head back to Cape Cod.

✠ ✠ ✠ ✠

Many days and leagues after that, Bellamy scanned the color-ripened waves off the coast of South Carolina. He went through the details of the trip in his mind, growing increasingly anxious as he did the calculations. They had less than a week of beer, three weeks of food and two rolls of canvas. The salt was water damaged, but the freshwater held. They would make it, he realized. The trip home would be a sober, hungry one, yet the joy of having a hold full of riches would satiate them, he hoped.

Then one morning there was a perfume scent on the wind. By noontime they were in Florida, off of Playa Verda. Bellamy's clothes clung to his flesh, and his forehead dripped incessantly. Under the hot weight of the sun, the deck radiated heat like the surface of a skillet. As he climbed the height of the mast, he felt giddy with his improving seamanship and the view of the wide, sparkling ocean before him. He could see schools of fish moving in shifting clouds in the water below. Dolphins occasionally rode with the sloop. Once he even saw a plume of water sprayed up from the translucent green and blue depths and the long, dark shape of a whale under the surface.

He was so distracted by the sights that he was startled when he heard Nickerson's cry from the bow, below him, "Ships ahead! Loads of them!"

Bellamy peered at the vague shapes in the distance and felt a strange chill at the sight.

As Bellamy scrambled down the mast, he saw Williams coming towards him.

A familiar ruddy glow colored Williams' face. He beamed his thick-lipped grin and said, "The cast of the die now looks well indeed. I wonder if I shall like you as much when you are well off and not so hungry for improvement." He slapped Bellamy good-naturedly on the back.

When they got closer, they saw vessels of all sizes and shapes amassed in a small section of water. Some were anchored over the dark, shimmering silhouettes of drowned ships on the bottom. Divers slipped over the side of the salvage ships.

Boom... Boom...

The sound of cannon fire came incongruously out of the palm-lined shore. In the deep rumble, rolling over the water, Bellamy heard threatening echoes of the pirate ship firing upon the *Josephine*, which had led to his rubicon step off the rail and eventually brought him to this spot.

Nearer to shore they could see three ships in a line, their decks covered in smoke, as they bombarded a small stone fort on land. Plumes of answering smoke wafted out of the building, and tiny shapes of men scurried along the distant walls and battlements.

"The fort's Spanish. The ships fly English colors, but they don't look like navy ships. I'll bet you they're a bunch of bloody pirates!" Paine spat. "Is this the wreck site? Are you sure it's here?" his voice escalated in panic as he spun to face Williams.

"I am sure."

"Then they're fools as much as we are!" Paine pointed madly out at the wreck site.

Bellamy glanced back at the score of ships that were working the waters, in almost purposeful oblivion to the fighting at the fort. If the Spanish shore was under siege by an English fleet, it left only one grim possibility, which Bellamy did not want to be the one to say. None of them did. The booming cannon fire resonated sickly in their stomachs as the crew of the *Neptune* each silently measured out what they had found and what its meaning was.

Finally Williams, who could not stay silent long, declared, "Our calculations suggested that we would have at least two or three days on the Spanish. But it seems the Spanish have reclaimed their prize. They have likely hidden it in that garrison. Whoever those ships are that attack the fort, they are well-armed and well-organized. We should give them a wide berth. We are tardy and outgunned."

A fierce spasm crossed Paine's face. Nickerson shrugged as if it were simply the sour end of a day's fishing journey rather than a one month long sojourn to change the fortune of his life. He began coiling line, looking ready to tack around and head home.

"Wait a moment! Only the easy pickings have been scooped up! Surely there was not enough time for the Spanish to salvage everything!" Bellamy cried. He gestured towards the wreck site. "Those other ships don't linger out of vain hope. There are vessels pulling up silver plates and doubloons as we sit here! Let those that fight over the fort do so while we grab what we can of what is left and be away before they are any the wiser!"

"Look at them all! The place will be picked clean!" Paine yelled.

"So what? Better a quarter share of what we thought we'd get than empty pockets! I say we try!" Bellamy urged, but the truth was that he felt shaken. Every roar of the guns seemed to jostle his guts more forcefully. War or not, they were too close to turn back now. That was impossible. There would be no going back empty-handed.

Next to him, Williams stood rocking back and forth on his heels like he was in the middle of telling himself a good joke. His face was beaming as if every complication of the plan made the trip more and more precious to him.

Finally Paine gave a stiff nod of agreement. "To the lines!" he hollered. "Nickerson! Tack to the port side! Every one keep a lookout for wrecks on the bottom!"

After several sweeps along the coast Nickerson, with his keen eyes, spotted one of the sunken treasure fleet. "Ship below!" he called.

"Coming about!" Paine yelled and skillfully spun the ship's wheel, swinging the boat around in a graceful, tight arc. "Ready to drop sail!" he shouted at the men at the mast.

At the bow of the ship, Williams stood with anchor ready.

"Now!" Paine commanded, and Williams let loose the anchor. It whirred through the lock like a saw before bringing the ship to a rocking stop. The men hurried to the rail, for a glimpse of treasure sparkling in the water. There was nothing visible but white sand, swaying seaweed and the flash of fish.

"We are right over the wreck. If there is treasure, it still may be trapped in its sunken hold," Paine explained as he stripped off his shirt and started to climb down into the water.

It was Bellamy who felt like he was holding his breath as he watched the man descend.

"You did not want the honor?" Williams asked Bellamy.

"I do not much care for the water."

"Is that so? Interesting that the likes of you and I have so little skill with the ocean, and yet we have the audacity to expect to take our fortune from it. Did you know that the ancient ones thought that success was measured out in equal measure to one's talent and courage? As fascinating as they are, I am not prone to such archaic notions. Otherwise, I would think that our experiences thus far do not bode well."

"I am not a superstitious man either," Bellamy said, his eyes locked on the shimmering form of Paine diving below the surface.

"So you've said. Yet I wonder if that matters to such power as *Fate*."

✠ ✠ ✠ ✠

The sky was bleaching out in the way that tropical days mellow and fade. Paine was down for what seemed like the hundredth time. The men had stopped counting after a while. He had come up to the surface, over and over, with nothing in hand.

Bellamy stared at the now silent fort. The attacking ships had sent longboats to shore. The longboats came back loaded with bound prisoners and cargo. The fort's empty flag pole stood bare and futile over the battlements. He hoped that the attackers would be too sated from their victory at the fort to bother with salvagers such as themselves, but he was not sure. All he needed was a little more time.

"He's got something!" Nickerson cried.

Bellamy peered into the water and saw the rising form of Paine. Sure enough, he held something in his arms. Hands reached down to haul Paine and his prize from the sea.

"This is all I found. I saw nothing else," he gasped. He held up a brown box with lime colored seaweed draped over it. Then he stood off to the side, catching his breath, while Nickerson pried the box open.

"This is it!" Bellamy said. "It is plenty big enough to hold a fortune. I once had a box a quarter of the size that was well filled with coin."

"Yes, I profited well from that box you had," Williams replied impishly.

"Well, this time I will keep my share," Bellamy said ebulliently.

"Open the damn box!" Paine yelled.

It sprang apart with a watery pop. The men crowded around for a glimpse of the treasure. But when Williams held it up, the deck was as silent as a graveyard.

It was filled with porcelain dishware.

"NO!" Paine screamed. He dove at the box and wildly threw out several plates, cups and small bowls, which fragmented on the deck in shards.

✠ ✠ ✠ ✠

The next morning the men were slow to wake. The anchors had held and so had the weather. The rising heat of late morning drew Bellamy to his feet, and he went to the stern to watch the shoreline.

Black smoke funneled out of the center of the fort on shore and gently lifted into the bright sky where its ominous color leached into the pastel colors of blue heavens, white clouds and tan pelicans. Aside from the smoldering fort, everything else was impossibly clear and resplendent.

They were informed by a passing ship that the Spanish salvagers had gotten to the wreck site first. Their native crewmen had dove and reclaimed the bulk of the prize and squirreled it away on shore. Then Henry Jennings, a privateer from Jamaica, had gathered two hundred mercenaries and besieged the fortress until the Spanish gave up their treasure.

As the sun rose and glanced wickedly off of the rippled water, Bellamy gradually came to resent the placid weather and rising heat. The sunny climate seemed to mock their defeat, like a maddeningly cheerful spotlight on their futility. Every ship that turned away from the wreck site and set sail for the sorrowful horizon seemed to pull on them to give up too. It did not matter whether the treasure had ended up with the Spanish or the privateers, either way, the dream of plucking a quick fortune from the sandy bottom was gone.

Bellamy went down into the dark hold where nothing but the shifting of the ship's haunches and the occasional squawk of a gull passing nearby gave indication of the watery world around him. He reviewed all of the events that had befallen him since his arrival in the colonies. The unyielding judgment and the pompous righteousness of the people of Eastham had forced him to this risky spot. Mostly, he thought about the girl for whom he had sailed. He pictured Maria's little, intimate twists of mouth and each expression of her eyes, trying to convince himself that he had found a treasure already. He struggled to hold Maria's face in his mind. To his horror, her beautiful visage kept dissolving into a terrible, bitter frown. It was the expression that she would greet him with if he came back empty-handed, he believed.

Something under him was growing discomforting. When he sat up to retrieve it, he found a dark woolen blanket that Maria had given him back when his bed was a clump of reeds by Eastham's Great Cove. He had slept under it until only a week ago when the southern air burned off the chill. He held the blanket in his hands, feeling its texture. He passed it under his nose and sniffed it. On the first leg of the journey, Maria's scent had clung to it, a most beautiful perfume that some nights almost tricked him into thinking that he lay in her soft embrace rather than upon the unforgiving boards of the ship. The wind and salt spray had driven her essence from the blanket and left it wet and black, like a warning of what should become of his heart should he not be careful.

Then an image began to take shape… He groped around for his sewing kit and set to work to fashion it exactly as he saw it.

✠ ✠ ✠ ✠

Bellamy strode into the center of the deck. Set apart from the rest of the men, his height and straight bearing gave him a dignity that outshone his grubby sailor's clothes. The hot sun had made his face dark, accentuating its strong, appealing lines but also making the hollow of his eyes seem like an impenetrable gouge. As those eyes swung around the tiny circle of men, they felt Bellamy's gaze like physical impact.

"My friends, this is a woeful position, make no mistake. I don't know exactly why we found such rotten luck…"

"You know as well as me that the bloody Spanish and *English* took that treasure! We need provisions if we are to make it home. I don't fancy dying in this place," Paine interrupted.

A strange half-smile played on Bellamy's lips. "The lure of riches brought us to this point. We thought that Florida was the end of our journey, but it could be the beginning if we want. I offer you another choice. To continue on. There!" Bellamy turned and pointed towards the southern horizon.

Instead of looking out to sea, the others gaped at Bellamy.

"With no provisions? With nothing to trade?" Paine asked.

"It seems like a death wish," Nickerson said with a shake of his head.

"Everything we need awaits us out there! Forget the wrecks below us! It is too easy! I see that now! These heroes and gods of old that you admire - this Neptune, for instance. He would not deliver a fortune without a trial, right? We have to *take* it for ourselves!" Bellamy said to Williams, causing the jeweler to chuckle.

Bellamy pulled something from beneath his jacket. He unfurled Maria's dark blanket. Upon it was a massive image. At first it looked like a jumble of broken bones, but as soon as he raised it to the top of the mast, the wind snatched at it as if, in its outrage, it meant to rip the affront from the pole. The bones fused and came together into a huge, leering skull with a white, knobby cross beneath it. It was an image of stark death. But the skull had an unmistakable grin to match Bellamy's as he stood proudly next to the pennant.

"Take that thing down!" Paine exclaimed. "Ships are but a league away!"

"If you care who sees now, then I doubt you'll be able to sail under this mark at all," Bellamy said with a caustic edge to his voice. "The sooner we vote, the sooner we take down the bones. Forget not that they'll stay branded into your own bones from then on!"

"Bellamy! Is this wise? Outlawry is far different than salvaging," Williams said. His fleshy face was pasty with anxiety. But there was an unmistakable quiver of excitement in his tone.

"I ask you: is it less dangerous than returning to Eastham? Facing the risk that a single storm may drown us on the next whaling voyage, leaving our loved ones destitute? Or that our lives play out their dull courses while Reverend Treat, Justice Doane and those other plump swine mold the town to their purpose, take the fruits of our labor for their stockpiles and laugh at us if we have the gall to ask for one of their daughters' hands in marriage? Aye, we'll be living on the edge. But the Spanish Main has plenty of gold too. A few fat merchant ships from now, we could sail back to Eastham with no one the wiser whether we got that coin from the Florida sea bottom or a Spanish brigantine."

"It is a fool's errand," Paine said.

"And this errand that we are on presently? I would not call this success," Bellamy replied. "What say you?" he asked Nickerson.

The Cape Codder ran a hand through his hair. "I suppose..."

The other crewmen nodded slowly in agreement.

Then Bellamy questioned the jeweler, "What say you? Does this have the feel of too much aimless drifting to you?"

"No, not at all. I'd say that it is just the thing that might take our minds off of the current disappointment... *Captain.*"

Chapter Five
"On Account"

Summer 1695 – Twenty Years Earlier...

All along the docks of Plymouth, England, ships stood rocking in a tangle of rigging. Here and there a vessel was raising canvas, setting the sails for departure or hauling the sails in to make anchor, the men laughing and boasting of how they would soon spend their wages in the dockside shops, taverns and whorehouses.

Crowds moved along the creaking boardwalk. They were filled with common sailors shuttling cargo or looking for a good ship to take berth on, crimps signing drunken fools onto the hellish voyages that decent sailors shied from, merchants checking wares, the men and women who feed on the fringes, offering more illicit goods and captains bellowing for their crews as they are wont to do.

A small boy moved among the throng. He felt like one of those strange monkeys that men were bringing back from Africa to do tricks, as he was pulled loping along by a man in a faded blue woolen suit. He could see the doings of the harbor in snatches when the crowd parted: hulls glinting with the reflection of rippling, sunlit water, gulls spinning around the tops of the masts, mean looking men shouldering through the crowd.

"Hurry!" said his uncle, tightening his grip. The boy could feel the calluses on his uncle's hand grinding into his own soft palm.

Captain Jameson pushed back roughly at a sailor who had knocked him with his sea-bag as he passed. The sailor tossed back a curse and looked ready to throw a fist as well until he saw the captain's colors.

Jameson waved away the seaman's stammered apology. "Mind where you walk, sailor! Had this been the deck of my ship rather than the harbor, you'd be unpacking your kit in irons!"

He looked down at the boy and winked, and the boy knew that his uncle was all bluster.

"Still feels like I am in the navy," Jameson told the young Sam Bellamy.

"You won't miss it?"

"Perhaps. But wait till you see my new ship, son! I told you that you'll wish it were your very own house when you lay eyes on it! She's the perfect partner to start life as a merchant man."

"Come on. I want to arrive before the quartermaster starts picking the crew. I'll have no layabouts on my brig," he added.

The boy beamed up into his uncle's face; the familiar twinkling eyes, the same color as a sun-streaked ocean, the lines of worry that made his skin look like ship's planking.

They had not taken two more steps when Jameson barged into a man coming the other way and fell over, taking the boy down with him.

The face that the boy saw towering over him gave him another image of a sailor altogether. The man's eyes, as ocean blue as his uncle's, took him in like they meant to swallow him. His face was lean, and the light brown wig he wore made his dark, waxed moustache stand out all the more. The man wore a long crimson coat, with all manner of colored silks tied around his neck and waist. It was a strange outfit, and the boy would have laughed if not for the intensity of the man's gaze.

He offered a hand to Jameson, but to the boy's surprise, his uncle just scowled.

"I'll mind myself, thank you! And you mind your course next time!"

The other man just smiled, a wide grin like a sword unsheathed. "Begging your pardon...*Captain*...but you came a-crashin' into me."

Then he reached down and hauled the boy up by his armpits and stood him next to his uncle.

"Unhand him! I don't want him mingling with the likes of you!"

The stranger laughed. "I'm afraid that we have already mingled! But don't fear! I won't trouble you further, not even for the apology you owe me."

"*Owe you?*"

"Ah! Seems that won't be forthcoming. And I thought navy men prided themselves on their honor."

Suddenly the boy saw a look more sinister than he had ever seen come across his uncle's face. His uncle was smaller than the other man but seemed by far the more dangerous of the two as he growled, "Look here, you. Honor demands recourse to insult. Push any further and I'll soon test whether you can handle your blade any better than you can dress yourself."

The boy looked from face to face, feeling shame at his uncle for the first time in his life, feeling a strange twist of guilt to think that his uncle seemed diminished in the face of this dashing stranger.

From under his moustache, the stranger's mouth twitched as if he were trying to suppress a smile. Instead he bowed. "Let us consider the matter closed. I am here for respite, not violence."

He turned to the boy. "There's a good lad. Don't let the petty squabbles of your elders cast clouds on this fine day!"

Before the boy knew what had happened to him, the stranger had his small hand in his own and was shaking it vigorously.

"Remember: in every chance meeting there is the promise of good fortune," the man said cryptically. Then he released the boy, leaving something hard and cold in his hand.

Jameson saw what it was before the boy did. "He'll not be accepting this!" he said, but when he turned to find the stranger, there was no sign of him in the crowd.

"It's a gold coin!" the boy exclaimed.

"Aye. Not honestly earned either."

The boy felt a strange surge of annoyance. "How do you know that?"

Jameson pulled the boy out of the stream of people and knelt before him. "Listen, son. Don't be deceived by the fancy clothes and loose talk. You don't want to befriend a man like him. I know his kind well. He is a pirate, son. Not an honest sailor like me or like you will be."

"*Pirate?*" the boy breathed. "How do you know?"

"Avery has been strutting these docks for much of the past week, acting like he is lord of this town. He has a lot of gall to be showing his face in public!"

"Avery is a Devonshire man. He is one of us! Everyone says he is a hero," the boy exclaimed. Everyone knew the name of Henry Avery even if they didn't know the man. Everyone knew where he got his wealth too, but that didn't stop folks from letting him stroll about town like a prince or taking an ale or two with him in town.

"He is an outlaw, not a hero. No one who has met him out there considers him a man to be proud to have met," Jameson said, pointing out to sea.

"Why isn't he arrested then?"

Jameson dropped his voice, "Good question, lad. The answer is not easy to hear. It is this: there are plenty of pirates on land as well as sea. Some even bear titles like Justice and Lord and Governor. Greed makes any man a pirate. But let's speak no more of this. Put him out of your mind. He'll not touch a hair on your head with me here."

Whether the law was finally closing in on him or not, Avery sailed away shortly thereafter and was never seen in Devon again. The boy couldn't put the image of Avery out of his head. Nor could he think of him other than an impressive figure. His uncle seemed to forget about the coin, and the boy slipped it into his pocket, even tucked it under his pillow at night, every once in a while reaching in to feel its solid promise.

Captain Jameson, the brother of Bellamy's mother, had been the highest reaching member of either side of Bellamy's family, one who John Bellamy hoped would be a great influence on his son. Even from his older vantage point, Bellamy knew that Captain Jameson was an exception to the rule, an honest, decent man at the ship's helm. But, like the fields took his father, the sea took Bellamy's uncle and any opportunity of using him to secure a berth in the navy. Yet his uncle had more to do with Bellamy's current life at sea than any of them had expected. He had literally introduced him to his first taste of piracy.

✠ ✠ ✠ ✠

April 1716

The memory of Henry Avery shimmered and burned away in the hard heat of the sun above Bellamy. By the calendar it was the beginning of spring, and Bellamy tried to imagine what life on Cape Cod was like at the moment. It took some effort to push the feel of the warm spray and the tangy smell of salt and fish from his mind, but he could conjure a whiff of peat smoke that he knew would be billowing from the Halletts' chimney back in Eastham and imagine the chill pressed against the glass, at night, as Maria huddled inside her house, awaiting him.

That thought sent its own kind of coldness through his veins. Had they found the coin in Florida, he would be back in Eastham by now. Instead, it was more than six months later. More and more he felt that there needed to be a large enough treasure to compensate him for all of this lost time. Bellamy guessed that the bleak New England winters would soon be pulling on Maria's heart. Too many months and she might even decide that he was lost. Maybe the girl had already found another. That fool Hopkins for instance. In some sense he was amazed that he still desired to go back to that little backwater town with all of its small-minded people, its desolation and narrow borders, penned in by the sea. Once again the ocean had shown him how massive the world was. All of it was waiting with adventure and reward, each wave pushing him farther away and splashing like laughter at his notions of returning and settling down.

They had spent the months sailing around the West Indies, harassing the shipping of the Spanish Empire and the English logging colonies of British Honduras. Their existence had seemed no more prideful than a gull hopping around, trying to get a beak into a man's meal. They had less to show for their efforts than a hungry bird would. They had been living off of spoils taken from small fishing craft, manned by poor working men who stared silent recrimination back along the barrels of the pirates' pistols as the crew of the *Neptune* climbed among their stores of rope, fish barrels and extra canvas. A bottle of wine was considered a significant find. But so far, everything, even the liquor, left a bitter taste in Bellamy's mouth. It was not his aim to come down here and thieve from men with as few worldly goods as himself. He kept scanning the distance for one of the great treasure ships that he had seen lying on the sea bottom in Florida. Yet he was not sure exactly what they would have done had they come upon one. He had seen the way that the English ships had subdued an entire fort with their guns, and he suspected that the treasure ships had even more artillery.

Along the way they picked up a few new recruits from the ships they pillaged. The only other thing of worth that they acquired was a name: *New Providence Island, Bahamas.* Some of the new men knew it well and described it as a pirate haven in which rum and carnal pleasure and all other manner of vice and indulgence flowed freely. As they spoke of the place, there was a glow in their eyes, like they were seeing a glimpse of paradise.

The approach to New Providence was a string of islands, which rose out of the brilliant blue and green sea. The image looked much like the jewels they were expecting to find.

Bellamy gazed at the leafy verdure blowing in the breeze like great fans, the bone white sand, the impossible lucidity of the water and the reefs strewn with carnival colored fish below. Any one of them could be a dream island come to life. For some time he nursed the daydream of standing with his girl, as the islands slipped by, and asking her to take her pick.

They cruised into the port of Nassau, the main town on the island, through a narrow channel, which cut between the main island and a smaller barrier beach sitting just off of it. Nestled in that vise-like harbor was a collection of the rattiest and most remarkable ships that the crew had ever seen. Masts and spars had been cut down. Cannon bristled from hand cut holes in the hulls. All manner of pennants and lines hung askew in the rigging. Men lounged all over the ships' decks, dressed in outlandish costumes, which made Bellamy think of Avery again.

"Now we see if we can play the game with authenticity," Palsgrave Williams remarked.

Bellamy eased the boat into a free berth along the dock and considered the statement. The hubbub of the port life was instantly familiar in essence, though it was makeshift, decrepit and shrouded in palms and leafy tropical shrubs rather than the cool green fields of home. There was a small fort and rows of tents and shacks, behind which stretched meager fields for planting.

Some ships busied themselves for departure as if they were loading cargo to take back to London or Bristol. But the lazy eyed sailors at work on these vessels would not fill their holds until they had given chase to legitimate shipping. These were the outlaw sloops that had the governor of nearby Jamaica writing near hysterical complaints to the king.

They could hear the din from the town drifting out on the warm, lazy current of wind. Waltzing, cursing and chortling along the waterfront went a citizenry that seemed composed almost entirely of pirates, gamblers and whores. It was well-known that the governor of the Bahamas colony ruled with a loose hand, but Bellamy wondered if the man himself was some sort of rogue.

The Red Squall was famous for its hard hitting liquor and soft feeling ladies. It was also a sort of unofficial customs house where incoming pirates announced their arrival and traded the latest news and stories of the day.

Inside the tavern, most of the decoration hung from the ceiling: lanterns, spent fishing nets, broken ship wheels and oars. Aside from that, there was little ornamentation or need for it. The business of any given day was distraction enough. Dice rolled incessantly across the table tops, leaving cheers and foul cries in their wake. The noise of the place was like steady waves roaring onto shore. Voices offered boasts and jests in one loud volume. Bar wenches hollered brazen compliments at the promising looking men, as they skirted around the crowded tables, like deft sailboats maneuvering through moorings. And there was an endless tromp of boots going up and down the stairs to the private rooms where the press of hard currency could take those compliments to their logical conclusion.

Standing on the threshold, the Cape Codders received no more than a passing glance from the patrons within. Bellamy had the distinct impression that they were not yet a sight to warrant much comment. At the same time he knew that he was among men whose measure of each other was something far different than any place he had been, and he relished it.

"*Good Lord, this place makes Higgins' and Smith's taverns seem like one of Treat's services*," Williams muttered.

"I'd imagine that gold gets one speedy service in a place such as this," Bellamy said, pushing into the throng.

At that moment the door swung open and on the threshold stood a man who was every inch the model of a fearsome pirate. He had none of the dash and charm of Henry Avery. With his tall, lean body, six pistols hanging off his vest and eyes that were as cavernous as an empty space of night sky, he looked like the worst kind of demon, stepping straight from the blackest pit of hell. It was his long black beard, twisted with ribbons, that really gave him his distinctive air. It was already becoming his namesake: *Blackbeard.*

Throughout the tavern there was a momentary hush, like a windless pocket on the ocean. Then the place erupted with boisterous cheering and foul, but welcoming, cursing.

Blackbeard went straight to the bar and slammed a pile of gold coins on its surface.

The tavern keeper, who was well-known to him, smirked mischievously. "Edward Teach! My favorite customer!"

"And your best!" Blackbeard boasted. "Do I not drink enough here on one night to keep you in business for the entire duration that I'm away on my errands?"

"Indeed you do, friend. If only I had twenty more like you."

"I'd kill them all!" Blackbeard shouted, causing appreciative laughter to ripple through the crowd.

Blackbeard nodded to the tavern keeper and rolled up his sleeves. A mug of rum was laid before him. Then he scanned the room until his eyes fell upon a pretty brunette-haired girl.

"Come here, my beautiful sea-lily!" he cooed.

Slowly, the girl swayed over. When she was next to him, he pointed down to the powder horn that hung on his belt. "Do you know what this is, fair one?"

"Of course, it's for the gunpowder," she said.

"Aye. It's my secret ingredient! Would you do the honors?"

She watched him quizzically. He grabbed her hand and guided it towards the powder horn but, at the last moment, moved it farther down and pressed it hard against his crotch. She squealed and pulled away, to the delight of the men around.

"Come, lass! I don't bite. Put the powder in the drink for me!"

She seductively grabbed the horn and poured a thick blob of gunpowder onto the surface of the rum, drawing more randy howls from the men around. Blackbeard took the horn and dumped even more on. "That'll get it really hot! Hotter than the Devil's own breath!"

He tipped back his head and drank in huge swallows until the mug was dry. He turned it upside-down to prove his mettle to the crowd. Then he threw the mug across the room, where it clattered against the wall, as he roared. Other pirates roared back, and the energy of the room surged like a tidal wave.

"Another!" Blackbeard shouted. On this one he put less gunpowder, a mere pinch of it, and touching a candle to it, set the top of the drink on fire. He pressed his face into the mug and drank. A hiss of smoke rose around his face as the liquid extinguished the blaze. When he had finished drinking, his face was black from soot and singeing.

"Who'll join me?" Blackbeard asked. His thunderous eyes dared the crowd. The jolly faces throughout the tavern looked suddenly sheepish. Men turned back to private jokes and conversations. But Blackbeard would not let them be. With a teasing leer on his face, he walked among those closest to him, flashing the blackened mug under their noses.

"Smells like a cannon muzzle, don't it? What say you stick your tongue down that hole?" he said to one pirate, who laughed nervously and did nothing but clap Blackbeard on the shoulder.

"Get off me, spineless jellyfish!" Blackbeard said, throwing the man's arm off. "Which of you are real men?"

"*You should not. He seeks only sport, not friendship. Drinks could lead to dueling, and I have not heard that you are anything of a marksman,*" Williams whispered to Bellamy when he caught the look in the sailor's eye.

"*But I can drink. I have proven that,*" Bellamy replied.

Meanwhile Blackbeard moved a step closer to them, coming to stand in front of a dandy looking pirate dressed in a velvet frock coat with lace protruding from every opening in the jacket.

"My dear Blackbeard," the man lisped like a country lord.

Blackbeard flashed his teeth at the man. "Is this how the young rogues are dressing themselves these days? Seems I have missed the latest fashion. You look more a doily than a drinking man. Might ruin your fine, fancy clothes there, *Squire*," Blackbeard said, smearing a soot-blackened hand across the man's lapel.

As he moved away, he gestured to the man once again. "Perhaps he's dressed for service! Is it Sabbath day already? I clean forgot! Seems I should spend more time with the Lord instead of that other fellow, Old Roger the Devil! But he's a friend to me!" Around Blackbeard, many glasses raised in salute.

"*We shan't get anything useful from this group. Perhaps we should return to the docks and try and talk to the men there to see if we can learn the manner of this trade,*" Williams suggested.

"I believe that we are seeing it in its very essence," Bellamy said. He wondered if Avery, had he been in this place, would have been prancing around like the dandies of the crowd or heckling and taunting like the malicious rogue that was moving steadily towards him. Long ago Bellamy had come to realize that most men were cut from about equal measures of natural strength and skill. He had seen enough farm workers, sailors and others whose life's work was carried on their backs to know that any man could push the plow, mend his own roof, fight for the meager crumbs of life, if that is what it took to survive. The true difference in men was merely of what they thought themselves capable. John Bellamy had believed that his son was able to conquer the sea, and now here Bellamy was, farther from Devon than he ever reckoned was possible. But it was just the beginning. As he watched Blackbeard parade around like a prince of these ragtag, drunken men, Bellamy felt more than able.

"Let's drink to the ladies! We drink with the Devil all day when we're out at sea!" Blackbeard roared.

It was at that moment that Bellamy stepped out from the crowd, enough that Blackbeard would walk right into him. As he did, Bellamy thought once more of his father and the dreams that he had inherited. He did not think that John Bellamy would have thought any better of Henry Avery had it been him, not his uncle, on the dock that day. Nor did he believe that his father would approve of this giant, black-bearded pirate. But he knew that his father would have been proud to see Bellamy stand up to life, in whatever form he found it.

"Whoa! Who's this who fancies himself also to be a Black-beard?" Blackbeard cried. His fingers fiddled with the ribbons in his beard as he inspected Bellamy and the growth on his chin. "Not a bad imitation... but tis but a scruff of ball hair yet!"

"Let us drink to your pretty speeches," Bellamy said.

The dark, beetle eyes across from his flickered dangerously. The shiny pistol barrels reflected the wan lantern light of the room, like memories of the last time their muzzles were flashing. But Bellamy was not afraid. He heard the sound of the tavern's approval roaring in his ears like surf. He felt men clapping him on the back, pressing him like a current away from the Cape Codders, towards the center of the tavern where the men had formed an open circle for the drinking. Then he and the big, black-bearded pirate were alone, mugs pressed together, which could have as easily been swords crossed, with the way that Blackbeard glared at him.

"The sea may look big, lad, but there's only room for one Blackbeard," the pirate whispered.

"He looks like naught but a fisherman to me," Blackbeard then told the assemblage.

Bellamy merely smiled. There was little difference in the height of the men. Bellamy was somewhat thicker, with a face less withered by the blasting wind and salt. His face was less battle scarred too, but that did little to endear him to the men in these quarters.

The serving girl brought two more drinks and handed one to each man. Blackbeard raised his mug and drained the explosive mix. When he finished, he blew flecks of it off of his moustache and hollered. The room erupted in a collective roar. He looked peevishly at Bellamy and tapped Bellamy's mug with his own empty one.

"To the ladies!"

Bellamy looked at his mug and then around the room, at the rapt faces of the crowd. Williams was nodding his head vigorously. Nickerson and Paine stared stiffly, forcing themselves to watch and feeling sure that this next drink would determine what kind of fate they would have to swallow.

Bellamy took a deep breath. He felt the swish of a dress as the bar maid leaned close and brought the flame up to his mug. "Drink it quick, handsome. Otherwise, you'll really feel the burn," she said.

The contents erupted hotly, and Bellamy closed his eyes and let the liquid pour down his throat. It burned like embers, searing into his sinuses and temples. He felt like screaming. He coughed up a little at the end, but when he turned the mug over, the crowd saw that it was empty and cheered.

"There's more iron in your belly than it appears," Blackbeard muttered.

"The *ladies* drive a hard bargain," Bellamy replied, wiping his moustache and hoping that there would not be another round.

Blackbeard laughed and thumped Bellamy on the back. "More than you know! Now pay the man for his rum. The gunpowder I offer freely!"

Bellamy laughed too, and later he was glad that he did. Despite all of Blackbeard's weaponry and his apparent willingness to use it, Bellamy's chuckle came out as natural as breathing. "I have not an honest penny to my name to pay with," he declared. It was the truest thing that he could have said, but it got the pirates howling so hard that they were almost crying. Even Blackbeard gave a wry grin, understanding that he had been bested in word if not in drink.

"Then I suppose you shall have to owe me! As the first man to have the guts to raise a glass of fire with me, I shall take on your debt without rancor. In fact, perhaps I shall take you and your crew on as well! We need more good men, unlike the cowardly bastards in this place!" Blackbeard scowled at the other patrons of *The Red Squall.*

Bellamy glanced at the Cape Codders. Nickerson shrugged, Paine seemed lost among the tavern full of rogues and Williams and the rest of the crew looked eager for the opportunity that Bellamy knew was being offered to them all. "You want us to sail with you?" Bellamy asked Blackbeard.

"Aye. But I sail under him!" Blackbeard pointed to a man sitting alone at a table, looking like a retired navy officer in his fading jacket of that station.

Blackbeard gave him a low bow that would have been mocking had it not been returned with a foul hand gesture.

"Captain Benjamin Hornigold..." Blackbeard chuckled. "Ever the most respectable gentleman of the island of New Providence."

"So..." Hornigold drawled, his eyes roving over them. "I wonder how you shall fare in the face of real cannon fire."

✠ ✠ ✠ ✠

The ship was but a nub on the horizon as Hornigold's fleet rushed towards it. Together, Hornigold's ships bore over one hundred men. A chatter of Dutch, Swedish, French, German and every dialect of the English language could be heard along their decks, all of it colored by the common, slurring vernacular of rum. The flagship was the grandest and under Hornigold's direct command. Blackbeard led another boat, and the third was captained by a Frenchman named Louis Lebous, or the *Buzzard*, a kind of foppish dandy similar to those Blackbeard had heckled at the tavern.

The vessels commanded by Blackbeard and Lebous were far afield, outpacing the flagship by half a league or more. By design, the two ships were going ahead to flank their prey. Hornigold described it as a purely tactical ploy, but Bellamy could not help wonder if there was something of entertainment to it as well. Several times he had turned to see Hornigold smiling and chuckling to himself as he watched the rest of his fleet in a way that seemed like he was betting on who would be first to the prize. It was clear by now that Blackbeard was his favorite to win.

Bellamy and the other former crewmen of the *Neptune* stood in a line in front of the captain. If their prey turned out to have a solid hull, Hornigold had promised that he would take the ship and put Bellamy up for election as the captain of the fourth member of the fleet. For now, he wanted the new men by his side so they could benefit from Hornigold's famous, unofficial school of piracy.

Thoughts raced through Bellamy's head with similar speed as the water streaming past the ship. Under Hornigold's hand nearly every pirate captain currently plaguing the West Indies had learned his trade. Without Hornigold the crew of the *Neptune* was a handful of men with no cannon. Bluster, bluff, swords and pistols would go only so far. It would never enable them to take a Spanish ship. Now they had eighteen guns in their ship's flanks. From the way that Hornigold spoke, it could be less than a month and Bellamy would be back to Maria, with his pockets filled with gold. Perhaps it had not unfolded the way that he had planned, but he knew that she would not care as long as he came back a rich man.

Hornigold unrolled a scroll, with a flourish, and thundered to the assembled crew, "For those of you who cannot read, this is not unlike the contract a man might sign if he is in the market for selling his soul."

"*To the Devil!*" the pirates yelled.

Those that looked out over the rail could see the prey coming larger into view, big and slow, like a meat laden sow wandering out into the open. Only half of the pirates listened to the captain speak. The rest leaned over the side of the ship, shouting imprecations that the fleeing vessel was too far away to hear. Bellamy could not take his eyes from the scene nor shake the strange feeling that he was watching some transplanted memory of his only previous experience with pirates, attacking the *Josephine*, from the other side of the rail. There was an ease and inevitability in the way that it unfolded. He was reminded that he did not know if the *Josephine* had escaped or not.

"Those bastards will begin their run any time now. Yes... see!" Hornigold said, pointing across the water to where the merchant ship was hoisting up extra sail. "They fly the English flag and so do we, but neither of us knows for certain. Most ships carry all manner of flags to disguise themselves if they think it is to their advantage, and so it is a guessing game to discern their true colors. Best to do is run when you see another ship on open water, for you never know who is coming towards you: a friend or the red flag of blood," Hornigold said with a chuckle. He glanced up at the red pennant that was now running up the mainmast. Its stained color told its victims what kind of bloody fate they would receive if they ran or resisted: no quarter. The fashion among the newer pirates was to fly the black flag, but Hornigold, in his appreciation for tradition, stayed with the ensign of his privateering days. *Jolie Rogue*. Jolly Red. Lately being corrupted by English tongues to say *Jolly Roger*, and applied to black flags as well. Either way, it was the Devil's mark.

Most of the men in Hornigold's fleet considered themselves pirates, but Hornigold still thought of himself as a privateer. A privateer was simply a pirate who preyed only upon the ships of his country's enemies while sparing his own compatriots. They were tolerated, even encouraged, by their mother countries during times of war. Their blows against enemy shipping aided the military effort, and their payment came from the spoils they collected. Hornigold, and many of his crew, had fought as privateers in Queen Anne's War, only a couple of years before. The war was over, and official sanction of privateers had ended. Those that kept sailing and looting were now just pirates. But Hornigold believed himself part of a larger drama between nations rather than a simple thief and cutthroat and, therefore, he would not give up his old title.

Hornigold looked back out to sea. "We shall catch them, of course. Then we shall see what kind of men they are."

They could be simple farm boys trying to find their fortunes, Bellamy thought. As such, they warranted mercy and consideration, for he knew the strength and desperation of their dreams. Yet the red flag, guns, weaponry, rum and chanting for blood was an intense brew, and he found himself swept away in it until he cared not who they were, only that they roll over and submit or else pay the consequences.

Hornigold pointed to the paper he held and declared, "Now, my brave fellows, these are what are known as the Articles. These are our rules. They are our solemn pledge to treat each other equally, with honor! I shall read them, and you shall give us your mark. After which, we shall be bonded together by word and deed and blood, and any violation of this code will be considered tantamount to treason, by agreement of all!"

"Each man is entitled to an equal share of all goods seized, including provisions and liquor, and each man may use those items at his pleasure, unless a period of scarcity requires retrenchment, which is decided by vote," Hornigold read.

"Each man has a vote in all matters that come before the crew, including electing the ship's officers, which may be done at any time if called and seconded by members of the crew. The captain alone has absolute power in times of warfare. The quartermaster has sole responsibility for warding, counting and distributing goods seized... Perhaps we shall vote on you becoming the new quartermaster, Williams. With your background you are perfectly suited for it. Thomas Clark had a similar mind. He was not one of mine, but I shared advice with him many a time in Nassau. He rose to be among the wealthiest privateers."

"I thank you for the compliment, Captain," Williams replied jauntily.

Hornigold beamed munificently and read on, "All manner of weapons must be kept clean for service at all times. No deserting the ship or shipmates during battle, or stealing from one another, under penalty of death or marooning. No fighting on deck among one another. Any irreconcilable disputes are to be settled on shore with dueling pistols or swords. No boys or women shall be taken among the crew or to sea, under penalty of death."

"No man shall refuse battle or else suffer death at the hands of his fellows..."

Boom! Boom!

A staccato of heavy thunder echoed across the water. The men rushed to the rail, cheering.

"*Blackbeard's taken out her mainsail!*" men shouted.

Bellamy could see the proud, pedagogical gleam in Horni-gold's eye as he aimed the spyglass towards the fray. "Ah! That Teach has ice for blood. He is coming along nicely... very nicely... No quarter. That is what builds reputations. Privateering is like a game of cards. Bluff, illusion and daring all play their part. That red flag alone should bring a ship to surrender. The only pity is that Teach had to put a hole in a perfectly good ship. Yet this time the waste is sufferable. She looks like a puny thing, not worth adding to our fleet."

A moment later a quill was in Bellamy's hand, and he spread the paper out on Nickerson's back and wrote his name, a signature that he was proud to know how to make.

Hornigold took the paper, rolled it up neatly and handed it to one of his men, who took it away to some place of storage. Bellamy watched the man shuffle off and wondered if he had indeed signed away something of eternal importance. All for a bit of gold.

Hornigold turned and snapped the spyglass into Bellamy's hands and said, "Look closely, Bellamy. There is much to be learned from others in this trade. It is a craft and a body of knowledge like any other. Teach has a lot of bluster to him. He reminds me of Edward England in that manner, one of my finest pupils. England put the fear into the Spanish but rarely drew his sword. Now Charles Vane, on the other hand, was an unruly cur from the beginning. The Devil himself could not leash him, let alone myself. We parted ways, and I heard that he went most foul in disposition afterwards, too much violence for my tastes. Teach straddles both the threat and the actual swing of the sword. He shall do very well, I should think."

While Hornigold's words poured over him, Bellamy watched the strange, silent pantomime play out in the round porthole of the spyglass. He could see the towering figure of Blackbeard, standing among rolling banks of smoke on deck, and he had to admire the man's courage as he waved to his crew to follow. He had tied twists of paper in his beard and lit them and stuck burning cannon fuses under his hat brim so that his very face seemed to emit foul black smoke. Lines held the two boats in a tight embrace, and many of the pirates themselves seemed to be in a close dance with the sailors aboard the taken ship. Only when a man, usually a sailor, spun away with an arching spray of red or sprang back as if stung and gripped the cherry stain growing on his belly or gave an awful wordless scream as he waved the stump of where an arm had just been, did Bellamy see the true rhythm of violence of the attack. Grenadoes, iron balls filled with metal shot and gunpowder, rolled along the deck and exploded at the merchant crew massed in the stern. A gaggle of white-wigged men stood by the forward hatch, surrounded by sailors, who were quickly falling under Blackbeard's blade.

Bellamy did not say it aloud, but he vowed to use different methods even if it meant that he became the one lily-livered student that Hornigold was too ashamed to name in his future fawning. All he could see were poor farm boys being gunned down for wealth that they would never see. It was not his aim to gather blood-stained gold, red flag above him or not.

"Come, let us join them. The fight will soon be finished. If not, we will help turn the tide," Hornigold said. There was no command given to adjust the sail and none needed. As soon as the captain strode onto the quarterdeck, the men knew the meaning of his position and pulled the sails around to catch a wind that would send them towards the battle.

When they reached the captured ship, it looked like a storm wave, rather than a group of men, had passed over it. The rigging hung like tangled vines. Lengths of wood were scattered everywhere like fallen branches. The mainmast leaned over against the wheelhouse like a cut tree. Men lay in contorted death throes across the deck. Blood stained the wood black as if someone had thrown tar across all portions of the ship. The stench was sickly sweet, particularly when mixed with the rum that was being downed by the victors in huge gulps.

The pirates shouted their victory in their discordant tongues. To Bellamy, it sounded like an awful braying, but the energy was palpable, and he took a bottle and drank, thankful for the numbing spread of liquor to ease his mind from the carnage around him.

"Speak, you Papist dogs! Where is the real treasure?" Hornigold stood at mid-deck, yelling into the florid face of a bewigged merchant man, whose white stockings were splattered red but the rest of him intact. "You see? They were not English at all! The flag was a ruse!" Hornigold cried to Bellamy.

Blackbeard hovered nearby, his beard still smoking like hell-fire. He raised a red sword to the merchant man's chest and smeared the color across the man's jacket, with the flat of the blade. "Spanish blood doesn't match well with a white vest," he remarked.

"You may humiliate us, but you shall all feel worse when you are taken to the gallows! No country stands for piracy anymore! And there is a treaty between our countries!" the merchant man shouted.

Hornigold slapped the man across the face. "I am a *privateer!* There is always war on the horizon between our countries, so I doubt that I shall be taken to task for this noble act!"

"You animals!"

"Tell us where the gold is! There is always some loose coin hidden about, by your type!"

"What *type?* I am a gentleman and an honest businessman. I would piss on you if I should pass you in the street!"

A moment later the man was wearing only half a wig. The top of it had been cropped by a quick stroke of Hornigold's sword, leaving a wispy, red-tinged line of wool and a clear view of the man's sweaty, bald pate.

"The *gold!*" Hornigold reminded him, and this time the Spaniard hurried off to the main cabin and soon was peeling up the boards of a concealed compartment.

Soon after, Hornigold held two bulging bags of coin aloft. "Good things come to he who is patient!" he cried to his crew and heard a roar of approval in return.

Behind Hornigold, the Spaniards scowled so pompously that Bellamy felt much of his sympathy for their plight diminishing. Whatever their tongue, merchant captains would rather see their crew slaughtered and their own necks tempt a blade than part with their precious treasures.

"Set fire to them," Hornigold pronounced the Spaniards' fate like it was an afterthought. Immediately the pirates pushed off from the doomed vessel and hurled firebrands into the other's sails and onto their deck.

Hornigold watched his victims racing to stamp and wash out the growing blaze. He shook his head as if he were watching the antics of hopeless fools. The flames clawed up the masts and across the deck, enveloping them so quickly that the Spaniards were soon springing off the ship into the water. Soon the vessel looked like a floating pyre drifting away into an ocean that would not quench the flames until they burned down to the waterline.

"God won't miss the loss of a few Papist dogs," Hornigold mused as he watched the death ship burning. Then he turned to Bellamy and said, "The French and Spanish are fair game, but all English are spared. We couldn't be certain until we seized them. But if they had turned out to be English, we would have released them. We work within English law so we will be spared by it. Those who declare themselves outlaws to every nation have no escape. Their road leads them to the gallows and nowhere else."

Bellamy nodded but he did not agree. Whether or not a ship was English had little to do with anything, he thought. He suspected that merchant ships the world over were owned and captained by greedy rogues, which made them all fair game. But he kept his thoughts to himself.

"The next one is yours," Hornigold added.

Around Bellamy, every eye seemed fastened to him, hundreds of them glowing devilishly red in the firelight. He felt no fear of them or of what he was about to do. The true meaning of his life was suddenly unfolding in his mind like a road map, one that cut through familiar terrain that had been there all along. He was to become a pirate, taking from men of ill gotten means and redistributing their wealth to the men around him, who had nothing but what they had taken with their own daring.

✠ ✠ ✠ ✠

A few days later there was another ship in sight of Hornigold's fleet. The view through the spyglass showed it to be of good wood. When they captured it, the boat would be Bellamy's, provided he won approval of the crew. He and the Cape Codders were aboard Blackbeard's ship, sent by Hornigold to reel in the prize. Hornigold had anointed Bellamy, but only through action would Bellamy be accepted and voted as a captain of their band.

Around Bellamy were men who did not value the things that were so prized on shore, like station, status and lineage. Wealth stirred them, but it too was worth only as much as the kinds of pleasures it could buy in the pirate towns like Nassau. The pirates measured men according to their boldness and nothing more. As

Bellamy watched the latest prize of the pirate fleet drifting towards them, he pondered this fact and knew that if ever he needed to make an impression, it was now.

"The first man over the rail is likely to be killed quick," Blackbeard said, coming up alongside of him.

"So I gathered," Bellamy said. Across the water was a wall of pikes and cutlasses.

"If you live, you get first choice of any weapon of the enemy. That's the code," Blackbeard went on. He cast a lazy eye at their quarry and added, "Seems there's plenty of weapons to choose from over there."

"That's not why I am doing this."

"I know," Blackbeard replied with a low chuckle.

The other boat drifted closer, drawn as if against its will into embrace with the outlaws.

"Prepare to board! Give them a good taste of Old Roger's medicine!" Blackbeard yelled to the crew. "Whenever you're ready, Bellamy. But if I was you, I'd do it quick and don't think about it for a second. There's lots of swords and pistols over there to cut short any musings if you should get caught up too much in daydreaming."

Bellamy walked down the deck until he reached one of the gunners who manned the small swivel cannon on the rail. As he moved, he saw men upon the other ship's deck keeping pace with him as if they had already chosen him as a mark. He wanted to think of them as Lord Radford's men, greedy louses who deserved receiving the punishment of pirates. As much as he could, he tried to put the faces that he remembered from his childhood on the sailors who were now scant feet away from him, aiming to cut him down.

"Give me that," Bellamy told the gunner. He plucked the flaming brand from the man's fist and held it above the fuse of the cannon.

There was no other way. The wreck site was empty. Maria's face was filled with wrath whenever he thought of it. He had not expected such a price to keep his promises, but there was nothing to do now but pay it. *They are Radford's men...* "Bastards," he muttered.

"Give it to them, lads!" Blackbeard shouted.

The screams for blood rose in Bellamy's ears. The force of the ships coming together nearly toppled him.

The flame touched the wick.

There was an explosion, and his ears went full of silence. He could see the smile on the gunner's lips but heard nothing of what the man was saying.

He felt his own throat stretching with a war cry. Sound was returning, slowly amplifying. Faint, seemingly harmless, pops of gunfire were coming across the bow.

As he stepped across the threshold between the ships, the rail felt thinner and more tenuous than when he had plunged off of the *Josephine* into Cape Cod waters.

Chapter Six
"St. George and the Dragon"

June 1716

In truth, the ocean was more often filled with empty blue waves than enticing merchant ships. For weeks Captain Hornigold and his men drifted aimlessly here and there and then tacked back the way they came, always hunting, always alert, but really no more in control of their course or destiny than the strings of seaweed that floated by in the water.

Gauged by the amount of rum drunk, freedom acquired and days whiled away with little to do but sing and gamble, the next few months were an unbridled success for Sam Bellamy. He was one of Hornigold's three sub-captains. As part of Hornigold's fleet, Bellamy drifted across the endlessly tranquil turquoise of the West Indies and came to feel its effect as a sleepy lullaby, occasionally interrupted by a burst of violent action in which he and the other pirates were the nightmare for some hapless ship's crew or other. Being disconnected from land freed him from the shackles of time too. Time itself seemed bound to terrestrial life and its plodding, grinding rhythm. Release from the calendar was an unexpected freedom for Bellamy, and he quickly realized that this pirate life demanded nothing of him, except the pursuit of any distant sail that came into sight.

Yet there were things with which to note the passage of time. The *Neptune* was gone, replaced by a newer, larger sloop that Bellamy named the *Maria*. Ebenezer Paine had fallen to the blade of another pirate in a Nassau tavern, in a drunken brawl that proved fatal. Jacob Nickerson and the other Cape Codders were seldom seen among a throng of new faces. Only Palsgrave Williams was still at Bellamy's side.

Despite serving in what was essentially a pirate armada, the spoils in the hold were little different than what the Cape Codders had amassed, themselves, in the first days out from Florida when their black flag had not yet faded to the thread-worn gray blanket that now hung on the mast.

So enticing was the freedom that the pirates offered, that Bellamy feared he might give in to it so completely that he would forget why he was here. Pirates' freedom was an outlaw freedom.

They lived as they wished, on the fringes and in the backwater lairs of life. The freedom Bellamy sought was one that was recognized by the merchants, ministers, lords and ladies of the land. They would not like it, but by God, they would have to acknowledge it and suffer it, he thought. He longed for a freedom like Henry Avery's, which enabled him to walk the waterfront of Plymouth or Eastham with independent spirit and finery.

Gradually Bellamy had come to actually feel like a captain. Whereas before he could only see the abuse that was so often associated with the position, now he understood that captaincy was merely a tool, which could be employed for higher purpose instead of misery.

At the same time Bellamy realized that pirates had their own lords. The sight of Hornigold's ship in the distance reminded him of that fact. He had quickly seen that, at heart, Hornigold was more akin to the lords of the land than the free men of the sea. Hornigold's Articles gave the illusion of freedom, but there were other rules that were not written on the page. Hornigold expected allegiance and devotion. Bellamy had seen what happened to the pirates who did not give Hornigold enough affection or dedication. They were forcibly released at the next port by Blackbeard. On a few occasions when men had openly cursed and complained about Hornigold's lofty position, Blackbeard had cast them off the ship in mid-motion in the middle of the West Indies.

As long as Hornigold produced enough rum, most men did not complain. Bellamy often wondered what would happen when the spoils were leaner, like they were becoming now.

"We'd have a lot more spoils if we started taking ships like that one," Bellamy mused as he watched a sloop in the distance, which was tacking away from his pirate ship.

"But it is English. See? The St. George's Cross flies from it," replied Peter Hoof, a tall, morose Swedish pirate, who had come up alongside Bellamy. Hoof pointed to the flag, an elongated red cross on a white backdrop, that flew from the fleeing ship's masthead.

"But they may not be English. The flag could be false," Bellamy replied. Then he turned and looked his companion in the eye. "Hornigold prohibits us from taking English ships, but you wouldn't care, would you?"

As usual, the Swede's face remained stoic and unreadable as he thought the matter over. "There is nothing in the Articles about not taking English ships," Hoof replied.

"Ah! That is true! If they are a pack of rascals, should we not fleece them one and the same?"

"There won't be any Swedish mothers crying if we do," Hoof said with a shrug.

Bellamy thumped Hoof on the back. "If only Hornigold was as wise as you!" He glanced once more behind the *Maria* and saw that Hornigold was farther away from him than the prey was before him. Hornigold was so far out of range that he likely could not even read the flag of the ship that Bellamy pursued.

"The islands will slow them down," Hoof said, pointing to the rocky outcroppings of the Exuma chain that were to the west of them. "We are faster than them. When we catch up, we can pin them against those islands. They will have to sail behind them and lose the wind or head out into the open sea. But they are too small for deep water."

Bellamy took one more glance back at Hornigold's ship and then made his decision, which he shouted down the length of the deck, "Gentlemen! The quarry is ahead! I say we bring her down! What say you?"

A roar answered him, and men sprang into motion, to tighten the sails and cut hard for their prey.

"Run up the black flag!" Bellamy cried.

The fleeing ship made a feint towards the open water of the ocean but then thought better of it and tacked back towards the islands. The maneuver allowed the pirates to considerably close the gap between the two ships.

"They are fools… They see that the reefs make it too dangerous to go between the islands, but they know they have nowhere else to go. They will give up soon if they have any sense," Hoof declared.

Sure enough, only a few minutes later, the fleeing ship dropped sail and prepared to surrender. Bellamy made sure that his pistols were loaded and easy to draw from the sash across his chest when the time came. The boarding was now only moments away. The fear of jumping over the rail, without knowing if death awaited him, had not gone away, but it had lessened. It had, in fact, become something of a thrill. In the back of his mind, he felt certain that there was no threat from any combat at sea, for he was not meant to die as a pirate. That is what he told himself before he went over the rail. After the ship had been taken, and Bellamy was still alive and breathless from the exertion, he chastised himself for believing in any sort of higher purpose or protection. Luck, he reminded himself, was a fickle companion. As far as his safety was concerned, he was on a good, long streak of luck, but that is all that it was.

The ship was quickly subdued. The brief scuffle that was the pirates' entrance was over without any fatalities, just a few wounded men, who sat groaning here and there on the deck. The captured captain and his crew were led to the center of the ship while pirates streamed down into the hold to investigate their prize.

As soon as Bellamy heard the groans and curses, he knew that this was no treasure ship.

"*Ah! Tis worms floating in here!*" he heard one pirate exclaim from below.

"*Where?*" another asked.

"*In the bloody water barrel!*"

"*Damn! You're right! I'll take nothing from this bloody rotten old tub of a ship. Ain't worth it!*"

Up on deck Bellamy scoffed at the exchange. "There is no curse from the damned water barrel! There is only the bad luck that this is a worthless prize!" he called down into the hold.

A pirate's head peered up at him. "And this ship is one of a string of such bad luck! That's what we're saying. Them worms prove that we sail under crossed stars. The next ship will likely be as empty as this one!"

"To the Devil with such talk!" Bellamy snorted and kicked the hatch shut over the man's head.

Bellamy then stomped over to the mainmast where the captain of the captured vessel was tied.

"Turn out your pockets!" Bellamy commanded as he strode towards the man, with his sword extended.

"There is nothing of importance in them!"

"Turn them out, nonetheless!"

"Not for the likes of filth like you!" the man replied.

With lightening swift strokes, Bellamy cut two lines across the captain's cheek. "If I asked your crew what kind of man you are, I wonder if they would say that you are the bigger pile of filth, eh?"

He meant to press the blade against the man's face, as a warning, but he felt fingers dig into his arm and yank his arm back. When he swiveled furiously around, he looked into the dark coals of Blackbeard's eyes.

Then Bellamy noticed that Hornigold's other ships had come up alongside of them. There were twice as many men aboard than before, and nearly all of them had fallen silent.

"Tisk, tisk, Black Sam," Blackbeard said jovially. With his free hand he pointed to the top of the mast where the St. George's Cross was hanging limply.

"What in *blazes* do you think you are doing, Bellamy?" Hornigold thundered as he charged down the deck. He too was pointing at the English flag. "Have you allegiance to nothing? Release this man! Release him!" he shouted and pointed at Bellamy's prisoner. "Can't you hear in his voice that he is English?"

"Every one of us aboard my ship is English or of one of our colonies," the captured captain added indignantly.

Blackbeard dropped Bellamy's arm, and Bellamy slammed his sword into its sheath. His face burned with shame and fury.

"Back to the boats!" Blackbeard cried. "This one is a king's man. Thanks to Bellamy he's got the red cross upon his cheek so the next privateers don't make the same mistake!"

The pirates laughed, thankful for a break in the tension. The captured ship's cargo was lumber, a loss hardly worth bemoaning.

"Go easy, my friend. You won't lack for sport here with us. But you ought play by old Horny's rules or else risk his foul, black temper..." Blackbeard whispered into Bellamy's ear.

Meanwhile Hornigold was untying the captured captain. "Your pardon, sir. We are privateers. Most of us are veterans of the King's Navy and Queen Anne's War. This is most unfortunate that we have erred against you in such fashion. My letter of marque allows me full latitude against foreign shipping. Yet I would not willingly harm one of my countrymen. Had my ship been in the lead..."

"I want him punished," the captured captain rasped, pointing at Bellamy. "He is a rogue, not a captain!"

"The name is *Captain Bellamy!*" Bellamy said.

"He is new to the trade and a slow learner!" Hornigold replied, casting a furious eye at his underling.

"I want him *punished!* Surely you can do so. You are the leader of these *privateers?*" the captured captain replied, yanking his feet out from the last coil of rope and looking around dubiously at the pirates around him.

Hornigold's jaw clenched. "We *are* privateers. You doubt the veracity of my speech?"

"Call yourself whatever you will. If you mean any of it truthfully, then I want to watch how you handle your crew!" the man said.

Bellamy could not fight off the smile that crept onto his lips, seeing Hornigold's pride become as bruised as his own.

"I grant you your ship, your crew and freedom to return on your way. Take that generosity and be gone. We deal in justice on our own terms."

"As I thought!" the man spat. "*Sam Bellamy...* I shall not forget you now, you rogue. I shall look forward to hearing your name again when there is news of your capture and hanging!"

"Pray that you do not come around another island, hence, and find me sailing alone," Bellamy replied.

At those words Hornigold jerked his head around, but Bellamy said nothing more.

"I'll make sure that your name is known far and wide, Sam Bellamy! Every customs man, Admiralty clerk, navy man, lord and judge who I meet shall hear of it!" the man roared as the pirates climbed back over onto their own vessel.

Hornigold did not immediately cross over to his own ship. He strode over towards Bellamy, a finger extended like he was offering a duel. "*You!* No one will have time to learn your name after I am finished with you! Come! I shall have a word with you in my quarters!"

☖ ☖ ☖ ☖

A few minutes later Hornigold stood in his private chambers on his own ship, staring into the amber depths of the rum that he swished in a glass. He continued to study the swirling liquid as he addressed his apprentice, "In a tin cup, this is just rum. But when it is put into a glass, it transforms into something refined. In the same way, men are transformed when their deeds are elevated by higher purpose. We are still serving the empire against her enemies. That is what we do out here."

"No, Hornigold. *This* is what we do!" Bellamy replied, plucking the rum bottle from the table and taking a long pull directly from the bottle.

"Damn you to hell, you arrogant pup!" Hornigold said. He slapped the bottle out of Bellamy's hand, and it flew against the wall and shattered in a cascade of glistening pieces.

Bellamy glared at the older pirate. "I am lucky to still be in good standing with my men. How are they to respect me if you come and chastise me like that in front of them? You might as well cut me down yourself, for they surely will if they come to believe that I am your lackey," Bellamy said.

"You are my *apprentice!* The men might have voted for you as a captain, but I assure you that they did so only after they saw that I had chosen you! I anointed you, Bellamy, and don't forget it!"

"I am no one's servant," Bellamy replied.

"You little…" Hornigold exclaimed, before he could stop himself. He breathed deep and stared at a map that was spread out on the table. The little islands on the map had coastlines that looked chewed upon by the sea. "I have seen many islands in my years. And I have had many men standing before me, with all manner of deceit, worship and greed playing out on their faces. You could be one of the great ones, Bellamy, if you were not so defiant! Stop acting like a deprived farm boy and start acting like a *captain!* You need to have more *sense* in this matter! Can you not see that all of these islands are bread crumbs leading back to the lairs of voracious beasts who live in London, Paris and Madrid. One does not go traipsing through the wilderness without leaving at least one trail back to safe quarters. Men who leave themselves no escape, those who truly go on account under the black flag, without pretense, end up on the gallows!" Hornigold thundered, slamming the map with his fist.

"All prey is equal in my mind. The crews and the cargo all hail from around the world. An English ship could carry Spanish timber. An English captain could be commanding a ship financed in Holland with a Swedish crew…" Bellamy recited his side of the old argument that had stood between them from the beginning.

"This is all academic! The truth of the matter is plain. English ships with English captains and crews are spared. I have *always* spared our own ships! You know this, fool!"

"You believe that just because a captain hails from Wapping or Bristol that he is beyond repute! England is filled with devils, as is everywhere else."

"We are *privateers*, damn it! Not pirates! We work within English law so we will be spared by it!"

Hornigold stood and walked over to where a copy of the Articles was posted. "Recall this promise: Each man is allotted an equal share," he read. "You will one day be sitting in a manor house while those devils that you speak of still man the tiller. Nothing is truly free or equal. Even here." His finger tapped on another phrase and he read again, "The punishment for mutiny or other blatant disregard for command, especially in battle, is death."

"The men decide that through vote," Bellamy replied, his hand moving to the butt of his pistol.

"I am not threatening you. These rules favor the likes of you and me. Yet we must set an example even if it deprives us of personal satisfaction here and there."

Hornigold went to a cabinet and withdrew another glass and another bottle. He filled the glass, and his own glass, with ruby colored liquid and handed it to Bellamy. "I did not appreciate the taste of things like Spanish wine when I was a young sailor. I was like them out there on deck or you, perhaps, satisfied with grog and ale and whatever scraps fell into my lap. With success comes refinement, for those who know the true worth of wealth. Riches are not meant to be squandered on cheap ale and whores. Some of us are out here in order to elevate ourselves. I know that you are such a man."

He watched Bellamy through his glass as he drained it and was pleased to see that the young captain appeared to be thoughtfully considering the good advice that he had given him. Settling things in a civilized manner was far more tasteful, he thought. He was sure that Bellamy could see that now.

"You're right. I am green, a bit young even. But I have fought, and I have been untouched. I am lucky, I guess," Bellamy said, dipping a finger into the wine and experimentally touching it to his tongue.

Hornigold smirked. "It is not poisoned, if that's what you're thinking! And yes, you have been lucky. But that you cannot count on, pup. I know your desires. Your ambition is as clear as that red waistcoat you're wearing. You are not in the same class as Avery yet."

"But perhaps Avery is my future."

"Ha! I know your true future! At the rate you are going, you will die unloved on the open water if you are lucky or in some rank brothel bed if you are not!"

Bellamy drank his wine in one gulp. "As I have heard the tale told, Avery took whatever ships crossed his bow, English or not."

Hornigold's grip on his glass turned white-knuckled.

"Get out! I don't take on apprentices lightly. And I don't give away my trade secrets for free! The next time we have some disagreement, there will be no hospitality, nothing but swords and pistols!" Hornigold screamed.

✠ ✠ ✠ ✠

Palsgrave Williams was making jewelry again. They were crude pieces, rough composites that he made over the fire. Mostly, he simply attached a new precious stone to an existing chain or widened a ring size so a new found treasure could be made to fit. It was not his most inspired work, but the pirates loved it. Everywhere he went among the crew, he was now offered a hard slap on the back, a slug of rum and a receptive ear.

Williams also knew something of foreign tongues. He did a secret count and discovered that, as he suspected, the men born under other flags were far less inclined to subscribe to Hornigold's policy of leniency towards his own homeland. Many of the colonials shared this opinion, feeling ostracized from their roots in the same way that Sam Bellamy did. The Atlantic Ocean was so large a barrier, and the colonies so huge and full of plenty, that many colonials felt as good as gone from under England's wing. Bellamy also had the sea between him and England although, in truth, the sensation of drifting away from the land of his birth had always been with him.

"There is little science to it and no guarantee. They are all drunk enough that were Hornigold to come along behind me and ask the same question, they might swear to him the opposite of what they said to me. Yet I am certain that the Frenchmen and Dutch would join us most enthusiastically. The Swedes, Danes and Germans are smaller in number and harder to fathom. The Scots and Irish are fiery and unpredictable as always...."

"Bollocks to them!" Bellamy said. "How many do you reckon we can count on?"

"Perhaps forty, maybe fifty. Maybe less if we wait too long..." Williams replied. He glanced towards the front of the boat where a half-dozen men were lying among the anchor lines, moaning and pleading with each bounce of the boat. Dr. Ferguson, an educated physician, Jacobite and member of Hornigold's band, was riding with Bellamy's ship, attending to the crew. Men were dropping left and right from some fever. He stuck one man with a brass syringe and then batted the knife out of the man's hand when it rose up in protest. Ferguson then moved to the next man, sighed and motioned to one of the healthy pirates to help him heave the dead man over the rail.

"Twas a bonny good rebel's death," Ferguson declared and then wiped his hands on his shirt and pulled a bottle of whisky from his coat pocket.

Bellamy did a quick calculation. Forty men out of a crew of some one hundred and forty. If it came to a fight, it would be a quick one and not in their favor. According to Hornigold's precious Articles, there was nothing to stop a pack of men from going off on their own. Surely some of Hornigold's former pupils had done the same, the very men that Hornigold now so often bragged about. He wondered what became of those students who Hornigold felt did not make the grade. He felt that he might soon find out. Ever since their meeting in Hornigold's cabin, Bellamy did not see the same proud shine in the old pirate captain's eyes when they looked at each other.

"How many of these men are on our ship?"

"Very few," Williams said, giving Bellamy the answer that he knew already.

Jacob Nickerson came up to where the two men were talking. He pointed to Ferguson and his makeshift ward of dead and dying. "That could be us."

"Leave or stay, we are susceptible to disease. The original sin ensures that," Williams chuckled.

"I know! But there's too many men here. I feel I can't breathe sometimes. All these sick bastards right up close to us makes it more likely we'll end up with the pox or some such curse. I feel chained to death."

"Ah! But at least you aren't married!" Williams chuckled.

Forty men... Bellamy kept saying the number in his head, hoping that it would sound more impressive after some repetition. "There are too many English ships on these waters to ignore them. Starving men do not turn away even a single morsel."

"Ah! I am glad that you are still so hungry. I was beginning to think that you fancied a full time occupation as a pirate," Williams replied.

"No, we are here for gold enough to rise above all occupation. That and nothing more." As it was, Bellamy still believed that a man must work as hard as he could, be his craft smithing, money counting or farming. After he reached as far as he could, then the best he could do was hope for luck to carry him the rest of the way to his dreams. For most men luck ran out as surely as dice eventually tumble wrong or a sea breeze wanes into nothing. But few of those men had ever had command of a pirate ship.

✠ ✠ ✠ ✠

There were four ships in the pirate fleet as they sailed off the coast of Cuba. Hornigold and his lieutenants sailed in a rough circular formation, with their latest prize penned between them. It was time for a respite on a small island called the Isle of Pines where they would clean up their boats, lay their feet in the sand and set about their latest capture, like it was a hog on a spit. Even staunch roving men of the sea occasionally needed firm ground to hold them.

Havana faded in the distance and in due course the Isle of Pines came into view. Green pine and other verdure covered the hilly terrain, the perfect camouflage for resting pirates. At the mouth of a river that burrowed into the island's interior, the pirates hid their ships.

Then they came streaming out on to the decks and into dinghies. Some of the men jumped straight into the water and swam for the nearby swath of sandy beach. Some were carried, laughing drunkenly, out by the current into a large harbor. The others watched and jeered, making no move to aid their drifting shipmates, who had to seize outcroppings of rock and haul themselves out of the water, lest they be pulled out to sea.

The men formed a loose gathering beside a wall of gently bobbing palms. The dozen men from the captured ship mingled freely with their captors. Hornigold stood in the shade. He tipped back his wide, feathered hat and addressed them, "First, some business. Specifically, the matter of the prisoners and their fate. Afterwards we will clean the ships and take a much needed rest!"

The ship had been captured so quickly and so close to their hideout that no one had yet interrogated the prisoners.

"Who is the captain here?" Hornigold demanded.

A tough looking, solid-built man stepped forward. "I am. Captain John Brett of London." There was no fear in his voice. He had a prickly demeanor and a rough, weather-beaten face, which made him indistinguishable from the rogues around him.

Hornigold assessed him slowly. "English, then?"

"Aye. And what of it?"

A groan escaped from a portion of the crowd. Bellamy looked to see which men had made the sound, for they were the ones who disapproved of releasing ships that had English captains. They would be his allies. But they seemed small in number.

"Show me your manifest," Hornigold commanded.

"Let's get this over with. Whatever you aim to do, I'd sooner be done with it," Brett said and handed him a stack of papers.

Hornigold did not answer the man. He handed the papers to Palsgrave Williams. "Will you double check this, my good man? Seems this issue has gotten too sticky to be cavalier about."

"Captain, home port, goods are all English..." Williams read.

Hornigold glanced at the assembled pirates and then back at the captured crew.

"Are you going to kill us? I did not fight in a bloody war only to be killed by pirates..." Brett said.

"Queen Anne's War?"

"Damned right."

Hornigold winced. "Come over to the shade and share a bottle, until the men's work is done. I would hear something of your travels, away from the men."

"What of the crew and cargo? What the bloody hell is in it?" Thomas Brown asked, before Sam Bellamy could stop him.

"We shall discuss it when Captain Brett and I are finished with the bottle," Hornigold said. With a glare at Bellamy, he added, "Have the guts to ask me yourself next time!"

Few of the other men responded one way or another. The ships needed to be hauled up for careening, and most wanted the chore done as quickly as possible so they could sooner get to their drinking.

Two by two, the ships were sailed as far as possible into the shallows and there anchored and unloaded of cargo. The outgoing tide then did the bulk of the work, stranding the vessels on the flats. The men used winches and ropes around nearby tree trunks to pull the ships onto their sides. Then they weighed them down with ballast of heavy rock. The masts were propped up to take the pressure off of them. The exposed hulls were scraped of barnacles and seaweed, which had cemented there during the ships' travels. Any holes or cracks were caulked and let dry in the sunlight. With one hundred and forty men in the fleet, they made speedy work of the chore. By high tide the ships were back afloat. At the next low tide, the other two ships in the fleet were similarly attended to.

Only Brett's ship was left untouched. That ship they let stand on anchor, until they had determined what to do with it and its crew. Bellamy, for one, was certain what their fate would be.

By nightfall, the men sat under a ripening moon. Hornigold's bottle was long empty, and his hands were still waving expressively, in what Bellamy recognized was a retelling of his glory years in Queen Anne's War. Next to him, Brett gesticulated just as enthusiastically. Bellamy would not have been surprised if the two men soon had their arms around each other's shoulders and were harmonizing in some old wartime song.

Bellamy slumped down in the sand next to Peter Hoof.

"May I join you?"

Hoof looked at him noncommittally. Then he turned his gaze back up at the illuminated night sky.

Bellamy took a slug from the rum bottle that he carried and felt the liquid burn a trail down the length of his throat. In the darkness beside him, Hoof took his own quiet pull. They sat looking up into the stars while Bellamy thought of the many roads available to him.

Hoof pointed to the sky. "The same stars can be seen over my house in Sweden. When I was a younger man, I thought that they would lead somewhere special where the land underneath them would be better. But we only have blood and death and this," he said, raising his bottle and then taking a long drink.

Talking with the Swede always depressed Bellamy. He suddenly felt as somber as Hoof. The Swede drank again, deeply, and Bellamy took his own drink and tried to change the subject, "When we find treasure, which is bound to be around the corner, seeing as though we are in the Spanish Empire, then you will see better paths in the stars. First, we have to decide what to do about this privateering business..."

Hoof shrugged and said, "In the wintertime in Sweden, it is dark for the whole day and night, except for a few hours in the middle. The stars sit there, blinking, the whole time."

Hoof drank again, and Bellamy forced himself to keep up. He felt someone flop down next to him. He turned and saw the grim expression on the face of Thomas Brown.

"They're letting Brett go," Brown observed, pointing to the ship that was emerging from behind a row of palms.

Brett's ship eased its way out of the channel and past the open beach where Bellamy and the other men sat.

"Damn Hornigold!" Bellamy spat.

"Give him some of this sharp medicine, eh?" Brown said, tapping his thumb on the edge of his knife blade to test its sharpness. "Brett, Hornigold, Blackbeard, all of them should get some sharp medicine. We are the better men, aren't we? No bloody favorites!" He sliced the knife through the air a few times. "Cut them down to a more humble size, I say!"

Bellamy scowled at Brown's viciousness. But he was not so naïve to believe that he and his supporters could simply walk away from Hornigold's band, unchallenged. Brown, Hoof, Nickerson, Williams... Bellamy considered them all to be his men, ones who had shown loyalty to him. There were at least a dozen more who he was sure he could count on if there was a confrontation. The numbers kept circling in his head. Some forty of the crew were not English born, another two dozen were slaves. Could he count on those origins to ensure the men's sympathy? Hornigold and Blackbeard had a strong hold. They were adept at providing wine at sea, women in port and enough ships to chase that many men might be content to keep their lot with what they had. How many of them had a deeper hunger, he mused? Maybe fifty? Maybe less? Not enough if it came to a fight…

Bellamy was surprised when Lebous plopped down in the sand beside him.

"*I have talked with Williams. I will sail with you when you go,*" the Frenchman whispered.

Bellamy hid his grin behind the bottle he was raising. "And your men? Will they follow you?"

"They have all the way from Marseilles to these islands. They are as loyal to me as Hornigold is to his country," Lebous said. He raised a finger and stabbed the air. "Were we to take more French ships, then perhaps you would see the same argument from us about a different mother country! But there are few of our ships in this sea these days." He shrugged and drank from his own bottle.

After another swig Lebous cried, "Out here in this ocean there is an opportunity for every man to be his own liege and master! Hornigold is so English. He wants to manage everything so there is no risk. Fortune favors the brave, and a rich life awaits he who is willing to throw off his yoke and run free. They call it *going on account*. See, we are merely borrowing against future payment. I'd rather enjoy the good life now while I still have my good French looks! Let's drink to that!" He clinked his bottle against Bellamy's. "To the Devil!"

"Aye. To the Devil…" Bellamy said and drank his whole bottle, all of the good life at once.

"Drink tonight and in the morning we shall see who is happy that the sow was let out of the pen," Lebous advised.

"And who will be captain, you or me?" Bellamy asked, his smile looking sly for a moment.

Lebous grinned back. "I will sail with you tomorrow, but after that, who knows? Fair is fair."

"Agreed," Bellamy replied. They clinked bottles again.

"But we still need more men," Lebous pointed out.

"What about them?" Bellamy said. He was looking at a group of Africans, freed from a heist of a slave ship only to be placed in a more limited form of service for the pirates. They were not bound and chained, so in that respect they had a semblance of freedom, but their tasks were the most menial that no other pirate wanted. In battle they were not given arms, for none of them had been offered a chance to sign the Articles.

"The slaves?" Lebous snorted.

"They would likely be grateful to the men who elevated them," Bellamy noted.

"And they would repay you with a dagger in the back!" Lebous replied.

"They aren't even sailors!" Brown protested.

"We shall see... They can carry a vote and even carry a sword. If Hornigold won't count their votes, he shall certainly notice their swords," Bellamy said, standing and walking over to where some two dozen men sat by themselves around their own private campfire.

Walking out of the light and laughter of the other pirates, Bellamy felt a shiver of fear. In the darkness the Africans looked all the more foreign. They sat together, mumbling in their own native tongue, occasionally rising to dance around the fire in some kind of ceremony.

Their leader was Daku, a fiery, impatient man, who came out to intercept Bellamy before he could reach the fire.

"This time is ours. We do not bother you when you are pirating or singing or drinking. You do not bother us when we talk and pray."

The press of the man's hand against Bellamy's chest gave hint of the kind of power that he and his brethren could add to Bellamy's cause. Yet Bellamy did not take another step forward. Something told him that the Africans' service was a fragile thing. They were too small to defeat the entire band of pirates, but Daku's gesture suggested that they would not let themselves be pushed too far.

"I come to make you a deal..."

"No! Go back to your friends! We are busy..."

"Listen! You come with us. You join those of us who are planning to leave Hornigold's band and start another, and we shall welcome you as one of us."

"You wish us to work for you rather than Hornigold?" Daku asked, his eyes narrowing.

"I wish you to join us as equals. To fight and drink and get bloody rich."

Daku's hand pressed harder. "We do not care about why you pirates fight with each other. Hornigold has promised to take us back home, in exchange for our service."

"He is lying... He is tricking you..."

"Perhaps you lie!" Daku raised his hand to Bellamy's throat. Bellamy reached for his pistol, but found it already snatched away by the African.

"Your homeland is far away. Come with me and become rich men. Then you can return as princes. You will even have your own boat."

"Ha! I am already a prince among my people!" Daku said, pushing Bellamy away and walking back to the other Africans, still carrying Bellamy's pistol.

"Think about it!" Bellamy called after him.

There was nothing else to do that night but wait and long for sleep. Deep into the night Bellamy could not get the sound of the waves, rolling in and out, from his head. It seemed an apt noise to accompany his own up and down thoughts.

The next morning, when Bellamy awoke, his back lay firmly upon the beach, but his head rolled as if on the waves. His mouth was full of sand, and the bright morning sun rapped upon his eyelids. He squeezed his eyelids shut and fought in vain to hold onto the last wisps of his dream. He had been standing next to a house on a bluff, which rolled down to a bright blue sea where a white vessel bobbed on a mooring. Maria was there, smiling, beside him as they held hands and looked out across vast tracts of land and sea where no one else but them resided.

"Alright then, we are ready to sail," Hornigold pronounced.

Bellamy got up and walked over to him. "Not quite yet."

It was only a few dozen feet across the sand, but to Bellamy it felt like miles, with so many men's eyes upon him, so much tension in the air.

Hornigold stared hard at his young protégé. "I think that we are," he said purposefully.

Bellamy turned to the crowd of pirates. Would the men back him, he wondered? He thought so, but he wasn't sure. The apple orchard in Eastham had produced great success, Florida had not. One never knew what each new chance would bring, he mused, but it had brought him farther than he had ever expected. He scanned the crowd for Williams, caught the jovial jeweler's eye and felt a surge of confidence, which he hoped was not ill-founded. "For a few months now, there has been some disagreement about whether or not English shipping is fair game."

"I, for one, am getting weary of this discussion," Hornigold said.

"So are we all! I propose that we end the debate right now."

Hornigold peered suspiciously at Bellamy. "How? Half think one way and half the other. Clearly, we have not been able to agree yet."

"Yet we continue the practice of favoring English shipping."

"Yes, because that is the way it has always been."

"With you as captain," Bellamy added.

Hornigold's eyes widened as if he was suddenly seeing a broadside aimed at him. For all of Bellamy's unbridled ambition and clear charisma, Hornigold was still a privateer at heart – a man of race, country, and rules. Bellamy was his student, a fellow Englishman. He had seen pirates come and go, but in truth, he had not thought it would come to this.

"I propose that we have a vote. Those that want to continue to spare English shipping, for no other reason than the miserable captain, who beats his wretched crew, is from the next village over from where you were born, can remain with Hornigold. As for those of you who want to be twice, nay, three times as rich and truly bound by no laws, then elect me captain, and we will steal from every fat hen that crosses us, no matter what tongue he speaks!"

The men were stunned. Even Blackbeard's mouth hung wide open.

"English or otherwise, all of those merchant men are all the same. Show me a merchant captain, and I will show you a heartless, greedy louse, who would bleed dry his own mother and beat his own sickly father if it gained him but a single penny more!" Bellamy said.

Blackbeard snorted thunderously.

"Look at this crew," Bellamy went on. "Only half of the men are English. If there is no preference for crew membership, why should there be partiality towards prey? The goods we seek are not English anyway. It's Spanish gold if it's worth anything."

"You disappoint me, Bellamy!" Hornigold roared, reaching for his sword. Then he addressed the crowd, "I elevated all of you higher than you could have ever reached on your own! This is my reward?"

Blackbeard ran a finger along the edge of his sword blade. "Lucky for you, Black Sam, that I don't kill my own or else your blood would run hot on this beach!"

"Bellamy," Hornigold snapped. "Should you lose, this could be a very long fall." He raised his weapon. Behind him many pirates drew their weapons and came to stand alongside of him.

All around Bellamy men were armed and shouting at each other. It was too late to turn back now, he realized. The thoughts flew through his head in quick succession: his dying father, Maria in the orchard, the image of a blade slicing through his red vest... He wondered how painful it was to die by the blade.

A pistol went off. And suddenly, all across the beach, the battle raged.

Chapter Seven
"The Pirate Prince"

June 1716

Sam Bellamy saw the surface of the water speeding towards him, but he could not even throw his hands out to break his fall because his arms were tied securely to his side. The water was so clear that he could see the white sandy bottom beneath the waves, but at the last second he squeezed his eyes closed and clamped one last breath into his mouth, before the sea engulfed him.

For a moment he felt pure terror.

He kicked his feet, which were also lashed together with rope. He thrashed his body within his binds and felt like a bait fish tied to a fishing line. The thought was brief. It was drowned out by an inner cry that resounded in his head. *Air!*

His lungs screamed as his breath seeped out. His eyes popped open and gave him a view of the sea floor, coming closer and closer. He squirmed more frantically, his body fighting against the deathly plunge, but the ropes held him fast.

There was nothing to do but wait and hope...

Then, suddenly, he felt himself being reeled back up through the depths. His chest still yowled with protest, his mind screamed for the motion of the line to go faster. *Faster!*

His feet broke through the water into the air above. The rest of his body soon followed, lastly his head, which throbbed from the breathless pressure of below.

Bellamy then heard voices shouting and hollering at him.

He blinked out the sea water, gulped in the precious air and watched the ship spin past him once... twice... three times as he twirled on the end of the rope. Upside-down, bearded pirate faces were grinning at him from the rail. Men were cheering, raising bottles.

Baptism at sea. That is what the old salts called it. For the pirates it was a ritual to celebrate their new camaraderie and their new captain. It was a rite of passage that Bellamy knew Hornigold would not have suffered. But Hornigold was now far away on the other side of the West Indies with Blackbeard and the rest of the crew who insisted on sparing English ships. Bellamy would not soon forget the shock and fury that had twisted Hornigold's face when the vote to part ways was called for. Neither would Bellamy forget staring into the deathly black eye of Hornigold's pistol barrel or the scores of weapons raised up in Bellamy's defense. One hundred and twenty men chose to try their luck with a new captain: Bellamy. Only twenty men sided with Hornigold. One and all, the men stood by the vote and the Articles. The battle on the beach ended almost as soon as it started. Hornigold soon realized that the numbers were sorely against him. In the end Bellamy suffered no more than a volley of curses from his mentor.

Bellamy had declared all ships prey in equal measure and all pirates under his banner true brethren of the sea. Brothers. He had been determined not to elevate himself over his crew although for the moment he did indeed dangle suspended above them.

His men had responded enthusiastically to the egalitarianism that Bellamy preached. One by one, they trussed their shipmates with rope, which was run off of the end of a yardarm, high upon the mainmast. There the men hung, bound hand and foot, in a crude approximation of the gibbets that proper society erected at the edge of ports and harbors to hold the bodies of pirates executed by the Crown for practicing their craft. In turn, the pirates enacted the mocking, black farce of their own destruction.

Bellamy motioned for his crew to haul him back aboard, feeling that any more time spent hung on this rope would indeed be a humiliation.

When he landed on the deck, hands slapped him on the back. Bottles were pressed into his hand, poured over his head and some even tossed over the rail.

"*Captain! Captain! Captain!*" the pirates chanted, and Bellamy indulged them by rushing to the quarterdeck and there uttering a feral roar. Then he stood there a while, grinning out over these mad, unbounded men as he thought about how they were all free to make up any new rites and customs that they could devise. In the same manner, they were at liberty to take any course that pleased them. And he, *Captain* Bellamy, was going to lead them.

In the ensuing weeks there were many more celebrations. Ships surrendered to the *Maria*, which was now Bellamy's flagship. They dropped sail like frightened lambs knee buckling to the ground in submission. For a while, ships seemed to come across Bellamy's bow every day or two. None delivered to him the sort of treasure that he longed for, but they had produced enough to keep the men's morale high. The men began to say that Bellamy had been blessed with unnatural luck. Although Bellamy was wary of such superstitious claims, he was nonetheless pleased with the good fortune.

✠ ✠ ✠ ✠

November 1716

The *Maria* moved across water so still that it seemed that something other than wind was moving her. Some breeze did indeed blow, but it left the water unruffled as if even weather had not the ability to disturb the endless tranquility of the West Indies. Day after day was measured by the slow drift of mountainous white clouds across an endless, bright sky. Hour after hour was spent gazing into clear water, which went fuzzy only when too much rum had been consumed. Months slipped quickly and painlessly under the keel until Bellamy found that he had completely lost track of them.

He did not see how any man could keep any kind of momentum for long in this torrid place. The fact that there were any lasting settlements at all in this part of the world sometimes astonished him. He would have thought that sooner or later every one of them would have dissolved as its men and women wandered aimlessly away, drawn by some idle daydream or other.

Bellamy leaned over the forward rail, his brown arms dangling over the water. He looked out at the turquoise tropical water. Out here there were no roads, no streets or other markers. Men picked a path of their own choosing, and it did not matter if that line was straight or jagged or went in circles. Nor was there any law except the Articles, which merely put into writing basic common sense that men should treat each other with decency, as long as it was warranted.

These days Bellamy looked as ostentatious as Henry Avery, in his red vest, lacey shirt, wide brim hat and three brace of pistols – all taken from various captains who had come under the pirates' swords. Not a single merchant captain had done anything to dissuade Bellamy from his belief that they were all a pack of rouges a thousand times worse than the men that Bellamy now sailed with.

He had been repaying himself for the humiliation that he had felt under Captain Pound's iron hand, and slowly he was beginning to feel that the score was being settled. He had done it with as little barbarity as possible. Of course, in the business of piracy, some blood was bound to be spilled. While his compatriots expressed little remorse should some of their quarry fall in the course of a heist, Bellamy himself was determined not to shed blood, even of merchant captains. There was too much avarice in the world as it was. The captains would repay him with fortune, and then he would walk among them as Avery did, in his display of finery, and they would have no choice but to take him seriously. He wanted them to live to bear witness to the way he intended to turn the world upside-down.

The only problem was that the merchant men were not paying fast enough. Bellamy had acquired little real wealth except for a few silver rings and a pocketful of coin.

They were in the Bahamas now, cruising through the Exuma chain. Islands started materializing out of the water in a row of little bumps, like the folds in a giant sea dragon's tail.

"Don't try to tally them," Palsgrave Williams' deep voice said close to Bellamy's shoulder. "There are hundreds of them. You could probably spend one day on each island and not see them all inside of a year."

"It has been more than a year that we have been down here. Already, I feel like I have seen each island twice over," Bellamy noted.

Williams' hand came down upon Bellamy's shoulder, and Bellamy saw that all of the whiteness and softness of it had been baked away. It was now as brown and leathery as any sailor's mitt. Williams' shirt sleeve hung loose off of an arm that, like the rest of his body, was much thinner than at the start of their voyage. Bellamy recalled his first days with the jeweler and marveled at the transformations in the man. Williams had become as hard-drinking, tough and brave as any of his fellow brethren. At the same time he retained some kind of in-born refinement that elevated him. It was not the kind of arrogance that the upper class exhibited. It was a sense of honor and dignity, which Bellamy had taken as a model. Without Williams, Bellamy might have found himself deep in the pack of starry-eyed pirates, shouldering each other out of the way in their push towards the front of the gang. Some were content to take their share of drink and profit and leave the chores of command to others. But there was enough ambition aboard to create competition. Plenty of men wanted their names to be on the trembling lips of sea captains, bankers, reverends and innocent, gossiping farm girls across the known world. Bellamy sometimes wondered how far his own name had traveled and whether it was yet being spoken of with hushed awe by the likes of Isaiah Higgins or Justice Doane.

"This place suits you. You look ten years younger. I never told you this, but you were so full of anger and reproach back in Eastham that you often seemed halfway to an early grave. Such weight crushes a man. It is far more desirable to live as carefree as we do now," Williams said.

"You look much older these days. The sun has boiled your skin like a blacken corn cob," Bellamy replied.

Williams eyed him for a second, the gaze hard and convincingly threatening. The look, along with the sword and pistols on his belt, had covered over any outward vestige of Williams' Newport origins. "I am quite older than you, lad. Old enough, almost, to be a father to you."

"Father? Have you ever even attempted to make an offspring? I have not noticed you go upstairs with the tavern girls of New Providence even once."

"Nor have I seen you there. Yet I know the reason for that…"

"And it will remain unsaid. Were it known, our brethren would think me as fettered as a married man."

"Instead, they wonder if you like the fairer sex at all. But at least you aren't married!" Williams chuckled.

"I don't care what any of them think. My mistress is the gold that is coming to us on one of these ships or other," Bellamy replied.

"Yes…and my mistress is the looking for it. You are young enough to be my nephew at least," Williams said.

Bellamy thumped the jeweler on the back. It had become a playful ritual with them, the teasing about age and impotence. Underneath was a fondness that was more avuncular than Bellamy would have liked to admit. Father, uncle, foster father, they were all dead now, and he had no intention of adding another, surrogate as Williams would be. Friendship would suffice. The jeweler was of that age when Bellamy suspected that childless men come to know regret. In place of descendants, Williams was trying to prolong his own youth.

At the same time Bellamy could admit that his own legacy was no more permanent than the wake of the ship. The easy, timeless lifestyle of the tropics sucked the ambition from him. *The next ship, the next day...* thoughts like this lapped like gentle waves on a shell strewn beach. There was no rush anymore.

✠ ✠ ✠ ✠

Bellamy found his own distinctive style of piracy, one that was as free as possible of innocent blood. Even the hardened rouges of his crew did not protest Bellamy's gentle conquests, for they had to admit that they had never sailed for a captain who had coaxed so many prizes from the sun-bathed horizon of the West Indies. But he had yet to capture the big prize. A treasure ship.

There were dark looks from certain crew members that told Bellamy that his supply of time was not endless. Among the dissatisfied was a contingent of Dutch convicts, lead by Thomas Baker, who sought out others of their race, to smoke and drink together, chattering in their native tongue and casting shifty glances that made Bellamy nervous. He could see the same lack of patience that he bore when chafing under the yoke of Hornigold's philosophy of privateering. Only the shine of gold would break through those clouded, mutinous eyes.

Bellamy's thoughts were interrupted by a snatch of song from nearby, *"Our queen was then at Tilbury, What could you more desire, For whose sweet sake Sir Francis Drake, Did set them all on fire! But let them look about themselves, For if they come again, They shall be served with that same sauce, As they were, I know when..."*

He turned and saw a pirate playing a fiddle. He could not recall when or how the fiddler had joined the crew, there were so many pirates among them now. Bellamy searched his mind for the man's name: Alfred. He was a skinny little man, with shaggy hair of indeterminate color and a beard, which hung like wet moss from his chin. Bending the bow over the strings, he made his instrument seem a living thing, one whose natural calling was the sweetest kind of music that Bellamy had heard. He had no idea that men could draw such sounds from a collection of wood and string. The sea shanties of the pirates had been well-sung, with much heart and lurid imagination to the lyrics. Alfred's music put such drunken warbling to shame.

"Since you are a Devonshire man, you must know that song about your countryman, the great rogue, Sir Francis Drake? A man of your kind of cloth!" Alfred said to Bellamy.

Bellamy smiled at the man's shameless flattery. "Everyone in England has heard of Drake."

"Yes! Of course. Twas the year 1588. The Spanish had just sent their dreaded Armada. And the heartbroken, virgin Queen Elizabeth had but one man to look for to save our land, the venerable Drake!" Alfred replied, striking a dramatic pose. "I suppose you have heard of Robin Hood as well?"

"Do you have a song about him too?" Bellamy asked, bemused by this odd little pirate.

Alfred peered at him thoughtfully as if he was feeling a song coming on at that very moment. "I was thinking of writing something in Robin Hood's spirit about our very crew."

"Indeed?"

"Think of it! We are men of little means, who have pulled ourselves up to wealth by fleecing the very ones who outlaw us, making their wealth and power our own. A fair turn of the tables, eh? Instead of greed, we are bonded by principle! The Articles. And we are, of course, brave in the face of insurmountable odds, fighting the ruling class for the good of all common men who are still bound to their lords, wishing they could be men such as us but able only to live vicariously through our valor!"

Bellamy felt himself nodding frantically, the words moving like living things through his mind. It was as if someone had finally told him the reason he lingered out at sea, letting the months drain away, hunting for ships the way other men hunted for fish, taking from those with means, yes, but at the same time spreading fear and violence among plenty who didn't deserve it. His sense of justice had been shrinking with each common sailor who had broken his heart, clinging to his horrid captain, like a beaten dog that won't leave his master. But the ones that really pained him were the men of visible strength of mind who denounced Bellamy as a rogue, who told him that they would rather die than sail with him. He used to think that they were fools and occasionally that they were right. Now he saw that they were simply blind to his crew's higher purpose. That purpose existed whether they accepted the freedom he offered them or not. And if they fell during a taking, their deaths did not bother him as much as they once did. They were weak, foolish and good as dead anyway. He would not let their blind allegiance to bondage get in the way of his freedom. It was a freedom that he meant to offer to all poor souls who crossed his path.

✠ ✠ ✠ ✠

On the deck of the next ship that they took, Bellamy strutted about as if he was on some stage.

"I am Robin Hood of the sea!" he told the imprisoned captain. The man looked back at him as if he was mad. Bellamy knew that he was thinking more clearly than ever before. At Bellamy's elbow was Alfred, playing the fiddle. The man launched into a tune, with such verve and inspiration that Bellamy thought that some of his prisoners looked on the verge of clapping.

"We are a company of free princes, in the way that all men are born! We do not sneak around, begging for scraps under the table from our so-called lords and masters! The meals on that table were set by our hands, grown on land that we tilled, squeezed from out of the sweat and blood of our lives. Why shouldn't we get the same portion as the idle fools who do nothing to earn it? In this spirit, we seize your cargo and return it to men who have slaved away their whole lives. With brotherhood we extend welcome to those of you who may wish to set your own course of freedom instead of bondage! We were long ago besieged by men who set their thrones upon us. They still occupy our land, but out here, they are nothing! We are the lords of the sea! And we have no flags but those of freedom!"

When he finished, he did a little bow. It was a worthy speech, he decided, and sure enough, several men stepped across the deck to join the pirates.

The musician's merry music continued as they transferred the other ship's cargo. When the boats drifted away, he was still playing and the pirates were singing gleefully, waving to their released captives as if it was the breakup of a most wonderful sort of party.

There was still not an ounce of coin in the hold, but it mattered less all of a sudden. What was there - silk, spice, rum – was infused with new meaning. It was cleansed with higher purpose. He was not really a thief at all, Bellamy realized. He was a liberator. Men like Robin Hood were recalled, by lord and serf alike, as the greatest of heroes.

✠ ✠ ✠ ✠

January 1717

The ships collided with a massive lurch. On the pirates' ship Thomas Baker joined the feral roar of combat and watched the lines tangle and the grappling hooks fly over the side to snare the other ship's rigging.

Flames clawed out from a hole in the captured ship where the pirates' cannon fire had struck true. For Baker, the image brought to mind cold nights in the little, broken-down hovel that his family owned in New Amsterdam. He could plainly see himself huddled in front of the hearth, with his brothers and sisters, his parents a few feet closer to the fire and his aging grandfather sitting right before the blaze, orange fingers of flame crackling around him as he told his hellish tales. He talked of Indian raids and the steady attacks of the English, a constant pressure that did not subside until the flag of St. George and a new name, New York, finally hung over the city. According to measurements of war, the final English takeover was a relatively placid thing, a show of such overwhelming brawn that the Dutch of New Amsterdam and their Swedish allies to the south had no choice but to submit. After all, the whole of the New World had become a feast for England, France and Spain to claw over, and the little Dutch colony was but a crumb, which would fall on the plate of one of those gluttonous powers sooner or later. By all accounts the polyglot population of the city came together with remarkable unity. But people like Baker's grandfather remembered the little cruelties that accompany even the most gentle of wars. He had passed those images on to his grandson. Now, when Baker saw the flames consuming the forward hold of a captured ship such as this, he saw the reflection of that long ago fire and recalled the tales of the English who took their fine city.

He saw Sam Bellamy laughing, a noise filled with arrogance and affectation, it seemed to Baker. He watched Bellamy brandish his sword and make a few menacing cuts in front of the face of the square-jawed man who Baker knew to be the first mate of the captured ship. Once his type crumbled, the rest would soon plead for mercy. Baker appreciated the strategy, but he still cared little for the man who was standing as if he was as grand as all of the nonsense that he told about himself. *Robin Hood,* even *Pirate Prince,* is what some were calling him now. The very thought made Baker spit on the deck in contempt.

Baker fingered his own weapon as he pushed through the crowd of captives, which was already subdued. He frisked the men roughly, hoping to draw some protest from one of them, which would justify him using his weapons. Fighting, as well as spoils and the delight of spending them, was the tonic of the regular pirate.

When he looked at Bellamy, he saw a farm boy who had likely never drawn a blade or shot a pistol, until he found himself on a pirate deck. Baker had done both by the time his apprenticeship as a tailor had run its course. He was born in view of the shanty bars and whorehouses of the city's port. His father told him that to survive in the city, one needed a trade. Yet Baker was not meant to be a tailor. Before his contract was over, Baker had already mastered a different kind of education, that of brawling, thieving and pleasure seeking. He owed seven years to the tailor but gave most of the sixth to the alehouses, until he was deep in debt and out of favor. He escaped to the sea where, to his amusement, he spent much of his time sewing sails and his sailor's shirt. Only once did he come home, when he heard that his grandfather was dying. He did not make it off the dock. The constable found him, and he spent the night that his grandfather died in jail and the next morning on a prison ship sent to the Jamaica colony. Before that ship had delivered him into bondage, the pirates found and liberated him. In that moment he had considered Bellamy to be the finest man he had ever met. Since then he had come to see that under Bellamy's performance was nothing but cowardice. Bellamy was content merely to act like a court jester rather than a true pirate, gritty and hungry.

Then came Bellamy's tiresome speech to the new recruits, the captured crewmen assembled on deck. Baker saw, with satisfaction, that a number of the men looked like the sort of ruffians who might eventually tip the scale in his favor. Bellamy could do nothing about it. The speech that was so carefully crafted to give sheen to his own inflated, fairy tale image drew in as many blackhearted thieves as it did idealists who wished to play Robin Hood. To turn down any man would tarnish Bellamy's reputation, perhaps even forfeit his captaincy. He was trapped by his own invitation.

"And marriage! That is the worst sort of imprisonment! Unfortunately, you fools who are presently in such fetters must be excluded from our merry band, for we cannot be burdened by the softhearted!" Palsgrave Williams added.

"Aye!" Bellamy agreed, and following the rules of his arbitrary code, he let the married men go, including one with a fine band of gold around his finger. Baker did not bother to make mention of it, knowing that Bellamy would only take it for himself.

Baker again mused about his journey on the prison ship, pitching back and forth in the dark hold, listening to the sounds of the unforgiving chains rattling around him and the imprisoned men spewing their wormy bread onto the floor. He kept imagining what he would do if he again tasted freedom. In that blackness he resolved to live every moment that he could snatch from life to its fullest offering. Freedom, he knew, was an action, not a flowery sentiment. Bellamy could drink and boast with the best of men, but he had grown caught up in the making of his own legend, making their pirating something noble whereas for most men it was simply a way to free drinking and whoring. There was too much talking, too much refrain from the kind of rough-housing that their trade demanded, too much love of status and not enough pillaging. When he was captain, all that would change, Baker thought. He did not care if anyone ever knew his name. In fact, the easy life was that much easier when a man lived in the shadows rather than strutted around the world like it was a stage. He just needed men to follow him in another direction.

Peter Hoof, the big Swede, burst onto the deck, dragging with him the captain of the captured ship.

"He was hiding in the hold," Hoof explained. The man tried to break Hoof's grip but only succeeded in losing his cap and having his shirt pulled up over his head in the struggle. For sport, some of the other pirates pricked him on the stomach and back, with the tips of their blades, while the captured man howled.

"Step away! Step away!" Bellamy roared. Baker spat again as he watched Bellamy charge across the deck to break up the fun.

The captain's head popped out of his shirt. His eyes, face, beard and hair were various shades of red.

"You!" Bellamy cried. To Baker's astonishment, Bellamy knocked the man down.

"What have you done?" Bellamy seethed. He pointed to the mainmast where another man was tied. The bound man's back was bare, except for a bumpy map of past punishment and a single red trail where the next line of pain was being drawn by the whip. The captured captain had been in the middle of the whipping when the pirates had come upon them. There was little else that could condemn a merchant man more than to catch him red-handed in such an act.

"What have *you* done, you mean! I'll tell you! You have just made the biggest mistake of your miserable life! You'll rot for this, you vermin!" the captain cried.

Bellamy glared at his captive. "Do you know me?" he asked.

"I do not deign to keep track of which of you criminals con-sider yourselves noteworthy. You are all nameless outlaws to me."

"Lift him up and tie him to the mast!" Bellamy commanded.

Peter Hoof clamped his large fingers around the nape of the captain's neck. With a swift stroke of the sword in his other hand, he cut the vest and shirt of the captain open from the back of his collar to his belt.

"Get off me, you brute! Get off me, you filth! I've earned my way on my own, made something of myself! You scum think it is your right to come and strip it away from me, without lifting a finger in honest work! It is not fair! You shall burn in hell for this! You shall all hang…" the man shouted until the Swede clubbed him with a fist that was as large and solid as a cudgel and the voice broke off.

A sword stroke severed the rope that held the prisoner to the mast. The man fell to the deck, and the pirates tied the captain in his place. Then Bellamy had Hoof pour sea water over the captain's head and slap him into sputtering consciousness.

Baker watched, amazed and fascinated, as Bellamy took the whip that Hoof handed to him. And soon the air was filled with the snap of the whip and the satisfying echo of the captain's pained cries. The pirates urged Bellamy on, and Bellamy swung faster and harder, even the sound of his prisoner's moaning seemed to propel him to more violence.

"You brought this on yourself! Remember that! Your conscious might be clear but your back will be a reminder! Damn you, Captain Pound! You shall remember the name of the Pirate Prince next time!" Bellamy hollered.

The beating continued until even water could not revive the bound man. Baker could not believe his eyes. Just when it seemed as though Bellamy's transformation was complete, Bellamy's next forward swing was brought up short in Williams' grasp.

"He is not Captain Pound," Williams said. He did not wince in the face of Bellamy's furious glare.

"I know very well who he is!"

Williams lifted the beaten captain's head to display his face. "Are you quite sure? I have read the manifest and queried the crew. All evidence suggests his name is Constable, not Pound."

The whip slipped out of Bellamy's hand, and with it went the fire that Baker had been on the verge of admiring. "You're right... They are as alike as brothers. But it is not Pound."

"Well, perhaps he deserved it all the same," Williams mused.

"What else did you find? What of the cargo?" Bellamy asked, still panting from exertion.

This time Hoof spoke, his dark eyes looking more moody than before. Even good news could sound morose coming from the depressed Swede. As soon as Baker heard the man's grim recounting of the contents of the hold - sugar, molasses, spice - he joined the collective groan of the crew.

"That's all?" Bellamy asked.

"That is all."

Baker watched Bellamy look furtively around the ship as the pirates cracked open the water barrels that lay on deck and trimmed off coils of rope and extra sails. It was the kind of labor meant to salvage what they could. There was considerably less yelling and carousing, almost to the point of silence. Baker could not stop the smile that spread across his face.

Chapter Eight
"The Bouncing Dice"

January 1717

New Providence. During past visits the name had not quite lived up to the promise, but the sight of the seedy pirate stronghold still drew a lusty cheer from Sam Bellamy's men. After all, it was much easier to wait for divine Providence with an ale in hand.

There were two ships in the pirate fleet. The *Sultana,* a captured merchant vessel that they had armed to the teeth with cannon, was under the command of Bellamy, and the *Maria* was now captained by the recently elected Palsgrave Williams.

Soon they were all sitting in the packed tavern room of *The Red Squall.* Bellamy noticed that he was receiving more attention than any other patron in the tavern. It amused him to gaze about the place and see the range of emotion directed at him. At the moment, he was observing the women, from whom he received adoring looks, which were so obviously counterfeit in their affection.

"They are trying to measure us by our money purses," Williams remarked, authority in his voice.

Bellamy agreed. It was, in fact, the attitude of his fellow pirates that most impressed him. In their eyes he saw looks of jealousy and longing, which gave him a good measurement of how high his fame had risen.

Men hovered near his table. Some of the braver, or more brazen, approached him and offered a few words of camaraderie or congratulations. Most of them stood forth for an audition to join the crew.

"The name's Roger Balfour," said a sandy-haired lad, whose face was covered with the pimples of youth. "I've two years merchant experience and one working with some pirates off of Cuba…"

"Three years! You hardly look old enough to be a cabin boy!" Alfred, the musician, said. He dealt a card onto the table, followed by Williams, Thomas Brown and Bellamy.

"I've killed four men with me bare hands!" the lad shouted. He puffed out his chest and drew a pistol, which he waved menacingly in the air.

"Easy, lad!" Alfred cried.

"And go away! Can't you see that the adults are playing cards," Brown added.

"I was talking to Black Bellamy, not you two!" Balfour responded.

At the sound of his name, Bellamy's head snapped around. "You know me?"

The lad smiled. "Of course! You have taken some forty ships already this past year, they say. Who does not know of you?"

Bellamy felt a smile of his own growing. Next to him, Alfred was winking. "A Prince among pirates... His name known across the sea..." he sang.

"Will you play your cards?" Williams asked irritably.

Alfred and Brown laid down their cards.

Bellamy cradled his and said to the lad, "Are you looking to join us?"

"Aye!"

"Come to my ship tomorrow morning, and we'll have you sign the Articles. Do you know where my ship is berthed?"

Balfour looked at him like he was kidding. "I'll be there!" He turned and signaled, encouragingly, to a table full of young pirates, who had watched the exchange avidly.

"You can bring them along if you wish. The more, the merrier," Bellamy called after him. The lad turned and bowed, then scampered away.

"What a bloody audience. Like you really are something special," Brown joked.

Bellamy did not answer. At another table he could see Baker and some fellow Dutchmen, Simon Van Vorst and Hendrick Quintor, sitting with shoulders hunched, talking to another group of new pirates.

"What are they up to?" he mused.

"Will you play already?" Williams groaned.

"They look to be recruiting their own crew," Bellamy said, quietly, still studying the Dutchmen.

"They are nothing to fret about, considering that they are a small minority! Now would you please play your cards?"

Bellamy tapped his cards, thoughtfully, on his bearded chin. "I suppose you are right... I am sure that my luck will hold!" His face turned impish as he laid his cards on the table. Three aces. Williams let out a choking sound.

"This is the last of it?" Bellamy asked, a smirk on his face as he pulled Williams' coin to his side of the table.

"Yes."

"But I raised the bet another five silver pennies. You are short," Bellamy said, watching with amusement as Williams patted down his empty pockets.

"I shall have to go into your debt."

"I'll take that locket instead..." Bellamy said, pointing to a gold medallion hanging from around Williams' neck.

"Not the locket."

"I don't remember seizing that. When did we take that? I am sure that I would have kept it for myself had you given me a chance to have a look. Which captain did you pinch it from?"

"You know very well that I've had this since we sailed from Great Island."

"Hmmm... I don't recall."

"Yes, well the memory does tend to wither in this rum-soaked, sun-burnt climate."

"Regardless of its origin, let's have it on the table."

"You are being quite an ass today. Are you enjoying having the shoe on the other foot?"

"If you are saying that you are broke, then I am enjoying myself."

"Well then, young rascal. Seems I feel the sting of poverty after all."

"Hardly. You still have the locket."

Alfred, grinning, leaned over and poked Williams on the arm. "Let's have it, jeweler. You can always forge another. The Pirate Prince demands that you bet with it."

"*Pirate Prince!* What sort of nonsense... And I resent the way you are looking at me, like some sort of lord to whom I owe allegiance!" Williams said to Bellamy.

"The locket..." Bellamy repeated and then glared at the jeweler until Williams' yielded and slid the locket across the table, with a hand that shook as much as his pained face.

"After you've licked your wounds for a time, I will let you play to get it back..." Bellamy said. He noticed a little clasp on the locket and began to pry it open, but he was suddenly distracted by a clicking sound in his ear and an accompanying pressure on his temple.

When he tried to pivot his head, a bear-like voice chuckled in his ear, "Tut, tut! Don't move another inch, unless the *Pirate Prince's* skull is so thick that it can stop a pistol shot. Although perhaps your head is so full of shit that the ball would pass through without causing harm at all!"

Bellamy was aware that most of the tavern had lapsed into silence. In part of his mind, he knew that he should be terrified. But the pressure of the gun barrel against his head felt irritating, not lethal. The irritation quickly swelled to fury as he moved his eyes around the room and saw that everyone in the tavern was witnessing his humiliation. He did not consider the possibility that he could be uttering his last words as he bellowed in scalding indignation, "By the sudden stench in the room and the cowardice of this attack, I'd say that it is none other than Blackbeard behind me! This is how you settle your scores? A shot in the back of the head!"

"Why not! Tis far easier that way. Less risk of getting shot myself!" Blackbeard cried.

"You would not dare! Do you know who this is? This man has founded a pirate empire. Robin Hood himself pales in deed and word to his exploits!" Alfred shouted.

Blackbeard's brow arched. "What's this? You have your own little monkey in tow?"

"We left you according to the tenants of the Articles," Williams pointed out.

"And here's the lawyer..." Blackbeard chuckled. "The damned daintiest pack of pirates I've ever seen. But I won't dirty *The Red Squall* with the worthless blood of you three. I value my seat at the bar more than my score with you. But should we meet on the ocean..."

"You would be the sorrier for it!" Alfred sang.

"Were you a man, not a monkey, you'd be howling hot right now for that kind of talk!" Blackbeard snarled. Then he lowered his pistol and bent again to Bellamy's ear, "*Gathering the praises of drunken would-be pirates ain't the same kind of reputation as being on the wanted list of the navies of the world. I have warships after me...*"

When Bellamy turned to face the other pirate, he was surprised to see that Blackbeard was grinning at him.

Then Blackbeard addressed the silent tavern room in general, "Did I scare the lot of you? Tis just two old friends meeting for a drink, you chickenhearted fools!"

Blackbeard motioned to the tavern keeper and pulled Bellamy over to the bar. "I've been planning to leave Hornigold myself all along. It just wasn't the time yet when you made your little mutiny. I'll wait till I'm good and strong before I make my own way. But I'll toast to you for making the first move! To the Devil!" he shouted and fired his pistol into the rafters.

The room erupted in cheers. All around Bellamy men were calling his name. The tavern girl was already pouring the rum. Blackbeard, up to his old tricks, was pressing her hand down to his powder horn. Another tavern girl looked to Bellamy as if prepared to find his horn as well. He stepped over to the bar and lifted his mug.

"To the Devil!" he said.

✠ ✠ ✠ ✠

St. Croix was a Danish Island, but the Danes treated it with such indifference that it had become a foremost hideout of pirates, smugglers and all manner of lascivious dwellers of the West Indies. The place was mostly dense jungle, whose very vines, tangled in thick clumps from every available tree branch, seemed a product of the Danes' neglect.

Aboard the *Sultana* the entire crew had amassed in boisterous revelry.

After a time, Bellamy disengaged from the rest of the pirates and went off to stand at the bow of the boat. There he listened to the sound of the wind and water sweeping by and wondered how he had come to be where he was now and whether it was a blessing or a curse. In the end piracy was mostly boredom and drinking. On the faces of the men gathered around the musician, in the middle of the deck, was fatigue so obvious that it was amazing that any of them were still standing. Who would have thought that living the free and easy life could be such a toil, Bellamy mused?

Bellamy recognized Williams' heavy, languid trod on the planks. Williams' voice called out in much the same tone, "One would think that you tire of our company, by the way that you slink off to be alone."

"I have nothing but company. Even the captain's quarters is open to one and all. You will soon learn that the position of captain is that of constant service and scrutiny. Why are you here? Have you already tired of your own ship and come to covet mine?" Bellamy asked.

Williams chuckled. "I have no intention of dethroning you, in case the thought has plagued you."

Bellamy shook his head. "No. I have more pressing matters to worry over." He twisted the gold ring on his finger, one that had been taken from the finger of one of his recent captives. "I have the men. I have the weapons. God knows that I have spent plenty of time in pursuit, yet still I have no real fortune. I have only a pittance of gold, silver and jewels. I am beginning to wonder if there is indeed some kind of curse upon me," Bellamy complained.

Williams arched a brow. "*Curse?* Did I hear that right?"

"Forget it! I rave is all! The talk of the men is getting to me," Bellamy growled. His hand held onto the neck of a bottle, the same thing that propped all of them up. He brought it to his lips and sucked out enough to make his throat smolder in a satisfying manner. Then he handed the bottle to the jeweler, a courtesy that he would have offered any man who had found him there.

Williams looked drained too. His hands were finally as scarred and marked as a man's should be. What remained of his hair was as stringy as frayed rope. And his face was gray and thin, making his age stand out. Now that he saw what pirate living had done to the man, Bellamy believed that Williams' full cheeks had seemed his natural, healthy state. Despite everything, the jeweler was still smiling. His inheritance was a thousand leagues away, and Bellamy had thought that sooner or later the jeweler would grouse about his unusually empty pockets. That he hadn't only gave Bellamy more grudging respect for the man.

"I want you to take Baker, Van Vorst and his lot onto your ship," Bellamy said.

Williams gaped at him. "That will not look well upon you. The men will think that you are afraid…"

"Damn it!" Bellamy slapped the rail with his palm. "I have men plotting behind my back at every turn! I cannot keep an eye on all of them. Do not forget who gave you your ship!"

"As I recall, I gave *you* your first ship. I thought that we were past this kind of pretentious rancor," Williams said, squaring himself to Bellamy.

"Do not mock me, Palsgrave! You have no idea the pressure I am under! The men want gold! They demand that of me! As yet I have given them little of it! Take those troublemakers from me or by the Devil…"

"I shall ask the men to vote on reorganizing the crews. But you know as well as I that it is up to them. You are too suspicious. Princes often fall prey to such vice."

"I told you that I do not wish to be mocked!"

Williams sighed. "Then give them their own ship. It is what they want, isn't it?"

"The rest of the men will not vote for that. They will not see what we are trying to accomplish. They will only see Baker being elevated above them, and they will not have it."

"Then give him something to do that will take his mind off of plotting. We are not finding much in the way of gold and silver, but we have an abundance of silk, wine, rope, lumber… Such goods can be converted into coin, as you well know. Rumor has it that there are plenty of men among these islands around us who will barter for such goods. Men of similar nature as our old friend Samuel Smith," Williams said.

"And what if Baker and his followers should double-cross us and take their leave on another ship with all of the coin?"

Williams shrugged. "It seems a reasonable price to be rid of them."

"The rest of the crew will be rid of us for being cheated of their due."

"No. Baker will have made a mockery out of all of us, to a man. The crew will want his head, not ours," Williams reasoned.

Bellamy gave an unconvinced grunt. Then, from his pocket, he fished out Williams' golden locket and flashed it in front of the jeweler. "Baker at least is open in his defiance. He is not smiling to my face, all the while full of deceit…"

"What do you mean?" Williams said, an uncharacteristic waver in his voice.

"The locket was hard to pry open, but I succeeded at last," Bellamy explained, giving the jeweler a stony glare. Bellamy popped the latch, with some difficulty. His fingernails could not find the narrow seam for some time. When they did, the locket unfolded and revealed two tiny silhouettes, one on each panel, under which were written *Palsgrave* and *Abigail*.

"You are married!" Bellamy exclaimed.

Williams trembled. "I deceived you only because I was deceiving myself too."

"You know the ban on married men joining the crew as well as I do!"

"I was married before we adopted the Articles!"

"That does not matter! We are an example to rest of the men!" Bellamy dropped his voice, "*Should anyone discover this, you know what they could call for...*"

"This isn't about the Articles! I am sorry that I lied to you. Don't you understand that I am not trying to hide anything from my shipmates, only myself? Samuel... I implore you... You yourself sailed because you were inspired by love, don't you remember?"

"Hold your tongue, Palsgrave! And damn you for lording yourself over us all of the time! I should call for a meeting right now and have this out in front of the entire crew. By your birth you consider yourself above our laws!"

"I do not! I sailed to be away from rules, as did we all."

"You left your wife to come wandering around the West Indies, looking for coin that you do not need!"

"You do not know what it was like, living in that household day after day, with the expectations, the demands, the duplicity of pretending to be that which I was not! Is that not why I am here? I too am a man without a place in this world that fits him... Besides, those portraits are not of my wife and me. They are two of my children."

"*What?* That is even worse! You left your children to come out here for adventure? When you have everything that poor men dream of, at home at your fingertips! They need you!"

"I did not treat them poorly."

"You left them! You could have given them the world rather than squandering it!"

"I keep trying to tell you that having *everything* does not ensure that one will inhabit a happy world! My legacy was to be a slow death in front of a ledger book. What will yours be? Are you still a man looking to steal a piece of fortune, with a few good rolls, and return in triumph? Or is your pursuit in aim of exacting payment for all of your scars? Perhaps you will not be happy until you have revenge."

"That is not true…"

"Isn't it? What other aim did Robin Hood have if not that?"

✠ ✠ ✠ ✠

Bellamy did not divulge Williams' secret. Instead, he mused over Williams' words as the ships cruised through the Virgin Islands. He did not accept Williams' accusation that some feud against the world propelled him. The compass was still affixed firmly on elusive wealth, the dreamy promise of Spanish gold, which the West Indies had long offered. However, ship after ship held nothing of the golden promise that had brought him here, just more of the same poor contents. He tallied all of the ships that they had taken, mentally sorting through the goods that never seemed to add up to enough. In that sense, Williams was correct. To get coin for the kind of lace, spice and other articles that they were seizing, they would have to deal with the smugglers in the port towns, men as slippery and greedy as old Samuel Smith of Billingsgate. The mere idea of it made Bellamy feel cheated, in some way that he could not calculate. He imagined that, somehow, a tithe made its way back to Smith even though his mind knew that no such wide ranging syndicate existed.

Finally Bellamy and Williams steered their ships to Virgin Gorda. Once there, they anchored off of the northern end of the island, opposite the small town of inhabitants to the south. A light breeze caressed them, and Bellamy was amazed as always that the wind and sea could be so warm. There was nothing of the hard edge of his English homeland. It was like sailing in a sun-warmed rain puddle, except that it was beautiful.

The lingering heat of the evening carried the sweet smell of papaya out from the island. Here and there, through the leaves,

Bellamy saw the dark shape of a slave, picking the ripening fruit for the market on the other side of the island. The cries of warblers and mockingbirds pierced through the canopy of trees on shore. Apart from that, there was little sound or movement, and it made Bellamy nervous.

They had arrived in the morning and sent Thomas Baker, Simon Van Vorst, Hendrick Quintor and a handful of other Dutchmen ashore. The men stole some untended wagons, which they found on the beach, and used them to cart their wares inland. They went searching for the local smugglers who they had heard about from their fellow pirates in *The Red Squall.* Although Virgin Gorda was home to a small colonial government and militia, those powers were known to overlook the illicit activities that flourished on the less populated fringes of the island. At least that was the rumor. But even a tiny force of men-at-arms could pose problems to pirate operations ashore. If the government of Virgin Gorda had a change of heart, already they had been given a full day to summon the nearest warship to come and corner the *Maria* and *Sultana* in their little harbor.

Bellamy paced the deck, noting with alarm how quickly the light waned after the sun went down. As the sun sank away, a full moon rose, like a giant red-tinged coin over the far side of the island. Behind him Alfred's music jangled softly across the deck, capturing the shimmering essence of the moonlight on the water. At Bellamy's side stood several pirates, including Williams, whom Bellamy had summoned from his own ship.

"Well? The night has almost arrived, and there is no sign of them. What say you?"

Williams stared thoughtfully at a cluster of small fishing boats heading around the corner of the island. "We should not fret over this. It could have taken some time for them to locate a trading partner. Or they have completed the deal but are nervous to venture through those unknown woods in the dark. Perhaps we shall see them at first light."

"Or maybe they have double-crossed us, found another ship and have already left this island," Bellamy countered.

"Then we are rid of them," Williams said.

"No! Then men all across the West Indies will know that I can be made a fool of," Bellamy said.

"You care about such things?" Williams asked.

Bellamy glowered at the jeweler. "A loss of reputation can kill a pirate captain as surely as a bullet!"

"Ah! Now, that statement reminds me of someone we once knew..."

"I will not be undercut as we did Hornigold! Get back to your ship and wait there at anchor! I will take the *Sultana* around the bend and see what we can discover..."

Williams wandered off without protest, and Bellamy hollered for the crew of the *Sultana* to raise sail and anchor.

Not long afterwards they were drifting alongside of the island, with Bellamy drumming his fingers on the rail and scanning the wall of trees for any sight of the Dutchmen.

It was Daku who now stood next to him. The Africans had proved their mettle. They had taken up Bellamy's offer of equality and showed that they deserved it, even excelled at it. Even among pirates, Daku was something to behold. His large and powerful frame was draped with shell necklaces, bones and bottles of odd color powder, which he claimed were part of a religion meant to summon spirits and make them do his bidding. His strength and sword were enough to dissuade most of those he met in combat. Few believed that he needed any extra assistance from the unseen world.

Daku was tracing symbols in the air with his finger. He made the same motion over and over, rhythmically chanting as he did so. When he finished, he inhaled deeply and drew his sword. "I am ready."

"What were you doing?" Bellamy said with a snicker.

"The same thing I do before any fight. I ask for protection. You know Vodun?"

"No."

"Vodun is our religion, our gods. They are everywhere - in the woods, in the sea, in the sky. Mine come from the sea. My ancestor spirits. We do not forget our fathers and brothers. Not even in death."

"Ah... I don't believe in ghosts. Even if they were about, I prefer to keep my eyes fixed upon *this* world. Whatever happens next, I shall get to it in due time. For now, I have plenty to keep me busy."

"You may not care about them, but that does not mean they do not care about you! They come out when the moon is full," Daku replied.

"Are you talking of the full moon? Tis bad tidings to kill a man under a full moon," Thomas Brown broke into the conversation.

"Where the hell did you hear that?" Bellamy asked.

"Tis common knowledge."

"I was once told that sharks in the water are bad luck."

"They are!"

"Down here we catch them and eat them," Bellamy observed.

"Bad luck might catch up with us yet!" Brown cried.

"In my land we too know the curse of the moon," Daku said. "When a moon rises red and a man kills another man under that moon, then the man who kills will be cursed... Did you not see it come over the trees this night? Blood red. So I will use this only to protect myself," he went on, patting the sword that hung from his belt. "As long as I only kill to protect myself, I think that the moon will spare me."

Brown adopted a ministerial air, something that his haggard, sun-beaten face did not hold well. "You ought to listen to him, Bellamy. You've taken many a ship. We've done many a sin. It is all bound to catch up with us sooner or later."

Bellamy snorted. "As you well know, I have cheated the sea itself and not been punished by fate for it. I am satisfied with my chances."

"We have but minutes left before we won't be able to see anything, even a rock on the sea floor. At least we ought to throw anchor and not risk going aground," Brown observed, drawing a laugh from Bellamy. "I don't find wrecking on this runt of a place very funny!"

"Nor do I! I am laughing at fate, not you! Look!" He pointed up ahead at a small fishing sloop, which was quickly losing ground to the pirate ship. Even in the growing twilight, they could see the Dutchmen riding upon it.

"Damn their blood!" Brown cried. "They are swindling us!"

"Aye! But they won't succeed," Bellamy said, turning and calling out to the sailing master of the *Sultana*, William Main, to cut across the smaller ship's bow.

The Dutchmen had seen the *Sultana* bearing down on them, and they tried to tack into the shallow water near the beach. Bellamy could see Baker, Van Vorst, Quintor and several other Dutchmen yanking in the sail and keeping tight to the wind as they raced towards shore. Another man was perched in the bow, scouting for hazards on the sea bottom and calling out whenever he spied a treacherous, dark shape in their path. There was something familiar about the man, and Bellamy squinted hard but could not place him.

On shore the line of palms came into sharper focus, looking implacable as a row of fence posts on the beach. Solid ground seemed to be reeling in the *Sultana*, but it was hauling in the Dutchmen that much faster because they were closer to shore.

"It's too shallow!" Brown cried, yanking on Bellamy's arm to get his attention.

Bellamy was well aware that the water was running out beneath them. They had only a few minutes before they would be stranded and Baker and his followers safely ashore.

"Shoot them down!" Bellamy hollered at the men around him.

For a second, nobody moved. Some pirates looked away. Others looked quizzically from Bellamy to their fleeing shipmates in the little sloop before them.

"*Brown! Get the cannon loaded and send that sloop to the bottom!*" Bellamy yelled. Then turning to the others, he shouted, "They are robbing from us all! Will you let them make fools out of us?"

"Go on!" he cried at Peter Hoof and Daku, sending them after Brown to load the guns.

Over the rail, they heard Baker whooping for joy, his escape almost within reach.

"*Fire! Fire! Fire!*" Bellamy yelled, and the cannon bellowed in answer.

Two shots went wide of the little sloop but close enough to send the Dutchmen sprawling.

The next round cracked through the wooden flank of the ship. Then the *Sultana* fired again, and this time the shots all found their mark, ripping across the sloop and leaving a trail of shattered mast, rail and spars.

"She will sink fast…" Brown observed.

Beside him Bellamy did not answer. He was staring towards shore where the local militia was stepping tentatively out of the waving palm fronds and onto the beach.

Brown glanced that way too and let out a curse. "Let's be away from here! We don't want to tangle with an army!"

"They are no army. In fact, in men and arms we have four times their number. Fire away!"

Brown's expression changed to one of awe. "You intend to take over the entire island…"

The words were blasted away by an explosion, which sent the sleeping island birds squawking towards the darkened heavens. There was a flash of light, which gave an eerie glow to the shoreline, making the trees at the water's edge look ghostly. In that burst of light, Bellamy saw Baker's small boat bathed in deadly illumination. The cannon fire flew over head, tearing through the trunks and leaves of the jungle, with a meaty sound, and putting the militia to flight.

The *Sultana* dropped anchor only a few yards from where the remains of Baker's sloop was sinking into the shallow water. Miraculously, the Dutchmen were unharmed. They shot furious glances at the now empty beach on one side and the line of leering, threatening pirates on the other. But they made no effort to resist.

Bellamy nodded to Daku. "Go haul them aboard and tie them to the masts for a whipping."

"Why not just shoot them where they are in the water and let the tide be rid of them once and for all?" Brown suggested.

"No! They will not escape that easy!" Bellamy said. There were other pirates who shared Brown's opinion, and they pointed out that the Articles themselves proscribed the harshest punishment for traitors, but Bellamy overrode them all. In the end the majority of the crew came to prefer the idea of having some rough sport with the Dutchmen over killing them off.

Bellamy did not even look at the Dutchmen when they were brought back aboard the *Sultana*. Instead, he stared at the body of the man that he had seen in the bow of Baker's boat. The man who he thought he recognized. Suddenly he had clear view of the man as his body thumped up against the side of Bellamy's ship. He had died in the cannonade and floated into a watery grave. Bellamy could now see that the man was not from the pirate crew. He was a local man, probably the rightful owner of the boat, who Baker had kept aboard to act as a pilot. Bellamy could not take his eyes from the man's face. He was not mesmerized by the frozen rictus of death. Some trick of the light altered the man's features. It was no doubt a distortion produced by the gloom of twilight. But the configuration of features conjured the ghost of another long-dead man. If he had not seen his father laid into the ground some twenty years ago, he would have thought he was looking at John Bellamy himself.

Bellamy's father looked out across time and death at his son, and his recrimination was undeniable. John Bellamy had steered his son towards the sea to get him away from the kind of bloodthirsty men of power who had been the death of him. Yet here Bellamy stood with innocent blood on his hands after all. The fights had been few because so much of the prey had quickly surrendered. But he had fired guns and cannon over the rail plenty of times. Every time the smoke from his weapons cleared, Bellamy felt that a different version of himself stepped out of the haze. How many stray shots, obscured by battle smoke, had taken the lives of men who Bellamy had not even seen fall, he wondered, feeling shameful all of a sudden.

Brown's voice suddenly interrupted Bellamy's thoughts. "Daku has them. Who is going to do the whipping?" Brown asked.

"No one. Put them in the hold," Bellamy replied, his voice sounding distant and dreamy even to his own ears.

Brown glanced at the assembled pirates waiting expectantly on deck and then back at Bellamy. *"Are you sure? The men might think you've gone soft,"* Brown whispered.

"Lock them up for now," Bellamy commanded.

Brown turned and gave a nod to Daku. "Put them in irons says the captain!"

Bellamy heard the rumble of discontent sweep through the crew. Baker's voice rose above the rest, loud and defiant, calling Bellamy a coward. But Bellamy turned away from the confused faces of his crew and watched the man in the water sink slowly into the depths. A last glimpse of the face that looked like his father's. This time there was no doubt. He had killed a man. On the other side of the sky, the moon was growing to a full red bloom.

✠ ✠ ✠

For the next few weeks, the *Sultana* and *Maria* sailed aimlessly throughout the West Indies. Bellamy stood on deck amidst the puzzled looks and muttered speculation of the crew. As a constant refrain to the general confusion of the pirates, the muffled voices of Baker and his cohorts rang out below as they shouted rowdy songs, day and night, in the hold. Eventually some of the pirates on deck began laughing at the scene. Others joined in a chorus here and there.

Bellamy watched men going up and down into the hold, and he knew that they were visiting the prisoners. He found himself counting their number and studying their faces as they came and went. Increasingly, he came to imagine that most of them were sympathetic to the Dutchmen and visiting them to express their support. He knew that something had to be done. An example had to be made or else he would become a laughingstock for the entire crew.

When they reached Hispaniola and the Windward Passage, the men's bewilderment and discontent became increasingly honed and focused on the fact that no ship had been taken in quite some time. Whispers became outright grumbling. Men talked openly about the lack of prey, the empty bottles that were piling up around them and their growing lust for booty of all sorts.

Bellamy paced the deck, feeling the pressure of mutinous eyes upon his back as strongly as the wind that pushed the ship along.

Above him a massive sail shifted in the wind. Blinding sunlight cascaded upon him. He squinted through the glare at the huge expanse of cloudless sky that stretched over the ship, as big as the ocean, like a smooth reflection of the water below. Sea and sky were both empty.

He saw Thomas Brown and called him over. "What are they talking of down in the hold? Are the Dutch calling for mutiny?"

"*You should act now and stamp out this little fire lest it grow too hot,*" Brown advised.

"So they do seek to cast me out..." Bellamy said. Brown nodded in agreement. "How many mutineers?"

Brown shrugged. "It is not too late. Let me bring them up here and then show them all what you are made of."

"Alright then. Drop anchor and hail Williams and the *Maria*. And then bring the Dutchmen up."

"Aye, aye!" Brown said eagerly. He shouted out Bellamy's orders, and then called to Daku and the other Africans, who had become Bellamy's loyal guard, and the group of them hurried down below deck.

A few minutes later they returned with the Dutch prisoners. All across the ship, men stopped and watched the procession, which ended at the mainmast where Bellamy stood and glared at the pirates, one and all.

Then Bellamy turned to Baker and his followers and shouted, "What say you to the charge of trying to steal our money? Every man here owned a share of the goods that we sent you ashore to sell, yet you saw fit to take it all for yourselves! You are lucky I don't turn you over to the crew, for I am sure that you would be begging for a simple whipping from me rather than what just punishment they would give you!"

Instead of replying, Baker and the others simply stared at Bellamy. Making matters worse for Bellamy, after a brief shout of encouragement from Brown and a few others, a heavy silence enveloped the entire ship. Baker noticed it too and began to smirk.

"You think that this is amusing, do you? You are a thief, and the Articles set forth a certain punishment for those who take from their shipmates! Brown! Hand me the whip!" Bellamy cried.

Bellamy's hand was shaking as he took the whip from Brown. He felt trapped in a course of events that seemed to hurry him towards doom with every word and action. He could not figure out exactly how he had come to be caught in this web. And he could not think of a way out, other than fighting his way through. Somehow the men had turned on him. After all of the rum, coin, women and good life that Bellamy had steered them towards, his thanks was a simmering uprising. He flexed the whip, wishing that he could use it on every ungrateful cur who stood around him. He longed to call them the fools that they were. He knew that few of them could withstand the pressure of endlessly providing spoils. Yet, like spoiled children, they rebelled, with the mad notion that they could find better fortune by blindly drifting off on their own.

"Thomas Baker! In the spirit of the Articles that bind us all together, I charge you and your supporters with treason against your brethren! For that, you shall be whipped and put off of this boat at the next island!"

To Bellamy's dismay, the Dutchman started chuckling. "I would be content to take a whipping if it gets me off of this ship so I might find a *real* captain, a real pirate, to sail with rather than the spineless coward we have in charge."

"Damn my blood, you have a crooked tongue, you traitorous rogue! We shall see if you find me so soft after I have laid the whip into you a few score times! Perhaps that will silence you!"

Baker leered balefully at Bellamy. "Then before I loose my voice, I call for a vote! For a new captain!"

"Damn you!" Bellamy roared, striking Baker across the face. "There is spine in that, wouldn't you say?" He raised the whip to strike, but he stopped when a familiar deep voice rang out and hit Bellamy like a musket shot.

"Wait a moment, Bellamy! A vote has been called!"

Bellamy was so shocked that words momentarily escaped him. But Palsgrave Williams went on to say, "I too am a captain here. Remember, Bellamy, that we hold these posts only by the good grace and judgment of our fellow brethren. We are not lords entitled to our titles and power. That's why we have the Articles, is it not?"

Amidst the widespread cheering of the crew, Bellamy whispered to the jeweler, *"All of this time I have been worrying about the Dutchmen when I should have been worrying about you! I assumed that you and I had become as close as kin. But it seems that our friendship is worth less to you than your pride and revenge!"*

"I admit that I was hurt by your recent treatment of me, but this is not about revenge, Bellamy. This is about preserving the freedom that we preach," Williams replied.

"You are just hiding behind more lies, Williams! It seems to me that you crave the entitlement that you left behind in Newport. Now you shall be the hero and the leader of this crew."

"No, I will vote for you because I will always be your friend," Williams said, laying a hand on Bellamy's shoulder.

"Let's vote then, damn you all!" Bellamy cried, casting Williams hand off of him as he strode to the middle of the deck where he began to clean his pistols and pack them with powder.

Chapter Nine
"Bird of Paradise"

February 24, 1717

The handle of his pistol felt solid in Sam Bellamy's hand. But he would only have a couple of shots before dozens of armed men turned on him. "Save at least one bullet, should you ever be voted off of the ship," Hornigold had once advised him. Dethroned pirate captains were usually marooned on some uninhabited island where the last shot was a mercy from a wasting illness or starvation.

All across the deck, men were cheering, cursing and arguing. Thomas Baker was shouting louder than the rest, making his case, "I am tired of stealing rope and trinkets! Perhaps we need a new hand on the tiller of this ship! Bellamy has had plenty of chances, but this *Prince* is a Prince of Paupers! We know that the Spanish haul endless amounts of gold and treasure through these waters. It is out there!"

"We've found plenty of rum, and also some coin here and there! It is only bad luck that we have found no great treasures!" Thomas Brown shouted back.

"Then we need a man in charge who luck favors. I call for a vote for a new captain! Me or him!" Baker said. "Who's for me, then?"

Many hands rose. There were too many hands to count, too many faces to remember, too many men to curse, thought Bellamy.

"You as well?" Bellamy cried when he saw Thomas Brown's hand lift up.

"*Ship!*" Brown responded.

Before Baker could complete the vote, half the crew was rushing to the rail. Bellamy followed them, his spyglass searching the wide swath of blue until it came to rest on a distant vessel.

Even from afar Bellamy was impressed. He swung the spyglass hard into the gut of the man next to him, and one by one, the pirates had a look at their quarry.

"Well then? Is this not a bit of good luck? A fine ship on the horizon!" He could hear the voices changing, the excitement coming into them.

Before Baker could speak, Bellamy roared, "Who will follow me?"

Men sprang to the lines, and the *Sultana* cut deftly towards her prey.

"This is not over!" Baker warned, struggling futilely to loosen the ropes that bound him.

"You can stay there and enjoy the view, tailor! We are heading towards a fight, and I am still your captain!" Bellamy snarled.

For the next two days, Bellamy kept his position as captain of the *Sultana*. All that while, the *Maria* and *Sultana* stalked the large, swift galley that fled before them.

Her power and stamina was like that of a racehorse, and although the pirate ships were light and speedy, Bellamy feared that she would outlast them and finally escape into the deeper ocean where he dared not follow.

Slowly, the pirates gained ground until they were close enough to observe the ship in all of her splendor. She was magnificent. One hundred feet long and three hundred tons in size.

Bellamy walked among his men. His own energy had revived. It was the finest ship he'd ever seen. Behind the outer plank what treasures might she hold, he wondered? How far did he dare dream?

As they got closer, Bellamy instinctively began counting the square cannon hatches in the hull of the fleeing ship. Nine. And that was just on one side. He could also see a number of small swivel cannon mounted on the rail. She was not only a fast ship, but she had teeth as well. He called for two shots to be fired across the fleeing ship's bow and waited to see how the prey would react to the little show of bluster.

Then he could see men from the fleeing ship clambering up the mainmast. A flag rose slowly from somewhere below them. At first he thought it was the St. George's cross and that it was twisted in the wind so that the red cross was obscured. Now he could see it plainly, but he did not believe his eyes. It was solid white. They were giving up.

Cheers began on either side of him. But what if it is a trap, Bellamy mused?

The guns worried him. Once they were alongside, the galley could shred the *Sultana* at point blank range with bristling cannon fire. It could not be this easy.

Then the ship before them was slowing down. They were loosening the sails and angling slightly into the wind.

A small plaque was nailed onto the stern. Bellamy said the name to himself, *Whydah*. There was a certain music to it.

Then, unbelievably, the ship pulled its cannon back. They would not fight.

"The cowards are through!" one of the pirates screamed. The cheering grew to a roar.

"Give them a show, lads!" Bellamy cautioned. "We still have to give them a show so they don't change their minds!" The men cheered again, raising their cutlasses and pistols. Baker had gotten someone to untie him, and he came up beside Bellamy.

"If it is a trap, then you are leading us to our deaths!" he said.

Bellamy looked into the Dutchman's face. "A short life and a merry one… Isn't that what I've often heard you say?"

Contempt spread across Baker's face. "Our vote has not yet been finished," he warned and moved away into the throng of pirates at the rail.

It was no trap. The *Whydah* swung into irons, lowered sail and was neatly pinned between the ships of Bellamy and Palsgrave Williams, like a great stag cornered by a pack of dogs.

The pirates surged aboard their prize, and the captives were soon disarmed and lined up in the stern.

Bellamy felt a tug on his sleeve and turned to look into Brown's worried face. "This is a slave ship. If it's all Negroes in the hold, then we don't make shit. We'll just end up with a hundred new crew to feed."

Brown did not notice that Daku, the African pirate, had come up behind him until he was cuffed on the side of the head by a large, dark hand. "I should put *you* in the hold of this ship and see how you like it! Nothing to eat, the water is dark and foul, men shit on their beds, they sleep in chains. And to you they are worth nothing?"

"Easy my friend…" Brown replied.

The next thing Bellamy knew, Daku and a small cadre of stern faced Africans had gone below deck to scout out the rest of the vessel and round up any stragglers. Bellamy watched them with trepidation, praying that none of their countrymen were below. He did not want any more revenge or bloodshed.

To distract himself, he strode over to the captured captain. "And you are?"

"Captain Prince," the man replied curtly.

"Good evening, Captain Prince. I trust that you are enjoying this endlessly warm weather?" Bellamy said, keeping an ear cocked to the sounds of his men foraging below.

Prince inhaled deeply as if trying to summon his frayed patience. "What is to become of us?"

"I am insulted, Captain. Will you not discuss the weather with me? I thought that the English captain class was the model of civility."

"In a civil world that is true."

"A civil world? Such as one that peddles in human traffic? One that enslaves the poor at home, to grind out fortunes for their masters, on their captive land? Yes, I see now where I was mistaken. This piracy of ours is nothing but sheer barbarism," Bellamy sneered.

"And what would you call your methods? Nobility? Restitution?"

"Fairness."

Prince fell silent. He was smoldering. His first mate shuffled nervously.

"The *Whydah*? What is the meaning of that name?"

"To the Africans, it means *The Paradise Bird*."

"Very appropriate. She is a beauty. So why didn't you run?"

Prince stared at Bellamy coldly. "If you weren't my captor, I'd not deign to explain my rationale."

"But I insist," Bellamy said. He was growing hot. Why were they all like this, he wondered? So arrogant. He was becoming furious at Prince for reviving his old anger at merchant captains.

"Very well. You have two ships and more men than I. If it came to a fight, I did not like my chances. As for escape, I did not think that the newness of my vessel favored me. I did not want to risk taking her into open water at full speed."

"You jest!"

Prince bit his lip and squinted his eyes in malice. "I am sure that I do not."

"Captain Prince, I may be your adversary, but I am not some simpleton or barbarian. I am a captain same as you." Bellamy ignored Prince's condescending scowl. "Let us drink to the shared life of the sea, like the sailors that we are. I am in no mood for strife today. We both just want to be on our separate ways. I don't plan to do anything with you, if it eases your mind. You are a pack of rascals and lackeys to me, and the quicker you are out of my sight, the better. In fact, you and your crew are free to go as soon as you like. And since I am in such a jolly mood, I am even going to give you the *Sultana*, for you to sail away on."

"*What?*" Prince exclaimed. "You are keeping the *Whydah?*"

Bellamy laughed. "Of course! The *Sultana* has served me well, but the *Whydah* is too fine a ship to pass up. She will be the envy of all other pirate crews!"

Suddenly Daku emerged from the hold. His face was twitching as if it was trying to simultaneously hold fury and delight.

"There are no men down here. They have been sold, and what is left is the payment for them!" he glared at Prince and his crew.

"What is left?" Bellamy demanded.

Daku smiled. "Come see…"

✠ ✠ ✠ ✠

What followed was like a waking dream to Bellamy. The images were fractured, fleeting things – watching his boots descending into the hold… hearing the celebration of the men who were deeper than he into the cargo area… looking in one direction and seeing a room filled with bales of silk… looking in the other direction and seeing piles of pale white ivory horn…

Already his heart was accelerating to match the pace of his hurried steps.

A hand landed upon his shoulder. "Not in a hundred years did I think that this would be happening to me!" Thomas Brown said, before being pulled away by a gang of reveling pirates who needed help prying open boxes that, when opened, spewed forth a rush of sugar.

Slow and dream-like, Bellamy followed Daku deeper into the hold. The big African was whistling a strange, haunting, altogether foreign, tune. If Bellamy closed his eyes, he might have thought himself in a dark jungle, cutting through a thin, leafy trail rather than stepping through rows of towering crates and boxes.

Beside him he heard Williams chuckling with delight and disbelief. He heard men's footsteps running down the opposite side of the vessel and voices howling in glee. One pirate walked rapidly along the row of cannon, counting each one as he passed, the man's mad giggling becoming increasing unrestrained as the number climbed higher and higher.

Bellamy could not believe it. The *Whydah* was a dream ship... *Could she be real?*

Daku brushed past another throng of boisterous pirates, and Bellamy followed, nodding to his shipmates, accepting slaps on the back, doling out his own although he knew not exactly what for.

Then he saw a group of pirates standing over casks filled with luminous powder, the cracked lids at their feet. They were clawing into the barrels, gold dust sparkling on their hairy arms.

A strong forearm suddenly blocked Bellamy's passage. Daku stopped and held Bellamy in place. He nodded at an open doorway next to them.

"See in there? This is where they made the slaves sleep," Daku snarled.

Bellamy peered into a murky chamber, the walls of which were filled with planks fitted as close together as shelves in some store keeper's shop.

"Aye. At least the profit of their suffering will not line some rich man's pockets," Bellamy said.

"But that does not help them now, does it?" Daku replied.

"Well... We cannot save everyone," Bellamy said and turned away from the look of challenge in Daku's eyes.

The next room ahead seemed to radiate golden light of its own accord although Bellamy knew that it had to be the illumination of some lantern. Yet some kind of spell emanated from the place, and he brushed past Daku to inspect it more closely.

Bellamy stepped across the threshold and nearly staggered. Wall to wall, row after row stood the glittering fantasy of all freebooters... Pieces of eight, sacks of gold coin, gold and silver bars stacked with neat precision. Bellamy dropped to his knees and pressed the coins against his face, feeling victory in their solid touch. They were cold, hard, bright and so very, very real.

It was a payload beyond any fantasy. The *Whydah* carried twenty-thousand pounds worth of coins as well as bags full of indigo dye, Jesuit's bark and piles of elephant tusks. The gold and coins would be divided by Williams into one hundred and eighty sacks of equal shares, one for each pirate. But for now, the coins rained around Bellamy and his cohorts as they showered themselves with their loot, some men rolling through the piles and laughing until they had tears in their eyes.

For a brief moment Bellamy felt the hot pressure of tears welling as he thought of the long, twisting course that had brought him to this point, from the disappointment of Florida and Honduras to the apprenticeship with Hornigold to ship after ship with nothing but rope in the hold, through scurvy, death and blaring headaches in the morning sun… Mostly he thought of the long, long nights and the days slipping off of the calendar. He had paid with his time, maybe with more than that if there was not a certain girl waiting back in Eastham for him. Bellamy stared at the coins and wondered if it was indeed time to go back to Cape Cod.

✠ ✠ ✠ ✠

The hold of the *Whydah* was something of a princely place with its wide beams and long length of open hull, creating a space that was cathedral-sized compared to the tight decks of the ships that Bellamy was used to. The fact that it had been created to hold men against their will did nothing to diminish its grandeur. There was little sign of that, anyway, since the men of Bellamy's crew had ripped out the crude, cramped bed slats where the slaves had been shackled.

Bellamy stood within a ring of light that projected downwards from the brass lantern that swung over head. The light cast by the lantern spread flickering illumination upon a pile that needed nothing to add to its shine. The effect of the arcing light was to make the coins and gems radiate with almost unbearable luster. In his mind Bellamy had always expected the gleam of treasure to be like a glimpse of a heavenly world. There was some of that feeling, to be sure, but there was also a hard cast to the reflection, which hit his eye like a knife.

Bellamy ran a finger through the pile and listened to its satisfying clink. If one did not look at the glittering mass showing at the top, the bags were similar to plump field sacks that could have been as easily filled with wheat as the stolen fruits of empire. Part of Bellamy noted that the money had likely not been honestly gained to begin with. If nothing else, it had been minted from the sweat of the poor and swindled by the idle lords above them. Yet he was not sure anymore that these men he sailed with were an improvement over any other kind.

Pirate Prince. He felt suddenly ashamed that he had ever taken such a title, or rather, that he had ever let men call him such. Once he had been a simple farm boy looking to the blue horizon for justice and advancement. Then he had been a newly elevated captain, hoping only to keep those in his command happy and satisfy meager dreams of wealth. He became Robin Hood after that, the simple acts of debauchery raised to something noble. Finally he had become nobility itself, and he could think of nothing that disgusted him more.

Bellamy's thoughts were sailing ahead of him, covering the leagues that he hoped would pass by quickly. Cape Cod. Never before had it seemed like such an alluring paradise. Williams would be the only one who knew of his true intentions. The rest could give him as much hell as they could muster when they learned of his plan. He didn't care. He would swim ashore if he had to, floating his share in behind him. For a brief second he was amazed to realize that even the gold didn't much matter to him anymore. Maria herself was more treasure than he could have plundered in a lifetime. However, he could not even picture Maria's face in all of its detail without some effort of mind. Too quickly it washed away, like the swing of lantern light, then he was back to darkness, with a bottle in hand, boastful songs that none outside of their little floating kingdom would prize and a long stretch of sea running through his mind, like a dream that would not end.

He wondered how much payment it would take to keep Samuel Smith quiet about how the treasure was gained. Would the elders of Eastham accept his sudden rise without question or intrigue? Would Maria leave her childhood home as readily as he had? Their talk of leaving had been one thing, but the doing of it was quite another.

Then there was the worst possibility of all: that she had taken another's hand in his absence. He drew up a pinch of coins and let them fall back into the bag, one by one, imagining them as days falling away. When his fingers were empty, he had accounted for little more than a week. The depth of the entire bag might come closer to the time that he had lost in parting from the girl, and the bag looked enormous at the moment.

Perhaps he deserved to be alone with his money, sharing it only with drunks, harlots and greedy tavern owners. He knew he was not the man who had left Maria with nothing more than promises. He did not know if the man who was returning was better or worse. The fact that he was returning to keep his word, no matter how tainted he had become in the process, had to count for something.

There was a rustle behind Bellamy, and he forced a smile and called out over his shoulder, "Who is there skulking in the shadows? Do not fear! Though I am a pirate, I am no thief! Your share is safe if that is what you've come to check on!"

He spun around, smirking at his joke and expecting to see the grin of one of his shipmates. Instead, he saw a humorless look, which brought all of his inner debate into sharp focus. Thomas Davis. A Welsh carpenter who the pirates had forced to join them because of his skill with the hammer.

"Damn you, Davis! What business have you sneaking up on me like a rat in the hold?" Bellamy sputtered. He had a notion to reach for one of his weapons, but the Welshman had never shown any sign of fighting. Bellamy did not think any defense was warranted. But until he was safely back in Eastham with his treasure, he did not intend to underestimate anyone. He was too close to success to risk losing everything now. He kept one hand upon one of the pistols that hung from his belt, his fingers drumming anxiously upon the handle, as he watched Davis approach.

"This is the result of your *labors*..." Davis said, his dark eyes passing by Bellamy and fastening onto the mound of loot.

"Aye. Tis work hunting it down too. I spent nearly two years collecting naught but lumber, trinkets and the likes of you before I was rewarded."

"May your reward sustain you, then."

"It shall! Damn your tongue for what you are really saying to me!" Bellamy replied. Despite the man's misplaced righteousness, Davis was a likeable fellow. The two were of similar background, and Bellamy had the sense that they might have been fast friends had they met in other circumstances.

Bellamy smiled. "The quartermaster has cut you a share." He patted one of the plump bags. "'Tis half your weight in gold," he added.

"I want none of it. I will not be bought and bound to you. Freedom is all I've asked for."

"Freedom!" Bellamy exploded. "This ship is its standard bearer! We are a new society of free men without flag or country! Are you so daft not to see it?"

Davis shook his head. "I've heard that dream spun out from your lips many a night. I see no new society here. It is the same face of the ancient sins of sloth and thievery and idolatry and murder and…"

"Shut up!" Bellamy shouted. His fist clenched out of habit, but his anger was burning away. There would be no more violence.

"Your ears cannot hear the truth! You say you are out to change the world into a better place? Is that why you sail to and fro, fleecing what ships come under your guns?" Davis' face shook. He was a fool, but no coward, Bellamy noted.

"*Shut up…* We may indulge in some of those sins, but the men who rule the world you long to return to have them mastered. Whatever pimp of a parson told you such drivel no doubt has a whore on the side. Let the man who is stain free dole out such judgment, and then I might listen a while."

"You promised that you would release me on the next ship that was seized, yet I remain here among you and your men," Davis went on, in a quiet and accusatory tone.

"I am truly sorry for that! It was the crew, not me, who voted to keep you aboard. I must abide by their vote, for we all have an equal say."

"So we are all equal, but we are not all free."

Bellamy was going to recite more lines about the injustice of the world, the suffering at the hands of hypocrites and lazy frauds, the downtrodden's miserable fate, the liberation he offered, man by man. But it all sounded too much like trumpets bleating out a march song. His words tasted as sour as the criticism Davis was giving him.

Davis gave a tiny sardonic smile. "Yes, why should you listen? You are the mighty Pirate Prince."

"I sailed only to find this!" Bellamy said and swung his sword over Davis' head and sent it crashing into one of the bags. The canvas rent neatly apart, and a line opened and drooped down, like a mouth hanging drunkenly ajar, spewing out a rush of gold.

"I will put you ashore when we next make port, as I promised. For I am finished," he added. Then, realizing the folly of the statement, he pressed the sharp edge of the blade against the carpenter's throat. "Repeat one word of that to anyone and your neck will be as neatly cut as that bag, and it will bleed a much different color!"

Boom! Boom! Boom!

The shots were muffled by the wood over head but there were many. *An attack*, Bellamy wondered?

He raced to the stairs and up onto the deck. He looked wildly to and fro, expecting to see some ship that had snuck up upon them, enemies swinging over the rail or even a full scale mutiny directed by Baker's hand.

Instead, he saw a deck full of reveling pirates. There were, of course, the usual drinking contests, games of dice and mock sword fighting. But this evening all of those regular amusements were infused with more zest and joy than ever before. Here and there groups of pirates stomped out crude country dances, which soon disintegrated into a collision of stumbling, laughing drunks. Others linked arms around each other's shoulders and swayed as they warbled out the chorus of all manner of lewd and victorious songs. Others fired off their pistols into the sky.

By the foremast the musician Alfred stood in front of an extra sail that had been hung up between the shrouds. It was painted with a crude scene of a shoreline bluff skirted by ocean waves upon which two ships rode. In front of this backdrop, a dozen pirates gathered around Alfred. They were draped in the rich colored silks and shawls that were part of the treasure.

Alfred drew his sword and shouted, "Grovel for me, Captain Prince, for I am the Pirate Prince, and the *Whydah* is now mine!"

Another pirate, wearing a stolen officer's jacket, growled and thumped Alfred hard in the chest. "To the Devil with you! If you want my ship, let's see you take it!"

"No! Those are not the words!" Alfred complained. Then, seeing Bellamy, his face lit up. "Ah! It is the *real* Pirate Prince! We are preparing a play, good Captain, to commemorate our dramatic seizure of this treasure! Tonight we shall perform it for the crew!"

"Well done," Bellamy said with little enthusiasm.

Boom! Boom! Boom!

Bellamy turned towards the stern of the ship, expecting to see more pirates discharging their guns in victory.

Boom!

The next shot whizzed past him, with a trail of hot wind, and punched into the rail behind him, with a splintering crack of wood.

Suddenly he realized that the great throng of pirates in the stern was not celebrating at all. Four members of the crew lay dead in their blood, and a half-dozen more men were writhing from wounds. Guns and swords were poised in all directions. Men cursed, shoved and beat upon one another.

"That one had extra gold in his pocket. He was taking more than his share!" Brown was screaming, pointing at one of the dead men.

"And whose share did he pinch it from? How do we know that you aren't skimming coins off the bags too?" Van Vorst shouted back.

"Because I just heard *him* telling his friends that he was pinching coins from the bags!"

"I say we bring all the bags up here right now and count every damned last one!" Van Vorst cried.

"Enough!" Bellamy shouted, heading towards the men. By the time that he reached the outer ring of the throng, another melee broke out in the center.

Boom! Boom!

Shouts, curses and cries rang out, and the entire mass of men pushed outward, throwing Bellamy backwards.

At once, a chorus of recriminations and protests broke out. A few more men grappled, and suddenly a fresh wave of violence swept through the ship. The fight swelled beyond all words or reason. For a moment Bellamy feared that the battle might consume the entire crew, dispatching them as effectively as a volley from a navy warship. Then he had an idea.

He turned and raced back below deck, flipped open a few of the cannon hatches and rolled the muzzles of the guns out through the holes. The guns were always kept loaded to be ready for use at a moment's notice. Bellamy thought that they had never been needed more so than now as he touched a torch to the flame in one of the swinging lanterns and then set it to the wicks of the guns.

BOOM! BOOM! BOOM!

The cannon fire rocked the ship, and when Bellamy reappeared on deck, the fighting had ceased. The crew stood in place, looking sober and chastised.

For a moment there was no noise but the groaning of the wounded. Bellamy held his tongue and let them all listen to the sound of their deadly folly. Then he demanded, "Is this what a pile of gold gets us? Every man's share will take years to spend, and yet we kill each other over a pocketful of coin? You are a bunch of filth and vermin if you wage war on each other for pennies! The greedy lords of the land would be proud of the likes of you butchers!"

"Well said!" Brown shouted. "If anyone else doubts the Pirate Prince…"

"Enough!" Bellamy roared. "Let whoever wants to count his coin go below. The rest can help wash the stains off the deck. Whoever killed a man, I hold you responsible for trussing him up in proper burial sheets and throwing him overboard! And throw his gold overboard too! God knows we should not split up such blood money!"

He glared at them, to see if anyone would protest. But none made a sound.

"We have paid with too much blood already," he added, to himself as much as the rest of them.

✠ ✠ ✠ ✠

Fog enveloped the boat, but it did little to muffle the sound of the screaming. Nor did the rum, which was usually so reliable for softening the edges of life.

Peter Hoof poured the liquid down the throat of Roger Balfour, one of the injured pirates, while four other men held him still.

"You are the best man with a saw," Bellamy had told Davis moments earlier.

"But you are the better butcher," Davis replied.

"Go perform your duties!" Bellamy said, pushing the carpenter towards the wounded man.

Davis drew the saw blade across Balfour's shattered arm, wishing that he had not had the misfortune of having to ply his trade on living flesh.

"Gather around me, men! I believe that we were in the midst of a vote not too long ago!" Bellamy cried out. The wind shifted and mist cleared like a curtain, revealing dark stains on the deck and splintered wood from stray shots. If he squinted, it did not take much imagination for Bellamy to see the shattered remains of his fate, should he stay too long in this trade. Sooner or later he would encounter a ship with more guns and determination than he and his pirates, assuming the pirates did not kill each other first.

He called for Baker, but the Dutchman did not emerge from the crowd. Bellamy did not feel like gloating at the moment. "Is there any man who would set himself against me as captain?"

Aside from Balfour's screaming, there was no response.

Then Bellamy urged them to set a course for Cape Cod, to find a New England smuggler who might offer them better prices than the thieves who conducted trade in the West Indies and to enjoy their gold for a moment before heading onward to wherever the wind might take them.

"We are too spent and half-mad with this never ending sea and sun to enjoy our gold! Let us rest if nothing else!" Bellamy concluded.

He had the gold. Now he had to find some purpose for it. Otherwise, he would end up like the fools whom he sailed with, waiting for the day that disease, cannon ball or some drunken pirate's cutlass was the end of him. All of it was but grim theater. It was time to bring down the curtain, he decided.

Most of the men were sober now, no matter how much they had been drinking. Some, like Williams, returned to the *Maria*, the second ship of the pirate fleet. The old jeweler was now a much admired captain. In his own unusual and gentlemanly way, he had won the respect of the hardened veterans under him and formed a crew that often seemed more easy and jovial than his own, Bellamy thought bitterly. Bellamy longed to serve under his old friend, like the rest of the happy drunks. He would likely be much better for it. Captaincy was fine for a spell, but when that spell wore off, it left a hangover the likes of which he had never felt before.

"If you look over at me once more, you will be cutting your own arm off next!" he yelled at Davis.

The carpenter's gaze deflected away, and Bellamy cursed. He had the gold. There was no need for violence. He had the gold...

Chapter Ten
"The Cursed Sea"

For the next week Sam Bellamy thought only of the hazards that lay between him and his destination. He gave wide berth to Bermuda and any other place that might cause him bitterness on the journey back. All of the months he had spent keeping out of reach of the roving Spanish and English warships should have annealed him to any fear of what lay ahead. Yet there was a weakness growing in his mind. Little things like sudden gales or rocks that just missed the ship's bottom gave him shivers worse than any combat he had experienced. Each seemed a portent of larger disaster looming. A bullet that grazed his jacket seemed a promise of future debt to pay. He dreamed of sea creatures like the one that had washed up with him that first day in Eastham. In his dream he and it were coupled together by eternal fate, bound together by some curse. Only the fact that he was nearly constantly drunk kept him from feeling chased by madness. When he was not inebriated, even the sudden snap of sail over head made his shoulders clench.

Each ship on the horizon was cause for new misery, a forced habit that worsened his guilt. As his shipmates cheered, he felt only hollowness in his gut at this duty that had become a burden. He had to admit now that luck might hide fate under its capricious gifts. If that were true, then one day or another, fate would want what was owed. The only question was how it would extract payment.

A week later the *Whydah* and the *Maria* anchored briefly off the coast of Virginia. Palsgrave Williams and Bellamy stood side by side on the deck of the *Whydah*, waiting for a party of the men to repair the rudder of the *Maria*. For some time they did not speak.

After a while Bellamy fished around in the pockets of his red vest and withdrew the locket that he had once won from Williams. He handed it to Williams and said, "I accused you of hypocrisy, Palsgrave, but in the end it seems as though you have remembered yourself better than I."

Williams solemnly took the locket and put it around his neck. "We came down here to make ourselves anew, didn't we? I know better than most what labor is required to fashion featureless metal into something exquisite. It always takes flame and perseverance," he mused, fingering the locket around his neck. "We have made something to behold, but I find myself thinking more and more about what we left behind."

"Aye. Me too."

The terrain of the land next to them looked foreign after all of their time in the tropics. Even though it was closer to the kind of land that each had spent the bulk of his life in, the thick pine trees and heavy shingled houses seemed cold and hard compared to the paradise of easy living.

When the crew voted to go to Cape Cod, Williams began thinking seriously about the comforts of his Newport home, for the first time a long while. His skin was hard and brown from adventure but, underneath, his bones felt brittle. A man of his years should be tending to his children, not sailing among child-age ruffians and acting out a perpetual youth. It was an unpleasant thought at first, a kind of defeat. But as the days stretched bright and unyielding towards the horizon, the idea of going home grew pleasantly, and soon he did not think he could stomach another taste of stale biscuit or swig of rum. Nonetheless, he was wise enough to keep drinking in front of the crew.

"My son is but twelve years old. I have had some of my captains, that is, the captains once in my employ, suggest that he will be old enough to serve before the mast in but two years. Two years... nearly the same length of time as we have been away," Williams mused.

Bellamy watched a pair of fishermen working on the small river that fed into the inlet in which the pirates were moored. The fishermen cast wary glances at the pirate ships but made no move to stop what they were doing. Their ambivalence was a relief to Bellamy, for he wanted to savor the last moments of this pirate life, with as much peace as was possible. It felt like a dream that was burning away in the morning sun.

"It seemed like a full lifetime down there in the West Indies," Bellamy remarked.

"Let us hope that our time is not finished because of it. I would like to live to see that lad of mine grown."

"And he will become a money lender and jeweler like his father?"

"Perhaps. That is his decision. I could not take that choice from him and consider myself an honorable man," Williams said.

The jeweler's steady hand clamped down on Bellamy's shoulder. "Were he to grow into a man like you, I would not be displeased at all. For a while it seemed that your dice would bounce off of the board itself, but you gambled well, my friend. You pulled it off."

Bellamy nodded gratefully. "That deserves a toast. But for once we have no bottle."

"No matter. It might be good for us to take a break from the bottle."

Bellamy frowned. "However we decide to celebrate, I shall thank you properly for setting me on this course. Without you, there would have been no voyage to Florida. I would not have been able to now afford my own mansion!"

"Yes, well... *I'm sure you would have found your way to the same place eventually*," Williams mumbled bashfully.

"So you are not coming back to visit old Samuel Smith?"

"Perhaps one day I will. But I cannot say when."

Bellamy nodded but said nothing. There was no need for comment. He understood perfectly. They were like two men coming to their senses after sitting too long at a table, rolling dice.

A group of women had come down to wash laundry in the running river and both men watched them for a while. The water curled around the women's ankles as if trying to sweep them away. Bellamy wondered if any of them ever dreamed of getting drawn into that stream's pull. He thought it strange and even funny that none of them likely had any idea of the far, distant places to which the water could carry them.

"Don't make the mistake that I did, Samuel. I ran away from my life, in order to hide in the waves. You are returning gloriously to love. That will be your next adventure."

"Even marriage?"

"It might work for some... As long as they are not marrying solely for political alliance," Williams chuckled.

Bellamy sighed. "They say that the sea is the place where a man loses his memory," he said, recalling what Daku had once told him.

"Yet you still remember why you came out on the sea. That is a powerful sign if you now believe in such notions."

Instead of answering, Bellamy looked into the distance. All around them the sky was dark and ominous, winds swirling as if in a cauldron coming to boil. It is just foul weather, he told himself. Nothing more than random weather.

☧ ☧ ☧ ☧

They seized five ships between Virginia and Rhode Island. As each vessel appeared on the horizon, Bellamy felt an invisible noose tighten around his neck.

Three of the five vessels carried rum or wine, but such drinks tasted suddenly bitter to Bellamy. Perhaps Palsgrave was right, he thought. He glanced around to make sure that he was not being observed, and then he dumped the contents of his bottle over the rail into the waves below.

He thought of the tall dunes of the Cape and it gave him hope. If he could make it within sight of the peninsula and the steeple of the Eastham meeting house, then he would be fine, he thought. *No more distractions.* It was time to head home. It startled him to hear the word *home* in his head. For the first time it seemed like he had finally found the place where he belonged. It was not at sea or in the tropics but in a non-descript hamlet full of feuding farms and fishermen where his girl was waiting.

The sixth prize, the *Mary Anne*, was loaded with Madeira wine. The small crew of the puny bark quickly raised what looked like a tattered, gray handkerchief to the top of the mast. Apparently, they had no white cloth to signal their surrender.

"Take it!" Bellamy said to Thomas Baker, knowing what the man's question would be as the Dutchman came to stand at his elbow.

"She'll do," Baker grumbled.

"Just remember that you are not officially captain until there is a vote! After your betrayal, I doubt that will occur! For now, I think most of us would agree that there is merit in simply getting you out of our sight for a while!" He felt no need to humiliate the mutineers, simply for the sake of his pride. There was a fifty pound sack of coin in the hold that pushed all thought of revenge from his mind.

The Dutchman's face darkened. "I heard Nickerson say that you worked for this fellow we're going to meet on Great Island... Smith... Is this some kind of plot? Are you and your friend planning to cheat us of our gold?"

"No."

"Well, I might linger off shore, with my share of the gold, while you deal with the smugglers. Don't worry. If any warships sneak up on us, I'll be sure to come fetch you."

"Take your lot with you. Van Vorst, Quintor, South, Shuan... And Hoof and Brown as well," Bellamy snapped.

Baker scowled at hearing the last two names, men loyal to Bellamy, but he could not hide his general excitement. He strode away, snapping commands. For a brief moment Bellamy thought of himself as a sire of pirates in the fashion of Hornigold. He wondered if the old pirate was dead and if Blackbeard or Lebous still sailed the waters or lay somewhere underneath them.

As the boarding party rowed over to the *Mary Anne*, a storm flared up as if in rebuttal to Bellamy's hope that Cape Cod would soon be his sanctuary.

When they set sail again, Bellamy had a fleet of ships. Baker took the latest ship, that of Captain Andrew Crumpstey of Dublin. The captured captain and most of his Irish crew were taken aboard the *Whydah* as prisoners. A handful of captives were left aboard with Baker to help the pirates learn the rigging of the new ship. Forty pirates sailed with Williams on the *Maria*. The bulk of the men, some one hundred and fifty, remained on the *Whydah*, along with the treasure.

The storm drove into them, and the ships departed too quickly, before their captains had a chance to share their collective knowledge of the formidable channels of Cape Cod and Nantucket Sound. Williams slipped behind the rest of the fleet and hugged the coast that he knew well from his youth in nearby Rhode Island. When the pummeling wind and waves threw him back, he eventually decided to wait out the storm on Block Island, home of his mother and cousins. Baker also knew the area well, having been a longtime resident of New York. His expertise had made it easy for Bellamy to justify giving him the *Mary Anne*. But he too quickly fell behind the swiftly flying *Whydah*. Bellamy's choice was not to wait, but to outrun the storm. He plowed into the swirling thickness of it and hoped that his fleet was right behind him.

A giddiness came over him when the flat lip of Cape Cod's underarm broke through the rainy mist, like light shining under a door. They were only off the coast of Yarmouth, still sixty miles and a treacherous turn around Cape Cod's elbow away from Eastham. Then they had to slip around the outer arm into the safety of Cape Cod Bay and Billingsgate.

Bellamy laughed. They were almost there. The big galley headed back out to sea to cut around the spit at Chatham, the elbow of the Cape. They would lose sight of land momentarily, but Bellamy was not worried as long as the *Whydah* kept outrunning the black clouds.

✠ ✠ ✠ ✠

April 26, 1717 – Night

As the *Whydah* lay anchored at the southern tip of Cape Cod, rain coursed down the masts and across the deck. The furious wind made the lines and sails snap and wail. Bellamy stood in the stern, wishing that he had drunk some of the captured wine. He could take a break from drinking after the gale had passed. All around him was a misty veil behind which the storm growled. The tumultuous weather had stirred up all of those thoughts of fate that had grown on him over the past months. Of all the times for a gale to strike, could it be pure chance, he wondered?

"I've heard about this coast of Cape Cod! There are shoals beneath these waves that could wreck even as fine a ship as the *Wolf of the Sea!*" John Lambert, the pilot, cried into Bellamy's ear.

Wolf of the Sea. It was the nickname that the men had taken to calling the *Whydah*. Right now, however, as the vessel convulsed in the frothing jaws of the waves, the name seemed a misnomer.

"I know something about this coast!" Bellamy shouted back. "And we had better pray that Renneux brings us back a man who knows it like the back of his hand!"

As they had approached the tip of Chatham, they had spied a lone fisherman. Bellamy had given the order to lay anchor, and a small crew of pirates, led by Jacques Renneux, had launched a boat over the rail, to chase the fisherman down. If they could catch him, he would become one of their number, likely the most important man in the crew while the storm lasted, for he would guide them to safety.

Bellamy looked out over the bow of the boat and saw nothing but gray, stormy winds wrapping around them, squeezing his ship, his treasure. *God, let this pilot guide us to safety,* he pleaded silently.

Soon they heard the voice of Renneux, carrying on the wind, *"We are in luck! He is a real local!"*

Bellamy gave a shout of triumph and slapped Lambert on the back. "Bring him up here straight away!" Bellamy called.

At first Bellamy saw only the top of the pilot's head as the man climbed aboard the *Whydah*. He was in the midst of saying, "Warm rum and fistful of coin will show you that you are not a prisoner..."

Then he saw the face of John Julian.

The native stood like an apparition before him. Bellamy's eyes went as wide as the ones staring into his own.

"You!" Bellamy cried. The wind whipped across the deck and beat about his ears as if howling retribution.

"Do you know this man, Captain?" Renneux asked.

Bellamy did not answer him. Fate swirled around him in the mounting wind. He took a step back from the native. "What are you doing out in this storm... No, no... There is no meaning in this meeting. There cannot be!" He fumbled to draw his pistol from his belt and aimed it at Julian.

"Did this man do something to you, Captain?" said Renneux, yanking out two pistols of his own.

Julian's eyes sat as unreadable as black stones in his face. Only his shaking lip betrayed that he was thinking the same thing as Bellamy.

"He saved me from the sea..." Bellamy muttered at last, lowering his weapon.

"And you want to shoot him?" Renneux exclaimed. "I say we let him live! Perhaps he will bring us luck!"

In response to that comment, both Bellamy and Julian scowled.

"In her dreams my aunt saw you come ashore. She knew you would come. She said that when you did, the land would be lost. I tried to save you anyway," Julian said with a despondent shrug of his shoulders.

"No, no… There are no curses nor fate nor prophecies! I have been among drunken, superstitious men too long! There is only this damned sea!" Bellamy cried, firing the pistol up into the dark cloud above him.

✠ ✠ ✠ ✠

In the gloom there were shapes. For a second they looked like a land mass, and then they diluted into the sheets of thick black rain and wind. Bellamy peered into the storm and tried to get his bearings. *Forgive me, Maria*, he thought, *I have risked everything. Too much…* Life itself, it seemed, had turned against him. He went over the events of the past few hours again in his mind. He could have sheltered in some harbor along a deserted section of coast. He probably should have. The storm came in so fast and with teeth. It was too dark to land now. Although all around him was howling mayhem, Bellamy's whole body was quiet and tense, waiting and hoping not to hear the ominous sound of breakers. For then he would know that they were too close to shore, and it would be too late.

"The pull is enormous! We're getting beaten onto shore!" William Main, the sailing master, shouted from where he stood at the wheel on the quarterdeck. He usually had a firm hand at steering the ship, but the pirates had never before set a course into such a tempest. Tonight he needed an extra pair of hands, those of the pilot James Lambert, to move the wheel.

"Cut east, out to sea, as hard as you can!" Bellamy replied.

"I can't! Look!" Main cried.

In the lightening flash Bellamy saw the wave coming towards them, like a black mountain top erupting out of the water. He had only enough time to wrap his arm through the shrouds of the mizzenmast before the water crashed onto them, filling his mouth with salty spume and hurling him into the solid bulwark of the ship. Several inches of water was swishing around the deck when he stood up. Main and Lambert were by the wheel, clutching it like a life raft.

"Turn the bow into each wave!" Bellamy ordered.

"I fear I'll rend us in two!" Main replied.

"Do it!" Bellamy yelled.

Then he saw John Julian coming along the gangway towards the quarterdeck. The native was drenched, of course, but he looked calm and surefooted as he approached. Occasionally he raised his head and let the rain soak his face. When he caught Bellamy's eye, a flicker of trepidation crossed his face. Julian's sudden consternation revived Bellamy's uncertainty for a moment. Along the same stretch of coast, in another storm, this same man had pulled him from the ocean. That could not be mere happenstance. In fact, Bellamy even dared to hope that it was a good sign. But he was not sure.

"Eastham," Julian said, pointing into the dark void that obscured the terrain alongside of them.

Somewhere out there in the blackness, Maria was sleeping in her bed, Bellamy realized. He almost asked Julian about the girl, but he did not. Too many pirates were standing within earshot.

The next time lightening lit up the sky, Bellamy strained to see through the darkness on the port side. He saw a high cliff of dunes clearly outlined by the flash.

His heart started pounding. "We're too close!" he screamed at Main and Lambert on the quarterdeck. The two men yanked hard on the wheel, but they could not stop the ship from drifting towards shore.

Just then the boatswain, Jeremiah Burke, came hurrying past. Bellamy grabbed the arm of the big Irishman and brought him to a stop. "Get the men ready to drop anchor!"

"I can't get them to do anything! Most of them huddle in the hold, waiting to die!" Burke said. When the lightening flashed, Bellamy could see the terror in Burke's square, ruddy face. A long white scar, a wound from an old fight, cut across Burke's cheek down to his chin, looking like a little bolt of lightening.

"Drop the anchor!" Bellamy screamed and pushed Burke away. Burke scurried off and was immediately swallowed by the darkness.

"Do you hear anything?" Bellamy cried to Julian, knowing that the native would know exactly what he meant. Any Cape Cod bred sailor knew that sandbars lurked all along the length of the arm of the coast. It made the sea surrounding the peninsula the most treacherous water in New England.

"No," Julian replied.

Bellamy felt relief. "Good. Nor do I."

"We're now by the Table Lands," Julian remarked.

"Northern parish already?"

"The cliffs are high. We are halfway up the arm."

Good, Bellamy thought. If they could get around the Province Lands, then they could make it. They just needed to reach the safety of the bay.

Lightening flashed again. Bellamy caught sight of Julian, whose eyes were huge and frightened. He was listening hard to something. Then Bellamy heard it too. A dull undercurrent of rumbling beneath the mad tumult of the storm. The deadly hiss of waves breaking on the shallows.

"Burke! Drop anchor!" Bellamy bellowed. There was still a chance, he thought, if they could pin themselves down and ride out the storm. But the *Whydah* was slipping, moment by moment, closer to the lethal chorus of the breakers.

"Come! We must drop the anchor ourselves!" he yelled to Julian. The two of them pushed towards the bow of the ship, through the screaming wind.

"Burke!" Bellamy shouted. He squinted into the wind-driven rain, which was thick and felt like needles on his face, but he could not see the bow of the ship.

Suddenly the ship went taut at the end of its anchor line and rocked back and forth in the waves. Bellamy threw himself against the rail for support. A few moments later he saw Burke come out of the darkness, clawing his way along the rail.

"Fine work, Burke!" The two men smiled at each other.

"There's still a lot of storm to get through!"

"Aye, but we'll make fast here and hope she holds. With luck we'll breakfast under blue skies on the shores of Cape Cod Bay come morning!"

Then Jacob Nickerson was there, frowning into the tempest.

"Almost at my bloody front door!" he yelled. "I've come home drunk before from Smith Tavern but never in this fashion!"

"Hold steady, Jacob! We'll have a homecoming to remember come tomorrow morning!"

A tremor in the deck undermined Bellamy's prediction. The anchors were pulling the ship's bow under the waves. The *Whydah* dangled on its tether in front of the inexorable press of water, each blow coming closer to swamping them.

"Damn!" Bellamy yelled. "Come help me! We must cut the line and heave away from the waves!" he said to Burke and Nickerson.

"No! It's madness! We'll be at the wind's mercy!" Burke yelled.

Bellamy was past the point of debate. He and Nickerson groped their way towards the bow. They had no axe to cut the anchor line, so Bellamy used his sword instead. The wet rope merely dented as Bellamy struck it again and again.

In the next illumination of lightening, they could all plainly see the sandbar. The waves formed a thin, bubbling white crust where the ground was highest.

"Oh God!" Nickerson screamed. He began chopping at the line as well.

Finally the rope frayed down to a single strand, which Bellamy severed with a sawing motion.

Then he turned and ran back along the gangway towards the quarterdeck, the wind pushing strongly from behind and making him feel like he was flying towards the stern.

When he could see Main and Lambert at the wheel, he roared, "Turn us to catch the wind!" It would be a gamble. They could not ride out the storm without being buried under it, and they could not sail through it without being smashed sideways into the shallows. They would have to run straight for shore and hope that the stormwater was high enough so they could slip over the breakers. Such high water would surely hit the shore with great force. As for the landing, Bellamy would have to trust in luck once again.

The boat gyrated in the surf. The huge mainsail and foresail were still hauling them rapidly towards the sandbar. Bellamy hurried back to the bow and slashed the lines to the spritsail, and the sail shot away, in a white streak, into the night like a ghost. He did not want them coming in too fast. The wind was pushing them along rapidly enough already.

Through the gloom Bellamy saw the faces of the crew. Some looked drunk, but most were frozen in terror or mesmerized by the raging sea around them.

"Hurry! Do you want to die like drowned rats in a barrel?" Bellamy yelled. He ran along the deck, rallying some of the men to climb the masts and trim or cut down the sails.

"*We're not going to die!*" Bellamy shouted. He looked up into the downpour and howled like a wolf into the storm.

Each time the thunder sounded, he raised his fist and boomed back, "Damn you, *Fate!* Damn your thunder! Damn this wretched wind! *Is this the best you can do?*"

Other men were shouting and crying out too. Some raged, others pleaded.

Soon the ship's topgallant sails puffed and jumped on the wild winds, like giant flags of surrender. The ship surged towards the dark shape of land in the near distance. Around them the breakers' roar grew to a scream.

"The ship's too heavy!" Lambert cried. "Let's dump cargo!"

At that moment men were emerging from the hold, their pants and vest pockets fat with gold. Some could hardly walk from the weight they carried.

"You are fools! Leave it! Leave the money!" Bellamy cried.

Swords and pistols rose up in response.

"If you touch my treasure, I'll dump you overboard!" the closest man yelled. His beard was scraggly, and his face had been ravaged by some old case of pox. Bellamy was not sure that he had ever seen the man before. He must have been one of the recent recruits. That meant that he had not been there during the early, lean times. In fact, he did not even deserve such riches, for the little he had likely done to earn them, Bellamy thought. In his purple silk garments and frilly lace, he looked like an idiot. They all did. In the face of the storm, Bellamy finally saw everything that they had been playing at during the past year and a half as a ridiculous game. It would have been laughably childish if not for the cost of it.

"Fine! Then you can hold onto your bags of gold! I hope they are comfortable pillows for you when you sleep on the sea bottom!" he cried out to the crew in general.

"Just hold us steady!" Bellamy then yelled to Lambert. Bellamy did not want to dump the treasure either, but he knew that

457

Lambert was correct. They were too heavy. So that was the punishment, he mused. He was being offered a choice of either the gold or his life. If he survived by ditching the treasure, then at least he would still have Maria, if he could trust that her love had stayed true. He had to gamble on that.

At that moment another tremendous wave blasted across the deck. Bellamy was washed along the quarterdeck. He reached out and managed to grab and wrap himself around the wheel, tangled up with Main and Lambert. The side of the ship dipped so far down that Bellamy's feet slid out from under him. He looked down at the seething water below him. But he held on tight to the wheel.

As the ship righted itself, Julian pointed frantically towards shore. "The breakers are right there!"

Bellamy did not need to be told. He could hear their gnashing sound growing louder. The ship was drifting towards shore faster now.

"We need to dump everything! Everything!" Bellamy screamed at Julian. "Get some men and go below. Start with the heaviest trunks!"

A moment later the boat slammed to a stop. Bellamy was hurled against the rail. Main and Lambert were thrown overboard into the furious sea, leaving the ship's wheel spinning unmanned in the wind. Only the fact that he was standing directly in front of the mizzenmast saved Julian from a similar fate.

Each ensuing wave drove the boat more tightly against the sandbar. The combination of wind and water was slowly turning the ship over onto its side. In the intermittent flashes of lightening, Bellamy could see the shore, some two hundred yards away on the other side of the sandbar, separated from him by angry waves. He knew that the only way to get there was by diving into the water. But he could not summon the courage to make the leap overboard.

When he looked up into the night sky, he saw a sheer cliff face of ocean, as tall as a dune, towering over the ship. As he closed his eyes, the sea came down on the ship, like a mallet on an anvil. The *Whydah* buckled and screamed like a wounded animal under the claws of a predator. Her mainmast snapped, and she sank deck first into the consuming waves.

Bellamy's head sank under the surface, and all of the terrible death sounds diminished. A torn sail from the ship drifted down over him, covering him like a shroud. For a second, in the sudden quiet, Bellamy thought that maybe, for some inexplicable reason, he was going to heaven and this was the peaceful cloud coming to take him. Then he heard a strange noise – a chiming. It was the ship's bell. It rang and rang like the steeple bell did on Sabbath day and, muffled as it was by the water, it sounded like eerie, gloating laughter...

BOOK FOUR

The Remains of a Curse

Chapter One
"Washashores"

By the time that the *Mary Anne* had circumnavigated Chatham, the pirates aboard were completely drunk. One by one, they took turns going up on deck to man the helm while the rest stayed in the hold, passing wine bottles back and forth.

"Stay close, lad," Alexander Mackconachy told young John Dunavan. The boy hadn't spoken since the pirates had seized them. Mackconachy, or *Mack* as his mates called him, had been a prisoner of the English and knew that it was good defense to go into one's shell in a situation like this, but not so far that you never came out. The boy worried him. He had that stare like he was looking through everything.

"What smells down here?" the pirate called Simon Van Vorst said. He sniffed the air near Mack. "You been rolling in the lard, Cookie?"

Mack said nothing. Fade into the woodwork, he told himself. But his silence only inflamed Van Vorst, who had come down into the hold not just to fill up on wine but to have a little fun with the captives. "Then cook us up something to feast on, God damn it! And you!" He swung towards Dunavan. "Ain't you a pretty young lad."

"Back off!" Mack roared. "Let the lad be!"

Van Vorst smiled. "You're his protector then? A sweet piece of property you got there. He must keep you warm at night." Van Vorst wrapped young Dunavan in a tight bear hug. The boy kept staring into nothingness.

Mack's face flushed. "He's like a son to me, you ape! He's just a boy!" The old cook was ready to fight, pirates or not.

Van Vorst let the insult slide off of him since none of his mates were present to hear it. He liked the way that the cook's face looked like a plump tomato when he got mad. He wondered if he could make the boy cry. "That's just what we like when there are no ladies about." He notched a finger in Dunavan's belt and tugged it. The boy tried to pull away but Van Vorst held him fast.

Then Mack raised his spoon, since the pirates had taken his knives away from him, and poked it at the pirate. "Away with you, loathsome cur! If you were a real sailor, I'd flog you myself, you buggering bastard!"

Van Vorst drew his pistol and pointed it at Mack's chest, "I should kill you for that!"

"Stop!" Dunavan yelled, surprising them both. "Let me fetch you some more wine."

Van Vorst smiled and lowered the pistol. "Smart and pretty. Yes, trot along, boy," he said and patted Dunavan on the rump. "I'm thirsty… and hungry." He glowered at Mack.

"We're the best of the seven seas," another pirate, Hendrick Quintor, bragged, wine running down the front of his white silk shirt in a purple flare. "It's your privilege to be raided by us. We took fifty ships this year alone."

"More than sixty," Van Vorst corrected.

"Aye, sixty, then. Will be one hundred next year."

"Have you ever killed anybody?" Thomas Fitzgerald, another young Irish seaman, asked.

The pirates looked at each other and laughed. Quintor leaned close to the boy. "See these gold chains?" he said, pointing to the many necklaces that hung around his neck. "I put on a new one for each of my victims. And I've got a sack full of knuckles in my bunk. Just tokens to remind me."

"It's all lies, lad," Mack told Fitzgerald. "These men are a bunch of sallies. Probably pee in their britches sooner than fire a shot."

"Like Hell!" Quintor roared and snatched the spoon from Mack's hand. "You've never killed more than a spider!"

"I've slain men in the honorable way – on a field of battle! Face to face! For God and country!"

Quintor spat. "Whose country? Not your own, I'll bet." He drank the bottle until it was empty.

"For the damned English. But it's better than stealing a man's valuables and then sticking him in the back for good measure. The French artillery in Quebec was like rain. I broke a man's neck with my bare hands."

Before anyone could respond, a huge boom shook the sides of the hull. The rain started anew as if they had sailed across the very edge of the waiting storm. They saw Thomas Baker's head in the stairwell. Thunder punched through the night sky behind him. He was already drenched even though the rain had only been falling for a few seconds. "Where the hell is my relief? I am the captain, don't you know?"

"Isn't Brown up there?" Van Vorst asked.

"Aye. But I don't trust him. He's Bellamy's man."

"I don't trust any man who won't drink with me," Van Vorst added, glancing again at the Irishmen.

"You go," Quintor nudged the quiet French pirate, Jean Shuan.

"*Qu'avez-vous dit?*"

"Go steer," Baker said, pulling Shuan up off of the floor. "Go steer the ship!" he shouted into Shuan's blank face. "We're just floating right now, damn it to hell!"

Lightening hit the sea, just off the bow, with an earsplitting snap. The ship lurched sickeningly. A burning smell wafted down into the hold from the deck.

"This is bad," Peter Hoof said darkly.

"We've been through worse," Baker replied. "We'll send the Irish boys up into the sails."

"That's murder!" Mack protested.

"We'll all die if we don't!"

"Just stay off shore!" Mack growled. Baker spun and struck the cook hard in the stomach, and Mack fell to the floor with a groan.

"I'm captain here," Baker explained.

"The cook is right," Hoof said, squaring himself to Baker. "We need the sails up and us as far from land as possible."

Baker considered Hoof's words for a second, until another deafening clap of thunder jolted them all. "We'll ride it out."

The waves were growing higher and stronger. The boat pitched violently. A bottle of wine toppled off of a crate and smashed on the floor, between the hands of several pirates who unsuccessfully dove for it at once. Cargo shifted with each roll of the waves, and even the most stalwart seamen were feeling queasy.

"Damn this storm and damn it all!" Van Vorst cried.

"No, no... This storm won't stop us! The Devil himself won't stop us!" Baker growled.

A moment later there was a brief pause in the staccato of thunder, and they all heard Quintor whisper, as if to himself, *"I'm not ready to die yet. I can't..."*

The storm renewed with another sharp report of thunder, but the pirates stood in stunned silence. Then the reflection of a flash of lightening flickered like fire on the stairs leading up to the deck.

Van Vorst gave Quintor a playful shove and asked, "Are you joking with us?"

"I never thought it would happen. Not in the battles at least. After I survived a few, I guess I thought myself to be protected. But how do you escape a storm such as this? On a deck, you can dodge the cutlasses, duck the bullets. Here, there is nowhere to go to get away from the wind but into the jaws of the sea!" Quintor said, slurring from the wine and wide-eyed with sudden panic.

A slap stopped any further lament. "Shut up, you weakling!" Van Vorst shouted, keeping his hand poised for another blow. "What's the matter with you?"

Quintor held up his hands to shield his face. "I don't know!"

"You drank too much, you fool! When you drink too much, you start sounding like *him!*" Van Vorst said, jerking a thumb towards Hoof.

Hoof frowned. "Every man alive is doomed. Just out of reach of destiny for a few moments," he said. Then he drained his bottle with a single gulp.

Mack smirked at Fitzgerald. He knew that they were just a bunch of sallies. "There were men in our regiment who survived the entire battle only to be knocked off the deck by a wayward boom on the ship ride home."

"Shut up!" Van Vorst shouted, lifting his pistol again.

Quintor looked searchingly at Fitzgerald. "Is there a Bible aboard?"

"Yes," the boy replied.

"And can you read it?"

"Some."

"Read it then! I need repenting!" Quintor pleaded.

When Fitzgerald returned with the Bible, the pirates gathered round him in the dim hold like a congregation. In the rocking quarters they clutched their wine bottles and listened to the words of salvation. "And the waters rose and struck the walls of the sinned city..."

Quintor shook his head in irritation. "Not that one, damn you! Something with green fields and blue skies."

The young Irishman flipped the book open randomly and read, "Behold, you trust in deceptive words to no avail. Will you steal, murder, commit adultery, swear falsely, burn incense to Baal and go after other gods that you have not known, and then come and stand before me in this house, which is called by my name, and say, 'We are delivered!' only to go on doing all these abominations?"

"Stop! Not that *shit!*" Quintor yelled, waving his pistol in the boy's face. "Pick something else! Something with angels, God damn it!"

The pistol and the boy's fingers shook to the same degree, as Fitzgerald tore through the book to find some safer passage. The gun barrel did not lower until the boy was saying, "And an angel of the Lord appeared to them..."

"Good," Quintor grunted.

"And the glory of the Lord shone around them, and they were filled with fear... And the angel said to them, 'Be not afraid, for behold, I bring you good news of a great joy, which will come to all the people...'" Fitzgerald hurried on.

The reading took on a lyrical drone, which put the men in an almost mellow mood. All except Baker, who was restless. He kept thinking that he ought to go on deck and check on the state of the ship. But he never got the chance. The boat was shaken by a terrific crash, followed by a jarring motion that threw everyone in the hold into a heap on one side.

"God damn it!" Baker cried. He sprinted up the steps to the deck where he was met by a wall of flying wind and water. Brown and Shuan pulled frantically on the wheel and lines, but Baker could tell that their efforts were useless. The ship was not moving at all. The hull sat motionless upon some sandbar beneath the relentless, buffeting water.

Bitterly, Baker realized that all they could do was wait for that one wave to drive them over. With that toppling wave, his captaincy would be finished too.

✠ ✠ ✠ ✠

April 26-27, 1717

Behind him the *Whydah* moaned in the dark. Although the wind and waves were too loud to hear it, Thomas Davis shuddered as he imagined the death cries and raw fear of the men trapped within the *Whydah's* fractured hull as the sea came for them. They weren't all bad men, he thought. Many had simply been swept up into a pirate's life, like himself. He wondered if the storm would cull the good from the bad, threshing out the pure and spinning the sinners away in the current like chaff. But that was up to God, not him.

He saw the shoreline before him, like a ridge of black teeth poised to chew the *Whydah* to pieces. When the lightening flashed, it revealed a line of towering dunes. Once he thought he spied another light, a smaller glow that danced along the crest of the ridge like a firefly, but the waves kept dunking him under, and when he looked again, it was gone.

The waves screeched in his ears. He heard them crashing in front of him, hitting shore. The sound grew louder and louder as he got closer to land. All thought slipped out of his mind except one: *Please, God, let me live!*

He felt the sea rising underneath him and then the pull of water rushing out from under his feet. For a moment he felt like he was in the air. Then his breath was snatched away as if by an undertow.

The wave curled around him, and he was thrust underwater. He slammed the bottom face-first, tasted sand in his mouth, slipped back into the suction of the waves and then was driven down again, water piling on top of him.

But this time he could dig his hands into the sand. Solid ground.

When the last wave rolled him up onto the beach, Davis started to cry. It was something he had not done since he was a child, but in a way, he felt like a little boy being swept up into his mother's arms.

It was too frigid to lie in the wet sand for long, so he stood up and looked around. He did not glance at the ship that was stuck on the reef. That was all behind him now, and he resolved to never look back.

The beach stretched on endlessly into the night, in either direction, and he knew not which way to travel. The entire length looked devoid of shelter. Just when he had committed himself to digging a pit at the foot of the dune and sleeping there, he spied a dim light on the highlands. A burst of lightening revealed the outline of a house. Someone was burning the midnight oil. For a moment he hesitated because the folk of his homeland were wary of answering a knock on the door after dark, for fear of the ghosts and devils of the night. But there was no other option. He began climbing the hill and praying that the folks in these parts were not a superstitious people.

Halfway up the slope, his muscles felt like string. They were aching from the ride in on the waves. His head swam with fatigue. He did not think that he could make it to the house. He needed to sleep. But at least it was not an eternal rest, he told himself.

✠ ✠ ✠ ✠

Samuel Harding, along with his wife and children, lived on the edge of the Devil's Pasture on the ocean side of Billingsgate. Theirs was the only house around for miles. Normally, it was a quiet and secluded spot. But tonight the wind came howling off of the thundering ocean and rattled the window shutters.

Harding tossed and turned for hours, before finally getting up and wondering how to pass the time until the storm broke. He didn't like reading to begin with, and he only had a Bible, anyway, which was his wife's diversion, not his. He was too weary to fix his tools, and he didn't want to start drinking, in case the storm caused some emergency that required him to think straight. So he lit a candle and watched the flame dance. That gave him some comfort. It was like a little promise of sunshine to come when the gale had blown itself out.

He listened to the wind and waves and, behind them, an odd thumping noise. Then he heard it again, and there was no doubt that it was not the shutters this time. He put on his boots and coat, lit a lantern and stepped out into the storm.

The wind plowed into Harding and sought to push him back, throwing salt spray and sand into his face. Yet the air was warm and had that strange crisp, earthy perfume that stormy weather brings. It made him feel invigorated and alive.

The noise was coming from the barn. He trudged towards the small, loose-board structure, thinking that the animals were stricken by fear and riled up from the storm. As he walked, he suddenly remembered the witch girl. He had chanced upon her crude hut several months ago while hunting rabbits through the Devil's Pasture. They had not met, but Harding was certain that she was well aware of his presence and did not approve of him. Strange things had been happening since he had encountered her lair such as tools disappearing and animals getting loose from the barn. His wife kept telling him that his own absent-mindedness was to blame, but he was not so sure about that. The keening wind spooked him, and he looked around nervously. When the lightening broke, the bushes seemed to loom out at him.

Apart from the lantern, he was totally unarmed, and that made him feel more vulnerable. For once, he wished he lived a little closer to his neighbors. He would have gladly suffered all of their gossiping and prying if it meant having a few folks on hand should something horrid come against him.

He creaked open the barn door and immediately smelled the staleness of stacked hay and animal odors. The cow snorted in the dark, but it was the overall stillness, combined with the walls shaking from the wind, that jarred him.

"*Easy there,*" he whispered as much to himself as the cow.

He suddenly realized that he was breathing hard. Then the heat drained from his skin as he comprehended that it wasn't his breath that he was hearing. It was coming from the next stall over. *Oh God, please,* he prayed silently, *protect me from the witch girl. Let guarding angels stand by me!*

"Leave me be! I am protected by angels!" Harding roared. "I cast you away, demon!"

He started backing towards the door. He didn't know whether he should return to the house or try and brave the long ride into town for help. All that he knew was that he had to get out of there fast.

He did not see or hear the two sheep that were sidling up next to him for warmth. When he turned, he walked right into them.

"Jesus!" he cried and dropped the lantern.

When he stooped to retrieve it, in the pool of light that spilled under the next stall, he saw boots.

"Good Lord," he said.

In reply he heard a pitiful groan.

Harding thrust his lantern over the partition wall and saw the hollow face of one who looked like he had been through extreme deprivation and was on the verge of death. The man's eyes flicked open when the light shone upon them.

"I mean you no harm," the man said hoarsely.

Harding remained guarded as he inspected the man. He looked real enough, but Harding wondered if it was a trick. Perhaps the man was some kind of apparition conjured by the witch girl, Harding thought. After all, it was said that she had great powers. However, the fellow looked like he could barely stand, let alone do any harm. His clothes were soaked as if he had borne the full brunt of the storm.

Soaked... Men did not willingly come to Eastham from the ocean side. There were too many unseen traps of sand and current to risk that.

"Your ship wrecked!" Harding exclaimed.

Thomas Davis nodded vigorously, almost thankfully. "Yes."

"How far out were ya?"

"About two hundred yards..."

Harding cracked a toothy smile. "Praise God! You survived! That's no easy feat! Plenty have been swallowed up over the years, mark my words!" he said and shook the man's shoulders.

Davis forced a smile. He wished only to talk of food and bed. All else could wait until morning. But the Cape Codder had other ideas.

"What is her name and what did she carry?"

"The *Whydah*. She carried..." Davis broke off, uncertain how much to say.

"Well, what did she carry?"

No rest for the wicked... The thought flickered in Davis' mind like a hot flame. His legs ached. The ground felt like it was buckling under him. Harding's eyes shown like two small, flickering lantern lights. It made him look very much like a pirate, Davis thought. But he had to trust this man. The truth, he hoped, would be his salvation. But would others believe it?

"I was captured by the men of that wrecked ship. They took me because of my skill as a carpenter."

"Aye. I know the tricks of the damned English navy. Pressing any man they find into service if they feel like it. But where is your uniform?"

"It was not the navy, but... pirates."

Harding's eyes became brighter. "How much stolen loot did you have?"

"I don't know..."

"Tell me the truth, and I will speak on your behalf when the justice arrives!"

When Davis told him, Harding's breath caught.

So many ships went down off of the fierce outer arm of Eastham. And folks around town knew that Harding would, likely as not, be the first one on the spot. In fact, some townsfolk referred to the outer bar as *Harding's Toll*, for all of the scavenging it had offered him. He had learned that one never knew what those waves might bring. But they had never brought in a gift such as this.

"*Gold...*" he muttered dreamily.

"All tainted with blood and trickery," Davis intoned, but he could tell that his new host was not listening. "Sir, they are well-armed and unprincipled. If any should come ashore in good stead, you would not find it an easy quarrel with them."

"There won't be any others coming ashore in this sea! You shouldn't be here neither for that matter," Harding said. "They hang any man who was on such a ship. Doesn't matter what kind of story he has to cover his sins," Harding added. He did not care what the man thought of the hard words. The sailor was in no position to challenge him.

"'Tis no tale."

"Hmmm," Harding mused. "It matters nothing to me. I'll shelter you for a time, on one condition." He pointed down towards the sea.

Davis at once understood his meaning and protested.

"If you help me, I'll help you on your way from here. If you have been wronged by these pirates, then it will be sweet revenge," Harding went on.

The carpenter did not think of it that way, but he had no other option than to help Harding load up his wagon and set off back to the beach even though he felt his body was about to collapse from fatigue.

"By the way, what was the captain's name?" Harding asked as they rolled through the slashing rain.

Davis hesitated for a moment. The ship and its crew seemed like a dream already, a nightmare cleansed away by the punishing storm. Surely, he owed nothing to any of those men. He did not condone the methods or the crimes, but how could he explain that within their outlawry, there was a certain admirable equality among the pirates. He could begrudgingly concede that point now that he was away from the *Whydah*. But he was exhausted. And what did it matter now?

"Captain Bellamy."

"Sam Bellamy?" Harding said, his jaw dropping.

Davis was equally surprised. "You know this man?"

Harding did not answer. Bellamy had done it after all, he mused, feeling at once impressed and amazed. He looked at the shipwrecked sailor and calculated. Day break would be here in a matter of hours. Before it came, this fellow was going to show him exactly where the cargo was.

✠ ✠ ✠ ✠

There had been many mornings after storms in the long history of the sea-beleaguered peninsula of Cape Cod, but few in which the waking folks of Eastham considered themselves so blessed to have survived. All across town, groggy, sleep deprived faces looked out of their windows and doors and were almost surprised to observe their town still standing. They half expected the sands to be whittled away to a bar the width of a razor clam.

On the farms across town, men set out on their normal rounds, bringing feed to the chickens and milking the cows, before the sun broke. But the sun would not appear at all today. The sky clasped the dark sea like a gray pot lid.

The prolonged darkness made Elder Knowles slow to rise. His bones felt heavy in the morning, especially with such moisture in the air. He no longer felt the fire in his mind that would send him springing out of his repose before the roosters crowed. He had been struggling with early morning nightmares, which plagued him frequently these days. Now that he was in charge of Eastham's salvation, he pictured people's souls slipping through his fingers. He did not know how Treat had carried such a burden for so long.

A few miles down the road, Mrs. Cole hummed gaily to herself as she plucked the lint off of her son's Sunday clothes, preparing them for tomorrow's service. Today she awoke feeling more religious than she had in a long while. She knelt in prayer while her husband took the canoe out fishing. She asked if God, in His grace and goodness, would allow her boy to one day lead the Eastham congregation.

Off of Great Island, Samuel Smith already had his men out in the bay because every good fisherman knows that a storm churns up the bottom and throws all kinds of fish to shore. The storm that had just blown through had enough force to herd half of the ocean into his lap, he reckoned. He glanced uneasily at the hooded sky and wondered if he should have heeded his wife's warning that this was the left punch of the gale and that the right fist was soon to follow. He resolved to stay close to shore. Should the storm rear up again, it would be a death sentence to get caught out on the open water. He pitied any man foolish or unlucky enough to be out there in the raging ocean.

Directly across from Smith, on the other side of the Cape, men and women hurried through the gray morning light towards a line of wreckage that astounded their eyes, for it seemed to them that the Lord had caused the waters to overflow with bounty.

Samuel Harding had already been working the shoreline for hours. He hauled another load of bales of silk to the barn. The beach was littered with pieces of planking, crates and canvas. Harding watched his neighbors approach and swore. Davis was sleeping inside the barn, and Harding too felt worn out. But he wouldn't stop until everything that he could carry had been hidden.

Part way out to sea, sticking out of the water, was a clutch of broken masts and spars, which seemed like a giant hand grasping out of the depths. The sad tatters of line and sail danced madly about the poles. As the sky lightened to a watery gray color, it revealed the remains of a smashed hull, flipped over and ripped apart as if something had taken a tremendous bite out of it.

Gulls jeered over head as the villagers assembled. The winged scavengers hopped among the human kind, all of them sifting through the broad swath of litter.

Barrels came rolling up in the frothy tide and then bounded back again. Children and women, hiking up their petticoats from the foam, chased after them and herded them towards the wagons that lined the beach. Some men coiled rope out of the churning water. Others picked through the bits of wood that floated in, finding them so plentiful that they threw the undesirable pieces back into the water. If anyone found anything more unusual than that, they were wise enough to slip it quietly into a pocket.

There was one among the beachcombers whom few paid heed to, although everyone there would have recognized her, had they given her more than a passing glance. Only Harding looked away from his foraging long enough to catch her eye.

"*The witch...*" he muttered, slipping in the soft sand as he sought to scurry behind his wagon. He considered pointing her out to his neighbors, if not to warn them, then at least to divert them with her menace and, hopefully, draw their greedy hands away from the rest of the spoils. But he was soon distracted with guarding the pile that he was amassing near his wagon. By the time he looked up again, she was gone.

He saw her again, a little while later. This time she was closer to him, bending over a dark shape that Harding first mistook for a stranded blackfish. He saw one and then another and was astounded that, in addition to the prized cargo, the ocean had disgorged a whole herd of whales.

Only when he nearly tripped upon one of the dead beasts did he realize what it was: a dead man.

Harding's eyes widened as he scanned the beach, focusing his attention only on the dead. There were more corpses in the shallows. Many more... *One... Two... Five... Ten...* There were over one hundred – as many as might litter a battlefield after the fight was lost. It was a beach full of dead men, and behind them their bone-broken ship was in a state of agonizing collapse just off shore. Everything around him was carnage. The sea kept pushing out more dead men, casting them on shore as if they were a scourge to be rid of.

Stepping away from the body, Harding's boot kicked a stiff, lace covered arm, and the dead man's hand fell open and dumped a sprinkle of coins into the sand, like he was laying a bet on a table.

Grimly and dutifully, Harding scooped them up and pocketed them, thinking that the tragedy would be all the worse if these coins were to be lost in the sand, with no one at all to profit from them.

Chapter Two
"All the King's Men"

April 27, 1717

If not eagerness, there was a certain sense of anticipation that Lieutenant John Cole felt when he woke up on the morning after the storm. He had witnessed enough gales sweep across Eastham to know that their passage could reshape the delicate landscape over night. As he pulled on his clothes, he stepped towards the front window of his house and looked out towards Pochet Island, some two hundred yards in the distance. He would not have been surprised to see some new cut of water surging through the sand dunes or a section of marshland covered with silt. However, there was nothing different about Pochet Island and the marsh around it except a large ship that lay stranded on an exposed patch of sand.

Not long after that, Cole paddled his canoe through the marshy inlets out towards the shipwreck. Approaching the wreck, he saw scattered cargo, toppled masts and the splintered pieces of spars sticking out of the flats.

As the canoe slid onto the beach with a hiss of sand, Cole noticed footprints among the wreckage. Tracks were everywhere, and some of the crates appeared to be pried open, their covers lying neatly beside them. Cole wondered if someone from town had been here before him and had already looted the remains.

"Hello?" Cole called. His voice seemed to roll away down the beach where it tumbled into the distant crunch of the incoming waves. Cole inspected the hull of the boat. It was good, solid wood. The name *Mary Anne* was painted onto the bow, and the figurehead of a woman, nymph-like with arms out-raised, was swinging off the end of the ship, like she was hanging on for dear life or praying for somebody to save her.

Voices called back to Cole. The survivors began lining up along the rail. He counted ten men in all. They told Cole that they were merchant men. But Cole noticed the men's clunky accents, the staggering about as if some of them were drunk and the mismatched fancy clothes.

"Where are you from?" Cole asked.

"I'm from New Amster… New York. Dutch is what you hear. I am Captain Baker," their leader replied, puffing out his chest.

"Well-armed, I see," Cole said. He noted all manner of knives, guns and clubs decorating the wrecked men's clothes.

For a moment a dark, suspicious look crossed Baker's face, but it dissolved into a crooked grin. "Can't be too careful out there. The seas are filled with pirates, you know."

Cole had no need to ask what the cargo was. The scent of it filled the air and made his head spin like it did after a night at Higgins Tavern.

The shipwrecked sailors began dismounting by way of the far end of the vessel where the side was so low that they had only to drop a few feet to reach ground. They were an edgy group of men, who kept looking at Cole, each other and all around.

One of them, a young boy, was shivering and looked quite frightened. "What happens to us now?" he asked. Another accent, this time Irish, Cole noted. A strange crew indeed, Cole thought. He decided that he would not ask anymore about it until he had Justice Doane and the militia beside him.

"You'll come with me back to my dwelling, right over that creek," Cole replied. He pointed back behind him. "I am sure that a hot breakfast will taste good, after what you have been through."

"Aye," another of the sailors piped up, in the same Dutch accent. "It is a great day to be alive! Ever go through a time when life suddenly seemed grander than you ever dreamed? That's what these days have been like. Even the angels answer to us…" he gushed before being cut off by a whack from Captain Baker.

"Be quiet, Quintor!"

"Hmmm," Cole mused. In truth, he had never experienced such bliss or ever heard a man utter such sentiment unless he was awash with ale. It made him wonder anew about what kind of men would be drunk in the middle of a gale.

Cole was not convinced by the tale of the shipwrecked men, but he led them back to his house. With his usual nonchalance Cole shrugged as he gave the men a tour of the house and an introduction to his wife, Mary, with a single sweeping gesture. He knew that his wife did not appreciate these unexpected visitors. He could read her displeasure plainly in the hard set of her mouth. Dutifully, she served them food. While she did, Cole watched the men eat greedily and work their way through the wine bottles they had brought with them. All the while Cole wondered what he would do next. If he could keep them here and occupied, maybe there was a way to send word to Justice Doane and the rest of the militia. He thanked God that they had trained so long and hard, for now they would have to put their military skills to the test it seemed.

Cole talked about fishing, the cut of ships, drinking rum at Higgins Tavern and anything else that he could think of. He talked and talked to the point where his glib tone made him feel that he too had been drinking at this hour of the morning. His wife wondered also, for she had never heard this amount of chitchat issue from him. However, the shipwrecked men merely thought that he was a small-town gabber, which is exactly what Cole hoped they would think.

Gradually Cole tried to glean what tidbits he could from the men, without arousing too much suspicion. It felt not unlike reeling in a fish, playing with the delicate tension of the line and drawing it in, inch by inch.

"So you are heading to Great Island? I take it you've been here to our shores before?"

"No. We've heard of it though," Baker said carefully.

"It's mostly whalers there. Do you know any man there?" Cole queried. Samuel Smith and his smugglers came to mind.

"The owner of our ship is a friend of the whalers. We are hoping that they might help us."

Cole tried to force all skepticism from his face as he met the Dutchman's eye. "Aye. Tis a good plan. The island is a good ways away, on the other side of the mainland, through the marsh channels, Great Cove, Jeremiah's Gutter and out into the great bay."

"Could you sail us there?"

"When the tide turns, I will be able to get you there," Cole said. Through the window, he could see the edge of the marsh and the water running back into it. He could not wait much longer, he realized.

The fire was growing low, and in its blackened embers he saw the spark of a plan. It was a damp, chilly morning due to the storm. No one would think it unusual for him to keep the hearth going, especially with company in the house.

"Johnny..." Cole motioned to his son, who had been lingering in the background the whole time. "The fire is almost out, and we're going to need you to go into the forest and gather wood while your mother and I stay here and entertain our guests."

"I'll just go to the wood pile," the boy responded.

Cole looked hard at his son. "The wood pile is empty. You'll have to go searching. Come outside and I'll show you what size sticks and logs I need." Cole worried about placing their safety in his son's hands. He was too young. Cole would have much preferred to make the trip himself, but he knew that was impossible. At least his son would be out of the house and safe. If the boy was truly watched over by God, they would find out soon enough one way or the other.

When they got outside he said, "Quick, boy, come to me!"

He kneeled down in front of his son. "I need you to find Justice Doane as fast as you can. Bring him here to the house. Tell him to get as many men as he can. Understand?"

There was not the look of steel that he would have expected from a preacher-to-be, but the boy was young yet and the situation confusing even to the likes of Cole. *Pirates? Here in Eastham?* What had brought them this far north to a place where few but the French ever harried, he wondered?

"What is going on, father?" Johnny asked, his voice quaking.

"No fear! Understand? This is a mission. Tis like a calling. Think of angels at your back because you are on an errand of Godliness and righteousness!" he said.

Those words, so foreign in his mouth, seemed to steady the boy.

"They are not kind men, son. Criminals…"

"Says you! You'd have seen things different if you'd been in my shoes!" came a sharp voice from the doorway.

Johnny screamed. The pistol in Simon Van Vorst's hand exploded in response. A pistol ball ripped through the cloud of smoke and slammed into the trunk of a tree behind Johnny, just above the boy's head, with a loud slap.

"Damn you!" Cole cried, launching himself at the pirate. As Van Vorst stepped out of the house, Cole shouldered into him and knocked him back against the stoop. He heard the hard thwack of the pirate's head against the foot of the stairs and then sickening silence. A moment later there was jerky laughter coming from where the man lay. Cole did not know whether to feel relief or disappointment that he had not hit the man harder. He did not know that the maniacal laugh was Van Vorst's battle cry.

Cole shooed his son away, clapping at the boy when he stood there frozen. "Get going! Run!" he cried.

Johnny Cole looked like he was going to cry, but his father raised his finger like it was itself a pistol. "GO!"

A split second later there was a shout from inside the house. The urgent cry of the Irish cook, *"These men are pirates!"*

The boy turned and ran across the fields as fast as he could.

John Cole heard the sound of Van Vorst rising behind him. Inside the house there was a commotion of men scuffling. Any minute now, he knew that the others would come outside to investigate the pistol shot. Turning quickly, his eyes searched for some kind of weapon. There was not even a single stick on the ground. His fastidious care of the homestead was now his undoing.

Cole stepped backwards. It had been a long time since he had been in a fight. Probably not since he was a young man, boxing Thomas Linnell over who was going to ask Mary Rogers for her hand in marriage. He had won that one, but this one would be different, he reckoned.

"You got me good, you old loose-lipped bastard, knocking me over like that. I'd be lying if I said I wasn't impressed," Van Vorst said. He wedged the pistol in the crook of his arm and began filling it with powder and shot as he talked. "Your tongue seems a little knotted now. Where did you send him? To the sheriff?"

Cole felt wrath building in him until it was a blind rage, beyond any recriminating words. The man would have killed his boy... *The man would have killed...*

Again he charged at his target, but he was no match for the battle-hardened pirate. Van Vorst looked up and frowned at the simplicity of repeating the move. Cole's momentum carried him headlong at the pirate, seeking to pin and crush him against the side of the stairs. Van Vorst leapt out of the way, onto the top step of the stairs, as agilely as climbing up the mast. Cole crashed into the footing of stairs and looked up, his eyes conveying every word of fury that was swirling inside of him.

The pirate understood that language better than most men, and it was that recognition that slowed his hand. Yet it did not stay the blow. He held the pistol by the barrel and brought the butt of it down like a gavel upon Cole's head. The Cape Codder had time only to blink in surprise, before he crumpled to the ground.

Van Vorst's next thought was about the woman inside. She was not a young, fetching lass like they had at the taverns in Nassau, but she would do. He thought about how long it had been since he had the soft pleasure of a woman, and his pants bulged uncomfortably at the memory. He started up the stairs, holstering the gun as he went. There would be no need for it. This was an entirely different sport than killing a man but equal in its pleasure.

He opened the door and collided, in a rough embrace, with the Irish cook, who he flung away, harder than was necessary. The burning lust in his mind ignited his anger once more. Mack landed on the floor with a groan.

Baker was right behind him. "Get the bloody hell up! All of you! Get out!"

He pushed Van Vorst back out through the door.

"What the Devil?"

"Let's go! We cannot stay here!" Baker said.

"We have time!" Van Vorst said. Over Baker's shoulder he could see the woman. She was cowering in the corner, clasping her hands as if she was praying. She was handsome enough already, but that act of piety made him long even more to defile her. Baker grabbed his face and turned his gaze into his own.

"We are in a fight, not a brothel, so I am captain!"

Van Vorst glared at him. The burn in his loins made him want to scream. He let Baker yank him out of the house, not quite knowing why. If this was their last stand, he would curse this moment later if a final fornication had been squandered. There would be no captain then, just each one of them swinging from his own rope.

"The next wench I meet will not get off so lucky!" he shouted into Baker's face as the pirates and sailors all poured out of the house.

"Think of your neck, not your dick!" Baker shot back. "Let's head for the tavern! There's bound to be horses there."

"No. We need a boat to get to Great Island straight away. There is no time!" Thomas Brown railed.

"I'm the bloody captain!" Baker snapped.

"I say it is time to vote for a new captain!" Brown said. He glanced at Peter Hoof, a young pirate named Thomas South and the Irishmen behind him as a show of strength. Baker did not have to count to know that the numbers were against him, but he believed that the three men who stood with him were worth twice their number, making things about even.

"Bellamy ain't here to protect you now, you arsehole! He cast you off with me, didn't he?" Baker gloated.

"To look after you, the evil, treasonous snake that you are!" Brown replied.

"But who's going to look after *you?*" Baker spat.

In a flash Brown's hands were around the Dutchman's throat and guns and knives were raised in every direction.

"Stop! Stop! We must flee! The sheriff will find us!" Hoof cut in. He brought his arms down like lumber across Brown's chokehold and broke it.

"Some of us are free men!" South added. "We ain't gonna go down with the rest of you. I was forced against my will!" He tried to step closer to the Irishmen, but they danced away.

"Hell you were! I saw you sign the Articles!" Baker shouted.

"I was *forced!*" South insisted, glancing in turn at the Irishmen, Brown and Hoof, but all of them looked away.

"Come on, Cookie, you're with us," Van Vorst said to Mack. "Or else I'll skin your hide for a mainsail to get us to Great Island!"

"We will dole out his medicine in short order, rest assured," Baker promised. "Follow me!"

"You aren't captain! What need is there for a captain without a ship? We are ashore, and we are each our own man now!" Brown shouted.

The fight erupted again and did not stop until a shot rent the air. The men all stopped at once while the echoes of the gunfire rippled away through the little grove of trees in which they stood, like a stone cast into a still pond.

"*Idiot!*" Baker whispered at Van Vorst.

They listened a moment and heard nothing but the plaintive cry of doves in the trees above them.

"Cole said that the tavern is that way. We go. All of us!" Baker commanded. Van Vorst raised another loaded pistol.

Baker pushed Mack ahead roughly, and Van Vorst aimed the gun at Brown, who otherwise would not move. The men tramped off towards the center of town. Anyone passing along the road that day would have stopped and looked twice at the line of ten wind-swept men wandering around the fields. But no one was there to see them.

When they finally found the tavern, they checked the stalls and found no horses. However, there was the unmistakable aroma of ale wafting out of the building.

✠ ✠ ✠ ✠

When Johnny Cole could not find Justice Doane, he did not know what to do until he thought of the tavern. He did not want to go back to his father empty-handed.

Mehitable Higgins only ruffled his hair when he told her about the pirates. "Aren't you a handsome young lad," she cooed.

Higgins Tavern was soon having the best day of business that anyone could remember. Mehitable did not know who these rough men were, other than that they had come from the wreck that everyone in the southern part of Eastham was talking about. Her father was, at the moment, heading towards the beach to look for anything of value among the wreckage. She knew that her father, had he been here, would have kept the ale flowing.

They were not the handsomest men, Mehitable thought. But they were new faces, and that meant new chances for laughs and maybe even love.

Johnny kept tugging on her sleeve. *"They are pirates! We've got to do something!"* he whispered.

"Let me go, little man. They are paying customers. We are the pirates tonight for taking so many coins from lonely sailors' pockets. Let them leave their coins, and then you can ambush them out back when they go, how about that?" She pulled away gently, and Johnny stamped his foot in frustration.

Van Vorst stared at the boy through a cloud of pipe smoke and thought that he looked very much like the lad who he had recently seen running away through a gunpowder haze. He was trying to determine for certain if this was the same boy, but he was not getting any help from his liquor-addled memory. Part of him wanted to shoot the boy, just to be on the safe side. Then an ale landed squarely in front of him, on the table, diverting his attention. The full bosom leaning over him distracted him further.

"Anything else you require? Must be lonely out there at sea," Mehitable's voice trilled, making his skin tingle.

"Aye..." he said.

"That your boy?" Quintor cut in. "You look too young to have a lad of his size."

Mehitable blushed. "He's not mine. I have none."

"I don't mind," Quintor said with a lewd grin. "I'd not turn you away just for having a little bum hugger."

Johnny followed behind Mehitable as she moved from table to table. He saw a hand flash out in front of him and whack her on the behind. Mehitable yelped and the pirates laughed.

"Boy's got good taste, following around this morsel," Quintor went on.

Mehitable went down into the cellar where her father kept the extra barrels of ale. They were piled in the corner, each one so heavy that she could do little but scrape it a few inches at a time towards the stairs. Some ten feet stood between the nearest barrel and the foot of the stairs. Covering that distance was the easy part. Carrying the barrel up to the main floor was the challenge, one that she knew was impossible on her own.

Dust trickled down from the eaves over head. She heard laughing, shouting and stomping that shook the boards so hard that at any moment she imagined that the floor would splinter and deposit a pile of inebriated sailors at her feet. That would be a good laugh, she supposed.

Mehitable reached into her apron and withdrew a hammer and tap. It would be much more of a bother, but she could tap the barrel here and make trips up and down the stairs to refill the mugs. Perhaps, if the reveling got wild enough, the entire party might move down here, she mused.

She placed the tap and gave it a few swift hammer strikes to drive it home. Then she stepped back and mopped her brow with her sleeve.

A moment later two thick forearms slid out from behind her and wrapped around her waist.

In her ear, a gravelly voice said, "Might I have the first taste?"

She screamed.

Van Vorst spun her around, danced a little jig in front of her and swung her arms up and down in time with his steps as if they were simply at a village fair together. Then he tipped back his head and screamed too, an awful cry that sounded like an Indian calling for blood.

"God, you scared the bloody hell out of me!" she cried, yanking her hand away and slapping his shoulder.

"I was thirsty and could only wait so long. As soon as I heard you tinkering, I knew where to come. Oh yes, I knew that this was the place to be!" he said. Even with his Dutch accent, his voice was thick with suggestion.

"I didn't hear you on the stairs," Mehitable said. He was not the best looking of the bunch. She would have preferred Captain Baker or the tall, quiet Swede, but this one would suffice. He had spirit. Besides, she had learned that looks could be a bitter seduction. That sailor, Sam Bellamy, had taught her that. She had sulked for a while after that rejection, but she knew now that he was not worth it. His choice of that crazy girl, Maria Hallett, had been proof enough of that. There were plenty of other sailors out there to pick from. That a pack of them had ended up on her doorstep seemed like some kind of divine nudge that her own ship was bound to come in. Perhaps it had arrived tonight, she thought. If not, at least this fellow had a funny accent.

"You came here to see me, didn't you?"

"Yes I did. Care for another dance?" he said, pulling her close to him.

"Aren't I giving you enough attention upstairs?"

"I am here, aren't I? The kind of attention I need is best done in private," he said, nuzzling her neck.

"For God sake! How long have you been at sea? Your courting is a tad rough!"

"There is no courting to it. I mean to be satisfied here and now, wench!"

It was not the sort of romance that Mehitable was used to, and when she tried to fend Van Vorst off a second time and he did not budge, she realized that the only pleasure he intended was for himself.

"Release me…"

"Now that you mention it, it has been a long time since I was with a woman," he said. He flashed a broken-toothed grin.

"Let me go!" she cried.

"Whoooo!" he cried with her. "Whoooo… *AHHH!*"

Van Vorst's arms dropped to his crotch to massage a sudden flaring pain. As soon as she was free, Mehitable fled to the stairs, dropping the hammer with which she had broken his grip.

"Damn you, *whore!*" he shouted after her.

The strike was a glancing blow, and soon he was nearly in reach of her again as he scrambled up the stairs behind her.

She dashed towards the main room, but he bolted out in front of her, between a table and the great fireplace, leaving nowhere for her to run but into his arms.

"If you prefer public wooing, then so be it!" he cried. "You are going to soothe that spot that you made ache. Yes, God damn it, you are going to keep at it until I feel all better!"

Mehitable scanned the room, looking for support from any local, but only her uncle was turned towards her. *Not him…* she thought, fearing for his safety more than her own. "Get those fellows at the far table to help!" she told him. Years in a tavern had given Mehitable a cool head. She had seen the underbelly of men many times and was always surprised at how many variations of it there were. She also knew that from that underbelly hung an organ that was always and single-mindedly in search of copulation.

Van Vorst flashed a knife in front of her face. "I don't need no help! I think I can handle you just fine on my own! And I got the Devil on my side if I need him!" he said in his most menacing voice. He slid the knife under the strap of her apron and cut through it.

"Help! Help!" Mehitable screamed.

"Let her be!" Barnabus Merrill said, rising from his table.

Van Vorst turned towards Mehitable's uncle and pulled back his jacket to show off his arsenal of pistols. "Tend to your ale, old man. Let the young have their fun!"

Barnabus did not back down. He took a step towards the Dutchman. The other pirates stood up, drawing weapons and looking around at the Cape Codders.

"Unhand her, you damned piece of filth!" Barnabus cried. To Mehitable's surprise, he whipped out a rusty old dagger, which she had never before seen him carry, from some hidden place in his jacket.

"No!" she cried.

Van Vorst released one hand and pulled out a pistol.

The old man moved faster than any of them imagined, surging past Van Vorst and tearing him across the face with the blade as he went.

"Damn!" Van Vorst exclaimed. He turned and fired blindly, then touched his knuckles to the blood forming on his cheek. "The old fool ain't strong enough to do anything but scratch me!"

"Uncle!" Mehitable cried at the prone figure lying on the floor behind her.

"Did I kill the old bugger?" Van Vorst asked.

Mehitable peered at her uncle but could see no blood, no sign that he had been hit. She wondered if the fall itself was enough to break his brittle, old bones.

Barnabus' body finally twitched, and he cracked open an eye. "Damned pirates never did fight fair, the bastards… But he missed me!"

Mehitable exhaled in relief, then spun towards Van Vorst and hit him as hard as she could in the teeth, before he could raise his weapon again. "Go to hell!"

It only shut him up for a second. Then he gave her a red-tinged smile that made her want to hit him again. The only consolation was that there was an extra gap in his teeth, which she was sure had not been there earlier.

"That's some spirit you got, wench. I can't wait to take a roll with you," he said.

Mehitable slapped the pirate's face again, and this time he did not smile. The fleshy sound rang through the room. It was followed by the hard clack of the pistol being cocked.

"Time for you to behave," Van Vorst said, taking aim.

Then there was a louder sound. The front door crashed in, and Justice Doane's voice boomed out, "In the name of the king and the authority of the town of Eastham, you men are hereby arrested for crimes of piracy against our kingdom!"

The militiamen, including many natives, surged past Doane and filled the tavern room.

The steely, dark faced natives silently gathered the pirates into tighter and tighter circles. When the pirates were rounded up into a frightened mob, toppled upon each other, Doane spoke again, "Had you killed anyone, we would weigh your crimes and punish them here and now, as we see fit. That you didn't, you will stay here until we take you to Barnstable. Then the Crown can administer its own justice. If you are well-mannered, we will put in a word for you. If not..." he left the rest up to the imagination. The pistol that he pointed at Van Vorst's head gave a clear indication of his meaning.

To Doane, the pirates looked more like a group of fishermen or whalers, who struggled like the rest of them to make a living. But he knew that this was big. Once the colonial government found out about it, things would be bigger still. Sooner or later someone would be pressing his seal into the wax on a letter that would ultimately bring the gaze of the whole English government to bear on this little town. A tidal wave was approaching.

Suddenly William Hopkins was standing in the doorway. "Another ship has come ashore up in the northern parish off the Table Lands."

Doane spun around. "What kind of vessel?"

"I don't know, sir. She looks huge, though. She's sitting less than a quarter mile out, on a sandbar."

The way the pirates chattered excitedly around him confirmed Doane's feeling that this was another one of their ships. *A pirate fleet*, Doane thought and shuddered.

It was as if fate had pushed Elder Knowles in at that very moment to hear Mack grumble, "That'd be the rest of Captain Bellamy's boys. I'd bet my life on it."

"Sam Bellamy?" Knowles asked incredulously.

"You've heard of us up here?" Baker exclaimed from the back table where the pirates were listening avidly.

Doane began buttoning his jacket, saying nothing but nodding to his men to follow him out the door.

However, Elder Knowles strode over to where the pirates sat. "I do not know your name. But I do know his. The name *Bellamy* is a curse, and this time we shall extinguish it for good!" he said and thumped a fist on the table.

✠ ✠ ✠ ✠

April 28, 1717- Boston.

Governor Samuel Shute stood by the window in his office in the State House, looking down at Long Wharf in the distance. Sailless masts stood like rows of stripped tree trunks, the mighty forest of Yankee economic power. He thought of it as the wooden heart of the New World empire, whose pulse began in his office and rippled out around the world. It was an empire worthy of an austere colonial palace like the glorious mansion that Shute planned to build on the outskirts of the city.

Shute paced between the window and the table, picking at the remnants of his supper of roasted pheasant. He was ruminating on this business in Eastham where what could be the biggest financial windfall in Massachusetts history had washed up on a desolate stretch of shore – a place which most men in Boston rarely thought about. Perhaps the Puritans of old had needed to keep an eye on their soil and fish-rich Pilgrim neighbors on Cape Cod, back when farming had been the foundation of the colonies. Now commerce ruled, and Shute had spent little time dwelling on the existence of his sparsely settled, philistine constituents in Eastham until today. Now he could not stop thinking about them.

His assistant, one of the few men he trusted, Christopher Lowell, stood on the other side of the table. In Lowell's hand was a letter, which had been delivered that morning. It was written and sent by a man named Nehemiah Hobart *of Boston and, lately, Eastham*, so it said. Neither Lowell nor Shute had ever heard of the man, and both regarded him contemptuously, considering him an obvious mercenary out for reward. Yet the facts of the letter, if true, were astounding.

Lowell spoke as he made a second pass of flipping through the pages, "Even if it is true, consider the fate of your predecessor, Governor Bellomont, thanks to his dealings with the pirate Captain Kidd. Damn unsightly. It almost lost the governor his office and freedom."

"Bellomont was a pompous rascal. As for myself, I was promised five hundred pounds for salary, but the legislature has given me but three hundred and fifty. I am owed, and it seems to me that the cargo of this ship will serve most justly to cover the difference."

"If this is played wrong, it could cost you a knighthood."

"How can it be played wrong? There is gold washing up on the beach and prisoners in hand. We'll hang the prisoners to make the admirals happy, save their souls to make Cotton Mather happy and give a cut to the Crown to make King George happy. I'll be happiest of all because my cut will be the biggest," Shute replied.

"Cheers to that!" Lowell said, raising his glass.

"You too, old friend." He popped another piece of pheasant into his mouth and came over to the table to clink wineglasses with Lowell.

"Have you considered anyone to carry out this mission?" Lowell asked.

"Southack. The man is a decorated captain. He will have no trouble dealing with these Cape Codders," Shute said and raised his glass again. "To reaping the bounty of the sea."

Chapter Three
"The Final Land Division"

May 1717

The spade dug into the dirt as fast as Samuel Smith could drive it. He was downstairs in the basement of his tavern, merely a rough hewn square of dirt upheld by walls of timber. There was a table made from the vertebrae of a large whale, the kind that does not wash up very often, and various crates and boxes full of things that he wanted kept out of sight.

Most of his living had been made on the bending inner arm of the Cape. But he had followed the rumors to the ocean side and there found a treasure that eclipsed any worth he had ever pulled from the bay. A godsend, a sack of gold, had come up in the storm. He laid it in a hole in the ground and covered it with dirt.

Upstairs, Smith looked at the sorry faces, bent over their soup bowls, of the whale men sitting at the long table in front of a massive fireplace.

The men ate in silence. Although they were but a dozen, they felt like an army as he watched his wife filling up the bowls. No whales had been sighted in weeks. Whale soup was beginning to sour in his belly anyway, he thought, as he pulled up his own chair and poked his spoon around in his portion. At least there was ale. Even that could not get much life out of this somber group.

The gold that Smith had found in the water had given him an idea. But he would not share it with anyone but his wife. The rest of the whale men had been to the wreck site too, but none had found hard currency there. Smith was sure that he would have heard such news, had it occurred, because none of the others were clever enough to keep quiet about it.

"What about this land division? We aren't leaving, that's for certain. What do you propose to do if they come to take this place? If we ask the others on the island to help, we'll have plenty more men than Doane. That should scare him off," Eleazer Snow said.

Some of the others nodded in quiet agreement.

Smith shrugged and finished his ale. "No one need leave this place."

"Aye... then what is the plan?" Snow asked. He wanted to ask about the digging in the basement too, but he would give Smith a chance to explain on his own. And if he did not do so soon, then they would all go down and have a peek.

"I don't know, alright?" Smith said, slamming his spoon onto the table. "Rebecca. This is cold," he added to his wife, stepping towards the fire while she wandered over and snatched up his bowl with a scowl.

The wood crackled and roared, wasting itself in a brilliant blaze, but he was not sorry for it. There was little left outside in the forest, perhaps enough for two or three more seasons. After that, whoever owned this tavern would just have to hope that he could make do by feeding scrub brush to the fire. The following year he would have to come up with something better.

Smith was under no delusion that he would end up with a share of Great Island. For a moment he pondered the long, tangled saga of the island. Years ago none of the town fathers had much cared about the place, although even then they claimed to own all of Billingsgate. They were fixated upon the rich fields of Eastham proper, not the few souls who ventured north and made their own deals with the natives. Then the town fathers saw Great Island's abundance of fish, whales and wood, and they tried to divide up the land and parcel it out to men of good standing, as they liked to refer to themselves and their closest friends and family. Yet the lines that they drew were on paper only. Many men had already staked a claim to parts of Great Island, many of which overlapped. Smith had already constructed his tavern. The rough men of the island turned their backs on the land divisions and pronouncements declared in Eastham proper, and the men of good standing dared not come and enforce them. They held more meetings to further divide and record their dubious claims over the island. They called on the residents of Great Island to produce proof of their ownership, knowing that most of those earlier purchases from the natives were sealed by handshake, not deed. However, Smith was an exception. He had insisted on documentation, affixed with the mark of the old native sachem. Dutifully, Smith had delivered his evidence to the Eastham town clerk. Then one day, shortly after Justice Doane had stood up in town meeting to deliver his most adamant pledge to rid Great Island of smuggling, Smith's deed had mysteriously disappeared. For once, Smith had followed the letter of the law, and it had proved to be the biggest loss of his career. Even he could appreciate the irony of it, as unpalatable as it was. Now he felt the fight going out of him. Hidden in his basement was his best chance of leaving this tavern and island with some profit in hand.

The fire felt hot on his eyes, making them water as if he was crying. It was a sensation that he hadn't felt in years, and for some reason it made him laugh. The whole thing was crazy, unbelievable. He did not get a chance to tell his wife about it until much later when the whale men were all asleep. Even then his whispers seemed to echo alarmingly in the little room that he and his wife shared. He was sure that he had only heard eleven pairs of footsteps head up to the loft for sleep, when there were, in fact, twelve whale men. Someone was out there listening. The thought made him grope along the surface of the table near the bed until, with a clink, his fingers found the key to the padlock he had placed on the cellar trapdoor, and he was filled with relief.

"*We must go soon. The men will not wait forever to know what is going on,*" he told his wife.

"Go where?" she demanded, not bothering to keep her voice down.

"*Quiet, woman! Who cares where we go? We shan't have worries anymore.*"

Rebecca snorted.

"*We can even get a servant, so you will no longer have any duties to fret over,*" he soothed.

"You must be talking in your sleep. But it is a good dream," she replied groggily.

The next morning Smith saw a ship prowling off of Great Island, the same ship that he had seen the evening before. The whale men had all gone down to the beach, after a surly, silent breakfast.

Rebecca came up behind him as he stared out of the wide windows at the craft circling out on the bay. She was pulling her apron tight and pinning up her hair, to get ready for baking. Her tone was far more subdued now, "It is Palsgrave, is it not?"

"So it appears…" Smith mused. His mind raced through the mass of details that had washed up out of the sea. He felt Rebecca's hand lock on his arm.

"They made it back after all. Perhaps the bastards did it," he told her.

✠ ✠ ✠ ✠

There was a thumping on the door of the tavern. Samuel Smith opened it to find Justice Doane and his men milling about in the yard.

"Your land has been bought by another," Doane declared.

"I did not sell it," Smith replied.

"You did not own it either."

Smith shrugged. "Says you!"

"Enough games! You were at town meeting. This land is forfeit under whatever pretense it was formally held."

"What sneaking devil bought it?"

"I bought it," Doane said flatly.

It was a rare moment when Smith had no reply, but his lips moved soundlessly as he struggled to comprehend the depths to which Doane had taken their dispute.

"*You bastard…*" he finally muttered.

"This time I will have a look inside," Doane stated.

"Who the hell is this?" Smith said, pointing at Cyprian Southack, a middle-aged man, puffed up with self-importance, who stood next to the justice.

Southack strode forward and pressed a piece of paper into Smith's hand. Smith immediately crumpled it.

"I know what this says, and I won't abide by it! If I am to leave, I will sell for a fair price first!"

Doane reached between the two men and snatched the paper out of the tavern keeper's hands and smoothed it back out.

"You have not read this!"

Southack stuck out his chest, making him resemble the solid soldier that he once was. "This is a proclamation from the *Captain General and Governor in Chief!*" he said and began reading in a loud voice, "I do, therefore, with the advice of His Majesty's council, strictly charge, command and require all Justices of the Peace, Sheriffs, Constables and other of His Majesty's officers and subjects within this Province, to use their utmost endeavors and diligence to seize and apprehend or cause to be seized and apprehended, any person or persons belonging to the said pirate ship, their accomplices and confederates, with the money, bullion, treasure, goods and merchandise taken out of said ship or any of her apparel that shall be found with them or in the possession of any others… All persons whomsoever are strictly forbidden to countenance, harbor, entertain, comfort, conceal or convey away any of the said ship's company or any of their money, treasure, goods or merchandise as they will answer the same at their utmost peril!"

As the words flowed over Smith, he watched Doane with malice. If he had only one more evening. He just needed darkness again, and then he could be away from here forever and the tavern could crumble into dust, for all he cared.

Doane, it turned out, was looking at something else. Smith turned and saw a triangular shape on the horizon, a patch of white sail cutting along the line from Race Point towards his island.

The justice tapped Southack on the arm, and the dreary monologue broke off.

"God damn! That's him!" Southack cried.

Doane snapped an order to his militia, and a group of them headed towards the barn, another towards the house. When Smith stepped to intercept them, Doane hurried forward. "Smith! We have no time for this! See that ship? Do you know who is upon it? The men of Sam Bellamy, the outlaw who you once harbored!"

It was Doane's hand on the butt of his pistol that silenced Smith. Captain Southack looked from one man to another, waiting for further explanation that never came.

Smith moved aside and watched the militiamen file past. Most were natives. There were one or two white men among the crowd, and he appealed to each of them, reminding them of the free ales they had received under his roof, for once wishing that he had doled out more of them. None of the men met his glance, Doane's hold on them was stronger than what came out of Smith's taps.

"Do something!" he hollered at Eleazer Snow and the others who were assembled on the bluff, watching the affair. The whale men stood in an unsmiling line, facing him. None moved or spoke a word. For the first time in his life, Smith saw Doane smile.

"Don't forget to search the whaleboats on the beach," Doane told the last group of militia and pointed them towards a path that led down to the strip of sand below. Turning to Smith, he said,

"I am not uncharitable. You may stay here in the tavern for a day or two, to gather all that is *rightfully* yours, before you are on your way."

Smith walked away from them all, to the viewing platform where he could see Palsgrave's ship growing larger. He did not know which was worse: the fact that the fool jeweler had pulled it off despite him or that he had gotten part of the treasure anyway, only to see it taken from his grasp. None of it mattered now, he thought bitterly.

A hand slid into his, and he felt the cool press of steel between the clasp.

Rebecca kissed his ear in a way that she had not in a very long time.

He felt the key in his hand, dropped it into his pocket and turned to redirect her lips towards his own. "You are a genius," he told her.

"We should be away as soon as they leave."

"Yes, we'll have to risk it in daylight," he said, kissing her again and noticing that she was out of breath. She grinned at his realization.

"I haven't moved so quickly in ages," she said, pressing against him.

He chuckled. "That's my girl. Doane will dig nothing but rocks from that basement! So where did you put the gold?"

"In one of the whaleboats. I put an extra sail there too. That's all I could manage…"

He pushed her away roughly. "You put it in a damned *whaleboat?*"

"What?"

He spun her around, so she could see Doane's men filing down towards the whaleboats lining the shore. "You might as well have handed it over to them and saved them the walk, you idiot!"

She put her hands on her hips and glared at him. "The next time I won't bother with the basement! Perhaps I should have locked you in it when I had the chance!"

As Rebecca stormed off, he heard the shouts of glee, from the barn, as the militia dragged out the sails, wooden beams and casks that he had pulled from the wreck. A few minutes later there was a louder shout down by the whaleboats.

"Now we are finally making progress!" he heard Southack declare as Doane's men loaded everything aboard the wagons that Doane had brought.

Later Smith went to the basement and sat down at the whale bone table, next to the empty hole, wondering if perhaps he should simply close the door over his head and rot away there, until he was as stripped and bare as that skeleton.

✠ ✠ ✠ ✠

Smith slept upstairs in the whale men's loft that night. Any hopes he had of a merry night with his wife under the covers had evaporated after the confrontation with Doane. Now he had nothing but the cold touch of the sheets and a tickle on his nose of frigid air coming through a seam in the eaves, testament to the draft that his men had been complaining about all winter. It was early May, but there was still ice in the air. As he lay there shivering in the sheets, he wondered whether it was his men or his wife who was getting the most satisfaction from his misery.

If he had not been upstairs, he would not have smelled the scent so quickly. His men, bunch of drunks that they were, had fallen too deep into ale-sodden stupors to raise the alarm. Smith's nose caught the acrid odor, and it brought fears of fresh nuisance to his sleepy mind. The whiff was that of wood burning, and he worried that the old hearth had cracked through, setting too much heat against the back wall.

He had just come grumbling out of bed when the window opposite him flared up in a sheet of orange fire.

The sight sent him tumbling back into bed. He was so shocked that he would not have been surprised if Satan himself had burst through the glass.

Instead, the other upstairs windows filled with flame.

A moment later the household came roaring to life. He could hear Rebecca's panicked cursing coming from the bedroom below.

Men fell out of bed, looking groggily around. The few with some clarity left in their drunken minds followed Smith down the stairs and outside where they had to dodge the licking fire that was crawling along the side of the tavern's outside wall towards them.

All around the building, flames climbed the walls. More crackled on the roof where he could see the dark shapes of firebrands, which had been thrown up there to set the blaze.

A host of villains came to mind: Smalley, Justice Doane, French pirates…

"The boards are too rotted and dry! I kept telling you to spend some of our money on fixing this place. Now the whole place will be naught but ashes in a few minutes!" Rebecca hollered.

"*What money?* I put everything I had back into our business affairs! The boats! The whaling equipment! Blood money for those blackhearted pirates in Helltown! The only break we got was down in that hole in the basement…"

"Don't you start, Samuel! If you say another word, you'll be sleeping alone forever! Now go get some water or else there will be nothing left!" Rebecca yelled.

Smith threw his hands up in the air. "Why should we care? This fire is Doane's problem now, not ours!"

"It is our problem because Doane will think that *we did it!* To spite him!" Then, without waiting for her husband to react, she turned and began shoving the whale men, who were gathered watching the blaze, towards the path to the beach. "*Go get water, you fools!*"

She left with them, but Samuel did not. He stood there, transfixed by the inferno. He knew that the place was already ruined. What did it matter, he thought? Soon it would not be his place anyway. If he kept fighting the verdict of the town meeting or Doane's purchase, he knew he would not win. If he petitioned to buy this place on their terms, even if they let him buy it, it would feel like a defeat after all of the claims that he had made on the island. It was over.

A branch snapped in the darkness behind the burning tavern, and Smith pivoted towards the sound. Suddenly he realized how unprepared and vulnerable he was, standing there in his underclothes. What if the blaze was merely a diversion and the true attack was meant for him, he wondered? Not joining the others might prove a fatal mistake.

A man stepped out of the gloom and stared at the conflagration of the tavern, apparently inspecting his handiwork. Then he sensed he was not alone, and he sprung around and faced Smith. He froze there for a moment, surprised to see the tavern keeper.

"Whatever you want, I got nothing left! Everything I owned was in that house. I got no money! Leave me be! I might have taken more than my fair share at times, but I never did real harm to any man!" Smith shouted.

His words seemed to incite the man. He took a step forward. As he approached the firelight, Smith could see the garish red, white and black streaks across his face and his naked chest. In his hair were tied some sort of feathers. Around his neck was a string of sharp teeth.

"What the hell... An Indian..." Smith said.

Raw fear seized him – crazy, horrible thoughts of invasion or uprising. Then he focused on the man's face. The features started to take familiar form in the light. Before he could put a name to the face, the native turned and disappeared into the night.

✠ ✠ ✠ ✠

The exigencies of the mission had prohibited leisurely sailing, so Cyprian Southack kept his sloop, *Nathaniel*, hitched fast to the wind on the journey from Boston to Cape Cod, too fast to properly appreciate the subtle curves in terrain and natural ocean channels. He hadn't been at sea for several years, enjoying his semi-retirement and pursuing his first love, cartography. But he sensed the governor's urgency, and that evoked his sense of duty. It would be good to get on the water again, he thought. Perhaps he would even have a chance to take some depth measurements.

When they broke into the expanse of Cape Cod Bay, a wall of wind from the south reduced their progress to a slow tacking back and forth, allowing Southack to admire the amazing flatness of the bay for some time, forgetting the pull of his mission for a while. The impression it made was similar to a frying pan, in that it was wide and almost uniformly shallow across its bottom. The incessant wind prevented them from reaching the Province Lands until the afternoon of the second day. Veteran seamen were lamenting the ill omen of contrary winds at the start of a voyage. Despite being delayed in schedule, Southack took several moments to gaze out at the empty plain of the bay when they were anchored at Cape Cod

Harbor. It looked as though a man could walk across the sandy surface of the bay from end to end at low tide.

Unfortunately, it seemed as though the veteran sailors had correctly read the omen. There were few men in the muggy desert of the Province Lands or its inhospitable little settlement. Those that were there did not offer provisions, aid or even a welcoming word. The king's law did not lay heavy on them. The land seemed more akin to the Barber Coast of Africa than a spit of Massachusetts Colony. No appeal to law or even payment would elicit their goodwill or rental of one of their vessels. All these observations Southack faithfully recorded in his journal as he and his assistants sat on deck, inspecting the barren land of dunes before them.

Southack needed a sturdy, wide ship to brave the rough spine of the outer cape, off of which lay the wreck. The ship that he took from Boston was too fragile for such work.

With the use of his writ from the governor, he finally succeeded in securing a whaleboat although he was not sure if it was more the paper, and its fancy signature and wax seal, or his blunderbuss and shining cutlass that had convinced the hard men of the Province Lands to provide the vessel.

He took Jeremiah's Gutter, which had recently been widened by the men of Eastham, from the bay through to the ocean. He did not have the inborn hesitation, which the local men had, to risk the sandbars on the ocean side of the channel. Besides, the twists and turns of the marshland called out to him for chronicling. He rowed the whaleboat right through the surf of the breakwater at the end of Nauset Harbor. Only then, when the seas rose up like a herd of galloping horses around him, did he see how easy it would be for a ship of any size to be dashed apart in these waters.

Eventually Southack came to stand on the beach overlooking the distant stump of the wreck, a small section of the *Whydah's* overturned hull, which protruded from the water. The rest of the ship had been smashed to pieces and scattered by the ocean.

He was tired. Mostly, he was sick of the sand. He could feel it in his teeth. His legs ached from trudging through it. He felt as though he had ballast rocks tied around his ankles.

He stared at the man standing before him and felt his irritation deepen. Samuel Harding, one of the most unhelpful locals in a community that had shown Southack nothing but ambiguity and defiance, nonchalantly watched the patter of small shorebirds in the surf. With all of the speculation about what the fate would be of the ten captured pirates from the wreck of the *Mary Anne*, it rankled Southack that no mention had been made about the audacity with which these Cape Codders blatantly snubbed the governor's mandate that the treasure should be collected and transported to Boston, *in its entirety*, as government property. It annoyed him that no one saw people like Harding for what he was: a pirate as bad as the dead men strewn along the beach.

"Let me make this plain in my mind, Mr. Harding," Southack said with strained patience. "You have absolutely *no* treasure in your possession." Southack held up a restraining hand as Harding began to vigorously shake his head for the umpteenth time. "*Even though* you, by your own admission, were the very first person to find the wreck as well as find the only known survivor of said wreck?"

"None," Harding growled.

"If I look in your barn or your home, as I am legally charged to do, I would find nothing to dispute your claim?"

"I said that I have none."

Southack unconsciously twisted the parchment that he held in his hands, the writ of permission to search any dwelling that he saw fit as a potential hiding place for loot from the *Whydah*.

"You'll forgive me for saying, Mr. Harding, that it appears as though there is some kind of conspiracy occurring in this town to keep me ignorant of the extent and content of the wreck site, the government's wreck site, I might add." His temper was rising and along with it his voice. "Any breech against me is also an affront to Governor Shute and constitutes a crime!"

Harding shrugged. "You rowed out there to the wreck every day for three days and you found nothing, right?"

Southack tried to repress the urge to rail at this unfathomably petulant man. "It was too cloudy to see anything because the bottom was stirred up by the storm! I *know* that items have washed up on shore. I have confiscated doubloons from Misters Smith, Mayo, Bassett and Atwood! Do you mean to tell me that those men, who claim to have visited the site two days after you, found precious coins when you yourself found only empty casks and the like!"

"Yes," Harding replied. He tapped his empty palm with a forefinger to emphasis his point. "I'm not saying there ain't any treasure, but I've seen none of it. I've seen enough wrecks to know that which floats comes to shore first and the heavy things get pushed up by the tide later, sometimes days, if at all."

He folded his arms and squared his jaw at Southack. In matters of shipwrecks, he was the expert and the wisdom he'd seen with his own eyes countless times was beyond dispute. Of course, he did not see the need to mention to Southack that he too had visited the wreck site on the second and third day as well.

"Very well, Mr. Harding. But what of the gold coins found in the pockets of the dead men themselves? Did you see none of that?"

Harding's blank stare pushed Southack over the edge. He poked Harding in the chest with the governor's writ. "Mr. Cutler!" he bellowed to his assistant. "Let us begin the house by house search of Billingsgate with the residence of Mr. Harding!"

Harding still did not blink. He picked at a blister on his thumb.

"You'll be in irons if I find evidence contrary to your statement, I promise you. I'll personally make sure that your bonds are welded shut forever! God save the king!" Southack shouted at Harding.

As he expected, Harding merely snorted in contempt.

"Sir?" Cutler queried.

"Yes?"

"The men at the trench..." he pointed a finger towards where a half-dozen local men stood with the Eastham coroner, Samuel Freeman, smoking pipes.

Freeman was a large man. He leaned against his shovel, resting ample weight against it. The faded, stained clothes he wore bagged around him, giving him a slovenly look, Southack thought.

The men had excavated a hundred-foot long trench, a mass grave in which several dozen pirates lay. An equal number of dead pirates were strewn about on the edges of the pit, disregarded by the laborers. It was as messy a sight as Southack had ever seen, and he almost felt a twinge of sympathy for the outlaws, for the indecency they had to suffer in death. Yet he imagined that during the course of the pirates' rampage, their victims had suffered far worse fates.

"Well?" Southack called out to Freeman. He felt like going over there and slapping the pipe from the man's teeth. His fingers drummed on the hilt of his sword, itching to do even worse.

"I haven't been paid yet," Freeman drawled. "You owe us eighty-three pounds, before we'll do any more shoveling!"

"You have likely gotten eighty-three pounds four times over, from their pockets, before I came! I did not have time to inspect the clothes of any of these men!" Southack shouted back.

The Cape Codders turned away.

Out on the water another pirate ship came cruising towards shore. Some people stood, and others sat on makeshift chairs of old logs and wreckage, to watch the graceful, stalking progression of the craft around the wreck site. The pirate ship circled once more, like a wild deer hovering around a wounded mate, and then turned back out to sea.

☒ ☒ ☒ ☒

Justice Doane looked out at the other pirate ship and wondered what he would do if it attempted to land. Most of the militia was close at hand. Elder Knowles was gathering additional volunteers in town, in case there were any survivors from the wreck who came out of the woodwork, with mischief on their minds. But Doane doubted that his people, farmers and fishermen, had enough strength and training to beat back a well-armed, determined landing party of pirates.

The solid, unflappable George Newcomb, one of his deputies, beckoned to him from farther along the beach. Doane caught up with Newcomb, and they walked together to where the bodies from the wreck lay.

"This fellow looks familiar," Newcomb said.

"An Eastham man?" Doane queried. "Were any of our boats out?"

"Not to my knowledge and not bloody likely in that storm. None of our boys are that dumb."

Doane squinted at the dead figure but did not recognize him.

"Down the way, some say that they've found Jacob Nickerson, Ephraim's boy," Newcomb went on. "Hard to tell, though. The face was so badly bruised."

"Take me to him."

With Newcomb trudging along in front of him, chewing thoughtfully on his thumbnail, Doane inspected the bodies they passed along the way. They were all wearing fancy clothes. The body that Newcomb identified as Nickerson was similarly dressed.

"How did Nickerson end up on a bloody pirate ship?" Newcomb asked. He held a fist full of gold, taken from Nickerson's pockets. He pushed the coins around thoughtfully in his palm, like he was inspecting no more than a handful of rocks from the tideline.

"I'll take those," Doane commanded.

"I was just looking at them! Don't see such things every day, do you?" Newcomb grumbled.

They were walking towards the pit where more pirate bodies had been laid. Around them, townsfolk, who were working the edge of the wreck site, watched their progress like jittery seagulls.

Doane felt a rush of anger. "Harding!" he cried and waved the sheepish scavenger over. He knew that in some nook of Samuel Harding's barn was likely the majority of the ship's cargo.

Meanwhile Doane and Newcomb had reached the ditch and peered into it. Many of the faces within were very young. In their death they seemed, to Doane, as peaceful as his own young sons. He had trouble imagining them as terrifying criminals out at sea. Yet he knew what men of any age were like without law to restrain them. "The sweet face of the Devil," Treat would have called it.

Newcomb whacked Doane's arm and pointed, "Look!"

Doane stepped closer to the long grave and peered in. Freeman and his men gathered around to look too.

"Move that one!" Doane commanded, and this time Freeman responded to the order without protest. He dragged a fearsome looking African away and exposed another body underneath. Like the others, the limbs were splayed in a painful contortion, the face gaping with watery shock at his bitter end. His dark hair and beard nearly covered his face. He was wearing a vest of dark velvet, the color of which was hard to tell since it was soaked by the sea. Several guns hung from a sash across his chest.

"Looks like Bellamy, doesn't it?" Newcomb said.

"I believe so," Doane replied.

"God have mercy on his wicked soul," Harding said over Doane's shoulder.

Doane spun around to face Harding. "*You! Is your soul any less soiled?*" he hissed.

Harding gave the justice a betrayed glance. "Me? Are you saying that I am as bad as them in the ditch?"

Doane shook his head savagely. "I am unhappy with *all* of the law breaking that is going on! It seems to have become our nature in this town to throw stones, thieve and lie!"

"Now, wait one minute! I didn't do anything!" Harding shot back.

"No, I will not listen to any more of your deceit. I am sure that you have some thing or other from the wreck hidden away. Perhaps that little shed of yours up there," Doane said, pointing towards the dune crest above them.

"That's not mine! That's the lair of that witch Goody Hallett," Harding responded.

"Really?" Doane said, momentarily taken aback. Everyone had heard that she had settled somewhere in the wilds of the north. A few had even mentioned that she had built a house on a patch of scrubland in the Table Lands. He had never thought to find out for himself or had much business to bring him to these parts until now.

The hut appeared eerily empty. "So that is where she ended up. Rather far away from the comforts of home," Doane mused.

"Too close for me," Harding said. "I've seen strange things on this beach. At night there's white lights flying around her hut on the cliff side. A witches' gathering, I swear it is. She lured this ship to shore, I reckon."

Doane frowned. "She was exonerated from the charge of witchcraft. You can attest to these allegations?"

"Yes."

"You who harbored an accused pirate?"

Harding turned white. "I knew it not!" he protested. "He was a man in need, who was hiding in my barn!"

Doane grit his teeth and looked up the length of the cliff. Directly above he could see the top of the door frame of Goody Hallett's hut. Bellamy was almost at her front door, he realized. It was eerie, true, but it did not elicit any superstitious shiver from him, only a fatigued sadness.

"We'll start by filling this section of trench," Doane said. He wanted Bellamy's body buried first, to be *finished* with this whole mess.

✠ ✠ ✠ ✠

A few weeks later Cyprian Southack was sailing home to Boston. This trip was not going to be remembered as the pinnacle of his career, he thought bitterly. The people of Eastham had turned out to be more formidable than a submerged reef or enemy marines. In the cursory search that he and his assistant, Cutler, had made of the village houses, cupboard after cupboard and barn after barn had been found to be bare. Whether they scowled, smiled or offered a pithy token like a belt buckle, copper pan or single doubloon, Southack could read their eyes like the fathom points of a channel. He knew that they were hiding something, deep in a backyard burrow or grove of trees or who knows where. This was confirmed in his mind when he saw children dashing from house to house ahead of his progress through town, like Indian scouts spreading warning. The promise of treasure was always a step out of reach, a mirage. Instead, his vessel was loaded with a mere pittance. It would have been next to nothing if not for the gold that he had confiscated from Samuel Smith. As it was, it was still barely enough to cover the expenses of this wild goose chase.

Southack had slowly and awkwardly learned something about politics over his long career. He did not fancy it. He put it in the same category as the collective duplicity exhibited by the townsfolk of Eastham. But he realized that his expedition would have farther reaching consequences than just balancing the ledger books. Newspaper editors, the politically ambitious and any number of gawkers would be waiting for him on Long Wharf in Boston. His half-filled hold would be an embarrassment, not only to him, but to Governor Shute as well.

"The wind is coming straight across the bay, sir. We're making good time to Boston," Cutler told him. Southack already knew that, but he was comforted to hear the relief in Cutler's voice. The young man was also eager to be away from the benighted peninsula of Cape Cod.

"Yes, good fortune is finally on our side," Southack said. Then he thought again of the mob waiting for him in Boston. "Or perhaps the winds blow strong in order to bring us more quickly to our final humiliation..."

Cutler, ever the good lieutenant, said nothing. Both men stared out at the flat, mirror-like bay.

After Plymouth the winds began pushing them back towards shore, so the pilot tacked into deeper water. It was there that Cutler pointed into the distance. "Sir, there is a vessel approaching. She's coming fast."

Southack looked out into the distance. "So there is. Hand me the glass."

What he saw in the small circle of the spyglass' lens made him disbelieve his own eyes.

"What are the colors, sir? I see some white in the pennant. I would think that she is one of ours. Especially this close to shore," Cutler said.

Southack tried to blink away the image. He had to wonder if he had been laden with some kind of curse. The ship was closing quickly, and unlike Southack's sloop, her sides were punctuated with gun portholes. Cutler was right – there was white in the flag. It was not the white backdrop of the St. George's cross but a leering white skull perched upon cross bones.

Pirates.

It was in fact the very ship that had been prowling just out of reach during his entire expedition. One of the companions of the *Whydah.*

His own ship was far too small and undermanned to flee or tackle the rogues. Recalling the grim faces and mass of weapons on the bodies of the dead men from the wreck, he was loathe to risk his own innocent and pithy crew.

"Strike the sail," he said sadly. There was nothing now to do but wait. Reaching into his pocket, he pulled out his sketch pad and recorded the details of the coming ship as it bore down upon them.

Chapter Four
"Days of Judgments and Revelations"

October 1717

To some present, the trial had been a farce. The members of the Admiralty Court, led by Governor Samuel Shute himself, sat on an upraised dais in their puffy, white wigs: Lt. Governor William Dummer, Vice-Admiralty Judge John Menzies, the captain of the *HMS Squirrel*, the Collector of Plantation Dues and seven other council members. Shute did little to disguise his disappointment with the results of Southack's mission. He did not care if the jury appeared to be the stacked deck that it was. Ensuring that their point of view was well-represented was a privilege of both office and empire. Shipping, part of the great economic gears of the English realm, would be protected. The pirate scoundrels would get the justice they deserved regardless of Southack's incompetence. This way, there would be no mistakes, Shute thought.

Yet the jury turned out to be not without mercy. Alexander Mackconachy, Thomas Fitzgerald, John Dunavan and Thomas Davis were judged to be forced men and, therefore, exonerated. Reverend Cotton Mather sat smiling angelically when even Thomas South was acquitted and walked penitently from the courtroom amidst the vociferous protest of Baker and the other condemned men.

Now those who had been found guilty were back in their dank cells in the Boston jail. Mather sat with them on the cold rock benches and stiff wooden chairs, appropriate material reminders of their coming contrition, Mather told them. All of the rebellious fire had been snuffed out of them. They sat in the near dark, listening to the droning, soporific voice of the reverend, like the seductive hum of breakers, each man alone in his thoughts. They looked younger now, not in their eyes, where most wore both the exhaustion of their tour of hedonism and the weight of their ordeal in the surf and courtroom, but in their faces, which seemed twenty-something again, like the final flicker of sunlight before it sets in the water.

"Your riches were achieved by sin, so they were punished by a devastating shipwreck, as is the will of God. There was no other way for you men to cleanse your souls because you refused to repent of your own accord! Do you still doubt the power of God?" Mather preached. Peter Hoof and Jean Shuan shook their heads remorsefully.

"*I repent. I reject all of my old ways. I love only God. I think only Godly thoughts now*," Thomas Baker whispered in what he hoped was a pious tone.

"Ah! A good overture! But you have been a great sinner, have you not?" Mather replied.

"Yes," Baker admitted. "But I am changed. God's storm stripped me clean of my sin. I feel anew and shamed and ready to live a better life."

Mather laid his own frail hand on the thick arm of the Dutchman. "My friend, the spirit of your words is admirable, yet the penance must be paid, and God does not care whether your debt is satisfied in ignorance, rebellion or supplication. All debt must be paid. Only then does He decide your eternal fate."

"You can't put in a good word for me, then? You can't save me?" Baker gasped. He had thought that he could cling to the old preacher's religious nonsense like a raft. Then, when he was safe and free, he would sail away forever.

Mather gave a sad smile. "I am here to save your soul, my friend. Your body is the price demanded of you to pay your great debt."

Baker fell silent. He had never protested his innocence. It was not simply about their pirate code but more so due to the fatalistic realization that no one would believe him. He had been a captain in the end. The common pirates would not try to shield him when the courts pounced to seize their required sacrifice. His biggest regret was that Sam Bellamy was not with them as he should be. The gallows pole was a more fitting end for him than falling into the deep sleep of the ocean.

His venomous thoughts were fueled by the decision that he knew was solely Bellamy's fault. Deep in his heart Baker knew that they should have kept sailing forever, never touching down where the other world might ambush them. They had come too close to land, and now the dream had vanished. He would have left Bellamy eventually had he been given the opportunity. He had simply run out of time.

"We were forced men!" Simon Van Vorst cried hysterically, startling Baker out of his meditation.

"No! Sin is never a matter of force. It is always a choice! If the choice was between death at the hands of the pirates who took you or joining their sinful ways, the Godly choice would have been to take death!" the old man's voice rose, straining, to its height.

"And you? What do you say for yourself?" Mather asked Hendrick Quintor even though it was obvious, by the way that the man was curled up on his bench, face towards the stone wall, that he would not speak.

"See! This one is so terrified of God's retribution that he can not even look an agent of God's mercy in the face. He sees only the dark wall of oblivion!" Mather went on. "He will be on the other side of that darkness soon and, I'm afraid, languishing in that pit of despair forever!"

Still Quintor did nothing but shake.

Next to Quintor, Thomas Brown was muttering to himself. There was no energy left to expend on any rivalry with Baker or the others, with the reverend in the room and the clack of the hammers building the gallows coming through the window.

Mather began to walk towards the door, but he stopped in front of Brown, "And you, Brown. Have you come to accept the sins of your ways?"

"Yes." Brown's voice seemed far away. The black flag had seemed to be a proclamation of freedom, but now he saw that the grinning skull assured nothing but death.

"Release your sins to the Lord!" Mather commanded.

Brown's eyes remained downcast. After a pause he said quietly, "Whoring, gambling, drinking, lying, thieving... A miserable life."

Mather wagged his head gravely, his white wig dancing upon his scalp. However, Baker heard something different in Brown's words. He heard the giggle of pretty, young women, the sound of liquor pouring out of the rum bottle and the jolly curse laid upon a far off ship of prey cutting through the wide, clear blue ocean. And it was all happiness.

✠ ✠ ✠ ✠

November 1717

On a cold gray day, the condemned men were put in a boat and rowed across Boston Harbor to the scaffold that had been erected on the shoreline of Charlestown. Baker tried not to look at the countless number of small boats filled with jeering spectators as he and his companions rode across the lapping harbor water, to where the nooses swung in the breeze. Instead, he tried to hold onto the image of sailing through the bright, West Indies sunshine.

Mather stood upon a boat anchored near the hanging platform, with the governor and members of the legislature next to him. The old preacher was still at it, but it was too late, and Baker was glad that the words were carried off in the wind. The only people that mattered now were himself and the hangman, who watched them approach, through the slits in his black hood. To himself, Baker promised to keep his dignity to the very end. He had heard that sometimes the condemned would press a gold coin or two into the hangman's palm, hoping to increase their odds of a hard and quick break on the rope. He would be damned if he would pay for his own killing. Not that he could anyway. After everything they had done in the tropics, he was here without a penny in his pocket. Such contemplation brought forth a macabre laugh. It had turned out to be quite a life, short as it was. With his final steps towards the gallows, Baker tried not to think about the executioner but instead raced to replay as many happy memories as he could.

Quintor was sniffling like a beaten child, distracting Baker and making him furious. He thrust away his irritation and clung to the image of the eyes of a serving girl in a smoky tavern room. She was looking at him, and he was looking at all of her... Love, not anger, is what he wanted to remember. Then the eyes became lanterns, swinging on their hinges on the back streets of the balmy town of Nassau, like cat's eyes...

There were more speeches, of course, by the governor, who thanked the Lord for stamping out the evil bane of piracy in society, and by Mather, who asked the Lord to now turn around and forgive that same evil.

Then Baker was surprised to hear Brown himself make a rambling, horrible, treasonous speech.

"All sailors must beware of the wicked life, such as the fate that came to me! God turned on me and let me fall into the hands of these evil men around me! Do not let pirates take you if you value your life and freedom! There is nothing but darkness hanging over those ships! Pirates took my fate and wrecked me..."

When it was over, Baker was steaming. He had been distracted by all of the talk and lost much precious time. He looked anxiously over at the hangman, hoping by force of will to stay his hand for a moment longer. He was trying to remember a party on New Providence, on that island where they say that all good pirates go when they die. Instead, he heard singing, in the language of his childhood. It was Van Vorst, acting like he was as drunk as ever and standing at the rail on a moonlit night, with nothing but the warm sea around them. This time, though, it was a song that the fool Mather would have liked if he could have discerned the words: *Loving God... Loving family...* Baker's daydreams were shifting, blowing away like smoke from a fire. He saw his mother and father standing in front of their tiny homestead in New Amsterdam. He saw his sisters dressed beautifully for church. Suddenly he too was crying. He couldn't stop even though he willed it away with all of his might. He had run away to get far away from all of those people, places and memories. How dare they show up now, after a lifetime of finally ridding himself of all that pain, he seethed. But they would not go away. The ships in his mind sunk over the horizon, and then all he could see was his family singing in his childhood parish church. Suddenly he realized that he too was singing. It grew louder and louder. So his final defiance was not some curse at the sky but a beautiful song from his youth. He was almost starting over. He was singing out for his own joys and love, against this brutality that was condemning him. So much in his life had been beautiful and totally his own, like arrows of sunlight through the sheets of darkness. He sang unashamed until he felt a rush of air beside him and, without looking, sensed the empty space where Van Vorst had just been standing. Don't look, he told himself, but out of the corner of his eye, he saw the hangman grab the next rope over, and it tugged gently around his Adam's apple. He sang as loud as he could although he suddenly realized, with a shock, that he would not make it to the next chorus...

BOOK FIVE

Of Tides and Shifting Sand

Justice Doane saw the mass of torches moving in his direction, and he let out a groan. He assumed that it was the posse of volunteers that Elder Knowles had promised to organize. Here it was, several weeks too late. Doane thanked the Lord that the other pirate ship had not decided to land.

From his dragging gait it was obvious that Knowles led the procession.

"You are too late, all of you! The pirates are all dead but those who are being sent onward to Boston for trial! There is no need for this assembly!" Doane shouted. Pivoting his head, he muttered a command to Deputy George Newcomb to be ready should the crowd turn unreasonable. He could see the fear in the man's face as if an order to fire on their friends and neighbors might actually be given. Something, however, needed to be done.

Men, women and even older children had dipped branches into tar buckets and lit them on the crackling bonfire that still roared farther down the beach. What they intended to do against armed pirates, had there been any, Doane could not fathom. He was grudgingly impressed that the elder had worked them into such a lather as to risk themselves so wantonly. Treat himself could hardly have done better.

"Elder Knowles, a word with you if I may?" Doane said. He knew that Knowles was at heart a reasonable man, so he fully expected him to step out of line and join him. But the man's pride was too damaged, Doane soon saw. He had taken the plight of the Hallett girl as slight on his own character. He knew too that there had been a run-in between Knowles and Bellamy.

Knowles held his torch aloft and shouted to the crowd, "We're not here for the pirates. We are here for Goody Hallett! Although, in truth, a witch and a gang of pirates are sprung from the same tainted seed! Was she not in communication with these pirates? Did she not bring them to us! Yes, she did! She is a devil's boil, who has been allowed to fester among us for far too long! We are all law-abiding citizens, but this malice has grown above the law! It has paralyzed the law!" He pointed over towards Doane, who was startled to observe hateful glances directed at him from the crowd.

"Now we the citizens of Eastham must act together and purge this evil from our town!"

Behind him the torches cast ghoulish red and orange shadows over the crowd.

"One and all of us recall Goody Hallett when she was an innocent maid in our midst. She was driven from us because she had ceased to be so. Now, left to her own devices in this *Devil's Pasture*, who knows what kind of deals she has made with Satan! Remember that, if you fear to strike. We must drive her out, along with all of the outlaws who she is in league with! Remember the warning of the great squid that came among us the summer before last! The seeds of wickedness that were planted then now do come to full, repugnant flower! That foul plant must be uprooted!" Knowles cried.

"Don't you remember that she was found innocent of the charge of witchcraft by our jury, our law!" Doane countered.

"It was not unanimous! There is still doubt! She is a murderess, who killed her child with her neglect! Such callousness towards life, particularly life that came from her own womb, suggests devilry to me!"

Only then did Doane see who stood at the elder's shoulder. She had no torch of her own, so when the light of the elder's flame swung towards her, Alice Hallett was illuminated and looked to Doane to be a forlorn, chilling sight, like a pale, mute statue.

"*Burn Goody Hallett out! Hang her!*" the crowd called, making Doane wince in sympathy for Alice's plight. If she felt similarly, she gave no outward sign.

The mob began climbing up the slope of the dune, heading towards Goody Hallett's hut on the crest. How they had discovered her dwelling place, Doane did not know, but it mattered little at the moment.

Knowles pointed towards the hut and said, "If the justice and the king's man, Southack, will not help us cleanse the town of devilry, then we will have to do it ourselves! We start there!"

"What should we do?" Newcomb asked Doane.

"Stay with them! Find those you know well and talk some sense into them!" Doane commanded. There was only one deputy on hand. The rest were farther along the beach where the wreckage was being guarded.

Alice Hallett saw the woeful, primitive structure that her daughter supposedly lived in, and it brought tears to her eyes. Horses in a stall or chickens in a coop had better shelter. The mound of moss-covered thatch and wind-bent branches seemed worthy only of a wild animal. Part of her, she had to admit, was not sorry to see it burn.

The torches took to their work with devastating speed, dropping through the cracks in the structure and filling it with fire. The crowd howled at the incineration, sounding despicably like beasts themselves, Alice thought. She had prayed that her daughter not be here, and thankfully, there was no sign of Maria. That too troubled Alice. She wondered if her daughter yet walked this earth or if her bones lay somewhere out here in this desolate plain. The hut looked long abandoned, but there was no way to tell for certain from such a crude construction.

Quicker than anyone expected, the hut was reduced to cinders, yet the mob's fever did not subside.

"Comb the area! She might be hiding in the trees, and we shall flush her out and then build another fire!" Knowles cried.

"You will kill my daughter?" Alice demanded. She was shaking all of a sudden.

"You did not protest when she was condemned or cast away! You did not seek her out! Nothing has changed for the better since then. If anything, her scourge has grown. She is no longer your daughter, but a minion of evil," Knowles said.

"If she is no longer my daughter, then you are no longer my husband. I say that in front of all of you, as witnesses. *I need no man who calls for the murder of my daughter!* For that is what this is!"

"Well said!" Doane's voice boomed over them. A half-dozen of his men now stood behind him, pistols drawn. "This exceeds any punishment that is warranted. Maria Hallett was exonerated from the charge of witchcraft. To be found guilty, new evidence is needed. Otherwise, this will indeed be blood on our hands. I want this town brought into *order!*"

"I am the minister of this town!" Knowles shouted.

Doane fished into his jacket pocket and drew out a scrap of paper, which was mostly burned away by fire. The justice brushed at the blackened edges and then cleared his throat. "This is not from this fire but from another recent blaze at Smith Tavern."

"You seek to divert us, Doane!" Knowles said.

"Plenty of sins have been uncovered recently. Many of us have been hiding things that will sooner or later see the light of day!" Doane's voice rose to compete with the torrent of protest around the fire.

"As reverend, I will seek atonement from any sinners," Knowles said.

"You will not!" Doane thundered. "This paper is a piece of evidence, miraculously spared from the fire. On it is a list of names that Smith writes were *receivers of said smuggled goods over the past five years.* Fate has erased all of the names on this list but one. As plain as day it reads, *Elder John Knowles.*"

"Everyone knows that Samuel Smith was a liar! You cannot seriously take the word of a *pirate* like him!" Knowles roared.

"I take this paper as proof. Smith had this list hidden in his home. He was not using it for blackmail. Perhaps it was once meant as insurance, but it proves him at fault as well. Regardless, it tells a sordid tale. We shall put this to a vote, of course, but I do not believe that we should employ a minister, or *acting* minister, who is proven to be involved in illegal trade."

"This is outrageous! Every other man here bought goods from Smith, just like everyone here took from the wreck! Why not arrest us all?"

"Only you are indicted by proof. Believe me, I do not relish this. But your conduct here makes me worry about your future deeds. I must consider the town's welfare."

"Samuel Harding bought from Smith. And John Cole, your lieutenant. And even our precious *Reverend Treat* did, for God's sake! And another two dozen men and women who I see standing *right before me!* This is prejudice to penalize me for our collective misdeed!" Knowles cried, spinning around and glaring at the crowd, which was quickly calming down and backing away, individual torches peeling away, like lightening bugs dancing out into the night.

Doane watched Knowles stand sulking by the smoking remains of Goody Hallett's hut and resolved to pay very close attention to the views of the next preacher before offering him a salary and land holdings.

Alice Hallett saw something moving in the bushes that no one else spied. She moved cautiously towards it, peeled back the leafy covering and looked at a young woman who she barely recognized.

"*Maria…*" she whispered.

For a few heartbeats mother and daughter observed each other through the tangle of branches. The dying flames of the fire occasionally flashed across Maria's face, allowing Alice to take measure of her. Her daughter's clothes had long since frayed and now were a patchwork of different colored bits of cloth and animal fur. A disturbing string of teeth hung around her daughter's neck. The look of Maria herself, with her wild eyes and unkempt hair and much of her prized splendor worn away like paint weathered off, made Alice gasp. Maria looked so far from the sweet girl who Alice had given birth to that she could not stop herself from crying at the waste of so precious and promising a beginning.

The branches snapped as Alice pushed through them, but she no longer cared who heard or saw. She gathered her daughter into her arms and heard her whisper, "*It was Sam Bellamy's ship. He came back.*"

Alice patted her daughter's head gently. She never wanted to hear the name *Sam Bellamy* again as long as she lived. "He is dead, my child. Justice Doane found the body."

"No, no. I looked at every man on the beach," Maria said.

In the darkness Alice could not tell if her daughter feared that the sailor still lived or dreaded that he had died. She offered no comment but a sigh.

Eventually the crowd moved away. Alice heard her husband calling out for her, a harsh cry devoid of warmth or worry. Then there was nothing but silence, and she knew at last that he would not be troubled should she be lost to the dark wilderness.

"Come. We have far to go this night." She lifted up her daughter and stood in the pitch black, wondering where to go. There were houses all along the King's Highway where people would know her and shelter her, but she did not think that she could look any of them in eye at the moment, perhaps never again. If her daughter had lived for over a year in the woods, then Alice knew that she could last a few nights out in the open, until she made it to her destination.

For several miles the thickness of the night seemed to silence them. The only sound was the crunch of their footsteps in the sand and the crumbling press of waves on the shore below. In the surf Alice saw flecks of shiny light, tricks of the eye to one who didn't know better. Alice had seen their like before and knew that if she went over and drew her finger in a line across the sand, a tiny trail of sparks would follow in the path, like the tail of a shooting star. Her father had once told her that it was the display of some tiny sea creature. As a girl, she had preferred to think of it as the washed up dust from the great moonbeam that falls across the surface of the sea. She smiled and marveled as much at the resurfaced, old memory as the glitter in the sand.

Finally, conversation came awkwardly out, like fits of wind blowing out of the night.

Alice told her daughter about the goings on at the farm, the strong herd of cattle this year and the fullest crops in a decade. She did not praise the extra hands in the Knowles family or any superior skill of that clan to explain the sudden fertility. Thankful was now married, she said, and had taken her place among her husband's family in Barnstable.

"I was to name the baby Samuel... after his father," Maria said suddenly.

Alice walked with breath held, sending her mind off among the hum of the insects in the shrubs on the dune crest. But she could not drown out the slow, sad chronicle of her daughter:

"He had dark hair and little brown eyes. When I held him, I felt as though if anything should happen to him, I could live no longer. I don't know what happened to me. This little person was suddenly there, and I felt like I had known him forever, better than his father even. Better than my own father. I cannot explain how much I loved him. I only knew him for one day... *oh God*, what have I done? *What have I done?* I left him to die in that barn. He was all alone in there, so scared. He must have been so, so scared..."

The words mesmerized Alice. They entered her like no words she had ever heard in her life, going right through her skin and into her inner organs. In truth, she had not thought much about Maria's baby, other than as an object of law breaking. Now she could picture him so clearly as if he was suspended right out in front of her. Try as she might, she could not blink him away even when her eyes became awash with tears.

Maria was crying too. She had no voice left for the rest of her story, but Alice knew it anyway. She had lived it.

"You would have had five brothers and sisters had God willed it. Did you know it was that many?"

"No…"

"Yes. They were all so beautiful. Like your little Sam, I am sure. In a way you were lucky. For you had your little one for a day whereas I had mine for scant minutes, if at all. None lived long enough even to be given names or christenings for their poor little souls."

"They are at peace. I do know that. Why it is said that God punishes the un-christened, I do not know. My little Sam does not burn in the eternal fire. My heart tells me this," Maria said.

"I believe you are right. That is why I named them anyway: Seth, Amaziah, Grace, Josiah and Prudence. I know that it is foolish. Elder Knowles would have called it so."

"But not father."

"No, he did not think it foolish. My poor husband. All I wanted was to bless our union with happy children. I never could do even that. Even you did not end up happy, my child. For that, I am so sorry."

She had left her own child out there in the dark wilderness of Billingsgate, all alone and scared. Who of them needed more forgiveness when all of their sins were measured out?

"I loved your father deeply… Did you know that?" Alice choked out. "No man ever made me feel so glad to wake up in the morning even if it was only to put bread in the oven and mend clothes all day. You did not see it because I did not show how much I looked forward to waking up over and over with him. I would give anything for just one morning back with him, to show him how happy and lucky I felt. I just assumed that we would be that way forever."

Maria's hand slipped into her mother's. "That is how I felt about Sam. You may say that I was too young for such love but so were you. Why couldn't it happen the same way for me?"

"It could, child. We may all find love again."

"I am sorry that Elder Knowles is furious with you. Do you care for him at all?"

"He should not reproach me for defending my child. In all other ways I have been a dutiful wife," Alice said, lapsing back into her stiff bearing.

"Men are the ruin of us," Maria said.

"Yet they do occasionally provide us with great gifts," Alice said, pulling her daughter into embrace. They had cut inland, through a long swath of trees, and come out at the King's Highway near the bridge at Blackfish Creek. There Maria hesitated.

"We go south," Alice declared.

"To the Knowles farm?"

"No. To Yarmouth and your father's kin. If they will not welcome us, then there is a cousin of mine in the New Jersey colony. He was always kindhearted towards me. Perhaps he will take us in."

"You will survive," Maria said softly, gently releasing herself from her mother. "And thank you for coming for me..."

Alice blinked at her daughter, not comprehending until Maria began walking in the other direction.

"What are you doing?"

In response Maria touched her disfigured cheek. "I do not know what is to become of me, but I know that there is no place for me in the places you speak of. No man would want me in his household."

"That's not true! They are kin! Where else would you go?"

Maria wiped her eyes on her shirt sleeve as she shrugged. "Helltown? Farther?"

"No, not after everything!"

"Because of everything is why we must part," Maria said. Then she pointed towards the west and said, "There is a Punonakanit village on Indian Neck. Follow the highway for a couple of miles. They are Christians and will welcome you. In the morning they can take you across to Yarmouth. They are good people from what I have heard."

"Maria..."

"You found me, and one day I will find you again," Maria added, giving a forlorn smile.

✠ ✠ ✠ ✠

Maria's mother would not turn to leave. Upon her face was the kind of emotion that could have changed things had she shared it with her daughter long ago.

"This is a chance for a new life. A better one," Alice pleaded, trying to follow Maria.

Maria backed away. "Please just go... There is no place for me in Yarmouth or New Jersey."

"You were right! I was weak! We do not need a man to shield us. There are colonies in which women fare better under the law. Should we not stick together, now that we have found each other? After all we have suffered?"

The tremble in her mother's voice brought fresh tears to Maria's eyes, but she increased the distance between them.

"I know I deserve your punishment, but please do not go!" Alice cried.

"I am not trying to punish you! I do not belong anywhere but out here now!" Maria said, throwing her arms out as if embracing the desolate, shadowy land around them. She did not think that she could go forward any easier than going back. In fact, she did not feel that she could go anywhere. Upon the King's Highway she felt suddenly vulnerable and exposed. All she wanted was some time to think, in some safe place. She hurried back towards the Devil's Pasture, like a creature returning to its den. She ran until she could no longer hear her mother plaintively shouting her name. She did not stop until she was deep into the inky socket of the night and the familiar, isolated silence that she was used to.

A cloud of smoke came rolling out of the shadows as if her hut was still burning nearby, although she knew her dwelling was nothing but a heap of charred wood. The smoke was actually fog creeping along the gullies of the Devil's Pasture. She felt the wet chill that floated in behind it, and she hugged her shoulders and hurried onward.

The remains of her hut were little bigger than the spent bed of a cook fire. She had expected her heart to throb at the sight, but all she felt was a twinge. Another part of her twisting fate had passed, and all she could think about was which ways the future might push and bend her down the road. If there was one thing that she had learned, it was that every twist of fate led her to more bitter surprises.

Her thoughts carried her over a ridge of dunes, and when she glanced back, all that was in view was an undulating plain of sand and scrub. Her hut was gone. The thought occurred to her that there was nothing left to inform future inhabitants of this place that she had ever lived here. In fact, her entire life gave her that feeling.

At least there was the monument. To other eyes, it would seem but a jumble of stones, but it would last for a little while at least, she hoped. And as long as she lived, she would understand its meaning.

She sat before it and said a prayer for little Sam, that he had indeed made it safely to heaven and found his grandfather waiting with open arms, the way that she had so often imagined it during those long nights sleeping alone on this bluff. Whether she had the right to ask for such blessings, she did not know. Nor was she sure what she was at heart, be it witch, medicine woman or simply an average woman who had been sent down a dark road. All she knew was that she felt a comfort here in the deep, quiet night, alone on a cliff overlooking the sea. The solitude was, perhaps, her curse. At times it seemed like justice. After all, so many of the lives that had touched hers had veered off towards their own disastrous ends. Sometimes it felt like she had a pile of guilt inside of her as heavy as the monument of stones.

In truth, she did not know where to go. She stood on the precipice where she had hurled her curse out at the sea and the world. Magic did indeed exist, she decided. She had witnessed power and mystery of all sorts. She had even contributed to it. What part God and spirits played in all of it, she did not know. It was the deeds of men and women that caused the most pain and havoc. Therefore, she decided to keep her distance from their dangerous world. Even as she held the thought, she also heard herself contradicting it. A view of the ocean, its vast stretch of moonlit waves, reminded her of what could be a long life before her. Would she be able to spend the rest of it hidden away in the dunes of this place?

For some reason John Julian came to mind. He had vanished weeks ago without a trace or word. Were he here in this moment of uncertainty, he would ask the spirit world for a sign. He had taught her to build a fire and give offerings to the unseen world, in exchange for advice, protection, even power. A few hours ago her hut would have provided flame enough to ask as big a question as she could imagine. She wondered if a whisper of some answer might still be lingering in the last puffs of smoke from the embers.

"Show me a place where there is a chance for me to have some happiness," she muttered into the night.

Then she waited and let the night wash over her, all of her senses alert for some response. But she heard and saw nothing unusual. She sighed and stood up. The spirits did not seem to care where she would go.

✠ ✠ ✠ ✠

John Julian had tried to live in peace. Then he had tried open war. He had tried to leave his land and had almost died, only to live to face his omen one more time. That fog off of Monomoyick was the smoke of the Great Spirit, the barrier between the worlds. What he had seen through that smoke made this world seem but a murky, smeared reflection in a puddle. But the spirit world was not ready for him. It had spit him out, back to shore, when it had swallowed the *Whydah*. It had left him standing on the beach, feeling profoundly humble and grateful that he alone seemed to have survived the destruction of the ship.

When he discovered that he was alive and, amazingly, deposited at the foot of the dune atop which the witch girl's hut perched, he did not know what to do next.

The girl's hut was empty, but later after the sun rose, he observed her among a large crowd of English, who were coming from all directions to investigate the wreck. For a time he lay among the dune grass on the ridge of dunes and watched the whites pick apart and horde the remains of the pirate ship. Their numbers were great, and he constantly worried that he would be discovered. Even the swamp seemed in danger of infiltration by the scavenging mob. It seemed as though every English man, woman and child who lived in these parts was congregating at the wreck site. Thus, it was the perfect time to visit his land on Great Island, with the desperate hope that the storm had done something magical to it, perhaps ripping it from the land and making it a free island unto itself.

As it turned out, the spit looked the same as it ever had. The only difference was a set of four poles that had been driven into the ground in the middle of the landscape. They were arranged in a square, and already two of them were connected by long boards. A great pile of lumber was stacked in the sand nearby. Julian ran to investigate and found no sign of any men, just a few mallets and saws, which had been dropped haphazardly on the ground. Julian guessed that the tools had been discarded in haste by men who had rushed off to the wreck site. The tools came in handy to tear the footings and boards apart.

When he had finished, Julian was panting from his furious exertion. His eyes roamed to the hillcrest where the tavern stood, and he knew that he had to strike back at least once…

After burning Smith Tavern, Julian had returned there briefly to collect what nails he could find among the charred remains of the building. These he planted on the north end of the island – his end – and murmured a spell over each one so that each nail would bring the same destructive fate to a similar English dwelling.

After that there was nothing else that he could think to do. His interpretation of the omen had been all wrong. Mittawa had told him about a fish, which she called a beast, and it had come. She had seen a man, and he had come too. The man, she said, might be mistaken for a fish. Julian had thought that she was referring to the sailor or perhaps the father fish spirit. But that is not what Mittawa had meant at all. Slowly, like a shoot breaking through the hard shell of a seed, the answer had crept into his mind. "Things are not always as they seem. A fish is not always a fish," she had once told him. The squid and sailor, they were simply messengers to tell Julian that the crucial time was at hand. And he, John Julian, was the omen. He was the man, trying to live with peace and respect, and also the beast, fighting tooth and nail. Either way, he was not able to save the land. That is how he had come to interpret his aunt's words.

His heart was heavy. All he could hope for was to be given another sign. Until then, he would wait… Waiting, it seemed, had become the essence of his life.

✠ ✠ ✠ ✠

In the end Julian returned to the swamp. For much of the time, he simply stared at the trees, which looked so much like wise village elders, but he heard nothing from them but an occasional, indiscernible murmur of wind through their branches. He left the swamp only to gather sustenance and medicine. Otherwise, he sat and waited in the gloomy, wet forest, cut off from sunlight and feeling much closer to the spirit world than the land of flesh-and-blood men and women. Sometimes a chill would scrape across his skin or the hairs on his arms would rustle even though there was no breeze among the cedars. The spirits were close, but they did not call to him, as if they too were waiting.

There was other company too in that watery den where Julian hibernated. Much of the food and herbs that he collected were in aid of a man who spent his first days rolling on a bed of moss, deliriously crying out commands to a crew that had left this world and a ship that lay under the waves.

Twice now Julian had pulled Sam Bellamy out of the surf, from death back into life. In the beginning he was not sure that Bellamy would survive his wounds and fever as readily as the storm, which in itself had been a close call. But the fever cleared, and the sailor found his senses and his voice, but not his legs. Bellamy's lower limbs had been badly broken in the wreck. It took weeks for the sailor to be able to haul himself to his feet, and that he could not do without hollering.

After that, Bellamy stepped gingerly among the roots of the ancient trees. It took only fifty paces for him to become sore and exhausted. Then Julian would start a fire and boil the herbs, forcing the sailor to drink for his health, ignoring Bellamy's complaints that he would be better served by a bottle of rum.

From time to time Julian saw a ship haunting the wreck site. After describing it to the sailor, Bellamy grew excited. "It is Palsgrave!" he exclaimed. From then on Bellamy drank the broth without complaint and forced himself to trudge fifty paces, then sixty, then more. He hatched a plan for his rescue, and Julian encouraged his progress towards that goal, fighting off a slight surge of jealousy that he did not have his own form of rescue lingering.

Bellamy asked endless questions, cursed when he learned about the arrest of his fellow survivors and blamed himself for the fate of the victims of the wreck. But mostly he wanted to know what had become of the witch girl. Julian had not seen her the few times he had been to her hut after the wreck. If he had, he was not sure if he would have informed her that the sailor lived. Julian had no doubt that she had some part to play in the swirling destruction of the *Whydah*. In the last fatal moments of the ship, he had looked to shore and seen her bonfire sputtering on the coast despite the slashing rain. He did not know if the sight of the sailor would please her or incite her to further violence. So when he did not find her, he did not search her out. To the sailor's repeated questions, he patiently answered only that she had been driven to the highland, lived here for a while and now was gone. After that he said that he did not know what had befallen her even though he had some idea. The last time that he had been to her dwelling, following the trail of a fat spring rabbit, he found nothing there but blackened sticks jumbled in a pile of soot. The image of Mittawa's ruined *wetu* flashed in his mind, and he suspected that another witch had met a fiery end.

Bellamy was not dissuaded. "Find her... She lives," he told Julian every time the native went out foraging. When Julian shrugged in doubt, Bellamy grew adamant and angry. "I have lost everything, but I have beaten death more than once! I will not let her be taken from me! She lives!"

✠ ✠ ✠ ✠

June 1717

It had been six weeks since the wreck of the Whydah, and throughout Eastham attention had returned to more predictable topics like planting the harvest and unpacking the salt hay from the foundations of the homesteads. With warm weather upon them, there was no more need to insulate against the cold, vicious wind that spent the winter sweeping over the fields and plains.

Normal small town rhythms returned. New courses were set in motion. Mehitable Higgins ran off with a sailor from Chatham. And Thankful Knowles Bearse was showing with child, the heir to a shipping fortune in Barnstable.

In the meeting house the new reverend, an itinerant pastor named Mr. Lord, preached a simmered down rant against hellfire, and people seemed embarrassed, if anything, by their previous fears. Yet there was still some cause to be vigilant. There were still occasional sightings of pirates off shore, which is why Jonathan

Hopkins was in the Devil's Pasture, guarding the northern parish shoreline.

His return to the Devil's Pasture reminded Hopkins painfully of his last images of the place. He thought of Elder Knowles' final blaze of righteousness before he quietly holed up in his homestead, without wife or Treat's lands or even respect, since he had been stripped of his posts. His erstwhile wife, Alice Hallett, had fled in shame and had not been heard from since. Most of all, he had Maria Hallett on his mind. He did not know why. Sometimes he felt that the feelings lingered because of her rejection of him. Other times he thought that she had indeed put some kind of spell on him.

He had asked for the Devil's Pasture to be his post, and Justice Doane had given him the duty. Something inside of him told him that Maria Hallett was not finished with Eastham and was preparing to bring fresh madness to town. God knew that her cursed hand had stirred up so much other evil already. He, for one, was not yet ready to concede that there was no threat left from dark forces. He believed that they were still out there, and they had not felt this close to the town's borders since the night of the wreck.

The fog gave a spooky cast to the gray afternoon. Hopkins squinted into the vapor, watching a silhouette disappear into the haze. It looked like a person walking away from the sea. A survivor perhaps, he wondered? *A pirate?*

He kicked his mount in the ribs, and horse and rider went stumbling into the mist, which parted around them as if they were wading in it. The touch of the mist on his face was as wet as the rub of a damp rag.

They tromped over the green and crimson carpet of bearberry. Scrub pines loomed dark and monstrous from the blanket of fog.

Before them the figure materialized again out of the vapor, closer than Hopkins had expected. He was gaining on it.

The sky above seemed to grow denser and gloomier as he approached the white cedar swamp. A few gulls wheeled in the sky, looking like cold white chips of ice caught in the towering clouds.

The path suddenly veered to the right, down an eroded embankment and into a thick wedge of blueberry bushes. He pulled the horse up short and assessed the black archway that the bushes formed and the foreboding wall of darkness within. He shivered. A crow jeered at him from within the inky murk, the surf growled in the distance, but other than those sounds, the entrance to the swamp was unnervingly silent.

He was not so sure about any of this now. Was the figure that he was chasing a man at all? Or was it some spirit going about its unfinished business? This place was named after the Devil after all. It was a home to one known witch, perhaps scores of vicious, desperate pirates and who knew what else.

"*Sam!*" came a cry in front of him. A woman's voice.

His courage returned, and he spurred ahead through the clasp of branches and into the cool air of the swamp. The fetid smell of leaves, decomposing in deep layers, mixed with the malodorous stink of mud. Moss coated the trees, and slicks of algae floated on the pools of water between the trees, except in some places where the water was a deep burgundy, like wine with leaves floating in it. The white cedar tree trunks contorted and bent as they rose into a thick, dark blanket of canopy above him. Sticking out from the sides of the trees were bulbous growths with cracks that formed faces. They seemed to watch him as he jumped the horse in between them, landing on the little islands of moss that had built up around their roots.

He saw the flicker of motion ahead, a shadow breaking apart from the general gloom.

"Sam," the figured called again.

"*Maria Hallett...*" Hopkins whispered, hardly daring to believe that such reckoning was at hand. Then he noticed another figure some distance in front of her. So they were both here, he thought, his excitement mounting. He had arrived just in time to catch them.

Hopkins slipped off of his horse into the soupy water. Deeper and deeper his quarry moved into the interior of the swamp. With a start he discovered that he could no longer remember the direction from which he came. Every view of the swamp around him looked the same, and he had no idea how big the place was. He might wander for days before finding dry land again. He had heard of men becoming snow-blind in blizzards and dying only a few yards from their front doors or in an ocean storm, passing right by a harbor obscured by a wall of solid rain. But there was no time to fret over such notions at the moment. His pursuit was all that mattered.

"Sam!" Maria hollered, up ahead, her words muffled up by the surrounding trees.

He sloshed up behind her, closer and closer, until finally she sensed him. She spun towards him, and he had barely time enough to dive behind the nearest mossy trunk. He was close enough now to see her face and was surprised to see it framed with as much fear as he felt himself. What kind of witch would be so disconcerted in a place of gloom and ghosts, he wondered?

Then the man she was chasing stepped out of a line of trees and turned to look at her. He was far enough away that all Hopkins could discern was his scraggly black hair. Slowly the far away figure looked at the girl and raised his hand in a wave.

Maria's body began trembling. "*Sam?*" she cried.

"*Good Lord... It really is the pirate,*" Hopkins muttered. He reached down to his hip, withdrew his pistol from his belt and lined up the barrel with the miraculous survivor in the distance.

Then the air shattered.

The pirate dropped down and knelt in the water.

"No!" Maria screamed. It took her some time to splash to-wards him, calling frantically as she did. However, Bellamy did not turn towards her. His eyes remained fixed on the interwoven branches over his head.

Hopkins watched her trudge as fast as she could against the sucking pull against her shins. He saw the defeated sag of his victim's body. She was still twenty yards away when Bellamy started to topple into the water. He heard her scream again, and then he heard the splash of the body. Face down.

Hopkins watched her agony as the water sloshed up on her, the trees seemingly perfectly positioned to block her progress. He counted in his head *One... Two... Three...*

She scrambled over the last hillock, pushing past the gnarled rooted feet of a cedar and splashed down next to the pirate.

Twenty-five... Twenty-six... Twenty-seven... Hopkins did not think that a living man could spend so many heartbeats underwater.

"Sam! No! No! No!" she hollered.

So it is done, Hopkins mused. He stood and looked back into the tangle of briars and shadowy tree trunks, and suddenly he did not feel lost at all. In fact, he felt that his path was clear for the first time in years. It had not been as he wanted it. But life did not always flow according to the paths that men set for it. These past couple of years had taught him that in hard terms. If nothing else, now that lesson was finished. And so was his longing for Maria. It would lie buried in this swamp, along with the dead pirate, forever. For too long he had let it fester, beyond all reason. With that single shot, he had expelled it at last. He felt relief. He did not relish taking a man's life, but that man was an outlaw, whose days would have soon come to an end at the end of a rope, if not by Hopkins' hand.

It occurred to him that Justice Doane and others might want to see Bellamy's body for themselves, and there would be much honor for the man who killed the pirate captain. But it was getting late, and he was filled with fatigue and a burning desire to be away from this hellish swamp and devilish pasture. He decided that the past was better left to rot in the swamp. He had no intention of informing the justice.

Tomorrow he would ride into town and look for a proper wife, as he should have done months ago. This time he would not be so choosy. All he needed was a real Eastham girl, a strong boned, softhearted woman who would pray loudly and speak quietly, and whose only notion of spells was how to properly spice an evening supper.

✠ ✠ ✠ ✠

John Julian opened his eyes under the murky water and saw faces looking up at him with anticipation, which Julian feared was a sort of welcome. The swamp was filling with his life's blood. The more that seeped out of him, the more that his fear went with it. By the time the girl had reached him and turned him over, he was almost disappointed to be blinking up into the dark tree canopy instead of the bright forever of the spirit world.

Her face pressed down close to his, and he could see the heartbreak and disappointment in it. He had heard whom she called. At last he felt that he should tell her that Sam Bellamy was not floating somewhere under the waves off shore, wherever the white men's spirits were gathering, but instead was at the other end of the swamp, waiting. The witch girl could then do whatever she wanted with the knowledge. Though in his head he could hear himself relaying this news to her, he soon realized that nothing but a grating noise was coming from his throat.

"Who did this to you?" Maria cried, her voice rising out of control. While she spoke, she examined him, found the spot on the right side of his chest where the bullet had gone through and felt the blood stick to her palm when she pressed it there.

"You're bleeding. Oh God! If I only had a cook fire and pot to make a broth... What plants can be used without boiling them? Tell me where they are in this swamp, and I shall fetch them!" Maria said, her voice wild and confused.

"Leave the wound," he commanded weakly.

Maria wrapped her wool shawl around his waist. "Your hurt is deep. There is much blood... That bastard! *That bastard...*" she said, her throat clenching. She looked around for a sign of the assailant but saw nothing.

Julian gasped for breath, but amazingly, the pain was receding. Underneath him he felt the spirits moving closer. "I am almost home. Where I belong."

Then he began coughing violently, and Maria laid her hands on his chest to steady him.

"I have seen the bodies. The men from the ship... It was my fault. I cursed them," she confessed.

"No curse... He is here... *There...*" It felt like it took his last bit of strength to reach out and point back into the swamp. He hoped that she would understand, but he could not say anymore. His head swam with a light, drifting feeling. Julian smiled benignly. Curses and omens. They seemed so different now. They were nothing but rot and decay, like the softness of wood that is left alone in the forest. Perhaps they had no power at all, unless one was foolish enough to believe in them. He smiled wider at the thought. What else could he do but laugh at the great trick of this earthly world? Life, he mused, is but a hard played joke by the spirits on their flesh and bone cousins. He wondered what his own life would have been like had he had the revelation sooner.

Julian grabbed one of Maria's hands. She was much more than he ever imagined. "You have healing hands. I feel it," he said weakly. Once again he had been wrong. She was not a destroyer but rather meant for good. He tried to apologize for encouraging her towards curses and to advise her not to fill her heart up with anger and darkness. Then he tried again to tell her about the sailor. But the words simply fell away in his mind, lost to a mist that was fogging his brain, like the mist of the Great Spirit off of Monomoyick. It was inside of him now. It had always been there, he realized with a laugh. The mist gathered in his eyes, obscuring everything but a few shafts of muted sunlight that penetrated the thick, gloomy leaf cover above. The sun reflected off the shallow pools of water and bounced back up into the branches where it played upon the foliage, like the breath of gold or coins soundlessly jangling.

"I am afraid that I can do nothing for you," Maria whimpered.

"There is no need now. I will get there on my own. My spirit knows the way."

She did not hear him, but she saw the wide smile stretch across his face.

"No!" she cried, slamming her hands upon his chest.

Julian did not feel them as blows. He barely felt them at all except for the heat of them.

The warmth of love... he thought. He no longer saw or thought about the witch girl. There was nothing left that he could do for her anyway. He did not even see the land itself. Not the land of his death, that is. Instead, he saw an earlier land. A beautiful one that surged around him with vivid smell, color and *feeling...* The sharpness of wet pine needles, the smoky odor of the leaf piles after a rain, the overwhelming, deep earthy fragrance of the land itself before stormy weather broke, the warmth of sitting in a block of sunshine on the flats while watching the seagulls fly... Feelings of being alive.

In that way John Julian finally returned to his homeland...

✠ ✠ ✠ ✠

Sam Bellamy considered the swamp to be a wretched place. His life for the past few weeks had been as cheery as wasting away in a stagnant ship's hold, with creaking tree limbs in place of shuddering planking.

Lying there, staring into the clasp of leaves high above his head, had given him plenty of time to let his mind drift. Finally he had come to realize that there were larger forces that flowed through a man's life, currents whose pull was too strong to resist. This peninsula, for instance, was destined to have him and break him too it seemed. Each arrival to these shores was a little more jarring and rough. He shuddered to think what would happen should he attempt to land at Eastham a third time. How broken would he be if he washed up yet again, he wondered? He did not intend to find out. He basically had his strength back, a miraculous recovery that enabled him to stand and walk gingerly around. Now he just needed the girl. That is all he wanted from this place. Then the next current could carry him where it would.

The native had some part to play in everything too, Bellamy believed. He wondered if they would always be intricately bound by fate. He decided to ask Julian about it when he next saw the man. When he heard sloshing in the distance, he almost shouted out the question, just to hear his voice echo through the drab, staid cedars. It was a little joke, which he knew would rankle his friend, but it would surely make Bellamy feel a little less bound by this bark and branch prison.

Then it occurred to Bellamy that there was reason to be cautious. In all the time that he had been recuperating in the swamp, no one else had ever come here. But Julian usually called out softly by now, announcing his return. This time Bellamy heard nothing but determined splashing, approaching quickly.

There was no time to clear the evidence of the campfire, only enough to grab the thickest, longest branch that he could find for a cudgel and wedge himself between two close growing trunks.

After a few minutes the sound stopped and was replaced by anxious breathing. Bellamy peeked from his hideout, debating whether to run screaming into the fight or wait and hope for a chance moment to surprise this interloper, should he prove hostile.

Then the stick fell out of his hands.

He could not believe his eyes. She was here...

A moment later he was holding Maria Hallett in his arms, wondering whether she would clasp him, strike him or level a curse at him. For he had heard about the child who had died, the trial and her summoning of thunder and lightening to do her bidding, although he did not believe in such power. After much badgering, he had gotten Julian to fill in many of the gaps for him, so he knew the grim picture of her existence in his absence. He saw it reflected in her poor ravaged face.

"*I am sorry...*" he muttered.

She squeezed him and held him that way while the swamp sat silently, like the space between heartbeats.

"You did indeed put a spell on me... I came back! I could not do otherwise."

When she looked up at him, her lips were trembling. "I am glad of it," she said.

He ran a gentle finger across the horrid mark on her cheek. "*They seek to ruin all that is beautiful...*" he muttered. "But they cannot."

Then she told him about Julian, and he could not believe it. This time, instead of saving Bellamy from death, Julian had taken Bellamy's place. It suddenly struck him how fond of the man he had grown. Julian had saved him, healed him and sent Maria back to him. The loss of Julian made him feel worse than that of all of the men with whom he had sailed.

With Julian gone, so too was his protection it seemed. It was time to leave, Bellamy reckoned. Palsgrave Williams' ship was out there, and he knew then that he and Maria would be heading to sea together at last.

"I saw our island more than once in my travels," he said.

"No more promises," she replied. She seemed at a loss for words, and he wondered if her seclusion had sucked them from her. Yet her eyes were full of hope and, unless it was some trick of the light, love... He felt that was almost more than he deserved.

Now all they had to do was get across the peninsula and wait for Williams' ship, which Julian told him had passed by Great Island several times during the past weeks. He just needed one more good role of the dice.

"We could go north and wait. No one will bother us there," Bellamy suggested, pointing towards Helltown.

Maria shivered into him. "No... I have been to that place and shall never return there."

"You have?" Bellamy asked, a murderous look in his eye. "Perhaps I should go there and make amends for you."

"No! We stay together. We go there to wait," she replied with a nod towards Indian Neck to the south. "It is closer. If Palsgrave comes, he will have to pass by there."

Bellamy smiled. "You're right! Besides, it doesn't matter where we go, does it?"

She shook her head. It was true. There was so much for both of them to say, and she was not sure how her half of it would come out of her mouth, but she did not want to speak of any of it at the moment. She simply wanted to keep ahold of her sailor. She did not intend to let this twist of fate slip out of her grasp.

A few hours later they were in the tiny village of the Punonakanits, surrounded by men and women who looked like John Julian. With that thought in mind, Bellamy sighed. "Poor bastard..."

Out of fear or respect, the natives kept their distance. It did not matter to Bellamy what was motivating them as long as they cleared out of the way. And if they ran to fetch Justice Doane, then he would take one of their canoes, and he and Maria would head straight out to sea, he thought grimly. He did not intend to let himself be brought back into the clutches of the petty fools of Eastham or lose Maria in the process. His luck would hold, he felt, yet his neck and forehead grew uncomfortably hot as he peered at the empty bay. *"Come on, Palsgrave..."* he whispered.

"Did an English woman pass through your village some months ago? Did anyone help her on her way from here?" Maria asked one of the members of the tribe.

"An English woman?" one of the men replied, looking warily at Maria's scar.

"Yes. She was alone. Lost. Trying to get across the bay."

"Yes... I remember. We took her to Nobscusset... What do you say? *Yarmouth.* Yes..." the man replied.

Maria sighed in relief. "That is good."

"And that is better!" Bellamy cried, whooping and throwing his hands in the air, causing the Punonakanits to step back even farther.

Coming around the headland of Great Island was a spread of gray sails, which puffed gently in the easy wind. Bellamy grabbed Maria's hand and ran down to the shoreline, shouting to the vessel. He could see a distinguished looking man, leaning upon the rail, whose uncharacteristically lean form was shaking with visible delight.

The ship anchored one hundred yards off shore, and dinghies were lowered over the side.

"Here. It is not much. It is all that Julian and I could find on the beach," Bellamy said, dropping a fistful of gold coins into Maria's hands.

"We will pillage and plunder and get more?" she asked, pointedly.

After a pause Bellamy replied, "We shall do and go where you want... Do you know yet what and where that is?"

"Not yet."

Bellamy did not either. He soon pushed the thought out of his mind. Familiar faces were alongside of him. Men were slapping him on the back. The sun blazed down on Great Island, the top of which looked strangely cropped without the tavern standing there.

"You are a lucky bastard..." Williams said, pulling Bellamy into embrace.

"And you are not in Newport?"

Williams shrugged. "Seems it is harder to return home than I thought."

Maria had walked to the rail and stood gazing at Cape Cod as it washed away from them. Bellamy imagined that she was saying her good-bye, a moment that he knew would leave a bittersweet taste. She waved and, in his bliss, he did the same, only then noting that there was a man on one of the dune crests of Great Island. The man seemed to be watching their departure.

"Is that a Punonakanit?" Bellamy asked, stepping over to Maria.

"Yes," she replied.

"For a moment I thought it looked like... No, it can't be."

"John Julian," she said, filling in the name for him.

The figure on the distant bluff waved and then seemed to disappear in a flash of sunlight, making Bellamy wonder if he had seen anyone there at all. Yet she had seen it too...

The train of thought was interrupted by Williams' hand thumping on his shoulder. "We've got forty men aboard, one hundred bottles of rum and only a single bag of coins to spare. Where to, Captain?"

Bellamy smiled. "I believe that we should vote on it."

"Yes, indeed!" Williams chuckled, adding, "Fear not! There is more treasure to be had!"

"Not for me. We sail only until we find the perfect island. Then you may drop us off..." Bellamy said and walked over to stand with Maria at the rail. Below them the water raced, bright with promise, and he did not much care where it took them.

THE END

ACKNOWLEDGMENTS

Most of all, I am indebted to my wife Lynne. A decade ago we stood on the overlook by the parking lot of the white cedar swamp in Wellfleet, and I recounted the story of Sam Bellamy and Maria Hallett. "Why don't you write a novel about it?" she asked. *Why not?* I thought. Since then it has been a journey of countless drafts, storylines, twists, turns and day jobs. Lynne helped me come up with many of the ideas, edits, plot twists and characterizations in *Pieces of Eight*. I am thankful for all of her inspiration, support, belief and love.

Many thanks and much appreciation goes to my parents, Richard & Karin Delaney, and in-laws, Bob & Sandy McLuckie, who supported me and this book every step of the way.

I am also grateful to my main readers: Nickey Burnell, Karin Delaney, Judy Fueyo, Rebecca Lach, Sandy McLuckie and Ron Thibodeau. Thank you for your insightful comments and helpful guidance.

Thanks to our vizsla Brady Delaney for keeping me focused and making sure that I put my time in on the computer - even lying across my lap while I type, if necessary.

Along the way, numerous friends, family and acquaintances have provided all manner of enthusiastic assistance for this endeavor - everything from reading excerpts to offering advice on the world of publishing and marketing to faithfully asking me, "How's your book going?" year after year... From the very beginning, this book has been more of a communal effort than I ever anticipated. I know that it is a better piece of work because of that. I could fill pages with the names of all those who helped and encouraged me along the way. Of those, the following deserve special mention: Dorothy Calkins, Boyd Christie, Max Delaney & Deb Monaghan, Kathy Doyle, Carey & Derek Hamilton, Dan Hamilton, Mike Lach, Doreen Leggett, Tom & Jane McLuckie, Dave Miller, Dan Milsky, John Murphy, Kris Rodanas, Seth Rolbein, Jeff Thibodeau, Jana Scholten & Dan Junkins, Peter Schuhknecht, Elaine O'Brien Sharron – and Alla Chekhova Kennedy for her beautiful painting that graces the cover of this book. I thank you all!

HISTORICAL NOTE

In order to piece together the atmosphere and details of the time period and historical roots of this story, I greatly benefited from many sources. The various town histories, articles and published works are too numerous to mention. However, I leaned on a few sources more heavily than others.

Any writing about Sam Bellamy and Goody Hallett must begin with the work of Barry Clifford, who found and excavated the *Whydah,* and Ken Kinkor, historian of Expedition Whydah. Many of their findings and research are contained in the books *Expedition Whydah* (by Barry Clifford with Paul Perry) and *The Pirate Prince* (by Barry Clifford with Peter Turchi), which are mandatory reading for the topic. *Whidah: Cape Cod's Mystery Treasure Ship,* by Edwin Dethlefsen and *Treasure Wreck: The Fortunes and Fate of the Pirate Ship Whydah,* by Arthur T. Vanderbilt were written in close observation of the excavation of the *Whydah* and also contain many valuable details.

A General History of The Pyrates, by Daniel Defoe, *Pirates and Buccaneers of the Atlantic Coast,* by Edward Rowe Snow, *The Narrow Land: Folk Chronicles of Old Cape Cod,* by Elizabeth Reynard, *Everyday Life in Truro, Cape Cod,* by Richard F. Whalen, *The Times of Their Lives: Life, Love, and Death in Plymouth Colony,* by James Deetz & Patricia Scott Deetz, *Historic Cultural Land Use Study of Lower Cape Cod,* by Richard D. Holmes, et al, *Historic and Archaeological Resources of Cape Cod and the Islands,* by James W. Bradley and the pirate research of David Cordingly were also particularly informative.

The wonderful history exhibits at Plimoth Plantation and the Hoxie House in Sandwich both provided a lot of texture about the living conditions of white settlers and Native Americans alike during the period of the book.

This novel is a blend of fact and fiction. It grew out of an old Cape Cod legend, which itself contains kernels of truth planted in broader swaths of speculation. I have endeavored to accurately portray much of the historical underpinning of the story, both the known details of the lives of Sam Bellamy, Maria Hallett and their contemporaries, and also the culture and atmosphere of the early eighteenth-century world in which they lived. At the same time I have not been shy about using the vague and uncertain elements of the story to my advantage. I have concocted, adapted and altered some of the plot and characters where I thought it necessary.

The basis for *Pieces of Eight* is the legend of Sam Bellamy and Maria Hallett. Many different versions of this tale exist in print and the collective memory and imagination of Cape Codders. The standard outline of the tale is that a dashing young Englishman, Sam Bellamy, arrives on Cape Cod and woos a young local girl named Maria Hallett. He leaves in search of treasure, and she remains at home, heartbroken, pregnant and ultimately persecuted after the townsfolk find out about her baby, who dies after choking on a piece of straw. Many of the locals think that Maria is a witch, so she is exiled to the bluffs of Wellfleet. Meanwhile Bellamy embarks upon a lucrative pirate career in the West Indies. He eventually returns to the Cape where his ship wrecks, either by some act of the ocean or curse levied by his spurned lover, Maria. The end of the tale has the most variation. In some versions Bellamy dies in the wreck. In others he survives and comes back to town in search of Maria. There is also a wide spectrum of fates for Maria, everything from suicide to a quiet retirement with some of the gold from the *Whydah* to a reunion with Bellamy.

The Sam Bellamy-Maria Hallett legend was first introduced to me by my father, who used to tell the tale to groups of friends, family and visitors, around campfires on the beaches of Wellfleet and Truro. My brother and I eventually became part of the act, hiding in the dune grass on the high bluffs above the beach. There we would wait for a cue from my father, when he reached the climax of the tale - *Goody Hallett still haunts this very spot to this day* - at which point we would howl, moan and stand up as dark silhouettes on the crest, sometimes holding a flashlight in place of Goody Hallett's lantern, with which she endlessly scans the water for signs of Bellamy's ship. My father's version of the tale included the torch-bearing mob that came to run Goody Hallett out of her hovel, after the wreck, and also her flight into the White Cedar Swamp in Wellfleet where some say she perished. In high school there were many of us kids who would use our freshly-minted driver's licenses to go up to the swamp in the dark of winter and scare ourselves half to death, wandering around among the bearded white cedars where it is said that her ghost still haunts.

In *Pieces of Eight* I use many of the most prominent and re-peated elements of the legend. These include Sam Bellamy's stay in Higgins Tavern, his meeting with Maria Hallett – said to be the most beautiful girl in Eastham – in the apple orchard, his learning of the Spanish wreck, his pursuit of the sunken treasure with Palsgrave Williams, his promise to return to Maria as a rich man, Maria's pregnancy, the death of her baby, the rumors of witchcraft around her, the trial and expulsion of Maria for the death of her baby, and her curse that sunk Bellamy's ship at the moment of his return.

Other scenes and storylines of *Pieces of Eight* are entirely my own inventions such as the washing up of the sea creature, the general tenor of fear in town, the death of Maria's father, Maria's premonitions, Elder Knowles' machinations to gain land and power, Julian's attempts to reacquire Great Island and Jonathan Hopkins' murder of Julian. These were concocted to propel the story along the lines that I envisioned and bridge various gaps in the legend.

In the same vein I also made some small, innocuous (I be-lieve) alterations of historical detail, for the sake of advancing my version of the story. I renamed the *Marianne,* the pirate ship that Bellamy receives from Hornigold (not to be confused with the similarly named ship that wrecked on Pochet Island), the *Maria.* I made Johnny Cole, who was actually nineteen-years-old, according to the historical record, a young boy, in keeping with the legend (and I do not mention any of the many siblings that the historical Johnny Cole had). The town records show that a "Mr. Lord" briefly preached in town after the death of Reverend Treat. I suggest that Elder Knowles became interim minister before Mr. Lord's arrival. Cyprian Southack's ship was robbed by pirates on the way to Cape Cod. I moved this encounter to his trip back to Boston, at the end of a virtually fruitless mission, to increase the drama and irony of the episode.

The ongoing research of Barry Clifford and Ken Kinkor continually adds new details and theories to the legend. Some of those details and theories were revised over the course of the ten years that I worked on this book. In some cases I incorporated the new discoveries into my version of the tale. In other cases I stuck with old, perhaps even outdated, understandings of the story and historical figures because I was already deeply committed to certain twists of plot and characterizations.

There was indeed a pirate named Sam Bellamy. It is believed that he hailed from Devonshire, England. The precise location of Bellamy's birth and youth is not known. I placed my version of Bellamy in view of Plymouth harbor in a fictitious lordship that is named after and loosely based on a real manor house, Radford Manor, in Plymstock.

The legends and historical tidbits about Bellamy suggest that he was apparently egalitarian and concerned with social and economic justice. That is the overall spirit that I have given to my version of him. Other research suggests a darker side of the man, befitting the culture of piracy and the demands of retaining a position of power among the tough men who constituted pirate crews.

Bellamy's exploits are well-documented. I had to leave out many, many events and long stretches of his career in order to streamline my plot and character development. Bellamy's flagship, the *Whydah*, did wreck upon the coast of modern day Wellfleet, Massachusetts on April 26, 1717. Bellamy's second ship, the *Mary Anne*, wrecked on that same night on Pochet Island in modern day Orleans.

Less is known about Bellamy's pirate cohorts and prisoners, but the names and some biographical details of such men as Palsgrave Williams, Thomas Baker, Hendrick Quintor, Peter Hoof, Thomas Brown, Thomas Davis, Alexander Mackconachy, John Dunavan, Thomas Fitzgerald, Benjamin Hornigold, Louis Lebous as well as many of the captains victimized by Bellamy and his pirates are taken from the historical record. I have tried to include and be faithful to whatever historical detail I could discover about these men. Some of the biographical details are uncertain, and most are unknown, so each pirate developed his own personality in the context of my tale. The most famous pirate who Bellamy crossed paths with is, of course, Edward "Blackbeard" Teach. He and Bellamy only interacted for a brief time, as far as can be determined, which is one reason that Blackbeard only gets a cameo role in this story.

Daku is based on the many African pirates who sailed with Bellamy and his crew. Liberated slaves, African freemen and men of African descent became pirates in great numbers and made up a sizeable percentage of Bellamy's crew.

The aftermath of the wrecks is probably the closest to historical reality. Governor Samuel Shute, Cyprian Southack and Cotton Mather were all real people, and many of the events related in Book Four are drawn from archival documents.

Many of the townsfolk of Eastham and Billingsgate are historical figures, including such people as Reverend Samuel Treat, Justice Joseph Doane, Lieutenant John Cole, Deacon John Paine and Samuel Harding. Others such as Elder John Knowles, Samuel Smith and Isaiah Higgins, the tavern keeper, derive from the legends, but are as likely as not based on real people and perhaps even correctly named although I could not pin-point them for certain in any historical documents. I invented many other townsfolk in order to advance the story. Nearly all of them were given local surnames of the families who were alive at that time and still live in the area today.

Maria Hallett is the most conspicuously absent from the historical record. There are theories as to her identity and fate. However, there is scant evidence of Halletts living in the Eastham area during the eighteenth-century. That family is usually associated with Yarmouth.

The apocalyptic atmosphere and witch craze in town mirror similar events in Europe and colonial America at roughly the same time period. Widow Chase is an invention, but she suffers the real fate of some midwives who had the misfortune of delivering one too many still-born babies.

Mittawa is also an invention. Her half-French ancestry is based on the frequent visits of the French and other Europeans to outer Cape Cod in the seventeenth and eighteenth centuries. Her herbal medicine and shamanic visions are a composite of my research and interpretation of native spiritual and healing practices. The unusual spring-like thaw in the winter of 1717, predicted by Mittawa in Maria's dream, did in fact occur.

John Julian is given brief mention in most of the legends as a local, native pilot, who was picked up by the *Whydah* to help the pirates navigate through unfamiliar, tricky waters. The research of Clifford and Kinkor suggests that Julian might have been a native of the West Indies or Central America, who joined Bellamy at a much earlier date. I have chosen to retain his local ancestry in order to explore the dynamic between natives and English settlers on colonial Cape Cod. The dwindling population of natives, conversion of most natives to Christianity, Treat's reputation as a missionary and the details of various native villages are drawn from historical texts. John Tom is a character of my devising, named after and loosely based on a native Christian preacher from roughly the same time period as the story.

The wrangling over the land on Great Island is based, in part, on fact. The area was a focal point for whaling, smuggling and land squatters. Several disputes over ownership and divisions of land appear in the records from the early eighteenth-century. In reality, the majority – if not all – of the land purchases would have been from the heirs of the original proprietors, from Eastham, who bought the land from the natives in the seventeenth-century. I suggest that some residents of Great Island, like Samuel Smith, were still negotiating directly with the natives to acquire land. Unfortunately, we'll never know for certain. When the Barnstable County Courthouse was destroyed by fire in 1827, most of the old deeds went with it. The uncertainty allowed me to use some imagination to flesh out the history, nature and ramifications of this nebulous ownership to create the dynamic of Julian's quest to reclaim his people's land.

In general, I strived to be true to the land itself. I attempted to create an authentic sense of place, in terms of the atmosphere and layout of Cape Cod in the early eighteenth-century, the organization of the community and the culture and beliefs of the time. As much as possible, I incorporated the known history of the time period and events relating to this particular story. Any inventions of plot or character or environment were crafted to be as realistic as possible.

COMING SOON...

Like most of America in the Fall of 1848, the people of Cape Cod are enthralled by tales of gold in the California hills. As expeditions are organized to go west in search of fortune, a body is found on an oyster bed offshore and, for gravestone carver Ephraim White, a mystery begins. In the beginning Ephraim believes that he is simply trying to determine if the death was by means fair or foul. He soon discovers himself entangled in a deeper web of greed and envy, which is woven into the fabric of his little fishing village. The more he listens to the whispered tales of ghosts and pirates of old, the more he is inspired to uncover the truth. But Ephraim's meddling, as some would say, brings to light some stories that others in town will go to great lengths to keep buried. The passions and rivalries that come to the surface in 1848 stretch back in time for over a century. And some of the original rivals from the past seem to reach out from beyond the grave to affect the fate of those living in Ephraim's time...

For more information visit: www.capecodlegends.com

TIMELINE

1715

June
✠ Sam Bellamy arrives in Eastham and meets Maria Hallett.
✠ Julian meets Mittawa, recalls her prophecy and starts questioning his ancestry.

September
✠ Bellamy flees to Great Island.
✠ Samuel Smith gives Julian a deed for part of Great Island.
✠ Julian converts to Christianity.

October
✠ Alice Hallett marries Elder Knowles.
✠ Maria discovers she is pregnant.
✠ Bellamy and Palsgrave Williams sail to Florida in search of treasure.
✠ Finding no gold in Florida, Bellamy declares himself a pirate.

1716

April
✠ Bellamy joins Hornigold's crew.

May
✠ The Town Elders meet in Hopkins' tannery to discuss their fears of witchcraft.

June
✠ Maria gives birth to a baby in Knowles' barn. She is put on trial for witchcraft.
✠ Bellamy leaves Hornigold to pursue his own pirate career.

July

✠ Maria is driven out of town to the Devil's Pasture in Billingsgate.

✠ John Julian is driven off of Great Island and goes to the Devil's Pasture where he meets Maria.

1717

February

✠ Unusual winter thaw.

March

✠ Reverend Treat dies.

April

✠ Maria curses Sam Bellamy from the dune crest.

✠ Julian declares war on Eastham. He then leaves the land and is picked up by the *Whydah*.

✠ The *Mary Anne* and *Whydah* wreck.

May

✠ Elder Knowles leads a torch-bearing mob to burn Maria's hut.

✠ Julian burns down Smith Tavern.

✠ In the name of the king, Southack comes to Cape Cod to collect the pirates' treasure.

June

✠ Deputy Jonathan Hopkins pursues two figures through Great Cedar Swamp.

October

✠ Pirate trial in Boston.

November

✠ Pirates executed in Boston.